PENGUIN BOOKS

THE PORTABLE BERNARD SHAW

Each volume in The Viking Portable Library either presents a representative selection from the works of a single outstanding writer or offers a comprehensive anthology on a special subject. Averaging 700 pages in length and designed for compactness and readability, these books fill a need not met by other compilations. All are edited by distinguished authorities, who have written introductory essays and included much other helpful material.

"The Viking Portables have done more for good reading and good writers than anything that has come along since I can remember."

—Arthur Mizener

Stanley Weintraub is Research Professor of English at Pennsylvania State University and director of its Institute for the Arts and Humanistic Studies as well as editor of *The Shaw Review*. He is author of two biographical studies of Shaw, *Private Shaw and Public Shaw* and *Journey to Heartbreak*, and has edited Shaw's autobiographical writings and *An Unfinished Novel by Bernard Shaw*. His *Beardsley: A Biography* was nominated for a National Book Award.

XX

The Portable
BERNARD
SHAW

Edited, with an Introduction and Notes, by
STANLEY WEINTRAUB

XXXXXXXXXXXXXXXXXXXXXXXXXXXXXXXXXXXXXXXXXX

Penguin Books

Penguin Books Ltd, Harmondsworth, Middlesex, England
Penguin Books, 625 Madison Avenue, New York, New York 10022, U.S.A.
Penguin Books Australia Ltd, Ringwood, Victoria, Australia
Penguin Books Canada Limited, 2801 John Street,
Markham, Ontario, Canada L3R 1B4
Penguin Books (N.Z.) Ltd, 182–190 Wairau Road,
Auckland 10, New Zealand

First published in the United States of America in simultaneous
hardbound and paperbound editions by The Viking Press and
Penguin Books 1977
Reprinted 1979, 1981, 1982

LIBRARY OF CONGRESS CATALOGING IN PUBLICATION DATA
Shaw, George Bernard, 1856–1950,
The portable Bernard Shaw.
(The Viking portable library)
Bibliography: p. 697
I. Weintraub, Stanley, 1929—   II. Title.
PR5361.W4   1977b   822'.9'12   77-7457
ISBN 0 14 015.090 0

Printed in the United States of America by
Kingsport Press, Inc., Kingsport, Tennessee
Set in Linotype Times Roman

The illustration on page 698 is by Feliks Topelski and is
from the first text of the film script of *Pygmalion*.

CONTENTS

EDITOR'S INTRODUCTION

In his preface to *Man and Superman*, one of his most ambitious works, Bernard Shaw declared, "This is the true joy in life, the being used for a purpose recognized by yourself as a mighty one; the being thoroughly worn out before you are thrown on the scrap heap; the being a force of Nature instead of a feverish selfish little clod of grievances complaining that the world will not devote itself to making you happy." Practicing what he preached, Shaw lived his ninety-four years fully and forcefully. Beginning late as a playwright, he became nevertheless the most significant English dramatist since the seventeenth century, although the theatre was only one of his many careers. And he was more than the best comic dramatist of his time, for some of his greatest work for the stage has a high purpose and a prose beauty unmatched by his theatrical contemporaries. Among his other roles he was the most trenchant pamphleteer since Swift, the most readable music critic in English, the best theatre critic of his generation, a prodigious lecturer and essayist on politics, economics, religion, and society, and possibly the most prolific letter writer in literature. All of these facets of G.B.S.—and more—are illuminated in this volume.

Born in Dublin on July 26, 1856, G.B.S. was the third child and only son of the middle-aged George Carr Shaw and his young wife, Lucinda. Technically he belonged to the Protestant "ascendancy"—the landed Irish gentry—but his father (first a sinecured civil servant and then an unsuccessful corn merchant) was little more than an amiable drunkard, and young Shaw grew up in a "downstart" atmosphere of genteel impecuniosity, which he felt was more humiliating than to be born poor and have pretensions to nothing more. After being tutored by a

clerical uncle, he attended—briefly—both Protestant and
Catholic day schools (the latter an experience repugnant to
him in the extreme), and before he was sixteen he was
working in a land agent's office, having derived his most
practical education outside the classroom.

The Shaw ménage was a curious one. George Carr
Shaw counted for little. His wife had turned for consolation not only to music, but also to her music teacher,
George John Vandeleur Lee, a mesmeric figure in Irish
music circles. By 1866 Lee shared a house in Dublin
with the Shaws as well as a cottage on Dalkey Hill, over-
looking Dublin Bay, a setting that provided the young
Shaw with the beginnings of an aesthetic sensibility. Art
he found in abundance at the National Gallery in Dublin
and music pervaded the household, since Lee trained singers
and rehearsed operas and oratorios. Shaw absorbed what
he could, often accompanying on the piano or acting as
Lee's factotum. At the estate office of Uniacke Townshend,
Shaw joylessly handled the collections and the accounts,
and sang arias to relieve the tedium. Escape finally came
when his mother and sisters abandoned George Carr Shaw
in Dublin and followed Lee to London in 1875. Determined to make his way in literature, but not knowing how
—except that London was the place in which to make the
attempt—G.B.S. followed the next year.

In his twenties Shaw endured unrelieved frustration and
poverty, yet he never became embittered. For a while he
produced ghost-written musical criticism for Lee, but his
only other job, which he found through an aunt late in
1879, was with the Edison Telephone Company of London. He seized the opportunity of the company's consolida-
tion with a competing firm to leave in mid-1880, and this
marked the end of his nonliterary employment. Living with
his mother and elder sister Lucy (Agnes had died in 1876),
he depended upon their pound a week from a family
bequest, mailed from Dublin by George Carr Shaw, and
his mother's earnings as a music teacher. He spent his days
in the British Museum Reading Room, writing novels and
reading what he had missed at school, and his nights in
search of additional self-education through the free lec-

tures and debates that characterized the intellectual ferment of contemporary middle-class London. And he became a vegetarian: such a diet was cheap and Shelley had subscribed to the philosophy. Eventually it became a passionate commitment.

Shaw's fiction failed, utterly. The semiautobiographical and aptly titled *Immaturity*, written in 1879 (but not published until 1930) was Shaw's own *David Copperfield*, with a flavor both reminiscent of Dickens and anticipatory of Gissing. Its sometimes sober, sometimes satirical evocation of the mid-Victorian milieu put off every publisher in London. The next four novels, similarly refused, soon padded out propagandist magazines edited by Shaw's socialist friends. *The Irrational Knot* (1880; serialized 1885–87) Shaw later pronounced a forerunner of Henrik Ibsen, of whom he had not yet heard, for the hero marries at the beginning and walks out on the heroine at the end. Its characters, hardly more than animated theories, were each endowed with an "original morality" that publishers' readers found "disagreeable," "perverse," and "crude." With half-hearted job hunting still fruitless, Shaw began *Love Among the Artists* (1881; serialized 1887–88), which reflected, in the neglect of "a British Beethoven" among dilettantes and mediocrities, Shaw's passionate belief in his own large talents and his frustration at being thwarted. Midway through the manuscript in 1881 he was stricken during a smallpox epidemic in London, but he stubbornly completed the unsalable novel and the next year began still another, *Cashel Byron's Profession* (1882; serialized 1885–86). Its exuberance belied Shaw's lack of success and its theme, "immoral" and "retrograde" professions— in this case, prizefighting—as an indictment of society, anticipated such early plays as *Mrs. Warren's Profession*. In 1901 Shaw spoofed his own novel in a burlesque Elizabethan blank-verse adaptation which he called *The Admirable Bashville*.

The socialism in *Cashel Byron* was an afterthought, most of it daubed in for its appearance in a magazine after an 1882 lecture by the radical American economist Henry George had spurred him to a reading of Marx. Shaw was ready to become a socialist disciple, but found difficulty in selecting a group to join from among many splinter parties in London. Meanwhile, the new gospel became the stimulus for his last novel, *An Unsocial Socialist* (1883; serialized 1884). Intended as "a gigantic grapple with the whole social problem," it broke down under the weight of its incongruities, which included a runaway husband, a finishing school for girls, and ponderous paraphrases from *Das Kapital* among passages of sparkling Shavian dialogue. A fragment written and abandoned in 1887–88 was his final false start in fiction, except for a few minor short stories and a witty, *Candide*-like novella he wrote in 1932, *The Adventures of the Black Girl in Her Search for God.* His strength, he had discovered, lay in dialogue. He was not, he later announced, "a plot-monger."

The story of the Black Girl, told simply in fable fashion, came to Shaw as a result of his meeting in England with an authentic female missionary, and then finding himself in South Africa in the appropriate setting for his story; but it summed up his own attitude toward religions, and his own faith, more accessibly than he had ever done before. He reviewed the gods of man from Jehovah to Science, and closed with a blending of rationalism and mysticism which had appeared in his plays and his "lay sermons" and essays since the turn of the century. Despite its unconventional religion and some denunciations from English pulpits, it was a Christmas season best-seller.

Notwithstanding his early failure in fiction, the 1880s was the decade in which Shaw found himself. He became a spell-binding orator, a polemicist, even tentatively a playwright. He became the force behind the newly founded (1884) Fabian Society, a middle-class Socialist group which aimed at the transformation of English society not through revolution but through "permeation" (in Sidney Webb's term) of the nation's intellectual and political life. Adept at committee work, Shaw involved himself in every aspect of Fabian activities, most visibly as editor of what proved to be one of the classics of British radicalism, *Fabian Essays in Socialism* (1889), to which he also contributed two sections. Through the Fabians, too, he assisted at the birth of the Labour Party in 1893 and helped Fabian-supported candidates campaign in municipal and parliamentary elections.

Shaw's experience as a pamphleteer and platform speaker helped forge the forceful prose of his missionary books *The Quintessence of Ibsenism* (1891, revised 1913), *The Perfect Wagnerite* (1898), *The Sanity of Art* (1895, revised 1908), *The Common Sense of Municipal Trading* (1904, revised 1908)—the result of his years, from 1897–1903, as Vestryman and Borough Councillor of St. Pancras Parish, London)—and of his later tracts and polemics as well as the prefaces and dialogue for his plays. His John Tanner of *Man and Superman* was good-humored Shavian satire of this political aspect of himself. Although Tanner combined the personalities of socialist theoretician Sidney Webb and socialist agitator Henry Hyndman, Shaw's protagonist (the Don Juan of the "Interlude in Hell") also combined the Don Juan and the polemical sides of his creator. Tall, pale, and red-bearded, G.B.S. was a striking figure in a debate or on the stump, and for years he not only attended every public lecture he could within commuting distance of London, but also spoke without fee two or three times a week to groups of any political or religious persuasion interested in hearing him, often paying his own expenses to get there. According to Beatrice Webb, nearly every "advanced" female in London "worshipped at the Shavian shrine," for his romantic Irish wit and charm won those not captured by his dialectical skill or his ideas. And he spoke on street corners, in parks and public squares, at the docks, or in the traditional London halls where liberal or radical causes could be espoused, offering—usually from note cards—extemporaneous treatises, lectures, and lay sermons on topics ranging from municipal reform to modern theology. In 1933, in his seventy-seventh year, Shaw gave his last public lecture—at the Metropolitan Opera House in New York, on a rare visit to the United States. "I regard the platform as obsolete," he told an interviewer; "the microphone's the thing. It is foolish to talk to a few hundred when you can talk to millions." By then he had already perfected his

radio speaking style, which was warm and informal and
directed at audiences of all ages and interests; one of his
talks, entitled "School" (reprinted here), was even intended
for Sixth Form students. At ninety he gave his last B.B.C.
broadcast—this time for television.

Although Shaw's journalism quickly became an extension of his platform role, he began writing book reviews in
the *Pall Mall Gazette* (1885–88) and art criticism in the
World (1886–88) because a young drama critic, William
Archer, who became a lifelong friend, provided the con-
tacts and because Shaw needed the bread-and-butter income. "I did not throw myself into the struggle for life,"
he once joked. "I threw my mother into it. I was not a
staff to my father's old age: I hung on to his coat tails."
Until his thirtieth year, he had lived off his mother's earnings as a music teacher while he struggled to make a
career as a writer, and it was finally music that made the
career possible, for Shaw finally found himself through
brilliant, and often brilliantly digressive, musical columns
in the *Star* (signed by "Corno di Bassetto"—basset horn)
from 1888 to 1890 and in the *World* (as "G.B.S.") from
1890 to 1894. In his reviews, he confessed, he was always
"electioneering. . . . Never in my life have I penned an
impartial criticism; and I hope I never may." He cam-
paigned for better music and better performances, and
declared that "a criticism written without personal feeling
is not worth reading. It is the capacity for making good
or bad art a personal matter that makes a man a critic."
But, he added, he went beyond personal feeling, for it
was the "passion for artistic perfection—the noblest beauty
of sight, sound and action—" that made him seem "diaboli-
cally unfair" to performers who were trying their best.

When Shaw transferred his attentions to the drama his
strategy remained the same. "If my head had not been
full of Ibsen and Wagner in the nineties," he confessed, "I
should have been kinder and more reasonable in my
demands. Also, perhaps, less amusing." Recruited by Frank
Harris to the *Saturday Review* as a theatre critic (1895–98),
Shaw carried on in its columns a campaign to displace the
artificialities and hypocrisies of the Victorian stage (or

"Sardoodledom" as he called it) with a theatre of vital ideas. It required also the unmasking of "Bardolatry," as Shaw described the pompous and reverential portrayal of Shakespeare, whom he admired beyond all other dramatists, but whose words, he insisted, were not holy writ but only lines for players to speak. It required a contemporary drama of wit and substance to replace the melodramas and farces which were the staple of the commercial theatre, but other than the comedies of Wilde and the dramas of Ibsen, there was little around which Shaw could rally.

With his talk about a "New Drama" threatening to conclude with the humiliating confession that in England, at least, modern theatre was "only a figment of the revolutionary imagination," Shaw determined that the situation could not be further endured: "I had rashly taken up the case; and rather than let it collapse I manufactured the evidence." That effort became his primary activity during the 1890s. The strain—for his critical and political work went on unabated—sapped his strength to such an extent, however, that a minor foot infection, haphazardly cared for in bachelor fashion, developed into necrosis of the bone and required serious surgery. Since playwriting had, by then, become more important to him than play criticism, the event provided him with an excuse for his "Valedictory" as drama columnist, a sprightly essay written from his bed and introducing his hand-picked successor, "the incomparable Max" Beerbohm, a young man in his middle twenties whose major piece of criticism had been two columns in the *Saturday Review* taking issue with Shaw's own *Mrs. Warren's Profession*.

In 1898, during his recuperation, Shaw married his unofficial nurse, Charlotte Payne-Townshend (1857–1943), an Irish heiress and friend of Beatrice and Sidney Webb. It was an unusual marriage, for at Charlotte's insistence it remained unconsummated. Although the couple was childless, they established a series of surrogate-parent relationships, with such men as actors Granville Barker and Robert Loraine and writer-soldier T. E. Lawrence, which seemed to satisfy an otherwise unfulfilled need. As Shaw confessed to Frank Harris, he had been financially unable as a young man to maintain a mistress or a marriage and his sexual initiation, with an aggressive widow, did not occur until he was twenty-nine. After that time, he enjoyed a number of affairs (two simultaneous ones are satirized in his play *The Philanderer* which was written in 1893 but not performed until 1903), but eventually his passions subsided, concentrating themselves into female friendships which were mostly epistolary. The chief exception was his relationship with Mrs. Stella Patrick Campbell (1865–1940), the Eliza Doolittle of his *Pygmalion* in 1914. His ardor for Mrs. Campbell nearly wrecked his marriage in 1912. Thereafter, however, his correspondences cooled, concluding with an almost fatherly flirtation with American actress Molly Tompkins, which began when Shaw was nearly seventy, and a nearly brotherly one (in every sense of the word) with Sister Laurentia McLachlan, a Benedictine nun, which ended only with Shaw's death. As he wrote in the preface to a volume of his correspondence with actress Ellen Terry (1931), ". . . only on paper has mankind ever yet achieved glory, beauty, truth, knowledge, virtue and abiding love."

The Shaws' marriage lasted until Charlotte's death in 1943. In many ways she had become a substitute mother who compensated for a childhood marked by neglect that G.B.S. in later years preferred to make light of rather than expose the wound, although his plays are replete with ineffective mothers—and fathers. When Charlotte died of a lingering illness, Shaw, who was frail and feeling the effects of World War II privations, made a permanent retreat from his apartment in bomb-wracked London to his country home at Ayot St. Lawrence, a village in Hertfordshire where he had lived since 1906. He died there at the age of 94 on November 2, 1950, having continued to write and to maintain the crusty "G.B.S." persona to the end.

"The Celebrated G.B.S.," Shaw once wrote, "is about as real as a pantomime ostrich. . . . I have played my game with a conscience. I have never pretended that G.B.S. was real: I have over and over again taken him to pieces before the audience to shew the trick of him." Yet having put on his jester's cap and bells to call attention to himself, he became the captive of his public reputation. The real Shaw, according to J. B. Priestley, "was courteous, kind, generous, shy rather than impudent, physically strong and courageous, yet rather timid and prudish in his relations with the world of food and drink, sex or hearty male companionship or conviviality, no dramatist for the Mermaid Tavern." Much of that real Shaw emerges in his private letters, which show a warm, waggish, witty human being, sometimes sentimental, often selfless, always sincere, whether his strategy utilized Irish blarney, Anglo-Saxon candor, or Shavian paradox. But G.B.S. to the outside world was ruthless as a critic, devastating in wit, irreverent about people, careless of feelings, impudent toward convention, iconoclastic toward institutions, hyperbolic for effect, cold-blooded about politics, second-hand as a thinker—a Mephistopheles-Machiavelli (as Andrew Undershaft in *Major Barbara* is charged) who boasted that he was better than Shakespeare. Few understood the humane vision that articulated what Shaw wrote and did better than his great friend and ideological opposite G. K. Chesterton, who still early in Shaw's career wrote, "Here was a man who could have enjoyed art among the artists, who could have been the wittiest of the flaneurs; who could have made epigrams like diamonds and drunk music like wine. He has instead labored in a mill of statistics and crammed his mind with all the most dreary and most filthy details, so that he can argue on the spur of the moment about sewing-machines or sewage, about typhus fever or twopenny tubes. . . ."

Although Shaw had been experimenting in the drama since his early twenties, not until William Archer suggested a collaboration in 1884 (he to supply the plot, G.B.S. the dialogue) did serious work begin. Even then the project was abandoned when Shaw used up all the projected plot in hardly more than half the play; but eight years later, in 1892, Shaw completed it on his own for J. T. Grein's fledgling Independent Theatre. *Widowers' Houses* had only two performances but created a newspaper sensation all out of proportion to its merits, for it was a dramatized socialist tract on slum landlordism redeemed in part by what Shaw had learned about ironic comedy from Ibsen and Dickens. The romantic predicament of the lovers (who find that both their incomes derive from exploitation of the poor) becomes an economic one and the "happy ending" in which they agree to live happily ever after on their tainted money could not please an audience expecting the threadbare sentimental conventions exploited even by the most daring new playwrights.

Unafraid to satirize himself, or even the new movements he championed, Shaw then in *The Philanderer* invented an "Isben Club" and ironically treated the "New Woman." But no one was willing to produce the play, and Shaw, undeterred, began a third, *Mrs. Warren's Profession* (1893; performed 1902). This time the Lord Chamberlain as Censor of Plays refused it a license, although its ostensible subject, organized commercial prostitution, was treated remorselessly and without the titillation afforded by fashionable comedies about "fallen women" which long had been the West End's stock in trade. To make his seriousness certain, Shaw drew his Mrs. Warren as a vulgarly flashy woman who found that being proprietor of her own body was more advantageous than sweating for a pittance in a factory or a pub, and turned her realization into a chain of profitable brothels. Her daughter Vivie, whose discovery of the facts behind her fashionable Newnham College education sets up the situation of the play, discovers, too, that she cannot look sentimentally for very long at daughterly duty or economic rationalizations. The result is a play with a sardonic thesis built upon the paradox of a form of prostitution meant to symbolize not just social and economic guilt but all the ways in which human beings prostitute their humanity for gain. Labeling as "unpleasant" three of the plays in his first collection, the two-volume edition *Plays, Pleasant and Unpleasant* (1898), Shaw explained that "their dramatic power is being used to force the spectator to face unpleasant facts. No doubt all plays which deal sincerely with humanity must wound the monstrous conceit which it is the business of romance to flatter."

The four "pleasant" plays of the companion volume were Shaw's attempt to find the producers and audiences his mordant comedies put off. "To me," he explained in the preface to the second volume, "[both] the tragedy and comedy of life lie in the consequences, sometimes terrible, sometimes ludicrous, of our persistent attempts to found our institutions on the ideals suggested to our imaginations by our half-satisfied passions, instead of on a genuinely scientific natural history." *Arms and the Man* (1894), in a spoof-Balkan setting, satirized romantic falsifications of love, war, and upward mobility, and was itself romanticized (unauthorized by Shaw) in the Oscar Straus operetta *Der tapfere Soldat* (1908), translated as *The Chocolate Soldier* (1909). *Candida* (1894, performed 1897) seemed to be a conventional comedy-drama about a husband, wife, and young interloper, complete with a happy ending in which the sanctity of the hearth is upheld and the interloper ejected into the night. Beneath the surface, however, the wife—who represents herself in a *tour de force* "auction scene" as being compelled to choose between her stuffy but high-minded clergyman husband (a well-meaning Christian Socialist) and a hysterical and immature young poet—chooses the best of all possible worlds for herself, and the poet renounces what Shaw later called "the small beer of domestic happiness" for the larger creative purpose he senses within himself. The two other "pleasant" plays were of lighter weight. The one-act *The Man of Destiny* (1895, performed 1897) Shaw described as "a bravura piece to display the virtuosity of two performers," but it was more than that. Shaw's antidote to the "older, coarser Napoleon" of earlier plays, this was his first study in greatness. In *You Never Can Tell* (1896, performed 1899) Shaw spun out his themes about parent-child relationships, the equality of women in society, and the power of the sex instinct—the latter bringing together an amorist of uncertain confidence and an impregnably rational New Woman.

Three Plays for Puritans (1901) packaged Shaw's continued output, again with what became the traditional Shavian preface—an introductory essay in an electric prose style dealing as much with the themes suggested by the plays as with the plays themselves. The texts of the plays, made available to the wider reading public for whom his plays were generally inaccessible even when produced, included—a Shaw innovation—stage directions and descriptions in narrative form rather than in brief directorial jargon. *The Devil's Disciple* (1896; performed 1897), a play set in New Hampshire during the American Revolution and written as an inversion of traditional Victorian melodrama, has been accepted by most audiences, eager to fulfill expectations, as authentic melodrama. Dick Dudgeon, however, the black sheep of his family because he rejects Puritan masochism and hypocrisy, appears to be heroically taking the place of a rebel minister whom the English condemn to the gallows, but he manages to do the right things for the wrong reasons. He acts, not in Sydney Carton fashion (Shaw's inspiration for the scene was the final episode of *A Tale of Two Cities*), out of love for the Rev. Anderson's wife, as she supposes, but spontaneously, out of some instinctive imperative. As with Caesar and other significant Shavian characters, virtue is a quality, not an achievement.

Caesar and Cleopatra (1898, performed 1901) was Shaw's first attempt at a play of Shakespearean scope for a heroic actor, in this case Sir Johnston Forbes-Robertson. By choosing a sixteen-year-old Cleopatra, rather than Shakespeare's thirty-eight-year-old temptress of Antony, and a Caesar in Egypt who has not yet been enticed into the domestic demagoguery against which Brutus reacts, Shaw seemingly evades the "Better than Shakespear?" challenge of his preface. His feline Cleopatra, however, is a logical precursor to Shakespeare's voluptuous one; and G.B.S.'s aging Caesar, as much philosopher as soldier in this mentor-disciple play, is meant to be a study in credible magnanimity and "original morality," rather than a superhuman hero on a stage pedestal—in Shaw's words, a hero "in whom we can recognize our own humanity." A seriocomic chronicle play which rises to prose-poetic eloquence and wisdom, it may be the best theatrical work written in English in the nineteenth century. Its companion piece in

Three Plays for Puritans, Captain Brassbound's Conversion (1899, performed 1900), is subtitled "An Adventure" and appears to be little more than that. Here, too, however, are serious themes, particularly that of revenge as misplaced justice, lurking amid the musical-comedy plot about an aristocratic Englishwoman (a role written for Ellen Terry) among brigands in turn-of-the-century Morocco.

In *Man and Superman* (1901–02, performed 1905) Shaw "took the legend of Don Juan in its Mozartian form and made it a dramatic parable of Creative Evolution. But being then at the height of my invention and comedic talent, I decorated it too brilliantly and lavishly. I surrounded it with a comedy of which it formed only one act, and that act was so episodical (it was a dream which did not affect the action of the piece) that the comedy could be detached and played by itself. . . . Also I supplied the published work with an imposing framework consisting of a preface, an appendix called *The Revolutionist's Handbook*, and a final display of aphoristic fireworks. The effect was so vertiginous, apparently, that nobody noticed the new religion in the centre of the intellectual whirlpool." Although Henri Bergson's *Creative Evolution* (1907) was still unwritten, Shaw used the term in a Bergsonian sense to describe the purposeful and eternal movement toward ever higher organisms he saw to be a more satisfactory explanation of the nature of things than "blind" Darwinian evolution, and one which restored a sense of divinity to the universe besides. Subtitled "A Comedy and a Philosophy," the play on the surface is Shaw's equivalent to Congreve's *The Way of the World* (1700), even to a brilliant last-act proposal scene, a comedy of manners about the relations between the sexes in which a resourceful young woman, Ann Whitefield, determines to capture her man, the reluctant John Tanner, who is a social philosopher and socialist propagandist. The action provides the basis for a series of interlocking debates and discussions in which Shaw explored the intellectual climate of the new century. It provides, too, the frame for the nonrealistic third act "Don Juan in Hell" dream scene, often played separately and independently, in which mythic counterparts to four characters in *Man and Superman*, Don Juan Tenorio, Doña Ana, the Commander (Ana's father), and the Devil play out a dramatic quartet that is spoken theatre at its most operatic. Shaw's early operatic education of the hands of his mother and Lee never left him, nor did the effect of his years as a music critic, and he often not only cast his own plays according to the timbre of voice needed, but also shaped his scenes into recitatives, arias, and vocal ensembles. In the duets and arias of the Devil and Don Juan, twentieth-century literature for the stage attained a height in its first years that it would seldom reach again.

At W. B. Yeats's request, Shaw wrote *John Bull's Other Island* (1904) for the Abbey Theatre, Dublin, but the Abbey directors, worried about audience reaction to the wit and honesty of its picture of Ireland, used the excuse of casting difficulties to avoid producing it. Yet Shaw had written into this play of contemporary Anglo-Irish relations, for exhibition to an Irish audience, a comic Englishman as absurd as the comic Irishmen so often seen on the London stage in those days. Although its politics have become dated, the play when performed as a period piece remains a shrewd examination of the Irish character, as well as—in Father Keegan—one of Shaw's earliest explorations of the religious rebel as saint. While performances of his earlier plays in Central Europe had already established him on the continent as a major dramatist, it was the Vedrenne-Barker London production of *John Bull*, including a Command Performance for Edward VII, which finally established Shaw's stage reputation in England. He had backed John Vedrenne's and Harley Granville Barker's management of the Royal Court Theatre, Sloane Square, not only with his own capital but with his own plays as well, and in the years of their association (1904 through 1907), with Barker both acting and directing, a skilled repertory group grew up which gave Shavian drama many of its finest moments. His plays soon drew box-office receipts to such an extent that the Court management, while experimenting with the work of other contemporary dramatists, found it necessary to produce Shaw 701 times (in eleven plays) out of 988 total performances. He had arrived.

Through the medium of high comedy Shaw continued to explore the religious consciousness and to point out society's complicity in its own evils. In *Major Barbara* (written and performed in 1905), Barbara Undershaft, a major in the Salvation Army, discovers that her estranged father, a munitions manufacturer, may be a dealer in Death, but that his principles and practice, however unorthodox, are religious in the highest sense, while those of the Salvation Army require the hypocrisies of often-false public confession and the donations of the distillers and the armorers against which it piously inveighs. Indebted to Plato (*The Republic*) and Euripides (*The Bacchae*) as well as to dozens of other sources, including the lives of such contemporary armaments makers as Nobel and Krupp, it is one of Shaw's most intellectually complex plays, yet ironically also one of his most moving, particularly in its second-act Salvation Army shelter scene (peopled with Dickensian characters) in which Barbara recants her adopted faith.

With his place in the English theatre secure, Shaw began shifting after *Major Barbara* to theatrical experiments already foreshadowed in earlier plays. In *The Doctor's Dilemma* (1906), he produced a comedy with a serio-comic death scene, a satire upon the medical profession (representing the self-protection of professions in general) and upon both the artistic temperament and the public's inability to separate it from the artist's achievement. If Shaw failed to create a convincing artistic genius in the tubercular and double-dealing painter Louis Dubedat, it may be not that he could not depict one, but rather that he aimed at depicting the self-advertising frauds who use the license of "genius" to bilk a world baffled by the artistic temperament.

Other plays of the prewar period ranged from self-described potboilers to an attempt to create a discussion-drama which might best be described as serious farce. *Getting Married* (1907–8), *Misalliance* (1909; performed

1910), and *Fanny's First Play* (1911) are examples of the genre—dramatized debates on marriage, parents and children, and women's rights, respectively. *Misalliance* has since shown remarkable vivacity in revival as a period farce, while the thinner *Fanny's First Play* set a first-run box-office record unequaled by any other Shavian play—622 performances. *The Shewing-up of Blanco Posnet* (1909), set in an improbable American "Wild West," concerned the conversion of a horse thief, aptly subtitled "A Sermon in Crude Melodrama." *Androcles and the Lion* (1912) more successfully handled true and false religious exaltation, combining the traditions of miracle play and Christmas pantomime and transforming the fable of the Greek slave and the Roman lions into a philosophical farce about early Christianity. Its central theme—recurrent in Shaw—is that one must have something worth dying for, a purpose outside oneself, in order to make life worth living. Lavinia, its heroine—like Father Keegan and Barbara Undershaft before her—is a step toward Shaw's Joan of Arc.

Pygmalion (1912; first performed 1913 in Vienna) was claimed by Shaw to be a didactic play about phonetics, and its anti-heroic middle-aged hero, Henry Higgins, is a fanatical phonetician; however, the play is a high and humane comedy about love and class and human dignity—the story of a Cockney flower girl trained to pass as a lady and of the repercussions of the "experiment's" success. Possibly Shaw's comedic masterpiece, and certainly his funniest and most popular play, *Pygmalion* has been both filmed (1938), winning an Academy Award for Shaw (who wrote the screenplay), and turned into a musical, in 1956, as *My Fair Lady*.

The play's London success in 1914 outraged as well as delighted Shaw. Sir Herbert Beerbohm Tree, the Henry Higgins of the production, having played a lifetime of romantic endings, had devised a way to distort Shaw's ironic and ambiguous conclusion without altering a word; in the interval between the last lines of the play and the last lowering of the curtain he would provide by demonstrative affection for Eliza a broad hint that matrimony was in store for the professor and his pupil. Shaw was furious at the Cinderella suggestion and wrote to Tree telling him what he thought of the performance. "My ending makes money; you ought to be grateful," Tree answered smugly. Shaw fired back, "Your ending is damnable: you ought to be shot." And to prevent future fairy-tale endings Shaw wrote an unsentimental short-story epilogue for the published play which "proved" that Eliza would marry the weak Freddy Eynsford Hill and open a successful flower shop with money proffered from Colonel Pickering. "It does not follow in the least," Shaw defended himself to his Edinburgh printer, William Maxwell, nearly twenty years later, "that Liza and Higgins were sexually insensible to each other, or that their sensibility took the form of repugnance . . . ; but the fact stands that their marriage would have been a revolting tragedy and that the marriage with Freddy is the natural and happy ending to the story." But no one acts an undramatized prose epilogue, and Shaw's bittersweet ending to the actual play leaves the Higgins-Eliza relationship more dramatically at its appropriate—and unsettled—point.

The 1914-18 war, which followed immediately upon the success of *Pygmalion*, was a watershed for Shaw. At first he stopped writing plays, producing instead in the first days of the war a lengthy Swiftian pamphlet, *Common Sense About the War* (1914), which called Britain and its allies equally culpable with the Germans and which argued for negotiation and peace. It sold more than 75,000 copies and made him internationally notorious. "It is an established tradition," Shaw wrote years afterward, that he was "a pro-German, a Pacifist, a Defeatist, a Conscientious Objector, and everything that any enemy of his country can be without being actually shot as a traitor. Nothing could be more absolutely wide of the truth." The common sense of his, and similar, arguments prevailed only when the nation was ground down by astronomical—and futile—casualties and home-front austerities, but until 1917 unreason reigned, even to the extent that some of his antiwar speeches were erased from history by newspaper censorship, and he himself was ejected from the Dramatists' Club, although he was its most distinguished member. As the

tide of public opinion turned, the Government's measure
of Shaw's usefulness shifted as well, and in early 1917 he
was even invited to Flanders to report from the front
(*Daily Sketch*, March 6–8, 1917, reprinted in *What I Really
Wrote About the War*, 1931). By the end of the war he
was not that persecuted but proud figure, a major prophet
whom his own people refused to honor, but a confirmed
oracle, a prophet who had survived into his own time. Explaining the metamorphosis, T. S. Eliot afterward remarked that "it might have been predicted that what he
said then would not seem so subversive or blasphemous
now. The public has accepted Mr. Shaw not by recognizing
the intelligence of what he said then, but by forgetting it;
we must not forget that at one time Mr. Shaw was a
very unpopular man. He is no longer the gadfly of the
commonwealth; but even if he has never been appreciated,
it is something that he should be respected."

The unforgetful Shaw translated his experience of
1914–18 (including a Zeppelin raid) into a dozen plays,
sometimes defiantly, sometimes unobtrusively. *Heartbreak
House* (written 1916–17, performed 1920) became the
classic Shavian presentation of the spiritual bankruptcy of
the generation responsible for the war, a departure for him
in that he combined high discursive comedy with an almost
Strindbergian symbolism, producing a somber vision owing
much in mood to Chekhov's *Cherry Orchard* while owing
its elderly leading figure, as well as much else, to Shakespeare's *Lear*. Captain Shotover is eighty-eight and half mad;
and although he tries to recall the heroine from a cynical
despair induced by disillusioned love, his own sense of fore-
boding (he warns that the country must "learn navigation") is expressed in his having turned his skills as an
inventor to military uses. At the end there is an air raid
which causes casualties and destruction, yet there is no
other sign (except for a character playing several bars of
"Keep the Home Fires Burning" on his flute in the last
act) that the action takes place in wartime. The drama's
culminating horror lies, however, not in exploding bombs,
but in the comments of two jaded and once lovesick
women at the curtain, one saying of the unseen and

anonymous raiders in the sky, "But what a glorious experience! I hope they'll come again tomorrow night," and the other ("*radiant at the prospect,*" in Shaw's stage directions) agreeing, "Oh, I hope so." Thanatos has replaced Eros.

Back to Methuselah (1918–20; performed 1922) was Shaw's attempt to keep from falling into "the bottomless pit of an utterly discouraging pessimism." A cycle of five linked plays (*In the Beginning, The Gospel of the Brothers Barnabas, The Thing Happens, The Tragedy of an Elderly Gentleman, As Far as Thought Can Reach*), it created a parable of "Creative Evolution" which progresses from the Garden of Eden to A.D. 31,920, a "Metabiological Pentateuch" which drew imaginatively upon *Genesis*, Plato, Swift, and dozens of other sources, including the war in progress (all but the last part was begun before 1918), with the aim of creating a work of the magnitude of Wagner's *Ring*. The first and most poetic play, from Adam and Eve (and the Serpent) to Cain and Abel, dramatizes the need to overcome death by the renewal of birth, and the need to have aspirations beyond mere subsistence. (Serpent: "You see things; and say 'Why?' But I dream things that never were; and I say 'Why not?' ") Cain, having killed his brother and resenting his plodding father, discovers that he does not know what he wants "except that I want to be something higher and nobler than this stupid old digger." "Man need not always live by bread alone," says Eve. "There is something else." Finding the something else—and the means to it—motivates the cycle.

The second part takes place in the years just after the First World War, and is an indictment of the generation that created the war ("Burge" is Lloyd George, and "Lubin" is Asquith). But in it, too, Conrad Barnabas makes the discovery that sufficient longevity to learn from experience—perhaps three hundred years—might be willed. (The superman is here no longer thought of as attainable through eugenic breeding, Shaw's earlier thesis, and comes with a leap in the third play.) Two undistinguished characters from the second play prove to be still alive in A.D. 2170, and longevity has given them wisdom. In the fourth

play, set in A.D. 3000, an elderly gentleman from the
now-shrinking race of short-livers confronts the conflicting
manners and motives of the passionless and ascetic long-
livers, who possess extraordinary powers over nature, but
—to the Gentleman—no soul. Nevertheless, although he
is warned that he will very likely die of discouragement,
he wants to remain in the land of his ancestors (the scene
is the shore of Galway Bay), rather than return to
the distant land in which his vanishing breed is confined.
"If I go back," he pleads, like Gulliver among the
Houyhnmnmns, "I will die of disgust and despair. . . . It
is the meaning of life, not of death, that makes banishment so terrible to me." He stays, and dies. In the remote
fifth play, with its science-fiction overtones, humans are
born fully developed from eggs and live lives of contem-
plative ecstasy achieved through creative use of intellect
after a brief adolescent phase of physical pleasure. Through
satire which ranges from bright to bleak and through
his futuristic characters, Shaw had progressed from examin-
ing in the first plays how mankind had found itself in its
present predicament to speculating in the closing parts of
the cycle about the uncertain values of escaping from "this
machinery of flesh and blood." An uneven work, it is
compounded of the prosaic as well as the poetic, and it
is dated as well as enlarged by the topical references in
the middle plays. *Back to Methuselah* is nevertheless ennobling in vision although awkward as a total theatre experience.

Convinced that the long cycle had exhausted his creative energies, Shaw anticipated, as he approached seventy,
that he had ended his career as a playwright; however, the
canonization of Joan of Arc in 1920 had reawakened
within him ideas for a chronicle play about the warrior
saint which had never quite been abandoned. For G.B.S.
it would not have been enough to depict Joan as the
sentimental heroine of a melodrama arrayed against a
stage full of stock villains. Neither the militant nor the
martyr in Joan were as important to him as her symbolizing
the possibilities of the race. Thus for Shaw, the Maid is
not only Catholic saint and martyr but Shavian saint and

martyr, a combination of practical mystic, heretical saint, and inspired genius. For this reason Shaw made the conflict as irreconcilable as did Sophocles in his *Antigone*. To give Joan's greatness of soul credibility he had to make her adversaries credible, which meant that Shaw—with more courage than the Vatican itself—had to rehabilitate Cauchon and his clerical colleagues much as Joan herself had been rehabilitated nearly five centuries earlier. As Hegel—whom Shaw had read—suggested, the truly tragic is not to be found in the conflict between right and wrong, but in that between right and right. Joan as the superior being (in the Inquisitor's words), "crushed between those mighty forces, the Church and the Law," is the personification of the tragic heroine, but to Shaw it was not sufficient for his theme. Tragedy was not enough: thus the Epilogue begins with Shavian wit and moves inexorably to litany, transforming the play from a tragedy of inevitability to the embodiment of the paradox that humankind fears—and often kills—its saints and its heroes and will go on doing so until the very qualities it fears become the general condition of man.

Acclaim for *Saint Joan* (1923; performed 1924) resulted in a Shavian apotheosis. Even the Nobel Prize committee could no longer look away, and Shaw received the Prize for Literature in 1925, an honor almost certainly given because of *Joan*. To the consternation of the grantors, he wrote to the Royal Swedish Academy to "discriminate between the award and the prize. For the award I have nothing but my best thanks. But after the most careful consideration I cannot persuade myself to accept the money. My readers and audiences provide me with more than sufficient money for my needs; and as to my renown it is greater than is good for my spiritual health. Under these circumstances the money is a lifebelt thrown to a swimmer who has already reached the shore in safety."

The dream-epilogue to *Saint Joan* had continued Shaw's explorations into tragicomic and nonrealistic symbolism. His last fourteen plays would intensify this aspect of his work, which involved broad, caricatured impersonations, sometimes of Aristophanic extravagance, on which Shaw based a theatre of disbelief. These characterizations were deliberately designed to destroy Ibsenesque verisimilitude by regularly reminding the audience that these were performances in a theatre, not life in a three-walled room or realistic exterior.

During a six-year theatrical silence Shaw worked on his Collected Edition of 1930–38 and the encyclopedic *Intelligent Woman's Guide to Socialism, Capitalism, Sovietism, and Fascism* (1928), an idiosyncratic essay on political economy replete with ironic Shavian asides on education, marriage, religion, law, population, patriotism—and himself. The emphasis upon government led to his Platonic "political extravaganza" *The Apple Cart* (1928; performed 1929), a futuristic comedy which emphasized Shavian inner conflicts between his lifetime of radical politics and his essentially conservative mistrust of the common man's ability to govern himself. Later plays even included apocalyptic imagery, Shaw warning that the 1914–18 war was about to be repeated. The deliberately absurd *Too True to be Good* (1931; performed 1932) is a dream-fantasy including a Bunyanesque prophet, a Lawrence of Arabia caricature, and a burglar-turned-preacher who (as the curtain closes upon him) suggests Shaw confronting his own obsolescence. *On the Rocks* (1933) predicts the collapse of parliamentary government in a proto-fascist, depression-ridden England. *The Simpleton of the Unexpected Isles* (1934; performed 1935), in a futuristic South Seas setting, satirizes a eugenic solution to human problems and ends with a spoof Day of Judgment. *The Millionairess* (1932–34; performed 1936), a "Jonsonian comedy" according to the subtitle, is a knockabout farce which probes the human type of "born boss," while *Geneva* (1936–38; revised 1947) translates the problem into contemporary political terms, lampooning the futile League of Nations as well as dictators Hitler, Mussolini, and Franco, all of whom appear on the stage under nearly invisible disguises. That the despots are treated so lightly suggests that Shaw's flirtation with dictatorships, which arose out of his 1914–18 disillusionment with democracies, was slow in dying, the one with Stalin stubbornly enduring to the end. *In Good*

King Charles's Golden Days (1938–39), his last prewar play, is a throwback to the mood of *The Apple Cart*, a warm yet discursive high comedy in which Charles II, Newton, Fox, Nell Gwynn, and others in "a true history which never happened" debate leadership, science, art, and religion. Eloquent, humorous, and intermittently moving, it dwells further upon the major preoccupation of Shaw's final period. "The riddle of how to choose a ruler is still unanswered," says Charles, "and it is the riddle of civilization." As a result, at eighty-eight he published his final long tract, the discursive yet incisive and aptly named *Everybody's Political What's What?* (1944).

After a second wartime stage hiatus Shaw produced several plays in his nineties. *Buoyant Billions* (begun 1936–1937; completed 1945–47; performed 1948), subtitled "a comedy of no manners," concerned the peregrinations of Junius, a self-styled "world-betterer." *Farfetched Fables* (1948; performed 1950) is a farce in six short scenes, in which Shaw attempted to see into a timeless future which, in his post-atomic outlook, is much different from that envisioned in the *As Far as Thought Can Reach* finale of *Back to Methuselah.*

Shakes versus Shav (1949) is a brief puppet play in which the two playwrights confront each other and gently challenge the greatness of each other's works, Shaw reaffirming his once-shaken evolutionary optimism in the face of Shakespeare's alleged pessimism. They even debate each other's lines, as Aristophanes in *The Frogs* once toyed with Aeschylus and Euripides. Still, at the curtain, "Shav" appeals, "Peace, jealous Bard:/We are both mortal. For a moment suffer/My glimmering light to shine." A last playlet, *Why She Would Not* (1950), a fantasy with flashes of the earlier Shaw in evidence, combines the "born boss" theme with the duel of sex, but has more historical than dramatic interest. As G.B.S. had written in the preface to *Buoyant Billions*, "As long as I live I must write." He did.

Visiting Shaw's house at Ayot St. Lawrence on behalf of the National Trust, to which G.B.S. had willed it, Sir Harold Nicolson was dubious about the government's accepting the unpretentious former rectory. "I am not

happy about it," he noted in his diary. "I do not think
that Shaw will be a great literary figure in 2000 A.D."
But despite that glum prediction in 1950, Bernard Shaw's
"glimmering light" is likely to illuminate stages—and
minds—well into the next century, and after.

STANLEY WEINTRAUB

BIBLIOGRAPHICAL NOTES

The most authoritative text of the plays and prefaces is
*The Bodley Head Bernard Shaw: Collected Plays with
Their Prefaces*, 7 volumes (1970–74), published in the
U.S. as *Complete Plays with their Prefaces* (1975). Penguin editions are being revised to conform with this text.
Shaw's major works, including his collected music and
drama reviews, major critical essays, and novels, and vari-
ous polemical works described in the foregoing biographical
introduction, have previously appeared in the Collected
Edition, 33 volumes (1930–38), and in the Constable
Standard Edition, 38 volumes (1931–50). Posthumous col-
lections of previously uncollected and/or unpublished
essays, speeches, and reviews continue to appear, and include *Shaw on Theatre*, ed. by E. J. West (1958; rev. by
Dan H. Laurence, 1961); *Shaw on Shakespeare*, ed. by
Edwin Wilson (1961); *How to Become a Musical Critic*,
ed. by Dan H. Laurence (1961); *Religious Speeches of
Bernard Shaw*, ed. by W. S. Smith (1963); *Shaw on
Language*, ed. by Abraham Tauber (1963); *Platform and
Pulpit*, ed. by Dan H. Laurence (1961); *The Matter with
Ireland*, ed. by Dan H. Laurence and David H. Greene
(1962); *Bernard Shaw's Nondramatic Literary Criticism*,
ed. by Stanley Weintraub (1972); *The Road to Equality*,
ed. by Louis Crompton (1971), early Socialist lectures;
Practical Politics: Twentieth Century Views on Politics

and Economics, ed. by Lloyd J. Hubenka (1976), post-1906 lectures and articles.

Shaw's *Collected Letters*—a four-volume collection of about 3000 of his most important letters, is in process of publication. The first two volumes, edited by Dan H. Laurence, cover the period 1872–97 (1964) and 1898–1910 (1972). Published individual correspondences include *Ellen Terry and Bernard Shaw*, ed. by Christopher St. John (1931); *Bernard Shaw and Mrs. Patrick Campbell*, ed. by Alan Dent (1952); *Advice to a Young Critic and Other Letters* (to R. Golding Bright), ed. by E. J. West (1955); *Shaw's Letters to Granville Barker*, ed. by C. B. Purdom (1956); "The Nun and the Dramatist" (correspondence with Dame Laurentia McLachlan), *Cornhill*, no. 1008, pp. 415–58 (1956), and *In a Great Tradition*, ed. by the Benedictines of Stanbrook (1956); *To a Young Actress* (Molly Tompkins), ed. by Peter Tompkins (1960).

Although Shaw never wrote an autobiography, *Sixteen Self Sketches* (1949) collects and revises some earlier pieces and adds several new ones; *Shaw: An Autobiography*, 2 vol., ed. by Stanley Weintraub (1969–70), creates a patchwork memoir from Shaw's myriad memoir writings and asides, and includes as appendix his last will and testament.

A Bibliography of Shaw's writings by Dan H. Laurence is in preparation. The earlier bibliographies are fragmentary and obsolete. A continuing bibliography appears in *The Shaw Review*. *A Concordance to the Plays and Prefaces of Bernard Shaw* by E. Dean Bevan (10 volumes, 1972) is based upon the Standard Edition.

Biography: Archibald Henderson, *George Bernard Shaw* (1911; rev. and augmented, 1932 and 1956); Frank Harris, *Bernard Shaw* (1931); Hesketh Pearson, *Bernard Shaw* (1943, augmented 1961); St. John Ervine, *Bernard Shaw* (1956); Allan Chappelow (ed.), *Shaw: The Villager and Human Being* (1961); B. C. Rosset, *Shaw of Dublin: The Formative Years* (1964); Stanley Weintraub, *Private Shaw and Public Shaw* (1963) and *Journey to Heartbreak: The Crucible Years of Bernard Shaw*, 1914–18 (1971);

Janet Dunbar, *Mrs. G. B. S.* (1963); J. P. Smith, *The Unrepentant Pilgrim* (1965).

Criticism: Early studies include: H. L. Mencken, *George Bernard Shaw: His Plays* (1905); G. K. Chesterton, *George Bernard Shaw* (1909, augmented 1935); Julius Bab, *Bernard Shaw* (1910, rev. 1926; in German); and P. P. Howe, *Bernard Shaw: A Critical Study* (1915). Later criticism includes E. Strauss, *Bernard Shaw: Art and Socialism* (1942); Stephen Winsten (ed.), *G.B.S. 90* (1946); Eric Bentley, *Bernard Shaw* (1947); William Irvine, *The Universe of G.B.S.* (1949); C. E. M. Joad, *Shaw* (1949); Alick West, *George Bernard Shaw: A Good Man Fallen Among Fabians* (1950); Desmond MacCarthy, *Shaw* (1951), a collection of his Shavian reviews over several decades; Arthur H. Nethercot, *Men and Supermen*, 2d ed. rev. (1966); Raymond Mander and Joe Mitchenson, *A Theatrical Companion to Shaw* (1954); Julian B. Kaye, *Bernard Shaw and the Nineteenth-Century Tradition* (1958); Richard M. Ohmann, *Shaw: The Style and the Man* (1962); Martin Meisel, *Shaw and the Nineteenth-Century Theatre* (1963); J. I. M. Stewart, in *Eight Modern Writers* (1963); Donald P. Costello, *The Serpent's Eye: Shaw and the Cinema* (1965); Louis Crompton, *Shaw the Dramatist* (1969); Bernard F. Dukore, *Bernard Shaw, Director* (1971) and *Bernard Shaw, Playwright* (1973); Margery Morgan, *The Shavian Playground* (1972); Maurice Valency, *The Cart and the Trumpet, The Plays of George Bernard Shaw* (1973); Charles A. Berst, *Bernard Shaw and the Art of Drama* (1973); Alfred Turco, *Shaw's Moral Vision: The Self and Salvation* (1976); Rodelle Weintraub, ed., *Fabian Feminist, Shaw and Woman* (1976), includes some of Shaw's own early feminist writings.

THE PORTABLE BERNARD SHAW

To Arnold White

XXXXXXXXXXXXXXXXXXXXXXXXXXXXXXXXXXXXXXXXXXXX

Arnold White was manager and secretary of the Edison Telephone Company of London, to whom Shaw received an introduction from his cousin Mrs. Cashel Hoey. The novel which he was revising was Immaturity, *which he had begun in March 1879 and which was completed on 28th September 1879.*

The testimonial mentioned in the postscript is dated 9th August 1878, and reads:

"Mr. George Shaw served in our office from 1st November, 1871 to 31st. March 1876 when he left at his own desire.

"He entered as a youth and left us having attained to the position of Cashier.

"He is a young man of great business capacity, strict accuracy, and was thoroughly reliable and trustworthy.

"Anything given him to do, was always accurately & well done. We parted from him with regret, and shall always be glad to hear of his welfare.

> *C. Uniacke Townshend & Co.*
> *Land Agents."*

> 13 Victoria Grove SW
> 5th October 1879

After our recent conversation, I think it best to tell you what my circumstances are, as your experience will enable you to judge of my position better probably than I can myself.

When I was fifteen, I left school—where I had learnt nothing—and entered the office of a leading firm of land-agents in Dublin as junior clerk, at a salary of £18 a year. In this post I sulkily distinguished myself so much that when, a year later, the cashier, an elderly man whose testimonials were quite as flattering as that which I enclose, absconded, I took his place, and kept it. Its duties were the receipt and payment of the rents, insurances, charges, private debts &c on many estates with occasional trips to the country to make collections. They acted also as private bankers, & to a certain extent, confidential agents to their clients, and hence I became accustomed to handling large sums of money and to meeting men of all conditions. I should mention that there were no bill transactions, and that therefore I know very little about this branch of business.

My post being the most active & responsible in the office, I resisted offers of promotion as being in the nature of kicking me upstairs. However, the firm desired to place a relative of theirs at the cash desk, and so I eventually became a general clerk, that is to say, I had nothing to do, and drew an increased salary for doing it. At this time, having learnt all that the office could teach me, and feeling uncomfortable in its narrow Irish atmosphere, I resigned, rejected an offer of reinstatement as cashier, and came to London, where my mother and sisters had been for some time. This was in April 1876. I at first prepared to enter the civil service, but as I was neither a linguist nor a mathematician, I had to study for a small berth. Whilst I was doing so, and getting very impatient of the society of schoolboys and the tutelage of a grinder, a friend of mine who was musical critic to a weekly paper, offered me the emoluments of the post if I would discharge its duties. I threw up my studies, and set to work to reform the musical profession. At the end of a year my friend was one of the most unpopular men in London, the paper was getting into difficulties, and complications were arising from the proprietor's doubts as to a critic who was not only very severe, but capable of being in two places at the same time. I gave up that too (making a virtue of necessity), and the proprietor presently retired, ruined.

In the last two years I have not filled any post, nor have I been doing anything specially calculated to qualify me for a business one. During the first half of that time, I was

unsettled, and much in that active, but unproductive vein
in which an immature man wanders about London at
night, plans extravagant social reforms, reads Shelley, and
so forth. I wrote a few unsuccessful articles, studied harmony and counterpoint, and wrote a novel, which I am
now revising. It cost me five months labour, and I have
no means of publishing it when it is finished.

My only reason for seeking commercial employment is
a pecuniary one. I know how to wait for success in literature, but I do not know how to live on air in the interim.
My family are in difficulties. I may be deceived as to my
literary capacity, and in any case, it is as well to be independent of a fine art if clean work is to be made in it.
Experience of the organisation & administration of such
an enterprise as yours, which is in some sort a tangible
part of civilization, would be worth working for. I have
no illusions on the subject of business, and although it is
exhilarating to make a clever stroke occasionally, the
everyday work is too serious, in my opinion, to be undertaken for the purpose (as in landagency) of enriching
an individual at the expense of the community. However,
I should be loth to press you for a place in which I might
not be the right man. If you can give me any hints as
to what I might do with myself elsewhere, I shall be well
satisfied, for I know you will be able [to] understand my
position. Hitherto I have disregarded so much advice from
well intentioned friends, that I am reputed almost as
impracticable as another member of the family with whom
you are acquainted.

Pray excuse the length of this letter. I understood that
you desired to get some idea of my character, and this I
could not have given you by confining myself to facts which
would not distinguish me from the next fifty clerks who
might apply to you. Narrative too, is a congenial form
to me.

It only remains to thank you again for your exceedingly
kind reception of my informal visit.

faithfully yrs
[G. B. Shaw]

P.S. The testimonial was obtained without my knowledge from Messrs Townshend more than two years after I had left there by my father. Doubtless you know how little such documents are worth.

To Macmillan & Co.

XXXXXXXXXXXXXXXXXXXXXXXXXXXXXXXXXXXXXXXXX

In rejecting Shaw's fifth and last-completed novel, An Un-social Socialist, *Macmillan had added consolingly that they "would be glad to look at anything else [Shaw] might write of a more substantial kind."*

36 Osnaburgh Street NW
14 January 1885

Many thanks for reading An Unsocial Socialist. Your demand for "something more substantial" takes my breath away. Your reader, I fear, thought the book not serious— perhaps because it was not dull. If so, he was an Englishman. I have only met one reviewer [J. M. Robertson] and one oral critic [William Archer] who really took the book in. They were both Scotchmen. You must admit that when one deals with two large questions in a novel, and throws in an epitome of modern German socialism as set forth by Marx as a makeweight, it is rather startling to be met with an implied accusation of triviality.

yours faithfully
George Bernard Shaw

"The Classes and Musical Culture"

XXXXXXXXXXXXXXXXXXXXXXXXXXXXXXXXXXXXXX

31 May 1889

Elsewhere you will find a letter on The Music of the People, by Mr Marshall-Hall, a young composer who is much spoken of among the young lions of Mr Hamish McCunn's generation. At one of Mr Henschel's concerts Mr Stanley sang some portions of an opera, the poem and music of which were by Mr Marshall-Hall. I was not at that concert, so I am quite out of it as far as Mr Marshall-Hall's music is concerned; but I am delighted to find him, as a representative of young genius, denouncing the stalls, trusting to the gallery, waving the democratic flag, and tearing round generally.

Young genius has rather a habit, by the way, of writing to my editor to denounce me as flippant and unenlightened, and to demand that I also shall tear round and proclaim the working man as the true knower and seer in Art. If I did, the working man would not think any the better of me; for he knows well enough that society is not divided into "animated clothes-pegs" on the one hand and lovers of Beethoven in ligatured corduroys on the other. For Beethoven purposes society is divided into people who can afford to keep a piano and go to operas and concerts, and people who cannot. Mr Marshall-Hall's idea that the people who cannot are nevertheless screwed up to concert pitch by honest, thorough, manly toil, shews that, though he be an expert in the music question, in the labor question he is a greenhorn.

Take a laborer's son; let him do his board-schooling mostly on an empty stomach; bring him up in a rookery tenement; take him away from school at thirteen; offer him the alternative of starvation or 12 to 16 hours work a day at jerry building, adulterated manufactures, coupling

railway waggons, collecting tramway fares, field labor, or
what not, in return for food and lodging which no "animated clothes-peg" would offer to his hunter; bully him;
slave-drive him; teach him by every word and look that
he is not wanted among respectable people, and that his
children are not fit to be spoken to by their children. This
is a pretty receipt for making an appreciator of Beethoven.

The truth is, that in the innumerable grades of culture
and comfort between the millionaire on the one hand,
and the casual laborer on the other, there is a maximum
of relish for art somewhere. That somewhere is certainly
not among the idle rich, whose appetites for enjoyment
are not sharpened by work, nor is it among those who,
worn out by heavy muscular toil, fall asleep if they sit
quiet and silent for five minutes of an evening. Professional
and business men of musical tastes who work hard, and
whose brains are of such a quality that a Beethoven
symphony is a recreation to them instead of an increased
strain on their mental powers, are keen patrons of music,
though, in outward seeming, they belong to the animated
clothes-peg section. Middle-class young ladies, to whom
there is no path to glory except that of the pianist or prima
donna, frequent St James's Hall with astonishing persis-
tence, and eventually form musical habits which outlast
their musical hopes.

The musical public is the shilling public, by which I
mean the people who can afford to pay not more than
a shilling once a week or so for a concert without going
short of more immediately necessary things. Music can
be better nourished on shilling, six-penny, and threepenny
seats than on the St James's Hall scale. The laborers are
so enormously numerous that the absolute number of their
exceptional men—men who will buy books out of 13s. a
week in the country and 18s. in a town, and find time to
read them while working 12 hours a day—is considerable.
The more comfortable members of the artisan class can
often afford a shilling much better than the poorer middle-
class families; but it has a certain customary and traditional scale of expenditure, in which concerts stand at
threepence or sixpence, shillings being reserved for the

gallery of a West-end theatre, and half-crowns for Sunday trips to Epping Forest and for extra refreshments.

After these come the innumerable "poor devils" of the middle class, always craving in an unaccountable way for music, and crowding the Promenade Concerts on classical nights, the Albert Hall gallery, and wherever else decent music is to be heard cheaply. To these three classes Mr Marshall-Hall must look for the little that is now possible in the way of a musical public. Even when we have supplied all three with as much music as they can stomach, the laborer in ligatured corduroys will still open his eyes to darkness, and the vapid snob grub like a blind puppy in the light. What we want is not music for the people, but bread for the people, rest for the people, immunity from robbery and scorn for the people, hope for them, enjoyment, equal respect and consideration, life and aspiration, instead of drudgery and despair. When we get that I imagine the people will make tolerable music for themselves, even if all Beethoven's scores perish in the interim.

Pending these millennial but perfectly practical measures, I must beg my readers not to blame me if the progress of the race makes it more and more apparent that the middle-class musical critic is the most ridiculous of human institutions. I do not take my function seriously, because it is impossible for an intelligent man to do so; and I am an eminently intelligent man. I often yield to quite romantic impulses. For instance, when Miss Adrienne Verity sent me a ticket for her concert at Collard's the other day, I went because Adrienne Verity struck me as being a pretty name. And I must own that I found her a pleasant-faced, well-grown lass, with refreshingly unceremonious ways and a healthy boisterousness which would make her the life and soul of a haymaking. But a singer! an artist! not yet. The way in which that young lady plunged into *Saper vorreste*, and rampaged through Be wise in time, and fired off Cherry Ripe at us, was bewildering. When ladies and children came forward with trophies of flowers, and did her floral homage as a Queen of Song, my brain reeled. And now I suppose that Miss Verity, having invited me to hear her sing, expects me to give her my opinion. My opinion is that she will either study hard with a competent teacher for a couple of years to come, learning to sing, to speak, to walk, to bow, and to abjure premature concerts and flower offerings, or else she will find a place in Mr D'Oyly Carte's or Mr Leslie's chorus, and there unskilfully scream her voice away in less than six months. And whoever gives her a more flattering opinion will do her a very cruel kindness.

Of the numerous concerts which I unavoidably missed, none caused me any particular regret, except the performance by pupils of the Royal Normal College for the Blind at the Crystal Palace, and a Board School contest at Hampstead, which the head master was quite right in bringing under my notice. It was, for example, much more important than Miss McKenzie's concert at Dudley House, which has been much written about, and concerning which I have nothing whatever to say except that it went off very successfully; that Mr Giddings amused me by his recitation; that the Dudley pictures interested me more than the music; and that the Dudley livery of black and yellow continually reminded me of the contrast between the gildings in Park-lane and the gloom of the coal pits wherein that gilding is made.

I need hardly say that my remarks about the Tonic Sol-Fa have brought letters upon me insisting on the attractive simplicity of the notation, and even inviting me to learn it myself forthwith. This reminds me of a sage whom I consulted in my youth as to how I might achieve the formation of a perfect character. "Young man" he said "are you a vegetarian?" I promptly said "Yes" which took him aback. (I subsequently discovered that he had a weakness for oysters.) "Young man" he resumed "have you mastered Pitman's shorthand?" I told him I could write it very nearly as fast as longhand, but that I could not read it; and he admitted that this was about the maximum of human attainment in phonography. "Young man" he went on "do you understand phrenology?"

This was a facer, as I knew nothing about it; but I was determined not to be beaten, so I declared that it was my favorite pursuit, and that I had been attracted to him by the noble character of his bumps. "Young man" he continued "you are indeed high on the Mount of Wisdom. There remains but one accomplishment to the perfection of your character. Are you an adept at the Tonic Sol-Fa system?" This was too much. I got up in a rage, and said: "Oh, dash the Tonic Sol-Fa system!" Then we came to high words; and our relations have been more or less strained ever since. I have always resolutely refused to learn the Tonic Sol-Fa, as I am determined to prove that it is possible to form a perfect character without it.

"Solemnity and Triviality"

XXXXXXXXXXXXXXXXXXXXXXXXXXXXXXXXXXXXXXXX

25 June 1890

I have been getting my mind improved at the Crystal Palace. Naturally that was not what I went for. My sole object in submitting to the unspeakable boredom of listening to St. Paul on Saturday afternoon was to gain an opening for an assault on the waste of our artistic resources—slender enough, in all conscience, even with the strictest economy—caused in England every year by the performance and publication of sham religious works called oratorios. In so far as these are not dull imitations of Handel, they are unstaged operettas on scriptural themes, written in a style in which solemnity and triviality are blended in the right proportions for boring an atheist out of his senses or shocking a sincerely religious person into utter repudiation of any possible union between art and religion. However, there is an intermediate class in England which keeps up the demand in the oratorio market. This class holds that the devil is not respectable (a most unsophisticated idea); but it deals with him in a spirit of extraordinary liberality in dividing with him the kingdom of the fine arts. Thus in literature it gives him all the novels, and is content to keep nothing but the tracts. In music it gives him everything that is played in a theatre, reserving the vapidities of the drawing room and the solemnities of the cathedral for itself. It asks no more in graphic art than a set of illustrations to its family Bible, cheerfully devoting all other subjects to the fiend. But people who make a bad bargain never stick to it. These ascetics smuggle fiction under the covers of the Society for the dissemination of their own particular sort of knowledge; drama in the guise of "entertainments"; opera in scores labelled "cantata" or "oratorio"; and Venus and

Apollo catalogued as Eve and Adam. They will not open
a novel of Boisgobey's, because novels are sinful; but
they will read with zest and gloating how The Converted
Collier used to beat his mother in the days when he was
an unregenerate limb of Satan. They console themselves
for Coquelin by Corney Grain; and, since they may not
go to Macbeth at the Lyceum, they induce Mr Irving to
dress the Thane in a frock-coat and trousers, and transport
him, Sullivan, Miss Terry, and all, to St James's Hall. It is
just the same with music. It is wrong to hear the Covent
Garden orchestra play Le Sommeil de Juliette; but if
Gounod writes just such another interlude, and calls it
The Sleep of the Saints before the Last Judgment, then
nothing can be more proper than to listen to it in the
Albert Hall. Not that Gounod is first favorite with the
Puritans. If they went to the theatre they would prefer
a melodramatic opera with plenty of blood in it. That
being out of the question, they substitute an oratorio with
plenty of damnation. The Count di Luna, grinding his
teeth and longing to "centuplicar la morte" of his rival
with "mille atroci spasimi," is a comparatively tame creature until he takes off his tunic and tights, hies to a
"festival," and, in respectable evening-dress, shouts that
"the Lord is angry with the wicked every day," and that
"if the wicked [meaning the people who go to the Opera]
turn not, the Lord will whet His sword and bend His bow."
What a day Sunday must be for the children of the oratorio
public! It was prime, no doubt, at the Crystal Palace on
Saturday, to hear the three thousand young ladies and
gentlemen of the choir, in their Sunday best, all shouting
"Stone him to death: stone him to death"; and one could
almost hear the satisfied sigh of Mr Chadband as St Paul's
"God shall surely destroy them" was followed in due
time by the piously fugal "See what love hath the Father
bestowed on us." But to me, constitutional scoffer that I
am, the prostitution of Mendelssohn's great genius to this
lust for threatening and vengeance, doom and wrath, upon
which he should have turned his back with detestation, is
the most painful incident in the art-history of the century.
When he saw Fra Diavolo, he was deeply scandalized at

the spectacle of Zerlina undressing herself before the looking-glass on her wedding eve, singing "Oui, c'est demain," with the three brigands peeping at her through the curtains. "I could not set such things to music," he said; and undoubtedly the theme was none too dignified. But was it half so ignoble and mischievous as the grovelling and snivelling of Stiggins, or the raging and threatening of Mrs Clennam, which he glorified in St Paul and Elijah? I do not know how it is possible to listen to these works without indignation, especially under circumstances implying a parallel between them and the genuine epic stuff of Handel, from which, in spite of their elegance, they differ as much as Booth does from Bunyan. The worst of it is that Mendelssohn's business is still a going concern, though his genius has been withdrawn from it. Every year at the provincial festivals some dreary doctor of music wreaks his counterpoint on a string of execrable balderdash with Mesopotamia or some other blessed word for a title. The author is usually a critic, who rolls his own log in his paper whilst his friendly colleagues roll it elsewhere. His oratorio, thus recommended, is published in the familiar buff cover, and played off on small choral societies throughout the country by simple-minded organists, who display their knowledge by analysing the fugues and pointing out the little bits of chorus in six real parts. In spite of the flagrant pedantry, imposture, corruption, boredom, and waste of musical funds which the oratorio system involves, I should not let the cat out of the bag in this fashion if I thought it could be kept in much longer; for who knows but that some day I might get into business myself as a librettist, and go down to posterity as the author of St Nicholas Without and St Walker Within, a sacred oratorio, founded on a legend alluded to by Charles Dickens, and favorably noticed in the columns of The World and other organs of metropolitan opinion? But I fear I was born too late for this. The game is up; and I may as well turn Queen's evidence whilst there is some credit to be got by it.

As for the performance at the Crystal Palace, it was, with the three thousand executants, a rare debauch of its kind; and except that it was dragged out to twice its

normal length by the slow *tempi* taken by Mr Manns—
unnecessarily slow, I think—the effect was not so inferior
to that of a performance on the proper scale as might have
been expected from so monstrous a piece of overdoing.
Edward Lloyd sang without a fault, and Mr Watkin Mills'
vocal style was excellent. Madame Albani pulled the music
about in her accustomed fashion by hanging on to every
note that shewed off her voice, and her intonation, compared with that of her three colleagues, was fallible, but
she was otherwise equal to the occasion. Madame Patey
was at her best, as she generally is at such functions.

"Bands and Bridges"

XXXXXXXXXXXXXXXXXXXXXXXXXXXXXXXXXXXXXXXXXXXXX

2 July 1890

The concert last week in aid of the project for establishing a municipal band in London reminded me of the late Edmund Gurney's demand for an orchestra for the East End. If I had my way in the matter the money should not be raised by a concert and a subscription list, as if the London County Council were a distressed widow: a fitter course would be to levy the cost by the strong hand of the tax-collector on the thousands of well-to-do people who never go to a concert because they are "not musical," but who enjoy, all the same, the health-giving atmosphere which music creates. Just as the river is useful to men who do not row, the bridges to West Enders who never cross them, and the railways to the bedridden, so the provision of good music and plenty of it smooths life as much for those who do not know the National Anthem from Rule Britannia, as for those who can whistle all the themes in the Ninth Symphony. Now that we have renounced the hideous absurdity of keeping up Waterloo Bridge out of the halfpence of the people who actually go over it, it is pitiable to have to go back to that ridiculous system for a town band. We certainly want such a band, though not because private enterprise has been behindhand in the matter. On the contrary, it is because private enterprise every Sunday sends a procession, religious or Radical, past my windows every five minutes or so, each headed by a band, that I feel the need for some model of excellence to hold up to these enthusiastic instrumentalists. In Lancashire and Yorkshire there are, it is computed, twenty thousand bandsmen.

When I was in Bristol some time ago, a fifteen minutes' walk through the working-class quarter on Sunday morn-

ing brought me across three bands, two of them by no
means bad ones. In London you can, on the occasion of
a big "demonstration," pass down a procession miles long
without ever being out of earshot of at least two bands.
The cultured class sometimes, when suffering from an
attack of nerves, wants the band-playing class to be dis-
persed and silenced; but this cannot now be effectively done
for the band-playing outnumber the cultured five to one,
and two-thirds of them have votes.

Whether we like the bands or not, we must put up with
them: let us therefore, in self-defence, help them to make
themselves fairly efficient. It is certain that they are not so
good as they might be at present, and that as long as they
never hear anything better than their own music they will
remain much as they are. Their instruments are not so
bad as might be supposed. They may not come from the
first-class stocks of Mahillon, Courtois, or Boosey; but the
competition between instrument-makers has resulted in
the production of fairly good brass instruments of the
simpler types (cornets, saxhorns, etc.) at reasonable prices
payable by instalments. Hence the fortuitous German
bombardon with cylinders, bought at a pawnshop, and
pitched nearly half-a-tone lower than its British com-
panions in the band, is now scarcer than it used to be,
though unhappily it is not yet extinct.

But even in bands in which the instruments are all
manufactured to English military pitch and of endurable
quality, with players whose ears are not satisfied until they
have adjusted their tuning-slides and their blowing so as
to get the notes made with the pistons tolerably in tune,
chaos sets in the moment the music goes beyond the
simplest diatonic harmonies. At the occurrence of one
of the series of tonic discords which are so freely used in
modern music, and which make the six old gentlemen who
form the anti-Wagner party in Paris put their fingers to
their ears, the working-class bandsman not only does not
know whether he is in tune or out, but he actually does not
know whether he is playing the right note, so strange is
the chord to his ear. Consequently he is limited to the banal
quicksteps and tiresome Boulanger marches which confirm

him in his vulgar and obvious style of execution. Even a Schubert march is beyond him, because the modulations, simple and brilliantly effective as they are, are not solely from tonic to dominant and back again. The only way to rescue him from his groove is to familiarize him with the sound of modern polyphony in all its developments. A gentleman can do this for himself at his pianoforte; but a wage-earner who has to buy a modest two-guinea cornet by laborious instalments is as likely to learn driving on his own four-in-hand as modern music at his own Steinway.

You must send round to Victoria Park, Finsbury Park, Battersea Park, Peckham Rye, Hampstead Heath, and Blackheath a numerous, well paid, honorably esteemed, highly skilled, and splendidly equipped band, with a conductor who puts music before applause, the chance of a knighthood, loyalty, morals, religion, and every other earthly or unearthly consideration—a municipal August Manns, in short. This is the only way to teach the bandsman of the street and his patrons how his quicksteps with their three chords and one modulation have been improved on by Schubert, Offenbach, Auber, and Rossini, by Weber, Mendelssohn, and Goetz, and finally by Beethoven and Wagner. Let him pick all this up through his ears, and he will come out with a much sounder knowledge than that of the literate person who knows that Wagner is "marvellous" by reading statements to that effect in the critical scriptures of the day. In the end he will pay back the outlay; for when he is qualified as a consumer and producer of good music, the resultant cheapness and plenty will bring down the exorbitant cost of even the Opera. Think of that, ye golden ones whose Oriental names I read on the box-doors as I stroll about Mr Harris' corridors of an evening during the *entr'actes*; and do not let the Municipal Band Fund fall through for lack of subscriptions. . . .

To Florence Farr Emery

XXXXXXXXXXXXXXXXXXXXXXXXXXXXXXXXXXXXXXX

Leaving a Fabian Society meeting early to call on Mrs. Emery, Shaw "found the place in darkness," noting in his diary, "Wandered about disappointed. . . ."

29 Fitzroy Square W.
4 May 1891

Miserable, ill starred woman, what have you done? When my need was at its highest, my weariness at its uttermost, my love at its holiest, I found darkness, emptiness, void. I cannot believe now that we shall ever meet again. Years have passed over me—long solemn years: I have fallen in with my boyhood's mistress, Solitude, and wandered aimlessly with her once more, drifting like the unsatisfied moon. Tears have dropped from my heart—tears of mortal disappointment, reminding me of the days when disappointment seemed my inevitable & constant lot. I have lost my faith in all the achievement & confidence since that time: whatever my dreams may have been, I have slept where I was born, in the valley of the shadow. How could you do this thing? Are there no subtle fluids, no telepathic wires, to tell you when the chapter of accidents sets me free from my chains? This was to have been the happiest of all my great happinesses, the deepest and restfullest of all my tranquillities, the very inmost of all my loves. And I was robbed of it in the moment of embracing it by your caprice, your wanton caprice—you told me you had nothing to do. And I contrived so ingeniously, so patiently; sent my mother to the opera; induced a colleague to break an engagement I was bound to keep with him; left one meeting early and gave another the slip; and for what? Wretch! selfish, indifferent, heartless wretch! A million reproaches on you for ever and ever. Farewell: all the

happiness I owe you is cancelled and the balance is now
on the other side—a huge balance, incalculable, unliquida-
table. You can never repay me.

GBS

"The Playwright on His First Play"
(An interview, drafted by Shaw, on *Widowers' Houses*.
The Star, 29 November 1892)

XXXXXXXXXXXXXXXXXXXXXXXXXXXXXXXXXXXXXXXX

I am an experienced interviewer; but I confess that when
The Star editor directed me to tackle Bernard Shaw on
the subject of the play he has written for the Independent
Theatre, I felt nervous. "Keep him to the point," said the
editor. "Be firm, or he will talk your head off without once
alluding to the play." Though quaking inwardly, I looked
bold as I assured my chief he might rely on me. Then I
went off to the well-known number in Fitzroy-sq., and
arrived there about half-past eleven in the morning. The
door was furnished with several bells, one of them bearing
the name SHAW. I performed on this instrument for
some 12 minutes in vain, concluding with a five minutes'
fantasia on all the other bells. Then I was joined by a
rather attractive young woman in an ulster, come, as I
gathered, to help the eminent Socialist by looking after
the household work. She informed me that it was extremely improbable that Mr. Shaw would be up at that
early hour, and, on my criticising the bells, remarked
apologetically that there was one of them that rang sometimes. However, she let me in, which was, after all, the
main thing; and brought me up some desolate stone steps
to the second floor,

WHERE I FOUND MR. SHAW
in a very small room, completely blocking up the narrow
passage between the wide-open window and the door as he
sat between the fire and the table in a substantial chair
fortified by a strong wooden rail, with a typewriter on its
stand before him. The table was untidy beyond belief: dusty
heaps of letters and papers in utter disorder were mixed up
with stationery, inkstands, *Stars, Chronicles*, butter, sugar,
stray apples, knives and spoons, a full breakfast cup of

cocoa, and a plate upon which Mr. Shaw, as I entered, was dumping down a helping of porridge which he had just extracted from a saucepan on the hob. I confess I felt embarrassed. Not so my host. He received me affably, with entire confidence in the propriety of his surroundings, and piloted me between the Scylla of the typewriter and the Charybdis of the blazing fire to a chair by the window. Before I was fairly seated he began a most brilliant account of the entire history of *The Star* newspaper from its inception to the present time. This gave me 15 minutes to make a note of two photographs—one of Mr. Toft's bust of Cunninghame Graham over the mantelshelf, and the other, over the table, of the well-known horse's head from the Naples museum. Also to study Mr. Shaw's costume, and to observe that he wore

A GRAY COLLAR AND SANDALS.

"And now, Mr. Shaw," I said, "what about 'Wendover's Horses'?"

"What do you mean?"

"Your play, Mr. Shaw. That is the title given by one of the evening papers."

"Nonsense. 'Widowers' Houses' is the title."

"Why 'Widowers' Houses' if I may ask?"

"I thought you would have recognised the allusion. I have been assured that in one of the sections of the Bible dealing with the land question there is a clause against the destruction of widows' houses. There is no widow in my play; but there is a widower who owns slum property. Hence the title. Perhaps you are not familiar with the Bible."

I apologised for not catching the reference. My next question was,

"To what genre does the play belong? Comedy, tragedy, farce, or melodrama?"

"To none of them. To Humanity solely. That is the only genre I recognize."

"Is it true, Mr. Shaw, that Sir Augustus Harris has consented to play one of the leading parts?"

"Unhappily, no. It's only an idle rumor. I wish it were

true. It would give me a practical opportunity of imparting my views on stage management to Sir Augustus, who
recognises my merits as an operatic critic."

"Have you heard that Mr. Clement Scott is returning
from the East to be present at the performance?"

"I have not heard it; but it is, of course, quite possible."

"I see that your play is announced by the Independent
Theatre as 'a didactic, realistic drama.' May I venture to
hope that it will

NOT BE TOO DIDACTIC?"

"Sir," said Mr. Shaw sternly, "it will be nothing else
than didactic. Do you suppose I have gone to all this
trouble to *amuse* the public? No, if they want that, there
is the Criterion for them, the Comedy, the Garrick, and
so on. My object is to instruct them."

"Quite so. Do you find that the stage manager takes
that view?"

"I am sorry to say that he does not. I cannot understand
it in so clever a man. You know him—Hermann de Lange,
who did that perfect bit of acting in 'Thérèse Raquin'—
an artist to the tip of his fingers, a master of nuances that
not one actor in ten can distinguish, one from whom even
I have learnt something—a man with such a confounded
vivacity of imagination that he conceives every character
in my play six times over at each rehearsal, and conceives it
differently every time. Well, I cannot make de Lange see
the importance of appealing to the audience on the solid
ground of political economy. There is a situation in the
second act—the climax of the play—which really requires
to be explained by one of the leading characters on a
blackboard by means of a diagram. They actually want to
cut out the blackboard. De Lange keeps saying, 'My dear
boy you can't get a blackboard over the footlights.' I
explain to him that I don't want to get it over the footlights—that I want it to stand on the stage, not to have it
handed round the stalls. But he only laughs at me and
says I don't understand the theatre. All I can say is that
I will not be responsible for the success of the scene

IF THE BLACKBOARD IS OMITTED.

The public cannot possibly understand the economic point without the diagram." (Here Mr. Shaw drew the diagram for me, and explained at great length the bearing on the play of the value theory of the late Professor Stanley Jevons. It was most interesting.)

"You must not suppose, however, that this is my only difficulty with the Independent Theatre. They have the most limited ideas as to the proper length for a play. They say two hours and a half. I say that this may be all very well for the idle pleasure-seekers, but that an audience of genuine enthusiasts, attending the theatre with serious aims, would not grudge five hours. That is clear, is it not?"

"Unquestionably, Mr. Shaw. And is the play to last five hours, if I may ask?"

"No. There is only time to learn three acts of it, which will occupy no more than the usual time."

"How many acts, then, are there in the whole play?"

"Seventeen. 'Widowers' Houses' is a mere episode in a historic drama." (Here Mr. Shaw held me spellbound for nearly an hour with a brilliant aperçu of the social and industrial development of England from the Reformation up to the twenty-second century, of which he has the clearest prevision.)

"May I ask for a sketch of the plot of your play, Mr. Shaw? As you do not wish to amuse the public, you need not, I presume, hesitate to disclose it."

"There is no plot. The hero, who has no conventionally heroic qualities, loves the heroine, who has no conventionally amiable ones. She has, in fact,

AN ABOMINABLE TEMPER.

Her father, a widower, offers to provide handsomely for the young couple. But the hero discovers that the widower's money comes from the rents of a slum property—a horrible example of house knacking. Like a true son of the middle-class, he recoils with horror from the idea of profiting by such an iniquity until he discovers that his own little income is equally compromised. He then sorrowfully admits that 'such things must be.' This is the point which I wanted to have demonstrated on the blackboard."

"May we anticipate some of your unrivalled touches of humor, Mr. Shaw?"

"Certainly not. I have removed with the greatest care every line that could possibly provoke a smile. I have been greatly misunderstood in this matter. Being an Irishman, I do not always see things exactly as an Englishman would: consequently my most serious and blunt statements sometimes raise a laugh and create an impression that I am intentionally jesting. I admit that some Irishmen do take advantage of the public in this way. Wilde, unquestionably the ablest of our dramatists, has done so in 'Lady Windermere's Fan.' There are lines in that play which were put in for no other purpose than to make the audience laugh."

" 'Widowers' Houses' will be quite free from that sort of thing, then?"

"Absolutely. However, I do not blame Wilde. He wrote for the stage as an artist. I am simply a propagandist."

"Has the play been refused by many London managers?"

"It has never been offered to one. Why should it? They are not interested in propaganda. Since I wrote it in 1885, I have been too busy to concern myself about its production. The entire credit of its appearance is due to Mr. Grein, the founder of the Independent Theatre."

"And the cast, Mr. Shaw?"

"Nothing can exceed the devotion of the cast. They are presenting their services to the Independent Theatre at considerable expense to themselves, and without the least prospect of making the sort of personal success which an ambitious actor might score in the work of a practised dramatist bent on a popular success. As the whole play is carried on by five persons, the parts are not only thankless but

VERY LONG AND TROUBLESOME.

The part of the widower is as difficult as that of Digby Grand in 'The Two Roses,' which first brought Mr. Irving to the front. It has been undertaken by Mr. T. W. Percyval, whom you may remember as Count Evitoff in 'Gloriana.' He finds the part the most difficult he has ever studied; and he is by no means a novice. I remember his telling me that he began his career by playing eight different parts in 'Hamlet.' "

"Do you mean on the same evening?"

"I am not sufficiently familiar with the play to know whether that is possible. Let us say on the same tour, not on the same evening. Then there is the hero. His part, strangely enough, revolted the moral sense of several actors who were asked to play it. They complained of his being 'a feeder'—I cannot think why, as I have made no allusion to his appetite, nor does he eat anything on the stage. Fortunately Mr. W. J. Robertson stepped in to save the performance from being postponed, and will do his best to sustain his reputation in this ungrateful part. But my great trouble is with Mr. Arthur Whittaker, the representative of the hero's confidant. Mr. Whittaker is, unfortunately, a practised and versatile comedian, who is accustomed to play the most popular parts of Mr. Penley, Mr. Hawtrey, and Mr. Hare. He has made me laugh several times at rehearsal; and I foresee great danger of his

UPSETTING THE GRAVITY OF THE AUDIENCE.

He seems only imperfectly sensible of the force of my remonstrances. By the bye, I am forgetting to mention the part that appeals most to the actor. It is that of the slum rent collector; and I shall be glad to have your opinion of it when it has been played by Mr. James Welch, whom you have seen as the Artful Dodger at the Olympic."

"I think you said something about a heroine, Mr. Shaw?"

"To be sure. There is a heroine and a housemaid. The housemaid was the great difficulty; for the part is small and yet so important that the end of the second act depends entirely on it. Mr. Grein said that nobody but a first-rate actress could be trusted with it. I said, 'Very good, let us have a first-rate actress: there is more hope for us in the modesty of a finished artist than in the vanity of a beginner.' And we boldly asked Miss Kate Phillips, who consented with the utmost goodnature. For the heroine I had

long before set my heart on Miss Florence Farr, if only
she could be persuaded to undertake so odious a task as
the impersonation of a rich upstart's wilful, violent
daughter, who hates the class from which her father sprang.
Miss Farr is an actress trained only in farcical comedy,
with obvious gifts for such stage work as demands a
lively sense of humor and personal grace and address, but
without the formidable physical equipment for tragedy
which distinguishes Miss Robins and Miss Achurch, for
instance. I first met Miss Farr in the days of the Ibsen controversy. The only Ibsen part which seemed at all within
her means was 'The Lady from the Sea,' which she was
about to attempt when I directed her attention to the
most difficult tragic part in the whole Ibsen repertory—
that of Rebecca West in 'Rosmersholm.' You remember
how she actually produced that extraordinary play, and
what an impression she made as Rebecca, and how, later
on, in spite of appalling difficulties created by our corrupt
censorship, she saved us from having to let the Shelley
centenary pass without at least a glimpse of Beatrice Cenci.
And all this, remember,

NOT AS PART OF HER ORDINARY BUSINESS;

for she is not a tragédienne, but a quite unassuming member of Mr. Hawtrey's company at the Comedy Theatre.
This sort of thing can only be done by a highly intelligent
woman. No mere genius—everybody on the stage is a
genius—could achieve it. I appealed to Miss Farr on the
ground that the play was impossible without her; and
she, too, consented, though her part is a specially hazardous
and disagreeable one."

"Do you really think the censorship is corrupt, Mr.
Shaw?"

"Of course. All irresponsible authorities are corrupt.
It is a law of nature—a commonplace of political philosophy. Besides, look at the second act of 'Incognita,' licensed
for a rich financier who was supposed at the time to have
bought up the *Pall Mall Gazette*, and compare it with
Brandes' 'Visit,' for which a license was refused to the
comparatively poor and socially uninfluential Independent

Theatre. Look at Mr. Pigott's evidence before the Royal Commission—how he assumed as a matter of course that Mr. William Archer was simply booming Ibsen to make money out of him. Corrupt!—the Lord Chamberlain's office is a sink of corruption. I do not mean that they take £50 notes there for licenses, though I have no guarantee whatever that they don't; but that they are respecters of persons and their pretence of keeping the theatre pure is an impudent sham are facts too flagrant to be overlooked. The only comfort is that as the censorship is

A DESPOTIC STATE DEPARTMENT,

the right to denounce them is part of the public right of free speech against the Government."

"As a playwright, Mr. Shaw, you are of course a follower of Ibsen?"

"What! *I* a follower of Ibsen! My good sir, as far as England is concerned, Ibsen is a follower of mine. In 1880, when I was only 24, I wrote a book called 'The Irrational Knot,' which reads nowadays like an Ibsenite novel. When I wrote the first two acts of 'Widowers' Houses' I had never heard of Ibsen. My 'Quintessence of Ibsenism' proved that I understood Ibsen's drift better than he understood it himself."

"Shakespeare is your model, perhaps?"

"Shakespeare! stuff! Shakespeare—a disillusioned idealist! a pessimist! a rationalist! a capitalist! If the fellow had not been a great poet, his rubbish would have been forgotten long ago. Molière, as a thinker, was worth a thousand Shakespeares. If my play is not better than Shakespeare, let it be damned promptly."

"I suppose there is no doubt that you are an exceptionally clever man, Mr. Shaw?"

"Not the slightest. Ah, if I had only realised that years ago!—if I had only had courage and faith in myself

AS WELL AS BRAINS!

Be warned by me—you are a young man still—beware of timidity and diffidence. They have done me a world of harm and very little good."

"I will bear it in mind, Mr. Shaw. Many thanks. I am afraid I have detained you unconscionably."

"Not at all. May I offer you some refreshment—a glass of water and few carrots?"

"Thanks, I never take anything at this hour. Have I your full permission to publish what has passed?"

"Verbatim, if you please. Tell the exact truth. Remember me to all at Stonecutter-st. Good day."

"Good day, Mr. Shaw. Again many thanks. Never mind coming down. By the bye, where and when is the performance to take place?"

"On the 9th, I believe. I don't know where—perhaps at the Avenue, or the Royalty. Ask Grein: he knows. Good-bye."

And I left him beaming flatteringly after me from the stairhead. He was the most copious talker I ever interviewed.

"Gilbert and Sullivan"

×××

11 October 1893

Pleasant it is to see Mr Gilbert and Sir Arthur Sullivan working together again full brotherly. They should be on the best of terms; for henceforth Sir Arthur can always say, "Any other librettist would do just as well: look at Haddon Hall"; whilst Mr Gilbert can retort, "Any other musician would do just as well: look at The Mountebanks." Thus have the years of divorce cemented the happy reunion at which we all assisted last Saturday. The twain still excite the expectations of the public as much as ever. How Trial by Jury and The Sorcerer surprised the public, and how Pinafore, The Pirates, and Patience kept the sensation fresh, can be guessed by the youngest man from the fact that the announcement of a new Savoy opera always throws the middle-aged playgoer into the attitude of expecting a surprise. As for me, I avoid this attitude, if only because it is a middle-aged one. Still, I expect a good deal that I could not have hoped for when I first made the acquaintance of comic opera.

Those who are old enough to compare the Savoy performances with those of the dark ages, taking into account the pictorial treatment of the fabrics and colors on the stage, the cultivation and intelligence of the choristers, the quality of the orchestra, and the degree of artistic good breeding, so to speak, expected from the principals, best know how great an advance has been made by Mr D'Oyly Carte in organizing and harmonizing that complex co-operation of artists of all kinds which goes to make up a satisfactory operatic performance. Long before the run of a successful Savoy opera is over Sir Arthur's melodies are dinned into our ears by every promenade band and street piano, and Mr Gilbert's sallies are quoted threadbare by conversationalists and journalists; but the whole work as presented to eye and ear on the Savoy stage remains un-hackneyed.

Further, no theatre in London is more independent of those executants whose personal popularity enables them to demand ruinous salaries; and this is not the least advantageous of the differences between opera as the work of a combination of manager, poet, and musician, all three making the most of one another in their concerted striving for the common object of a completely successful representation, and opera as the result of a speculator picking up a libretto, getting somebody with a name to set it to music, ordering a few tradesmen to "mount" it, and then, with a stage manager hired here, an acting manager hired there, and a popular prima donna, comedian, and serpentine dancer stuck in at reckless salaries like almonds into an underdone dumpling, engaging some empty theatre on the chance of the affair "catching on."

If any capitalist wants to succeed with comic opera, I can assure him that he can do so with tolerable security if he only possesses the requisite managerial ability. There is no lack of artistic material for him to set to work on: London is overstocked with artistic talent ready to the hand of anyone who can recognize it and select from it. The difficulty is to find the man with this power of recognition and selection. The effect of the finer artistic temperaments and talents on the ordinary speculator is not merely nil (for in that case he might give them an engagement by accident), but antipathetic. People sometimes complain of the indifference of the public and the managers to the highest elements in fine art. There never was a greater mistake. The Philistine is not indifferent to fine art: he *hates* it.

The relevance of these observations will be apparent when I say that, though I enjoyed the score of Utopia more than that of any of the previous Savoy operas, I am quite prepared to hear that it is not as palatable to the majority of the human race—otherwise the mob—as it was to me. It is written with an artistic absorption and enjoyment of which Sir Arthur Sullivan always had moments, but which seem to have become constant with him only since he was knighted, though I do not suggest that the two things stand in the relation of cause and effect. The orchestral work is charmingly humorous; and as I happen to mean by this only what I say, perhaps I had better warn my readers not to infer that Utopia is full of buffooneries with the bassoon and piccolo, or of patter and tum-tum.

Whoever can listen to such caressing wind parts—zephyr parts, in fact—as those in the trio for the King and the two Judges in the first act, without being coaxed to feel pleased and amused, is not fit even for treasons, stratagems, and spoils; whilst anyone whose ears are capable of taking in more than one thing at a time must be tickled by the sudden busyness of the orchestra as the city man takes up the parable. I also confidently recommend those who go into solemn academic raptures over themes "in diminution" to go and hear how prettily the chorus of the Christy Minstrel song (borrowed from the plantation dance Johnnie, get a gun) is used, very much in diminution, to make an exquisite mock-banjo accompaniment. In these examples we are on the plane, not of the bones and tambourine, but of Mozart's accompaniments to Soave sia il vento in Cosi fan tutte and the entry of the gardener in Le Nozze di Figaro. Of course these things are much thrown away on people who are not musicians as a copy of Fliegende Blätter on people who do not read German, whereas anyone can understand mere horseplay with the instruments.

But people who are not musicians should not intrude into opera-houses: indeed, it is to me an opera question whether they ought to be allowed to exist at all. As to the score generally, I have only one fault to find with Sir Arthur's luxurious ingenuity in finding pretty timbres of all sorts, and that is that it still leads him to abuse the human voice most unmercifully. I will say nothing about the part he has written for the unfortunate soprano, who might as well leave her lower octave at home for all the relief she gets from the use of her upper one. But take the case of Mr Scott Fishe, one of Mr Carte's most promising discoveries, who did so much to make the ill-fated Jane Annie endurable.

What made Mr Fishe's voice so welcome was that it was neither the eternal callow baritone nor the growling bass: it rang like a genuine "singing bass"; and one felt that here at last was a chance of an English dramatic *basso cantante*, able to "sing both high and low," and to contrast his high D with an equally fine one an octave below. Unfortunately, the upper fifth of Mr Fishe's voice, being flexible and of excellent quality, gives him easy command (on occasion) of high passages; and Sir Arthur has ruthlessly seized on this to write for him an excessively specialized baritone part, in which we get not one of those deep, ringing tones which relieved the Jane Annie music so attractively. I have in my time heard so many singers reduced by parts of this sort, in the operas of Verdi and Gounod, to a condition in which they could bawl F sharps *ad lib.* at high pressure, but could neither place a note accurately nor produce any tolerable tone from B flat downwards, that I always protest against vocal parts, no matter what voice they are written for, if they do not employ the voice all over its range, though lying mainly where the singer can sing continuously without fatigue.

A composer who uses up young voices by harping on the prettiest notes in them is an ogreish voluptuary; and if Sir Arthur does not wish posterity either to see the stage whitened with the bones of his victims or else to hear his music transposed wholesale, as Lassalle transposes Rigoletto, he should make up his mind whether he means to write for a tenor or a baritone, and place the part accordingly. Considering that since Santley retired from the stage and Jean de Reszke turned tenor all the big reputations have been made by *bassi cantanti* like Edourd de Reszke and Lassalle, and that all the great Wagner parts in which reputations of the same calibre will be made for some time to come are impossible to completely specialized baritones, I venture, as a critic who greatly enjoys Mr Fishe's performance, to recommend him to ask the composer politely not to treat him worse than Mozart treated Don Giovanni, than Wagner treated Wolfram, or than Sir Arthur himself would treat a clarinet. Miss Nancy McIntosh, who was introduced to us, it will be remembered, by Mr Henschel at the London Symphony Concerts, where she sang in a selection from Die Meistersinger and in the Choral Symphony, came through the trials of a most inconsiderate vocal part very cleverly, evading the worst of the strain by a treatment which, if a little flimsy, was always pretty. She spoke her part admirably, and, by dint of natural tact, managed to make a positive advantage of her stage inexperience, so that she won over the audience in no time. As to Miss Brandram, Mr Barrington (who by means of a remarkable pair of eyebrows transformed himself into a surprising compound of Mr Goschen and the late Sir William Cusins), Messrs Denny, Kenningham, Le Hay, Gridley, and the rest, everybody knows what they can do; and need only particularize as to Miss Owen and Miss Florence Perry, who gave us some excellent pantomime in the very amusing lecture scene, contrived by Mr Gilbert, and set to perfection by Sir Arthur, in the first act.

The book has Mr Gilbert's lighter qualities without his faults. Its main idea, the Anglicization of Utopia by a people boundlessly credulous as to the superiority of the English race, is as certain of popularity as that reference to England by the Gravedigger in Hamlet, which never yet failed to make the house laugh. There is, happily, no plot; and the stage business is fresh and well invented—for instance, the lecture already alluded to, the adoration of the troopers by the female Utopians, the Cabinet Council "as held at the Court of St James's Hall," and the quadrille, are capital strokes. As to the "Drawing Room," with *débutantes,* cards, trains, and presentations all complete, and the little innovation of a cup of tea and a plate of cheap biscuits, I cannot vouch for its verisimilitude, as I have never, strange as it may appear, been present at a Drawing Room; but that is exactly why I enjoyed it, and why the majority of the Savoyards will share my appreciation of it.

To William Archer

XXXXXXXXXXXXXXXXXXXXXXXXXXXXXXXXXXXXXXXXXX

Shaw wrote after midnight, following the opening of his play Arms and the Man, *clearly anticipating an unfavorable review from his friend Archer. And he was correct. The notice in the* Pall Mall Gazette *was exactly as anticipated.*

29 Fitzroy Square W
23 April 1894

I must really clear that Gilbert notion out of your head before you disgrace yourself over Arms & The Man. You have a perfect rag shop of old ideas in your head which prevent your getting a step ahead.

Gilbert is simply a paradoxically humorous cynic. He accepts the conventional ideals implicitly, but observes that people do not really live up to them. This he regards as a failure on their part at which he mocks bitterly. This position is precisely that of Sergius in the play, who, when disilluded, declares that life is a farce. It is a perfectly barren position: nothing comes of it but cynicism, pessimism, & irony.

I do not accept the conventional ideals. To them I oppose in the play the practical life & morals of the efficient, realistic man, unaffectedly ready to face what risks must be faced, considerate but not chivalrous, patient and practical; and I not only represent the woman as instinctively falling in love with all this even whilst all her notions of finemannishness are being outraged; but I dot the i's by making him say in audible words—"You mean, dont you, that I am the first man that has ever taken you *quite* seriously &c"—"Now that you've found out that life isnt a farce, but something quite sensible & serious &c" and so on. You will not find a trace of this in Gilbert, and only some broken

glimpses of it in Ibsen, who is by old habit a pessimist. My
whole secret is that I have got clean through the old cate-
gories of good & evil, and no longer use them even for
dramatic effect. Sergius is ridiculous through the breakdown
of his ideals, not odious from his falling short of them. As
Gilbert sees, they dont work; but what Gilbert does not see
is that there is something else that does work, and that in
that something else there is a completely satisfactory
asylum for the affections. It is this positive element in my
philosophy that makes Arms & The Man a perfectly
genuine play about real people, with a happy ending and
hope & life in it, instead of a thing like [Gilbert's] "Engaged" which is nothing but a sneer at people for not being
what Sergius & Raina play at being before they find one
another out. Every touch in Engaged is false: not one
speech or action in it is possible. In the first act of Arms
& The Man there is not one speech of Bluntschli's that is
not faithful in fact & spirit to the realities of soldiering. All
the effect is got out of facts stated in the simplest terms.
The chocolate, the effect of a third day under fire, the dirt,
the sleepiness, the cavalry charge are prosaically accurate.
The effect is produced by an adroit contrast of their reality
with the unreality of the woman's notions. If you could only
rid yourself of the intense unreality of your own precon-
ceptions, and of your obsession by the ideals which you
grow pessimistic over, you would not find that an effect due
to the ridiculous obviousness and common sense of realism
breaking through the mist & glamor of idealism, was a mere
mechanical topsyturvyism.

But my chief object in writing this letter is to call your
attention to the fact that last night, whether it leads to a
commercial success or not, totally shatters your theory that
I cannot write for the stage. Your notice of Widowers'
Houses was one of the stupidest things you ever perpetrated,
except perhaps your notice of Arms & The Man, which will
no doubt explain matters virtually on the old ground that I
am a supernatural being. Now the theory of *my* dramatic
incompetence was part of a general theory involving *your*
dramatic incompetence too. If you write a play, which you

can do if you will sit down sincerely to amuse yourself, it
will get produced as easily as Arms & The Man. And I still
think that you ought to try. You dont intend to spend the
rest of your life reviewing for the P.M.G., do you?

                                                        GBS

"Yvette Guilbert"

XXXXXXXXXXXXXXXXXXXXXXXXXXXXXXXXXXXXXXXXX

16 May 1894

Another great artist has come. I suppose I ought to have been quite familiar with her performances already when I went to her reception of the English Press (musical critics *not* included) at the Savoy Hotel last week; but as a matter of fact I had never heard her before. The fact is I am a very bad Parisian. I have never been to the Chat Noir: I have looked at its advertisements on the Boulevards time after time without the least conviction that my sense of being in the fastest forefront of the life of my age would culminate there. To me, going to Paris means going back fifty years in civilization, spending an uncomfortable night, and getting away next morning as soon as possible. I know, of course, that there must be places and circles in Paris which are not hopelessly out of date; but I have never found them out; and if I did, what figure could I make in them with my one weapon, language, broken in my hand?

Hence it is that I had never seen Mlle Yvette Guilbert when Monsieur Johnson, of the Figaro, introduced her to a carefully selected audience of the wrong people (mostly) at the Savoy Hotel as aforesaid. Monsieur Johnson, as a veteran, will not feel hurt at any comment which only goes to prove that "the power of beauty he remembers yet"; therefore I need have no delicacy in saying that the remarks which he addressed to the audience by way of introducing Mlle Guilbert were entirely fatuous when his emotion permitted them to be heard. When the young lady appeared, it needed only one glance to see that here was no mere music-hall star, but one of the half-dozen ablest persons in the room. It is worth remarking here, that in any society whatever of men and women there is always a woman among the six cleverest; and this is why I, who have a some-

what extensive experience of work on the committees of
mixed societies, have been trained to recognize the fact that
the Efficient Person in this world is occasionally female,
though she must not on that account be confounded with
the ordinary woman—or the ordinary man, for that matter
—whom one does not privately regard as a full-grown
responsible individual at all.

You do not waste "homage" on the female Efficient
Person; you regard her, favorably or unfavorably, much as
you regard the male of the Efficient species, except
that you have a certain special fear of her, based on her
freedom from that sickliness of conscience, so much depre-
cated by Ibsen, which makes the male the prey of unreal
scruples; and you have at times to defend yourself against
her, or, when she is an ally, to assume her fitness for active
service of the roughest kinds, in a way which horrifies the
chivalrous gentlemen of your acquaintance who will not
suffer the winds of heaven to breathe on a woman's face
too harshly lest they should disable her in her mission of
sewing on buttons.

In short, your chivalry and gallantry are left useless on
your hands, unless for small-talk with the feminine rank
and file, who must be answered according to their folly,
just like the male rank and file. But then you get on much
better with the female master-spirits, who will not stand
chivalry, or gallantry, or any other form of manly patronage. Therefore let others, who have not been educated as I
have been, pay Mlle Guilbert gallant compliments: as for
me, no sooner had the lady mounted the platform with that
unmistakable familiarity with the situation and command
of it which shews itself chiefly by the absence of all the
petty affectations of the favorite who has merely caught the
fancy of the public without knowing how or why, than I
was on the alert to see what an evidently very efficient
person was going to do.

And I was not at all deceived in my expectancy. It
amuses her to tell interviewers that she cannot sing, and
has no gestures; but I need not say that there would be very
little fun for her in that if she were not one of the best
singers and pantomimists in Europe. She divided her pro-

gram into three parts: Ironic songs, Dramatic songs, and—
but perhaps I had better use the French heading here, and
say Chansons Legères. For though Mlle Guilbert sings the
hymns of a very ancient faith, profusely endowed and
sincerely upheld among us, we deny it a name and an
establishment. Its Chansons Ironiques are delivered by her
with a fine intensity of mordant expression that would not
be possible without profound conviction beneath it; and if
there is anything that I am certain of after hearing her
sing Les Vierges, it is the perfect integrity of her self-
respect in an attitude towards life which is distinctly not
that of the British matron.

To kindle art to the whitest heat there must always be
some fanaticism behind it; and the songs in which Mlle
Guilbert expresses her immense irony are the veil of a
propaganda which is not the propaganda of asceticism. It
is not my business here to defend that propaganda against
the numerous and highly respectable British class which
conceives life as presenting no alternative to asceticism but
licentiousness: I merely describe the situation to save people
of this way of thinking from going to hear Mlle Yvette,
and proposing to treat her as their forefathers treated Joan
of Arc.

Perhaps, however, they would only laugh the innocent
laugh of the British lady who, not understanding French,
and unwilling to let that fact appear, laughs with the rest
at the points which prevented Mlle Guilbert from inviting
the episcopal bench as well as the Press to her reception.
In spite of her superb diction, I did not understand half her
lines myself. Part of what I did understand would have
surprised me exceedingly if it had occurred in a drawing-
room ballad by Mr Cowan or Sir Arthur Sullivan; but I
am bound to add that I was not in the least shocked or disgusted, though my unlimited recognition of an artist's right
to take any side of life whatsoever as subject-matter for
artistic treatment makes me most indignantly resentful of
any attempt to abuse my tolerance by coarse jesting.

The fact is, Mlle Guilbert's performance was for the
most part much more serious at its base than an average
Italian opera scena. I am not now alluding to the avowedly

dramatic songs like Le Conscrit and Morphinée, which any
ordinary actress could deliver in an equally effective, if
somewhat less distinguished, manner. I am thinking of Les
Vierges, Sur la Scène, and the almost frightful La Pierreuse.
A *pierreuse*, it appears, is a garrotter's decoy. In the song
she describes how she prowls about the fortifications of
Paris at night, and entraps some belated bourgeois into
conversation. Then she summons her principal with a
weird street cry; he pounces on his prey; and the subsequent
operations are described in a perfect war dance of a refrain.

Not so very horrible, perhaps; but the last verse describes
not a robbery, but the guillotining of the robber; and so
hideously exquisite is the singing of this verse that you see
the woman in the crowd at La Roquette; you hear the half-
choked repetition of the familiar signal with which she
salutes the wretch as he is hurried out; you positively see
his head flying off; above all, you feel with a shudder how
the creature's impulses of terror and grief are overcome by
the bestial excitement of seeing the great State show of
killing a man in the most sensational way.

Just as people would not flog children if they could
realize the true effect of the ceremony on the child's pet
playmates, to whom it is supposed to be a wholesome
warning, so the French Government would certainly
abolish public executions *sans phrase* (and perhaps private
ones too) if only they would go and hear Mlle Guilbert
sing La Pierreuse.

Technically, Mlle Guilbert is a highly accomplished
artist. She makes all her effects in the simplest way, and
with perfect judgment. Like the ancient Greeks, not to
mention the modern music-hall artists, she relies on the
middle and low registers of her voice, they being the best
suited for perfectly well-controlled declamation; but her
cantabile is charming, thanks to a fine ear and a delicate
rhythmic faculty. Her command of every form of expression is very remarkable, her tones ranging from the purest
and sweetest pathos to the cockniest Parisian cynicism.

There is not a trace of the rowdy restlessness and forced
"go" of the English music-hall singer about her; and I suggest to those members of the London County Council who

aim at the elevation of the music-hall, that they could not do better than offer Mlle Guilbert handsome terms to follow up her reception of *la Presse anglaise* by a series of receptions of Miss Marie Lloyd, Miss Katie Lawrence, and other eminent English prima donnas, in order that they might be encouraged to believe that there is room in music-hall singing for art of classic self-possession and delicacy without any loss of gaiety, and that the author of a music-hall song may not be the worse for being a wit, or even a poet. . . .

"Taking Wagner Seriously"

×××××××××××××××××××××××××××××××××××××××

Shaw ends this review with the suggestion that he was not yet done with the subject at hand; but he was. It would be his last musical review for The World. *He had already resigned the post on the death of his editor and friend, Edmund Yates, but remained on at the new editor's request until the end of the season. With this review the season, and his tenure as a regular music critic, ended.*

8 August 1894

Sitting, as I am today, in a Surrey farmhouse with the sky overcast, and a big fire burning to keep me from shivering, it seems to me that it must be at least four or five months since I was breathing balmy airs in the scented pine-woods on the hills round Bayreuth. If I could only see the sun for five minutes I could better recall what I have to write about. As it is, I seem to have left it all far behind with the other vanities of the season. I no longer feel any impulse to describe Lohengrin and Tannhäuser as I promised, or to draw morals for Frau Wagner on the one hand, or Sir Augustus Harris on the other. For months I have held the whole subject of musical art in an intense grip, which never slackened even when I was asleep; but now the natural periodicity of my function asserts itself, and compels me to drop the subject in August and September, just as hens moult in November (so they tell me here in the farmhouse).

What I feel bound to record concerning the Bayreuth Lohengrin—remember that this is the first time the work has been done there, and probably the first time it has ever been thoroughly done at all, if we except the earliest attempt under Liszt at Weimar—is that its stage framework is immensely more entertaining, convincing, and natural than it has ever seemed before. This is mainly because the stage management is so good, especially with regard to the chorus. In Lohengrin there are only two comparatively short scenes in which the chorus is not present and in constant action.

The opera therefore suffers fearfully on ordinary occasions from the surprising power of the average Italian chorister to destroy all stage illusion the moment he shambles on the scene with his blue jaws, his reach-me-down costume, his foolish single gesture, his embarrassed eye on the prompter, and his general air of being in an opera chorus because he is fit for nothing better. At Covent Garden he is, in addition, generally an old acquaintance: it is not only that he is destroying the illusion of the opera you are looking at, but that he has destroyed the illusion of nearly all the operas you have ever seen; so that the conflict of his claim upon you as one of "the old familiar faces" with the claims of the art which he outrages finally weakens your mind and disturbs your conscience until you lose the power of making any serious effort to get rid of him. As to the ladies of our opera chorus, they have to be led by competent, sensible women; and as women at present can only acquire these qualities by a long experience as mothers of large families, our front row hardly helps the romance of the thing more than the men do.

Now I am not going to pretend that at Bayreuth the choristers produce an overwhelming impression of beauty and chivalry, or even to conceal the fact that the economic, social, and personal conditions which make the Covent Garden chorus what it is in spite of the earnest desire of everybody concerned that it should be something quite different, dominate Frau Wagner just as they dominate Sir Augustus Harris, and compel her to allot to Elsa a bevy of maidens, and to Henry the Fowler a band of warriors, about whose charms and prowess a good deal of make-believe is necessary. The stouter build of the men, the prevalence of a Teutonic cast among them, and their reinforcement by a physically and artistically superior class of singers who regard it as an honor to sing at Bayreuth, even in the chorus, certainly help the illusion as far as the Saxon and Brabantine warriors in Lohengrin are concerned; but

this difference in raw material is as nothing compared with
the difference made by the intelligent activity of the stage-
manager.

One example of this will suffice. Those who know the
score of Lohengrin are aware that in the finale to the first
act there is a section, usually omitted in performance, in
which the whole movement is somewhat unexpectedly repeated in a strongly contrasted key, the modulation being
unaccountable from the point of view of the absolute musician, as it is not at all needed as a relief to the principal
key. At Bayreuth its purpose is made clear. After the com-
bat with Telramund and the solo for Elsa which serves
musically as the exposition of the theme of the finale, the
men, greatly excited and enthusiastic over the victory of
the strange knight, range themselves in a sort of wheel
formation, of which Lohengrin is the centre, and march
round him as they take up the finale from Elsa in the prin-
ciple key. When the modulation comes, the women in their
white robes, break into this triumphal circle, displace the
men, and march round Elsa in the same way, the striking
change of key being thus accompanied by a correspondingly
striking change on the stage, one of the incidents of which
is a particularly remarkable kaleidoscoping of the scheme
of color produced by the dresses.

Here you have a piece of stage management of the true
Wagnerian kind, combining into one stroke a dramatic
effect, a scenic effect, and a musical effect, the total result
being a popular effect the value of which was proved by
the roar of excitement which burst forth as the curtains
closed in. A more complex example of the same combination was afforded by the last act of Tannhäuser, which
produced the same outburst from the audience, and which
was all the more conclusive because none of the enthusiasm
could be credited to the principal artists, who had, in the
first two acts, effectually cleared themselves of all suspicion
of being able to produce any effect except one of portentous
boredom.

Here, then, we have the point at which Bayreuth beats
Drury Lane and Covent Garden in staging Wagner and
every other composer whose works have been for some

years in our repertory. I have over and over again pointed out the way in which the heroic expenditure of Sir Augustus Harris gets wasted for want of a stage-manager who not only studies the stage picture as it is studied, for instance, at the Savoy Theatre, or at any of our music-halls where ballets form part of the entertainment, but who studies the score as well, and orders the stage so that the spectator's eye, ear, and dramatic sense shall be appealed to simultaneously.

I have sometimes had to point out, in the case of old stock operas, that there is often reason to suspect that the stage-manager either does not even know the story of the opera he has in hand, or has become cynically convinced that an opera is in itself such a piece of nonsense that an extra absurdity or two cannot matter much. This is of course quite a tenable view argumentatively; but it is not the understanding upon which the public pays for its seats. The moment you take a guinea, or half-a-crown, or whatever it may be, from an individual for a performance of an opera, you are bound to treat the performance as a serious matter, whatever your private philosophic convictions may be.

At Bayreuth they do take the performance seriously in all its details: the heroine does not die in the middle of the street on a lodging-house sofa, nor does the tenor step out of a window with a rope ladder attached to it, and openly walk off at the level of the chamber floor. The rank and file are carefully instructed as to what they are supposed to be doing; and nobody dreams of taking any liberties with the work or with the public. It is quite a mistake to suppose that the makeshifts which circumstances force upon Covent Garden are unknown at Bayreuth, or that the stock works are as well rehearsed and prepared as the new works; but there is, at any rate, always the habit of discipline; and though things may be left undone for want of time or ill done for want of rehearsal, nothing is let slide on the assumption that it is not worth doing. I have been tortured there by bad singing, and bored by solemnly prosaic acting; but I have never been offended by wanton trifling.

I have sufficiently explained in my last article how Bayreuth's scrupulous artistic morality is heavily counter-balanced by the callousness of its musical sensibility. The cure for this, however, is not the writing of homilies about it, but the cultivation of the German ear by actual experience of something better than the singing they are accustomed to tolerate. Already the popularity of Van Dyck, a Belgian singer with none of the German bluntness about him, whose charm of voice and style was sufficient, when he appeared as Des Grieux at Covent Garden, to produce on Jean de Reszke, who was at that time taking his supremacy for granted somewhat too lazily, the effect popularly known as "making him sit up," is rendering the Bayreuth stage more accessible to foreigners, who will finally, if the Germans do not realize their own deficiencies, make it difficult for a German singer to get an engagement there. This year we have Nordica and Miss Brema as well as Van Dyck; and it is probable that Frau Wagner will look for more help in the same direction—across the frontier, that is—on future occasions.

I am not quite done with the subject even yet; but as this farmhouse is beyond the sphere of the Post Office, I must conclude, in order to allow three or four days for the journey of thirty miles or so which my communication must make before it reaches London.

To Henry Arthur Jones

✕✕✕✕✕✕✕✕✕✕✕✕✕✕✕✕✕✕✕✕✕✕✕✕✕✕✕✕✕✕✕

Philosophically the two playwrights were opposed; technically they were equally opposed. Jones preferred conservatism, compromise—and commercial success.

West Cliff Hotel. Folkestone
2nd December 1894
(Beastly wet day)

Here I am at the seaside between the finishing of one play and the beginning of another, just the time to send back the ball to you.

All that you say is quite true statically. Dynamically, it is of no virtue whatever. Like you, I write plays because I like it, and because I cannot remember any period in my life when I could help inventing people and scenes. I am not a storyteller: things occur to me as scenes, with action and dialogue—as moments, developing themselves out of their own vitality. I believe you will see as I go on that the conception of me as a doctrinaire, or as a sort of theatrical Joyce (of *Scientific Dialogues* fame), is a wrong one. On the contrary, my quarrel with the conventional drama is that it is doctrinaire to the uttermost extreme of dogmatism—that the dramatist is so strait-jacketted in theories of conduct that he cannot even state his conventional solution clearly, but leaves it to be vaguely understood, and so for the life of him cannot write a decent last act. I find that when I present a drama of pure feeling, wittily expressed, the effect when read by me to a picked audience of people in a room is excellent. But in a theatre, the mass of the people, too stupid to relish the wit, and too convention-ridden to sympathise with real as distinct from theatrical feeling, simply cannot see any drama or fun there at all; whilst the clever people feel the discrepancy between the real and theatrical feeling only as a Gilbertian satire on the latter, and, appreciating the wit well enough, are eager to shrew their cleverness by proclaiming me as a monstrously clever sparkler in the cynical line. These clever people predominate in a first night audience; and, accordingly, in "Arms and The Man," I had the curious experience of witnessing an apparently insane success, with the actors and actresses almost losing their heads with the intoxication of laugh after laugh, and of going before the curtain to tremendous applause, the only person in the theatre who knew that the whole affair was a ghastly failure. The same thing is occurring now in Boston, Philadelphia, &c—there is about as much of me in the affair as there is of Shakespeare in Garrick's "Katherine and Petruchio." Here and there, of course, I come across a person who was *moved* by the play, or by such portions of it as got played any better than a pantomime opening; but for the general paying public there needs a long fight, during which my plays will have to be produced in spite of all economic considerations, sometimes because the parts are too fascinating to be resisted, sometimes because Pinero is not ready with his commissioned play, sometimes because I am willing to forgo an advance, sometimes because Nature will not submit wholly to the box office.

Now here you will at once detect an enormous assumption on my part that I am a man of genius. But what can I do—on what other assumption am I too proceed if I am to write plays at all? You will detect the further assumption that the public, which will still be the public twenty years hence, will nevertheless see feeling and reality where they see nothing now but mere intellectual swordplay and satire. But that is what always happens. You must remember my musical experience. I remember well when even cultivated musicians could hear no melody in Lohengrin, not to mention Die Meistersinger, and when they thought Spohr's and Mendelssohn's oratorios, and "Mozart's 12th Mass" the summit of musical sublimity and profundity. The public is still as great an ass (to speak in that way) as it was then; but it now knows that Wagner's work is all melody and feeling, and that the other stuff is nine tenths formality and twaddle. Consequently I am absolutely confident that *if my work is good* (the only assumption on which I can go on with it) all the miracles will happen, and it will be quite well worth my while to make £150 a play, or even to make nothing and starve, or play Wagner to your Liszt in the sense of borrowing all your spare cash.

And now as to the barrenness of politics. What conviction can you really have as to their barrenness unless you have fallen in love with them and found that no child came of their embraces?—or unless you have actually worked in the arena with politicians all through their apprenticeship. You have to swallow all the formulas if you are to know what they really taste like and what effect they have on the constitution. Politics are just as much a part of life as gambling or poetry; and it is extremely instructive to see how impotent the political opinions which men *think*, are to produce action, and how potent the political prejudices which men *feel*, are to produce it. I am a politician because life only realises itself by functioning energetically in all directions; and I find on the platform and in council opportunities for functioning away like mad with faculties that would otherwise be atrophied from disuse. My passion, like that of all artists, is for efficiency, which means intensity of life and breadth and variety of experience; and already I find, as a dramatist, that I can go at one stroke to the centre of matters that reduce the purely literary man to colorless platitudes.

Do you now begin to understand, oh Henry Arthur Jones, that you have to deal with a man who habitually thinks of himself as one of the great geniuses of all time?—just as you necessarily do yourself. We may be deceiving ourselves; but why add to the heavy chances of that the absolute certainty of such a deception as would be involved in the notion that we thought ourselves common fellows with a bit of talent.

Have you ever considered the case of Dickens carefully? Don't you think his last (and greatest) works would have been much greater if he had had something of the systematic philosophical, historical, economic, and above all, artistic training of Goethe? I grant you it is a difficult question; but surely so fine a spirit could have been rescued from the reproach of being a Philistine, a guzzler, and an ignorantly contemptuous reporter-politician?

G. Bernard Shaw

To Reginald Golding Bright

XXXXXXXXXXXXXXXXXXXXXXXXXXXXXXXXXXXXXX

*Bright was the young man of the famous solitary "Boo!"
when the author came on stage after the opening night
performance of* Arms and the Man. *Since the outburst
gave Shaw the opportunity for his most famous rejoinder
("I quite agree with you, sir; but who are we among so
many?"), he harbored no grudge, and indeed assisted the
aspiring young critic. The notice he sent to Shaw for comment was a review of Sardou's* Odette.

29 Fitzroy Square W
2 December 1894

The best service I can do you is to take your notice and jot
down on it without ceremony the comments which occur to
me. You will find first certain alterations in black ink. In
them I have tried to say, as well as I can off hand, what
you were trying to say: that is, since it was evident you
were dodging round some point or other, I have considered
the only point there was to make, and have made it. It
came quite easy when I had altered your statement about
Frenchmen at large to what you really meant—the conventional stage Frenchman. Always find out rigidly and
exactly what you mean, and never strike an attitude,
whether national or moral or critical or anything else. You
struck a national attitude when you wrote that about the
Frenchman and Englishman; and you struck a moral attitude when you wrote "She has sunk low enough in all
conscience." Get your facts right first: that is the foundation of all style, because style is the expression of yourself;
and you cannot express yourself genuinely except on a basis
of precise reality.

In red ink you will find some criticisms which you may

confidently take as expressing what an experienced editor would think of your sample of work.

You have not at all taken in my recommendation to you to write a book. You say you are scarcely competent to write books just yet. That is just why I recommend you to learn. If I advised you to learn to skate, you would not reply that your balance was scarcely good enough yet. A man learns to skate by staggering about and making a fool of himself. Indeed he progresses in all things by resolutely making a fool of himself. You will never write a good book until you have written some bad ones. If they sent you my Scottish article, you will see that I began by writing some abominably bad criticisms. I wrote five long books before I started again on press work. William Archer wrote a long magnum opus on the life and works of Richard Wagner, a huge novel [*The Doom of the Destroyed*], and a book on the drama [*English Dramatists of Today*, 1882], besides an essay on Irving [*Henry Irving, Actor and Manager*, 1883] and a good deal of leader work for a Scotch paper [*Edinburgh Evening News*] before he began his victorious career on The World. He also perpetrated about four plays in his early days. (By the way, you mustn't publish this information). You must go through that mill too; and you can't possibly start too soon. Write a thousand words a day for the next five years for at least nine months every year. Read all the great critics—Ruskin, Richard Wagner, Lessing, Lamb and Hazlitt. Get a ticket for the British Museum reading room, and live there as much as you can. Go to all the first rate orchestral concerts and to the opera, as well as to the theatres. Join debating societies and learn to speak in public. Haunt little Sunday evening political meetings and exercise that accomplishment. Study men and politics in this way. As long as you stay in the office, try and be the smartest hand in it: I spent four and a half years in an office before I was twenty. Be a teetotaller; don't gamble; don't lend; dont borrow; dont for your life get married; make the attainment of EFFICIENCY your sole object for the next fifteen years; and if the city can teach you nothing more, or demands more time than you can spare from your apprenticeship, tell your father that you prefer to cut loose and starve, and *do it*. But it will take you at least a year or two of tough work before you will be able to build up for yourself either the courage or the right to take heroic measures. Finally, since I have given you all this advice, I add this crowning precept, the most valuable of all. NEVER TAKE ANYBODY'S ADVICE.

And now, to abandon the role of your guide, philosopher and friend, which I don't propose to revert to again until you report progress in ten years or so, let me thank you for the paragraph in the Sun, which was quite right and appropriate. I have no more news at present, except that I have nearly finished a new play, the leading part in which I hope to see played by Miss Janet Achurch, of whose genius I have always had a very high opinion. It is quite a sentimental play, which I hope to find understood by women, if not by men; and it is so straightforward that I expect to find it pronounced a miracle of perversity. This is my fifth dramatic composition. The first was "Widowers' Houses," of Independent Theatre fame. The second was "The Philanderer," a topical comedy in which the New Woman figured before Mr Grundy discovered her. The third was "Mrs Warren's Profession," a play with a purpose, the purpose being much the same as that of my celebrated letter to the Pall Mall Gazette on the Empire controversy. The fourth was "Arms and The Man," which was so completely misunderstood that it made my reputation as a playwright both here and in New York. The Independent Theatre has already announced "Mrs Warren's Profession" for its forthcoming season. "The Philanderer" was written originally for that society; but on its completion I threw it aside and wrote another more suitable for the purposes of the society—Mrs Warren. Wyndham asked me to do something for him on seeing "Arms and The Man"; and I tried to persuade him to play The Philanderer; but whilst the project was under consideration, Wyndham made such a decisive success with "Rebellious Susan" that he resolved to follow up the vein of comedy opened by Henry Arthur Jones to the end before venturing upon the Shawian quicksand. But this involved so long a delay that I withdrew the play, and am now looking round to see whether the world contains another actor who can philander as well as Wyndham. As I have always said that if I did not write six plays before I was forty I would never write one after, I must finish the work now in hand and another as well before the 26th July 1896; but I hope to do much more than that, since I have managed to get through the present play within three months, during which I have had to take part in the Schoolboard and Vestry elections, to keep up my work in the Fabian Society, to deliver nearly two dozen lectures in London and the provinces, and to fire off various articles and criticisms. The fact is, I took a good holiday in Germany, Italy, and in Surrey; and I accumulated a stock of health which I am dissipating at a frightful rate. The Christmas holidays will come just in time to save my life.

If any of this stuff is of use to you for paragraphing purposes—and remember that the world will not stand too much Bernard Shaw—you are welcome to work it up by all means when it suits you. Only, don't quote it as having been said by me. That is an easy way out which I bar.

I find that you have got an atrociously long letter out of me. I have been blazing away on the platform this evening [at Kentish Town, on "The Limits of Democracy"] for an hour and a half, and ought to be in bed instead of clattering at this machine.

> yours, half asleep
> G. Bernard Shaw

"Henry James and Oscar Wilde"

This was Shaw's first column for Frank Harris's Saturday Review.

×××××××××××××××××××××××××××××××××××××

GUY DOMVILLE. A play in three acts. By Henry James. St. James's Theatre, 5 January 1895.

AN IDEAL HUSBAND. A new and original play of modern life. By Oscar Wilde. Haymaker Theatre, 3 January 1895.

[12 January 1895]

The truth about Mr James's play is no worse than that it is out of fashion. Any dramatically disposed young gentleman who, cultivating sentiment on a little alcohol, and gaining an insight to the mysteries of the eternal feminine by a couple of squalid intrigues, meanwhile keeps well aloof from art and philosophy, and thus preserves his innocence of the higher life of the senses and of the intellect, can patch up a play tomorrow which will pass as real drama with the gentlemen who deny that distinction to the works of Mr Henry James. No doubt, if the literary world were as completely dominated by the admirers of Mr Rider Haggard as the dramatic world is by their first cousins, we should be told that Mr James cannot write a novel. That is not criticism: it is a mere begging of the question. There is no reason why life as we find it in Mr James's novels— life, that is, in which passion is subordinate to intellect and to fastidious artistic taste—should not be represented on the stage. If it is real to Mr James, it must be real to others; and why should not these others have their drama instead of being banished from the theatre (to the theatre's great loss) by the monotony and vulgarity of drama in which passion is everything, intellect nothing, and art only brought in by the incidental outrages upon it. As it happens, I am not myself in Mr James's camp: in all the life that has energy enough to be interesting to me, subjective volition, passion, will, make intellect the merest tool. But there is in

the centre of the cyclone a certain calm spot where cultivated ladies and gentlemen live on independent incomes or
by pleasant artistic occupations. It is there that Mr James's
art touches life, selecting whatever is graceful, exquisite, or
dignified in its serenity. It is not life as imagined by the pit
or gallery, or even by the stalls: it is, let us say, the ideal
of the balcony; but that is no reason why the pit and gallery
should excommunicate it on the ground that it has no blood
and entrails in it, and have its sentence formulated for it by
the fiercely ambitious and willful professional man in the
stalls. The whole case against its adequacy really rests on
its violation of the cardinal stage convention that love is
the most irresistible of all the passions. Since most people
go to the theatre to escape from reality, this convention is
naturally dear to a world in which love, all powerful in the
secret, unreal, day-dreaming life of the imagination, is in
the real active life the abject slave of every trifling habit,
prejudice, and cowardice, easily stifled by shyness, class
feeling, and pecuniary prudence, or diverted from what is
theatrically assumed to be its hurricane course by such
obstacles as a thick ankle, a cockney accent, or an un-
fashionable hat. In the face of this, is it good sense to accuse
Mr Henry James of a want of grip of the realities of life
because he gives us a hero who sacrifices his love to a
strong and noble vocation for the Church? And yet when
some unmannerly playgoer, untouched by either love or
religion, chooses to send a derisive howl from the gallery
at such a situation, we are to sorrowfully admit, if you
please, that Mr James is no dramatist, on the general
ground that "the drama's laws the drama's patrons give."
Pray, which of its patrons?—the cultivated majority who,
like myself and all the ablest of my colleagues, applauded
Mr James on Saturday, or the handful of rowdies who
brawled at him? It is the business of the dramatic critic to
educate these dunces, not to echo them.

Admitting, then, that Mr James's dramatic authorship is
valid, and that his plays are *du théâtre* when the right
people are in the theatre, what are the qualities and faults
of Guy Domville? First among the qualities, a rare charm
of speech. Line after line comes with such a delicate turn

and fall that I unhesitatingly challenge any of our popular dramatists to write a scene in verse with half the beauty of Mr James's prose. I am not now speaking of the verbal fitness, which is a matter of careful workmanship merely. I am speaking of the delicate inflexions of feeling conveyed by the cadences of the line, inflexions and cadences which, after so long a course of the ordinary theatrical splashes and daubs of passion and emphasis, are as grateful to my ear as the music of Mozart's Entführung aus dem Serail would be after a year of Ernani and Il Trovatore. Second, Guy Domville is a story, and not a mere situation hung out on a gallows of plot. And it is a story of fine sentiment and delicate manners, with an entirely worthy and touching ending. Third, it relies on the performers, not for the brute force of their personalities and popularities, but for their finest accomplishments in grace of manner, delicacy of diction, and dignity of style. It is pleasant to be able to add that this reliance, rash as it undeniably is in these days, was not disappointed. Mr Alexander, having been treated little better than a tailor's dummy by Mr Wilde, Mr Pinero, and Mr Henry Arthur Jones successively, found himself treated as an artist by Mr James, and repaid the compliment, not only, as his manager, by charming eighteenth-century stage setting of the piece, but, as actor, by his fine execution of the principal part, which he touched with great skill and judgment. Miss Marion Terry, as Mrs Peveril, was altogether charming, every movement, every tone, harmonized perfectly with the dainty grace and feeling of her lines. In fact, had the second act been equal to the first and third, and the acting as fine throughout as in the scenes between Mr Alexander and Miss Terry (in which, by the way, they were well supported by Mr Waring), the result would have been less doubtful. It will be a deplorable misfortune if Guy Domville does not hold the stage long enough to justify Mr Alexander's enterprise in producing it.

Unfortunately, the second act dissolved the charm rather badly; and what was more, the actors felt it. The Falstaffian make-up of Mrs Saker, and the senseless drunken scene, which Mr Alexander played with the sobriety of desperation, made fuss instead of drama; and the dialogue, except for a brief and very pretty episode in which Miss Millard and Mr Esmond took part, fell off into mere rococo. Little of this act can be remembered with pleasure except Miss Millard's "Forgive me a little," and a few cognate scraps of dialogue. It had better have been left out, and the wanderings of the prodigal taken for granted. And, to weight it still further, it contained a great deal of the gentleman who played Lord Devenish, and played him just as he might have played an elderly marquis in a comic opera, grimacing over a snuff-box, and withering all sense and music out of Mr James's lines with a diction which I forbear to describe. He was very largely responsible for the irritation which subsequently vented itself on the author; and I am far from sure that I ought not to borrow a weapon from the Speaker of the House of Commons, and go to the extreme length of naming him.

Guy Domville is preceded by a farce (called in the bill a comedy) by Julian Field, entitled Too Happy by Half. It is deftly turned out from old and seasoned materials, and is capital fun for the audience and for Mr Esmond and Miss Millard. Miss Millard is not yet quite experienced enough to do very easy work quite well: she is the least bit crude occasionally.

Mr Oscar Wilde's new play at the Haymarket is a dangerous subject, because he has the property of making his critics dull. They laugh angrily at his epigrams, like a child who is coaxed into being amused in the very act of setting up a yell of rage and agony. They protest that the trick is obvious, and that such epigrams can be turned out by the score by any one lightminded enough to condescend to such frivolity. As far as I can ascertain, I am the only person in London who cannot sit down and write an Oscar Wilde play at will. The fact that his plays, though apparently lucrative, remain unique under these circumstances, says much for the self-denial of our scribes. In a certain sense Mr Wilde is to me our only thorough playwright. He plays with everything: with wit, with philosophy, with drama, with actors and audience, with the whole theatre. Such a feat scandalizes the Englishman, who can no more play with wit and philosophy than he can with a football or a cricket bat. He works at both, and has the consolation, if he cannot make people laugh, of being the best cricketer and footballer in the world. Now it is the mark of the artist that he will not work. Just as people with social ambitions will practise the meanest economies in order to live expensively; so the artist will starve his way through incredible toil and discouragement sooner than go and earn a week's honest wages. Mr Wilde, an arch-artist, is so colossally lazy that he trifles even with the work by which an artist escapes work. He distils the very quintessence, and gets as product plays which are so unapproachably playful that they are the delight of every playgoer with twopenn'orth of brains. The English critic, always protesting that the drama should not be didactic, and yet always complaining if the dramatist does not find sermons in stones and good in everything, will be conscious of a subtle and pervading levity in An Ideal Husband. All the literary dignity of the play, all the imperturbable good sense and good manners with which Mr Wilde makes his wit pleasant to his comparatively stupid audience, cannot quite overcome the fact that Ireland is of all countries the most foreign to England, and that to the Irishman (and Mr Wilde is almost as acutely Irish an Irishman as the Iron Duke of Wellington) there is nothing in the world quite so exquisitely comic as an Englishman's seriousness. It becomes tragic, perhaps, when the Englishman acts on it; but that occurs too seldom to be taken into account, a fact which intensifies the humor of the situation, the total result being the Englishman's utterly unconscious of his real self, Mr Wilde keenly observant of it and playing on the self-unconsciousness with irresistible humor, and finally, of course, the Englishman annoyed with himself for being amused at his own expense, and for being unable to convict Mr Wilde of what seems an obvious misunderstanding of human nature. He is shocked, too, at the danger to the foundations of society when seriousness is publicly laughed at. And to complete the oddity of the situation, Mr Wilde, touching what he himself reverences, is absolutely the most sentimental dramatist of the day.

It is useless to describe a play which has no thesis: which is, in the purest integrity, a play and nothing less. The six worst epigrams are mere alms handed with a kind smile to the average suburban playgoer; the three best remain secrets between Mr Wilde and a few choice spirits. The modern note is struck in Sir Robert Chiltern's assertion of the individuality and courage of his wrongdoing as against the mechanical idealism of his stupidly good wife, and in his bitter criticism of a love that is only the reward of merit. It is from the philosophy on which this scene is based that the most pregnant epigrams in the play have been condensed. Indeed, this is the only philosophy that ever has produced epigrams. In contriving the stage expedients by which the action of the piece is kept going, Mr Wilde has been once or twice a little too careless of stage illusion: for example, why on earth should Mrs Cheveley, hiding in Lord Goring's room, knock down a chair? That is my sole criticism.

The performance is very amusing. The audience laughs conscientiously: each person comes to the theatre prepared, like a special artist, with the background of a laugh ready sketched in on his or her features. Some of the performers labor intensely at being epigrammatic. I am sure Miss Vane Featherstone and Miss Forsyth could play Lady Macbeth and Medea with less effort than Lady Basildon and Mrs Marchmont, who have nothing to do but sit on a sofa and be politely silly for ten minutes. There is no doubt that these glimpses of expensive receptions in Park Lane, with the servants announcing titles *ad libitum*, are enormously attractive to social outsiders (say ninety-nine hundredths of us); but the stage reproduction is not convincing: everybody has an outrageous air of being at a party; of not being used to it; and, worst of all, of enjoying themselves immensely. Mr Charles Hawtrey has the best of the fun among the principals. As everyone's guide, philosopher, and friend, he has moments in which he is, I think, intended to be deep, strong, and tender. These moments, to say the least, do not quite come off; but his lighter serious episodes are excellent, and his drollery conquers without effort. When Miss Neilson sits still and lets her gifts of beauty and grace be eloquent for her, she is highly satisfying; but I cannot say the same for the passages in which she has to take the stage herself and try to act. She becomes merely artificial and superficially imitative. Miss Fanny Brough makes Lady Markby, an eminently possible person, quite impossible; and Miss Maude Millet, playing very well indeed as Mabel Chiltern, nevertheless occasionally spoils a word by certain vowel sounds which are only permissible to actresses of the second rank. As an adventuress who, like the real and unlike the stage adventuress, is not in love with any one, and is simply selfish, dishonest, and third rate, Miss Florence West is kinetoscopically realistic. The portrait is true to nature; but it has no artistic character: Miss West has not the art of being agreeably disagreeable. Mr Brookfield, a great artist in small things, makes the valet in the third act one of the heroes of the performance. And Mr Waller is handsome and dignified as the ideal husband, a part easily within his means. His management could not have been more auspiciously inaugurated.

"Poor Shakespear!"

×××××××××××××××××××××××××××××××××××××××

ALL'S WELL THAT ENDS WELL. Performance by the Irving Dramatic Club at St George's Hall, 22 and 24 January 1895.

[2 *February* 1895]

What a pity it is that the people who love the sound of Shakespear so seldom go on the stage! The ear is the sure clue to him: only a musician can understand the play of feeling which is the real rarity in his early plays. In a deaf nation these plays would have died long ago. The moral attitude in them is conventional and secondhand: the borrowed ideas, however finely expressed, have not the overpowering human interest of those original criticisms of life which supply the rhetorical element in his later works. Even the individualization which produces that old-established British speciality, the Shakespearean "delineation of character," owes all its magic to the turn of the line, which lets you into the secret of its utterer's mood and temperament, not by its commonplace meaning, but by some subtle exaltation, or stultification, or slyness, or delicacy, or hesitancy, or what not in the sound of it. In short, it is the score and not the libretto that keeps the work alive and fresh; and this is why only musical critics should be allowed to meddle with Shakespear—especially early Shakespear. Unhappily, though the nation still retains its ears, the players and playgoers of this generation are for the most part deaf as adders. Their appreciation of Shakespear is sheer hypocrisy, the proof being that where an early play of his is revived, they take the utmost pains to suppress as much of it as possible, and disguise the rest past recognition, relying for success on extraordinary scenic attractions; on very popular performers, including, if possible, a famously beautiful actress in the leading part; and, above all, on Shakespear's reputation and the consequent submission of the British public to be mercilessly bored by each of his plays once in their lives, for the sake of being able to say they have seen it. And not a soul has the hardihood to yawn in the face of the imposture. The manager is praised; the bard is praised; the beautiful actress is praised; and the free list comes early and comes often, not without a distinct sense of conferring a handsome compliment on the acting manager. And it certainly is hard to face such a disappointment without being paid for it. For the more enchanting the play is at home by the fireside in winter, or out on the heather of a summer evening—the more the manager, in his efforts to realize this enchantment by reckless expenditure on incidental music, colored lights, dances, dresses, and elaborate rearrangements and dislocations of the play—the more, in fact, he departs from the old platform with its curtains and its placards inscribed "A street in Mantua," and so forth, the more hopelessly and vulgarly does he miss his mark. Such crown jewels of dramatic poetry as Twelfth Night and A Midsummer Night's Dream, fade into shabby colored glass in his purse: and sincere people who do not know what the matter is, begin to babble insufferably about plays that are meant for the study and not for the stage.

Yet once in a blue moon or so there wanders on to the stage some happy fair whose eyes are lodestars and whose tongue's sweet air's more tunable than lark to shepherd's ear. And the moment she strikes up the true Shakespearean music, and feels her way to her part altogether by her sense of that music, the play returns to life and all the magic is there. She may make nonsense of the verses by wrong conjunctions and misplaced commas, which shew that she has never worked out the logical construction of a single sentence in her part; but if her heart is in the song, the protesting commentator-critic may save his breath to cool his porridge: the soul of the play is there, no matter where the sense of it may be. We have all heard Miss Rehan perform this miracle with Twelfth Night, and turn it, in spite of the impossible Mr Daly, from a hopelessly ineffective actress show into something like the exquisite poem its author left it. All I can remember of the last performance I witnessed of A Midsummer Night's Dream is that Miss Kate Rorke got on the stage somehow and began to make some music with Helena's lines, with the result that Shakespear, who had up to that moment lain without sense or motion, immediately began to stir uneasily and shew signs of quickening, which lasted until the others took up the word and struck him dead.

Powerful among the enemies of Shakespear are the commentator and the elocutionist: the commentator because, not knowing Shakespear's language, he sharpens his reasoning faculty to examine propositions advanced by an eminent lecturer from the Midlands, instead of sensitizing his artistic faculty to receive the impression of moods and inflexions of feeling conveyed by word-music; the elocutionist because he is a born fool, in which capacity, observing with pain that poets have a weakness for imparting to their dramatic dialogue a quality which he describes and deplores as "sing-song," he devotes his life to the art of breaking up verse in such a way as to make it sound like insanely pompous prose. The effect of this on Shakespear's earlier verse, which is full of the naïve delight of pure oscillation, to be enjoyed as an Italian enjoys a barcarolle, or a child a swing, or a baby a rocking-cradle, is destructively stupid. In the later plays, where the barcarolle measure has evolved into much more varied and complex rhythms, it does not matter so much, since the work is no longer simple enough for a fool to pick to pieces. But in every play from Love's Labour Lost to Henry V, the elocutionist meddles simply as a murderer, and ought to be dealt with as such without benefit of clergy. To our young people studying for the stage I say, with all solemnity, learn how to pronounce the English alphabet clearly and beautifully from some person who is at once an artist and a phonetic expert. And then leave blank verse patiently alone until you have experienced emotion deep enough to crave for poetic expression, at which point verse will seem an absolutely natural and real form of speech to you. Meanwhile, if any pedant, with an uncultivated heart and a theoretic ear, proposes to teach you to recite, send instantly for the police.

Among Shakespear's earlier plays, All's Well that Ends Well stands out artistically by the sovereign charm of the young Helena and the old Countess of Rousillon, and intellectually by the experiment, repeated nearly three hundred years later in A Doll's House, of making the hero a perfectly ordinary young man, whose unimaginative prejudices and selfish conventionality make him cut a very fine mean figure in the atmosphere created by the nobler nature of his wife. That is what gives a certain plausibility to the otherwise doubtful tradition that Shakespear did not succeed in getting his play produced (founded on the absence of any record of a performance of it during his lifetime). It certainly explains why Phelps, the only modern actor-manager tempted by it, was attracted by the part of Parolles, a capital study of the adventurous yarn-spinning society-struck coward, who also crops up again in modern fiction as the hero of Charles Lever's underrated novel, A Day's Ride: a Life's Romance. When I saw All's Well announced for performance by the Irving Dramatic Club, I was highly interested, especially as the performers were free, for once, to play Shakespear for Shakespear's sake. Alas! at this amateur performance, at which there need have been none of the miserable commercialization compulsory at the regular theatres, I suffered all the vulgarity and absurdity of that commercialism without its efficiency. We all know the stock objection of the Brixton Family Shakespear to All's Well—that the heroine is a lady doctor, and that no lady of any delicacy could possibly adopt a profession which involves the possibility of her having to attend cases such as that of the king in this play, who suffers from a fistula. How any sensible and humane person can have ever read this sort of thing without a deep sense of its insult to every charitable woman's humanity and every sick man's suffering is, fortunately, getting harder to understand nowadays than it once was. Nevertheless All's Well was minced with strict deference to it for the members of the Irving Dramatic Club. The rule for expurgation was to omit everything that the most

pestiferously prurient person could find improper. For
example, when the non-commissioned officer, with quite
becoming earnestness and force, says to the disgraced
Parolles: "If you could find out a country where but
women were that had received so much shame, you might
begin an impudent nation," the speech was suppressed as
if it were on all fours with the obsolete Elizabethan badi-
nage which is and should be cut out as a matter of course.
And to save Helena from anything so shocking as a reference to her virginity, she was robbed of that rapturous outburst beginning.

> There shall your master have a thousand loves—
> A mother and a mistress and a friend, etc.

But perhaps this was sacrificed in deference to the opinion
of the editor of those pretty and handy little books called
the Temple Shakespear, who compares the passage to "the
nonsense of some foolish conceited player"—a criticism
which only a commentator could hope to live down.

The play was, of course, pulled to pieces in order that
some bad scenery, totally unconnected with Florence or
Rousillon, might destroy all the illusion which the simple
stage directions in the book create, and which they would
equally have created had they been printed on a placard
and hung up on a curtain. The passage of the Florentine
army beneath the walls of the city was managed in the
manner of the end of the first act of Robertson's Ours,
the widow and the girls looking out of their sitting-room
window, whilst a few of the band gave a precarious selection from the orchestral parts of Berlioz's version of the
Rackoczy March. The dresses were the usual fancy ball
odds and ends, Helena especially distinguishing herself by
playing the first scene partly in the costume of Hamlet and
partly in that of a waitress in an Aerated Bread shop, set
off by a monstrous auburn wig which could by no stretch
of imagination be taken for her own hair. Briefly, the
whole play was vivisected, and the fragments mutilated,
for the sake of accessories which were in every particular
silly and ridiculous. If they were meant to heighten the
illusion, they were worse than failures, since they rendered

illusion almost impossible. If they were intended as illustrations of place and period, they were ignorant impostures. I have seen poetic plays performed without costumes before a pair of curtains by ladies and gentlemen in evening dress with twenty times the effect: nay, I will pledge my reputation that if the members of the Irving Dramatic Club will take their books in their hands, sit in a Christy Minstrel semicircle, and read the play decently as it was written, the result will be a vast improvement on this St George's Hall travesty.

Perhaps it would not be altogether kind to leave these misguided but no doubt well-intentioned ladies and gentlemen without a word of appreciation from their own point of view. Only, there is not much to be said for them even from that point of view. Few living actresses could throw themselves into the sustained transport of exquisite tenderness and impulsive courage which makes poetry the natural speech of Helena. The cool young woman, with a superior understanding, excellent manners, and a habit of reciting Shakespear, presented before us by Miss Olive Kennett, could not conceivably have been even Helena's thirty-second cousin. Miss Lena Heinekey, with the most beautiful old woman's part ever written in her hands, discovered none of its wonderfully pleasant good sense, humanity, and originality: she grieved stagily all through in the manner of the Duchess of York in Cibber's Richard III. Mr Lewin-Mannering did not for any instant make it possible to believe that Parolles was a real person to him. They all insisted on calling him *parole*, instead of Parolles, in three syllables, with the *s* sounded at the end, as Shakespear intended: consequently, when he came to the couplet which cannot be negotiated on any other terms:

> Rust, sword; cool, blushes; and, Parolles, thrive;
> Theres place and means for every man alive,

he made a desperate effort to get even with it by saying:

> Rust, rapier; cool, blushes; and, *parole*, thrive,

and seemed quite disconcerted when he found that it would not do. Lafeu is hardly a part that can be acted: it comes right if the right man is available: if not, no acting can conceal the makeshift. Mr Herbert Everitt was not the right man; but he made the best of it. The clown was evidently willing to relish his own humor if only he could have seen it; but there are few actors who would not have gone that far. Bertram (Mr Patrick Munro), if not the most intelligent of Bertrams, played the love scene with Diana with some passion. The rest of the parts, not being character studies, are tolerably straightforward and easy of execution; and they were creditably played, the king (Mr Ernest Meads) carrying off the honors, and Diana (Mrs Herbert Morris) acquitting herself with comparative distinction. But I should not like to see another such performance of All's Well or any other play that is equally rooted in my deeper affections.

"Pinero and Wilde"

×××

THE IMPORTANCE OF BEING EARNEST. A trivial comedy for serious people. By Oscar Wilde. St James's Theatre, 14 February 1895.
? A play in ? acts. By ?. Opera Comique, 16 February 1895.
THE SECOND MRS TANQUERAY. A play in four acts. By Arthur W. Pinero. London: W. Heinemann. 1895.

[23 February 1895]

It is somewhat surprising to find Mr Oscar Wilde, who does not usually model himself on Mr Henry Arthur Jones, giving his latest play a five-chambered title like The Case of Rebellious Susan. So I suggest with some confidence that The Importance of Being Earnest dates from a period long anterior to Susan. However it may have been re-touched immediately before its production, it must certainly have been written before Lady Windermere's Fan. I do not suppose it to be Mr Wilde's first play: he is too susceptible to fine art to have begun otherwise than with a strenuous imitation of a great dramatic poem, Greek or Shakespearean; but it was perhaps the first which he designed for practical commercial use at the West End theatres. The evidence of this is abundant. The play has a plot—a gross anachronism; there is a scene between the two girls in the second act quite in the literary style of Mr Gilbert, and almost inhuman enough to have been conceived by him; the humor is adulterated by stock mechanical fun to an extent that absolutely scandalizes one in a play with such an author's name to it; and the punning title and several of the more farcical passages recall the epoch of the late H. J. Byron. The whole has been varnished, and here and there veneered, by the author of A

Woman of no Importance; but the general effect is that of a farcical comedy dating from the seventies, unplayed during that period because it was too clever and too decent, and brought up to date as far as possible by Mr Wilde in his now completely formed style. Such is the impression left by the play on me. But I find other critics, equally entitled to respect, declaring that The Importance of Being Earnest is a strained effort of Mr Wilde's at ultra-modernity, and that it could never have been written but for the opening up of entirely new paths in drama last year by Arms and The Man. At which I confess to a chuckle.

I cannot say that I greatly cared for The Importance of Being Earnest. It amused me, of course; but unless comedy touches me as well as amuses me, it leaves me with a sense of having wasted my evening. I go to the theatre to be moved to laughter, not to be tickled or bustled into it; and that is why, though I laugh as much as anybody at a farcical comedy, I am out of spirits before the end of the second act, and out of temper before the end of the third, my miserable mechanical laughter intensifying these symptoms at every outburst. If the public ever becomes intelligent enough to know when it is really enjoying itself and when it is not, there will be an end of farcical comedy. Now in The Importance of Being Earnest there is plenty of this rib-tickling: for instance, the lies, the deceptions, the cross purposes, the sham mourning, the christening of the two grown-up men, the muffin eating, and so forth. These could only have been raised from the farcical plane by making them occur to characters who had, like Don Quixote, convinced us of their reality and obtained some hold on our sympathy. But that unfortunate moment of Gilbertism breaks our belief in the humanity of the play. Thus we are thrown back on the force and daintiness of its wit, brought home by an exquisitely grave, natural, and unconscious execution on the part of the actors. Alas! the latter is not forthcoming. Mr Kinsey Peile as a man-servant, and Miss Irene Vanbrugh as Gwendolen Fairfax, alone escaped from a devastating consciousness of Mr Wilde's reputation, which more or less preoccupied all the rest, except perhaps Miss Millard, with whom all comedy is a preoccupation, since she is essentially a sentimental actress. In such passages as the Gilbertian quarrel with Gwendolen, her charm rebuked the scene instead of enhancing it. The older ladies were, if they will excuse my saying so, quite maddening. The violence of their affectation, the insufferable low comedy soars and swoops of the voice, the rigid shivers of elbow, shoulder, and neck, which are supposed on the stage to characterize the behavior of ladies after the age of forty, played havoc with the piece. In Miss Rose Leclerq a good deal of this sort of thing is only the mannerism of a genuine if somewhat impossible style; but Miss Leclerq was absent through indisposition on the night of my visit; so that I had not her style to console me. Mr Aynesworth's easy-going Our Boys style of play suited his part rather happily; and Mr Alexander's graver and more refined manner made the right contrast with it. But Mr Alexander, after playing with very nearly if not quite perfect conviction in the first two acts, suddenly lost confidence in the third, and began to spur up for a rattling finish. From the moment that began, the play was done with. The speech in which Worthing forgives his supposed mother, and the business of searching the army lists, which should have been conducted with subdued earnestness, was bustled through to the destruction of all verisimilitude and consequently all interest. That is the worst of having anyone who is not an inveterate and hardened comedian in a leading comedy part. His faith, patience, and relish begin to give out after a time; and he finally commits the unpardonable sin against the author of giving the signal that the play is over ten minutes before the fall of the curtain, instead of speaking the last line as if the whole evening were still before the audience. Mr Alexander does not throw himself genuinely into comedy: he condescends to amuse himself with it; and in the end he finds that he cannot condescend enough. On the whole I must decline to accept The Importance of Being Earnest as a day less than ten years old; and I am altogether unable to perceive any uncommon excellence in its presentation.

I am in a somewhat foolish position concerning a play

at the Opera Comique, whither I was bidden this day
week. For some reason I was not supplied with a program;
so that I never learnt the name of the play. I believe I
recognized some of the members of the company—generally a very difficult thing to do in a country where, with
a few talented exceptions, every actor is just like every
other actor—but they have now faded from my memory.
At the end of the second act the play had advanced about
as far as an ordinary dramatist would have brought it five
minutes after the first rising of the curtain; or, say, as far
as Ibsen would have brought it ten years before that event.
Taking advantage of the second interval to stroll out into
the Strand for a little exercise, I unfortunately forgot all
about my business, and actually reached home before it
occurred to me that I had not seen the end of the play.
Under these circumstances it would ill become me to
dogmatize on the merits of the work or its performance.
I can only offer the management my apologies.

I am indebted to Mr Heinemann for a copy of The
Second Mrs Tanqueray, which he has just published in a
five-shilling volume, with an excellent photographic portrait
of the author by Mr Hollyer. Those who did not see the
play at the St James's Theatre can now examine the literary
basis of the work that so immoderately fascinated playgoing London in 1893. But they must not expect the play
to be as imposing in the library as it was on the stage. Its
merit there was relative to the culture of the playgoing
public. Paula Tanqueray is an astonishingly well-drawn
figure as stage figures go nowadays, even allowing for the
fact that there is no cheaper subject for the character
draughtsman than the ill-tempered sensual woman seen
from the point of view of the conventional man. But off the
stage her distinction vanishes. The novels of Anthony
Trollope, Charles Lever, Bulwer Lytton, Charles Reade,
and many other novelists, whom nobody praised thirty
years ago in the terms in which Mr Pinero is praised now,
are full of feats of character-drawing in no way inferior—
to say the least—to Mr Pinero's. The theatre was not ready
for that class of work then: it is now; and accordingly Mr
Pinero, who in literature is a humble and somewhat be-

lated follower of the novelists of the middle of the nineteenth century, and who has never written a line from which it could be guessed that he is a contemporary of Ibsen, Tolstoi, Meredith, or Sarah Grand, finds himself at the dawn of the twentieth hailed as a man of new ideas, of daring originality, of supreme literary distinction, and even—which is perhaps oddest—of consummate stage craft. Stage craft, after all, is very narrowly limited by the physical conditions of stage representation; but when one turns over the pages of The Second Mrs Tanqueray, and notes the naïve machinery of the exposition in the first act, in which two whole actors are wasted on sham parts, and the hero, at his own dinner party, is compelled to get up and go ignominiously into the next room "to write some letters" when something has to be said behind his back; when one follows Cayley Drummle, the confidant to whom both Paula and her husband explain themselves for the benefit of the audience; when one counts the number of doors which Mr Pinero needs to get his characters on and off the stage, and how they have finally to be supplemented by the inevitable "French windows" (two of them); and when the activity of the postman is taken into consideration, it is impossible to avoid the conclusion that what most of our critics mean by mastery of stage craft is recklessness in the substitution of dead machinery and lay figures for vital action and real characters. I do not deny that an author may be driven by his own limitations to ingenuities which Shakespear had no occasion to cultivate, just as a painter without hands or feet learns to surpass Michael Angelo in the art of drawing with the brush held in the mouth; but I regard such ingenuity as an extremity to be deplored, not as an art to be admired. In The Second Mrs. Tanqueray I find little except a scaffold for the situation of a step-daughter and step-mother finding themselves in the positions respectively of affianced wife and discarded mistress to the same man. Obviously, the only necessary conditions of this situation are that the persons connected shall be respectable enough to be shocked by it, and that the step-mother shall be an improper person. Mr Pinero has not got above this minimum. He is, of course, sufficiently skilled in fiction to give Ellean, Mrs Cortelyon, Ardale, Tanqueray, and Cayley Drummle a passable air of being human beings. He has even touched up Cayley into a Thackerayan *flâneur* in order to secure toleration of his intrusiveness. But who will pretend that any of these figures are more than the barest accessories to the main situation? To compare them with the characters in Robertson's Caste would be almost as ridiculous as to compare Caste with A Doll's House. The two vulgar characters produce the requisite jar—a pitilessly disagreeable jar—and that is all. Still, all the seven seem good as far as they go; and that very little way may suggest that Mr Pinero might have done good creative work if he had carried them further. Unfortunately for this surmise, he has carried Paula further; and with what result? The moment the point is reached at which the comparatively common gift of "an eye for character" has to be supplemented by the higher dramatic gift of sympathy with character—of the power of seeing the world from the point of view of others instead of merely describing or judging them from one's own point of view in terms of the conventional systems of morals, Mr Pinero breaks down. I remember that when I saw the play acted I sat up very attentively when Tanqueray said to Paula, "I know what you were at Ellean's age. You hadnt a thought that wasnt a wholesome one; you hadnt an impulse that didnt tend towards good; you never harbored a notion you couldnt have gossiped about to a parcel of children. And this was a very few years back, etc. etc." On the reply to that fatuous but not unnatural speech depended the whole question of Mr Pinero's rank as a dramatist. One can imagine how, in a play by a master-hand, Paula's reply would have opened Tanqueray's foolish eyes to the fact that a woman of that sort is already the same at three as she is at thirty-three, and that however she may have found by experience that her nature is in conflict with the ideals of differently constituted people, she remains perfectly valid to herself, and despises herself, if she sincerely does so at all, for the hypocrisy that the world forces on her instead of for being what she is. What reply does Mr Pinero put into her mouth? Here it is, with the stage directions: "A few—years ago! (*She walks slowly towards the door, then suddenly drops upon the ottoman in a paroxysm of weeping.*) O God! A few years ago!" That is to say, she makes her reply from the Tanqueray-Ellean-Pinero point of view, and thus betrays the fact that she is a work of prejudiced observation instead of comprehension, and that the other characters only owe their faint humanity to the fact that they are projections of Mr Pinero's own personal amiabilities and beliefs and conventions. Mr Pinero, then, is no interpreter of character, but simply an adroit describer of people as the ordinary man sees and judges them. Add to this a clear head, a love of the stage, and a fair talent for fiction, all highly cultivated by hard and honorable work as a writer of effective stage plays for the modern commercial theatre; and you have him on his real level. On that level he is entitled to all the praise. The Second Mrs Tanqueray has won him; and I very heartily regret that the glamor which Mrs Patrick Campbell cast round the play has forced me to examine pretensions which Mr Pinero himself never put forward rather than to acknowledge the merits with which his work is so concisely packed.

"Sardoodledom"

✕✕✕✕✕✕✕✕✕✕✕✕✕✕✕✕✕✕✕✕✕✕✕✕✕✕✕✕✕✕✕✕✕✕

FEDORA (Herman Merivale's English version). By Victorien Sardou. Haymarket Theatre, 25 May 1895. GISMONDA. By Victorien Sardou. Daly's Theatre, 27 May 1895.

[1 June 1895]

Up to this day week I had preserved my innocence as a playgoer sufficiently never to have seen Fedora. Of course I was not altogether new to it, since I had seen Diplomacy Dora, and Theodora, and La Toscadora, and other machine dolls from the same firm. And yet the thing took me aback. To see that curtain go up again and again only to disclose a bewildering profusion of everything that has no business in a play, was an experience for which nothing could quite prepare me. The postal arrangements, the telegraphic arrangements, the police arrangements, the names and addresses, the hours and seasons, the tables of consanguinity, the railway and shipping time-tables, the arrivals and departures, the whole welter of Bradshaw and Baedeker, Court Guide and Post Office Directory, whirling round one incredible little stage murder and finally vanishing in a gulp of impossible stage poison, made up an entertainment too Bedlamite for any man with settled wits to preconceive. Even the murder was arranged, in pure wantonness, flatly contrary to common sense. The hero is suspected by the heroine of having been a Nihilist at a period when matters were so bad in Russia that refugees who made no secret of their sympathy with the Terrorists were sympathetically welcomed by the strictest Constitutionalists in every other country in Europe. He completely regains her sympathy by proving to her that he is no Nihilist at all, but a common assassin who has deliberately murdered a man out of jealousy. Surely, if dramatists are bent on the fundamentally impossible task of inventing pardonable assassinations, they should recognize that the man who, for no reward or satisfaction to his direct personal instincts, but at the risk of his own life, kills for the sake of an idea, believing that he is striking in the cause of the general weal, is at any rate more respectable than the dehumanized creature who stabs or shoots to slake a passion which he has in common with a stag. I strongly object to heroic criminals, whether political or personal; but if the stage cannot yet get on without its illustrated police news, let us at least shun the most repulsive motives for the stage crimes we are expected to condone. This Loris Ipanoff is a vulgar scoundrel as far as he is credibly human at all; and Fedora, who has at first the excuse of being the avenger of blood, sinks to his level when, on learning that her husband preferred another woman to her, she gloats over his murder, and is disappointed because Loris did not kill his wife on the spot too. Why need plays be so brutally, callously, barbarously immoral as this? I wish Sir Henry Irving would give us at least a matinée of The Lady from the Sea to shew the playgoing public how a humane gentleman acts when he finds he has had the misfortune to lose the affection of his wife. Miss Terry as Ellida would be quite as worthy of the Lyceum Theatre as Nance Oldfield as Miss Terry.

It is greatly to Mrs Patrick Campbell's credit that, bad as the play was, her acting was worse. It was a masterpiece of failure. Not, pray observe, that Mrs Campbell herself did not succeed. The moment she was seen, our reason collapsed and our judgment fled. Every time the curtain fell there was a delirious roar. If the play was not tragic, our infatuation was. I solemnly warn all and sundry that no common man's opinion of the artistic merits of that performance was worth a farthing after the first flash of the heroine's eyes. It was not Fedora; but it was Circe; and I, as sworn critic, must make the best attempt I can to be Ulysses.

It cannot, I think, be disputed now that Mrs Campbell's force, which is intense enough, has only one mode, and

that one the vituperative. This was proved at one stroke
in the first act, when Fedora goes to her husband's bedside
and discovers him dead. Mrs Campbell uttered a shriek,
as any actress would; but it was a shriek that suggested
nothing of grief, or mortally wounded tenderness, or even
horror. What it did suggest very strongly was that Fedora
had surprised the secret which Loris reveals to her in the
third act. In short, it was a scream of rage. Again in the
second act, when Loris admitted the killing of Vladimir,
her cry of "Murderer, assassin," might have been any
abusive term hurled at a man, appropriately or not, under
an impulse of violent anger. Last week I politely attributed
to Mrs Campbell's sense of character her catching, as Mrs
Ebbsmith, what Miss Nethersole misses: namely, the tone
of invective in "Trafalgar Squaring" the Duke of St
Olpherts. But it now appears that, her emotion declines to
take any other form than that of invective. When she is
not abusing somebody, she sits visibly concentrating her
forces to restrain the vituperative pressure which is struggling to expand in reckless aggression, the general effect
being that of a magnificent woman with a magnificent temper, which she holds in or lets loose with exciting uncertainty. This of course means that Mrs Campbell is not yet
mistress of her art, though she has a rare equipment for
it. Even her diction is technically defective. In order to
secure refinement of tone, she articulates with the tip of her
tongue against her front teeth as much as possible. This
enters for what it is worth and no more into the method
of every fine speaker; but it should not suggest the snobbish
Irishman who uses it as a cheap recipe for speaking genteel
English; and once or twice Mrs Campbell came dangerously
near to producing this mincing effect. For instance, "One
absorbing thought which meeks a sleeve of me," is clearly
not the excess of a genuine refinement of diction, like Sir
Henry Irving's pure vowel method, which would lead him
to say "One ap-sorbing thot which me̽ks a slèv of me" (the
p in absorbing being a German b, and the italic letters
pronounced as in the French *fidèle*). I am only moderately
pedantic in this matter, and do not object at all to Mrs
Campbell's saying "Forgimme" for "Forgive me," or the

traditional and ugly "Be't so" for the correct and pretty "Be it so"; but I protest against "hatrid" and "disseived," which are pure inaccuracies produced by that Irish recipe. I make no apology for going into these details; for stage usage is one of our few standards of diction; and it is rather alarming to hear the extent to which our younger actresses are left to pick up the stage trick of speech without in the least understanding the phonetic part of it.

The death scene begins like a feeble drawing room plagiarism of the murder of Nancy by Bill Sykes, and ends with the Gilbertian absurdity of the woman, as she realizes with disgust that her husband actually proposes to commit the vulgarity of strangling her, rising with a dignity which paralyzes him, and saying, "Oh, if you are determined to behave in that way, I will poison myself like a lady; and you, I hope, will look on quietly like a gentleman," or words to that effect. Here Mrs Campbell did for a moment produce the effect which Sardou has so tediously and laboriously lath-and-plastered up, and produce it in a way which shewed unmistakably that she is quite capable of the modern equivalents of the whole Bernhardtian range of sensational effects—effects so enormously popular and lucrative that, though their production is hardly more of a fine art than lion-taming, few women who are able for them can resist the temptation to devote their lives to them. At every other point, Mrs Campbell threw Sardou out of the window and substituted her own personal magnetism for the stale mechanical tragedy of Fedora. It was irrelevant; but it was effective.

Sardou's latest edition of the Kiralfian entertainment which Madame Bernhardt has for years past dragged from sea to sea in her Armada of transports, is called Gismonda, and is surpassingly dreary, although it is happily relieved four times by very long waits between the acts. The scene being laid in the Middle Ages, there are no newspapers, letters, or telegrams; but this is far from being an advantage, as the characters tell each other the news all through except when a child is dropped into a tiger's cage as a cue for Madame Bernhardt's popular scream; or when the inevitable stale, puerile love scene is turned on to shew off that "voix céleste" stop which Madame Bernhardt, like a sentimental New England villager with an American organ, keeps always pulled out; or when, in a paroxysm of the basest sensationalism, we are treated to the spectacle of Gismonda chopping a man to death with a hatchet as a preliminary to appearing as a mediæval saint with a palm in her hand at the head of a religious procession. What does it matter whether such an entertainment is called Gismonda, or Theodora, or Venice, or Constantinople, or The Orient, or Captain Boyton's water show? Personally, I prefer the water show, because the sixty-foot header interested me, which Madame Bernhardt has long ceased to do; and the sensation of shooting the chute thrilled me, which Gismonda does not. As a pageant the affair may pass very well with people who, never having been touched by the peculiar spiritual beauty of the art of the Middle Ages, compare the scene-painter's titivated imitations with the Lord Mayor's Show and the architecture of Regent Street instead of with the originals; but it is no more to be compared to the pageantry of King Arthur at the Lyceum than the clever but thoroughly shoppy stage business of Madame Bernhardt is to be compared to the acting of Miss Ellen Terry. I confess I regard with a certain jealousy the extent to which this ex-artist, having deliberately exercised her unquestioned right to step down from the national theatre in which she became famous to posture in a travelling show, is still permitted the privileges and courtesies proper to her former rank. It is open to all actresses to say either, "Give me a dignified living wage and let me work at my art," or, "Give me as much money and applause as can possibly be got out of me, and let my art go hang." Only, when the choice is made, it is the business of the critic to see that the chooser of the lower level does not take precedence of the devoted artist who takes the higher one. Madame Bernhardt has elected to go round the world pretending to kill people with hatchets and hairpins, and making, I presume, heaps of money. I wish her every success; but I shall certainly not treat her as a dramatic artist of the first rank unless she pays me well for it. As a self-respecting critic I decline to be bought for nothing.

It seems a strange thing to me that we should still be so little awake to the fact that in these plays which depend wholly on poignant intensity of expression for the simple emotions the sceptre has passed to the operatic artist. What surprises me is not that this exhibition of Madame Bernhardt's should be flagrantly vulgar and commercial, or that it should be hackneyed and old-fashioned, but that we should dream of going to see it now that we have seen Calvé as Carmen and La Navarraise. In the front ranks of art there is a place for the methods of Duse, and for the drama in which emotion exists only to make thought live and move us, but none for Sarah Bernhardt and the claptraps which Sardou contrives for her. To me, at least, the whole affair seems antiquated and ridiculous, except when I regard it as a high modern development of the circus and the waxworks. I have seen it, just as I have seen, in my time, Madame Celeste in Green Bushes and The Red Woman. Though I always preferred Buckstone to Sardou as a tragic dramatist, and still do, I used to think Madame Bernhardt a greater actress than Celeste. But I almost believe now that this must have been a delusion of the departed days when Madame Bernhardt was so slim that when she went for a trip in a captive balloon, it was said that her stepping into the car had the same effect as throwing out ballast. At all events, I am quite sure that if I had to choose between seeing Miami and Gismonda again, I should vote eagerly for Miami, who was at least amusing.

To revert for a moment to Fedora, I hope Mrs Campbell will note that Sarah Bernhardt's career cannot be repeated now—that her art is out of date and her dramas dead. The proof is that Mrs Campbell cannot act Fedora, although to any actress over forty-five Fedora is more natural than Mrs Tanqueray. By the way, I have forgotten to say that Mrs Bancroft is in the cast, and is as amusing and skilful as ever. Mr Tree, confronted with the impossible Loris Ipanoff, was forced to take the part seriously, and, with the help of a Polish make-up, try to pull it through by a creditably awkward attempt at conventional melodramatic acting. Besides, Mrs Campbell ruined his clothes. Wherever

her beautiful white arms touched him they left their mark.
She knelt at his feet and made a perfect zebra of his left
leg with bars across it. Then she flung her arms convulsively right round him; and the next time he turned his
back to the footlights there was little to choose between
his coatback and his shirtfront. Before the act was over a
gallon of benzine would hardly have set him right again.
Mr Tree had his revenge at the end of the play, when, in
falling on Fedora's body, he managed to transfer a large
black patch to her cheek, which was strikingly in evidence
when she bowed her acknowledgment of the frantic
applause with which the evening ended; but he was still so
unhinged by the futility of Loris and the ill-treatment of
his garments, that when the audience called for Mr
Bancroft he informed them that Mr Bancroft was prevented from coming forward by modesty, but that Mrs
Bancroft—and here Mrs Bancroft came forward smiling;
and the audience naturally chuckled hugely.

May I suggest that soap and water is an excellent
cosmetic for the arms, and that it does not mark coats?
Also that this white-washing malpractice has become an
intolerable absurdity, and that there is at least one critic
who means to try whether ridicule can kill it.

"Dear Harp of My Country!"

×××

THE COLLEEN BAWN; OR, THE BRIDES OF GARRYOWEN. Dion
Boucicault's Great Drama (*sic*), in three acts. Princess's
Theatre, 25 January 1896.

[1 February 1896]
I have lived to see The Colleen Bawn with real water in
it; and perhaps I shall live to see it some day with real
Irishmen in it, though I doubt if that will heighten its
popularity much. The real water lacks the translucent
cleanliness of the original article, and destroys the illusion
of Eily's drowning and Myles na Coppaleen's header to a
quite amazing degree; but the spectacle of the two performers taking a call before the curtain, sopping wet, and
bowing with miserable enjoyment of the applause, is one
which I shall remember with a chuckle whilst life remains.

When I imply, as above, that the Irishmen in The
Colleen Bawn are not real Irishmen, I do not mean for a
moment to challenge the authenticity of Mr Richard
Purdon, who succeeds Dion Boucicault as Myles. Nor do
I even accuse him of demonstrating the undeniable fact
that the worst stage Irishmen are often real Irishmen.
What I mean is that Dion Boucicault, when he invented
Myles, was not holding the mirror up to nature, but blar-
neying the British public precisely as the Irish car-driver,
when he is "cute" enough, blarneys the English tourist.
To an Irishman who has any sort of social conscience, the
conception of Ireland as a romantic picture, in which the
background is formed by the Lakes of Killarney by moon-
light, and a round tower or so, whilst every male figure is
"a broth of a bhoy," and every female one a colleen in a
crimson Connemara cloak, is as exasperating as the conception of Italy as a huge garden and art museum, in-

habited by picturesque artists' models, is to a sensible
Italian. The Kerry peasant is no more a Myles na Coppaleen
(his real name is Smith, or, at most, Ryan) than the
real Wiltshire peasant is a Mark Tapley; and as for Eily,
Dolly Varden as a typical English tradesman's daughter is
a masterpiece of realism in comparison. The occupation
of the Irish peasant is mainly agricultural; and I advise the
reader to make it a fixed rule never to allow himself to
believe in the alleged Arcadian virtues of the half-starved
drudges who are sacrificed to the degrading, brutalizing,
and, as far as I can ascertain, entirely unnecessary pursuit
of unscientific farming. The virtues of the Irish peasant are
the intense melancholy, the surliness of manner, the incapacity for happiness and self-respect that are the tokens
of his natural unfitness for a life of wretchedness. His
vices are the arts by which he accommodates himself to
his slavery—the flattery on his lips which hides the curse
in his heart; his pleasant readiness to settle disputes by
"leaving it all to your honor," in order to make something
out of your generosity in addition to exacting the utmost
of his legal due from you; his instinctive perception that by
pleasing you he can make you serve him; his mendacity
and mendicity; his love of a stolen advantage; the superstitious fear of his priest and his Church which does not
prevent him from trying to cheat both in the temporal
transactions between them; and the parasitism which
makes him, in domestic service, that occasionally convenient but on the whole demoralizing human barnacle,
the irremovable old retainer of the family. Of all the tricks
which the Irish nation have played on the slow-witted
Saxon, the most outrageous is the palming off on him of
the imaginary Irishman of romance. The worst of it is, that
when a spurious type gets into literature, it strikes the
imagination of boys and girls. They form themselves by
playing up to it; and thus the unsubstantial fancies of the
novelists and music-hall song-writers of one generation are
apt to become the unpleasant and mischievous realities of
the next. The obsoletely patriotic Englishman of today is
a most pestilent invention of this sort; and ever since the
formation of the German Empire, the German has been

dramatized with such success that even the Emperor spends most of his time in working up the character. Ireland, always foremost in the drama, may claim the credit of having invented the Irishman out of nothing— invented him without the stimulus of empire, national independence, knowledge of her own history, united population, common religion, or two-pennorth of prestige of any sort, her very rebellions having only attained eminence by giving the national genius for treachery an opportunity of surpassing all recorded achievements in that important department of revolutionary politics. Fortunately the same talent that enabled Ireland to lead the way in inventing and dramatizing national types now keeps her to the front in the more salutary work of picking them to pieces, a process which appeals to her barbarous humor on the one hand, and on the other to her keen common sense and intelligent appreciation of reality. Of course it sacrifices the advantages which the imposture secured, as I have good reason to feel; for nobody can be better aware than I am of the convenience to an Irishman in England of being able, by an occasional cunning flourish of his nationality, to secure all the privileges of a harmless lunatic without forfeiting the position of a responsible member of society. But there is a point at which shams become so deadly tiresome that they produce ungovernable nausea, and are rejected at all risks. There are signs that Ireland, never very tolerant of the stage Irishman within her own coasts, is disaffected to him even in the literature by which her scribes habitually impose on England and America. Quite lately a London publisher, Mr Arnold, sent me a novel with the suggestive title of Misther O'Ryan, who turned out to be the traditional blend of Myles na Coppaleen, Robert Emmett, Daniel O'Connell, Thomas Moore, Fin McCoul, and Brian Boru, as compounded and impersonated by a vulgar rascal—an Irish Silas Wegg— whose blackguardism and irremediable worthlessness the writer, evidently that very rare literary bird, an Irish author living in Ireland, had sketched with a vengeful zest that was highly refreshing and, I should say, very wholesome just at present. Take any of the pictures Balzac or

Maupassant have painted for us of the spiritual squalor of
the routine of poor middle-class life, in which the education, the income, the culture of the family are three-
quarters abject pretence; and you will not find it more
depressing and even appalling than those which break
through the usually imaginative atmosphere of Mr T. P.
O'Connor's reviews when the book in hand happens to
touch Irish life. I shewed my own appreciation of my
native land in the usual Irish way by getting out of it as
soon as I possibly could; and I cannot say that I have the
smallest intention of settling there again as long as the
superior attractions of St Helena (not to mention London)
are equally available; but since I cannot disguise from
myself the helpless dependence of the British Empire on us
for vital elements of talent and character (without us the
English race would simply die of respectability within two
generations), I am quite ready to help the saving work of
reducing the sham Ireland of romance to a heap of un-
sightly ruins. When this is done, my countrymen can consider the relative merits of building something real in the
old country, or taking a hint from that other clever
people, the Jews, and abandoning their Palestine to put on
all the rest of the world as a shepherd putteth on his garment, beginning with English journalism and American
politics as a convenient intermediary stage to soften the
transition from their present habits.

These considerations, though they bear more or less on
the performance at the Princess's, are not absolutely indispensable to a reasonable enjoyment of it. I have always
had a special respect for Mr Richard Purdon because his
father was Lord Mayor of Dublin when I was an impres-
sionable boy; and I am, therefore, probably apt to overrate
his talent as a comedian. Still, I can see that his Myles is
not the inimitable Myles of Dion Boucicault. It is a case
of the words of Mercury being harsh after the songs of
Apollo. Boucicault had a charming brogue: not even the
speech of the eminent journalist and M.P. named in a
former paragraph of this article is more musical in sound
or irresistible in insinuation—"sloothering" would be the
right word, were it current here—than his. But Mr Purdon

unhappily did not learn to speak in Galway or Kerry. He bewrays the respectable Dublin citizen, whose knowledge of the brogue is derived from domestic servants drawn chiefly from the neighboring counties, and corrupted by the tongue of Dublin itself, which, like all crowded capitals, somehow evolves a peculiar villainous accent of its own. With such opportunities Mr Purdon, having a strong sense of fun, and being a born mimic, has no difficulty in producing a brogue; but it is not a pretty one. Further, his voice, a little coarsened, perhaps, by many years' vigorous exploitation in the interests of the aforesaid sense of fun, which seems unchastened by any very vigilant sense of beauty, is rougher than that of the late author. He has to omit the song in which Boucicault effortlessly persuaded us to accept the statement that "old Ireland was his country, and his name it was Malloy," as a complete and satisfying *apologia pro sua vita*. And the attempt to humbug Father Tom is an obvious and blundering evasion instead of what it used to be—an artless outpouring of the innocence of a poor lad who had not the wit to understand what the priest was asking, much less tell a lie to his reverence. Boucicault was a coaxing, blandandhering sort of liar, to whom you could listen without impatience long enough to allow the carpenters time to set the most elaborate water-scene behind the front cloth. Mr Purdon is just half a trifle too grating and boisterous, though of course the generation which does not recollect Boucicault hardly feels this. On the other hand, Miss Beaumont Collins is a much better Eily than Mrs Boucicault, who now plays Mrs Cregan, used to be. Mrs Boucicault was always hopelessly ladylike, and usually made Hardress Cregan's complaints of her rusticity ridiculous by being more refined than he. Miss Collins speaks the part, which is really an engaging and almost poetic one, very prettily, and is always right about the feeling of it. Mr Cockburn does nothing with Father Tom; but as the character happens to suit his personality, his performance passes, and is even highly praised. Mr Tom Terriss does capitally for Hardress, besides being in earnest about his work, and so sustaining the reputation of his name. Miss Agnes Hewitt does all that can be done with the part of Anne Chute, an Irish edition of Lady Gay Spanker, and therefore one of the dreariest of Boucicault's pet vulgarities. Miss Clifton as Shelah, and Messrs Kenney and Rochelle as Corrigan and Danny Mann, were fully equal to the occasion, though Danny did not shew any of Charles II's sense of the tediousness of a prolonged death agony. Mrs Boucicault's competence in the stagey work to which Mrs Cregan is condemned goes without saying. The play, as a whole, in spite of an obsolete passage or two, and of the stupid mutilations imposed by the censorship of its day, is so far superior to the average modern melodrama, that I shall not be surprised if it repays the management handsomely for reviving it.

I regret to say that the patrons of the gallery at the Princess's, being admitted at half the usual west end price, devote the saving to the purchase of sausages to throw at the critics. I appeal to the gentleman or lady who successfully aimed one at me to throw a cabbage next time, as I am a vegetarian, and sausages are wasted on me.

To Charlotte Payne-Townshend

XXXXXXXXXXXXXXXXXXXXXXXXXXXXXXXXXXXXXXXX

This early love letter to his future wife suggests—as later letters do as well—that the marriage followed a romantic courtship, despite Charlotte's apparent insistence that the marriage be celibate.

29 Fitzroy Square W
7 November 1896

I am all in the dark as to Paris—cannot find out for certain when the performance is to take place. If I learn tomorrow that it is to be on Monday, I'll start at once.

No: you don't love me one little bit. All that is nature, instinct, sex: it proves nothing beyond itself. Don't fall in love: be your own, not mine or anyone else's. From the moment that you can't do without me, you're lost, like Bertha [Newcombe]. Never fear: if we want one another we shall find it out. All I know is that you made the autumn very happy, and that I shall always be fond of you for that. About the future I do not concern myself: let us do what lies to our hands & wait for events. My dearest!

GBS

"Little Eyolf"

×××××××××××××××××××××××××××××××××××××

LITTLE EYOLF. A play in three acts, by Henrik Ibsen. Avenue Theatre, 23 November 1896.

[28 November 1896]

The happiest and truest epithet that has yet been applied to the Ibsen drama in this country came from Mr Clement Scott when he said that Ibsen was "suburban." That is the whole secret of it. If Mr Scott had only embraced his discovery instead of quarrelling with it, what a splendid Ibsen critic he would have made! Suburbanity at present means modern civilization. The active, germinating, life in the households of today cannot be typified by an aristocratic hero, an ingenious heroine, a gentleman-forager abetted by an Artful Dodger, and a parlormaid who takes half-sovereigns and kisses from the male visitors. Such interiors exist on the stage, and nowhere else: therefore the only people who are accustomed to them and at home in them are the dramatic critics. But if you ask me where you can find the Helmer household, the Allmers household, the Solness household, the Rosmer household, and all the other Ibsen households, I reply, "Jump out of a train anywhere between Wimbledon and Haslemere; walk into the first villa you come to; and there you are." Indeed you need not go so far: Hampstead, Maida Vale, or West Kensington will serve your turn; but it is as well to remind people that the true suburbs are now the forty-mile radius, and that Camberwell and Brixton are no longer the suburbs, but the overflow of Gower Street—the genteel slums, in short. And this suburban life, except in so far as it is totally vegetable and undramatic, is the life depicted by Ibsen. Doubtless some of our critics are quite sincere in thinking it a vulgar life, in considering the conversations which men hold with their wives in it improper, in finding

its psychology puzzling and unfamiliar, and in forgetting
that its bookshelves and its music cabinets are laden with
works which did not exist for them, and which are the
daily bread of young women educated very differently
from the sisters and wives of their day. No wonder they
are not at ease in an atmosphere of ideas and assumptions
and attitudes which seem to them bewildering, morbid,
affected, extravagant, and altogether incredible as the common currency of suburban life. But Ibsen knows better.
His suburban drama is the inevitable outcome of a suburban civilization (meaning a civilization that appreciates
fresh air); and the true explanation of Hedda Gabler's
vogue is that given by Mr Grant Allen—"I take her in to
dinner twice a week."

Another change that the critics have failed to reckon
with is the change in fiction. Byron remarked that

> Romances paint at full length people's wooings,
> But only give a bust of marriages.

That was true enough in the days of Sir Walter Scott, when
a betrothed heroine with the slightest knowledge of what
marriage meant would have shocked the public as much
as the same ignorance today would strike it as tragic if
real, and indecent if simulated. The result was that the
romancer, when he came to a love scene, had frankly to
ask his "gentle reader" to allow him to omit the conversation as being necessarily too idiotic to interest anyone.
We have fortunately long passed out of that stage in
novels. By the time we had reached Vanity Fair and Mid-
dlemarch—both pretty old and prim stories now—marriage had become the starting point of our romances. Love
is as much the romancer's theme as ever; but married love
and the courtships of young people who are appalled by
the problems of life and motherhood have left the gover-
nesses and curates, the Amandas and Tom Joneses of other
days, far out of sight. Ten years ago the stage was as far
behind Sir Walter Scott as he is behind Madame Sarah
Grand. But when Ibsen took it by the scruff of the neck
just as Wagner took the Opera, then, willy nilly, it had to
come along. And now what are the critics going to do? The

Ibsen drama is pre-eminently the drama of marriage. If dramatic criticism receives it in the spirit of the nurse's husband in Romeo and Juliet, if it grins and makes remarks about "the secrets of the alcove," if it pours forth columns which are half pornographic pleasantry and the other half sham propriety, then the end will be, not in the least that Ibsen will be banned, but that dramatic criticism will cease to be read. And what a frightful blow that would be to English culture!

Little Eyolf is an extraordinarily powerful play, although none of the characters are as fascinatingly individualized as Solness or Rosmer, Hedda or Nora. The theme is a marriage—an ideal marriage from the suburban point of view. A young gentleman, a student and an idealist, is compelled to drudge at teaching to support himself. He meets a beautiful young woman. They fall in love with one another; and by the greatest piece of luck in the world (suburbanly considered) she has plenty of money. Thus he is set free by his marriage to live his own life in his own way. That is just where an ordinary play leaves off, and just where an Ibsen play begins. The husband begins to make those discoveries which everybody makes, except, apparently, the dramatic critics. First, that love, instead of being a perfectly homogeneous, unchanging, unending passion, is of all things the most mutable. It will pass through several well-marked stages in a single evening, and, whilst seeming to slip back to the old starting point the next evening, will yet not slip quite back; so that in the course of years it will appear that the moods of an evening were the anticipation of the evolution of a lifetime. But the evolution does not occur in different people at the same time or in the same order. Consequently the hero of Little Eyolf, being an imaginative, nervous, thoughtful person, finds that he has had enough of caresses, and wants to dream alone among the mountain peaks and solitudes, whilst his wife, a warm-blooded creature, has only found her love intensified to a fiercely jealous covetousness of him. His main refuge from this devouring passion is in his peacefully affectionate relations with his sister, and in certain suburban dreams very common among literary ama-

teurs living on their wives' incomes: to wit, forming the
mind and character of his child, and writing a great book
(on Human Responsibility if you please). Of course the
wife, in her jealousy, hates the sister, hates the child, hates
the book, hates her husband for making her jealous of
them, and hates herself for her hatreds with the frightful
logic of greedy, insatiable love. Enter then our old friend,
Ibsen's divine messenger. The Ratwife, alias the Strange
Passenger, alias the Button Moulder, alias Ulrik Brendel,
comes in to ask whether there are any little gnawing things
there of which she can rid the house. They do not understand—the divine messenger in Ibsen is never understood,
especially by the critics. So the little gnawing thing in the
house—the child—follows the Ratwife and is drowned,
leaving the pair awakened by the blow to a frightful consciousness of themselves, the woman as a mere animal, the
man as a moonstruck nincompoop, keeping up appearances as a suburban lady and gentleman with nothing to
do but enjoy themselves. Even the sister has discovered
now that she is not really a sister—also a not unprecedented suburban possibility—and sees that the passionate
stage is ahead of her too; so though she loves the husband,
she has to get out of his way by the pre-eminently suburban expedient of marrying a man whom she does not
love, and who, like Rita, is warm-blooded and bent on the
undivided, unshared possession of the object of his passion.
At last the love of the woman passes out of the passionate
stage; and immediately, with the practical sense of her sex,
she proposes, not to go up into the mountains or to write
amateur treatises, but to occupy herself with her duties as
landed proprietress, instead of merely spending the reve-
nues of her property in keeping a monogamic harem. The
gentleman asks to be allowed to lend a hand; and immediately the storm subsides, easily enough, leaving the
couple on solid ground. This is the play, as actual and near
to us as the Brighton and South Coast Railway—this is the
mercilessly heart-searching sermon, touching all of us
somewhere, and some of us everywhere, which we, the
critics, have summed up as "secrets of the alcove." Our
cheeks, whose whiteness Mr Arthur Roberts has assailed

in vain, have mantled at "the coarseness and vulgarity
which are noted characteristics of the author" (I am quoting, with awe, my fastidiously high-toned colleague of the
Standard). And yet the divine messenger only meant to
make us ashamed of ourselves. That is the way divine
messengers always do muddle their business.

The perfomance was of course a very remarkable one.
When, in a cast of five, you have the three best yet discovered actresses of their generation, you naturally look
for something extraordinary. Miss Achurch was the only
one who ran any risk of failure. The Ratwife and Asta are
excellent parts; but they are not arduous ones. Rita, on the
other hand, is one of the heaviest ever written: any single
act of it would exhaust an actress of no more than ordinary resources. But Miss Achurch was more than equal to
the occasion. Her power seemed to grow with its own expenditure. The terrible outburst at the end of the first act
did not leave a scrape on her voice (which appears to have
the compass of a military band) and threw her into victorious action in that tearing second act instead of wreck-
ing her. She played with all her old originality and success,
and with more than her old authority over her audience.
She had to speak some dangerous lines—lines of a kind
that usually find out the vulgar spots in an audience and
give an excuse for a laugh—but nobody laughed or wanted
to laugh at Miss Achurch. "There stood your champagne;
but you tasted it not," neither shirked nor slurred, but
driven home to the last syllable, did not elicit an audible
breath from a completely dominated audience. Later on I
confess I lost sight of Rita a little in studying the surprising capacity Miss Achurch shewed as a dramatic instrument. For the first time one clearly saw the superfluity of
power and the vehemence of intelligence which make her
often so reckless as to the beauty of her methods of expression. As Rita she produced almost every sound that a
big human voice can, from a creak like the opening of a
rusty canal lock to a melodious tenor note that the most
robust Siegfried might have envied. She looked at one
moment like a young, well-dressed, very pretty woman: at
another she was like a desperate creature just fished

dripping out of the river by the Thames Police. Yet another moment, and she was the incarnation of impetuous, ungovernable strength. Her face was sometimes winsome, sometimes listlessly wretched, sometimes like the head of a statue of Victory, sometimes suffused, horrible, threatening, like Bellona or Medusa. She would cross from left to right like a queen, and from right to left with, so to speak, her toes turned in, her hair coming down, and her slippers coming off. A more utter recklessness, not only of fashion, but of beauty, could hardly be imagined: beauty to Miss Achurch is only one effect among others to be produced, not a condition of all effects. But then she can do what our beautiful actresses cannot do: attain the force and terror of Sarah Bernhardt's most vehement explosions without Sarah's violence and abandonment, and with every appearance of having reserves of power still held in restraint. With all her cleverness as a realistic actress she must be classed technically as a heroic actress; and I very much doubt whether we shall see her often until she comes into the field with a repertory as highly specialized as that of Sir Henry Irving or Duse. For it is so clear that she would act an average London success to pieces and play an average actor-manager off the stage, that we need not expect to see much of her as that useful and pretty auxiliary, a leading lady.

Being myself a devotee of the beautiful school, I like being enchanted by Mrs Patrick Campbell better than being frightened, harrowed, astonished, conscience-stricken, devastated, and dreadfully delighted in general by Miss Achurch's untamed genius. I have seen Mrs Campbell play the Ratwife twice, once quite enchantingly, and once most disappointingly. On the first occasion Mrs Campbell divined that she was no village harridan, but the messenger of heaven. She played supernaturally, beautifully: the first notes of her voice came as from the spheres into all that suburban prose: she played to the child with a witchery that might have drawn him not only into the sea, but into her very bosom. Nothing jarred except her obedience to Ibsen's stage direction in saying "Down where all the rats are" harshly, instead of getting the effect, in harmony with her own inspired reading, by the most magical tenderness. The next time, to my unspeakable fury, she amused herself by playing like any melodramatic old woman, a profanation for which, whilst my critical life lasts, never will I forgive her. Of Miss Robins's Asta it is difficult to say much, since the part, played as she plays it, does not exhibit anything like the full extent of her powers. Asta is a study of temperament—the quiet, affectionate, enduring, reassuring, faithful, domestic temperament. That is not in the least Miss Robins's temperament: she is nervous, restless, intensely self-conscious, eagerly energetic. In parts which do not enable her to let herself loose in this, her natural way, she falls back on pathos, on mute misery, on a certain delicate plaintive note in her voice and grace in her bearing which appeal to our sympathy and pity without realizing any individuality for us. She gave us, with instinctive tact and refinement, the "niceness," the considerateness, the ladylikeness, which differentiate Asta from the wilful, passionate, somewhat brutal Rita. Perhaps only an American playing against an Englishwoman could have done it so discriminately; but beyond this and the pathos there was nothing: Asta was only a picture, and, like a picture, did not develop. The picture, being sympathetic and pretty, has been much admired; but those who have not seen Miss Robins play Hilda Wangel have no idea of what she is like when she really acts her part instead of merely giving an urbanely pictorial recommendation of it. As to Allmers, how could he recommend himself to spectators who saw in him everything that they are ashamed of in themselves? Mr Courtenay Thorpe played very intelligently, which, for such a part, and in such a play, is saying a good deal; but he was hampered a little by the change from the small and intimate auditorium in which he has been accustomed to play Ibsen, to the Avenue, which ingeniously combines the acoustic difficulties of a large theatre with the pecuniary capacity of a small one. Master Stewart Dawson, as Eyolf, was one of the best actors in the company. Mr Lowne, as Borgheim, was as much out of tone as a Leader sunset in a Rembrandt picture—no fault of his, of course (the audience evidently liked him), but still a blemish on the play.

And this brings me to a final criticism. The moment I put myself into my old attitude as musical critic, I at once perceive that the performance, as a whole, was an unsatisfactory one. You may remonstrate, and ask me how I can say so after admitting that the performers shewed such extraordinary talent—even genius. It is very simple, nevertheless. Suppose you take Isaye, Sarasate, Joachim, and Hollmann, and tumble them all together to give a scratch performance of one of Beethoven's posthumous quartets at some benefit concert. Suppose you also take the two De Reszkes, Calvé, and Miss Eames, and set them to sing a glee under the same circumstances. They will all shew prodigious individual talent; but the resultant performances of the quartet and glee will be inferior, as wholes, to that of an ordinary glee club or group of musicians who have practised for years together. The Avenue performance was a parallel case. There was nothing like the atmosphere which Lugné-Poë got in Rosmersholm. Miss Achurch managed to play the second act as if she had played it every week for twenty years; but otherwise the performance, interesting as it was, was none the less a scratch one. If only the company could keep together for a while! But perhaps that is too much to hope for at present, though it is encouraging to see that the performances are to be continued next week, the five matinees—all crowded, by the way—having by no means exhausted the demand for places.

Several performances during the past fortnight remain to be chronicled; but Ibsen will have his due; and he has not left me room enough to do justice to any one else this week.

To Ellen Terry

×××××××××××××××××××××××××××××××××××××

*Shaw's courtship of Ellen Terry (nearly a decade his elder)
was intended to woo her to the New Drama, and was almost entirely epistolary. He admired her acting, especially
in Shakespeare, and met her only a few times in his life
other than at the rehearsals of his* Captain Brassbound's
Conversion *(1899), for which the Lady Cicely role had
been written to furnish Miss Terry with a romantic lead for
a mature woman. Shaw had been trying, also, to lure her
into a romantic role (as The Strange Lady) in his
Napoleonic* The Man of Destiny *(1895) but Sir Henry
Irving, her acting partner, would find the role unsuitable
for his Bardolatrous talents. The role Ellen Terry had
really wanted was the lead in* Candida *(1894), but Shaw
had written that for Janet Achurch. The script for William
Terriss would be* The Devil's Disciple, *but at his citadel of
melodrama, the Adelphi Theatre, the actor-manager was
murdered by a spurned job-seeker.*

29 Fitzroy Square W
30 November 1896

I must write at least three lines to you. Do not be afraid of
wasting my time: you are, on the contrary, saving my life.
Here is the proof.

1st. I finished my play today—what do you think of that?
Does that look like wasting my time? Three acts, six scenes,
a masterpiece all completed in a few weeks, with a trip to
Paris and those Ibsen articles thrown in—articles which
were so overwritten that I cut out & threw away columns.
Not to mention the Bradford election.

2nd. I am the centre of a boiling whirlpool of furious
enquiries from insulted editors, indignant secretaries of
public bodies (wanting orations) all over the country, the

management of the Haymarket, & innumerable private persons, who have written me letters upon letters, enclosing stamped envelopes, reply paid telegram forms, and every other engine for extracting instant replies in desperate emergencies. For months I haven't answered one of them. Why? Because I could write to no one but Ellen, Ellen, Ellen: all other correspondence was intolerable when I could write to her instead. And what is the result? Why, that I am not killed with lecturing and with the writing of magazine articles. (What the pecuniary result will be presently I decline to think; but now that the play is finished (in the rough) I shall try to earn a little supplemental money—not that I really want it; but I have always been so poor as to coin that nothing can persuade me now that I am not on the verge of bankruptcy.) I am saved these last inches of fatigue which kept me chronically overworked for ten years. The Socialist papers denounce me bitterly—my very devotees call me aristocrat, Tory, capitalist scribe & so on; but it is really all Ellen, Ellen, Ellen, Ellen, Ellen, the happiness, the rest, the peace, the refuge, the consolation of loving (oh, dearest Ellen, add "and being loved by"—a lie costs so little) my great treasure Ellen.

What did I want so particularly to say?—oh yes: it was this. I have written to Terriss to tell him that I have kept my promise to him & have "a strong drama" with a part for him; but I want your opinion; for I have never tried melodrama before; and this thing, with its heroic sacrifice, its impossible court martial, its execution (imagine W. T. *hanged* before the eyes of the Adelphi!), its sobbings & speeches & declamations, may possibly be the most monstrous piece of farcical absurdity that ever made an audience shriek with laughter. And yet I have honestly tried for dramatic effect. I think you could give me a really *dry* opinion on it; for it will not tickle you, like "Arms & The Man" & "You Never Can Tell," nor get your sympathetic side, like Candida (the heroine is not the hero of the piece this time); and you will have to drudge conscientiously through it like a stage carpenter & tell me whether it is a burlesque or not.

But now that I think of it, all this is premature. The play only exists as a tiny scrawl in my note books—things I

carry about in my pockets. I shall have to revise it & work
out all the stage business, besides reading up the history of
the American War of Independence before I can send it
to the typist to be readily copied. Meanwhile I can read it
to Terriss, and to other people, but not to—well, no matter:
I don't ask that the veil of the temple shall be rent: on the
contrary, I am afraid, in my very soul, to come stumping
in my thickbooted, coarse, discordant reality, into that
realm where a magic Shaw, a phantasm, a thing who looks
delicate and a boy (twelve stalls and a bittock off) poses
fantastically before a *really* lovely Ellen (Remember, I
have stood where I could have stolen your hairpins without
unbending my elbow, and you were talking like mad all the
time). But when the thing *is* typed, then you will read it for
me, won't you? Perhaps before then I shall have been
forced to break the spell by teaching you the words of The
Strange Lady.

What shall I write next?—comic opera?

Ask Janet whether I am not a patient teacher when words
have to be articulated by an undisciplined actress.

I have sat up again to write to you. Now the fire begins
to burn low; and Iachimo in his trunk gets intolerable pins
& needles. This grim cold is good for me, I suppose, since
I am by complexion & constitution a Northman; but you
I hope are warm as a summer island lying fast asleep in the
Mediterranean. This sounds like a flower of literature; but
I have bathed in the Mediterranean; and it was 80°
Fahrenheit.

Now I have finished my play, nothing remains but to kiss
my Ellen once and die.

GBS

"Robertson Redivivus"

CASTE. By T. W. Robertson. Revival. Court Theatre, 10 June 1897.

[19 June 1897]

The revival of Caste at the Court Theatre is the revival of an epoch-making play after thirty years. A very little epoch and a very little play, certainly, but none the less interesting on that account to mortal critics whose own epochs, after full deductions for nonage and dotage, do not outlast more than two such plays. The Robertsonian movement caught me as a boy; the Ibsen movement caught me as a man; and the next one will catch me as a fossil.

It happens that I did not see Mr Hare's revival of Caste at the Garrick, nor was I at his leave-taking at the Lyceum before his trip to America; so that until last week I had not seen Caste since the old times when the Hare-Kendal management was still in futurity, and the Bancrofts had not left Tottenham Court Road. During that interval a great many things have happened, some of which have changed our minds and morals more than many of the famous Revolutions and Reformations of the historians. For instance, there was supernatural religion then; and eminent physicists, biologists, and their disciples were "infidels." There was a population question then; and what men and women knew about one another was either a family secret or the recollection of a harvest of wild oats. There was no social question—only a "social evil"; and the educated classes knew the working classes through novels written by men who had gathered their notions of the subject either from a squalid familiarity with general servants in Pentonville kitchens, or from no familiarity at all with the agricultural laborer and the retinues of the country house and west end mansion. Today the "infidels" are bishops and church-wardens, without change of view on their part. There is no population question; and the young lions and lionesses of Chronicle and Star, Keynote and Pseudonym, without suspicion of debauchery, seem to know as much of erotic psychology as the most liberally educated Periclean Athenians. The real working classes loom hugely in middle-class consciousness, and have pressed into their service the whole public energy of the time; so that now even a Conservative Government has nothing for the classes but "doles," extracted with difficulty from its preoccupation with instalments of Utopian Socialism. The extreme reluctance of Englishmen to mention these changes is the measure of their dread of a reaction to the older order which they still instinctively connect with strict applications of religion and respectability.

Since Caste has managed to survive all this, it need not be altogether despised by the young champions who are staring contemptuously at it, and asking what heed they can be expected to give to the opinions of critics who think such stuff worth five minutes' serious consideration. For my part, though I enjoy it more than I enjoyed The Notorious Mrs Ebbsmith, I do not defend it. I see now clearly enough that the eagerness with which it was swallowed long ago was the eagerness with which an ocean castaway, sucking his bootlaces in an agony of thirst in a sublime desert of salt water, would pounce on a spoonful of flat salutaris and think it nectar. After years of sham heroics and superhuman balderdash, Caste delighted everyone by its freshness, its nature, its humanity. You will shriek and snort, O scornful young men, at this monstrous assertion. "Nature! Freshness!" you will exclaim. "In Heaven's name [if you are not too modern to have heard of Heaven], where is there a touch of nature in Caste?" I reply, "In the windows, in the doors, in the walls, in the carpet, in the ceiling, in the kettle, in the fireplace, in the ham, in the tea, in the bread and butter, in the bassinet, in the hats and sticks and clothes, in the familiar phrases, the quiet, unpumped, everyday utterance: in short, the commonplaces that are now spurned because they are commonplaces, and were then inexpressibly welcome because they were the most unexpected of novelties."

And yet I dare not submit even this excuse to a detailed examination. Charles Mathews was in the field long before Robertson and Mr Bancroft with the art of behaving like an ordinary gentleman in what looked like a real drawing room. The characters are very old stagers, very thinly "humanized." Captain Hawtrey may look natural now in the hands of Mr Fred Kerr; but he began by being a very near relation of the old stage "swell," who pulled his moustache, held a single eyeglass between his brow and cheekbone, said "Haw, haw" and "By Jove," and appeared in every harlequinade in a pair of white trousers which were blacked by the clown instead of his boots. Mr Henry Arthur Jones, defending his idealized early impressions as Berlioz defended the forgotten Dalayrac, pleads for Eccles as "a great and vital tragi-comic figure." But the fond plea cannot be allowed. Eccles is caricatured in the vein and by the methods which Dickens had made obvious; and the implied moral view of his case is the common Pharisaic one of his day. Eccles and Gerridge together epitomize mid-century Victorian shabby-genteel ignorance of the working classes. Polly is comic relief pure and simple; George and Esther have nothing but a milkcan to differentiate them from the heroes and heroines of a thousand sentimental dramas; and though Robertson happens to be quite right—contrary to the prevailing opinion among critics whose conception of the aristocracy is a theoretic one—in representing the "Marquizzy" as insisting openly and jealously on her rank, and, in fact, having an impenitent and resolute flunkeyism as her class characteristic, yet it is quite evident that she is not an original study from life, but simply a ladyfication of the conventional haughty mother whom we lately saw revived in all her original vulgarity and absurdity at the Adelphi in Maddison Morton's All that Glitters is not Gold, and who was generally associated on the stage with the swell from whom Captain Hawtrey is evolved. Only, let it not be forgotten that in both there really is a humanization, as humanization was understood in the 'sixties;

that is, a discovery of saving sympathetic qualities in
personages thitherto deemed beyond redemption. Even
theology had to be humanized then by the rejection of the
old doctrine of eternal punishment. Hawtrey is a good
fellow, which the earlier "swell" never was; the Marquise
is dignified and affectionate at heart, and is neither made
ridiculous by a grotesque headdress nor embraced by the
drunken Eccles; and neither of them is attended by a
supercilious footman in plush whose head is finally
punched powderless by Sam Gerridge. And if from these
hints you cannot gather the real nature and limits of the
tiny theatrical revolution of which Robertson was the
hero, I must leave you in your perplexity for want of
time and space for further exposition.

Of the performance I need say nothing. Caste is a task
for amateurs: if its difficulties were doubled, the Court
company could without effort play it twice as well as it
need by played. Mr Hare's Eccles is the *tour de force* of
a refined actor playing a coarse part; but it is all the more
enjoyable for that. Of the staging I have one small criticism
to offer. If George D'Alroy's drawing room is to be dated
by a cluster of electric lights, Sam Gerridge must not come
to tea in corduroy trousers, dirty shirt-sleeves, and a huge
rule sticking out of his pocket. No "mechanic" nowadays
would dream of doing such a thing. A stockbroker in
moleskins would not be a grosser solecism.

To Mrs Richard Mansfield

×××

Richard Mansfield, like William Terriss, specialized in swaggering melodrama. Baron Chevrial, in A Parisian Romance, *was one of his most popular roles.*

29 Fitzroy Square W
8 January 1897

I have arrived at the end of the year with a frightful debt of correspondence against me. I cleared off all my arrears last Easter during my holiday. Since then I have broken down utterly. Every letter that could wait for a moment of happy leisure—and some that couldn't—has waited, and waited in vain. But then I have written much more than 100,000 words to everybody in the Saturday Review; and I've written two plays, not to mention various articles. At this moment I am simply beaten by three weeks continuous work—you can see it in my handwriting. I crawl to you for sympathy.

My last completed play (Op. 8) is called "The Devil's Disciple," and is just the play for America, as it occurs as an incident in the War of Independence. It is exactly the play for Richard—a splendid leading part, powerful life and death situations, any amount of singularity and individuality, simple enough for a village, and subtle enough for New York. Need I add that he is just the last person in the world to whom it would be of any use offering it? Besides the hero there is an older man—a Presbyterian minister of 50 who holds his own with the hero all through—and a very clever and effective part (General Burgoyne) in the last act. In both, the actors would make successes; and Richard would object to that. He couldn't play with an eyeglass, or a limp, or work in Chevrial or Cibber's Richard or Randegger or any of his pet nonsense.

He couldn't be Richard Mansfield acting: he would have
to be my man living. In short, he would have to be born
over again; and though that may conceivably happen to
him someday, just at present he would treat "The Devil's
Disciple" exactly as he treated "Candida." Why don't you
run away from him with somebody, just to give him a
shock? I will send you a copy of "The D's D." someday,
just to shew you what I can do in melodrama. I can't do
it just now because I have not time to work out the stage
business so as to have the MS ready for the typist; but
later on I hope to have a copy to send, unless you see it
performed first, or let me read it to you on one of your
visits.

"The D's D's" predecessor, "You Never Can Tell," is a
four act comedy, and is *tout ce qu'il y a de plus* Shaw-
esque. It requires a brilliant company—eight parts, all immense, the leading man a fine comedian. It is to follow the
Red Robe at the Haymarket; and I have promised to keep
the American rights unsold until after the production, both
Frohmanns being in the field for it.

Irving is to produce "The Man of Destiny" in the course
of this year. I have reserved the first turn in America for
him with it up to the end of 99; but after that, though he
can always play it when he wants to, his rights are not
exclusive.

Give my respects to Richard. He wrote me a letter in
August which created a sensation in the country house I
was staying at, as it was so amusing that I read it aloud at
breakfast. They all voted him the most original & interesting of geniuses. If only he had any conscience! Are there
signs of the growth of one yet? It would be such a convenience for me.

                                        yours sincerely
                                        G. Bernard Shaw

To Mrs Richard Mansfield

XXXXXXXXXXXXXXXXXXXXXXXXXXXXXXXXXXXXXXX

Mrs Mansfield was playing the role of Judith Anderson, the Rev Anthony Anderson's young wife. Mansfield was Dick Dudgeon, the Devil's Disciple.

29 Fitzroy Square W
10 December 1897

Thank you for the Philadelphia notices. I informed myself as to the New York production by private reports from trustworthy eye-witnesses, with the result that I very nearly wrote to you about the way in which your business has been spoiled by your monster of a husband. Get divorced, my dear Mrs Mansfield, get divorced. However, you shall have your revenge. In the next play, it is you that shall have the actor-proof part, and he that shall have the uphill work. We shall see then whether he will fascinate New York by carrying hot kettles about the stage. I shall cross the Atlantic someday and play the executioner myself; and on that occasion *Anderson will arrive too late.*

You may take the extreme and tender care with which he lays you down on the stage after the kiss as the measure of his sense of the tremendous effect you would make by carrying out my directions. Observe how everyone admires his acting—*his* acting, if you please, with the coat—the business which I arranged for him and which would produce its effect equally if it were done by a roasting jack. But when it comes to *your* effect: oh no, thank you! And then I am told that *you* spoiled the scene at its climax. Fortunately I asked how, and learnt that the actor-manager had suddenly lost faith in my stagecraft when it went to somebody else's credit. What is to be done with such a man? Can you wonder at my disowning, disclaiming, repudiating him?

I find also that Anderson, who should gain strong sympathy from his first word onward, is introduced as a canting snuffling burlesque Plymouth Brother in the beginning. But that *may* be Mr Whatshisname's fault. The business of the kiss is Richard's and nobody else's—except of course yours. You could have remonstrated—are there no pokers or carving knives in the house to give emphasis to your protests?

I strongly recommend you to drop the part & play Essie, or retire from the play altogether. Without that particular stroke it is a thankless business. If the end of the second act produces the right effect, the sympathy goes from the woman for her mistake about Anderson: whenever I have read it here the women have always been disgusted at her little faith. It is extremely difficult to hold up the horror of the court-martial scene against Burgoyne & the rest, and to be made the butt of such a cruel effect as his "that will do very nicely" when she takes refuge in agonized prayer under the gallows (I understand that this has been totally missed, though it is one of the most appalling things in the play). Nevertheless, these scenes would be worth the labor they must cost, if you could fix the audience's interest in you by striking home in the scene of the arrest. As it is— well, as it is, I say again, divorce him, divorce him, divorce him. And then you shall have a play all to yourself, cramful of irresistible effects.

yrs sincerely
G. Bernard Shaw

THE DEVIL'S DISCIPLE

XXXXXXXXXXXXXXXXXXXXXXXXXXXXXXXXXXXXXXXXXXX

When The Devil's Disciple *(1897) was published in 1900, it was in tandem with* Caesar and Cleopatra *and* Captain Brassbound's Conversion *as* Three Plays for Puritans. *That part of the preface relating to* The Devil's Disciple *follows.*

ON DIABOLONIAN ETHICS

There is a foolish opinion prevalent that an author should allow his works to speak for themselves, and that he who appends and prefixes explanations to them is likely to be as bad an artist as the painter cited by Cervantes, who wrote under his picture This is a Cock, lest there should be any mistake about it. The pat retort to this thoughtless comparison is that the painter invariably does so label his picture. What is a Royal Academy catalogue but a series of statements that This is The Vale of Rest, This The Shaving of Samson, This Chill October, This H.R.H. the Prince of Wales, and so on? The reason most playwrights do not publish their plays with prefaces is that they cannot write them, the business of intellectually conscious philosopher and skilled critic being no necessary part of their craft. Naturally, making a virtue of their capacity, they either repudiate prefaces as shameful, or else, with a modest air, request some popular critic to supply one, as much as to say, Were I to tell the truth about myself I must needs seem vainglorious: were I to tell less than the truth I should do myself an injustice and deceive my readers. As to the critic thus called in from the outside, what can he do but imply that his friend's transcendent ability as a dramatist is surpassed only by his beautiful nature as a man? Now what I say is, why should I get another man to praise me when I can praise myself? I have no disabilities to plead: produce me your best critic, and I will criticize

his head off. As to philosophy, I taught my critics the little
they know in my Quintessence of Ibsenism; and now they
turn their guns—the guns I loaded for them—on me, and
proclaim that I write as if mankind had intellect without
will, or heart, as they call it. Ingrates: who was it that
directed your attention to the distinction between Will and
Intellect? Not Schopenhauer, I think, but Shaw.

Again, they tell me that So-and-So, who does not write
prefaces, is no charlatan. Well, I am. I first caught the ear
of the British public on a cart in Hyde Park, to the blaring
of brass bands, and this not at all as a reluctant sacrifice of
my instinct of privacy to political necessity, but because,
like all dramatists and mimes of genuine vocation, I am a
natural-born mountebank. I am well aware that the ordinary British citizen requires a profession of shame from
all mountebanks by way of homage to the sanctity of the
ignoble private life to which he is condemned by his
incapacity for public life. Thus Shakespear, after proclaiming that Not marble nor the gilded monuments of
Princes should outlive his powerful rhyme, would apologize, in the approved taste, for making himself a motley
to the view; and the British citizen has ever since quoted
the apology and ignored the fanfare. When an actress
writes her memoirs, she impresses on you in every chapter
how cruelly it tried her feelings to exhibit her person to
the public gaze; but she does not forget to decorate the
book with a dozen portraits of herself. I really cannot respond to this demand for mock-modesty. I am ashamed
neither of my work nor of the way it is done. I like explaining its merits to the huge majority who dont know
good work from bad. It does them good; and it does me
good, curing me of nervousness, laziness, and snobbish-
ness. I write prefaces as Dryden did, and treatises as
Wagner, because I *can*; and I would give half a dozen of
Shakespear's plays for one of the prefaces he ought to
have written. I leave the delicacies of retirement to those
who are gentlemen first and literary workmen afterwards.
The cart and trumpet for me.

This is all very well; but the trumpet is an instrument
that grows on one; and sometimes my blasts have been so

strident that even those who are most annoyed by them
have mistaken the novelty of my shamelessness for novelty
in my plays and opinions. Take, for instance, the first play
in this volume, entitled The Devil's Disciple. It does not
contain a single even passably novel incident. Every old
patron of the Adelphi pit would, were he not beglamored
in a way presently to be explained, recognize the reading
of the will, the oppressed orphan finding a protector, the
arrest, the heroic sacrifice, the court martial, the scaffold,
the reprieve at the last moment, as he recognizes beefsteak
pudding on the bill of fare at his restaurant. Yet when the
play was produced in 1897 in New York by Mr Richard
Mansfield, with a success that proves either that the melodrama was built on very safe old lines, or that the American public is composed exclusively of men of genius, the
critics, though one said one thing and another another as
to the play's merits, yet all agreed that it was novel—
original, as they put it—to the verge of audacious eccentricity.

Now this, if it applies to the incidents, plot, construction,
and general professional and technical qualities of the
play, is nonsense; for the truth is, I am in these matters a
very old-fashioned playwright. When a good deal of the
same talk, both hostile and friendly, was provoked by my
last volume of plays, Mr Robert Buchanan, a dramatist
who knows what I know and remembers what I remember
of the history of the stage, pointed out that the stage tricks
by which I gave the younger generation of playgoers an
exquisite sense of quaint unexpectedness, had done duty
years ago in Cool as a Cucumber, Used Up, and many
forgotten farces and comedies of the Byron-Robertson
school, in which the imperturbably impudent comedian,
afterwards shelved by the reaction to brainless sentimen-
tality, was a stock figure. It is always so more or less: the
novelties of one generation are only the resuscitated fashions of the generation before last.

But the stage tricks of The Devil's Disciple are not, like
some of those of Arms and The Man, the forgotten ones of
the sixties, but the hackneyed ones of our own time. Why,
then, were they not recognized? Partly, no doubt, because

of my trumpet and cartwheel declamation. The critics were the victims of the long course of hypnotic suggestion by which G.B.S. the journalist manufactured an unconventional reputation for Bernard Shaw the author. In England as elsewhere the spontaneous recognition of really original work begins with a mere handful of people, and propagates itself so slowly that it has become a commonplace to say that genius, demanding bread, is given a stone after its possessor's death. The remedy for this is sedulous advertisement. Accordingly, I have advertized myself so well that I find myself, whilst still in middle life, almost as legendary a person as the Flying Dutchman. Critics, like other people, see what they look for, not what is actually before them. In my plays they look for my legendary qualities, and find originality and brilliancy in my most hackneyed claptraps. Were I to republish Buckstone's Wreck Ashore as my latest comedy, it would be hailed as a masterpiece of perverse paradox and scintillating satire. Not, of course, by the really able critics—for example, you, my friend, now reading this sentence. The illusion that makes *you* think me so original is far subtler than that. The Devil's Disciple has, in truth, a genuine novelty in it. Only, that novelty is not any invention of my own, but simply the novelty of the advanced thought of my day. As such, it will assuredly lose its gloss with the lapse of time, and leave The Devil's Disciple exposed as the threadbare popular melodrama it technically is.

Let me explain (for, as Mr A. B. Walkley has pointed out in his disquisitions on Frames of Mind, I am nothing if not explanatory). Dick Dudgeon, the devil's disciple, is a Puritan of the Puritans. He is brought up in a household where the Puritan religion has died, and become, in its corruption, an excuse for his mother's master passion of hatred in all its phases of cruelty and envy. This corruption has already been dramatized for us by Charles Dickens in his picture of the Clennam household in Little Dorrit: Mrs Dudgeon being a replica of Mrs Clennam with certain circumstantial variations, and perhaps a touch of the same author's Mrs Gargery in Great Expectations. In such a home the young Puritan finds himself starved of

religion, which is the most clamorous need of his nature.
With all his mother's indomitable selffulness, but with Pity
instead of Hatred as his master passion, he pities the devil;
takes his side; and champions him, like a true Covenanter,
against the world. He thus becomes, like all genuinely
religious men, a reprobate and an outcast. Once this is
understood, the play becomes straightforwardly simple.

The Diabolonian position is new to the London playgoer of today, but not to lovers of serious literature. From
Prometheus to the Wagnerian Siegfried, some enemy of
the gods, unterrified champion of those oppressed by them,
has always towered among the heroes of the loftiest poetry. Our newest idol, the Superman, celebrating the death
of godhead, may be younger than the hills; but he is as
old as the shepherds. Two and a half centuries ago our
greatest English dramatizer of life, John Bunyan, ended
one of his stories with the remark that there is a way to
hell even from the gates of heaven, and so led us to the
equally true proposition that there is a way to heaven
even from the gates of hell. A century ago William Blake
was, like Dick Dudgeon, an avowed Diabolonian: he
called his angels devils and his devils angels. His devil is a
Redeemer. Let those who have praised my originality in
conceiving Dick Dudgeon's strange religion read Blake's
Marriage of Heaven and Hell, and I shall be fortunate if
they do not rail at me for a plagiarist. But they need not go
back to Blake and Bunyan. Have they not heard the recent
fuss about Nietzsche and his Good and Evil Turned Inside
Out? Mr Robert Buchanan has actually written a long
poem of which the Devil is the merciful hero, which poem
was in my hands before a word of The Devil's Disciple
was written. There never was a play more certain to be
written than The Devil's Disciple at the end of the nineteenth century. The age was visibly pregnant with it.

I grieve to have to add that my old friends and colleagues the London critics for the most part shewed no
sort of connoisseurship either in Puritanism or in Dia-
bolonianism when the play was performed for a few weeks
at a suburban theatre (Kennington) in October 1899 by
Mr Murray Carson. They took Mrs Dudgeon at her own

valuation as a religious woman because she was detestably disagreeable. And they took Dick as a blackguard on her authority, because he was neither detestable nor disagreeable. But they presently found themselves in a dilemma. Why should a blackguard save another man's life, and that man no friend of his, at the risk of his own? Clearly, said the critics, because he is redeemed by love. All wicked heroes are, on the stage; that is the romantic metaphysic. Unfortunately for this explanation (which I do not profess to understand) it turned out in the third act that Dick was a Puritan in this respect also: a man impassioned only for saving grace, and not to be led or turned by wife or mother, Church or State, pride of life or lust of the flesh. In the lovely home of the courageous, affectionate, practical minister who marries a pretty wife twenty years younger than himself, and turns soldier in an instant to save the man who has saved him, Dick looks round and understands the charm and the peace and the sanctity, but knows that such material comforts are not for him. When the woman nursed in that atmosphere falls in love with him and concludes (like the critics, who somehow always agree with my sentimental heroines) that he risked his life for her sake, he tells her the obvious truth that he would have done as much for any stranger—that the law of his own nature, and no interest nor lust whatsoever, forbad him to cry out that the hangman's noose should be taken off his neck only to be put on another man's.

But then, said the critics, where is the motive? *Why* did Dick save Anderson? On the stage, it appears, people do things for reasons. Off the stage they dont: that is why your penny-in-the-slot heroes, who only work when you drop a motive into them, are so oppressively automatic and uninteresting. The saving of life at the risk of the saver's own is not a common thing; but modern populations are so vast that even the most uncommon things are recorded once a week or oftener. Not one of my critics but has seen a hundred times in his paper how some policeman or fireman or nurse maid has received a medal, or the compliments of a magistrate, or perhaps a public funeral, for risking his or her life to save another's. Has he ever seen it added that the saved was the husband of the woman the saver loved, or was that woman herself, or was even known to the saver as much as by sight? Never. When we want to read of the deeds that are done for love, whither do we turn? To the murder column; and there we are rarely disappointed.

Need I repeat that the theatre critic's professional routine so discourages any association between real life and the stage, that he soon loses the natural habit of referring to the one to explain the other? The critic who discovered a romantic motive for Dick's sacrifice was no mere literary dreamer, but a clever barrister. He pointed out that Dick Dudgeon clearly did adore Mrs Anderson; that it was for her sake that he offered his life to save her beloved husband; and that his explicit denial of his passion was the splendid mendacity of a gentleman whose respect for a married woman, and duty to her absent husband, sealed his passion-palpitating lips. From the moment that this fatally plausible explanation was launched, my play became my critic's play, not mine. Thenceforth Dick Dudgeon every night confirmed the critic by stealing behind Judith, and mutely attesting his passion by surreptitiously imprinting a heartbroken kiss on a stray lock of her hair whilst he uttered the barren denial. As for me, I was just then wandering about the streets of Constantinople, unaware of all these doings. When I returned all was over. My personal relations with the critic and the actor forbad me to curse them. I had not even the chance of publicly forgiving them. They meant well by me; but if they ever write a play, may I be there to explain!

THE DEVIL'S DISCIPLE

ACT I

At the most wretched hour between a black night and a wintry morning in the year 1777, Mrs Dudgeon, of New Hampshire, is sitting up in the kitchen and general dwelling room of her farm house on the outskirts of the town of Websterbridge. She is not a prepossessing woman. No woman looks her best after sitting up all night; and Mrs Dudgeon's face, even at its best, is grimly trenched by the channels into which the barren forms and observances of a dead Puritanism can pen a bitter temper and a fierce pride. She is an elderly matron who has worked hard and got nothing by it except dominion and detestation in her sordid home, and an unquestioned reputation for piety and respectability among her neighbors, to whom drink and debauchery are still so much more tempting than religion and rectitude, that they conceive goodness simply as self-denial. This conception is easily extended to others-denial, and finally generalized as covering anything disagreeable. So Mrs Dudgeon, being exceedingly disagreeable, is held to be exceedingly good. Short of flat felony, she enjoys complete license except for amiable weaknesses of any sort, and is consequently, without knowing it, the most licentious woman in the parish on the strength of never having broken the seventh commandment or missed a Sunday at the Presbyterian church.

The year 1777 is the one in which the passions roused by the breaking-off of the American colonies from England, more by their own weight than by their own will, boiled up to shooting point, the shooting being idealized to the English mind as suppression of rebellion and maintenance of British dominion, and to the American as defence of liberty, resistance to tyranny, and self-sacrifice on the altar of the Rights of Man. Into the merits of these idealizations it is not here necessary to inquire: suffice it to say, without

*prejudice, that they have convinced both Americans and
English that the most high-minded course for them to pursue is to kill as many of one another as possible, and that
military operations to that end are in full swing, morally
supported by confident requests from the clergy of both
sides for the blessing of God on their arms.*

*Under such circumstances many other women besides
this disagreeable Mrs Dudgeon find themselves sitting up
all night waiting for news. Like her, too, they fall asleep
towards morning at the risk of nodding themselves into the
kitchen fire. Mrs Dudgeon sleeps with a shawl over her
head, and her feet on a broad fender of iron laths, the step
of the domestic altar of the fireplace, with its huge hobs
and boiler, and its hinged arm above the smoky mantel-
shelf for roasting. The plain kitchen table is opposite the
fire, at her elbow, with a candle on it in a tin sconce. Her
chair, like all the others in the room, is uncushioned and
unpainted; but as it has a round railed back and a seat
conventionally moulded to the sitter's curves, it is comparatively a chair of state. The room has three doors, one
on the same side as the fireplace, near the corner, leading
to the best bedroom; one, at the opposite end of the opposite
wall, leading to the scullery and washhouse; and the house-
door, with its latch, heavy lock, and clumsy wooden bar,
in the front wall, between the window in its middle and the
corner next to the bedroom door. Between the door and the
window a rack of pegs suggests to the deductive observer
that the men of the house are all away, as there are no hats
or coats on them. On the other side of the window the clock
hangs on a nail, with its white wooden dial, black iron
weights, and brass pendulum. Between the clock and the
corner, a big cupboard, locked, stands on a dwarf dresser
full of common crockery.*

*On the side opposite the fireplace, between the door
and the corner, a shamelessly ugly black horsehair sofa
stands against the wall. An inspection of its stridulous surface shews that Mrs Dudgeon is not alone. A girl of sixteen
or seventeen has fallen asleep on it. She is a wild, timid
looking creature with black hair and tanned skin. Her frock,
a scanty garment, is rent, weather-stained, berrystained,*

*and by no means scrupulously clean. It hangs on her with
a freedom which, taken with her brown legs and bare feet,
suggests no great stock of underclothing.*

*Suddenly there comes a tapping at the door, not loud
enough to wake the sleepers. Then knocking, which disturbs
Mrs Dudgeon a little. Finally the latch is tried, whereupon
she springs up at once.*

MRS DUDGEON [*threateningly*] Well, why don't you open the
door? [*She sees that the girl is asleep, and immediately
raises a clamor of heartfelt vexation*]. Well, dear, dear
me! Now this is—[*shaking her*] wake up, wake up: do
you hear?

THE GIRL [*sitting up*] What is it?

MRS DUDGEON. Wake up; and be ashamed of yourself, you
unfeeling sinful girl, falling asleep like that, and your
father hardly cold in his grave.

THE GIRL [*half asleep still*] I didnt mean to. I dropped off—

MRS DUDGEON [*cutting her short*] Oh yes, youve plenty of
excuses, I daresay. Dropped off! [*Fiercely, as the knocking recommences*] Why dont you get up and let your
uncle in? after me waiting up all night for him! [*She
pushes her rudely off the sofa*]. There: I'll open the door:
much good you are to wait up. Go and mend that fire
a bit.

*The girl, cowed and wretched, goes to the fire and puts
a log on. Mrs Dudgeon unbars the door and opens it,
letting into the stuffy kitchen a little of the freshness and
a great deal of the chill of the dawn, also her second son
Christy, a fattish, stupid, fair-haired, roundfaced man
of about 22, muffled in a plaid shawl and grey overcoat.
He hurries, shivering, to the fire, leaving Mrs Dudgeon
to shut the door.*

CHRISTY [*at the fire*] F—f—f! but it is cold. [*Seeing the girl,
and staring lumpishly at her*] Why, who are you?

THE GIRL [*shyly*] Essie.

MRS DUDGEON. Oh, you may well ask. [*To Essie*] Go
to your room, child, and lie down, since you havnt
feeling enough to keep you awake. Your history isnt
fit for your own ears to hear.

ESSIE. I——

MRS DUDGEON [*peremptorily*] Dont answer me, Miss; but
shew your obedience by doing what I tell you. [*Essie,
almost in tears, crosses the room to the door near the
sofa*]. And dont forget your prayers. [*Essie goes out*].
She'd have gone to bed last night just as if nothing had
happened if I'd let her.

CHRISTY [*phlegmatically*] Well, she cant be expected to feel
Uncle Peter's death like one of the family.

MRS DUDGEON. What are you talking about, child? Isnt
she his daughter—the punishment of his wickedness and
shame? [*She assaults her chair by sitting down*].

CHRISTY [*staring*] Uncle Peter's daughter!

MRS DUDGEON. Why else should she be here? D'ye think
Ive not had enough trouble and care put upon me bringing up my own girls, let alone you and your good-for-
nothing brother, without having your uncle's bastards —

CHRISTY [*interrupting her with an apprehensive glance at
the door by which Essie went out*] Sh! She may hear you.

MRS DUDGEON [*raising her voice*] Let her hear me. People
who fear God dont fear to give the devil's work its right
name. [*Christy, soullessly indifferent to the strife of Good
and Evil, stares at the fire, warming himself*]. Well, how
long are you going to stare there like a stuck pig? What
news have you for me?

CHRISTY [*taking off his hat and shawl and going to the rack
to hang them up*] The minister is to break the news to
you. He'll be here presently.

MRS DUDGEON. Break what news?

CHRISTY [*standing on tiptoe, from boyish habit, to hang
his hat up, though he is quite tall enough to reach the
peg, and speaking with callous placidity, considering the
nature of the announcement*] Father's dead too.

MRS DUDGEON [*stupent*] Your father!

CHRISTY [*sulkily, coming back to the fire and warming himself again, attending much more to the fire than to his
mother*] Well, it's not my fault. When we got to Nevinstown we found him ill in bed. He didn't know us at
first. The minister sat up with him and sent me away.
He died in the night.

MRS DUDGEON [*bursting into dry angry tears*] Well, I do
think this is hard on me—very hard on me. His brother,
that was a disgrace to us all his life, gets hanged on the
public gallows as a rebel; and your father, instead of
staying at home where his duty was, with his own
family, goes after him and dies, leaving everything on
my shoulders. After sending this girl to me to take care
of, too! [*She plucks her shawl vexedly over her ears*].
It's sinful, so it is: downright sinful.

CHRISTY [*with a slow, bovine cheerfulness, after a pause*]
I think it's going to be a fine morning, after all.

MRS DUDGEON [*railing at him*] A fine morning! And your
father newly dead! Wheres your feelings, child?

CHRISTY [*obstinately*] Well, I didnt mean any harm. I suppose a man may make a remark about the weather
even if his father's dead.

MRS DUDGEON [*bitterly*] A nice comfort my children are to
me! One son a fool, and the other a lost sinner thats
left his home to live with smugglers and gypsies and
villains, the scum of the earth!

Someone knocks.

CHRISTY [*without moving*] Thats the minister.

MRS DUDGEON [*sharply*] Well, arnt you going to let Mr
Anderson in?

*Christy goes sheepishly to the door. Mrs Dudgeon
buries her face in her hands, as it is her duty as a widow
to be overcome with grief. Christy opens the door, and
admits the minister, Anthony Anderson, a shrewd, genial, ready Presbyterian divine of about 50, with something of the authority of his profession in his bearing.
But it is an altogether secular authority, sweetened by a
conciliatory, sensible manner not at all suggestive of a
quite thorough-going other-worldliness. He is a strong,
healthy man too, with a thick sanguine neck; and his
keen, cheerful mouth cuts into somewhat fleshy corners.
No doubt an excellent parson, but still a man capable
of making the most of this world, and perhaps a little
apologetically conscious of getting on better with it than
a sound Presbyterian ought.*

ANDERSON [*to Christy, at the door, looking at Mrs Dudgeon whilst he takes off his cloak*] Have you told her?

CHRISTY. She made me. [*He shuts the door; yawns; and loafs across to the sofa, where he sits down and presently drops off to sleep*].

    Anderson looks compassionately at Mrs Dudgeon. Then he hangs his cloak and hat on the rack. Mrs Dudgeon dries her eyes and looks up at him.

ANDERSON. Sister: the Lord has laid his hand very heavily upon you.

MRS DUDGEON [*with intensely recalcitrant resignation*] It's His will, I suppose; and I must bow to it. But I do think it hard. What call had Timothy to go to Springtown, and remind everybody that he belonged to a man that was being hanged?—and [*spitefully*] that deserved it, if ever a man did.

ANDERSON [*gently*] They were brothers, Mrs Dudgeon.

MRS DUDGEON. Timothy never acknowledged him as his brother after we were married: he had too much respect for me to insult me with such a brother. Would such a selfish wretch as Peter have come thirty miles to see Timothy hanged, do you think? Not thirty yards, not he. However, I must bear my cross as best I may: least said is soonest mended.

ANDERSON [*very grave, coming down to the fire to stand with his back to it*] Your eldest son was present at the execution, Mrs Dudgeon.

MRS DUDGEON [*disagreeably surprised*] Richard?

ANDERSON [*nodding*] Yes.

MRS DUDGEON [*vindictively*] Let it be a warning to him. He may end that way himself, the wicked, dissolute, godless— [*she suddenly stops; her voice fails; and she asks, with evident dread*] Did Timothy see him?

ANDERSON. Yes.

MRS DUDGEON [*holding her breath*] Well?

ANDERSON. He only saw him in the crowd: they did not speak. [*Mrs Dudgeon, greatly relieved, exhales the pent up breath and sits at her ease again*] Your husband was greatly touched and impressed by his brother's awful death. [*Mrs Dudgeon sneers. Anderson breaks off to demand with some indignation*] Well, wasnt it only natural, Mrs Dudgeon? He softened towards his prodigal son in that moment. He sent for him to come to see him.

MRS DUDGEON [*her alarm renewed*] Sent for Richard!

ANDERSON. Yes; but Richard would not come. He sent his father a message; but I'm sorry to say it was a wicked message—an awful message.

MRS DUDGEON. What was it?

ANDERSON. That he would stand by his wicked uncle and stand against his good parents, in this world and the next.

MRS DUDGEON [*implacably*] He will be punished for it. He will be punished for it—in both worlds.

ANDERSON. That is not in our hands, Mrs Dudgeon.

MRS DUDGEON. Did I say it was, Mr. Anderson? We are told that the wicked shall be punished. Why should we do our duty and keep God's law if there is to be no difference made between us and those who follow their own likings and dislikings, and make a jest of us and of their Maker's word?

ANDERSON. Well, Richard's earthly father had been merciful to him; and his heavenly judge is the father of us all.

MRS DUDGEON [*forgetting herself*] Richard's earthly father was a softheaded—

ANDERSON [*shocked*] Oh!

MRS DUDGEON [*with a touch of shame*] Well, I am Richard's mother. If I am against him who has any right to be for him? [*Trying to conciliate him*] Wont you sit down, Mr. Anderson? I should have asked you before; but I'm so troubled.

ANDERSON. Thank you. [*He takes a chair from beside the fireplace, and turns it so that he can sit comfortably at the fire. When he is seated he adds, in the tone of a man who knows that he is opening a difficult subject*] Has Christy told you about the new will?

MRS DUDGEON [*all her fears returning*] The new will! Did Timothy— ? [*She breaks off, gasping, unable to complete the question*].

ANDERSON. Yes. In his last hours he changed his mind.

MRS DUDGEON [*white with intense rage*] And you let him rob me?

ANDERSON. I had no power to prevent him giving what was his to his own son.

MRS DUDGEON. He had nothing of his own. His money was the money I brought him as my marriage portion. It was for me to deal with my own money and my own son. He dare not have done it if I had been with him; and well he knew it. That was why he stole away like a thief to take advantage of the law to rob me by making a new will behind my back. The more shame on you, Mr Anderson,—you, a minister of the gospel—to act as his accomplice in such a crime.

ANDERSON [*rising*] I will take no offence at what you say in the first bitterness of your grief.

MRS DUDGEON [*contemptuously*] Grief!

ANDERSON. Well, of your disappointment, if you can find it in your heart to think that the better word.

MRS DUDGEON. My heart! My heart! And since when, pray, have you begun to hold up our hearts as trustworthy guides for us?

ANDERSON [*rather guiltily*] I—er—

MRS DUDGEON [*vehemently*] Dont lie, Mr Anderson. We are told that the heart of man is deceitful above all things, and desperately wicked. My heart belonged, not to Timothy, but to that poor wretched brother of his that has just ended his days with a rope round his neck—aye, to Peter Dudgeon. You know it: old Eli Hawkins, the man to whose pulpit you succeeded, though you are not worthy to loose his shoe latchet, told it you when he gave over our souls into your charge. He warned me and strengthened me against my heart, and made me marry a Godfearing man—as he thought. What else but that discipline has made me the woman I am? And you, you, who followed your heart in your marriage, you talk to me of what I find in my heart. Go home to your pretty wife, man; and leave me to my prayers. [*She turns from him and leans with her elbows on the table, brooding over her wrongs and taking no further notice of him*].

ANDERSON [*willing enough to escape*] The Lord forbid that
I should come between you and the source of all comfort! [*He goes to the rack for his coat and hat*].

MRS DUDGEON [*without looking at him*] The Lord will know
what to forbid and what to allow without your help.

ANDERSON. And whom to forgive, I hope—Eli Hawkins
and myself, if we have ever set up our preaching against
His law. [*He fastens his cloak, and is now ready to go*].
Just one word—on necessary business, Mrs Dudgeon.
There is the reading of the will to be gone through; and
Richard has a right to be present. He is in the town; but
he has the grace to say that he does not want to force
himself in here.

MRS DUDGEON. He shall come here. Does he expect us to
leave his father's house for his convenience? Let them
all come, and come quickly, and go quickly. They shall
not make the will an excuse to shirk half their day's
work. I shall be ready, never fear.

ANDERSON [*coming back a step or two*] Mrs Dudgeon: I
used to have some little influence with you. When did
I lose it?

MRS DUDGEON [*still without turning to him*] When you married for love. Now youre answered.

ANDERSON. Yes: I am answered. [*He goes out, musing*].

MRS DUDGEON [*to herself, thinking of her husband*] Thief!
Thief! [*She shakes herself angrily out of her chair;
throws back the shawl from her head; and sets to work
to prepare the room for the reading of the will, beginning by replacing Anderson's chair against the wall and
pushing back her own to the window. Then she calls, in
her hard, driving, wrathful way*] Christy. [*No answer: he
is fast asleep*]. Christy. [*She shakes him roughly*]. Get up
out of that; and be ashamed of yourself—sleeping, and
your father dead! [*She returns to the table; puts the
candle on the mantelshelf; and takes from the table
drawer a red table cloth which she spreads*].

CHRISTY [*rising reluctantly*] Well, do you suppose we are
never going to sleep until we are out of mourning?

MRS DUDGEON. I want none of your sulks. Here: help me
to set this table. [*They place the table in the middle of

the room, with Christy's end towards the fireplace and
Mrs Dudgeon's towards the sofa. Christy drops the table
as soon as possible, and goes to the fire, leaving his
mother to make the final adjustments of its position]. We
shall have the minister back here with the lawyer and
all the family to read the will before you have done
toasting yourself. Go and wake that girl; and then light
the stove in the shed: you cant have your breakfast here.
And mind you wash yourself, and make yourself fit to
receive the company. [*She punctuates these orders by*
going to the cupboard; unlocking it; and producing a
decanter of wine, which has no doubt stood there un-
touched since the last state occasion in the family, and
some glasses, which she sets on the table. Also two green
ware plates, on one of which she puts a barnbrack with
a knife beside it. On the other she shakes some biscuits
out of a tin, putting back one or two, and counting the
rest]. Now mind: there are ten biscuits there: let there
be ten there when I come back after dressing myself.
And keep your fingers off the raisins in that cake. And
tell Essie the same. I suppose I can trust you to bring
in the case of stuffed birds without breaking the glass?
[*She replaces the tin in the cupboard, which she locks,*
pocketing the key carefully].

CHRISTY [*lingering at the fire*] Youd better put the ink-
stand instead, for the lawyer.

MRS DUDGEON. Thats no answer to make to me, sir. Go
and do as youre told. [*Christy turns sullenly to obey*].
Stop: take down that shutter before you go, and let the
daylight in: you cant expect me to do all the heavy
work of the house with a great lout like you idling about.

Christy takes the window bar out of its clamps, and
puts it aside; then opens the shutter, shewing the grey
morning. Mrs Dudgeon takes the sconce from the mantle-
shelf; blows out the candle; extinguishes the snuff by
pinching it with her fingers, first licking them for the
purpose: and replaces the sconce on the shelf.

CHRISTY [*looking through the window*] Heres the minister's
wife.

MRS DUDGEON [*displeased*] What! Is she coming here?

CHRISTY. Yes.

MRS DUDGEON. What does she want troubling me at this hour, before I am properly dressed to receive people?

CHRISTY. Youd better ask her.

MRS DUDGEON [*threateningly*] Y o u d better keep a civil tongue in your head. [*He goes sulkily towards the door. She comes after him, plying him with instructions*]. Tell that girl to come to me as soon as she's had her breakfast. And tell her to make herself fit to be seen before the people. [*Christy goes out and slams the door in her face*]. Nice manners, that! [*Someone knocks at the house door: she turns and cries inhospitably*] Come in. [*Judith Anderson, the minister's wife, comes in. Judith is more than twenty years younger than her husband, though she will never be as young as he is in vitality. She is pretty and proper and ladylike, and has been admired and petted into an opinion of herself sufficiently favorable to give her a self-assurance which serves her instead of strength. She has a pretty taste in dress, and in her face the pretty lines of a sentimental character formed by dreams. Even her little self-complacency is pretty, like a child's vanity. Rather a pathetic creature to any sympathetic observer who knows how rough a place the world is. One feels, on the whole, that Anderson might have chosen worse, and that she, needing protection, could not have chosen better*]. Oh, it's you, is it, Mrs Anderson?

JUDITH [*very politely—almost patronizingly*] Yes. Can I do anything for you, Mrs Dudgeon? Can I help to get the place ready before they come to read the will?

MRS DUDGEON [*stiffly*] Thank you, Mrs Anderson, my house is always ready for anyone to come into.

MRS ANDERSON [*with complacent amiability*] Yes, indeed it is. Perhaps you had rather I did not intrude on you just now.

MRS DUDGEON. Oh, one more or less will make no difference this morning, Mrs Anderson. Now that youre here, youd better stay. If you wouldnt mind shutting the door! [*Judith smiles, implying "How stupid of me!" and shuts it with an exasperating air of doing something*] *pretty and becoming*]. Thats better. I must go and tidy myself a bit. I suppose you dont mind stopping here to receive anyone that comes until I'm ready.

JUDITH [*graciously giving her leave*] Oh yes, certainly. Leave that to me, Mrs Dudgeon; and take your time. [*She hangs her cloak and bonnet on the rack*].

MRS DUDGEON [*half sneering*] I thought that would be more in your way than getting the house ready. [*Essie comes back*]. Oh, here y o u are! [*Severely*] Come here: let me see you. [*Essie timidly goes to her. Mrs Dudgeon takes her roughly by the arm and pulls her round to inspect the result of her attempt to clean and tidy herself—results which shew little practice and less conviction*]. Mm! Thats what you call doing your hair properly, I suppose. It's easy to see what you are, and how you were brought up. [*She throws her arm away, and goes on, peremptorily*] Now you listen to me and do as youre told. You sit down there in the corner by the fire; and when the company comes dont dare to speak until youre spoken to. [*Essie creeps away to the fireplace*]. Your father's people had better see you and know youre there: theyre as much bound to keep you from starvation as I am. At any rate they might help. But let me have no chattering and making free with them, as if you were their equal. Do you hear?

ESSIE. Yes.

MRS DUDGEON. Well, then go and do as youre told. [*Essie sits down miserably on the corner of the fender furthest from the door*]. Never mind her, Mrs. Anderson: you know who she is and what she is. If she gives you any trouble, just tell me; and I'll settle accounts with her. [*Mrs. Dudgeon goes into the bedroom, shutting the door sharply behind her as if even it had to be made do its duty with a ruthless hand*].

JUDITH [*patronizing Essie, and arranging the cake and wine on the table more becomingly*] You must not mind if your aunt is strict with you. She is a very good woman, and desires your good too.

ESSIE [*in listless misery*] Yes.

JUDITH [*annoyed with Essie for her failure to be consoled*

and edified, and to appreciate the kindly condescension of the remark] You are not going to be sullen, I hope, Essie.

ESSIE. No.

JUDITH. Thats a good girl! [*She places a couple of chairs at the table with their backs to the window, with a pleasant sense of being a more thoughtful housekeeper than Mrs Dudgeon*]. Do you know any of your father's relatives?

ESSIE. No. They wouldnt have anything to do with him: they were too religious. Father used to talk about Dick Dudgeon; but I never saw him.

JUDITH [*ostentatiously shocked*] Dick Dudgeon! Essie: do you wish to be a really respectable and grateful girl, and to make a place for yourself here by steady good conduct?

ESSIE [*very half-heartedly*] Yes.

JUDITH. Then you must never mention the name of Richard Dudgeon—never even think about him. He is a bad man.

ESSIE. What has he done?

JUDITH. You must not ask questions about him, Essie. You are too young to know what it is to be a bad man. But he is a smuggler; and he lives with gypsies; and he has no love for his mother and his family; and he wrestles and plays games on Sunday instead of going to church. Never let him into your presence, if you can help it, Essie; and try to keep yourself and all womanhood unspotted by contact with such men.

ESSIE. Yes.

JUDITH [*again displeased*] I am afraid you say Yes and No without thinking very deeply.

ESSIE. Yes. At least I mean—

JUDITH [*severely*] What do you mean?

ESSIE [*almost crying*] Only—my father was a smuggler; and— [*Someone knocks*].

JUDITH. They are beginning to come. Now remember your aunt's directions, Essie; and be a good girl. [*Christy comes back with the stand of stuffed birds under a glass case, and an ink-stand, which he places on the table*]. Good morning, Mr Dudgeon. Will you open the door, please: the people have come.

CHRISTY. Good morning. [*He opens the house door*].

The morning is now fairly bright and warm; and Anderson, who is the first to enter, has left his cloak at home. He is accompanied by Lawyer Hawkins, a brisk, middleaged man in brown riding gaiters and yellow breeches, looking as much squire as solicitor. He and Anderson are allowed precedence as representing the learned professions. After them comes the family, headed by the senior uncle, William Dudgeon, a large, shapeless man, bottle-nosed and evidently no ascetic at table. His clothes are not the clothes, nor his anxious wife the wife, of a prosperous man. The junior uncle, Titus Dudgeon, is a wiry little terrier of a man, with an immense and visibly purseproud wife, both free from the cares of the William household.

Hawkins at once goes brisky to the table and takes the chair nearest the sofa, Christy having left the inkstand there. He puts his hat on the floor beside him, and produces the will. Uncle William comes to the fire and stands on the hearth warming his coat tails, leaving Mrs William derelict near the door. Uncle Titus, who is the lady's man of the family, rescues her by giving her his disengaged arm bringing her to the sofa, where he sits down warmly between his own lady and his brother's. Anderson hangs up his hat and waits for a word with Judith.

JUDITH. She will be here in a moment. Ask them to wait. [*She taps at the bedroom door. Receiving an answer from within, she opens it and passes through*].

ANDERSON [*taking his place at the table at the opposite end to Hawkins*] Our poor afflicted sister will be with us in a moment. Are we all here?

CHRISTY [*at the house door, which he has just shut*] All except Dick.

The callousness with which Christy names the reprobate jars on the moral sense of the family. Uncle William shakes his head slowly and repeatedly. Mrs Titus catches her breath convulsively through her nose. Her husband speaks.

UNCLE TITUS. Well, I hope he will have the grace not to come. I h o p e so.

The Dudgeons all murmur assent, except Christy, who goes to the window and posts himself there, looking out. Hawkins smiles secretively as if he knew something that would change their tune if they knew it. Anderson is uneasy: the love of solemn family councils, especially funeral ones, is not in his nature. Judith appears at the bedroom door.

JUDITH [*with gentle impressiveness*] Friends, Mrs Dudgeon. [*She takes the chair from beside the fireplace; and places it for Mrs Dudgeon, who comes from the bedroom in black, with a clean handkerchief to her eyes. All rise, except Essie. Mrs Titus and Mrs William produce equally clean handkerchiefs and weep. It is an affecting moment*].

UNCLE WILLIAM. Would it comfort you, sister, if we were to offer up a prayer?

UNCLE TITUS. Or sing a hymn?

ANDERSON [*rather hastily*] I have been with our sister this morning already, friends. In our hearts we ask a blessing.

ALL [*except Essie*] Amen.

They all sit down, except Judith, who stands behind Mrs Dudgeon's chair.

JUDITH [*to Essie*] Essie: did you say Amen?

ESSIE [*scaredly*] No.

JUDITH. Then say it, like a good girl.

ESSIE. Amen.

UNCLE WILLIAM [*encouragingly*] Thats right: thats right. We know who you are; but we are willing to be kind to you if you are a good girl and deserve it. We are all equal before the Throne.

This republican sentiment does not please the women, who are convinced that the Throne is precisely the place where their superiority, often questioned in this world, will be recognized and rewarded.

CHRISTY [*at the window*] Heres Dick.

*Anderson and Hawkins look round sociably. Essie,
with a gleam of interest breaking through her misery,
looks up. Christy grins and gapes expectantly at the door.
The rest are petrified with the intensity of their sense of
Virtue menaced with outrage by the approach of flaunt-
ing Vice. The reprobate appears in the doorway, graced
beyond his alleged merits by the morning sunlight. He is
certainly the best looking member of the family; but his
expression is reckless and sardonic, his manner defiant
and satirical, his dress picturesquely careless. Only, his
forehead and mouth betray an extraordinary steadfastness; and his eyes are the eyes of a fanatic.*

RICHARD [*on the threshold, taking off his hat*] Ladies and
gentlemen: your servant, your very humble servant.
[*With this comprehensive insult, he throws his hat to
Christy with a suddenness that makes him jump like a
negligent wicket keeper, and comes into the middle of
the room, where he turns and deliberately surveys the
company*]. How happy you all look! how glad to see me!
[*He turns towards Mrs Dudgeon's chair; and his lip rolls
up horribly from his dog tooth as he meets her look of
undisguised hatred*]. Well, mother: keeping up appearances as usual? thats right, thats right. [*Judith pointedly
moves away from his neighborhood to the other side of
the kitchen, holding her skirt instinctively as if to save
it from contamination. Uncle Titus promptly marks his
approval of her action by rising from the sofa, and placing a chair for her to sit down upon*]. What! Uncle
William! I havnt seen you since you gave up drinking.
[*Poor Uncle William, shamed, would protest; but Richard claps him heartily on his shoulder, adding*] you have
given it up, havnt you? [*releasing him with a playful
push*] of course you have: quite right too: you overdid
it. [*He turns away from Uncle William and makes for
the sofa*]. And now, where is that upright horsedealer
Uncle Titus? Uncle Titus: come forth. [*He comes upon
him holding the chair as Judith sits down*]. As usual,
looking after the ladies!

UNCLE TITUS [*indignantly*] Be ashamed of yourself, sir—

RICHARD [*interrupting him and shaking his hand in spite of him*] I am: I am; but I am proud of my uncle—proud of all my relatives— [*again surveying them*] who could look at them and not be proud and joyful? [*Uncle Titus, overborne, resumes his seat on the sofa. Richard turns to the table*]. Ah, Mr Anderson, still at the good work, still shepherding them. Keep them up to the mark, minister, keep them up to the mark. Come! [*with a spring he seats himself on the table and takes up the decanter*] clink a glass with me, Pastor, for the sake of old times.

ANDERSON. You know, I think, Mr Dudgeon, that I do not drink before dinner.

RICHARD. You will, some day, Pastor: Uncle William used to drink before breakfast. Come: it will give your sermons unction. [*He smells the wine and makes a wry face*]. But do not begin on my mother's company sherry. I stole some when I was six years old; and I have been a temperate man ever since. [*He puts the decanter down and changes the subject*]. So I hear you are married, Pastor, and that your wife has a most ungodly allowance of good looks.

ANDERSON [*quietly indicating Judith*] Sir: you are in the presence of my wife. [*Judith rises and stands with stony propriety*].

RICHARD [*quickly slipping down from the table with instinctive good manners*] Your servant, madam: no offence. [*He looks at her earnestly*]. You deserve your reputation; but I'm sorry to see by your expression that youre a good woman. [*She looks shocked, and sits down amid a murmur of indignant sympathy from his relatives. Anderson, sensible enough to know that these demonstrations can only gratify and encourage a man who is deliberately trying to provoke them, remains perfectly good-humored*]. All the same, Pastor, I respect you more than I did before. By the way, did I hear, or did I not, that our late lamented Uncle Peter, though unmarried, was a father?

UNCLE TITUS. He had only one irregular child, sir.

RICHARD. O n l y one! He thinks one a mere trifle! I blush for you, Uncle Titus.

ANDERSON. Mr Dudgeon: you are in the presence of your mother and her grief.

RICHARD. It touches me profoundly, Pastor. By the way, what has become of the irregular child?

ANDERSON [*pointing to Essie*] There, sir, listening to you.

RICHARD [*shocked into sincerity*] What! Why the devil didnt you tell me that before? Children suffer enough in this house without— [*He hurries remorsefully to Essie*]. Come, little cousin! never mind me: it was not meant to hurt you. [*She looks up gratefully at him. Her tear-stained face affects him violently; and he bursts out, in a transport of wrath*] Who has been making her cry? Who has been ill-treating her? By God —

MRS DUDGEON [*rising and confronting him*] Silence your blasphemous tongue. I will bear no more of this. Leave my house.

RICHARD. How do you know it's your house until the will is read? [*They look at one another for a moment with intense hatred; and then she sinks, checkmated, into her chair. Richard goes boldly up past Anderson to the window, where he takes the railed chair in his hand*]. Ladies and gentlemen: as the eldest son of my late father, and the unworthy head of this household, I bid you welcome. By your leave, Minister Anderson: by your leave, Lawyer Hawkins. The head of the table for the head of the family. [*He places the chair at the table between the minister and the attorney; sits down between them; and addresses the assembly with a presidential air*]. We meet on a melancholy occasion: a father dead! an uncle actually hanged, and probably damned. [*He shakes his head deploringly. The relatives freeze with horror*]. T h a t s right: pull your longest faces [*his voice suddenly sweetens gravely as his glance lights on Essie*] provided only there is hope in the eyes of the child. [*Briskly*] Now then, Lawyer Hawkins: business, business. Get on with the will, man.

TITUS. Do not let yourself be ordered or hurried, Mr. Hawkins.

HAWKINS [*very politely and willingly*] Mr Dudgeon means no offence, I feel sure. I will not keep you one second,

Mr Dudgeon. Just while I get my glasses—[*he fumbles for them. The Dudgeons look at one another with misgiving*].

RICHARD. Aha! They notice your civility, Mr Hawkins. They are prepared for the worst. A glass of wine to clear your voice before you begin. [*He pours out one for him and hands it; then pours one for himself*].

HAWKINS. Thank you, Mr Dudgeon. Your good health, sir.

RICHARD. Yours, sir. [*With the glass half way to his lips, he checks himself, giving a dubious glance at the wine, and adds, with quaint intensity*] Will anyone oblige me with a glass of water?

Essie, who has been hanging on his every word and movement, rises stealthily and slips out behind Mrs Dudgeon through the bedroom door, returning presently with a jug and going out of the house as quietly as possible.

HAWKINS. The will is not exactly in proper legal phraseology.

RICHARD. No: my father died without the consolations of the law.

HAWKINS. Good again, Mr Dudgeon, good again. [*Preparing to read*] Are you ready, sir?

RICHARD. Ready, aye ready. For what we are about to receive, may the Lord make us truly thankful. Go ahead.

HAWKINS [*reading*] "This is the last will and testament of me Timothy Dudgeon on my deathbed at Nevinstown on the road from Springtown to Websterbridge on this twenty-fourth day of September, one thousand seven hundred and seventy seven. I hereby revoke all former wills made by me and declare that I am of sound mind and know well what I am doing and that this is my real will according to my own wish and affections."

RICHARD [*glancing at his mother*] Aha!

HAWKINS [*shaking his head*] Bad phraseology, sir, wrong phraseology. "I give and bequeath a hundred pounds to my younger son Christopher Dudgeon, fifty pounds to be paid to him on the day of his marriage to Sarah Wilkins if she will have him, and ten pounds on the birth of each of his children up to the number of five."

RICHARD. How if she wont have him?

CHRISTY. She will if I have fifty pounds.

RICHARD. Good, my brother. Proceed.

HAWKINS. "I give and bequeath to my wife Annie Dudgeon, born Annie Primrose"—you see he did not know the law, Mr Dudgeon: your mother was not born Annie: she was christened so—"an annuity of fifty-two pounds a year for life [*Mrs Dudgeon, with all eyes on her, holds herself convulsively rigid*] to be paid out of the interest on her own money"—t h e r e ' s a way to put it, Mr Dudgeon! Her own money!

MRS DUDGEON. A very good way to put God's truth. It was every penny my own. Fifty-two pounds a year!

HAWKINS. "And I recommend her for her goodness and piety to the forgiving care of her children, having stood between them and her as far as I could to the best of my ability."

MRS DUDGEON. And this is my reward! [*Raging inwardly*] You know what I think, Mr Anderson: you know the word I gave to it.

ANDERSON. It cannot be helped, Mrs. Dudgeon. We must take what comes to us. [*To Hawkins*]. Go on, sir.

HAWKINS. "I give and bequeath my house at Websterbridge with the land belonging to it and all the rest of my property soever to my eldest son and heir, Richard Dudgeon."

RICHARD. Oho! The fatted calf, Minister, the fatted calf.

HAWKINS. "On these conditions—"

RICHARD. The devil! Are there conditions?

HAWKINS. "To wit: first, that he shall not let my brother Peter's natural child starve or be driven by want to an evil life."

RICHARD [*emphatically, striking his fist on the table*] Agreed.

Mrs Dudgeon, turning to look malignantly at Essie, misses her and looks quickly round to see where she has moved to; then, seeing that she has left the room without leave, closes her lips vengefully.

HAWKINS. "Second, that he shall be a good friend to my old horse Jim"— [*again shaking his head*] he should have written James, sir.

RICHARD. James shall live in clover. Go on.

HAWKINS. —"and keep my deaf farm labourer Prodger Feston in his service."

RICHARD. Prodger Feston shall get drunk every Saturday.

HAWKINS. "Third, that he make Christy a present on his marriage out of the ornaments in the best room."

RICHARD [*holding up the stuffed birds*] Here you are, Christy.

CHRISTY [*disappointed*] I'd rather have the china peacocks.

RICHARD. You shall have both. [*Christy is greatly pleased*]. Go on.

HAWKINS. "Fourthly and lastly, that he try to live at peace with his mother as far as she will consent to it."

RICHARD [*dubiously*] Hm! Anything more, Mr Hawkins?

HAWKINS [*solemnly*] "Finally I give and bequeath my soul into my Maker's hands, humbly asking forgiveness for all my sins and mistakes, and hoping that He will so guide my son that it may not be said that I have done wrong in trusting to him rather than to others in the perplexity of my last hour in this strange place."

ANDERSON. Amen.

THE UNCLES AND AUNTS. Amen.

RICHARD. My mother does not say Amen.

MRS DUDGEON [*rising, unable to give up her property without a struggle*] Mr Hawkins: is that a proper will? Remember, I have his rightful, legal will, drawn up by yourself, leaving all to me.

HAWKINS. This is a very wrongly and irregularly worded will, Mrs Dudgeon: though [*turning politely to Richard*] it contains in my judgment an excellent disposal of his property.

ANDERSON [*interposing before Mrs Dudgeon can retort*] That is not what you are asked, Mr Hawkins. Is it a legal will?

HAWKINS. The courts will sustain it against the other.

ANDERSON. But why, if the other is more lawfully worded?

HAWKINS. Because, sir, the courts will sustain the claim of a man—and that man the eldest son—against any woman, if they can. I warned you, Mrs Dudgeon, when you got me to draw that other will, that it was not a wise will, and that though you might make him sign it, he would never be easy until he revoked it. But you wouldnt take advice; and now Mr Richard is cock of the walk. [*He takes his hat from the floor; rises; and begins pocketing his papers and spectacles*].

This is the signal for the breaking-up of the party. Anderson takes his hat from the rack and joins Uncle William at the fire. Titus fetches Judith her things from the rack. The three on the sofa rise and chat with Hawkins. Mrs Dudgeon, now an intruder in her own house, stands inert, crushed by the weight of the law on women, accepting it, as she has been trained to accept all monstrous calamities, as proofs of the greatness of the power that inflicts them, and of her own wormlike insignificance. For at this time, remember, Mary Wollstonecraft is as yet only a girl of eighteen, and her Vindication of the Rights of Women is still fourteen years off. Mrs Dudgeon is rescued from her apathy by Essie, who comes back with the jug full of water. She is taking it to Richard when Mrs Dudgeon stops her.

MRS DUDGEON [*threatening her*] Where have you been? [*Essie, appalled, tries to answer, but cannot*]. How dare you go out by yourself after the orders I gave you?

ESSIE. He asked for a drink— [*she stops, her tongue cleaving to her palate with terror*].

JUDITH [*with gentler severity*] W h o asked for a drink? [*Essie, speechless, points to Richard*].

RICHARD. What! I!

JUDITH [*shocked*] Oh Essie, Essie!

RICHARD. I believe I did. [*He takes a glass and holds it to Essie to be filled. Her hand shakes*]. What! afraid of me?

ESSIE [*quickly*] No. I— [*She pours out the water*].

RICHARD [*tasting it*] Ah, youve been up the street to the market gate spring to get that. [*He takes a draught*]. Delicious! Thank you. [*Unfortunately, at this moment he chances to catch sight of Judith's face, which expresses the most prudish disapproval of his evident attraction for Essie, who is devouring him with her grateful eyes. His mocking expression returns instantly. He puts down the glass; deliberately winds his arm round Essie's shoulders;*

*and brings her into the middle of the company. Mrs
Dudgeon being in Essie's way as they come past the
table, he says]* By your leave, mother [*and compels her
to make way for them*]. What do they call you? Bessie?

ESSIE. Essie.

RICHARD. Essie, to be sure. Are you a good girl, Essie?

ESSIE [*greatly disappointed that he, of all people, should
begin at her in this way*] Yes. [*She looks doubtfully at
Judith*]. I think so. I mean I— I hope so.

RICHARD. Essie: did you ever hear of a person called the
devil?

ANDERSON [*revolted*] Shame on you, sir, with a mere child—

RICHARD. By your leave, Minister: I do not interfere with
your sermons: do not you interrupt mine. [*To Essie*] Do
you know what they call me, Essie?

ESSIE. Dick.

RICHARD [*amused: patting her on the shoulder*] Yes, Dick;
but something else too. They call me the Devil's
Disciple.

ESSIE. Why do you let them?

RICHARD [*seriously*] Because it's true. I was brought up in
the other service; but I knew from the first that the Devil
was my natural master and captain and friend. I saw that
he was in the right, and that the world cringed to his conqueror only through fear. I prayed secretly to him; and
he comforted me, and saved me from having my spirit
broken in this house of children's tears. I promised him
my soul, and swore on oath that I would stand up for
him in this world and stand by him in the next.
[*Solemnly*] That promise and that oath made a man of
me. From this day this house is his home; and no child
shall cry in it: this hearth is his altar; and no soul shall
ever cower over it in the dark evenings and be afraid.
Now [*turning forcibly on the rest*] which of you good
men will take this child and rescue her from the house
of the devil?

JUDITH [*coming to Essie and throwing a protecting arm
about her*] I will. You should be burnt alive.

ESSIE. But I dont want to. [*She shrinks back, leaving Richard and Judith face to face*].

RICHARD [*to Judith*] Actually doesnt want to, most virtuous
lady!

UNCLE TITUS. Have a care, Richard Dudgeon. The law —

RICHARD [*turning threateningly on him*] Have a care, you.
In an hour from this there will be no law here but
martial law. I passed the soldiers within six miles on
my way here: before noon Major Swindon's gallows for
rebels will be up in the market place.

ANDERSON [*calmly*] What have we to fear from that, sir?

RICHARD. More than you think. He hanged the wrong man
at Springtown: he thought Uncle Peter was respectable,
because the Dudgeons had a good name. But his next
example will be the best man in the town to whom he
can bring home a rebellious word. Well, we're all rebels;
and you know it.

ALL THE MEN [*except Anderson*] No, no, no!

RICHARD. Yes, you are. You havnt damned King George
up hill and down dale as I have; but youve prayed for
his defeat; and you, Anthony Anderson, have conducted
the service, and sold your family bible to buy a pair of
pistols. They maynt hang me, perhaps; because the
moral effect of the Devil's Disciple dancing on nothing
wouldnt help them. But a minister! [*Judith, dismayed,
clings to Anderson*] or a lawyer! [*Hawkins smiles like a
man able to take care of himself*] or an upright horsedealer! [*Uncle Titus snarls at him in rage and terror*] or
a reformed drunkard! [*Uncle William, utterly unnerved,
moans and wobbles with fear*] eh? Would that shew that
King George meant business—ha?

ANDERSON [*perfectly self-possessed*] Come, my dear: he is
only trying to frighten you. There is no danger. [*He
takes her out of the house. The rest crowd to the door to
follow him, except Essie, who remains near Richard*].

RICHARD [*boisterously derisive*] Now then: how many of
you will stay with me; run up the American flag on the
devil's house; and make a fight for freedom? [*They
scramble out, Christy among them, hustling one another
in their haste*] Ha ha! Long live the devil! [*To Mrs
Dudgeon, who is following them*] What, mother! Are you
off too?

MRS DUDGEON [*deadly pale, with her hand on her heart as if she had received a deathblow*] My curse on you! My dying curse! [*She goes out*].

RICHARD [*calling after her*] It will bring me luck. Ha ha ha!

ESSIE [*anxiously*] Maynt I stay?

RICHARD [*turning to her*] What! Have they forgotten to save your soul in their anxiety about their own bodies? Oh yes: you may stay. [*He turns excitedly away again and shakes his fist after them. His left fist, also clenched, hangs down. Essie seizes it and kisses it, her tears falling on it. He starts and looks at it*]. Tears! The devil's baptism! [*She falls on her knees, sobbing. He stoops good-naturedly to raise her, saying*] Oh yes, you may cry that way, Essie, if you like.

ACT II

Minister Anderson's house is in the main street of Webster-bridge, not far from the town hall. To the eye of the eighteenth century New Englander, it is much grander than the plain farmhouse of the Dudgeons; but it is so plain itself that a modern house agent would let both at about the same rent. The chief dwelling room has the same sort of kitchen fireplace, with boiler, toaster hanging on the bars, movable iron griddle socketed to the hob, hook above for roasting, and broad fender, on which stand a kettle and a plate of buttered toast. The door, between the fireplace and the corner, has neither panels, fingerplates nor handles: it is made of plain boards, and fastens with a latch. The table is a kitchen table, with a treacle colored cover of American cloth, chapped at the corners by drap-ing. The tea service on it consists of two thick cups and saucers of the plainest ware, with milk jug and bowl to match, each large enough to contain nearly a quart, on a black japanned tray, and, in the middle of the table, a wooden trencher with a big loaf upon it, and a square half pound block of butter in a crock. The big oak press facing the fire from the opposite side of the room, is for use and storage, not for ornament; and the minister's house coat hangs on a peg from its door, shewing that he is out; for when he is in, it is his best coat that hangs there. His big riding boots stand beside the press, evidently in their usual place, and rather proud of themselves. In fact, the evolution of the minister's kitchen, dining room and drawing room into three separate apartments has not yet taken place; and so, from the point of view of our pampered period, he is no better off than the Dudgeons.

But there is a difference, for all that. To begin with, Mrs Anderson is a pleasanter person to live with than Mrs Dudgeon. To which Mrs Dudgeon would at once reply, with reason, that Mrs Anderson has no children to look after; no poultry, pigs nor cattle; a steady and sufficient income not directly dependent on harvests and prices at fairs; an affectionate husband who is a tower of strength to her: in short, that life is as easy at the minister's house as it is hard at the farm. This is true; but to explain a fact is not to alter it; and however little credit Mrs Anderson may deserve for making her home happier, she has certainly succeeded in doing it. The outward and visible signs of her superior social pretensions are, a drugget on the floor, a plaster ceiling between the timbers, and chairs which, though not upholstered, are stained and polished. The fine arts are represented by a mezzotint portrait of some Presbyterian divine, a copperplate of Raphael's St Paul preaching at Athens, a rococo presentation clock on the mantel-shelf, flanked by a couple of miniatures, a pair of crockery dogs with baskets in their mouths, and, at the corners, two large cowrie shells. A pretty feature of the room is the low wide latticed window, nearly its whole width, with little red curtains running on a rod half way up it to serve as a blind. There is no sofa; but one of the seats, standing near the press, has a railed back and is long enough to accommodate two people easily. On the whole, it is rather the sort of room that the nineteenth century has ended in struggling to get back to under the leadership of Mr Philip Webb and his disciples in domestic architecture, though no genteel clergyman would have tolerated it fifty years ago.

The evening has closed in; and the room is dark except for the cosy firelight and the dim oil lamps seen through

*the window in the wet street, where there is a quiet, steady,
warm, windless downpour of rain. As the town clock strikes
the quarter, Judith comes in with a couple of candles in
earthenware candlesticks, and sets them on the table. Her
self-conscious airs of the morning are gone: she is anxious
and frightened. She goes to the window and peers into the
street. The first thing she sees there is her husband, hurrying home through the rain. She gives a little gasp of relief,
not very far removed from a sob, and turns to the door.
Anderson comes in, wrapped in a very wet cloak.*

JUDITH [*running to him*] Oh, here you are at last, at last!
    [*She attempts to embrace him*].
ANDERSON [*keeping her off*] Take care, my love: I'm wet.
    Wait till I get my cloak off. [*He places a chair with its
    back to the fire; hangs his cloak on it to dry; shakes the
    rain from his hat and puts it on the fender; and at last
    turns with his hands outstretched to Judith*]. Now!
    [*She flies into his arms*]. I am not late, am I? The town
    clock struck the quarter as I came in at the front door.
    And the town clock is always fast.
JUDITH. I'm sure it's slow this evening. I'm so glad youre
    back.
ANDERSON [*taking her more closely in his arms*] Anxious,
    my dear?
JUDITH. A little.
ANDERSON. Why, youve been crying.
JUDITH. Only a little. Never mind: it's all over now. [*A
    bugle call is heard in the distance. She starts in terror
    and retreats to the long seat, listening*]. Whats that?
ANDERSON [*following her tenderly to the seat and making
    her sit down with him*] Only King George, my dear. He's
    returning to barracks, or having his roll called, or getting
    ready for tea, or booting or saddling or something.
    Soldiers dont ring the bell or call over the banisters when
    they want anything: they send a boy out with a bugle
    to disturb the whole town.
JUDITH. Do you think there is really any danger?
ANDERSON. Not the least in the world.

JUDITH. You say that to comfort me, not because you believe it.

ANDERSON. My dear: in this world there is always danger for those who are afraid of it. Theres a danger that the house will catch on fire in the night, but we shant sleep any the less soundly for that.

JUDITH. Yes, I know what you always say; and youre quite right. Oh, quite right: I know it. But—I suppose I'm not brave: thats all. My heart shrinks every time I think of the soldiers.

ANDERSON. Never mind that, dear: bravery is none the worse for costing a little pain.

JUDITH. Yes, I suppose so. [*Embracing him again*] Oh how brave you are, my dear! [*With tears in her eyes*] Well, I'll be brave too: you shant be ashamed of your wife.

ANDERSON. Thats right. Now you make me happy. Well, well! [*He rises and goes cheerily to the fire to dry his shoes*]. I called on Richard Dudgeon on my way back; but he wasnt in.

JUDITH [*rising in consternation*] You called on that man!

ANDERSON [*reassuring her*] Oh, nothing happened, dearie. He was out.

JUDITH [*almost in tears, as if the visit were a personal humiliation to her*] But why did you go there?

ANDERSON [*gravely*] Well, it is all the talk that Major Swindon is going to do what he did in Springtown—make an example of some notorious rebel, as he calls us. He pounced on Peter Dudgeon as the worst character there; and it is the general belief that he will pounce on Richard as the worst here.

JUDITH. But Richard said—

ANDERSON [*goodhumoredly cutting her short*] Pooh! Richard said! He said what he thought would frighten you and frighten me, my dear. He said what perhaps (God forgive him!) he would like to believe. It's a terrible thing to think of what death must mean for a man like that. I felt that I must warn him. I left a message for him.

JUDITH [*querulously*] What message?

ANDERSON. Only that I should be glad to see him for a

moment on a matter of importance to himself, and that
if he would look in here when he was passing he would
be welcome.

JUDITH [*aghast*] You asked that man to come here!

ANDERSON. I did.

JUDITH [*sinking on the seat and clasping her hands*] I hope
he wont come! Oh, I pray that he may not come!

ANDERSON. Why? Dont you want him to be warned?

JUDITH. He must know his danger. Oh, Tony, is it wrong
to hate a blasphemer and a villain? I do hate him. I cant
get him out of my mind: I know he will bring harm with
him. He insulted you: he insulted me: he insulted his
mother.

ANDERSON [*quaintly*] Well, dear, lets forgive him; and then
it wont matter.

JUDITH. Oh, I know it's wrong to hate anybody; but—

ANDERSON [*going over to her with humorous tenderness*]
Come, dear, youre not so wicked as you think. The worst
sin towards our fellow creatures is not to hate them, but
to be indifferent to them; thats the essence of inhumanity.
After all, my dear, if you watch people carefully, you'll
be surprised to find how like hate is to love. [*She starts,
strangely touched—even appalled. He is amused at her*].
Yes; I'm quite in earnest. Think of how some of our
married friends worry one another, tax one another, are
jealous of one another, cant bear to let one another out
of sight for a day, are more like jailers and slave-owners
than lovers. Think of those very same people with their
enemies, scrupulous, lofty, self-respecting, determined to
be independent of one another, careful of how they speak
of one another—pooh! havnt you often thought that if
they only knew it, they were better friends to their
enemies than to their own husbands and wives? Come:
depend on it, my dear, you are really fonder of Richard
than you are of me, if you only knew it. Eh!

JUDITH. Oh, dont say that: dont say that, Tony, even in
jest. You dont know what a horrible feeling it gives me.

ANDERSON [*laughing*] Well, well: never mind, pet. He's a
bad man; and you hate him as he deserves. And youre
going to make the tea, arnt you?

JUDITH [*remorsefully*] Oh yes, I forgot. Ive been keeping
   you waiting all this time. [*She goes to the fire and puts
   on the kettle*].

ANDERSON [*going to the press and taking his coat off*] Have
   you stitched up the shoulder of my old coat?

JUDITH. Yes, dear. [*She goes to the table, and sets about
   putting the tea into the teapot from the caddy*].

ANDERSON [*as he changes his coat for the older one hanging
   on the press, and replaces it by the one he has just taken
   off*] Did anyone call when I was out?

JUDITH. No, only— [*Someone knocks at the door. With a
   start which betrays her intense nervousness, she retreats
   to the further end of the table with the tea caddy and
   spoon in her hand, exclaiming*] Who's that?

ANDERSON [*going to her and patting her encouragingly on
   the shoulder*] All right, pet, all right. He wont eat you,
   whoever he is. [*She tries to smile, and nearly makes herself cry. He goes to the door and opens it. Richard is
   there, without overcoat or cloak*]. You might have raised
   the latch and come in, Mr Dudgeon. Nobody stands on
   much ceremony with us. [*Hospitably*] Come in. [*Richard
   comes in carelessly and stands at the table, looking
   round the room with a slight pucker of his nose at the
   mezzotinted divine on the wall. Judith keeps her eyes on
   the tea caddy*]. Is it still raining? [*He shuts the door*].

RICHARD. Raining like the very [*his eye catches Judith's as
   she looks quickly and haughtily up*] —I beg your pardon;
   but [*shewing that his coat is wet*] you see— !

ANDERSON. Take it off, sir; and let it hang before the fire a
   while: my wife will excuse your shirtsleeves. Judith: put
   in another spoonful of tea for Mr Dudgeon.

RICHARD [*eyeing him cynically*] The magic of property,
   Pastor! Are even you civil to me now that I have succeeded to my father's estate?

   Judith throws down the spoon indignantly.

ANDERSON [*quite unruffled, and helping Richard off with
   his coat*] I think, sir, that since you accept my hospitality,
   you cannot have so bad an opinion of it. Sit down. [*With
   the coat in his hand, he points to the railed seat. Richard,
   in his shirtsleeves, looks at him half quarrelsomely for a*

*moment; then, with a nod, acknowledges that the
minister has got the better of him, and sits down on the
seat. Anderson pushes his cloak into a heap on the seat
of the chair at the fire, and hangs Richard's coat on the
back in its place].*

RICHARD. I come, sir, on your own invitation. You left
word you had something important to tell me.

ANDERSON. I have a warning which it is my duty to give
you.

RICHARD [*quickly rising*] You want to preach to me. Excuse
me: I prefer a walk in the rain [*he makes for his coat*].

ANDERSON [*stopping him*] Dont be alarmed, sir: I am no
great preacher. You are quite safe. [*Richard smiles in
spite of himself. His glance softens: he even makes a
gesture of excuse. Anderson, seeing that he has tamed
him, now addresses him earnestly*] Mr Dudgeon: you are
in danger in this town.

RICHARD. What danger?

ANDERSON. Your uncle's danger. Major Swindon's gallows.

RICHARD. It is you who are in danger. I warned you—

ANDERSON [*interrupting him goodhumoredly but authoritatively*] Yes, yes, Mr Dudgeon; but they do not think so
in the town. And even if I were in danger, I have duties
here which I must not forsake. But you are a free man.
Why should you run any risk?

RICHARD. Do you think I should be any great loss, Minister?

ANDERSON. I think that a man's life is worth saving, whoever it belongs to. [*Richard makes him an ironical bow.
Anderson returns the bow humorously*]. Come: youll
have a cup of tea, to prevent you catching cold?

RICHARD. I observe that Mrs Anderson is not quite so
pressing as you are, Pastor.

JUDITH [*almost stifled with resentment, which she has been
expecting her husband to share and express for her at
every insult of Richard's*] You are welcome for my husband's sake. [*She brings the teapot to the fireplace and
sets it on the hob*].

RICHARD. I know I am not welcome for my own, madam.
[*He rises*]. But I think I will not break bread here,
Minister.

ANDERSON [*cheerily*] Give me a good reason for that.

RICHARD. Because there is something in you that I respect, and that makes me desire to have you for my enemy.

ANDERSON. Thats well said. On those terms, sir, I will accept your enmity or any man's. Judith: Mr Dudgeon will stay to tea. Sit down: it will take a few minutes to draw by the fire. [*Richard glances at him with a troubled face; then sits down with his head bent, to hide a convulsive swelling of his throat*]. I was just saying to my wife, Mr Dudgeon, that enmity— [*She grasps his hand and looks imploringly at him, doing both with an intensity that checks him at once*]. Well, well, I mustnt tell you, I see; but it was nothing that need leave us worse friends—enemies, I mean. Judith is a great enemy of yours.

RICHARD. If all my enemies were like Mrs. Anderson, I should be the best Christian in America.

ANDERSON [*gratified, patting her hand*] You hear that, Judith? Mr Dudgeon knows how to turn a compliment.

The latch is lifted from without.

JUDITH [*starting*] Who is that?

Christy comes in.

CHRISTY [*stopping and staring at Richard*] Oh, are y o u here?

RICHARD. Yes. Begone, you fool: Mrs Anderson doesnt want the whole family to tea at once.

CHRISTY [*coming further in*] Mother's very ill.

RICHARD. Well, does she want to see me?

CHRISTY. No.

RICHARD. I thought not.

CHRISTY. She wants to see the minister—at once.

JUDITH [*to Anderson*] Oh, not before youve had some tea.

ANDERSON. I shall enjoy it more when I come back, dear. [*He is about to take up his cloak*].

CHRISTY. The rain's over.

ANDERSON [*dropping the cloak, and picking up his hat from the fender*] Where is your mother, Christy?

CHRISTY. At Uncle Titus's.

ANDERSON. Have you fetched the doctor?

CHRISTY. No: she didnt tell me to.

ANDERSON. Go on there at once: I'll overtake you on his doorstep. [*Christy turns to go*]. Wait a moment. Your brother must be anxious to know the particulars.

RICHARD. Psha! not I: he doesnt know; and I dont care. [*Violently*] Be off, you oaf. [*Christy runs out. Richard adds, a little shamefacedly*] We shall know soon enough.

ANDERSON. Well, perhaps you will let me bring you the news myself. Judith: will you give Mr Dudgeon his tea, and keep him here until I return.

JUDITH [*white and trembling*] Must I—

ANDERSON [*taking her hands and interrupting her to cover her agitation*] My dear: I can depend on you?

JUDITH [*with a piteous effort to be worthy of his trust*] Yes.

ANDERSON [*pressing her hand against his cheek*] You will not mind two old people like us, Mr Dudgeon. [*Going*] I shall not say good evening: you will be here when I come back. [*He goes out*].

> They watch him pass the window, and then look at each other dumbly, quite disconcerted. Richard, noting the quiver of her lips, is the first to pull himself together.

RICHARD. Mrs Anderson: I am perfectly aware of the nature of your sentiments towards me. I shall not intrude on you. Good evening. [*Again he starts for the fireplace to get his coat*].

JUDITH [*getting between him and the coat*] No, no. Dont go: please dont go.

RICHARD [*roughly*] Why? You dont want me here.

JUDITH. Yes, I— [*Wringing her hands in despair*] Oh, if I tell you the truth, you will use it to torment me.

RICHARD [*indignantly*] Torment! What right have you to say that? Do you expect me to stay after that?

JUDITH. I want you to stay; but [*suddenly raging at him like an angry child*] it is not because I like you.

RICHARD. Indeed!

JUDITH. Yes: I had rather you did go than mistake me about that. I hate and dread you; and my husband knows it. If you are not here when he comes back, he will believe that I disobeyed him and drove you away.

RICHARD [*ironically*] Whereas, of course, you have really

been so kind and hospitable and charming to me that I
only want to go away out of mere contrariness, eh?

> *Judith, unable to bear it, sinks on the chair and bursts
> into tears.*

RICHARD. Stop, stop, stop, I tell you. Dont do that. [*Putting
his hands to his breasts as if to a wound*] He wrung my
heart by being a man. Need you tear it by being a
woman? Has he not raised you above my insults, like
himself? [*She stops crying, and recovers herself somewhat, looking at him with a scared curiosity*]. There:
thats right. [*Sympathetically*] Youre better now, arnt
you? [*He puts his hand encouragingly on her shoulder.
She instantly rises haughtily, and stares at him defiantly.
He at once drops into his usual sardonic tone*]. Ah, thats
better. You are yourself again: so is Richard. Well, shall
we go to tea like a quiet respectable couple, and wait for
your husband's return?

JUDITH [*rather ashamed of herself*] If you please. I—I am
sorry to have been so foolish. [*She stoops to take up the
plate of toast from the fender*].

RICHARD. I am sorry, for your sake, that I am—what I am.
Allow me. [*He takes the plate from her and goes with it
to the table*].

JUDITH [*following with the teapot*] Will you sit down? [*He
sits down at the end of the table nearest the press. There
is a plate and knife laid there. The other plate is laid
near it: but Judith stays at the opposite end of the table,
next the fire, and takes her place there, drawing the tray
towards her*]. Do you take sugar?

RICHARD. No: but plenty of milk. Let me give you some
toast. [*He puts some on the second plate, and hands it to
her, with the knife. The action shews quickly how well
he knows that she has avoided her usual place so as to
be as far from him as possible*].

JUDITH [*consciously*] Thanks. [*She gives him his tea*]. Wont
you help yourself?

RICHARD. Thanks. [*He puts a piece of toast on his own
plate; and she pours out tea for herself*].

JUDITH [*observing that he tastes nothing*] Dont you like it?
You are not eating anything.

RICHARD. Neither are you.

JUDITH [*nervously*] I never care much for my tea. Please dont mind me.

RICHARD [*looking dreamily round*] I am thinking. It is all so strange to me. I can see the beauty and peace of this home: I think I have never been more at rest in my life than at this moment; and yet I know quite well I could never live here. It's not in my nature, I suppose, to be domesticated. But it's very beautiful: it's almost holy. [*He muses a moment, and then laughs softly*].

JUDITH [*quickly*] Why do you laugh?

RICHARD. I was thinking that if any stranger came in here now, he would take us for man and wife.

JUDITH [*taking offence*] You mean, I suppose, that you are more my age than he is.

RICHARD [*staring at this unexpected turn*] I never thought of such a thing. [*Sardonic again*]. I see there is another side to domestic joy.

JUDITH [*Angrily*] I would rather have a husband whom everybody respects than—than—

RICHARD. Than the devil's disciple. You are right; but I daresay your love helps him to be a good man, just as your hate helps me to be a bad one.

JUDITH. My husband has been very good to you. He has forgiven you for insulting him, and is trying to save you. Can you not forgive him for being so much better than you are? How dare you belittle him by putting yourself in his place?

RICHARD. Did I?

JUDITH. Yes, you did. You said that if anybody came in they would take us for man and— [*She stops, terror-stricken, as a squad of soldiers tramps past the window*]. The English soldiers! Oh, what do they—

RICHARD [*listening*] Sh!

A VOICE [*outside*] Halt! Four outside: two in with me.

Judith half rises, listening and looking with dilated eyes at Richard, who takes up his cup prosaically, and is drinking his tea when the latch goes up with a sharp click, and an English sergeant walks into the room with two privates, who post themselves at the door. He comes promptly to the table between them.

THE SERGEANT. Sorry to disturb you, mum. Duty! Anthony Anderson: I arrest you in King George's name as a rebel.

JUDITH [*pointing at Richard*] But that is not— [*He looks up quickly at her, with a face of iron. She stops her mouth hastily with the hand she has raised to indicate him, and stands staring affrightedly*].

THE SERGEANT. Come, parson: put your coat on and come along.

RICHARD. Yes: I'll come. [*He rises and takes a step towards his own coat; then recollects himself, and with his back to the sergeant, moves his gaze slowly round the room without turning his head until he sees Anderson's black coat hanging up on the press. He goes composedly to it; takes it down; and puts it on. The idea of himself as a parson tickles him: he looks down at the black sleeve on his arm, and then smiles slyly at Judith, whose white face shews him that what she is painfully struggling to grasp is not the humor of the situation but its horror. He turns to the sergeant, who is approaching him with a pair of handcuffs hidden behind him, and says lightly*] Did you ever arrest a man of my cloth before, Sergeant?

THE SERGEANT [*instinctively respectful, half to the black coat, and to Richard's good breeding*] Well, no sir. At least, only an army chaplain. [*Shewing the handcuffs*]. I'm sorry sir; but duty—

RICHARD. Just so, Sergeant. Well, I'm not ashamed of them: thank you kindly for the apology. [*He holds out his hands*].

SERGEANT [*not availing himself of the offer*] One gentleman to another, sir. Wouldnt you like to say a word to your missis, sir, before you go?

RICHARD [*smiling*] Oh, we shall meet again before—eh? [*meaning "before you hang me"*].

SERGEANT [*loudly, with ostentatious cheerfulness*] Oh, of course, of course. No call for the lady to distress herself. Still— [*in a lower voice, intended for Richard alone*] your last chance, sir.

*They look at one another significantly for a moment.
Then Richard exhales a deep breath and turns toward
Judith.*

RICHARD [*very distinctly*] My love. [*She looks at him, pitiably pale, and tries to answer, but cannot—tries also to
come to him, but cannot trust herself to stand without
the support of the table*]. This gallant gentleman is good
enough to allow us a moment of leavetaking. [*The
sergeant retires delicately and joins his men near the
door*]. He is trying to spare you the truth; but you had
better know it. Are you listening to me? [*She signifies
assent*]. Do you understand that I am going to my death?
[*She signifies that she understands*]. Remember, you
must find our friend who was with us just now. Do you
understand? [*She signifies yes*]. See that you get him
safely out of harm's way. Dont for your life let him know
of my danger; but if he finds it out, tell him that he cannot save me: they would hang him; and they would not
spare me. And tell him that I am steadfast in my religion
as he is in his, and that he may depend on me to the
death. [*He turns to go, and meets the eyes of the sergeant,
who looks a little suspicious. He considers a moment, and
then, turning roguishly to Judith with something of a
smile breaking through his earnestness, says*] And now,
my dear, I am afraid the sergeant will not believe that
you love me like a wife unless you give one kiss before
I go.

*He approaches her and holds out his arms. She quits
the table and almost falls into them.*

JUDITH [*the words choking her*] I ought to—it's murder—

RICHARD. No: only a kiss [*softly to her*] for his sake.

JUDITH. I cant. You must—

RICHARD [*folding her in his arms with an impulse of com-
passion for her distress*] My poor girl!

*Judith, with a sudden effort, throws her arms round
him; kisses him; and swoons away, dropping from his
arms to the ground as if the kiss had killed her.*

RICHARD [*going quickly to the sergeant*] Now, Sergeant:
quick, before she comes to. The handcuffs. [*He puts out
his hands*].

SERGEANT [*pocketing them*] Never mind, sir: I'll trust you. Youre a game one. You ought to a bin a soldier, sir. Between them two, please. [*The soldiers place themselves one before Richard and one behind him. The sergeant opens the door*].

RICHARD [*taking a last look round him*] Goodbye, wife: goodbye, home. Muffle the drums, and quick march!

The sergeant signs to the leading soldier to march. They file out quickly. ****************** *When Anderson returns from Mrs Dudgeon's, he is astonished to find the room apparently empty and almost in darkness except for the glow from the fire; for one of the candles has burnt out, and the other is at its last flicker.*

ANDERSON. Why, what on earth— ? [*Calling*] Judith, Judith! [*He listens: there is no answer*]. Hm! [*He goes to the cupboard; takes a candle from the drawer; lights it at the flicker of the expiring one on the table; and looks wonderingly at the untasted meal by its light. Then he sticks it in the candlestick: takes off his hat; and scratches his head, much puzzled. This action causes him to look at the floor for the first time; and there he sees Judith lying motionless with her eyes closed. He runs to her and stoops beside her, lifting her head*]. Judith.

JUDITH [*waking; for her swoon has passed into the sleep of exhaustion after suffering*] Yes. Did you call? Whats the matter?

ANDERSON. Ive just come in and found you lying here with the candles burnt out and the tea poured out and cold. What has happened?

JUDITH [*still astray*] I dont know. Have I been asleep? I suppose— [*She stops blankly*], I dont know.

ANDERSON [*groaning*] Heaven forgive me, I left you alone with that scoundrel. [*Judith remembers. With an agonized cry, she clutches his shoulders and drags herself to her feet as he rises with her. He clasps her tenderly in his arms*]. My poor pet!

JUDITH [*frantically clinging to him*] What shall I do? Oh my God, what shall I do?

ANDERSON. Never mind, never mind, my dearest dear: it was my fault. Come: youre safe now; and youre not hurt, are you? [*He takes his arms from her to see whether she can stand*]. There: thats right, thats right. If only you are not hurt, nothing else matters.

JUDITH. No, no, no: I'm not hurt.

ANDERSON. Thank Heaven for that! Come now: [*leading her to the railed seat and making her sit down beside him*] sit down and rest: you can tell me about it tomorrow. Or [*misunderstanding her distress*] you shall not tell me at all if it worries you. There, there! [*Cheerfully*] I'll make you some fresh tea: that will set you up again. [*He goes to the table, and empties the teapot into the slop bowl*].

JUDITH [*in a strained tone*] Tony.

ANDERSON. Yes, dear?

JUDITH. Do you think we are only in a dream now?

ANDERSON [*glancing round at her for a moment with a pang of anxiety, though he goes on steadily and cheerfully putting fresh tea into the pot*] Perhaps so, pet. But you may as well dream a cup of tea when youre about it.

JUDITH. Oh stop, stop. You dont know— [*Distracted, she buries her face in her knotted hands*].

ANDERSON [*breaking down and coming to her*] My dear, what is it? I cant bear it any longer: you must tell me. It was all my fault: I was mad to trust him.

JUDITH. No: dont say that. You mustnt say that. He—oh no, no: I cant. Tony: dont speak to me. Take my hands —both my hands. [*He takes them, wondering*]. Make me think of you, not of him. Theres danger, frightful danger; but it is your danger; and I cant keep thinking of it: I cant, I cant: my mind goes back to his danger. He must be saved—no: you must be saved: you, you, you. [*She springs up as if to do something or go somewhere, exclaiming*] Oh, Heaven help me!

ANDERSON [*keeping his seat and holding her hands with resolute composure*] Calmly, calmly, my pet. Youre quite distracted.

JUDITH. I may well be. I dont know what to do. I dont know what to do. [*Tearing his hands away*]. I must save him. [*Anderson rises in alarm as she runs wildly to the*

*door. It is opened in her face by Essie, who hurries in
full of anxiety. The surprise is so disagreeable to Judith
that it brings her to her senses. Her tone is sharp and
angry as she demands]* What do you want?

ESSIE. I was to come to you.

ANDERSON. Who told you to?

ESSIE [*staring at him, as if his presence astonished her*] Are
you here?

JUDITH. Of course. Dont be foolish, child.

ANDERSON. Gently, dearest: youll frighten her. [*Going between them*]. Come here, Essie. [*She comes to him*]. Who
sent you?

ESSIE. Dick. He sent me word by a soldier. I was to come
here at once and do whatever Mrs Anderson told me.

ANDERSON [*enlightened*] A soldier! Ah! I see it all now!
They have arrested Richard. [*Judith makes a gesture of
despair*].

ESSIE. No. I asked the soldier. Dick's safe. But the soldier
said you had been taken.

ANDERSON. I! [*Bewildered, he turns to Judith for an explanation*].

JUDITH [*coaxingly*] All right, dear: I understand. [*To Essie*]
Thank you, Essie, for coming: but I dont need you now.
You may go home.

ESSIE [*suspicious*] Are you sure Dick has not been touched?
Perhaps he told the soldier to say it was the minister.
[*Anxiously*] Mrs Anderson: do you think it can have been
that?

ANDERSON. Tell her the truth if it is so, Judith. She will
learn it from the first neighbor she meets in the street.
[*Judith turns away and covers her eyes with her hands*].

ESSIE [*wailing*] But what will they do to him? Oh, what will
they do to him? Will they hang him? [*Judith shudders
convulsively, and throws herself into the chair in which
Richard sat at the tea table*].

ANDERSON [*patting Essie's shoulder and trying to comfort
her*] I hope not. I hope not. Perhaps if youre very quiet
and patient, we may be able to help him in some way.

ESSIE. Yes—help him—yes, yes, yes. I'll be good.

ANDERSON. I must go to him at once, Judith.

JUDITH [*springing up*] Oh no. You must go away—far away, to some place of safety.

ANDERSON. Pooh!

JUDITH [*passionately*] Do you want to kill me? Do you think I can bear to live for days and days with every knock at the door—every footstep—giving me a spasm of terror? to lie awake for nights and nights in an agony of dread, listening for them to come and arrest you?

ANDERSON. Do you think it would be better to know that I had run away from my post at the first sign of danger?

JUDITH [*bitterly*] Oh, you wont go. I know it. Youll stay; and I shall go mad.

ANDERSON. My dear, your duty—

JUDITH [*fiercely*] What do I care about my duty?

ANDERSON [*shocked*] Judith!

JUDITH. I am doing my duty. I am clinging to my duty. My duty is to get you away, to save you, to leave him to his fate. [*Essie utters a cry of distress and sinks on the chair at the fire, sobbing silently*]. My instinct is the same as hers — to save him above all things, though it would be so much better for him to die! so much greater! But I know you will take your own way. as he took it. I have no power. [*She sits down sullenly on the railed seat*] I'm only a woman: I can do nothing but sit here and suffer. Only, tell him I tried to save you—that I did my best to save you.

ANDERSON. My dear, I am afraid he will be thinking more of his own danger than of mine.

JUDITH. Stop: or I shall hate you.

ANDERSON [*remonstrating*] Come, come, come! How am I to leave you if you talk like this? You are quite out of your senses. [*He turns to Essie*] Essie.

ESSIE [*eagerly rising and drying her eyes*] Yes?

ANDERSON. Just wait outside a moment, like a good girl: Mrs Anderson is not well. [*Essie looks doubtful*]. Never fear: I'll come to you presently; and I'll go to Dick.

ESSIE. You are sure you will go to him? [*Whispering*]. You wont let her prevent you?

ANDERSON [*smiling*] No, no: it's all right. All right. [*She goes*]. Thats a good girl. [*He closes the door, and returns to Judith*].

JUDITH [*seated—rigid*] You are going to your death.

ANDERSON [*quaintly*] Then I shall go in my best coat, dear. [*He turns to the press, beginning to take off his coat*]. Where— ? [*He stares at the empty nail for a moment; then looks quickly round to the fire; strides across to it; and lifts Richard's coat*]. Why, my dear, it seems that he has gone in my best coat.

JUDITH. [*still motionless*] Yes.

ANDERSON. Did the soldiers make a mistake?

JUDITH. Yes: they made a mistake.

ANDERSON. He might have told them. Poor fellow, he was too upset, I suppose.

JUDITH. Yes: he might have told them. So might I.

ANDERSON. Well, it's all very puzzling—almost funny. It's curious how these little things strike us even in the most — [*He breaks off and begins putting on Richard's coat*] I'd better take him his own coat. I know what he'll say— [*imitating Richard's sardonic manner*] "Anxious about my soul, Pastor, and also about your best coat." Eh?

JUDITH. Yes, that is just what he will say to you. [*Vacantly*] It doesnt matter: I shall never see either of you again.

ANDERSON [*rallying her*] Oh pooh, pooh, pooh! [*He sits down beside her*]. Is this how you keep your promise that I shant be ashamed of my brave wife?

JUDITH. No: this is how I break it. I cannot keep my promises to him: why should I keep my promises to you?

ANDERSON. Dont speak so strangely, my love. It sounds insincere to me. [*She looks unutterable reproach at him*]. Yes, dear, nonsense is always insincere; and my dearest is talking nonsense. Just nonsense. [*Her face darkens into dumb obstinacy. She stares straight before her, and does not look at him again, absorbed in Richard's fate. He scans her face; sees that his rallying has produced no effect; and gives it up, making no further effort to conceal his anxiety*]. I wish I knew what has frightened you so. Was there a struggle? Did he fight?

JUDITH. No. He smiled.

ANDERSON. Did he realize his danger, do you think?

JUDITH. He realized yours.

ANDERSON. Mine!

JUDITH [*monotonously*] He said "See that you get him safely out of harm's way." I promised: I cant keep my promise. He said, "Dont for your life let him know of my danger." Ive told you of it. He said that if you found it out, you could not save him—that they will hang him and not spare you.

ANDERSON [*rising in generous indignation*] And you think that I will let a man with that much good in him die like a dog, when a few words might make him die like a Christian. I'm ashamed of you, Judith.

JUDITH. He will be steadfast in his religion as you are in yours; and you may depend on him to the death. He said so.

ANDERSON. God forgive him! What else did he say?

JUDITH. He said goodbye.

ANDERSON [*fidgeting nervously to and fro in great concern*] Poor fellow, poor fellow! You said goodbye to him in all kindness and charity, Judith, I hope.

JUDITH. I kissed him.

ANDERSON. What! Judith!

JUDITH. Are you angry?

ANDERSON. No, no. You were right: you were right. Poor fellow, poor fellow! [*Greatly distressed*] To be hanged like that at his age! And then did they take him away?

JUDITH [*wearily*] Then you were here: thats the next thing I remember. I suppose I fainted. Now bid me goodbye, Tony. Perhaps I shall faint again. I wish I could die.

ANDERSON. No, no, my dear: you must pull yourself together and be sensible. I am in no danger—not the least in the world.

JUDITH [*solemnly*] You are going to your death, Tony— your sure death, if God will let innocent men be murdered. They will not let you see him: they will arrest you the moment you give your name. It was for you the soldiers came.

ANDERSON [*thunderstruck*] For me!!! [*His fists clinch; his neck thickens; his face reddens; the fleshy purses under his eyes become injected with hot blood; the man of peace vanishes, transfigured into a choleric and formidable man of war. Still, she does not come out of her absorption to look at him: her eyes are steadfast with a mechanical reflection of Richard's steadfastness].*

JUDITH. He took your place: he is dying to save you. That is why he went in your coat. That is why I kissed him.

ANDERSON [*exploding*] Blood an' owns! [*His voice is rough and dominant, his gesture full of brute energy*]. Here! Essie, Essie!

ESSIE [*running in*] Yes.

ANDERSON [*impetuously*] Off with you as hard as you can run, to the inn. Tell them to saddle the fastest and strongest horse they have [*Judith rises breathless, and stares at him incredulously*] —the chestnut mare, if she's fresh—without a moment's delay. Go into the stable yard and tell the black man there that I'll give him a silver dollar if the horse is waiting for me when I come, and that I am close on your heels. Away with you. [*His energy sends Essie flying from the room. He pounces on his riding boots; rushes with them to the chair at the fire; and begins pulling them on*].

JUDITH [*unable to believe such a thing of him*] You arc not going to him!

ANDERSON [*busy with the boots*] Going to him! What good would that do? [*Growling to himself as he gets the first boot on with a wrench*] I'll go to them, so I will. [*To Judith peremptorily*] Get me the pistols: I want them. And money, money: I want money—all the money in the house. [*He stoops over the other boot, grumbling*]. A great satisfaction it would be to him to have my company on the gallows. [*He pulls on the boot*].

JUDITH. You are deserting him, then?

ANDERSON. Hold your tongue, woman; and get me the pistols. [*She goes to the press and takes from it a leather belt with two pistols, a powder horn, and a bag of bullets attached to it. She throws it on the table. Then she unlocks a drawer in the press and takes out a purse. Anderson grabs the belt and buckles it on, saying*] If they took

him for me in my coat, perhaps theyll take me for him in
his. [*Hitching the belt into its place*] Do I look like him?

JUDITH [*turning with the purse in her hand*] Horribly unlike him.

ANDERSON [*snatching the purse from her and emptying it
on the table*] Hm! We shall see.

JUDITH [*sitting down helplessly*] Is it of any use to pray, do
you think, Tony?

ANDERSON [*counting the money*] Pray! Can we pray Swindon's rope off Richard's neck?

JUDITH. God may soften Major Swindon's heart.

ANDERSON [*contemptuously—pocketing a handful of
money*] Let him, then. I am not God; and I must go to
work another way. [*Judith gasps at the blasphemy. He
throws the purse on the table*]. Keep that. Ive taken 25
dollars.

JUDITH. Have you forgotten even that you are a minister?

ANDERSON. Minister be—faugh! My hat: wheres my hat?
[*He snatches up hat and cloak, and puts both on in hot
haste*] Now listen, you. If you can get a word with him
by pretending youre his wife, tell him to hold his tongue
until morning: that will give me all the start I need.

JUDITH [*solemnly*] You may depend on him to the death.

ANDERSON. Youre a fool, a fool, Judith. [*For a moment
checking the torrent of his haste, and speaking with
something of his old quiet and impressive conviction*]
You dont know the man youre married to. [*Essie returns.
He swoops at her at once*]. Well: is the horse ready?

ESSIE [*breathless*] It will be ready when you come.

ANDERSON. Good. [*He makes for the door*].

JUDITH [*rising and stretching out her arms after him involuntarily*] Wont you say goodbye?

ANDERSON. And waste another half minute! Psha! [*He
rushes out like an avalanche*].

ESSIE [*hurrying to Judith*] He has gone to save Richard,
hasnt he?

JUDITH. To save Richard! No: Richard has saved him. He
has gone to save himself. Richard must die.

  Essie screams with terror and falls on her knees, hiding

her face. Judith, without heeding her, looks rigidly
straight in front of her, at the vision of Richard, dying.

ACT III

Early next morning the sergeant, at the British headquarters
in the Town Hall, unlocks the door of a little empty
panelled waiting room, and invites Judith to enter. She has
had a bad night, probably a rather delirious one; for even
in the reality of the raw morning, her fixed gaze comes back
at moments when her attention is not strongly held.

The sergeant considers that her feelings do her credit,
and is sympathetic in an encouraging military way. Being
a fine figure of a man, vain of his uniform and of his rank,
he feels specially qualified, in a respectful way, to console
her.

SERGEANT. You can have a quiet word with him here, mum.

JUDITH. Shall I have long to wait?

SERGEANT. No, mum, not a minute. We kep him in the
  Bridewell for the night: and he's just been brought over
  here for the court martial. Dont fret, mum: he slep like
  a child, and has made a rare good breakfast.

JUDITH [*incredulously*] He is in good spirits!

SERGEANT. Tip top, mum. The chaplain looked in to see
  him last night; and he won seventeen shillings off him at
  spoil five. He spent it among us like the gentleman he is.
  Duty's duty, mum, of course; but youre among friends
  here. [*The tramp of a couple of soldiers is heard*
  approaching]. There: I think he's coming. [*Richard*
  comes in, without a sign of care or captivity in his
  bearing. The sergeant nods to the two soldiers, and shews
  them the key of the room in his hand. They withdraw].
  Your good lady, sir.

RICHARD [*going to her*] What! My wife. My adored one.
  [*He takes her hand and kisses it with a perverse, raffish*
  gallantry]. How long do you allow a brokenhearted husband for leave-taking, Sergeant?

SERGEANT. As long as we can, sir. We shall not disturb you till the court sits.

RICHARD. But it has struck the hour.

.SERGEANT. So it has, sir; but theres a delay. General Burgoyne's just arrived—Gentlemanly Johnny we call him, sir—and he wont have done finding fault with everything this side of half past. I know him, sir: I served with him in Portugal. You may count on twenty minutes, sir; and by your leave I wont waste any more of them. [*He goes out, locking the door. Richard immediately drops his raffish manner and turns to Judith with considerate sincerity*].

RICHARD. Mrs Anderson: this visit is very kind of you. And how are you after last night? I had to leave you before you recovered; but I sent word to Essie to go and look after you. Did she understand the message?

JUDITH [*breathless and urgent*] Oh, dont think of me: I havnt come here to talk about myself. Are they going to —to— [*meaning "to hang you"*]?

RICHARD [*whimsically*] At noon, punctually. At least, that was when they disposed of Uncle Peter. [*She shudders*]. Is your husband safe? Is he on the wing?

JUDITH. He is no longer my husband.

RICHARD [*opening his eyes wide*] Eh?

JUDITH. I disobeyed you. I told him everything. I expected him to come here and save you. I wanted him to come here and save you. He ran away instead.

RICHARD. Well, thats what I meant him to do. What good would his staying have done? Theyd only have hanged us both.

JUDITH [*with reproachful earnestness*] Richard Dudgeon: on your honor, what would you have done in his place?

RICHARD. Exactly what he has done, of course.

JUDITH. Oh, why will you not be simple with me—honest and straightforward? If you are so selfish as that, why did you let them take you last night?

RICHARD [*gaily*] Upon my life, Mrs Anderson, I dont know. Ive been asking myself that question ever since; and I can find no manner of reason for acting as I did.

JUDITH. You know you did it for his sake, believing he was a more worthy man than yourself.

RICHARD [*laughing*] Oho! No: thats a very pretty reason, I must say; but I'm not so modest as that. No: it wasnt for his sake.

JUDITH [*after a pause, during which she looks shamefacedly at him, blushing painfully*] Was it for my sake?

RICHARD [*gallantly*] Well, you had a hand in it. It must have been a little for your sake. You let them take me, at all events.

JUDITH. Oh, do you think I have not been telling myself that all night? Your death will be at my door. [*Impulsively, she gives him her hand, and adds, with intense earnestness*] If I could save you as you saved him, I would do it, no matter how cruel the death was.

RICHARD [*holding her hand and smiling, but keeping her almost at arms length*] I am very sure I shouldnt let you.

JUDITH. Dont you see that I c a n save you?

RICHARD. How? by changing clothes with me, eh?

JUDITH [*disengaging her hand to touch his lips with it*] Dont [*meaning 'Dont jest'*]. No: by telling the Court who you really are.

RICHARD [*frowning*] No use: they wouldnt spare me; and it would spoil half his chance of escaping. They are determined to cow us by making an example of somebody on that gallows today. Well, let us cow them by showing that we can stand by one another to the death. That is the only force that can send Burgoyne back across the Atlantic and make America a nation.

JUDITH [*impatiently*] Oh, what does all that matter?

RICHARD [*laughing*] True: what does it matter? what does anything matter? You see, men have these strange notions, Mrs Anderson; and women see the folly of them.

JUDITH. Women have to lose those they love through them.

RICHARD. They can easily get fresh lovers.

JUDITH [*revolted*] Oh! [*Vehemently*] Do you realize that you are going to kill yourself?

RICHARD. The only man I have any right to kill, Mrs Anderson. Dont be concerned: no woman will lose her

lover through my death. [*Smiling*] Bless you, nobody
cares for me. Have you heard that my mother is dead?

JUDITH. Dead!

RICHARD. Of heart disease—in the night. Her last word to
me was her curse: I dont think I could have borne her
blessing. My other relatives will not grieve much on my
account. Essie will cry for a day or two; but I have provided for her: I made my own will last night.

JUDITH [*stonily, after a moment's silence*] And I!

RICHARD [*surprised*] You?

JUDITH. Yes, I. Am I not to care at all?

RICHARD [*gaily and bluntly*] Not a scrap. Oh, you expressed
your feelings towards me very frankly yesterday. What
happened may have softened you for the moment; but
believe me, Mrs Anderson, you dont like a bone in my
skin or a hair on my head. I shall be as good a riddance
at 12 today as I should have been at 12 yesterday.

JUDITH [*her voice trembling*] What can I do to shew you
that you are mistaken.

RICHARD. Dont trouble. I'll give you credit for liking me
a little better than you did. All I say is that my death
will not break your heart.

JUDITH [*almost in a whisper*] How do you know? [*She puts
her hands on his shoulders and looks intently at him*].

RICHARD [*amazed—divining the truth*] Mrs Anderson! [*The
bell of the town clock strikes the quarter. He collects
himself, and removes her hands, saying rather coldly*]
Excuse me: they will be here for me presently. It is too
late.

JUDITH. It is not too late. Call me as witness: they will
never kill you when they know how heroically you have
acted.

RICHARD [*with some scorn*] Indeed! But if I dont go through
with it, where will the heroism be? I shall simply have
tricked them; and theyll hang me for that like a dog.
Serve me right too!

JUDITH [*wildly*] Oh, I believe you w a n t to die.

RICHARD [*obstinately*] No I dont.

JUDITH. Then why not try to save yourself? I implore you—
listen. You said just now that you saved him for my sake

—yes [*clutching him as he recoils with a gesture of denial*] a little for my sake. Well, save yourself for my sake. And I will go with you to the end of the world.

RICHARD [*taking her by the wrists and holding her a little way from him, looking steadily at her*] Judith.

JUDITH [*breathless—delighted at the name*] Yes.

RICHARD. If I said—to please you—that I did what I did ever so little for your sake, I lied as men always lie to women. You know how much I have lived with worthless men—aye, and worthless women too. Well, they could all rise to some sort of goodness and kindness when they were in love [*the word love comes from him with true Puritan scorn*]. That has taught me to set very little store by the goodness that only comes out red hot. What I did last night, I did in cold blood, caring not half so much for your husband, or [*ruthlessly*] for you [*she droops, stricken*] as I do for myself. I had no motive and no interest: all I can tell you is that when it came to the point whether I would take my neck out of the noose and put another man's into it, I could not do it. I dont know why not: I see myself as a fool for my pains; but I could not and I cannot. I have been brought up standing by the law of my own nature; and I may not go against it, gallows or no gallows. [*She has slowly raised her head and is now looking full at him*]. I should have done the same for any other man in the town, or any other man's wife. [*Releasing her*] Do you understand that?

JUDITH. Yes: you mean that you do not love me.

RICHARD [*revolted—with fierce contempt*] Is that all it means to you?

JUDITH. What more—what worse—can it mean to me? [*The sergeant knocks. The blow on the door jars on her heart*]. Oh, one moment more. [*She throws herself on her knees*]. I pray to you—

RICHARD. Hush! [*Calling*] Come in. [*The sergeant unlocks the door and opens it. The guard is with him*].

SERGEANT [*coming in*] Time's up, sir.

RICHARD. Quite ready, Sergeant. Now, my dear. [*He attempts to raise her*].

JUDITH [*clinging to him*] Only one thing more—I entreat, I
    implore you. Let me be present in the court. I have seen
    Major Swindon: he said I should be allowed if you asked
    it. You will ask it. It is my last request: I shall never ask
    you anything again. [*She clasps his knee*]. I beg and pray
    it of you.

RICHARD. If I do, will you be silent?

JUDITH. Yes.

RICHARD. You will keep faith?

JUDITH. I will keep— [*She breaks down, sobbing*].

RICHARD [*taking her arm to lift her*] Just—her other arm,
    Sergeant.

    *They go out, she sobbing convulsively, supported by
    the two men.*

    *Meanwhile, the Council Chamber is ready for the
    court martial. It is a large, lofty room, with a chair of
    state in the middle under a tall canopy with a gilt crown,
    and maroon curtains with the royal monogram G.R. In
    front of the chair is a table, also draped in maroon, with
    a bell, a heavy ink-stand, and writing materials on it.
    Several chairs are set at the table. The door is at the
    right hand of the occupant of the chair when it has an
    occupant: at present it is empty. Major Swindon, a pale,
    sandy-haired, very conscientious looking man of about
    45, sits at the end of the table with his back to the door,
    writing. He is alone until the sergeant announces the
    General in a subdued manner which suggests that
    Gentlemanly Johnny has been making his presence felt
    rather heavily.*

SERGEANT. The General, sir.

    *Swindon rises hastily. The general comes in: the
    sergeant goes out. General Burgoyne is 55, and very well
    preserved. He is a man of fashion, gallant enough to
    have made a distinguished marriage by an elopement,
    witty enough to write successful comedies, aristocratically
    connected enough to have had opportunities of high
    military distinction. His eyes, large, brilliant, apprehen-
    sive, and intelligent, are his most remarkable feature:
    without them his fine nose and small mouth would sug-
    gest rather more fastidiousness and less force than go to*

the making of a first rate general. Just now the eyes are
angry and tragic, and the mouth and nostrils tense.

BURGOYNE. Major Swindon, I presume.

SWINDON. Yes. General Burgoyne, if I mistake not. [*They*
bow to one another ceremoniously]. I am glad to have
the support of your presence this morning. It is not particularly lively business, hanging this poor devil of a
minister.

BURGOYNE [*throwing himself into Swindon's chair*] No, sir,
it is not. It is making too much of the fellow to execute
him: what more could you have done if he had been a
member of the Church of England? Martyrdom, sir, is
what these people like: it is the only way in which a man
can become famous without ability. However, you have
committed us to hanging him; and the sooner he is
hanged the better.

SWINDON. We have arranged it for 12 o'clock. Nothing
remains to be done except to try him.

BURGOYNE [*looking at him with suppressed anger*] Nothing
—except to save your own necks, perhaps. Have you
heard the news from Springtown?

SWINDON. Nothing special. The latest reports are satisfactory.

BURGOYNE [*rising in amazement*] Satisfactory, sir! Satisfactory!! [*He stares at him for a moment, and then adds,*
with grim intensity] I am glad you take that view of them.

SWINDON [*puzzled*] Do I understand that in your opinion—

BURGOYNE. I do not express my opinion. I never stoop to
that habit of profane language, which unfortunately
coarsens our profession. If I did, sir, perhaps I should be
able to express my opinion of the news from Springtown
—the news which you [*severely*] have apparently not
heard. How soon do you get news from your supports
here?—in the course of a month, eh?

SWINDON [*turning sulky*] I suppose the reports have been
taken to you, sir, instead of to me. Is there anything
serious?

BURGOYNE [*taking a report from his pocket and holding it*
up] Springtown's in the hands of the rebels. [*He throws*
the report on the table].

SWINDON [*aghast*] Since yesterday!

BURGOYNE. Since two o'clock this morning. Perhaps we shall be in their hands before two o'clock tomorrow morning. Have you thought of that?

SWINDON [*confidently*] As to that, General, the British soldier will give a good account of himself.

BURGOYNE [*bitterly*] And therefore, I suppose, sir, the British officer need not know his business: the British soldier will get him out of all his blunders with the bayonet. In future, sir, I must ask you to be a little less generous with the blood of your men, and a little more generous with your own brains.

SWINDON. I am sorry I cannot pretend to your intellectual eminence, sir. I can only do my best, and rely on the devotion of my countrymen.

BURGOYNE [*suddenly becoming suavely sarcastic*] May I ask are you writing a melodrama, Major Swindon?

SWINDON [*flushing*] No, sir.

BURGOYNE. What a pity! What a pity! [*Dropping his sarcastic tone and facing him suddenly and seriously*] Do you at all realize, sir, that we have nothing standing between us and destruction but our own bluff and the sheepishness of these colonists? They are men of the same English stock as ourselves: six to one of us [*repeating it emphatically*] six to one, sir; and nearly half our troops are Hessians, Brunswickers, German dragoons, and Indians with scalping knives. These are the countrymen on whose devotion you rely! Suppose the colonists find a leader! Suppose the news from Springtown should turn out to mean that they have already found a leader! What shall we do then? Eh?

SWINDON [*sullenly*] Our duty, sir, I presume.

BURGOYNE [*again sarcastic—giving him up as a fool*] Quite so, quite so. Thank you, Major Swindon, thank you. Now you've settled the question, sir—thrown a flood of light on the situation. What a comfort to me to feel that I have at my side so devoted and able an officer to support me in this emergency! I think, sir, it will probably relieve both our feelings if we proceed to hang this dissenter without further delay [*he strikes the bell*] especially as I am debarred by my principles from the customary military vent for my feelings. [*The sergeant appears*]. Bring your man in.

SERGEANT. Yes, sir.

BURGOYNE. And mention to any officer you may meet that the court cannot wait any longer for him.

SWINDON [*keeping his temper with difficulty*] The staff is perfectly ready, sir. They have been waiting your convenience for fully half an hour. Perfectly ready, sir.

BURGOYNE [*blandly*] So am I. [*Several officers come in and take their seats. One of them sits at the end of the table furthest from the door, and acts throughout as clerk of the court, making notes of the proceedings. The uniforms are those of the 9th, 20th, 21st, 24th, 47th, 53rd, and 62nd British Infantry. One officer is a Major General of the Royal Artillery. There are also German officers of the Hessian Rifles, and of German dragoon and Brunswicker regiments*]. Oh, good morning, gentlemen. Sorry to disturb you, I am sure. Very good of you to spare us

SWINDON. Will you preside, sir?

a few moments.

BURGOYNE [*becoming additionally polished, lofty, sarcastic, and urbane now that he is in public*] No, sir: I feel my own deficiencies too keenly to presume so far. If you will kindly allow me, I will sit at the feet of Gamaliel. [*He takes the chair at the end of the table next the door, and motions Swindon to the chair of state, waiting for him to be seated before sitting down himself*].

SWINDON [*greatly annoyed*] As you please, sir, I am only trying to do my duty under excessively trying circumstances. [*He takes his place in the chair of state*].

Burgoyne, relaxing his studied demeanor for the moment, sits down and begins to read the report with knitted brows and careworn looks, reflecting on his desperate situation and Swindon's uselessness. Richard is brought in. Judith walks beside him. Two soldiers precede and two follow him, with the sergeant in command. They cross the room to the wall opposite the door; but when Richard has just passed before the chair of state the sergeant stops him with a touch on the arm,

*and posts himself behind him, at his elbow. Judith stands
timidly at the wall. The four soldiers place themselves
in a squad near her.*

BURGOYNE [*looking up and seeing Judith*] Who is that
woman?

SERGEANT. Prisoner's wife, sir.

SWINDON [*nervously*] She begged me to allow her to be
present; and I thought—

BURGOYNE [*completing the sentence for him ironically*] You
thought it would be a pleasure for her. Quite so, quite so.
[*Blandly*] Give the lady a chair; and make her thoroughly
comfortable.

The sergeant fetches a chair and places it near Richard.

JUDITH. Thank you, sir. [*She sits down after an awestricken
curtsy to Burgoyne, which he acknowledges by a dignified bend of his head*].

SWINDON [*to Richard, sharply*] Your name, sir?

RICHARD [*affable, but obstinate*] Come: you dont mean to
say that youve brought me here without knowing who I
am?

SWINDON. As a matter of form, sir, give your name.

RICHARD. As a matter of form then, my name is Anthony
Anderson, Presbyterian minister in this town.

BURGOYNE [*interested*] Indeed! Pray, Mr Anderson, what
do you gentlemen believe?

RICHARD. I shall be happy to explain if time is allowed me.
I cannot undertake to complete your conversion in less
than a fortnight.

SWINDON [*snubbing him*] We are not here to discuss your
views.

BURGOYNE [*with an elaborate bow to the unfortunate
Swindon*] I stand rebuked.

SWINDON [*embarrassed*] Oh, not you, I as—

BURGOYNE. Dont mention it. [*To Richard, very politely*]
Any political views, Mr Anderson?

RICHARD. I understand that that is just what we are here
to find out.

SWINDON [*severely*] Do you mean to deny that you are a
rebel?

RICHARD. I am an American, sir.

SWINDON. What do you expect me to think of that speech, Mr Anderson?

RICHARD. I never expect a soldier to think, sir.

Burgoyne is boundlessly delighted at this retort, which almost reconciles him to the loss of America.

SWINDON [*whitening with anger*] I advise you not to be insolent, prisoner.

RICHARD. You cant help yourself, General. When you make up your mind to hang a man, you put yourself at a disadvantage with him. Why should I be civil to you? I may as well be hanged for a sheep as a lamb.

SWINDON. You have no right to assume that the court has made up its mind without a fair trial. And you will please not address me as General. I am Major Swindon.

RICHARD. A thousand pardons. I thought I had the honor of addressing Gentlemanly Johnny.

Sensation among the officers. The sergeant has a narrow escape from a guffaw.

BURGOYNE [*with extreme suavity*] I believe I am Gentlemanly Johnny, sir, at your service. My more intimate friends call me General Burgoyne. [*Richard bows with perfect politeness*]. You will understand, sir, I hope, since you seem to be a gentleman and a man of some spirit in spite of your calling, that if we should have the misfortune to hang you, we shall do so as a mere matter of political necessity and military duty, without any personal ill-feeling.

RICHARD. Oh, quite so. That makes all the difference in the world, of course.

They all smile in spite of themselves; and some of the younger officers burst out laughing.

JUDITH [*her dread and horror deepening at every one of these jests and compliments*] How c a n you?

RICHARD. You promised to be silent.

BURGOYNE [*to Judith, with studied courtesy*] Believe me, madam, your husband is placing us under the greatest obligation by taking this very disagreeable business so thoroughly in the spirit of a gentleman. Sergeant: give

Mr Anderson a chair. [*The sergeant does so. Richard sits down*]. Now, Major Swindon: we are waiting for you.

SWINDON. You are aware, I presume, Mr Anderson, of your obligations as a subject of His Majesty King George the Third.

RICHARD. I am aware, sir, that His Majesty King George the Third is about to hang me because I object to Lord North's robbing me.

SWINDON. That is a treasonable speech, sir.

RICHARD [*briefly*] Yes. I mean it to be.

BURGOYNE [*strongly deprecating this line of defence, but still polite*] Dont you think, Mr Anderson, that this is rather—if you will excuse the word—a vulgar line to take? Why should you cry out robbery because of a stamp duty and a tea duty and so forth? After all, it is the essence of your position as a gentleman that you pay with a good grace.

RICHARD. It is not the money, General. But to be swindled by a pig-headed lunatic like King George—

SWINDON [*scandalized*] Chut, sir—silence!

SERGEANT [*in stentorian tones, greatly shocked*] Silence!

BURGOYNE [*unruffled*] Ah, that is another point of view. My position does not allow of my going into that, except in private. But [*shrugging his shoulders*] of course, Mr Anderson, if you are determined to be hanged [*Judith flinches*] theres nothing more to be said. An unusual taste! however [*with a final shrug*] — !

SWINDON [*To Burgoyne*] Shall we call witnesses?

RICHARD. What need is there of witnesses? If the townspeople here had listened to me, you would have found the streets barricaded, the houses loopholed, and the people in arms to hold down the town against you to the last man. But you arrived, unfortunately, before we had got out of the talking stage; and then it was too late.

SWINDON [*severely*] Well, sir, we shall teach you and your townspeople a lesson they will not forget. Have you anything more to say?

RICHARD. I think you might have the decency to treat me

as a prisoner of war, and shoot me like a man instead of hanging me like a dog.

BURGOYNE [*sympathetically*] Now there, Mr Anderson, you talk like a civilian, if you will excuse my saying so. Have you any idea of the average marksmanship of the army of His Majesty King George the Third? If we make you up a firing party, what will happen? Half of them will miss you: the rest will make a mess of the business and leave you to the provo-marshal's pistol. Whereas we can hang you in a perfectly workmanlike and agreeable way. [*Kindly*] Let me persuade you to be hanged, Mr Anderson?

JUDITH [*sick with horror*] My God!

RICHARD [*To Judith*] Your promise! [*To Burgoyne*] Thank you, General: that view of the case did not occur to me before. To oblige you, I withdraw my objection to the rope. Hang me, by all means.

BURGOYNE [*smoothly*] Will 12 o'clock suit you, Mr Anderson?

RICHARD. I shall be at your disposal then, General.

BURGOYNE [*rising*] Nothing more to be said, gentlemen. [*They all rise*].

JUDITH [*rushing to the table*] Oh, you are not going to murder a man like that, without a proper trial—without thinking of what you are doing—without— [*she cannot find words*].

RICHARD. Is this how you keep your promise?

JUDITH. If I am not to speak, you must. Defend yourself: save yourself: tell them the truth.

RICHARD [*worriedly*] I have told them truth enough to hang me ten times over. If you say another word you will risk other lives; but you will not save mine.

BURGOYNE. My good lady, our only desire is to save unpleasantness. What satisfaction would it give you to have a solemn fuss made, with my friend Swindon in a black cap and so forth? I am sure we are greatly indebted to the admirable tact and gentlemanly feeling shewn by your husband.

JUDITH [*throwing the words in his face*] Oh, you are mad.

Is it nothing to you what wicked thing you do if only you
do it like a gentleman? Is it nothing to you whether you
are a murderer or not, if only you murder in a red coat?
[*Desperately*] You shall not hang him: that man is not
my husband.

*The officers look at one another, and whisper: some of
the Germans asking their neighbors to explain what the
woman had said. Burgoyne, who has been visibly shaken
by Judith's reproach, recovers himself promptly at this
new development. Richard meanwhile raises his voice
above the buzz.*

RICHARD. I appeal to you, gentlemen, to put an end to
this. She will not believe that she cannot save me. Break
up the court.

BURGOYNE [*in a voice so quiet and firm that it restores
silence at once*] One moment, Mr Anderson. One
moment, gentlemen. [*He resumes his seat. Swindon and
the officers follow his example*]. Let me understand you
clearly, madam. Do you mean that this gentleman is not
your husband, or merely—I wish to put this with all
delicacy—that you are not his wife?

JUDITH. I dont know what you mean. I say that he is not
my husband—that my husband has escaped. This man
took his place to save him. Ask anyone in the town—
send out into the street for the first person you find there,
and bring him in as a witness. He will tell you that the
prisoner is not Anthony Anderson.

BURGOYNE [*quietly, as before*] Sergeant.

SERGEANT. Yes, sir.

BURGOYNE. Go out into the street and bring in the first
townsman you see there.

SERGEANT [*making for the door*] Yes, sir.

BURGOYNE [*as the sergeant passes*] The first clean, sober
townsman you see.

SERGEANT. Yes, sir. [*He goes out*].

BURGOYNE. Sit down, Mr Anderson—if I may call you so
for the present. [*Richard sits down*]. Sit down, madam,
whilst we wait. Give the lady a newspaper.

RICHARD [*indignantly*] Shame!

BURGOYNE [*keenly, with a half smile*] If you are not her

husband, sir, the case is not a serious one—for h e r [*Richard bites his lip, silenced*].   ·

JUDITH [*to Richard, as she returns to her seat*] I couldnt help it. [*He shakes his head. She sits down*].

BURGOYNE. You will understand of course, Mr Anderson, that you must not build on this little incident. We are bound to make an example of somebody.

RICHARD. I quite understand. I suppose theres no use in my explaining.

BURGOYNE. I think we should prefer independent testimony, if you dont mind.

The sergeant, with a packet of papers in his hand, returns conducting Christy, who is much scared.

SERGEANT [*giving Burgoyne the packet*] Dispatches, sir. Delivered by a corporal of the 33rd. Dead beat with hard riding, sir.

Burgoyne opens the dispatches, and presently becomes absorbed in them. They are so serious as to take his attention completely from the court martial.

THE SERGEANT [*to Christy*] Now then. Attention; and take your hat off. [*He posts himself in charge of Christy, who stands on Burgoyne's side of the court*].

RICHARD [*in his usual bullying tone to Christy*] Dont be frightened, you fool: youre only wanted as a witness. Theyre not going to hang you.

SWINDON. Whats your name?

CHRISTY. Christy.

RICHARD [*impatiently*] Christopher Dudgeon, you blatant idiot. Give your full name.

SWINDON. Be silent, prisoner. You must not prompt the witness.

RICHARD. Very well. But I warn you youll get nothing out of him unless you shake it out of him. He has been too well brought up by a pious mother to have any sense or manhood left in him.

BURGOYNE [*springing up and speaking to the sergeant in a startling voice*] Where is the man who brought these?

SERGEANT. In the guard-room, sir.

Burgoyne goes out with a haste that sets the officers exchanging looks.

SWINDON [*to Christy*] Do you know Anthony Anderson, the Presbyterian minister?

CHRISTY. Of course I do [*implying that Swindon must be an ass not to know it*].

SWINDON. Is he here?

CHRISTY [*staring round*] I dont know.

SWINDON. Do you see him?

CHRISTY. No.

SWINDON. You seem to know the prisoner?

CHRISTY. Do you mean Dick?

SWINDON. Which is Dick?

CHRISTY [*pointing to Richard*] Him.

SWINDON. What is his name?

CHRISTY. Dick.

RICHARD. Answer properly, you jumping jackass. What do they know about Dick?

CHRISTY. Well, you are Dick, aint you? What am I to say?

SWINDON. Address me, sir; and do you, prisoner, be silent. Tell us who the prisoner is.

CHRISTY. He's my brother Dick—Richard—Richard Dudgeon.

SWINDON. Your brother!

CHRISTY. Yes.

SWINDON. You are sure he is not Anderson.

CHRISTY. Who?

RICHARD [*exasperatedly*] Me, me, me, you—

SWINDON. Silence, sir.

SERGEANT [*shouting*] Silence.

RICHARD [*impatiently*] Yah! [*To Christy*] He wants to know am I Minister Anderson. Tell him, and stop grinning like a zany.

CHRISTY [*grinning more than ever*] Y o u Pastor Anderson! [*To Swindon*] Why, Mr Anderson's a minister—a very good man; and Dick's a bad character: the respectable people wont speak to him. He's the bad brother: I'm the good one. [*The officers laugh outright. The soldiers grin*].

SWINDON. Who arrested this man?

SERGEANT. I did, sir. I found him in the minister's house, sitting at tea with the lady with his coat off, quite at home. If he isnt married to her, he ought to be.

SWINDON. Did he answer to the minister's name?

SERGEANT. Yes. sir. but not to a minister's nature. You ask the chaplain sir.

SWINDON [*to Richard, threateningly*] So, sir, you have attempted to cheat us. And your name is Richard Dudgeon?

RICHARD. Youve found it out at last, have you?

SWINDON. Dudgeon is a name well known to us, eh?

RICHARD. Yes: Peter Dudgeon, whom you murdered, was my uncle.

SWINDON. Hm! [*He compresses his lips, and looks at Richard with vindictive gravity*].

CHRISTY. Are they going to hang you, Dick?

RICHARD. Yes. Get out: theyve done with you.

CHRISTY. And I may keep the china peacocks?

RICHARD [*jumping up*] Get out. Get out, you blithering baboon, you. [*Christy flies, panicstricken*].

SWINDON [*rising—all rise*] Since you have taken the minister's place, Richard Dudgeon, you shall go through with it. The execution will take place at 12 o'clock as arranged; and unless Anderson surrenders before then, you shall take his place on the gallows. Sergeant: take your man out.

JUDITH [*distracted*] No, no—

SWINDON [*fiercely, dreading a renewal of her entreaties*] Take that woman away.

RICHARD [*springing across the table with a tiger-like bound, and seizing Swindon by the throat*] You infernal scoundrel—

> *The sergeant rushes to the rescue from one side, the soldiers from the other. They seize Richard and drag him back to his place. Swindon, who has been thrown supine on the table, rises, arranging his stock. He is about to speak, when he is anticipated by Burgoyne, who has just appeared at the door with two papers in his hand: a white letter and a blue dispatch.*

BURGOYNE [*advancing to the table, elaborately cool*] What is this? Whats happening? Mr Anderson: I'm astonished at you.

RICHARD. I am sorry I disturbed you, General. I merely

wanted to strangle your understrapper there. [*Breaking out violently at Swindon*] Why do you raise the devil in me by bullying the woman like that? You oatmeal faced dog, I'd twist your cursed head off with the greatest satisfaction. [*He puts out his hands to the sergeant*] Here: handcuff me, will you; or I'll not undertake to keep my fingers off him.

> *The sergeant takes out a pair of handcuffs and looks to Burgoyne for instructions.*

BURGOYNE. Have you addressed profane language to the lady, Major Swindon?

SWINDON [*very angry*] No, sir, certainly not. That question should not have been put to me. I ordered the woman to be removed, as she was disorderly; and the fellow sprang at me. Put away those handcuffs. I am perfectly able to take care of myself.

RICHARD. Now you talk like a man, I have no quarrel with you.

BURGOYNE. Mr Anderson——

SWINDON. His name is Dudgeon, sir, Richard Dudgeon. He is an imposter.

BURGOYNE [*brusquely*] Nonsense, sir: you hanged Dudgeon at Springtown.

RICHARD. It was my uncle, General.

BURGOYNE. Oh, your uncle. [*To Swindon, handsomely*] I beg your pardon, Major Swindon. [*Swindon acknowledges the apology stiffly. Burgoyne turns to Richard*]. We are somewhat unfortunate in our relations with your family. Well, Mr Dudgeon, what I wanted to ask you is this. Who is [*reading the name from the letter*] William Maindeck Parshotter?

RICHARD. He is the Mayor of Springtown.

BURGOYNE. Is William——Maindeck and so on——a man of his word?

RICHARD. Is he selling you anything?

BURGOYNE. No.

RICHARD. Then you may depend on him.

BURGOYNE. Thank you, Mr——'m Dudgeon. By the way, since you are not Mr Anderson, do we still——eh, Major Swindon? [*meaning "do we still hang him?"*]

RICHARD. The arrangements are unaltered, General.

BURGOYNE. Ah, indeed. I am sorry. Good morning, Mr Dudgeon. Good morning, madam.

RICHARD [*interrupting Judith almost fiercely as she is about to make some wild appeal, and taking her arm resolutely*] Not one word more. Come.

She looks imploringly at him, but is overborne by his determination. They are marched out by the four soldiers: the sergeant very sulky, walking between Swindon and Richard, whom he watches as if he were a dangerous animal.

BURGOYNE. Gentlemen: we need not detain you. Major Swindon: a word with you. [*The officers go out. Burgoyne waits with unruffled serenity until the last of them disappears. Then he becomes very grave, and addresses Swindon for the first time without his title*]. Swindon: do you know what this is [*shewing him the letter*]?

SWINDON. What?

BURGOYNE. A demand for a safe-conduct for an officer of their militia to come here and arrange terms with us.

SWINDON. Oh, they are giving in.

BURGOYNE. They add that they are sending the man who raised Springtown last night and drove us out; so that we may know that we are dealing with an officer of importance.

SWINDON. Pooh!

BURGOYNE. He will be fully empowered to arrange the terms of—guess what.

SWINDON. Their surrender, I hope.

BURGOYNE. No: our evacuation of the town. They offer us just six hours to clear out.

SWINDON. What monstrous impudence!

BURGOYNE. What shall we do, eh?

SWINDON. March on Springtown and strike a decisive blow at once.

BURGOYNE [*quietly*] Hm! [*Turning to the door*] Come to the adjutant's office.

SWINDON. What for?

BURGOYNE. To write out that safe-conduct. [*He puts his hand to the door knob to open it*].

SWINDON [*who has not budged*] General Burgoyne.

BURGOYNE [*returning*] Sir?

SWINDON. It is my duty to tell you, sir, that I do not consider the threats of a mob of rebellious tradesmen a
sufficient reason for our giving way.

BURGOYNE [*imperturbable*] Suppose I resign my command
to you, what will you do?

SWINDON. I will undertake to do what we have marched
south from Quebec to do, and what General Howe has
marched north from New York to do: effect a junction
at Albany and wipe out the rebel army with our united
forces.

BURGOYNE [*enigmatically*] And will you wipe out our
enemies in London, too?

SWINDON. In London! What enemies?

BURGOYNE [*forcibly*] Jobbery and snobbery, incompetence
and Red Tape. [*He holds up the dispatch and adds, with
despair in his face and voice*] I have just learnt, sir, that
General Howe is still in New York.

SWINDON [*thunderstruck*] Good God! He has disobeyed
orders!

BURGOYNE [*with sardonic calm*] He has received no orders,
sir. Some gentleman in London forgot to dispatch them:
he was leaving town for his holiday, I believe. To avoid
upsetting his arrangements, England will lose her
American colonies; and in a few days you and I will be
at Saratoga with 5,000 men to face 18,000 rebels in an
impregnable position.

SWINDON [*appalled*] Impossible!

BURGOYNE [*coldly*] I beg your pardon?

SWINDON. I can't believe it! What will History say?

BURGOYNE. History, sir, will tell lies, as usual. Come: we
must send the safe-conduct. [*He goes out*].

SWINDON [*following distractedly*] My God, my God! We
shall be wiped out.

    *As noon approaches there is excitement in the market
place. The gallows which hangs there permanently for
the terror of evildoers, with such minor advertizers and
examples of crime as the pillory, the whipping post, and
the stocks, has a new rope attached, with the noose*

*hitched up to one of the uprights, out of reach of the
boys. Its ladder, too, has been brought out and placed in
position by the town beadle, who stands by to guard it
from unauthorized climbing. The Websterbridge townsfolk are present in force, and in high spirits; for the news
has spread that it is the devil's disciple and not the
minister that King George and his terrible general are
about to hang: consequently the execution can be enjoyed
without any misgiving as to its righteousness, or to the
cowardice of allowing it to take place without a struggle.
There is even some fear of a disappointment as midday
approaches and the arrival of the beadle with the ladder
remains the only sign of preparation. But at last reassuring shouts of Here they come: Here they are, are
heard; and a company of soldiers with fixed bayonets,
half British infantry, half Hessians, tramp quickly into
the middle of the market place, driving the crowd to the
sides.*

THE SERGEANT. Halt. Front. Dress. [*The soldiers change
their column into a square enclosing the gallows, their
petty officers, energetically led by the sergeant, hustling
the persons who find themselves inside the square out at
the corners*]. Now then! Out of it with you: out of it.
Some o youll get strung up yourselves presently. Form
that square there, will you, you damned Hoosians. No
use talkin German to them: talk to their toes with the
butt ends of your muskets: theyll understand that. Get
out of it, will you. [*He comes upon Judith, standing near
the gallows*]. Now then: y o u v e no call here.

JUDITH. May I not stay? What harm am I doing?

SERGEANT. I want none of your argufying. You ought to be
ashamed of yourself, running to see a man hanged thats
not your husband. And he's no better than yourself. I told
my major he was a gentleman; and then he goes and tries
to strangle him, and calls his blessed Majesty a lunatic.
So out of it with you, double quick.

JUDITH. Will you take these two silver dollars and let me
stay?

*The sergeant, without an instant's hesitation, looks
quickly and furtively round as he shoots the money*

dexterously into his pocket. Then he raises his voice in virtuous indignation.

THE SERGEANT. Me take money in the execution of my duty! Certainly not. Now I'll tell you what I'll do, to teach you to corrupt the Kings' officer. I'll put you under arrest until the execution's over. You just stand there; and dont let me see you as much as move from that spot until youre let. [*With a swift wing at her he points to the corner of the square behind the gallows on his right, and turns noisily away, shouting*] Now then, dress up and keep em back, will you.

Cries of Hush and Silence are heard among the townsfolk; and the sound of a military band, playing the Dead March from Saul, is heard. The crowd becomes quiet at once; and the sergeant and petty officers, hurrying to the back of the square, with a few whispered orders and some stealthy hustling cause it to open and admit the funeral procession, which is protected from the crowd by a double file of soldiers. First come Burgoyne and Swindon, who, on entering the square, glance with distaste at the gallows, and avoid passing under it by wheeling a little to the right and stationing themselves on that side. Then Mr Brudenell, the chaplain, in his surplice, with his prayer book open in his hand, walking beside Richard, who is moody and disorderly. He walks doggedly through the gallows framework, and posts himself a little in front of it. Behind him comes the executioner, a stalwart soldier in his shirtsleeves. Following him, two soldiers haul a light military waggon. Finally comes the band, which posts itself at the back of the square, and finishes the Dead March. Judith, watching Richard painfully, steals down to the gallows, and stands leaning against its right post. During the conversation which follows, the two soldiers place the cart under the gallows, and stand by the shafts, which point backwards. The executioner takes a set of steps from the cart and places it ready for the prisoner to mount. Then he climbs the tall ladder which stands against the gallows, and cuts the string by which the rope is hitched up; so that the

*noose drops dangling over the cart, into which he steps
as he descends.*

RICHARD [*with suppressed impatience, to Brudenell*] Look
here, sir: this is no place for a man of your profession.
Hadnt you better go away?

SWINDON. I appeal to you, prisoner, if you have any sense
of decency left, to listen to the ministrations of the chaplain, and pay due heed to the solemnity of the occasion.

THE CHAPLAIN [*gently reproving Richard*] Try to control
yourself, and submit to the divine will. [*He lifts his book
to proceed with the service*].

RICHARD. Answer for your own will, sir, and those of your
accomplices here [*indicating Burgoyne and Swindon*]: I
see little divinity about them or you. You talk to me of
Christianity when you are in the act of hanging your
enemies. Was there ever such blasphemous nonsense! [*To
Swindon, more rudely*] Youve got up the solemnity of the
occasion, as you call it, to impress the people with your
own dignity—Handel's music and a clergyman to make
murder look like piety! Do you suppose *I* am going to
help you? Youve asked me to choose the rope because
you dont know your own trade well enough to shoot me
properly. Well, hang away and have done with it.

SWINDON [*to the chaplain*] Can you do nothing with him,
Mr Brudenell?

CHAPLAIN. I will try, sir. [*Beginning to read*] Man that is
born of woman hath—

RICHARD [*fixing his eyes on him*] "Thou shalt not kill."
     The book drops in Brudenell's hands.

CHAPLAIN [*confessing his embarrassment*] What am I to
say, Mr Dudgeon?

RICHARD. Let me alone, man, cant you?

BURGOYNE [*with extreme urbanity*] I think, Mr Brudenell,
that as usual professional observations seem to strike
Mr Dudgeon as incongruous under the circumstances,
you had better omit them until—er—until Mr Dudgeon
can no longer be inconvenienced by them. [*Brudenell,
with a shrug, shuts his book and retires behind the
gallows*]. You seem in a hurry, Mr Dudgeon.

RICHARD [*with the horror of death upon him*] Do you think
    this is a pleasant sort of thing to be kept waiting for?
    Youve made up your mind to commit murder: well, do
    it and have done with it.

BURGOYNE. Mr Dudgeon: we are only doing this—

RICHARD. Because youre paid to do it.

SWINDON. You insolent— [*he swallows his rage*].

BURGOYNE [*with much charm of manner*] Ah, I am really
    sorry that you should think that, Mr Dudgeon. If you
    knew what my commission cost me, and what my pay is,
    you would think better of me. I should be glad to part
    from you on friendly terms.

RICHARD. Hark ye, General Burgoyne. If you think that I
    like being hanged, youre mistaken. I dont like it; and I
    dont mean to pretend that I do. And if you think I'm
    obliged to you for hanging me in a gentlemanly way,
    youre wrong there too. I take the whole business in
    devilish bad part; and the only satisfaction I have in it is
    that youll feel a good deal meaner than I'll look when it's
    over. [*He turns away, and is striding to the cart when
    Judith advances and interposes with her arms stretched
    out to him. Richard, feeling that a very little will upset
    his self-possession, shrinks from her, crying*] What are
    you doing here? This is no place for you. [*She makes a
    gesture as if to touch him. He recoils impatiently*]. No:
    go away, go away; youll unnerve me. Take her away,
    will you.

JUDITH. Wont you bid me goodbye?

RICHARD [*allowing her to take his hand*] Oh goodbye, good-
    bye. Now go—go—quickly. [*She clings to his hand—
    will not be put off with so cold a last farewell—at last,
    as he tries to disengage himself, throws herself on his
    breast in agony*].

SWINDON [*angrily to the sergeant, who, alarmed at Judith's
    movement, has come from the back of the square to pull
    her back, and stopped irresolutely on finding that he is
    too late*] How is this? Why is she inside the lines?

SERGEANT [*guiltily*] I dunno, sir. She's that artful—cant
    keep her away.

BURGOYNE. You were bribed.

SERGEANT [*protesting*] No, sir—

SWINDON [*severely*] Fall back. [*He obeys*].

RICHARD [*imploringly to those around him, and finally to Burgoyne, as the least stolid of them*] Take her away. Do you think I want a woman near me now?

BURGOYNE [*going to Judith and taking her hand*] Here, madam: you had better keep inside the lines; but stand here behind us; and dont look.

> *Richard, with a great sobbing sigh of relief as she releases him and turns to Burgoyne, flies for refuge to the cart and mounts into it.. The executioner takes off his coat and pinions him.*

JUDITH [*resisting Burgoyne quietly and drawing her hand away*] No: I must stay. I wont look. [*She goes to the right of the gallows. She tries to look at Richard, but turns away with a frightful shudder, and falls on her knees in prayer. Brudenell comes towards her from the back of the square*].

BURGOYNE [*nodding approvingly as she kneels*] Ah, quite so. Do not disturb her, Mr Brudenell: that will do very nicely. [*Brudenell nods also, and withdraws a little, watching her sympathetically. Burgoyne resumes his former position, and takes out a handsome gold chronometer*] Now then, are those preparations made? We must not detain Mr Dudgeon.

> *By this time Richard's hands are bound behind him; and the noose is round his neck. The two soldiers take the shafts of the waggon, ready to pull it away. The executioner, standing in the cart behind Richard, makes a sign to the sergeant.*

SERGEANT [*to Burgoyne*] Ready, sir.

BURGOYNE. Have you anything more to say, Mr Dudgeon? It wants two minutes of twelve still.

RICHARD [*in the strong voice of a man who has conquered the bitterness of death*] Your watch is two minutes slow by the town clock, which I can see from here, General. [*The town clock strikes the first stroke of twelve. Involuntarily the people flinch at the sound, and a subdued groan breaks from them*]. Amen! my life for the world's future!

ANDERSON [*shouting as he rushes into the market place*]
Amen; and stop the execution. [*He bursts through the
line of soldiers opposite Burgoyne, and rushes, panting,
to the gallows*]. I am Anthony Anderson, the man you
want.

> *The crowd, intensely excited, listens with all its ears.
> Judith, half rising, stares at him; then lifts her hands like
> one whose dearest prayer has been granted.*

SWINDON. Indeed. Then you are just in time to take your
place on the gallows. Arrest him.

> *At a sign from the sergeant, two soldiers come forward
> to seize Anderson.*

ANDERSON [*thrusting a paper under Swindon's nose*] Theres
my safe-conduct, sir.

SWINDON [*taken aback*] Safe-conduct! Are you— !

ANDERSON [*emphatically*] I am. [*The two soldiers take him
by the elbows*]. Tell these men to take their hands off me.

SWINDON [*to the men*] Let him go.

SERGEANT. Fall back.

> *The two men return to their places. The townsfolk
> raise a cheer; and begin to exchange exultant looks, with
> a presentiment of triumph as they see their Pastor speak-
> ing with their enemies in the gate.*

ANDERSON [*exhaling a deep breath of ˙relief, and dabbing
his perspiring brow with his handkerchief*] Thank God,
I was in time!

BURGOYNE [*calm as ever, and still watch in hand*] Ample
time, sir. Plenty of time. I should never dream of hanging
any gentleman by an American clock. [*He puts up his
watch*].

ANDERSON. Yes: we are some minutes ahead of you already,
General. Now tell them to take the rope from the neck of
that American citizen.

BURGOYNE [*to the executioner in the cart—very politely*]
Kindly undo Mr Dudgeon.

> *The executioner takes the rope from Richard's neck,
> unties his hands, and helps him on with his coat.*

JUDITH [*stealing timidly to Anderson*] Tony.

ANDERSON [*putting his arm round her shoulders and banter-*

ing her affectionately] Well, what do you think of your husband now, eh?—eh??—eh—???

JUDITH. I am ashamed— [*she hides her face against his breast*].

BURGOYNE [*to Swindon*] You look disappointed, Major Swindon.

SWINDON. You look defeated, General Burgoyne.

BURGOYNE. I am, sir; and I am humane enough to be glad of it. [*Richard jumps down from the cart, Brudenell offering his hand to help him, and runs to Anderson, whose left hand he shakes heartily, the right being occupied by Judith*]. By the way, Mr Anderson, I do not quite understand. The safe-conduct was for a commander of the militia. I understand you are a— [*He looks as pointedly as his good manners permit at the riding boots, the pistols, and Richard's coat, and adds*] —a clergyman.

ANDERSON [*between Judith and Richard*] Sir: it is in the hour of trial that a man finds his true profession. This foolish young man [*placing his hand on Richard's shoulder*] boasted himself the Devil's Disciple; but when the hour of trial came to him, he found that it was his destiny to suffer and be faithful to the death. I thought myself a decent minister of the gospel of peace; but when the hour of trial came to me, I found that it was my destiny to be a man of action, and that my place was amid the thunder of the captains and the shouting. So I am starting life at fifty as Captain Anthony Anderson of the Springtown militia; and the Devil's Disciple here will start presently as the Reverend Richard Dudgeon, and wag his pow in my old pulpit, and give good advice to this silly sentimental little wife of mine [*putting his other hand on her shoulder. She steals a glance at Richard to see how the prospect pleases him*]. Your mother told me, Richard, that I should never have chosen Judith if I'd been born for the ministry. I am afraid she was right; so, by your leave, you may keep my coat and I'll keep yours.

RICHARD. Minister—I should say Captain. I have behaved like a fool.

JUDITH. Like a hero.

RICHARD. Much the same thing, perhaps. [*With some bitterness towards himself*] But no: if I had been any good, I should have done for you what you did for me, instead of making a vain sacrifice.

ANDERSON. Not vain, my boy. It takes all sorts to make a world—saints as well as soldiers. [*Turning to Burgoyne*] And now, General, time presses; and America is in a hurry. Have you realized that though you may occupy towns and win battles, you cannot conquer a nation?

BURGOYNE. My good sir, without a Conquest you cannot have an aristocracy. Come and settle the matter at my quarters.

ANDERSON. At your service, sir. [*To Richard*] See Judith home for me, will you, my boy. [*He hands her over to him*]. Now, General. [*He goes busily up the market place towards the Town Hall, leaving Judith and Richard together. Burgoyne follows him a step or two; then checks himself and turns to Richard*].

BURGOYNE. Oh, by the way, Mr Dudgeon, I shall be glad to see you at lunch at half-past one. [*He pauses a moment, and adds, with politely veiled slyness*] Bring Mrs Anderson, if she will be so good. [*To Swindon, who is fuming*] Take it quietly, Major Swindon: your friend the British soldier can stand up to anything except the British War Office. [*He follows Anderson*].

SERGEANT [*to Swindon*] What orders, sir?

SWINDON [*savagely*] Orders! What use are orders now! Theres no army. Back to quarters; and be d—— [*He turns on his heel and goes*].

SERGEANT [*pugnacious and patriotic, repudiating the idea of defeat*] 'Tention. Now then: cock up your chins, and shew em you dont care a damn for em. Slope arms! Fours! Wheel! Quick march!

The drums mark time with a tremendous bang; the band strikes up British Grenadiers; and the Sergeant, Brudenell, and the English troops march off defiantly to their quarters. The townsfolk press in behind, and follow them up the market, jeering at them; and the town band, a very primitive affair, brings up the rear, playing

*Yankee Doodle. Essie, who comes in with them, runs to
Richard.*

ESSIE. Oh, Dick!

RICHARD [*good humoredly, but wilfully*] Now, now: come,
come! I dont mind being hanged: but I will not be cried
over.

ESSIE. No, I promise. I'll be good. [*She trys to restrain her
tears, but cannot*]. I—I want to see where the soldiers are
going to. [*She goes a little way up the market, pretending
to look after the crowd*].

JUDITH. Promise me you will never tell him.

RICHARD. Dont be afraid.

They shake hands on it.

ESSIE [*calling to them*] Theyre coming back. They want you.

*Jubilation in the market. The townsfolk surge back
again in wild enthusiasm with their band, and hoist
Richard on their shoulders, cheering him.*

"Trials of a Military Dramatist"

(*Review of the Week*, London, 4 November 1899)

×××××××××××××××××××××××××××××××××××××

On returning from a trip to the South of Europe, where I have found the two soundly beaten nations, Spain and Greece, so effectually brought back to the sober realities of national character and industry that I am almost in love with defeat, I find myself for the second time in my life enjoying a nine days' infamy as a malignant scoffer at everything that is noblest in war: in other words, at the British Army. This situation, however flattering to my private sense of my own importance, would not in time of peace have any interest for the public at large. As it is, with every newspaper full of cannon and trumpet, drum and death-roll, the most trivial instance of the cloud of melodramatic illusions which constitutes the military consciousness of the country, has its significance.

As I write, news comes in that a couple of British battalions concerning whom our general naïvely telegraphed yesterday that they were "expected that evening, but had not yet returned," have surrendered, and are prisoners. And our editors, appalled into seriousness, observe that nothing of the kind has happened since Burgoyne surrendered to the Americans at Saratoga 122 years ago. Now, it is but the other day that I called up on the stage the ghost of this very Burgoyne, and was told that he was nothing but my own sardonic self in an eighteenth century uniform. This was natural enough; for instead of simply putting on the stage the modern conception of a British general, half idealised prize-fighter, half idealised music-hall chairman, I had taken some pains to ascertain what manner of person the real Burgoyne was, and had found him a wit, a rhetorician, and a successful dramatic author. Also, of course, an eighteenth century gentleman, independent of a public of grown-up schoolboys. He was sent out to quell the American rebellion with a force of Hessians, English, and Indians. It was arranged that he should march from Boston to Albany, and there join a force marching thither simultaneously from New York. Unfortunately the civil servant in London, whose duty it was to send the necessary orders to the New York force, went down to Brighton and forgot all about it (observe how farcical history can be), much as somebody appears to have forgotten to send troops to South Africa in time for war the other day, or stores to the Crimea forty-five years ago. Burgoyne marched into the wilderness, where, instead of meeting his colleague's battalions, he met the Americans in overwhelming numbers, and in an impregnable position. He fought until his sense of dramatic effect was satisfied, and then capitulated. The Americans thereupon propounded articles of surrender to him; and the dramatic style and character of the man are in his answers. For example, it was set forth by way of preamble that he was completely beaten. His written comment was: — "Lieut.-General Burgoyne's army, however reduced, will never admit that their retreat is cut off while they have arms in their hands." The Americans further said that they would imprison British officers who broke their parole. Burgoyne replied, "There being no officer in this army under, or capable of being under, the description of breaking parole, this article needs no answer." And finally, in reply to Article VI., "This article is inadmissible in any extremity. Sooner than this army will consent to ground their arms in their encampments, they will rush on the enemy determined to take no quarter." In the final scene, when he handed his sword to the "rebel" commander, he played that worthy man, who was awkward and nervous, clean off the stage, although, as the defeated general, his part was painfully secondary. Finding himself, on his return to England, made a scapegoat, in the matter of the loss of America, for the king and the gentleman [Lord George Germain] who went to Brighton, he took refuge in the House of Commons and there exercised his rhetorical talents to his heart's content.

This is authentic history; but like all authentic histories

of great events enacted by men not great, its details produce an effect of comic opera on the multitude, who can recognise tragedy only when she brandishes her bowl and dagger. Its central event, the surrender at Saratoga, was just such an event as the surrender of last Monday. The Americans, like the Boers, were farmers who could shoot. They systematically picked off the English officers, Burgoyne himself narrowly escaping with bullet holes in his hat and waistcoat. My stage Burgoyne convulsed the playgoers of Kennington by asking a rebel who demanded to be "shot like a man instead of hanged like a dog," whether he had any idea of the average marksmanship of the British Army, and earnestly recommending him to be hanged. Everybody shrieked with laughter, and exclaimed that this was not General Burgoyne, but myself disguised as General Boum.* And yet, like all my wildest extravagances, it was an uncooked "slice of life." In my youth I was conversing one day, I and others, with a British general, who prophesied rain on the authority of a bullet in his shoulder which had served him faithfully for many years as a barometer. We set him talking about the campaign in which he acquired this instrument, and found, among other things, that he had conducted many military executions. On our assuming that these were carried out by shooting parties, he told us, with great earnestness, what indeed the famous case of the Mexican Maximilian should have suggested to us already, that no humane person who had ever seen an execution by shooting—horrible, sanguinary, and demoralising even when it was successful (which seldom happened)—would ever adopt it if a rope, a tree, and camp table were equally available for the swift and certain death, and comparatively bearable spectacle, of an execution by hanging. He declared that he would infinitely prefer hanging himself, and recommended us, as an elderly man speaking to his juniors, to choose it without hesitation should the alternative be presented to us. A moment's reflection will convince anybody that this

* A character in Offenbach's *La Grande Duchesse de Gérolstein*.

is not comic opera, but common-sense. Unhappily, in this country the people who reflect do not go to the theatre.

In transferring the counsels of my military acquaintance to Burgoyne, I incurred reprobation, not only for wilful farce, but for insulting the British Army by disparaging its marksmanship. From the many generous excuses made for me by my fellow critics, I select the following as typical: — "Of Mr. Shaw's remarks, put into the mouth of General Burgoyne, as to the marksmanship of the army, I think nothing as a matter of patriotism. To begin with, the army can scarcely be called a British Army at all; and, in addition, it was and is notorious that up to the time of the Crimea it took a ton of lead to kill a man." Up to the time of the Crimea! *Sancta simplicitas!* is any man so ignorant as to suppose that now, or at any other period, it has been possible to make the British taxpayer pay for cartridges enough to make the British soldier an efficient shooter? Why, only the other day, at Omdurman, the whole British and Egyptian forces of the Sirdar, blazing away for twenty minutes with modern magazine rifles, machine guns and field artillery, and using bullets each capable of penetrating several men, did not score more hits than a single machine gun might have done in skilful hands in half the time. The Crimean ton of lead is now a mountain. During the Dreyfus case, we had some grotesque instances of the French deference to "the honour of the army"; but the silliest of them must yield the palm to the assumption that Tommy Atkins is a marksman. It is just about as possible for him to be a marksman as it is for him to play the fiddle like Sarasate. How exquisitely English it is to refuse him the money for practice cartridges, and then pretend that he is a dead shot; to enlist him at twenty-five years of age with a 31 inch chest, and pretend that he is a youth of eighteen who will grow up to the standard; to tell him that flogging is abolished in the Army, and then flog him soundly the moment he gets into a military prison; to deprive him of our common political rights, and leave him to the mercy of the worst form of lynch law in the world (recognised as such lately at Rennes); to promise him a shilling a day, and filch pennies back from him under mean pretexts: in short, to take every conceivable shabby advantage of him until we are at last actually face to face with conscription—flat slavery—because we will not pay another sixpence a day and get an invincible army for it as Cromwell did. And, if you please, I, the dramatist, knowing all this, am to join the War Office in persuading the foolish man in the street that the British Army is perfect. Pray, why should I? The War Office may reply, Because it pays. But suppose I am of a perverse disposition, and get as much satisfaction out of exposing perilous humbug and befriending the unfortunate soldier, as a War Office apologist gets out of a large official salary, or a popular melodramatist out of the royalties on "One of the Best" or "In the Ranks"! Suppose, even, I were a military enthusiast and British patriot! Nobody will question the sincerity of Mr. Arnold Foster in both capacities. I wonder what would be said if I dramatised everything in Mr. Arnold Foster's Army letters to the *Times*, representing "the views of at least nine-tenths of the officers and men actually serving or on the retired list." Dreyfus's fate would be considered too merciful for me.

I remain astonished at my moderation.

"Tappertit on Cæsar"

XXXXXXXXXXXXXXXXXXXXXXXXXXXXXXXXXXXXXXX

JULIUS CÆSAR. Her Majesty's Theatre, 22 January 1898.

[29 January 1898]

The truce with Shakespear is over. It was only possible whilst Hamlet was on the stage. Hamlet is the tragedy of private life—nay, of individual bachelor-poet life. It belongs to a detached residence, a select library, an exclusive circle, to no occupation, to fathomless boredom, to impenitent mugwumpism, to the illusion that the futility of these things is the futility of existence, and its contemplation philosophy: in short, to the dream-fed gentlemanism of the age which Shakespear inaugurated in English literature: the age, that is, of the rising middle class bringing into power the ideas taught it by its servants in the kitchen, and its fathers in the shop—ideas now happily passing away as the onslaught of modern democracy offers to the kitchen-taught and home-bred the alternative of achieving a real superiority or going ignominiously under in the class conflict.

It is when we turn to Julius Cæsar, the most splendidly written political melodrama we possess, that we realize the apparently immortal author of Hamlet as a man, not for all time, but for an age only, and that, too, in all solidly wise and heroic aspects, the most despicable of all the ages in our history. It is impossible for even the most judicially minded critic to look without a revulsion of indignant contempt at this travestying of a great man as a silly braggart, whilst the pitiful gang of mischief-makers who destroyed him are lauded as statesmen and patriots. There is not a single sentence uttered by Shakespear's Julius Cæsar that is, I will not say worthy of him, but even worthy of an average Tammany boss. Brutus is nothing but a familiar type of English suburban preacher: politically he would hardly impress the Thames Conservancy Board. Cassius is a vehemently assertive nonentity. It is only when we come to Antony, unctuous voluptuary and self-seeking sentimental demagogue, that we find Shakespear in his depth; and in his depth, of course, he is superlative. Regarded as a crafty stage job, the play is a triumph: rhetoric, claptrap, effective gushes of emotion, all the devices of the popular playwright, are employed with a profusion of power that almost breaks their backs. No doubt there are slips and slovenliness of the kind that careful revisers eliminate; but they count for so little in the mass of accomplishment that it is safe to say that the dramatist's art can be carried no further on that plane. If Goethe, who understood Cæsar and the significance of his death—"the most senseless of deeds" he called it—had treated the subject, his conception of it would have been as superior to Shakespear's as St John's Gospel is to the Police News; but his treatment could not have been more magnificently successful. As far as sonority, imagery, wit, humor, energy of imagination, power over language, and a whimsically keen eye for idiosyncrasies can make a dramatist, Shakespear was the king of dramatists. Unfortunately, a man may have them all, and yet conceive high affairs of state exactly as Simon Tappertit did. In one of the scenes in Julius Cæsar a conceited poet bursts into the tent of Brutus and Cassius, and exhorts them not to quarrel with one another. If Shakespear had been able to present his play to the ghost of the great Julius, he would probably have had much the same reception. He certainly would have deserved it.

When it was announced that Mr Tree had resolved to give special prominence to the character of Cæsar in his acting version, the critics winked, and concluded simply that the actor-manager was going to play Antony and not Brutus. Therefore I had better say that Mr Tree must stand acquitted of any belittlement of the parts which compete so strongly with his own. Before going to Her Majesty's I was curious enough to block out for myself a division of the play into three acts; and I found that Mr Tree's division

corresponded exactly with mine. Mr Waller's opportunities
as Brutus, and Mr McLeay's as Cassius, are limited only
by their own ability to take advantage of them; and Mr
Louis Calvert figures as boldly in the public eye as he did
in his own production of Antony and Cleopatra last year
at Manchester. Indeed, Mr Calvert is the only member of
the company who achieves an unequivocal success. The
preference expressed in the play by Cæsar for fat men
may, perhaps, excuse Mr Calvert for having again permitted himself to expand after his triumphant reduction of
his girth for his last appearance in London. However, he
acted none the worse: in fact, nobody else acted so skilfully or originally. The others, more heavily burdened, did
their best, quite in the spirit of the man who had never
played the fiddle, but had no doubt he could if he tried.
Without oratory, without style, without specialized vocal
training, without any practice worth mentioning, they as-
saulted the play with cheerful self-sufficiency, and gained
great glory by the extent to which, as a masterpiece of the
playwright's trade, it played itself. Some small successes
were not lacking. Cæsar's nose was good: Calpurnia's bust
was worthy of her: in such parts Garrick and Siddons could
have achieved no more. Miss Evelyn Millard's Roman
matron in the style of Richardson—Cato's daughter as
Clarissa—was an unlooked-for novelty; but it cost a good
deal of valuable time to get in the eighteenth century between the lines of the first B.C. By operatic convention—
the least appropriate of all conventions—the boy Lucius
was played by Mrs Tree, who sang Sullivan's ultra-nine-
teenth-century Orpheus with his Lute, modulations and all,
to a pizzicato accompaniment supposed to be played on
a lyre with eight open and unstoppable strings, a feat com-
plexly and absurdly impossible. Mr Waller, as Brutus, failed
in the first half of the play. His intention clearly was to
represent Brutus as a man superior to fate and circumstance; but the effect he produced was one of insensibility.
Nothing could have been more unfortunate; for it is
through the sensibility of Brutus that the audience have to
learn what they cannot learn from the phlegmatic pluck
of Casca or the narrow vindictiveness of Cassius: that is,

the terrible momentousness, the harrowing anxiety and
dread, of the impending catastrophe. Mr Waller left that
function to the thunderstorm. From the death of Cæsar
onward he was better; and his appearance throughout was
effective; but at best his sketch was a water-color one. Mr
Franklyn McLeay carried off the honors of the evening by
his deliberate staginess and imposing assumptiveness: that
is, by as much of the grand style as our playgoers now
understand; but in the last act he was monotonously violent, and died the death of an incorrigible poseur, not of
a noble Roman. Mr Tree's memory failed him as usual;
and a good deal of the technical part of his work was
botched and haphazard, like all Shakespearean work nowadays; nevertheless, like Mr Calvert, he made the audience
believe in the reality of the character before them. But it
is impossible to praise his performance in detail. I cannot
recall any single passage in the scene after the murder that
was well done: in fact, he only secured an effective curtain
by bringing Calpurnia on the stage to attitudinize over
Cæsar's body. To say that the demagogic oration in the
Forum produced its effect is nothing; for its effect is inevitable, and Mr Tree neither made the most of it nor handled
it with any pretence of mastery or certainty. But he was
not stupid, nor inane, nor Bard-of-Avon ridden; and he
contrived to interest the audience in Antony instead of
trading on their ready-made interest in Mr Beerbohm Tree.
And for that many sins may be forgiven him nowadays,
when the playgoer, on first nights at all events, goes to
see the cast rather than the play.

What is missing in the performance, for want of the
specific Shakespearean skill, is the Shakespearean music.
When we come to those unrivalled grandiose passages in
which Shakespear turns on the full organ, we want to hear
the sixteen-foot pipes booming, or, failing them (as we
often must, since so few actors are naturally equipped with
them), the ennobled tone, and the tempo suddenly steadied
with the majesty of deeper purpose. You have, too, those
moments when the verse, instead of opening up the depths
of sound, rises to its most brilliant clangor, and the lines
ring like a thousand trumpets. If we cannot have these

effects, or if we can only have genteel drawing room arrangements of them, we cannot have Shakespear; and that
is what is mainly the matter at Her Majesty's: there are
neither trumpets nor pedal pipes there. The conversation is
metrical and emphatic in an elocutionary sort of way; but
it makes no distinction between the arid prairies of blank
verse which remind one of Henry VI at its crudest, and
the places where the morass suddenly piles itself into a
mighty mountain. Cassius in the first act has a twaddling
forty-line speech, base in its matter and mean in its measure, followed immediately by the magnificent torrent of
rhetoric, the first burst of true Shakespearean music in the
play, beginning—

> Why, man, he doth bestride the narrow world
> Like a Colossus, and we petty men
> Walk under his huge legs and peep about
> To find ourselves dishonorable graves.

I failed to catch the slightest change of elevation or reinforcement of feeling when Mr McLeay passed from one to
the other. His tone throughout was dry; and it never
varied. By dint of energetic, incisive articulation, he drove
his utterances harder home than the others; but the best
lines seemed to him no more than the worst: there were
no heights and depths, no contrast of black thunder-cloud
and flaming lightning flash, no stirs and surprises. Yet he
was not inferior in oratory to the rest. Mr Waller certainly
cannot be reproached with dryness of tone; and his delivery
of the speech in the Forum was perhaps the best piece of
formal elocution we got; but he also kept at much the
same level throughout, and did not at any moment attain
to anything that could be called grandeur. Mr Tree, except
for a conscientiously desperate effort to cry havoc and
let slip the dogs of war in the robustious manner, with no
better result than to all but extinguish his voice, very sensibly left oratory out of the question, and tried conversational sincerity, which answered so well that his delivery
of "This was the noblest Roman of them all" came off
excellently.

The real hero of the revival is Mr Alma Tadema. The

scenery and stage coloring deserve everything that has been said of them. But the illusion is wasted by want of discipline and want of thought behind the scenes. Every carpenter seems to make it a point of honor to set the cloths swinging in a way that makes Rome reel and the audience positively seasick. In Brutus's house the door is on the spectators' left: the knocks on it come from the right. The Roman soldiers take the field each man with his two javelins neatly packed up like a fishing-rod. After a battle, in which they are supposed to have made the famous Roman charge, hurling these javelins in and following them up sword in hand, they come back carrying the javelins still undisturbed in their rug-straps, in perfect trim for a walk-out with the nursery-maids of Philippi.

The same want of vigilance appears in the acting version. For example, though the tribunes Flavius and Marullus are replaced by two of the senators, the lines referring to them by name are not altered. But the oddest oversight is the retention in the tent scene of the obvious confusion of the original version of the play, in which the death of Portia was announced to Brutus by Messala, with the second version, into which the quarrel scene was written to strengthen the fourth act. In this version Brutus, already in possession of the news, reveals it to Cassius. The play has come down to us with the two alternative scenes strung together; so that Brutus's reception of Messala's news, following his own revelation of it to Cassius, is turned into a satire on Roman fortitude, the suggestion being that the secret of the calm with which a noble Roman received the most terrible tidings in public was that it had been carefully imparted to him in private beforehand. Mr Tree has not noticed this; and the two scenes are gravely played one after the other at Her Majesty's. This does not matter much to our playgoers, who never venture to use their comon sense when Shakespear is in question; but it wastes time. Mr Tree may without hesitation cut out Pindarus and Messala, and go straight on from the bowl of wine to Brutus's question about Philippi.

The music, composed for the occasion by Mr Raymond Roze, made me glad that I had already taken care to acknowledge the value of Mr Roze's services to Mr Tree; for this time he has missed the Roman vein rather badly. To be a Frenchman was once no disqualification for the antique, because French musicians used to be brought up on Gluck as English ones were brought up on Handel. But Mr Roze composes as if Gluck had been supplanted wholly in his curriculum by Gounod and Bizet. If that prelude to the third act were an attempt to emulate the overtures to Alceste or Iphigenia I could have forgiven it. But to give us the soldiers' chorus from Faust, crotchet for crotchet and triplet for triplet, with nothing changed but the notes, was really too bad. . . .

I am sorry I must postpone until next week all consideration of Mr. Pinero's Trelawney of the Wells. The tragic circumstances under which I do are as follows. The manager of the Court Theatre, Mr Arthur Chudleigh, did not honor the Saturday Review with the customary invitation to the first performance. When a journal is thus slighted, it has no resource but to go to its telephone and frantically offer any terms to the box-offices for a seat for the first night. But on fashionable occasions the manager is always master of the situation: there are never any seats to be had except from himself. It was so on this occasion; and the Saturday Review was finally brought to its knees at the feet of the Sloane Square telephone. In response to a humble appeal, the instrument scornfully replied that "three lines of adverse criticism were of no use to it." Naturally my curiosity was excited to an extraordinary degree by the fact that the Court Theatre telephone, which knew all about Mr Pinero's comedy, should have such a low opinion of it as to be absolutely certain that it would deserve an unprecedentedly contemptuous treatment at my hands. I instantly purchased a place for the fourth performance, Charlotte Corday and Julius Cæsar occupying my time on the second and third nights; and I am now in a position to assure that telephone that its misgivings were strangely unwarranted, and that, if it will excuse my saying so, it does not know a good comedietta when it sees one. Reserving my reasons for next week, I offer Mr Pinero my apologies for a delay which is not my own fault. (Will the Mining Journal please copy, as Mr Pinero reads no other paper during the current fortnight?)

I find this article has already run to such a length that I must postpone consideration of Charlotte Corday also, merely remarking for the present that I wish the play was as attractive as the heroine.

"Mr Charles Frohman's Mission"

XXXXXXXXXXXXXXXXXXXXXXXXXXXXXXXXXXXXXXXXXXXX

THE HEART OF MARYLAND. A drama in four acts. By David Belasco. Adelphi Theatre, 9 April 1898.

[16 April 1898]

After The Heart of Maryland, at the Adelphi, I begin to regard Mr Charles Frohman as a manager with a great moral mission. We have been suffering of late years in England from a wave of blackguardism. Our population is so large that even its little minorities of intellectual and moral dwarfs form a considerable body, and can make an imposing noise, so long as the sensible majority remain silent, with its clamor for war, for "empire," for savage sports, savage punishments, flogging, duelling, prizefighting, 144 hours' bicycle races, national war dances to celebrate the cautious pounding of a few thousand barbarians to death with machine projectiles, followed by the advance of a whole British brigade on the wretched survivors under "a withering fire" which kills twenty-three men, and national newspaper paragraphs in which British heroes of the rank and file, who will be flung starving on our streets in a year or two at the expiration of their short service, proudly describe the sport of village-burning, remarking, with a touch of humorous Cockney reflectiveness, on the amusing manner in which old Indian women get "fairly needled" at the spectacle of their houses and crops being burnt, and mentioning with honest pride how their officers were elated and satisfied with the day's work. My objection to this sort of folly is by no means purely humanitarian. I am quite prepared to waive the humanitarian point altogether, and to accept, for the sake of argument, the position that we must destroy or be destroyed. But I do not believe in the destructive force of a combination of de-

scriptive talent with delirium tremens. I do not feel safe
behind a rampart of music-hall enthusiasm: on the contrary, the mere thought of what these poor, howling, half-
drunk patriots would do if the roll of a hostile drum
reached their ears, brings out a cold sweat of pity and
terror on me. Imagine going to war, as the French did in
1870, with a stock of patriotic idealism and national enthusiasm instead of a stock of military efficiency. The
Dervishes have plenty of racial idealism and enthusiasm,
with religious fanaticism and personal hardihood to boot;
and much good it has done them! What would have happened to them if they had been confronted by the army of
the future is only conceivable because, after all, the limit
of possibility is annihilation, which is conceivable enough.
I picture that future army to myself dimly as consisting of
half-a-dozen highly paid elderly gentlemen provided with a
picnic basket and an assortment of implements of wholesale destruction. Depend upon it, its first meeting with our
hordes of Continental enslaved conscripts and thriftless
English "surplus population," disciplined into combining
all the self-helplessness of machinery with the animal dis-
advantages of requiring food and being subject to panic,
and commanded by the grown-up boyishness for which
the other professions have no use, will be the death of
military melodrama. It is quite clear, at all events, that
the way out of the present militaristic madness will be
found by the first nation that takes war seriously, or, as the
melodramatizers of war will say, cynically. It has always
been so. The fiery Rupert, charging for God and the King,
got on excellently until Cromwell, having some experience
as a brewer, made the trite experiment of raising the wages
of the Parliamentary soldier to the market value of respectable men, and immediately went over Rupert like a
steam-roller. Napoleon served out enthusiasm, carefully
mixed with prospects of loot, as cold-bloodedly as a pirate
captain serves out rum, and never used it as an efficient
substitute for facts and cannon. Wellington, with his characteristic Irish common sense, held a steadfast opinion of
the character of the average British private and the capacity
of the average British officer which would wreck the Adel-

phi theatre if uttered there; but he fed them carefully, and carried our point with them against the enemy. At the present time, if I or anyone else were to propose that enough money should be spent on the British soldier to make him an efficient marksman, to attract respectable and thrifty men to the service, to escape the necessity for filling the ranks with undersized wasters and pretending to believe the glaring lies as to their ages which the recruiting sergeant has to suggest to them, and to abolish the military prison with its cat-o'-nine-tails perpetually flourishing before our guardsmen in Gibraltar "fortress orders" and the like, there would be a howl of stingy terror from the very taxpayers who are now weeping with national enthusiasm over the heroism of the two Dargai pipers who, five years hence, will probably be cursing, in their poverty, the day they ever threw away their manhood on the British War Office.

The question for the dramatic critic is, how is it possible to knock all this blood-and-thunder folly out of the head of the British playgoer? Satire would be useless: sense still more out of the question. Mr Charles Frohman seems to me to have solved the problem. You cannot make the Britisher see that his own bunkum is contemptible. But shew him the bunkum of any other nation, and he sees through it promptly enough. And that is what Mr Frohman is doing. The Heart of Maryland is an American melodrama of the Civil War. As usual, all the Southern commanders are Northern spies, and all the Northern commanders Southern spies—at least that is the general impression produced. It may be historically correct; for obviously such an arrangement, when the troops once got used to it, would not make the smallest difference; since a competition for defeat, if earnestly carried out on both sides, would be just as sensible, just as exciting, just as difficult, just as well calculated to call forth all the heroic qualities, not to mention the Christian virtues, as a competition for victory. Maryland Cawlvert (spelt Calvert) is "a Southern woman to the last drop of her blood," and is, of course, in love with a Northern officer, who has had the villain drummed out of the Northern army for infamous conduct.

The villain joins the Southerns, who, in recognition no doubt of his high character and remarkable record, at once make him a colonel, especially as he is addicted to heavy drinking. Naturally, he is politically impartial, and, as he says to the hysterical Northerner (who is, of course, the hero of the piece), fights for his own hand. "But the United States!" pleads the hysterical one feebly. "Damn the United States" replies the villain. Instantly the outraged patriot assaults him furiously, shouting "Take back that. Take it back." The villain prudently takes it back; and the honor of America is vindicated. This is clearly the point at which the audiences should burst into frantic applause. No doubt American audiences do. Perhaps the Adelphi audience would too if the line were altered to "Damn the United Kingdom." But we are sensible enough about other people's follies; and the incontinent schoolboyishness of the hero is received with the coolest contempt. This, then, is the moral mission of Mr Charles Frohman. He is snatching the fool's cap from the London playgoer and shewing it to him on the head of an American. Meanwhile, our foolish plays are going to America to return the compliment. In the end, perhaps, we shall get melodramas in which the heroism is not despicable, puerile, and blackguardly, nor the villainy mere mechanical criminality.

For the rest, The Heart of Maryland is not a bad specimen of the American machine-made melodrama. The actors know the gymnastics of their business, and work harder and more smartly, and stick to it better than English actors. Mrs Leslie Carter is a melodramatic heroine of no mean powers. Her dresses and graces and poses cast a glamor of American high art on Mr Belasco's romance; and her transports and tornadoes, in which she shews plenty of professional temperament and susceptibility, give intensity to the curtain situations, and secure her a flattering series of recalls. She disdains the silly and impossible sensation scene with the bell, leaving it to a lively young-lady athlete who shews with every muscle in her body that she is swinging the bell instead of being swung by it. Mr Morgan as the villain is received with special favor; and

Mr Malcolm Williams pretends to be a corpse in such a life-like manner that he brings down the house, already well disposed to him for his excellent acting before his decease. Nobody else has much of a chance.

"Valedictory"

[21 May 1898]
As I lie here, helpless and disabled, or, at best, nailed by
one foot to the floor like a doomed Strasburg goose, a
sense of injury grows on me. For nearly four years—to be
precise, since New Year 1895—I have been the slave of
the theatre. It has tethered me to the mile radius of foul
and sooty air which has its centre in the Strand, as a goat
is tethered in the little circle of cropped and trampled grass
that makes the meadow ashamed. Every week it clamors
for its tale of written words; so that I am like a man fighting a windmill: I have hardly time to stagger to my feet
from the knock-down blow of one sail, when the next
strikes me down. Now I ask, is it reasonable to expect me
to spend my life in this way? For just consider my position. Do I receive any spontaneous recognition for the
prodigies of skill and industry I lavish on an unworthy institution and a stupid public? Not a bit of it: half my time is
spent in telling people what a clever man I am. It is no use
merely doing clever things in England. The English do not
know what to think until they are coached, laboriously and
insistently for years, in the proper and becoming opinion.
For ten years past, with an unprecedented pertinacity and
obstination, I have been dinning into the public head that
I am an extraordinarily witty, brilliant, and clever man.
That is now part of the public opinion of England; and
no power in heaven or on earth will ever change it. I may
dodder and dote; I may potboil and platitudinize; I may
become the butt and chopping-block of all the bright, original spirits of the rising generation; but my reputation shall
not suffer: it is built up fast and solid, like Shakespear's,
on an impregnable basis of dogmatic reiteration.

Unfortunately, the building process has been a most

painful one to me, because I am congenitally an extremely modest man. Shyness is the form my vanity and self-consciousness take by nature. It is humiliating, too, after making the most dazzling displays of professional ability, to have to tell people how capital it all is. Besides, they get so tired of it, that finally, without dreaming of disputing the alleged brilliancy, they begin to detest it. I sometimes get quite frantic letters from people who feel that they cannot stand me any longer.

Then there are the managers. Are *they* grateful? No: they are simply forbearing. Instead of looking up to me as their guide, philosopher, and friend, they regard me merely as the author of a series of weekly outrages on their profession and their privacy. Worse than the managers are the Shakespeareans. When I began to write, William was a divinity and a bore. Now he is a fellow-creature; and his plays have reached an unprecedented pitch of popularity. And yet his worshippers overwhelm my name with insult.

These circumstances will not bear thinking of. I have never had time to think of them before; but now I have nothing else to do. When a man of normal habits is ill, everyone hastens to assure him that he is going to recover. When a vegetarian is ill (which fortunately very seldom happens), everyone assures him that he is going to die, and that they told him so, and that it serves him right. They implore him to take at least a little gravy, so as to give himself a chance of lasting out the night. They tell him awful stories of cases just like his own which ended fatally after indescribable torments; and when he tremblingly inquires whether the victims were not hardened meat-eaters, they tell him he must not talk, as it is not good for him. Ten times a day I am compelled to reflect on my past life, and on the limited prospect of three weeks or so of lingering moribundity which is held up to me as my probable future, with the intensity of a drowning man. And I can never justify to myself the spending of four years on dramatic criticism. I have sworn an oath to endure no more of it. Never again will I cross the threshold of a theatre. The subject is exhausted; and so am I.

Still, the gaiety of nations must not be eclipsed. The

long string of beautiful ladies who are at present in the square without, awaiting, under the supervision of two gallant policemen, their turn at my bedside, must be reassured when they protest, as they will, that the light of their life will go out if my dramatic articles cease. To each of them I will present the flower left by her predecessor, and assure her that there are as good fish in the sea as ever came out of it. The younger generation is knocking at the door; and as I open it there steps spritely in the incomparable Max.

For the rest, let Max speak for himself. I am off duty for ever, and am going to sleep.

To Beatrice Webb

×××

All manner of extraordinary events have happened to me
in consequence of your departure. After you left, there
was nothing to take me out of town or away from my
work. Adelphi Terrace was closed by the visit [of Charlotte]
to Rome. I simply worked straight on end at all times &
all hours, and gave up half my eating because I got no
change or exercise to give me an appetite, & large meals
disturbed my digestion without one. However, I got the
book finally off my hands, gave the Saturday notice to quit,
& generally prepared myself for a better life later on. If
I had gone away at Easter, I should have saved the situation; but I had nowhere to go and nobody to go to; and
the theatres were very exacting; so I ventured to let the
opportunity slip. By this time I was in an almost superhuman condition—fleshless, bloodless, vaporous, ethereal,
and stupendous in literary efficiency. Then the bolt fell. I
rode out one night to Ealing & back on the bike; and when

I returned, my left foot was like this ⎰⎰🖐. Even then I

had it all but cured with simple hot water fomentation
when the Vestry Election caught me & induced me to
walk to a meeting & back. That settled it. The thing became
an abscess, and after a few more days of fomenting, I had
to deliver myself over to the knife & the ether bag. One of
my ancient flames acted as nurse; & her husband operated.
The anaesthetist was in the last agonies of influenza; but
he managed to perform his function without inconvenienc-
ing me: I wasnt sick afterwards, only rather drunk, in
which condition, when the anaesthetist had gone home to
bed, & the surgeon had left the room to talk to my mother,

I pretended to be delirious and raved all sorts of love to the nurse, who was deeply affected.

The surgeon did not trouble himself in the least about my etherized philanderings, but kicked up a tremendous row about my health. He said I was killing myself. When he cut into the foot he not only found no blood—"only some wretched sort of ichor" he said—but the bone was necrosed. He swore it was tubercular caries; drew up a dietary of the most butcherly kind; and told me flatly that I had to choose between it & death.

As it happened, somebody before the operation suggested the possibility of my dying under the anæsthetic, and I then found that the prospect was not in the least disagreeable to me—rather too tempting to be dwelt on, if anything. I backed vegetarianism to the extent of my life without a moment's hesitation. It did well enough too: I soon began to pull myself together. Sharpe (the doctor) no doubt took the case by the ordinary standard of breakdown deferred to the utmost point by the abuse of stimulants, whereas it was really a perfectly simple case of exhaustion & starvation (of fresh air & rest as much as food). But matters were left in a detestable way. Sharpe had not been prepared for a necrosis operation; and though he scraped away the bad bit of bone as well as he could, there is still a bit that will not heal & that must some day exfoliate and come away. Meanwhile the hole in my foot has to be packed afresh every day with iodoform gauze & treated constantly with boracic fomentations.

Meanwhile Charlotte had returned from Rome & was on the scene. It was now plain that I must go away to the country the moment I could be moved, & that somebody must seriously take in hand the job of looking after me. Equally plain, of course, that Charlotte was the inevitable & predestined agent appointed by Destiny. To have let her do this in any other character than that of my wife would (in the absence of your chaperonage) have involved our whole circle and its interests in a senseless scandal. You may wonder why I did not find that out long ago, instead of exploiting the chaperonage with complete selfishness. I can only say that I dont know—that the situation was changed by a change in my own consciousness. I found that my objection to my own marriage had ceased with my objection to my own death. This was the main change: there were of course many other considerations which we shall probably discuss at some future time. Possibly one of them was that the relation between us had never until then completely lost its inevitable preliminary character of a love affair. She had at last got beyond that corrupt personal interest in me, just as "The Devil's Disciple" had relieved me of the appearance of a pecuniary interest (more than was reasonable) in her. The thing being cleared thus of all such illusions as love interest, happiness interest, & all the rest of the vulgarities of marriage, I changed right about face on the subject and hopped down to the Registrar, who married me to her on one leg, after beginning the ceremony with [Graham] Wallas, who had a new coat on [.]

The papers noticed the event as eagerly as the death of Gladstone. Mrs Chumly (I forget the full length spelling) wrote to Charlotte, "Do not ask me to meet This Man. And as a last kindness to me, & for my sake, I ask you to secure your money."

At last, after much nursing, we secured this house, on the south slope of Hindhead, until October. I came down on crutches. The air was so fine that our troubles seemed to be over; but they had only just begun. The moment I began to get strong, I recklessly returned to work on a Quintessence of Wagner which I had begun earlier; and in a few days I was at it as savagely as ever. Sharpe wrote vehemently commanding me not to tempt the gods. Before his letter arrived I found out, after dictating Wagner criticism one morning for half an hour, that I was myself conscious that all the strain was on again. I called a halt, and went upstairs on the crutches (a foolish feat) to get something from my bedroom. Coming down again, the crutches got planted behind my centre of gravity & shot me into the air. I snatched at a bannister on the landing above, and caught it in my right hand; but it snapped like an Argoed tree; and I was precipitated fifty fathom or thereabout into the hall, with my left arm doubled up in ruin under me—like this

Imagine poor Charlotte's feelings! She got a pair of butter pats & made splints of them. The local doctor, who did not come for half an hour, during which I lay in the hall with all the strain gone, perfectly relieved and happy, was fortunately a capable man; and the setting was a success. But fancy my condition *now* (this happened four days ago[)]. I am helpless—a nurse (disciple of Honnor Morten) has to wash and dress and all but feed me. I have a wheeled chair, which I cannot wheel, since when worked with one hand only, it simply spins round & round. Heaven knows what will happen to Charlotte when the anxiety about me is over. Last night a cat, shut up accidentally in the pantry, simulated a burglar so successfully that I sallied out, walking recklessly on the bad foot, at three in the morning, & thereby did myself as much harm as possible. I no longer feel any confidence in my ultimate recovery: it seems certain to me that I shall presently break all my other limbs as well.

I am sitting in my wheeled chair on the lawn, looking over the hills through a gap in the trees to a bit of heather which reminds me of the Argoed, and of all my previous honeymoons, with respect to which I may now, as a correctly married man, speak to you, dear Beatrice, with frank sentiment. Not until you left me a widower was I driven to be unfaithful to your fireside.

                                                          G. Bernard Shaw

DON JUAN IN HELL

(Distributed with program at the Royal Court Theatre, London, 4 June 1907)

xxxxxxxxxxxxxxxxxxxxxxxxxxxxxxxxxxxxxxxxx

As this scene may prove puzzling at a first hearing to those who are not to some extent skilled in modern theology, the Management have asked the Author to offer the Court audience the same assistance that concert goers are accustomed to receive in the form of an analytical programme:

The scene, an abysmal void, represents hell; and the persons of the drama speak of hell, heaven, and earth as if they were separate localities, like "the heavens above, the earth beneath, and the waters under the earth." It must be remembered that such localizations are purely figurative, like our fashion of calling a treble voice "high" and a bass voice "low." Modern theology conceives heaven and hell, not as places, but as states of the soul; and by the soul it means, not an organ like the liver, but the divine element common to all life, which causes us "to do the will of God" in addition to looking after our individual interests, and to honor one another solely for our divine activities and not at all for our selfish activities.

Hell is popularly conceived not only as a place, but as a place of cruelty and punishment, and heaven as a paradise of idle pleasure. These legends are discarded by the higher theology, which holds that this world, or any other, may be made a hell by a society in a state of damnation: that is, a society so lacking in the higher orders of energy that it is given wholly to the pursuit of immediate individual pleasure, and cannot even conceive the passion of the divine will. Also that any world can be made a heaven by a society of persons in whom that passion is the master passion—a "communion of saints" in fact.

In the scene presented to-day, hell is this state of damnation. It is personified in the traditional manner by

the devil, who differs from the modern plutocratic voluptuary only in being "true to himself": that is, he does not
disguise his damnation either from himself or others, but
boldly embraces it as the true law of life, and organizes his
kingdom frankly on a basis of idle pleasure seeking, and
worships love, beauty, sentiment, youth, romance, etc.,
etc., etc.

Upon this conception of heaven and hell the author
has fantastically grafted the XVIIth century legend of
Don Juan Tenorio, Don Gonzalo of Ulloa, Commandant
of Calatrava, and the Commandant's daughter Doña Ana,
as told in the famous drama by Tirso de Molina and in
Mozart's opera. Don Gonzalo, having, as he says, "always
done what it was customary for a gentleman to do" until
he died defending his daughter's honor, went to heaven.
Don Juan, having slain him, and become infamous by his
failure to find any permanent satisfaction in his love affairs,
was cast into hell by the ghost of Don Gonzalo, whose
statue he had whimsically invited to supper.

The ancient melodrama becomes the philosophic comedy
presented to-day, by postulating that Don Gonzalo was a
simple-minded officer and gentleman who cared for nothing
but fashionable amusement, whilst Don Juan was consumed with a passion for divine contemplation and creative activity, this being the secret of the failure of love to
interest him permanently. Consequently we find Don
Gonzalo, unable to share the divine ecstasy, bored to distraction in heaven; and Don Juan suffering amid the
pleasures of hell an agony of tedium.

At last Don Gonzalo, after paying several reconnoitring
visits to hell under color of urging Don Juan to repent,
determines to settle there permanently. At this moment his
daughter Ana, now full of years, piety, and worldly honors,
dies, and finds herself with Don Juan in hell, where she
is presently the amazed witness of the arrival of her sainted
father. The devil hastens to welcome both to his realm.
As Ana is no theologian, and believes the popular legends
as to heaven and hell, all this bewilders her extremely.

The devil, eager as ever to reinforce his kingdom by

adding souls to it, is delighted at the accession of Don Gonzalo, and desirous to retain Doña Ana. But he is equally ready to get rid of Don Juan, with whom he is on terms of forced civility, the antipathy between them being fundamental. A discussion arises between them as to the merits of the heavenly and hellish states, and the future of the world. The discussion lasts more than an hour, as the parties, with eternity before them, are in no hurry. Finally, Don Juan shakes the dust of hell from his feet, and goes to heaven.

Doña Ana, being a woman, is incapable both of the devil's utter damnation and of Don Juan's complete supersensuality. As the mother of many children she has shared in the divine travail, and with care and labor and suffering renewed the harvest of eternal life; but the honor and divinity of her work have been jealously hidden from her by Man, who, dreading her domination, has offered her for reward only the satisfaction of her senses and affections. She cannot, like the male devil, use love as mere sentiment and pleasure; nor can she, like the male saint, put love aside when it has once done its work as a developing and enlightening experience. Love is neither her pleasure nor her study: it is her business. So she, in the end, neither goes with Don Juan to heaven nor with the devil and her father to the palace of pleasure, but declares that her work is not yet finished. For though by her death she is done with the bearing of men to mortal fathers, she may yet, as Woman Immortal, bear the Superman to the Eternal Father.

DON JUAN IN HELL
[Extracted from Act III of *Man and Superman,* 1903]

Stillness settles on the Sierra; and the darkness deepens. The fire has again buried itself in white ash and ceased to glow. The peaks shew unfathomably dark against the starry firmament; but now the stars dim and vanish; and the sky seems

*to steal away out of the universe. Instead of the Sierra there
is nothing: omnipresent nothing. No sky, no peaks, no light,
no sound, no time nor space, utter void. Then somewhere
the beginning of a pallor, and with it a faint throbbing buzz
as a ghostly violoncello palpitating on the same note end-
lessly. A couple of ghostly violins presently take advantage
of this bass*

*and therewith the pallor reveals a man in the void, an
incorporeal but visible man, seated, absurdly enough, on
nothing. For a moment he raises his head as the music
passes him by. Then, with a heavy sigh, he droops in utter
dejection; and the violins, discouraged, retrace their melody
in despair and at last give it up, extinguished by wailings
from uncanny wind instruments, thus:*

*It is all very odd. One recognizes the Mozartian strain;
and on this hint, and by the aid of certain sparkles of violet
light in the pallor, the man's costume explains itself as that
of a Spanish nobleman of the XV–XVI century. Don Juan,
of course; but where? why? how? Besides, in the brief lifting
of his face, now hidden by his hat brim, there was a curious
suggestion of Tanner. A more critical, fastidious, handsome
face, paler and colder, without Tanner's impetuous credulity
and enthusiasm, and without a touch of his modern plutocratic vulgarity, but still a resemblance, even an identity.
The name too: Don Juan Tenorio, John Tanner. Where on
earth—or elsewhere—have we got to from the XX century
and the Sierra?*

Another pallor in the void, this time not violet, but a disagreeable smoky yellow. With it, the whisper of a ghostly clarionet turning this tune into infinite sadness:

Donna Ana's song to Ottavia

The yellowish pallor moves: there is an old crone wandering in the void, bent and toothless; draped, as well as one can guess, in the coarse brown frock of some religious order. She wanders and wanders in her slow hopeless way, much as a wasp flies in its rapid busy way, until she blunders against the thing she seeks: companionship. With a sob of relief the poor old creature clutches at the presence of the man and addresses him in her dry unlovely voice, which can still express pride and resolution as well as suffering.

THE OLD WOMAN. Excuse me; but I am so lonely; and this place is so awful.

DON JUAN. A new comer?

THE OLD WOMAN. Yes: I suppose I died this morning. I confessed; I had extreme unction; I was in bed with my family about me and my eyes fixed on the cross. Then it grew dark; and when the light came back it was this light by which I walk seeing nothing. I have wandered for hours in horrible loneliness.

DON JUAN [*sighing*] Ah! you have not yet lost the sense of time. One soon does, in eternity.

THE OLD WOMAN. Where are we?

DON JUAN. In Hell.

THE OLD WOMAN [*proudly*] Hell! I in Hell! How dare you?

DON JUAN [*unimpressed*] Why not, Señora?

THE OLD WOMAN. You do not know to whom you are speaking. I am a lady, and a faithful daughter of the Church.

DON JUAN. I do not doubt it.

THE OLD WOMAN. But how then can I be in Hell? Purgatory, perhaps: I have not been perfect: who has? But Hell! oh, you are lying.

DON JUAN. Hell, Señora, I assure you; Hell at its best: that is, its most solitary—though perhaps you would prefer company.

THE OLD WOMAN. But I have sincerely repented; I have confessed—

DON JUAN. How much?

THE OLD WOMAN. More sins than I really committed. I loved confession.

DON JUAN. Ah, that is perhaps as bad as confessing too little. At all events, Señora, whether by oversight or intention, you are certainly damned, like myself; and there is nothing for it now but to make the best of it.

THE OLD WOMAN [*indignantly*] Oh! and I might have been so much wickeder! All my good deeds wasted! It is unjust.

DON JUAN. No: you were fully and clearly warned. For your bad deeds, vicarious atonement, mercy without justice. For your good deeds, justice without mercy. We have many good people here.

THE OLD WOMAN. Were you a good man?

DON JUAN. I was a murderer.

THE OLD WOMAN. A murderer! Oh, how dare they send me to herd with murderers! I was not as bad as that: I was a good woman. There is some mistake: where can I have it set right?

DON JUAN. I do not know whether mistakes can be corrected here. Probably they will not admit a mistake even if they have made one.

THE OLD WOMAN. But whom can I ask?

DON JUAN. I should ask the Devil, Señora: he understands the ways of this place, which is more than I ever could.

THE OLD WOMAN. The Devil! *I* speak to the Devil!

DON JUAN. In Hell, Señora, the Devil is the leader of the best society.

THE OLD WOMAN. I tell you, wretch, I know I am not in Hell.

DON JUAN. How do you know?

THE OLD WOMAN. Because I feel no pain.

DON JUAN. Oh, then there is no mistake: you are intentionally damned.

THE OLD WOMAN. Why do you say that?

DON JUAN. Because Hell, Señora, is a place for the wicked. The wicked are quite comfortable in it: it was made for them. You tell me you feel no pain. I conclude you are one of those for whom Hell exists.

THE OLD WOMAN. Do you feel no pain?

DON JUAN. I am not one of the wicked, Señora; therefore it bores me, bores me beyond description, beyond belief.

THE OLD WOMAN. Not one of the wicked! You said you were a murderer.

DON JUAN. Only a duel. I ran my sword through an old man who was trying to run his through me.

THE OLD WOMAN. If you were a gentleman, that was not a murder.

DON JUAN. The old man called it murder, because he was, he said, defending his daughter's honor. By this he meant that because I foolishly fell in love with her and told her so, she screamed; and he tried to assassinate me after calling me insulting names.

THE OLD WOMAN. You were like all men. Libertines and murderers, all, all, all!

DON JUAN. And yet we meet here, dear lady.

THE OLD WOMAN. Listen to me. My father was slain by just such a wretch as you, in just such a duel, for just such a cause. I screamed: it was my duty. My father drew on my assailant: his honor demanded it. He fell: that was the reward of honor. I am here: in Hell, you tell me: that is the reward of duty. Is there justice in Heaven?

DON JUAN. No; but there is justice in Hell: Heaven is far above such idle human personalities. You will be welcome in Hell, Señora. Hell is the home of honor, duty, justice, and the rest of the seven deadly virtues. All the wickedness on earth is done in their name: where else but in Hell should they have their reward? Have I not told you that the truly damned are those who are happy in Hell?

THE OLD WOMAN. And are you happy here?

DON JUAN [springing to his feet] No; and that is the enigma

on which I ponder in darkness. Why am I here? I, who repudiated all duty, trampled honor underfoot, and laughed at justice!

THE OLD WOMAN. Oh, what do I care why you are here? Why am *I* here? I, who sacrificed all my inclinations to womanly virtue and propriety!

DON JUAN. Patience, lady: you will be perfectly happy and at home here. As saith the poet, "Hell is a city much like Seville."

THE OLD WOMAN. Happy! here! where I am nothing! where I am nobody!

DON JUAN. Not at all: you are a lady; and wherever ladies are is Hell. Do not be surprised or terrified: you will find everything here that a lady can desire, including devils who will serve you from sheer love of servitude, and magnify your importance for the sake of dignifying their service—the best of servants.

THE OLD WOMAN. My servants will be devils!

DON JUAN. Have you ever had servants who were not devils?

THE OLD WOMAN. Never: they were devils, perfect devils, all of them. But that is only a manner of speaking. I thought you meant that my servants here would be real devils.

DON JUAN. No more real devils than you will be a real lady. Nothing is real here. That is the horror of damnation.

THE OLD WOMAN. Oh, this is all madness. This is worse than fire and the worm.

DON JUAN. For you, perhaps, there are consolations. For instance, how old were you when you changed from time to eternity?

THE OLD WOMAN. Do not ask me how old I was—as if I were a thing of the past. I a m 77.

DON JUAN. A ripe age, Señora. But in Hell old age is not tolerated. It is too real. Here we worship Love and Beauty. Our souls being entirely damned, we cultivate our hearts. As a lady of 77, you would not have a single acquaintance in Hell.

THE OLD WOMAN. How can I help my age, man?

DON JUAN. You forget that you have left your age behind you in the realm of time. You are no more 77 than you are 7 or 17 or 27.

THE OLD WOMAN. Nonsense!

DON JUAN. Consider, Señora: was not this true even when you lived on earth? When you were 70, were you really older underneath your wrinkles and your grey hairs than when you were 30?

THE OLD WOMAN. No, younger: at 30 I was a fool. But of what use is it to feel younger and look older?

DON JUAN. You see, Señora, the look was only an illusion. Your wrinkles lied, just as the plump smooth skin of many a stupid girl of 17, with heavy spirits and decrepit ideas, lies about her age! Well, here we have no bodies: we see each other as bodies only because we learnt to think about one another under that aspect when we were alive; and we still think in that way, knowing no other. But we can appear to one another at what age we choose. You have but to will any of your old looks back, and back they will come.

THE OLD WOMAN. It cannot be true.

DON JUAN. Try.

THE OLD WOMAN. Seventeen!

DON JUAN. Stop. Before you decide, I had better tell you that these things are a matter of fashion. Occasionally we have a rage for 17; but it does not last long. Just at present the fashionable age is 40—or say 37; but there are signs of a change. If you were at all good-looking at 27, I should suggest your trying that, and setting a new fashion.

THE OLD WOMAN. I do not believe a word you are saying. However, 27 be it. [*Whisk! the old woman becomes a young one, magnificently attired, and so handsome that in the radiance into which her dull yellow halo has suddenly lightened one might almost mistake her for Ann Whitefield.*]

DON JUAN. Doña Ana de Ulloa!

ANA. What? You know me!

DON JUAN. And you forget me!

ANA. I cannot see your face. [*He raises his hat.*] Don Juan

Tenorio! Monster! You slew my father! even here you pursue me.

DON JUAN. I protest I do not pursue you. Allow me to withdraw [*going*].

ANA [*seizing his arm*] You shall not leave me alone in this dreadful place.

DON JUAN. Provided my staying be not interpreted as pursuit.

ANA [*releasing him*] You may well wonder how I can endure your presence. My dear, dear father!

DON JUAN. Would you like to see him?

ANA. My father here! ! !

DON JUAN. No: he is in Heaven.

ANA. I knew it. My noble father! He is looking down on us now. What must he feel to see his daughter in this place, and in conversation with his murderer!

DON JUAN. By the way, if we should meet him—

ANA. How can we meet him? He is in Heaven.

DON JUAN. He condescends to look in upon us here from time to time. Heaven bores him. So let me warn you that if you meet him he will be mortally offended if you speak of me as his murderer! He maintains that he was a much better swordsman than I, and that if his foot had not slipped he would have killed me. No doubt he is right: I was not a good fencer. I never dispute the point; so we are excellent friends.

ANA. It is no dishonor to a soldier to be proud of his skill in arms.

DON JUAN. You would rather not meet him, probably.

ANA. How dare you say that?

DON JUAN. Oh, that is the usual feeling here. You may remember that on earth—though of course we never confessed it—the death of anyone we knew, even those we liked best, was always mingled with a certain satisfaction at being finally done with them.

ANA. Monster! Never, never.

DON JUAN [*placidly*] I see you recognize the feeling. Yes: a funeral was always a festivity in black, especially the funeral of a relative. At all events, family ties are rarely

kept up here. Your father is quite accustomed to this: he
will not expect any devotion from you.

ANA. Wretch: I wore mourning for him all my life.

DON JUAN. Yes: it became you. But a life of mourning is
one thing: an eternity of it quite another. Besides, here
you are as dead as he. Can anything be more ridiculous
than one dead person mourning for another? Do not look
shocked, my dear Ana; and do not be alarmed: there is
plenty of humbug in Hell (indeed there is hardly anything else); but the humbug of death and age and change
is dropped because here we are all dead and all eternal.
You will pick up our ways soon.

ANA. And will all the men call me their dear Ana?

DON JUAN. No. That was a slip of the tongue. I beg your
pardon.

ANA [*almost tenderly*] Juan: did you really love me when
you behaved so disgracefully to me?

DON JUAN [*impatiently*] Oh, I beg you not to begin talking
about love. Here they talk of nothing else but love: its
beauty, its holiness, its spirituality, its devil knows what!
—excuse me; but it does so bore me. They dont know
what theyre talking about: I do. They think they have
achieved the perfection of love because they have no
bodies. Sheer imaginative debauchery! Faugh!

ANA. Has even death failed to refine your soul, Juan? Has
the terrible judgment of which my father's statue was the
minister taught you no reverence?

DON JUAN. How is that very flattering statue, by the way?
Does it still come to supper with naughty people and
cast them into this bottomless pit?

ANA. It has been a great expense to me. The boys in the
monastery school would not let it alone: the mischievous
ones broke it; and the studious ones wrote their names
on it. Three new noses in two years, and fingers without
end. I had to leave it to its fate at last; and now I fear
it is shockingly mutilated. My poor father!

DON JUAN. Hush! Listen! [*Two great chords rolling on
syncopated waves of sound break forth. D minor and its
dominant: a sound of dreadful joy to all musicians.*] Ha!

Mozart's statue music. It is your father. You had better disappear until I prepare him. [*She vanishes.*]

[*From the void comes a living statue of white marble, designed to represent a majestic old man. But he waives his majesty with infinite grace; walks with a feather-like step; and makes every wrinkle in his war worn visage brim over with holiday joyousness. To his sculptor he owes a perfectly trained figure, which he carries erect and trim; and the ends of his moustache curl up, elastic as watch-springs, giving him an air which, but for its Spanish dignity, would be called jaunty. He is on the pleasantest terms with Don Juan. His voice, save for a much more distinguished intonation, is so like the voice of Roebuck Ramsden that it calls attention to the fact that they are not unlike one another in spite of their very different fashions of shaving.*]

DON JUAN. Ah, here you are, my friend. Why dont you learn to sing the splendid music Mozart has written for you?

THE STATUE. Unluckily he has written it for a bass voice. Mine is a counter tenor. Well: have you repented yet?

DON JUAN. I have too much consideration for you to repent, Don Gonzalo. If I did, you would have no excuse for coming from Heaven to argue with me.

THE STATUE. True. Remain obdurate, my boy. I wish I had killed you, as I should have done but for an accident. Then I should have come here: and you would have had a statue and a reputation for piety to live up to. Any news?

DON JUAN. Yes: your daughter is dead.

THE STATUE [*puzzled*] My daughter? [*Recollecting*] Oh! the one you were taken with. Let me see: what was her name?

DON JUAN. Ana.

THE STATUE. To be sure: Ana. A goodlooking girl, if I recollect aright. Have you warned Whatshisname? her husband.

DON JUAN. My friend Ottavio? No: I have not seen him since Ana arrived.

[*Ana comes indignantly to light.*]

ANA. What does this mean? Ottavio here and your friend! And you, father, have forgotten my name. You are indeed turned to stone.

THE STATUE. My dear: I am so much more admired in marble than I ever was in my own person that I have retained the shape the sculptor gave me. He was one of the first men of his day: you must acknowledge that.

ANA. Father! Vanity! personal vanity! from you!

THE STATUE. Ah, you outlived that weakness, my daughter: you must be nearly 80 by this time. I was cut off (by an accident) in my 64th year, and am considerably your junior in consequence. Besides, my child, in this place, what our libertine friend here would call the farce of parental wisdom is dropped. Regard me, I beg, as a fellow creature, not as a father.

ANA. You speak as this villain speaks.

THE STATUE. Juan is a sound thinker, Ana. A bad fencer, but a sound thinker.

ANA [*horror creeping upon her*] I begin to understand. These are devils, mocking me. I had better pray.

THE STATUE [*consoling her*] No, no, no, my child: do not pray. If you do, you will throw away the main advantage of this place. Written over the gate here are the words "Leave every hope behind, ye who enter." Only think what a relief that is! For what is hope? A form of moral responsibility. Here there is no hope, and consequently no duty, no work, nothing to be gained by praying, nothing to be lost by doing what you like. Hell, in short, is a place where you have nothing to do but amuse yourself. [*Don Juan sighs deeply.*] You sigh, friend Juan; but if you dwelt in Heaven, as I do, you would realize your advantages.

DON JUAN. You are in good spirits today, Commander. You are positively brilliant. What is the matter?

THE STATUE. I have come to a momentous decision, my boy. But first, where is our friend the Devil? I must consult him in the matter. And Ana would like to make his acquaintance, no doubt.

ANA. You are preparing some torment for me.

DON JUAN. All that is superstition, Ana. Reassure yourself. Remember: the devil is not so black as he is painted.

THE STATUE. Let us give him a call.

[*At the wave of the statue's hand the great chords roll out again; but this time Mozart's music gets grotesquely adulterated with Gounod's. A scarlet halo begins to glow; and into it the Devil rises, very Mephistophelean, and not at all unlike Mendoza, though not so interesting. He looks older; is getting prematurely bald; and, in spite of an effusion of goodnature and friendliness, is peevish and sensitive when his advances are not reciprocated. He does not inspire much confidence in his powers of hard work or endurance, and is, on the whole, a disagreeably self-indulgent looking person: but he is clever and plausible, though perceptibly less well bred than the two other men, and enormously less vital than the woman.*]

THE DEVIL [*heartily*] Have I the pleasure of again receiving a visit from the illustrious Commander of Calatrava? [*Coldly*] Don Juan, your servant. [*Politely*] And a strange lady? My respects, Señora.

ANA. Are you—

THE DEVIL [*bowing*] Lucifer, at your service.

ANA. I shall go mad.

THE DEVIL [*gallantly*] Ah, Señora, do not be anxious. You come to us from earth, full of the prejudices and terrors of that priest-ridden place. You have heard me ill spoken of; and yet, believe me, I have hosts of friends there.

ANA. Yes: you reign in their hearts.

THE DEVIL [*shaking his head*] You flatter me, Señora; but you are mistaken. It is true that the world cannot get on without me; but it never gives me credit for that: in its heart it mistrusts and hates me. Its sympathies are all with misery, with poverty, with starvation of the body, and of the heart. I call on it to sympathize with joy, with love, with happiness, with beauty—

DON JUAN [*nauseated*] Excuse me: I am going. You know I cannot stand this.

THE DEVIL [*angrily*] Yes: I know that you are no friend of mine.

THE STATUE. What harm is he doing you, Juan? It seems to me that he was talking excellent sense when you interrupted him.

THE DEVIL [*warmly patting the statue's hand*] Thank you, my friend: thank you. You have always understood me: he has always disparaged and avoided me.

DON JUAN. I have treated you with perfect courtesy.

THE DEVIL. Courtesy! What is courtesy? I care nothing for mere courtesy. Give me warmth of heart, true sincerity, the bond of sympathy with love and joy—

DON JUAN. You are making me ill.

THE DEVIL. There! [*Appealing to the statue*] You hear, sir! Oh, by what irony of fate was this cold selfish egotist sent to my kingdom, and you taken to the icy mansions of the sky!

THE STATUE. I cant complain. I was a hypocrite; and it served me right to be sent to Heaven.

THE DEVIL. Why, sir, do you not join us, and leave a sphere for which your temperament is too sympathetic, your heart too warm, your capacity for enjoyment too generous?

THE STATUE. I have this day resolved to do so. In future, excellent Son of the Morning, I am yours. I have left Heaven for ever.

THE DEVIL [*again touching the marble hand*] Ah, what an honor! What a triumph for our cause! Thank you, thank you. And now, my friend—I may call you so at last— could you not persuade him to take the place you have left vacant above?

THE STATUE [*shaking his head*] I cannot conscientiously recommend anybody with whom I am on friendly terms to deliberately make himself dull and uncomfortable.

THE DEVIL. Of course not; but are you sure he would be uncomfortable? Of course you know best: you brought him here originally; and we had the greatest hopes of him. His sentiments were in the best taste of our best people. You remember how he sang? [*He begins to sing in a nasal operatic baritone, tremulous from an eternity of misuse in the French manner*]

Vivan le femmine!
Viva il buon vino!

THE STATUE [*taking up the tune an octave higher in his counter tenor*]

Sostegno e gloria
D'umanità.

THE DEVIL. Precisely. Well, he never sings for us now.

DON JUAN. Do you complain of that? Hell is full of musical amateurs: music is the brandy of the damned. May not one lost soul be permitted to abstain?

THE DEVIL. You dare blaspheme against the sublimest of the arts!

DON JUAN [*with cold disgust*] You talk like a hysterical woman fawning on a fiddler.

THE DEVIL. I am not angry. I merely pity you. You have no soul; and you are unconscious of all that you lose. Now you, Señor Commander, are a born musician. How well you sing! Mozart would be delighted if he were still here; but he moped and went to Heaven. Curious how these clever men, whom you would have supposed born to be popular here, have turned out social failures, like Don Juan!

DON JUAN. I am really very sorry to be a social failure.

THE DEVIL. Not that we dont admire your intellect, you know. We do. But I look at the matter from your own point of view. You dont get on with us. The place doesnt suit you. The truth is, you have—I wont say no heart; for we know that beneath all your affected cynicism you have a warm one—

DON JUAN [*shrinking*] Dont, please dont.

THE DEVIL [*nettled*] Well, youve no capacity for enjoyment. Will that satisfy you?

DON JUAN. It is a somewhat less insufferable form of cant than the other. But if youll allow me, I'll take refuge, as usual, in solitude.

THE DEVIL. Why not take refuge in Heaven? Thats the proper place for you. [*To Ana*] Come, Señora! could you not persuade him for his own good to try change of air?

ANA. But can he go to Heaven if he wants to?

THE DEVIL. Whats to prevent him?

ANA. Can anybody—can *I* go to Heaven, if I want to?

THE DEVIL [*rather contemptuously*] Certainly, if your taste lies that way.

ANA. But why doesnt everybody go to Heaven, then?

THE STATUE [*chuckling*] *I* can tell you that, my dear. It's because Heaven is the most angelically dull place in all creation: thats why.

THE DEVIL. His excellency the Commander puts it with military bluntness; but the strain of living in Heaven is intolerable. There is a notion that I was turned out of it; but as a matter of fact nothing could have induced me to stay there. I simply left it and organized this place.

THE STATUE. I dont wonder at it. Nobody could stand an eternity of Heaven.

THE DEVIL. Oh, it suits some people. Let us be just, Commander: it is a question of temperament. I dont admire the heavenly temperament: I dont understand it: I dont know that I particularly want to understand it; but it takes all sorts to make a universe. There is no accounting for tastes: there are people who like it. I think Don Juan would like it.

DON JUAN. But—pardon my frankness—could you really go back there if you desired to; or are the grapes sour?

THE DEVIL. Back there! I often go back there. Have you never read the book of Job? Have you any canonical authority for assuming that there is any barrier between our circle and the other one?

ANA. But surely there is a great gulf fixed.

THE DEVIL. Dear lady: a parable must not be taken literally. The gulf is the difference between the angelic and the diabolic temperament. What more impassable gulf could you have? Think of what you have seen on earth. There is no physical gulf between the philosopher's class room and the bull ring; but the bull fighters do not come to the class room for all that. Have you ever been in the country where I have the largest following? England. There they have great racecourses, and also concert rooms where they play the classical compositions of his

Excellency's friend Mozart. Those who go to the race-courses can stay away from them and go to the classical concerts instead if they like: there is no law against it; for Englishmen never will be slaves: they are free to do whatever the Government and public opinion allow them to do. And the classical concert is admitted to be a higher, more cultivated, poetic, intellectual, ennobling place than the racecourse. But do the lovers of racing desert their sport and flock to the concert room? Not they. They would suffer there all the weariness the Commander has suffered in Heaven. There is the great gulf of the parable between the two places. A mere physical gulf they could bridge; or at least I could bridge it for them (the earth is full of Devil's Bridges); but the gulf of dislike is impassable and eternal. And that is the only gulf that separates my friends here from those who are invidiously called the blest.

ANA. I shall go to Heaven at once.

THE STATUE. My child: one word of warning first. Let me complete my friend Lucifer's similitude of the classical concert. At every one of these concerts in England you will find rows of weary people who are there, not because they really like classical music, but because they think they ought to like it. Well, there is the same thing in Heaven. A number of people sit there in glory, not because they are happy, but because they think they owe it to their position to be in Heaven. They are almost all English.

THE DEVIL. Yes: the Southerners give it up and join me just as you have done. But the English really do not seem to know when they are thoroughly miserable. An Englishmen thinks he is moral when he is only uncomfortable.

THE STATUE. In short, my daughter, if you go to Heaven without being naturally qualified for it, you will not enjoy yourself there.

ANA. And who dares say that I am not naturally qualified for it? The most distinguished princes of the Church have never questioned it. I owe it to myself to leave this place at once.

THE DEVIL [*offended*] As you please, Señora. I should have expected better taste from you.

ANA. Father: I shall expect you to come with me. You cannot stay here. What will people say?

THE STATUE. People! Why, the best people are here—princes of the Church and all. So few go to Heaven, and so many come here, that the blest, once called a heavenly host, are a continually dwindling minority. The saints, the fathers, the elect of long ago are the cranks, the faddists, the outsiders of today.

THE DEVIL. It is true. From the beginning of my career I knew that I should win in the long run by sheer weight of public opinion, in spite of the long campaign of misrepresentation and calumny against me. At bottom the universe is a constitutional one; and with such a majority as mine I cannot be kept permanently out of office.

DON JUAN. I think, Ana, you had better stay here.

ANA [*jealously*] You do not want me to go with you.

DON JUAN. Surely you do not want to enter Heaven in the company of a reprobate like me.

ANA. All souls are equally precious. You repent, do you not?

DON JUAN. My dear Ana, you are silly. Do you suppose Heaven is like earth, where people persuade themselves that what is done can be undone by repentance; that what is spoken can be unspoken by withdrawing it; that what is true can be annihilated by a general agreement to give it the lie? No: Heaven is the home of the masters of reality: that is why I am going thither.

ANA. Thank you: I am going to Heaven for happiness. I have had quite enough of reality on earth.

DON JUAN. Then you must stay here; for Hell is the home of the unreal and of the seekers for happiness. It is the only refuge from Heaven, which is, as I tell you, the home of the masters of reality, and from earth, which is the home of the slaves of reality. The earth is a nursery in which men and women play at being heroes and heroines, saints and sinners; but they are dragged down from their fool's paradise by their bodies: hunger and cold and thirst, age and decay and disease, death above

all, make them slaves of reality: thrice a day meals
must be eaten and digested: thrice a century a new generation must be engendered: ages of faith, of romance,
and of science are all driven at last to have but one
prayer: "Make me a healthy animal." But here you
escape this tyranny of the flesh; for here you are not
an animal at all: you are a ghost, an appearance, an
illusion, a convention, deathless, ageless: in a word,
bodiless. There are no social questions here, no political
questions, no religious questions, best of all, perhaps, no
sanitary questions. Here you call your appearance beauty,
your emotions love, your sentiments heroism, your aspirations virtue, just as you did on earth; but here there are
no hard facts to contradict you, no ironic contrast of
your needs with your pretensions, no human comedy,
nothing but a perpetual romance, a universal melodrama.
As our German friend put it in his poem, "the poetically
nonsensical here is good sense; and the Eternal Feminine
draws us ever upward and on"—without us getting a
step farther. And yet you want to leave this paradise!

ANA. But if Hell be so beautiful as this, how glorious must
Heaven be!

[*The Devil, the Statue, and Don Juan all begin to
speak at once in violent protest; then stop, abashed.*]

DON JUAN. I beg your pardon.

THE DEVIL. Not at all. I interrupted you.

THE STATUE. You were going to say something.

DON JUAN. After you, gentlemen.

THE DEVIL [*to Don Juan*] You have been so eloquent on the
advantages of my dominions that I leave you to do equal
justice to the drawbacks of the alternative establishment.

DON JUAN. In Heaven, as I picture it, dear lady, you live
and work instead of playing and pretending. You face
things as they are; you escape nothing but glamor; and
your steadfastness and your peril are your glory. If the
play still goes on here and on earth, and all the world
is a stage, Heaven is at least behind the scenes. But
Heaven cannot be described by metaphor. Thither I shall
go presently, because there I hope to escape at last from

lies and from the tedious, vulgar pursuit of happiness, to spend my eons in contemplation—

THE STATUE. Ugh!

DON JUAN. Señor Commander: I do not blame your disgust: a picture gallery is a dull place for a blind man. But even as you enjoy the contemplation of such romantic mirages as beauty and pleasure; so would I enjoy the contemplation of that which interests me above all things: namely, Life: the force that ever strives to attain greater power of contemplating itself. What made this brain of mine, do you think? Not the need to move my limbs; for a rat with half my brains moves as well as I. Not merely the need to do, but the need to know what I do, lest in my blind efforts to live I should be slaying myself.

THE STATUE. You would have slain yourself in your blind efforts to fence but for my foot slipping, my friend.

DON JUAN. Audacious ribald: your laughter will finish in hideous boredom before morning.

THE STATUE. Ha ha! Do you remember how I frightened you when I said something like that to you from my pedestal in Seville? It sounds rather flat without my trombones.

DON JUAN. They tell me it generally sounds flat with them, Commander.

ANA. Oh, do not interrupt with these frivolities, father. Is there nothing in Heaven but contemplation, Juan?

DON JUAN. In the Heaven I seek, no other joy! But there is the work of helping Life in its struggle upward. Think of how it wastes and scatters itself, how it raises up obstacles to itself and destroys itself in its ignorance and blindness. It needs a brain, this irresistible force, lest in its ignorance it should resist itself. What a piece of work is man! says the poet. Yes; but what a blunderer! Here is the highest miracle of organization yet attained by life, the most intensely alive thing that exists, the most conscious of all the organisms; and yet, how wretched are his brains! Stupidity made sordid and cruel by the realities learnt from toil and poverty: Imagination resolved to

starve sooner than face these realities, piling up illusions
to hide them, and calling itself cleverness, genius! And
each accusing the other of its own defect: Stupidity
accusing Imagination of folly, and Imagination accusing
Stupidity of ignorance: whereas, alas! Stupidity has all
the knowledge, and Imagination all the intelligence.

THE DEVIL. And a pretty kettle of fish they make of it between them. Did I not say, when I was arranging that
affair of Faust's, that all Man's reason has done for him
is to make him beastlier than any beast. One splendid
body is worth the brains of a hundred dyspeptic, flatulent
philosophers.

DON JUAN. You forget that brainless magnificence of body
has been tried. Things immeasurably greater than man
in every respect but brain have existed and perished. The
megatherium, the ichthyosaurus have paced the earth
with seven-league steps and hidden the day with cloud
vast wings. Where are they now? Fossils in museums, and
so few and imperfect at that, that a knuckle bone or a
tooth of one of them is prized beyond the lives of a
thousand soldiers. These things lived and wanted to live:
but for lack of brains they did not know how to carry
out their purpose, and so destroyed themselves.

THE DEVIL. And is Man any the less destroying himself for
all this boasted brain of his? Have you walked up and
down upon the earth lately? I have; and I have examined
Man's wonderful inventions. And I tell you that in the
arts of life man invents nothing; but in the arts of death
he outdoes Nature herself, and produces by chemistry
and machinery all the slaughter of plague, pestilence, and
famine. The peasant I tempt today eats and drinks what
was eaten and drunk by the peasants of ten thousand
years ago; and the house he lives in has not altered as
much in a thousand centuries as the fashion of a lady's
bonnet in a score of weeks. But when he goes out to
slay, he carries a marvel of mechanism that lets loose at
the touch of his finger all the hidden molecular energies,
and leaves the javelin, the arrow, the blowpipe of his
fathers far behind. In the arts of peace Man is a bungler. I have seen his cotton factories and the like, with

machinery that a greedy dog could have invented if it had wanted money instead of food. I know his clumsy typewriters and bungling locomotives and tedious bicycles: they are toys compared to the Maxim gun, the submarine torpedo boat. There is nothing in Man's industrial machinery but his greed and sloth: his heart is in his weapons. This marvellous force of Life of which you boast is a force of Death: Man measures his strength by his destructiveness. What is his religion? An excuse for hating me. What is his law? An excuse for hanging you. What is his morality? Gentility! an excuse for consuming without producing. What is his art? An excuse for gloating over pictures of slaughter. What are his politics? Either the worship of a despot because a despot can kill, or parliamentary cock-fighting. I spent an evening lately in a certain celebrated legislature, and heard the pot lecturing the kettle for its blackness, and ministers answering questions. When I left I chalked up on the door the old nursery saying "Ask no questions and you will be told no lies." I bought a sixpenny family magazine, and found it full of pictures of young men shooting and stabbing one another. I saw a man die: he was a London bricklayer's laborer with seven children. He left seventeen pounds club money; and his wife spent it all on his funeral and went into the workhouse with the children next day. She would not have spent sevenpence on her children's schooling: the law had to force her to let them be taught gratuitously; but on death she spent all she had. Their imagination glows, their energies rise up at the idea of death, these people: they love it; and the more horrible it is the more they enjoy it. Hell is a place far above their comprehension: they derive their notion of it from two of the greatest fools that ever lived, an Italian and an Englishman. The Italian described it as a place of mud, frost, filth, fire, and venomous serpents: all torture. This ass, when he was not lying about me, was maundering about some woman whom he saw once in the street. The Englishman described me as being expelled from Heaven by cannons and gunpowder; and to this day every Briton believes that the whole of his

silly story is in the Bible. What else he says I do not
know; for it is all in a long poem which neither I nor
anyone else ever succeeded in wading through. It is the
same in everything. The highest form of literature is the
tragedy, a play in which everybody is murdered at the
end. In the old chronicles you read of earthquakes and
pestilences, and are told that these shewed the power and
majesty of God and the littleness of Man. Nowadays
the chronicles describe battles. In a battle two bodies
of men shoot at one another with bullets and explosive
shells until one body runs away, when the others chase
the fugitives on horseback and cut them to pieces as
they fly. And this, the chronicle concludes, shews the
greatness and majesty of empires, and the littleness of
the vanquished. Over such battles the people run about
the streets yelling with delight, and egg their Governments on to spend hundreds of millions of money in the
slaughter, whilst the strongest Ministers dare not spend
an extra penny in the pound against the poverty and
pestilence through which they themselves daily walk. I
could give you a thousand instances; but they all come
to the same thing: the power that governs the earth is
not the power of Life but of Death; and the inner need
that has nerved Life to the effort of organizing itself
into the human being is not the need for higher life but
for a more efficient engine of destruction. The plague,
the famine, the earthquake, the tempest were too spas-
modic in their action; the tiger and crocodile were too
easily satiated and not cruel enough: something more
constantly, more ruthlessly, more ingeniously destructive
was needed; and that something was Man, the inventor
of the rack, the stake, the gallows, the electric chair; of
sword and gun and poison gas: above all, of justice, duty,
patriotism, and all the other isms by which even those
who are clever enough to be humanely disposed are persuaded to become the most destructive of all the de-
stroyers.

DON JUAN. Pshaw! all this is old. Your weak side, my
diabolic friend, is that you have always been a gull: you
take Man at his own valuation. Nothing would flatter

him more than your opinion of him. He loves to think of himself as bold and bad. He is neither one nor the other: he is only a coward. Call him tyrant, murderer, pirate, bully; and he will adore you, and swagger about with the consciousness of having the blood of the old sea kings in his veins. Call him liar and thief; and he will only take an action against you for libel. But call him coward; and he will go mad with rage: he will face death to outface that stinging truth. Man gives every reason for his conduct save one, every excuse for his crimes save one, every plea for his safety save one: and that one is his cowardice. Yet all his civilization is founded on his cowardice, on his abject tameness, which he calls his respectability. There are limits to what a mule or an ass will stand; but Man will suffer himself to be degraded until his vileness becomes so loathsome to his oppressors that they themselves are forced to reform it.

THE DEVIL. Precisely. And these are the creatures in whom you discover what you call a Life Force!

DON JUAN. Yes; for now comes the most surprising part of the whole business.

THE STATUE. Whats that?

DON JUAN. Why, that you can make any of these cowards brave by simply putting an idea into his head.

THE STATUE. Stuff! As an old soldier I admit the cowardice: it's as universal as sea sickness, and matters just as little. But that about putting an idea into a man's head is stuff and nonsense. In a battle all you need to make you fight is a little hot blood and the knowledge that it's more dangerous to lose than to win.

DON JUAN. That is perhaps why battles are so useless. But men never really overcome fear until they imagine they are fighting to further a universal purpose—fighting for an idea, as they call it. Why was the Crusader braver than the pirate? Because he fought, not for himself, but for the Cross. What force was it that met him with a valor as reckless as his own? The force of men who fought, not for themselves, but for Islam. They took Spain from us, though we were fighting for our very hearths and homes; but when we, too, fought for that

mighty idea, a Catholic Church, we swept them back
to Africa.

THE DEVIL [*ironically*] What! you a Catholic, Señor Don
Juan! A devotee! My congratulations.

THE STATUE [*seriously*] Come, come! as a soldier, I can
listen to nothing against the Church.

DON JUAN. Have no fear, Commander: this idea of a
Catholic Church will survive Islam, will survive the
Cross, will survive even that vulgar pageant of incom-
petent schoolboyish gladiators which you call the Army.

THE STATUE. Juan: you will force me to call you to account
for this.

DON JUAN. Useless: I cannot fence. Every idea for which
Man will die will be a Catholic idea. When the Spaniard
learns at last that he is no better than the Saracen, and
his prophet no better than Mahomet, he will arise, more
Catholic than ever, and die on a barricade across the
filthy slum he starves in, for universal liberty and equality.

THE STATUE. Bosh!

DON JUAN. What you call bosh is the only thing men dare
die for. Later on, Liberty will not be Catholic enough:
men will die for human perfection, to which they will
sacrifice all their liberty gladly.

THE DEVIL. Ay: they will never be at a loss for an excuse
for killing one another.

DON JUAN. What of this? It is not death that matters, but
the fear of death. It is not killing and dying that degrades
us, but base living, and accepting the wages and profits
of degradation. Better ten dead men than one live slave
or his master. Men shall yet rise up, father against son
and brother against brother, and kill one another for
the great Catholic idea of abolishing slavery.

THE DEVIL. Yes, when the Liberty and Equality of which
you prate shall have made free white Christians cheaper
in the labor market than black heathen slaves sold by
auction at the block.

DON JUAN. Never fear! the white laborer shall have his
turn too. But I am not now defending the illusory forms
the great ideas take. I am giving you examples of the

fact that this creature Man, who in his own selfish affairs is a coward to the backbone, will fight for an idea like a hero. He may be abject as a citizen; but he is dangerous as a fanatic. He can only be enslaved whilst he is spiritually weak enough to listen to reason. I tell you, gentlemen, if you can shew a man a piece of what he now calls God's work to do, and what he will later on call by many new names, you can make him entirely reckless of the consequences to himself personally.

ANA. Yes: he shirks all his responsibilities, and leaves his wife to grapple with them.

THE STATUE. Well said, daughter. Do not let him talk you out of your common sense.

THE DEVIL. Alas! Señor Commander, now that we have got on to the subject of Woman, he will talk more than ever. However, I confess it is for me the one supremely interesting subject.

DON JUAN. To a woman, Señora, man's duties and responsibilities begin and end with the task of getting bread for her children. To her, Man is only a means to the end of getting children and rearing them.

ANA. Is that your idea of a woman's mind? I call it cynical and disgusting animalism.

DON JUAN. Pardon me, Ana: I said nothing about a woman's whole mind. I spoke of her view of Man as a separate sex. It is no more cynical than her view of herself as above all things a Mother. Sexually, Woman is Nature's contrivance for perpetuating its highest achievement. Sexually, Man is Woman's contrivance for fulfilling Nature's behest in the most economical way. She knows by instinct that far back in the evolutional process she invented him, differentiated him, created him in order to produce something better than the single-sexed process can produce. Whilst he fulfils the purpose for which she made him, he is welcome to his dreams, his follies, his ideals, his heroisms, provided that the keystone of them all is the worship of woman, of motherhood, of the family, of the hearth. But how rash and dangerous it was to invent a separate creature whose sole function was her own impregnation! For mark what has happened. First Man has multiplied on her hands until there are as many men as women; she that has been unable to employ for her purposes more than a fraction of the immense energy she has left at his disposal by saving him the exhausting labor of gestation. This superfluous energy has gone to his brain and to his muscle. He has become too strong to be controlled by her bodily, and too imaginative and mentally vigorous to be content with mere self-reproduction. He has created civilization without consulting her, taking her domestic labor for granted as the foundation of it.

ANA. That is true, at all events.

THE DEVIL. Yes; and this civilization! what is it, after all?

DON JUAN. After all, an excellent peg to hang your cynical commonplaces on; but before all, it is an attempt on Man's part to make himself something more than the mere instrument of Woman's purpose. So far, the result of Life's continual effort not only to maintain itself, but to achieve higher and higher organization and completer self-consciousness, is only, at best, a doubtful campaign between its forces and those of Death and Degeneration. The battles in this campaign are mere blunders, mostly won, like actual military battles, in spite of the commanders.

THE STATUE. That is a dig at me. No matter: go on, go on.

DON JUAN. It is a dig at a much higher power than you, Commander. Still, you must have noticed in your profession that even a stupid general can win battles when the enemy's general is a little stupider.

THE STATUE [*very seriously*] Most true, Juan, most true. Some donkeys have amazing luck.

DON JUAN. Well, the Life Force is stupid; but it is not so stupid as the forces of Death and Degeneration. Besides, these are in its pay all the time. And so Life wins, after a fashion. What mere copiousness of fecundity can supply and mere greed preserve, we possess. The survival of whatever form of civilization can produce the best rifle and the best fed riflemen is assured.

THE DEVIL. Exactly! the survival, not of the most effective means of Life but of the most effective means of Death.

You always come back to my point, in spite of your wrigglings and evasions and sophistries, not to mention the intolerable length of your speeches.

DON JUAN. Oh, come! who began making long speeches? However, if I overtax your intellect, you can leave us and seek the society of love and beauty and the rest of your favorite boredoms.

THE DEVIL [*much offended*] This is not fair, Don Juan, and not civil. I am also on the intellectual plane. Nobody can appreciate it more than I do. I am arguing fairly with you, and, I think, successfully refuting you. Let us go on for another hour if you like.

DON JUAN. Good: let us.

THE STATUE: Not that I see any prospect of your coming to any point in particular, Juan. Still, since in this place, instead of merely killing time we have to kill eternity, go ahead by all means.

DON JUAN [*somewhat impatiently*] My point, you marble-headed old masterpiece, is only a step ahead of you. Are we agreed that Life is a force which has made innumerable experiments in organizing itself; that the mammoth and the man, the mouse and the megatherium, the flies and the fleas and the Fathers of the Church, are all more or less successful attempts to build up that raw force into higher and higher individuals, the ideal individual being omnipotent, omniscient, infallible, and withal completely, unilludedly self-conscious: in short, a god?

THE DEVIL. I agree, for the sake of argument.

THE STATUE. I agree, for the sake of avoiding argument.

ANA. I most emphatically disagree as regards the Fathers of the Church; and I must beg you not to drag them into the argument.

DON JUAN. I did so purely for the sake of alliteration, Ana; and I shall make no further allusion to them. And now, since we are, with that exception, agreed so far, will you not agree with me further that Life has not measured the success of its attempts at godhead by the beauty or bodily perfection of the result, since in both these respects the birds, as our friend Aristophanes long ago pointed out, are so extraordinarily superior, with their power of flight

and their lovely plumage, and, may I add, the touching
poetry of their loves and nestings, that it is inconceivable
that Life, having once produced them, should, if love
and beauty were her object, start off on another line and
labor at the clumsy elephant and the hideous ape, whose
grandchildren we are?

ANA. Aristophanes was a heathen; and you, Juan, I am
afraid, are very little better.

THE DEVIL. You conclude, then, that Life was driving at
clumsiness and ugliness?

DON JUAN. No, perverse devil that you are, a thousand
times no. Life was driving at brains—at its darling
object: an organ by which it can attain not only self-
consciousness but self-understanding.

THE STATUE. This is metaphysics, Juan. Why the devil
should—[to the Devil] I beg your pardon.

THE DEVIL. Pray dont mention it. I have always regarded
the use of my name to secure additional emphasis as
a high compliment to me. It is quite at your service,
Commander.

THE STATUE. Thank you: thats very good of you. Even in
Heaven, I never quite got out of my old military habits
of speech. What I was going to ask Juan was why Life
should bother itself about getting a brain. Why should
it want to understand itself? Why not be content to
enjoy itself?

DON JUAN. Without a brain, Commander, you would enjoy
yourself without knowing it, and so lose all the fun.

THE STATUE. True, most true. But I am quite content with
brain enough to know that I'm enjoying myself. I dont
want to understand why. In fact, I'd rather not. My experience is that one's pleasures dont bear thinking about.

DON JUAN. That is why intellect is so unpopular. But to
Life, the force behind the Man, intellect is a necessity,
because without it he blunders into death. Just as Life,
after ages of struggle, evolved that wonderful bodily
organ the eye, so that the living organism could see
where it was going and what was coming to help or
threaten it, and thus avoid a thousand dangers that
formerly slew it, so it is evolving today a mind's eye that

shall see, not the physical world, but the purpose of
Life, and thereby enable the individual to work for that
purpose instead of thwarting and baffling it by setting up
shortsighted personal aims as at present. Even as it is,
only one sort of man has ever been happy, has ever
been universally respected among all the conflicts of
interests and illusions.

THE STATUE. You mean the military man.

DON JUAN. Commander: I do n o t mean the military man.
When the military man approaches, the world locks up
its spoons and packs off its womankind. No: I sing, not
arms and the hero, but the philosophic man: he who
seeks in contemplation to discover the inner will of the
world, in invention to discover the means of fulfilling that
will, and in action to do that will by the so-discovered
means. Of all other sorts of men I declare myself tired.
They are tedious failures. When I was on earth, professors of all sorts prowled round me feeling for an unhealthy spot in me on which they could fasten. The doctors of medicine bade me consider what I must do to
save my body, and offered me quack cures for imaginary
diseases. I replied that I was not a hypochondriac; so
they called me Ignoramus and went their way. The doctors of divinity bade me consider what I must do to
save my soul; but I was not a spiritual hypochondriac any
more than a bodily one, and would not trouble myself
about that either; so they called me Atheist and went
their way. After them came the politician, who said
there was only one purpose in nature, and that was to
get him into parliament. I told him I did not care whether
he got into parliament or not; so he called me Mugwump
and went his way. Then came the romantic man, the
Artist, with his love songs and his paintings and his
poems; and with him I had great delight for many years,
and some profit; for I cultivated my senses for his sake;
and his songs taught me to hear better, his paintings to
see better, and his poems to feel more deeply. But he
led me at last into the worship of Woman.

ANA. Juan!

DON JUAN. Yes: I came to believe that in her voice was all

the music of the song, in her face all the beauty of the
painting, and in her soul all the emotion of the poem.

ANA. And you were disappointed, I suppose. Well, was it
her fault that you attributed all these perfections to her?

DON JUAN. Yes, partly. For with a wonderful instinctive
cunning, she kept silent and allowed me to glorify her: to
mistake my own visions, thoughts, and feelings for hers.
Now my friend the romantic man was often too poor or
too timid to approach those women who were beautiful
or refined enough to seem to realize his ideal; and so he
went to his grave believing in his dream. But I was more
favored by nature and circumstance. I was of noble
birth and rich; and when my person did not please, my
conversation flattered, though I generally found myself
fortunate in both.

THE STATUE. Coxcomb!

DON JUAN. Yes; but even my coxcombry pleased. Well, I
found that when I had touched a woman's imagination,
she would allow me to persuade myself that she loved
me; but when my suit was granted she never said "I am
happy; my love is satisfied": she always said, first, "At
last, the barriers are down," and second, "When will you
come again?"

ANA. That is exactly what men say.

DON JUAN. I protest I never said it. But all women say it.
Well, these two speeches always alarmed me; for the first
meant that the lady's impulse had been solely to throw
down my fortifications and gain my citadel; and the
second openly announced that henceforth she regarded
me as her property, and counted my time as already
wholly at her disposal.

THE DEVIL. That is where your want of heart came in.

THE STATUE [shaking his head] You shouldnt repeat what a
woman says, Juan.

ANA [severely] It should be sacred to you.

THE STATUE. Still, they certainly do say it. I never minded
the barriers; but there was always a slight shock about
the other, unless one was very hard hit indeed.

DON JUAN. Then the lady, who had been happy and idle
enough before, became anxious, preoccupied with me,

always intriguing, conspiring, pursuing, watching, waiting, bent wholly on making sure of her prey: I being the prey, you understand. Now this was not what I had bargained for. It may have been very proper and very natural; but it was not music, painting, poetry, and joy incarnated in a beautiful woman. I ran away from it. I ran away from it very often: in fact I became famous for running away from it.

ANA. Infamous, you mean.

DON JUAN. I did not run away from you. Do you blame me for running away from the others?

ANA. Nonsense, man. You are talking to a woman of 77 now. If you had had the chance, you would have run away from me too—if I had let you. You would not have found it so easy with me as with some of the others. If men will not be faithful to their home and their duties, they must be made to be. I daresay you all want to marry lovely incarnations of music and painting and poetry. Well, you cant have them, because they dont exist. If flesh and blood is not good enough for you, you must go without: thats all. Women have to put up with flesh-and-blood husbands—and little enough of that too, sometimes; and you will have to put up with flesh-and-blood wives. [*The Devil looks dubious. The Statue makes a wry face.*] I see you dont like that, any of you; but it's true, for all that; so if you dont like it, you can lump it.

DON JUAN. My dear lady, you have put my whole case against romance into a few sentences. That is just why I turned my back on the romantic man with the artist nature, as he called his infatuation. I thanked him for teaching me to use my eyes and ears; but I told him that his beauty worshipping and happiness hunting and woman idealizing was not worth a dump as a philosophy of life; so he called me Philistine and went his way.

ANA. It seems that Woman taught you something, too, with all her defects.

DON JUAN. She did more: she interpreted all the other teaching for me. Ah, my friends, when the barriers were down for the first time, what an astounding illumination!

I had been prepared for infatuation, for intoxication, for all the illusions of love's young dream; and lo! never was my perception clearer, nor my criticism more ruthless. The most jealous rival of my mistress never saw every blemish in her more keenly than I. I was not duped: I took her without chloroform.

ANA. But you did take her.

DON JUAN. That was the revelation. Up to that moment I had never lost the sense of being my own master; never consciously taken a single step until my reason had examined and approved it. I had come to believe that I was a purely rational creature: a thinker! I said, with the foolish philosopher, "I think; therefore I am." It was Woman who taught me to say "I am; therefore I think." And also "I would think more; therefore I must be more."

THE STATUE. This is extremely abstract and metaphysical, Juan. If you would stick to the concrete, and put your discoveries in the form of entertaining anecdotes about your adventures with women, your conversation would be easier to follow.

DON JUAN. Bah! what need I add? Do you not understand that when I stood face to face with Woman, every fibre in my clear critical brain warned me to spare her and save myself. My morals said No. My conscience said No. My chivalry and pity for her said No. My prudent regard for myself said No. My ear, practised on a thousand songs and symphonies; my eye, exercised on a thousand paintings; tore her voice, her features, her color to shreds. I caught all those tell-tale resemblances to her father and mother by which I knew what she would be like in thirty years' time. I noted the gleam of gold from a dead tooth in the laughing mouth: I made curious observations of the strange odors of the chemistry of the nerves. The visions of my romantic reveries, in which I had trod the plains of Heaven with a deathless, ageless creature of coral and ivory, deserted me in that supreme hour. I remembered them and desperately strove to recover their illusion; but they now seemed the emptiest of inventions: my judgment was not to be corrupted: my brain still said

No on every issue. And whilst I was in the act of framing my excuse to the lady, Life seized me and threw me into her arms as a sailor throws a scrap of fish into the mouth of a seabird.

THE STATUE. You might as well have gone without thinking such a lot about it, Juan. You are like all the clever men: you have more brains than is good for you.

THE DEVIL. And were you not the happier for the experience, Señor Don Juan?

DON JUAN. The happier, no: the wiser, yes. That moment introduced me for the first time to myself, and, through myself, to the world. I saw then how useless it is to attempt to impose conditions on the irresistible force of Life; to preach prudence, careful selection, virtue, honor, chastity—

ANA. Don Juan: a word against chastity is an insult to me.

DON JUAN. I say nothing against your chastity, Señora, since it took the form of a husband and twelve children. What more could you have done had you been the most abandoned of women?

ANA. I could have had twelve husbands and no children: thats what I could have done, Juan. And let me tell you that that would have made all the difference to the earth which I replenished.

THE STATUE. Bravo Ana! Juan, you are floored, quelled, annihilated.

DON JUAN. No: for though that difference is the true essential difference—Doña Ana has, I admit, gone straight to the real point—yet it is not a difference of love or chastity, or even constancy; for twelve children by twelve different husbands would have replenished the earth perhaps more effectively. Suppose my friend Ottavio had died when you were thirty, you would never have remained a widow: you were too beautiful. Suppose the successor of Ottavio had died when you were forty, you would still have been irresistible; and a woman who marries twice marries three times if she becomes free to do so. Twelve lawful children borne by one highly respectable lady to three different fathers is not impossible nor condemned by public opinion. That such a lady may

be more law abiding than the poor girl whom we used
to spurn into the gutter for bearing one unlawful infant
is no doubt true; but dare you say she is less self-
indulgent?

ANA. She is more virtuous: that is enough for me.

DON JUAN. In that case, what is virtue but the Trade
Unionism of the married? Let us face the facts, dear Ana.
The Life Force respects marriage only because marriage
is a contrivance of its own to secure the greatest number
of children and the closest care of them. For honor,
chastity, and all the rest of your moral figments it cares
not a rap. Marriage is the most licentious of human
institutions—

ANA. Juan!

THE STATUE [*protesting*] Really!—

DON JUAN [*determinedly*] I say the most licentious of
human institutions: that is the secret of its popularity.
And a woman seeking a husband is the most unscrupu-
lous of all the beasts of prey. The confusion of marriage
with morality has done more to destroy the conscience
of the human race than any other single error. Come,
Ana! do not look shocked: you know better than any of
us that marriage is a mantrap baited with simulated accomplishments and delusive idealizations. When your
sainted mother, by dint of scoldings and punishments,
forced you to learn how to play half a dozen pieces on
the spinet—which she hated as much as you did—had
she any other purpose than to delude your suitors into
the belief that your husband would have in his home
an angel who would fill it with melody, or at least play
him to sleep after dinner? You married my friend
Ottavio: well, did you ever open the spinet from the
hour when the Church united him to you?

ANA. You are a fool, Juan. A young married woman has
something else to do than sit at the spinet without any
support for her back; so she gets out of the habit of
playing.

DON JUAN. Not if she loves music. No: believe me, she
only throws away the bait when the bird is in the net.

ANA [*bitterly*] And men, I suppose, never throw off the

mask when their bird is in the net. The husband never
becomes negligent, selfish, brutal—oh, never!

DON JUAN. What do these recriminations prove, Ana? Only
that the hero is as gross an imposture as the heroine.

ANA. It is all nonsense: most marriages are perfectly comfortable.

DON JUAN. "Perfectly" is a strong expression, Ana. What
you mean is that sensible people make the best of one
another. Send me to the galleys and chain me to the
felon whose number happens to be next before mine;
and I must accept the inevitable and make the best of
the companionship. Many such companionships, they
tell me, are touchingly affectionate; and most are at least
tolerably friendly. But that does not make a chain a
desirable ornament nor the galleys an abode of bliss.
Those who talk most about the blessings of marriage
and the constancy of its vows are the very people who
declare that if the chain were broken and the prisoners
left free to choose, the whole social fabric would fly
asunder. You cannot have the argument both ways. If
the prisoner is happy, why lock him in? If he is not, why
pretend that he is?

ANA. At all events, let me take an old woman's privilege
again, and tell you flatly that marriage peoples the world
and debauchery does not.

DON JUAN. How if a time come when this shall cease to
be true? Do you not know that where there is a will
there is a way? that whatever Man really wishes to do
he will finally discover a means of doing? Well, you have
done your best, you virtuous ladies, and others of your
way of thinking, to bend Man's mind wholly towards
honorable love as the highest good, and to understand
by honorable love romance and beauty and happiness in
the possession of beautiful, refined, delicate, affectionate
women. You have taught women to value their own
youth, health, shapeliness, and refinement above all
things. Well, what place have squalling babies and household cares in this exquisite paradise of the senses and
emotions? Is it not the inevitable end of it all that the
human will shall say to the human brain: Invent me a

means by which I can have love, beauty, romance, emotion, passion, without their wretched penalties, their expenses, their worries, their trials, their illnesses and agonies and risks of death, their retinue of servants and nurses and doctors and schoolmasters.

THE DEVIL. All this, Señor Don Juan, is realized here in my realm.

DON JUAN. Yes, at the cost of death. Man will not take it at that price: he demands the romantic delights of your Hell whilst he is still on earth. Well, the means will be found: the brain will not fail when the will is in earnest. The day is coming when great nations will find their numbers dwindling from census to census; when the six roomed villa will rise in price above the family mansion; when the viciously reckless poor and the stupidly pious rich will delay the extinction of the race only by degrading it; whilst the boldly prudent, the thriftily selfish and ambitious, the imaginative and poetic, the lovers of money and solid comfort, the worshippers of success, of art, and of love, will all oppose to the Force of Life the device of sterility.

THE STATUE. That is all very eloquent, my young friend; but if you had lived to Ana's age, or even to mine, you would have learned that the people who get rid of the fear of poverty and children and all the other family troubles, and devote themselves to having a good time of it, only leave their minds free for the fear of old age and ugliness and impotence and death. The childless laborer is more tormented by his wife's idleness and her constant demands for amusement and distraction than he could be by twenty children; and his wife is more wretched than he. I have had my share of vanity; for as a young man I was admired by women; and as a statue I am praised by art critics. But I confess that had I found nothing to do in the world but wallow in these delights I should have cut my throat. When I married Ana's mother—or perhaps, to be strictly correct, I should rather say when I at last gave in and allowed Ana's mother to marry me—I knew that I was planting thorns in my pillow, and that marriage for me, a swaggering young officer thitherto unvanquished, meant defeat and capture.

ANA [*scandalized*] Father!

THE STATUE. I am sorry to shock you, my love; but since Juan has stripped every rag of decency from the discussion I may as well tell the frozen truth.

ANA. Hmf! I suppose I was one of the thorns.

THE STATUE. By no means: you were often a rose. You see, your mother had most of the trouble you gave.

DON JUAN. Then may I ask, Commander, why you have left Heaven to come here and wallow, as you express it, in sentimental beatitudes which you confess would once have driven you to cut your throat?

THE STATUE [*struck by this*] Egad, thats true.

THE DEVIL [*alarmed*] What! You are going back from your word! [*To Don Juan*] And all your philosophizing has been nothing but a mask for proselytizing! [*To the Statue*] Have you forgotten already the hideous dullness from which I am offering you a refuge here? [*To Don Juan*] And does your demonstration of the approaching sterilization and extinction of mankind lead to anything better than making the most of those pleasures of art and love which you yourself admit refined you, elevated you, developed you?

DON JUAN. I never demonstrated the extinction of mankind. Life cannot will its own extinction either in its blind amorphous state or in any of the forms into which it has organized itself. I had not finished when His Excellency interrupted me.

THE STATUE. I begin to doubt whether you ever will finish, my friend. You are extremely fond of hearing yourself talk.

DON JUAN. True; but since you have endured so much, you may as well endure to the end. Long before this sterilization which I described becomes more than a clearly foreseen possibility, the reaction will begin. The great central purpose of breeding the race: ay, breeding it to heights now deemed superhuman: that purpose which is now hidden in a mephitic cloud of love and romance and prudery and fastidiousness, will break

through into clear sunlight as a purpose no longer to be
confused with the gratification of personal fancies, the
impossible realization of boys' and girls' dreams of bliss,
or the need of older people for companionship or money.
The plain-spoken marriage services of the vernacular
Churches will no longer be abbreviated and half suppressed as indelicate. The sober decency, earnestness,
and authority of their declaration of the real purpose of
marriage will be honored and accepted, whilst their
romantic vowings and pledging and until-death-do-us-
partings and the like will be expunged as unbearable
frivolities. Do my sex the justice to admit, Señora, that
we have always recognized that the sex relation is not
a personal or friendly relation at all.

ANA. Not a personal or friendly relation! What relation is
more personal? more sacred? more holy?

DON JUAN. Sacred and holy, if you like, Ana, but not personally friendly. Your relation to God is sacred and holy:
dare you call it personally friendly? In the sex relation
the universal creative energy, of which the parties are
both the helpless agents, overrides and sweeps away all
personal consideration, and dispenses with all personal
relations. The pair may be utter strangers to one another,
speaking different languages, differing in race and color,
in age and disposition, with no bond between them but a
possibility of that fecundity for the sake of which the Life
Force throws them into one another's arms at the exchange of a glance. Do we not recognize this by allowing
marriages to be made by parents without consulting the
woman? Have you not often expressed your disgust at the
immorality of the English nation, in which women and
men of noble birth become acquainted and court each
other like peasants? And how much does even the peasant
know of his bride or she of him before he engages
himself? Why, you would not make a man your lawyer
or your family doctor on so slight an acquaintance as you
would fall in love with and marry him!

ANA. Yes, Juan, we know the libertine's philosophy. Always
ignore the consequences to the woman.

DON JUAN. The consequences, yes: they justify her fierce

grip of the man. But surely you do not call that attachment a sentimental one. As well call the policeman's
attachment to his prisoner a love relation.

ANA. You see you have to confess that marriage is necessary,
though, according to you, love is the slightest of all
human relations.

DON JUAN. How do you know that it is not the greatest of
all human relations? far too great to be a personal matter. Could your father have served his country if he had
refused to kill any enemy of Spain unless he personally
hated him? Can a woman serve her country if she refuses
to marry any man she does not personally love? You
know it is not so: the woman of noble birth marries as
the man of noble birth fights, on political and family
grounds, not on personal ones.

THE STATUE [*impressed*] A very clever point that, Juan: I
must think it over. You are really full of ideas. How did
you come to think of this one?

DON JUAN. I learnt it by experience. When I was on earth,
and made those proposals to ladies which, though universally condemned, have made me so interesting a hero
of legend, I was not infrequently met in some such way
as this. The lady would say that she would countenance
my advances, provided they were honorable. On inquir-
ing what that proviso meant, I found that it meant that I
proposed to get possession of her property if she had any,
or to undertake her support for life if she had not; that
I desired her continual companionship, counsel, and conversation to the end of my days, and would take a most
solemn oath to be always enraptured by them: above all,
that I would turn my back on all other women for ever
for her sake. I did not object to these conditions because
they were exorbitant and inhuman: it was their extraordinary irrelevance that prostrated me. I invariably
replied with perfect frankness that I had never dreamt of
any of these things; that unless the lady's character and
intellect were equal or superior to my own, her conversation must degrade and her counsel mislead me; that
her constant companionship might, for all I knew, become intolerably tedious to me; that I could not answer

for my feelings for a week in advance, much less to the
end of my life; that to cut me off from all natural and
unconstrained intercourse with half my fellowcreatures
would narrow and warp me if I submitted to it, and if
not, would bring me under the curse of clandestinity;
that, finally, my proposals to her were wholly unconnected with any of these matters, and were the outcome
of a perfectly simple impulse of my manhood towards
her womanhood.

ANA. You mean that it was an immoral impulse.

DON JUAN. Nature, my dear lady, is what you call immoral. I blush for it; but I cannot help it. Nature is a
pandar, Time a wrecker, and Death a murderer. I have
always preferred to stand up to those facts and build institutions on their recognition. You prefer to propitiate
the three devils by proclaiming their chastity, their thrift,
and their loving kindness; and to base your institutions
on these flatteries. Is it any wonder that the institutions
do not work smoothly?

THE STATUE. What used the ladies to say, Juan?

DON JUAN. Oh, come! Confidence for confidence. First tell
me what you used to say to the ladies.

THE STATUE. I! Oh, I swore that I would be faithful to the
death; that I should die if they refused me; that no
woman could ever be to me what she was—

ANA. She! Who?

THE STATUE. Whoever it happened to be at the time, my
dear. I had certain things I always said. One of them was
that even when I was eighty, one white hair of the
woman I loved would make me tremble more than the
thickest gold tress from the most beautiful young head.
Another was that I could not bear the thought of anyone else being the mother of my children.

DON JUAN [*revolted*] You old rascal!

THE STATUE [*stoutly*] Not a bit; for I really believed it with
all my soul at the moment. I had a heart: not like you.
And it was this sincerity that made me successful.

DON JUAN. Sincerity! To be fool enough to believe a
ramping, stamping, thumping lie: that is what you call

sincerity! To be so greedy for a woman that you deceive
yourself in your eagerness to deceive her: sincerity, you
call it!

THE STATUE. Oh, damn your sophistries! I was a man in
love, not a lawyer. And the women loved me for it,
bless them!

DON JUAN. They made you think so. What will you say
when I tell you that though I played the lawyer so callously, they made me think so too? I also had my moments of infatuation in which I gushed nonsense and
believed it. Sometimes the desire to give pleasure by
saying beautiful things so rose in me on the flood of
emotion that I said them recklessly. At other times I
argued against myself with a devilish coldness that drew
tears. But I found it just as hard to escape when I was
cruel as when I was kind. When the lady's instinct was
set on me, there was nothing for it but lifelong servitude
or flight.

ANA. You dare boast, before me and my father, that every
woman found you irresistible.

DON JUAN. Am I boasting? It seems to me that I cut the
most pitiable of figures. Besides, I said 'when the lady's
instinct was set on me'. It was not always so; and then,
heavens! what transports of virtuous indignation! what
overwhelming definance to the dastardly seducer! what
scenes of Imogen and Iachimo!

ANA. I made no scenes. I simply called my father.

DON JUAN. And he came, sword in hand, to vindicate outraged honor and morality by murdering me.

THE STATUE. Murdering! What do you mean? Did I kill
you or did you kill me?

DON JUAN. Which of us was the better fencer?

THE STATUE. I was.

DON JUAN. Of course you were. And yet you, the hero of
those scandalous adventures you have just been relating
to us, you had the effrontery to pose as the avenger of
outraged morality and condemn me to death! You would
have slain me but for an accident.

THE STATUE. I was expected to, Juan. That is how things

were arranged on earth. I was not a social reformer; and
I always did what it was customary for a gentleman to
do.

DON JUAN. That may account for your attacking me, but
not for the revolting hypocrisy of your subsequent proceedings as a statue.

THE STATUE. That all came of my going to Heaven.

THE DEVIL. I still fail to see, Señor Don Juan, that these
episodes in your earthly career and in that of the Señor
Commander in any way discredit my view of life. Here, I
repeat, you have all that you sought without anything
that you shrank from.

DON JUAN. On the contrary, here I have everything that
disappointed me without anything that I have not already
tried and found wanting. I tell you that as long as I can
conceive something better than myself I cannot be easy
unless I am striving to bring it into existence or clearing
the way for it. That is the law of my life. That is the
working within me of Life's incessant aspiration to
higher organization, wider, deeper, intenser self-consciousness, and clearer self-understanding. It was the supremacy of this purpose that reduced love for me to the
mere pleasure of a moment, art for me to the mere
schooling of my faculties, religion for me to a mere
excuse for laziness, since it had set up a God who looked
at the world and saw it was good, against the instinct in
me that looked through my eyes at the world and saw
that it could be improved. I tell you that in the pursuit
of my own pleasure, my own health, my own fortune,
I have never known happiness. It was not love for
Woman that delivered me into her hands: it was fatigue,
exhaustion. When I was a child, and bruised my head
against a stone, I ran to the nearest woman and cried
away my pain against her apron. When I grew up, and
bruised my soul against the brutalities and stupidities
with which I had to strive, I did again just what I had
done as a child. I have enjoyed, too, my rests, my
recuperations, my breathing times, my very prostrations
after strife; but rather would I be dragged through all

the circles of the foolish Italian's Inferno than through the pleasures of Europe. That is what has made this place of eternal pleasures so deadly to me. It is the absence of this instinct in you that makes you that strange monster called a Devil. It is the success with which you have diverted the attention of men from their real purpose, which in one degree or another is the same as mine, to yours, that has earned you the name of The Tempter. It is the fact that they are doing your will, or rather drifting with your want of will, instead of doing their own, that makes them the uncomfortable, false, restless, artificial, petulant, wretched creatures they are.

THE DEVIL [*mortified*] Señor Don Juan: you are uncivil to my friends.

DON JUAN. Pooh! why should I be civil to them or to you? In this Palace of Lies a truth or two will not hurt you. Your friends are all the dullest dogs I know. They are not beautiful: they are only decorated. They are not clean: they are only shaved and starched. They are not dignified: they are only fashionably dressed. They are not educated: they are only college passmen. They are not religious: they are only pewrenters. They are not moral: they are only conventional. They are not virtuous: they are only cowardly. They are not even vicious: they are only "frail." They are not artistic: they are only lascivious. They are not prosperous: they are only rich. They are not loyal, they are only servile; not dutiful, only sheepish; not public spirited, only patriotic; not courageous, only quarrelsome; not determined, only obstinate; not masterful, only domineering; not self-controlled, only obtuse; not self-respecting, only vain; not kind, only sentimental; not social, only gregarious; not considerate, only polite; not intelligent, only opinionated; not progressive, only factious; not imaginative, only superstitious; not just, only vindictive; not generous, only propitiatory; not disciplined, only cowed; and not truthful at all: liars every one of them, to the very backbone of their souls.

THE STATUE. Your flow of words is simply amazing, Juan. How I wish I could have talked like that to my soldiers.

THE DEVIL. It is mere talk, though. It has all been said
before; but what change has it ever made? What notice
has the world ever taken of it?

DON JUAN. Yes, it is mere talk. But why is it mere talk?
Because, my friend, beauty, purity, respectability, religion, morality, art, patriotism, bravery, and the rest are
nothing but words which I or anyone else can turn inside
out like a glove. Were they realities you would have to
plead guilty to my indictment; but fortunately for your
self-respect, my diabolical friend, they are not realities.
As you say, they are mere words, useful for duping barbarians into adopting civilization, or the civilized poor
into submitting to be robbed and enslaved. That is the
family secret of the governing caste; and if we who are of
that caste aimed at more Life for the world instead of at
more power and luxury for our miserable selves, that
secret would make us great. Now, since I, being a
nobleman, am in the secret too, think how tedious to me
must be your unending cant about all these moralistic
figments, and how squalidly disastrous your sacrifice
of your lives to them! If you even believed in your moral
game enough to play it fairly, it would be interesting to
watch; but you dont: you cheat at every trick; and if
your opponent outcheats you, you upset the table and
try to murder him.

THE DEVIL. On earth there may be some truth in this,
because the people are uneducated and cannot appreciate my religion of love and beauty; but here—

DON JUAN. Oh yes: I know. Here there is nothing but love
and beauty. Ugh! it is like sitting for all eternity at the
first act of a fashionable play, before the complications
begin. Never in my worst moments of superstitious terror
on earth did I dream that Hell was so horrible. I live,
like a hairdresser, in the continual contemplation of
beauty, toying with silken tresses. I breathe an atmosphere of sweetness, like a confectioner's shopboy. Commander: a r e there any beautiful women in Heaven?

THE STATUE. None. Absolutely none. All dowdies. Not two
pennorth of jewellery among a dozen of them. They
might be men of fifty.

DON JUAN. I am impatient to get there. Is the word beauty
ever mentioned; and are there any artistic people?

THE STATUE. I give you my word they wont admire a fine
statue even when it walks past them.

DON JUAN. I go.

THE DEVIL. Don Juan: shall I be frank with you?

DON JUAN. Were you not so before?

THE DEVIL. As far as I went, yes. But I will now go
further, and confess to you that men get tired of everything, of Heaven no less than of Hell; and that all history
is nothing but a record of the oscillations of the world between these two extremes. An epoch is but a swing of the
pendulum; and each generation thinks the world is pro-
gressing because it is always moving. But when you are
as old as I am; when you have a thousand times wearied
of Heaven, like myself and the Commander, and a thousand times wearied of Hell, as you are wearied now, you
will no longer imagine that every swing from Heaven to
Hell is an emancipation, every swing from Hell to
Heaven an evolution. Where you now see reform, progress, fulfilment of upward tendency, continual ascent by
Man on the stepping stones of his dead selves to higher
things, you will see nothing but an infinite comedy of
illusion. You will discover the profound truth of the
saying of my friend Koheleth, that there is nothing new
under the sun. Vanitas vanitatum—

DON JUAN [out of all patience] By Heaven, this is worse
than your cant about love and beauty. Clever dolt that
you are, is a man no better than a worm, or a dog than a
wolf, because he gets tired of everything? Shall he give
up eating because he destroys his appetite in the act of
gratifying it? Is a field idle when it is fallow? Can the
Commander expend his hellish energy here without ac-
cumulating heavenly energy for his next term of blessed-
ness? Granted that the great Life Force has hit on the
device of the clockmaker's pendulum, and uses the
earth for its bob; that the history of each oscillation,
which seems so novel to us the actors, is but the history
of the last oscillation repeated; nay more, that in the un-
thinkable infinitude of time the sun throws off the earth

and catches it again a thousand times as a circus rider throws up a ball, and that our agelong epochs are but the moments between the toss and the catch, has the colossal mechanism no purpose?

THE DEVIL. None, my friend. You think, because you have a purpose, Nature must have one. You might as well expect it to have fingers and toes because you have them.

DON JUAN. But I should not have them if they served no purpose. And I, my friend, am as much a part of Nature as my own finger is a part of me. If my finger is the organ by which I grasp the sword and the mandoline, my brain is the organ by which Nature strives to understand itself. My dog's brain serves only my dog's purposes; but my own brain labors at a knowledge which does nothing for me personally but make my body bitter to me and my decay and death a calamity. Were I not possessed with a purpose beyond my own I had better be a ploughman than a philosopher; for the ploughman lives as long as the philosopher, eats more, sleeps better, and rejoices in the wife of his bosom with less misgiving. This is because the philosopher is in the grip of the Life Force. This Life Force says to him "I have done a thousand wonderful things unconsciously by merely willing to live and following the line of least resistance: now I want to know myself and my destination, and choose my path; so I have made a special brain—a philosopher's brain—to grasp this knowledge for me as the husbandman's hand grasps the plough for me. And this" says the Life Force to the philosopher "must thou strive to do for me until thou diest, when I will make another brain and another philosopher to carry on the work."

THE DEVIL. What is the use of knowing?

DON JUAN. Why, to be able to choose the line of greatest advantage instead of yielding in the direction of the least resistance. Does a ship sail to its destination no better than a log drifts nowhither? The philosopher is Nature's pilot. And there you have our difference: to be in Hell is to drift: to be in Heaven is to steer.

THE DEVIL. On the rocks, most likely.

DON JUAN. Pooh! which ship goes oftenest on the rocks or

to the bottom? the drifting ship or the ship with a pilot on board?

THE DEVIL. Well, well, go your way, Señor Don Juan. I prefer to be my own master and not the tool of any blundering universal force. I know that beauty is good to look at; that music is good to hear; that love is good to feel; and that they are all good to think about and talk about. I know that to be well exercised in these sensations, emotions, and studies is to be a refined and cultivated being. Whatever they may say of me in churches on earth, I know that it is universally admitted in good society that the Prince of Darkness is a gentleman; and that is enough for me. As to your Life Force, which you think irresistible, it is the most resistible thing in the world for a person of any character. But if you are naturally vulgar and credulous, as all reformers are, it will thrust you first into religion, where you will sprinkle water on babies to save their souls from me; then it will drive you from religion into science, where you will snatch the babies from the water sprinkling and inoculate them with disease to save them from catching it accidentally; then you will take to politics, where you will become the catspaw of corrupt functionaries and the henchman of ambitious humbugs; and the end will be despair and decrepitude, broken nerve and shattered hopes, vain regrets for that worst and silliest of wastes and sacrifices, the waste and sacrifice of the power of enjoyment: in a word, the punishment of the fool who pursues the better before he has secured the good.

DON JUAN. But at least I shall not be bored. The service of the Life Force has that advantage, at all events. So fare you well, Señor Satan.

THE DEVIL [amiably] Fare you well, Don Juan. I shall often think of our interesting chats about things in general. I wish you every happiness: Heaven, as I said before, suits some people. But if you should change your mind, do not forget that the gates are always open here to the repentant prodigal. If you feel at any time that warmth of heart, sincere unforced affection, innocent enjoyment, and warm, breathing, palpitating reality—

DON JUAN. Why not say flesh and blood at once, though we have left those two greasy commonplaces behind us?

THE DEVIL [*angrily*] You throw my friendly farewell back in my teeth, then, Don Juan?

DON JUAN. By no means. But though there is much to be learnt from a cynical devil, I really cannot stand a sentimental one. Señor Commander: you know the way to the frontier of Hell and Heaven. Be good enough to direct me.

THE STATUE. Oh, the frontier is only the difference between two ways of looking at things. Any road will take you across it if you really want to get there.

DON JUAN. Good. [*Saluting Doña Ana*] Señora: your servant.

ANA. But I am going with you.

DON JUAN. I can find my own way to Heaven, Ana; not yours [*he vanishes*].

ANA. How annoying!

THE STATUE [*calling after him*] Bon Voyage, Juan! [*He wafts a final blast of his great rolling chords after him as a parting salute. A faint echo of the first ghostly melody comes back in acknowledgment.*] Ah! there he goes. [*Puffing a long breath out through his lips*] Whew! How he does talk! They'll never stand it in Heaven.

THE DEVIL [*gloomily*] His going is a political defeat. I cannot keep these Life Worshippers: they all go. This is the greatest loss I have had since that Dutch painter went: a fellow who would paint a hag of 70 with as much enjoyment as a Venus of 20.

THE STATUE. I remember: he came to Heaven. Rembrandt.

THE DEVIL. Ay, Rembrandt. There is something unnatural about these fellows. Do not listen to their gospel, Señor Commander: it is dangerous. Beware of the pursuit of the Superhuman: it leads to an indiscriminate contempt for the Human. To a man, horses and dogs and cats are mere species, outside the moral world. Well, to the Superman, men and women are a mere species too, also outside the moral world. This Don Juan was kind to women and courteous to men as your daughter here

was kind to her pet cats and dogs; but such kindness is
a denial of the exclusively human character of the soul.

THE STATUE. And who the deuce is the Superman?

THE DEVIL. Oh, the latest fashion among the Life Force
fanatics. Did you not meet in Heaven, among the new
arrivals, that German Polish madman? what was his
name? Nietzsche?

THE STATUE. Never heard of him.

THE DEVIL. Well, he came here first, before he recovered
his wits. I had some hopes of him; but he was a confirmed Life Force worshipper. It was he who raked up
the Superman, who is as old as Prometheus; and the 20th
century will run after this newest of the old crazes when
it gets tired of the world, the flesh, and your humble
servant.

THE STATUE. Superman is a good cry; and a good cry is
half the battle. I should like to see this Nietzsche.

THE DEVIL. Unfortunately he met Wagner here, and had
a quarrel with him.

THE STATUE. Quite right, too. Mozart for me!

THE DEVIL. Oh, it was not about music. Wagner once
drifted into Life Force worship, and invented a Superman called Siegfried. But he came to his senses afterwards. So when they met here, Nietzsche denounced him
as a renegade; and Wagner wrote a pamphlet to prove
that Nietzsche was a Jew; and it ended in Nietzsche's
going to heaven in a huff. And a good riddance too. And
now, my friend, let us hasten to my palace and celebrate
your arrival with a grand musical service.

THE STATUE. With pleasure: youre most kind.

THE DEVIL. This way, Commander. We go down the old
trap [*he places himself on the grave trap*].

THE STATUE. Good. [*Reflectively*]: All the same, the Superman is a fine conception. There is something statuesque
about it. [*He places himself on the grave trap beside The
Devil. It begins to descend slowly. Red glow from the
abyss.*] Ah, this reminds me of old times.

THE DEVIL. And me also.

ANA. Stop! [*The trap stops.*]

THE DEVIL. You, Señora, cannot come this way. You will
have an apotheosis. But you will be at the palace before
us.

ANA. That is not what I stopped you for. Tell me: where
can I find the Superman?

THE DEVIL. He is not yet created, Señora.

THE STATUE. And never will be, probably. Let us proceed:
the red fire will make me sneeze. [*They descend.*]

ANA. Not yet created! Then my work is not yet done.
[*Crossing herself devoutly*] I believe in the Life to Come.
[*Crying to the universe*] A father! a father for the Super-
man!

    [*She vanishes into the void; and again there is nothing.*]

To Max Beerbohm

XXXXXXXXXXXXXXXXXXXXXXXXXXXXXXXXXXXXXXXXX

Beerbohm's article, "Mr. Shaw's New Dialogues," in the Saturday Review *on 12th September was a review of* Man and Superman, *in which Max stated that Shaw "cannot create living human characters," but added, "This is his masterpiece, so far. Treasure it as the most complete expression of the most distinct personality in current literature."*

Shaw's reference to Beerbohm's "Jewish genius" elicited the reply on 21st September: "I am not a Jew. My name was originally Beerboom. The family can be traced back through the centuries in Holland. Nor is there, so far as one can tell, any Hebraism on the distaff side. Do I look like a Jew? (The question is purely rhetorical.)"

Strachur
15 September 1903

This wont do. Your article in the Saturday is most laborious, most conscientious: the spasms of compliment almost draw tears; but the whole thing is wrong: the *gene* of offended academicism makes it almost unreadable.

Suppose you published a collection of drawings which had to be criticized not only by "the press" in the usual sense, but by the drawing masters of England. You would find every one of them complaining that your figures, though clever, were unnatural, untrue, unlifelike. You would perhaps retort by saying contemptuously: "Of course I know perfectly well that R. L. Stevenson was not an animated candle, and that William Archer is not twice & a half as tall as Pinero." But you would soon recognize that this was not what the drawingmasters meant. Again, they would point to your caricatures of yourself, and shew that beneath all your pretences of caricaturing other people the same treatments, the same trick of the hand, the same fantastic line, the same untruth to nature could be detected: in short, that all your King Edwards & Roseberys & Bernard Shaws & so on were merely thinly disguised Maxes, & that when they ceased to be so they ceased to be entertaining. And you would again exclaim impatiently: "Of course I have my style, like Velasquez or Rembrandt; and my pictures are all Maxes just as Turner's Dovers & Nottinghams & Venices & Schaffhausens are all Turners." But you would soon find that they knew all about that too, and that this was not the real confusion in their minds. And you would at last find that what they missed in your work was not life nor truth nor any other vital quality, but "the antique," and that your works, considered in terms of this overwhelming defect, were all reduced to a common level of failure. This too, in all honesty, their belief being that every man strips to the Hermes, Laocoön or Farnese Hercules, & every woman to the Venus of Milo.

Just so have you become convinced, as all the "dramatic critics" do sooner or later (for no man can long resist either absinthe or environment), that the fantoccini of romance are real, & the tax collector & the district visitor either mere human utensils or comic relief—that Rosalind the pantomime "leading boy" is a real woman, & Isabella of Measure for Measure a failure. Years ago Stead said eloquently of Marie Bashkirtseff "A woman she was NOT." You laughed; but you are now explaining my creations away in the same fashion. In vain do I give you a whole gallery of perfectly miraculous life studies. Not even your Jewish genius enables you to recognize my two types of Englishwomen. They are reduced, for you, to the same barren Shavian formula by the fact that they are not Italian prima donnas. The chauffeur, the Irishman & his American son are positively labelled for you as Hogarthian life studies—in vain: they are not "the antique," and so your nerves refuse to conduct them to your brain. Most astonishing of all, you have before you in Bashville the Gay & Superman the Serious two terrific displays of literary bravura—the by-product of a quarter of a century of struggling for the mastery of words on top of a born capacity for them—and yet you make the

usual gull's apology—you, Max, a gull on such a point!—
for complimenting me on my art. You idiot, do you suppose
I dont know my own powers? I tell you in this book as
plainly as the thing can be told, that the reason Bunyan
reached such a pitch of mastery in literary art (and knew
it) whilst poor Pater could never get beyond a nerveless
amateur affectation which had not even the common workaday quality of vulgar journalism (and, alas! didnt know it,
though he died of his own futility), was that it was life or
death with the tinker to make people understand his message and see his vision, whilst Pater had neither message
nor vision & only wanted to cultivate style, with the result
that of the two attempts I have made to read him the first
broke down at the tenth sentence & the second at the first.
Pater took a genteel walk up Parnassus: Bunyan fled from
the wrath to come: that explains the difference in their pace
& in the length they covered.

And now, what is to be done with you? The answer is
indicated by the one piece of sense in your article. You
have yourself a certain command of the living word: you
can make a page talk (when it's not about me); and you
have found by experience that this leads to the platform,
and can be developed by it so as to give a man twenty
forms and appositions of phrase for every one possessed
by the mere book & pen man. But your evil angel has led
you to the one platform where your academicism gets confirmed & indurated—the Playgoers Club. Ten minutes on
the Drainage Sub Committee of the St Pancras Borough
Council, which has taken many an afternoon on days when
the Superman took the morning, would shatter that
academicism for ever.

As to your reviews of Woman, lovely Woman, you were
false to them when you omitted to say a good word for
Octavius. You say some women pursue men—meaning
those of whom Stead says "Woman she was NOT." The
truth is very simple. Walk down Piccadilly, and ask yourself
at every woman that passes you, could I bear to have her
as my mistress? You will be astonished at your own virtue:
99.99999999999999 per cent of them will leave you
cold—perhaps 100%. It is just so with Miss Ann Whitefield.

Her behaviour with regard to 99% of the men she meets will exactly confirm your Octavian conceptions of a womanly woman and a Paffick Lidy. But what if the 1% come along? Imogen refused Iachimo & Joseph Potiphar's wife; but what if the Life Force had short-circuited them?

There will be a Borough Council election in November. *Verb. sap.* Quit the theatre & *draw* for a living. Shake the Playgoers' dust off your shoes. Abjure Academicism. Urgent. Important. Forward immediately.

yrs ever
G.B.S.

To Archibald Henderson

XXXXXXXXXXXXXXXXXXXXXXXXXXXXXXXXXXXXXXXXXXX

Henderson (1877–1963), an Assistant Professor of Mathematics at the University of North Carolina at the time, had become a Shaw enthusiast after seeing a production of You Never Can Tell. *He wrote to Shaw in June 1904 asking for permission to write a biography and for a detailed list of Shaw's early uncollected writings.*

10 Adelphi Terrace W C
30 June 1904

I am afraid there is no way of getting at the mass of critical articles which I wrote between 1885 & 1898 except by coming to London & misspending several weeks at the British Museum library. . . . Total, over a million words, most of them about matters long since stone dead, and many of them become absolutely unintelligible now that they can no longer be read with the context of the events of the week in which they appeared.

Then there are my economic & political essays—my Socialist manifestoes, my defence of the value theory of Marx against that of Jevons, ending in my own conversion and my demolition of Marx on Jevonian lines with my own hand. All this is quite unknown to the admirers of my plays; but my first play "Widowers' Houses" could only have been written by a Socialistic economist; and the same thing is true of "Mrs Warren's Profession." Indeed, in all the plays my economic studies have played as important a part as a knowledge of anatomy does in the works of Michael Angelo.

I believe my career as a public speaker was also an important part of my training. There was a period of twelve years during which I delivered about three harangues every fortnight, many of them in the open air at the street

corners and before audiences of all sorts, from university
dons & British Association committees to demonstrations
of London washerwomen, always followed by questions &
discussion.

I never lived the literary life, or belonged to a literary
club; and though I brought all my powers unsparingly to the
criticism of the fine arts, I never frequented their social
surroundings. My time was fully taken up (when I was not
actually writing or attending performances) by public work,
in which I was fortunate enough to be associated with a
few men of exceptional ability and character. I got the
committee habit, the impersonality and imperturbability of
the statesman, the constant and unceremonious criticism
of men who were at many points much abler & better informed than myself, a great deal of experience which cannot be acquired in conventional grooves, and that "behind
the scenes" knowledge of the mechanism & nature of
political illusion which seems so cynical to the spectators in
front.

I advise you in anything you write to insist on this training of mine, as otherwise you will greatly exaggerate my
natural capacity. It has enabled me to produce an impression of being an extraordinarily clever, original, & brilliant
writer, deficient only in feeling, whereas the truth is that
though I am in a way a man of genius—otherwise I suppose
I would not have sought out & enjoyed my experience, and
been simply bored by holidays, luxury & money—yet I am
not in the least naturally "brilliant" and not at all ready or
clever. If literary men generally were put through the mill
I went through & kept out of their stuffy little coteries,
where works of art breed in and in until the intellectual &
spiritual product becomes hopelessly degenerate, I should
have a thousand rivals more brilliant than myself. There is
nothing more mischievous than the notion that my works
are the mere play of a delightfully clever & whimsical hero
of the salons: they are the result of perfectly straightforward drudgery, beginning in the ineptest novel writing
juvenility, and persevered in every day for 25 years. Anybody can get my skill for the same price; and a good many
people could probably get it cheaper. Man & Superman no

doubt sounds as if it came from the most exquisite atmosphere of art. As a matter of fact, the mornings I gave to it
were followed by afternoons & evenings spent in the committee rooms of a London Borough Council, fighting
questions of drainage, paving, lighting, rates, clerk's salaries
&c &c &c &c; and that is exactly why it is so different from
the books that are conceived at musical at homes. My latest
book, The Common Sense of Municipal Trading, is in its
way one of the best and most important I have ever written.
I beg you, if you write about my "extraordinary career,"
to make it clear to all young aspirants, that its extraordi-
nariness lies in its ordinariness—that, like a greengrocer &
unlike a minor poet, I have lived instead of dreaming and
feeding myself with artistic confectionery. With a little
more courage & a little more energy I could have done
much more; and I lacked these because in my boyhood I
lived on my imagination instead of my work.

Excuse all this twaddle; but it is probably what you require to help you out if you pursue the subject.

Widowers' Houses is out of print, thank Heaven, in the
original edition; but the preface & appendices were probably better reading than the text of the play in its original
foolishness. I do not know where a copy is to be had. . . .

It is quite true that the best authority on Shaw is Shaw.
My activities have lain in so many watertight compartments
that nobody has yet given anything but a sectional and
inaccurate account of me except when they have tried to
piece me out of my own confessions.

> yours faithfully
> G. Bernard Shaw

To Josephine Preston Peabody

⨯⨯⨯⨯⨯⨯⨯⨯⨯⨯⨯⨯⨯⨯⨯⨯⨯⨯⨯⨯⨯⨯⨯⨯⨯⨯⨯⨯⨯⨯⨯⨯

The Old House. Harmer Green
29th December 1904

That is a very energetic letter; and I hope you feel better now that it is off your mind. But it does not tell me anything except what I knew before: namely, that many people have a thoughtless and extremely wicked habit of calling the sexual instinct bestial. Until you get beyond that point there is no use in my writing to you or for you.

You do not seem to have quite taken in the very important passage in my preface [to *Man and Superman*] in which you yourself, as what you call (rightly) an Artist Woman, are put out of court in this matter. The ordinary woman lets you write about her, and laughs at you, having quite another purpose in life than yours. And she will not even read you unless your central theme is what you call her bestiality.

You talk of the Mother Woman as if she could be bracketed with the Artist Woman. You might as well bracket her with the mere pleasure fancier. Ann is the Mother Woman. She is not an artist aiming at the production of poems & romances like Octavius, or at the formulation of a philosophy of life, like Tanner. She is not a moralist, like Ramsden, nor a sensualist like nobody in the play. She is a breeder of men, specialized by Nature to that end and endowed with enormous fascination for it; and all the twaddling little minor moralities that stand between her and her purpose—as, for instance, that she must not be a naughty girl and tell fibs, and that she must not be what you (I rub in this reproach purposely) call "bestial"—all become the merest inpertinences. As she says in her transfiguration "I believe in the life to come"; and when you feel the mightiness of that belief and the vital Force of All

Forces that is behind it, you will blush at having had no more to say to it than "How unladylike!" (on five sheets of paper).

You are quite right in what you say about laughter: I should probably not have answered your letter but for that flash of insight in it. You will find it, if you want to see it in print, in the preface to my Plays Pleasant & Unpleasant.

I daresay you have been repelled somewhat by the fact that Ann, being a person in a comedy, has to have a particular as well as a universal character, and that one of her particularities is that she is an Englishwoman. As an American or an Irishwoman she would be impossible unless she surrounded her instinct with a halo of illusions and called it her Purity (the American formula) or refused to discuss it at all (the Irish practice). The Englishwoman looks her function in the face in an astonishingly business-like manner; and the American who hastily concludes that this is an inferiority should think three times before saying so.

You must not ask me to put Candida into every play. When Ann is married she will look after Tanner exactly as Candida looks after Morell. But when Candida was capturing Morell, and had not yet become his housekeeper and his nurserymistress, she was Ann. The author of Candida is clearly the author of Ann.

Dont, I beg of you, write to me again until you have learnt to respect your sex, and to appreciate that very vital protest of Don Juan against the degradation of the sex relation into a personal & sentimental romance. And whenever you write again on the subject to a person who does not know you, will you please mention your age. It is at least as important as the number of your house, which, by the way, I see you have not given me.

yours faithfully
G. Bernard Shaw

"The New Theology"

XXXXXXXXXXXXXXXXXXXXXXXXXXXXXXXXXXXXXXXXXXXX

A transcription of a lay sermon Shaw delivered at Kensington Town Hall, London, on 16 May 1907, as printed in the Christian Commonwealth *on 23 and 30 May 1907. The first sentence of the talk apparently refers to a previous lay sermon delivered at Essex Hall on 29 November 1906, "Some Necessary Repairs to Religion," which the Bishop of London attacked as "in contradiction to the Christian faith."*

When I last stood on this platform, I said there was not a single established religion in the world in which an intelligent or educated man could believe. Some feeling has been shown by those who have quoted that statement that somehow or other it is my fault, and I am not altogether disposed to deny it. A person who points out a thing of which the mass of people are unconscious really does to some extent create the thing which he points out. I remember not very long ago rolling up my sleeves to the elbow in order to wash my hands, and, as I have a great deal to think about, including the New Theology, I am sometimes rather absent minded. The consequence was that I forgot to roll down my sleeves, and walked about two miles in the west of London until I met a friend, who said, "What on earth are you going about in that fashion for?" Now, as I did not know that my sleeves were rolled up, they were not rolled up so far as I was concerned until that intrusive friend came and quite unnecessarily called my attention to the fact, covering me with blushes and confusion. And so my remark here last year may have destroyed the authenticity of established religions for many persons who up to that moment had believed that those religions, being established, were all right.

I want to see whether there is any possibility of our arriving at a religion on which we can agree, because it is very important we should have a religion of some kind. I know that that is quite a fashionable opinion, but we have got out of the habit of thinking that we ought to believe in the religion we have. Hardly any person in London believes in the religion he professes. Now let us come to the New Theology. It is not my habit, nor the habit of any really judicious lecturer, to begin by definitions, and when I do, I decline to be held by them. I do not address myself to your logical faculties, but as one human mind trying to put himself in contact with other human minds. By theology I really do mean the science of godhead, and I want to examine whether we have made any advance in the science, whether there is a science of it in which we can believe and on which we can get a pretty general agreement. I shall have to go back a considerable distance, because I want to make you aware of the state of your mind on the question. I am quite certain that you do not know it, unless you are familiar with the religious history of the nineteenth century, perhaps the wickedest in all human history.

When I came to London, at about the beginning of the last quarter of the nineteenth century, I found people in a very curious state as regards their religious belief. This was illustrated by something that happened at a bachelor party I attended in Kensington not far from this hall a short time after I arrived. I found myself in the company of a number of young men who either belonged to, or were qualifying for, one of the liberal professions, and they got into a dispute about religion. At that time the late Charles Bradlaugh was very notorious for the militant campaign he was carrying on as an atheist. One of the persons present, representing what was supposed to be the pious and religious side in the controversy, accused Bradlaugh of having publicly taken out his watch and challenged the Almighty, if he had the power and will to do so, to strike him dead in five minutes. An admirer and adherent of Bradlaugh vehemently denied that story, saying it was a gross calumny. The gentleman who made the accusation took the old-fashioned view; it had prevailed in this country for about three hundred years, that very dark period in which Christians, instead of being Christians in any reasonable sense, worshiped the Bible as a talisman. For instance, in tract shops you saw copies of the Bible exhibited with the dent of a bullet in them, and you were given to understand that the soldier who had in his pocket a testament given him by his mother had been saved from death because the book had stopped the enemy's bullet. The gentleman who told the story about Mr. Bradlaugh was a Bible worshiper, and believed, among other things, the story in the Bible that when Elisha the prophet was mocked because of his bald head by some young children, God sent a couple of bears out of a wood to eat those children. And the extraordinary thing is that the gentleman worshiped the God who did that! If you or I confessed doing such a thing as that probably we should be torn to pieces. But it was a common article of belief at that time that the universe was ruled by a God who was that particular sort of person, an exceedingly spiteful person, capable of taking the most ferocious revenge.

I was very much puzzled by the impassioned way in which the gentleman who was a secularist defended Charles Bradlaugh against the imputation of having taken out his watch and made this challenge, and when my turn came to speak, or rather when I spoke—I am not always in the habit of waiting for my turn exactly—I said that if the question which Charles Bradlaugh was dealing with was whether a God of that kind existed, the reported experiment seemed to me perfectly legitimate and natural and to deny the existence of such a God appeared to me to be a far more genuine religious position than that of the people who affirmed belief in him. I say it seemed to me perfectly natural and proper, if the ruler of the universe were really the petty, spiteful criminal he was represented to be, for a man who denied his existence to take his watch out of his pocket and, instead of troubling about what happened many centuries ago, to ask him to strike him dead at the end of five minutes. I said, "Since it appears that Mr. Bradlaugh never made this experiment, I, regarding it as a perfectly legitimate one, will try it myself," and with that I took my watch out of my pocket.

I have never done anything in public or private which produced such an instantaneous and extraordinary effect. Up to that moment the company had been divided into a pious and a sceptical party, but it now appeared that there were no sceptics present at all. Everyone of them felt it to be extremely probable that before the five minutes were up I should be taken at my word. One of the party appealed to us to turn the conversation to a more lively channel, and a gentleman present who had a talent for singing comic songs sat down at the piano and sang the most melancholic comic song I ever heard in my life.

That incident has its amusing side, but it also has its tragic side. It is a frightful thing that it should have been possible so recently as twenty-five years ago for a party of educated men to be in that state of superstition. I am not at all certain that I have not made some of those I address very uncomfortable by what I have just said. Well, I intend to go on making people who hold such views uncomfortable. I want to make them understand in a very vivid way that it is quite impossible at this time of day to unite the world or appeal to our highest intelligence or better natures by preaching that particular sort of God. It was the preaching of that kind of tribal idol that accounted for Charles Bradlaugh calling himself an atheist, and, disbelieving with my whole soul in such a being, I always did what Charles Bradlaugh did: made myself intelligible to those people who worship such a monster by saying that I was an atheist. And in that sense I still am an atheist, as it must seem to me every humane person must be. That kind of God is morally inconceivable. The God who would send bears to eat up little children would be a wicked God—what Shelley called an Almighty Fiend. Why did not Shelley's protest produce very much impression on the people of this country? Because, believing he was an Almighty Fiend, they feared and obeyed him very largely as such and supposed that if they told him the truth to his face he would probably strike them dead for blasphemy. They saw that there was a great deal of terrible cruelty in the world, which rather confirmed the idea that the force at the back of things was wicked and cruel, and therefore the denunciations of Shelley and others of the current conception of God as immoral did not remove the presumption that he existed.

There was another reason why these people had to believe in God: Everywhere in nature they saw evidence of design. It was no use telling them the universe was the result of blind chance. They said, "If you look around, if you note all that we are told even by scientific men about the marvelous adaptation of means to end, if you consider such a miraculous thing as the human eye, it is impossible for us to believe that these things came into existence without a designer, and we cannot blind ourselves to the fact that the designer is apparently cruel. We see plague, pestilence, and famine, battle, murder, and sudden death; we see our parents dying of cancer, our children dying of diptheria. We may not dare to say that the power that wills that is cruel; it might bring worse consequences on us. But the cruelty is no reason for our ceasing to believe in its existence." And so, neither science on the one hand, nor the moral remonstrances of Shelley and his school on the other, were able to shake the current belief in that old theology that came back to the old tribal idol, Jehovah.

I hope that I have produced a sufficiently gloomy impression upon you! The reason I have been putting the matter as I have is that I want to bring into your minds very strongly the fact that in the middle of the last century all the mind, conscience, and intelligence of the best part of mankind was in revolt against the old-fashioned conception of God, and yet at the same time finding itself intellectually unable to get away from the conception of God the Designer. They were in a dilemma. There must be what they called God, and yet they could not make him responsible for the good in the world without making him also responsible for the evil, because they never questioned one thing about him: that, being the designer of the universe, he must be necessarily omnipotent. This being the situation, is it not clear that if at the time any man had risen up and said, "All this wonderful adaptation of means to end, all this design which seems to imply a designer, is an illusion; it may have all come about by the operation of what we call blind chance," the most intelligent and best part of the human race, without stopping to criticize his argument very closely, would spring at that man and take him to their arms as their moral savior, saying, "You have lifted from our minds this horrible conception that the force that is governing us all and is managing the whole world is hideous, criminal, cruel"? That is exactly what happened when Charles Darwin appeared and the reason why he had such an enormous success that the religion of the last half of the nineteenth century became Darwinian. Many people are under the impression that Darwinism meant that the world had been converted to a belief in evolution. That is a mistake; exactly the contrary has happened. Darwin was really the man who completely turned the attention of mankind from the doctrine of evolution.

Evolution is a vital part of the New Theology, but it sprang into something like completeness as a conception at the end of the eighteenth century, when all the great evolutionists, including Erasmus Darwin, grandfather of Charles Darwin, brought out their books and developed the whole system. The main thing by which they astonished the world was by attacking the old conception of creation in the Garden of Eden. The amazing conception that thought of all life on this planet as having evolved from a little speck of slime in a ditch struck the world dumb. Erasmus Darwin justified the theology of it by saying, "Is not the conception that men have been developed from a speck of protoplasm much more wonderful than that the world and everything in it was made in six days?" The conception took hold of people, and its chief exponent was the great philosopher Lamarck, a Frenchman who began life as a soldier and ended it as a naturalist. In one of his books Lamarck gave an illustration of the process of evolution. He said the reason that the giraffe had a long neck is that this creature wanted to feed on the soft herbage on the top of tall trees, and by dint of generations of giraffes stretching their necks, they gradually made their necks longer, until they could reach the requisite height.

Now, that means that the giraffe got a long neck because it wanted a long neck—just in the same way that you learn to ride a bicycle or to speak French because you want to do so.

Well, in the year 1830, the scientific world got tired of generalizing and, instead of forming great cosmic theories, devoted itself to the study of isolated phenomena, assisted by the microscope, and shortly after this time Charles Darwin came on the scene. I am convinced that the accusations made against Darwin of having deliberately suppressed the debt that civilization owed to his grandfather for the discovery of evolution were entirely unjust, because I don't believe that Charles Darwin knew anything about evolution, or that to the end of his life he ever understood the whole theory or what it meant. From boyhood he delighted in frogs and pigeons and was the greatest pigeon fancier that ever lived. The real thing that enabled Charles Darwin to come to different conclusions from other naturalists was that between the time of the evolutionists of 1790–1830 and Charles Darwin's discovery in his book, *The Origin of Species*, the researches of the great biologist Lyell led him to teach the world that the stratification and formation of rocks and mountains in order to be scientifically accounted for forced us to assign a much greater age to the earth than had hitherto been assigned. Our grandfathers had always been taught, on the authority of Archbishop Ussher, that the world was 6,006 years old, and some people had actually discovered the actual day of the month when creation began. This present of millions of years gave time for Darwin's theory of natural selection. Now let us apply this theory to the case of the giraffe. Lamarck's theory implied purpose and will, and, remember, if there is purpose and will in a microbe there must be purpose and will through the whole universe. But Darwin said, in effect, "I can explain the giraffe's long neck without implying the slightest purpose or will. What really happened was this: The number of giraffes multiplied until they began to prey on the means of subsistence—until they bit off all the leaves on the trees within their reach, and then they found themselves starving. But suppose, by one of those little accidents and variations that will always occur—we do not know how—a few giraffes happened to have necks a little longer than the others, they would be able to reach vegetation, while their less fortunate fellows starved. Consequently the longer-necked giraffes would survive while the others perished and produce a race of giraffes with necks a little longer, and this without any purpose or design."

My difficulty in putting this apparently commonplace story of the giraffe before a modern audience is to make them understand the unspeakable and frightful prospect opened to the world by Darwin. He abolished adaptation and design, and, as Samuel Butler said, banished mind from the universe, which was a great relief to many Englishmen who greatly dislike anything in the shape of reflection. Considering that there are and necessarily must be a large number of consciously religious men always living, and that everyone of us has a considerable religious element in him and could not exist without it, why was it that the naked horror of Darwin's conception did not strike them? I have already given you the explanation; it is Elisha and the bears again. The world had got so horrified by the old theology, with its conception of a spiteful, narrow, wicked, personal God, who was always interfering and doing stupid things—often cruel things—that for a moment it could feel nothing but relief at having got rid of such a God altogether. It did not feel the void at first. A man with a bad toothache only thinks of getting rid of the tooth; it is not till afterwards he discovers that he must have a new tooth if he is to go on eating and keep his digestion in order. So people said, "Now that we have got rid of the old conception of religion we will believe in science and evolution." Of course, they knew nothing about evolution; they thought that natural selection, Darwin's discovery, was evolution. Darwin merely turned the attention of mankind to the effects of natural selection; he did not deal with the real problem of evolution. Samuel Butler and others were very soon able to show that it was no use denying the existence of purpose and will in the universe; they were conscious themselves of having purpose, will, design. Then came the discovery of the weak point of the natural selection theory: that it not only did away with

the necessity for design and purpose, but with the necessity
for consciousness. Men were able to demonstrate that,
according to the theory of natural selection, it was perfectly
possible that all the books in the British Museum might
have been written, all the pictures in the National Gallery
might have been painted, all the cathedrals of Europe might
have been built, automatically, without one person concerned in the process having been conscious of what he was
doing. Some of the natural selectionists used to make the
demonstration themselves with a certain pride in doing so.
But the common sense of mankind said, "If all the operations of the species can be accounted for without consciousness, intelligence, or design, you have still got to
account for the consciousness, intelligence, and design that
undoubtedly exist in man." The religious people naturally
turn this argument to account, saying, "It is all very well
to say that life is a mere pursuit of pleasure and gain, but
many men do not live in order to get a balance of pleasure
over pain; you see everywhere men doing work that does
not benefit them—they call it God's work; natural selection
cannot account for that. There is behind the universe an
intelligent and driving force of which we ourselves are a
part—a divine spark."

After the Darwins and Lyell and Samuel Butler had had
their say, the difficulty presented was this: How are we to
retain the notion of design without going back to the idea
that the design is the work of a cruel designer? The trouble,
as usual, was that we had been making the entirely gratui-
tous assumption that the force behind the universe is
omnipotent. Now, you cannot prove that that force is at
once omnipotent and benevolent. If omnipotent, why did it
create us? If there are three orders of existence—man as we
know him, the angels higher than man, and God higher
than the angels—why did God first create something lower
than himself, the angels, and then actually create something
lower than the angels, man? I cannot believe in a God who
would do that. If I were God, I should try to create something higher than myself, and then something higher than
that, so that, beginning with a God the higher thing in
creation, I should end with a God the lowest thing in

creation. This is the conception you must get into your head if you are to be free from the horrible old idea that all the cruelty in the world is the work of an omnipotent God, who if he liked could have left the cruelty out of creation, who instead of creating us . . . Just think about yourselves, ladies and gentlemen. I do not want to be uncomplimentary, but can you conceive God deliberately creating you if he could have created anything better?

What you have got to understand is that somehow or other there is at the back of the universe a will, a life-force. You cannot think of him as a person, you have to think of him as a great purpose, a great will, and, furthermore, you have to think of him as engaged in a continual struggle to produce something higher and higher, to create organs to carry out his purpose; as wanting hands, and saying, "I must create something with hands"; arriving at that very slowly, after innumerable experiments and innumerable mistakes, because this power must be proceeding as we proceed, be- cause if there were any other way it would put us in that way: we know that in all the progress we make we proceed by way of trial and error and experiment. Now conceive of the force behind the universe as a bodiless, impotent force, having no executive power of its own, wanting instruments, something to carry out its will in the world, making all manner of experiments, creating reptiles, birds, animals, trying one thing after another, rising higher and higher in the scale of organism, and finally producing man, and then inspiring that man, putting his will into him, getting him to carry out his purpose, saying to him, "Remember, you are not here merely to look after yourself. I have made your hand to do my work; I have made your brain, and I want you to work with that and try to find out the purpose of the universe; and when one instrument is worn out, I will make another, and another, always more and more intelli- gent and effective." One difficulty is that so many of the earlier efforts of this world-force—for example, the tiger— remain, and the incompatibility between them and man exists in the human being himself as the result of early experiments, so that there are certain organs in your body which are perishing away and are of no use and actually interfere with your later organs. And here you have, as it seems to me, the explanation of that great riddle which used to puzzle people—evil and pain.

Numbers of things which are at present killing and maiming us in our own organism have got to be evolved out of that organism, and the process is painful. The object of the whole evolutionary process is to realize God; that is to say, instead of the old notion that creation began with a God, a personal being, who, being perfect, created something lower than himself, the aim of the New Theology is to turn that process the other way and to conceive of the force behind the universe as working up through imperfection and mistake to a perfect, organized being, having the power of fulfilling its highest purposes. In a sense there is no God as yet achieved, but there is that force at work making God, struggling through us to become an actual organized existence, enjoying what to many of us is the greatest conceivable ecstasy, the ecstasy of a brain, an intelligence, actually conscious of the whole, and with executive force capable of guiding it to a perfectly benevolent and harmonious end. That is what we are working to. When you are asked, "Where is God? Who is God?" stand up and say, "I am God and here is God, not as yet completed, but still advancing towards completion, just in so much as I am working for the purpose of the universe, working for the good of the whole of society and the whole world, instead of merely looking after my personal ends." In that way we get rid of the old contradiction, we begin to perceive that the evil of the world is a thing that will finally be evolved out of the world, that it was not brought into the world by malice and cruelty, but by an entirely benevolent designer that had not as yet discovered how to carry out its benevolent intention. In that way I think we may turn towards the future with greater hope.

It had been my intention when I began to make the few introductory remarks which I have just delivered the first part of my lecture and then to go on applying that to existing religion, to deal with the actual articles of the Church of England, and to show how much of this truth that I have been teaching tonight is to be found in them. You will find a great deal of this truth in them and in your Bible and in all the religious books of the world. You will find it in the modern poets. When you once seize this you will find that this idea is no idle heresy or paradox of mine, but that it has been germinating in people's minds for a century past and for much more than that in the great poets and leaders of mankind.

"Mr. Bernard Shaw on His New Play"

(An interview drafted by Shaw for the *Daily Telegraph*, London, 7 May 1908)

XXXXXXXXXXXXXXXXXXXXXXXXXXXXXXXXXXXXXXX

Yesterday (writes a representative of *The Daily Telegraph*) I claimed from Mr. Bernard Shaw the fulfilment of an old promise that he would tell me something about his new play over and above what has to be told to everybody through the usual official communications. From these it is already known that the piece is entitled "Getting Married"; that it is to be produced at the Haymarket Theatre on the afternoon of the 12th; that it will, in performance, last nearly three hours; that it is in form a perfect Greek play with the unities of time and place strictly preserved; that the action is supposed to take place on the afternoon of the day on which the play is produced, provided the weather be suitable, and that it is neither a tragedy nor a comedy, but simply "an instructive conversation."

REVENGE ON THE CRITICS

"The attraction of a new play by you must have been irresistible?"

"Not a bit of it. This play is my revenge on the critics for their gross ingratitude to us, their arrant Philistinism, their shameless intellectual laziness, their low tastes, their hatred of good work, their puerile romanticism, their disloyalty to dramatic literature, their stupendous ignorance, their susceptibility to cheap sentiment, their insensibility to honour, virtue, intellectual honesty, and everything that constitutes strength and dignity in human character—in short, for the vices and follies and weaknesses of which Vedrenne and Barker have been trying to cure them for four years past."

In face of such a cyclonic outburst, what could the overwhelmed interviewer do but murmur a few words of acknowledgment of the unsolicited tribute to the majesty of the Press, and inquire the exact nature of the revenge to be wrought by the new play?

"It is very simple," said Mr. Shaw. "You remember 'A Dream of Don Juan in Hell,' at the Court. You remember the tortured howl of rage and anguish with which it was received in the Press. Yet that lasted only 110 minutes; and it was made attractive by music and by the magically fascinating stage pictures contrived by Mr. Charles Ricketts —a stroke of art which would have made a sensation in any other capital in Europe, and which was here passed over with complete unintelligence. Well, this time the 110 minutes of discussion will be stretched out to 150 minutes. There will be no costumes by Mr. Ricketts, nothing but a bishop in an apron. There will be no music by Mr. Theodore Stier or Mozart or anyone else. There will be nothing but talk, talk, talk, talk, talk—Shaw talk. The characters will seem to the wretched critics to be simply a row of Shaws, all arguing with one another on totally uninteresting subjects. Shaw in a bishop's apron will argue with Shaw in a general's uniform. Shaw in an alderman's gown will argue with Shaw dressed as a beadle. Shaw dressed as a bridegroom will be wedded to Shaw in petticoats. The whole thing will be hideous, indescribable—an eternity of brain-racking dulness. And yet they will have to sit it out. I see that one or two of them have been trying to cheer themselves with futile guesses at something cheerful to come. They are mistaken; they will suffer horribly, inhumanely—suffer all the more because when, at last, the final fall of the curtain releases them, and they stagger away to pen their maddened protest, and to assure the public that 'Getting Married' is not a play, and not even a bearable experience, they will do so at the risk of being reminded by their editors that they said all this before— said it of 'John Bull's Other Island'—said it of 'Arms and The Man,' and of 'Caesar and Cleopatra'—said it when they had plenty of fun, plenty of scenery, plenty of music, plenty of brilliant costumes; so that now, when their worst terrors have been realised, and all the delights for which they were so grossly ungrateful have been taken away from them, the tale of their suffering will not be believed. Well, serve them right! I am not a vindictive man; but there is such a thing as poetic justice; and on next Tuesday afternoon it will assume its sternest retributive form."

TOUCHES OF MERCY

"Then, will no concessions be made to human weakness?"

"Yes, a few. We shall not be altogether merciless. The curtains will be dropped casually from time to time to allow of first-aid to the really bad cases in the seats allotted to the Press. And Mr. Harrison has very kindly arranged with the authorities of the Charing Cross Hospital to have an ambulance available in case of need."

"Am I to understand that in order to revenge yourself on the Press you have deliberately written a bad play?"

"Good heavens, no; there is nothing they would like better. I have deliberately written a good play; that is the way to make the Press suffer. Besides, you will please observe that the enterprise in which we are engaged is not one to be fooled with. My play is the very best I can write; the cast is the very best available in London; and, what is equally important, the audiences will be the best audiences in London. Those audiences will enjoy the play and admire the acting keenly. But if we are to please such audiences, we cannot please everybody. If you turned a Tivoli or London Pavilion audience into the Queen's Hall and inflicted Beethoven's Ninth Symphony on them, they would remember the experience with horror to the end of their lives. That is what is the matter with most of our critics— they are very decent fellows, but they are Tivoli critics, and the Vedrenne and Barker authors are on the Beethovenian plane. Hence, naturally, ructions! We appear to be wantonly mocking and insulting the wrong people, when we are simply doing our best most earnestly to cater for the right people. There is not a single artist concerned in the production who would consent to be made a party to any wanton eccentricity or tomfoolery. The satisfaction of the people for whom we really work will be as keen as the sufferings of the others will be hideous."

THE PLOT

"Would it be indiscreet to ask you to lift a corner of the curtain prematurely, and give some notion of the plot of the play?"

"The play has no plot. Surely nobody expects a play by me to have a plot. I am a dramatic poet, not a plot-monger."

"But at least there is a story?"

"Not at all. If you look at any of the old editions of our classical plays, you will see that the description of the play is not called a plot or a story, but an argument. That exactly describes the material of my play. It is an argument—an argument lasting nearly three hours, and carried on with unflagging cerebration by twelve people and a beadle. They are all honourable, decent, nice people. You will find the materials for their argument in the Church Catechism, the Book of Common Prayer, Mr Sidney Webb's Letters to the *Times* on the subject of the birth-rate, the various legal text-books on the law of marriage, the sermons and table-talk of the present Bishop of Birmingham and the late Bishop of London [Mandell Creighton], 'Whitaker's Almanack,' 'The Statesman's Year-Book,' 'The Statistical Abstract,' the Registrar-General's returns, and other store-houses of fact and succulent stores of contemporary opinion. All who are intelligent enough to make these their daily reading will have a rare treat; but I am bound to add that people who prefer novelettes will have to pay repeated visits to the play before they acquire a thoroughly un-affected taste for it. If you would like me to go into the subject of the play in detail, I shall be delighted to do so."

"Thank you," said the interviewer, hurriedly, "I am quite satisfied, and space even in *The Daily Telegraph* is limited. I have no doubt that we shall have a most enjoyable after-noon on the 12th, although some of us may, as you suggest, have to spend the following day in Charing Cross Hospital. The dramatic critic, of course, is always open to such risks, but in the cause of duty he never refuses to face them. That accounts for the heavy death-rate among them, a fact which so comprehensive an observer of life as yourself cannot have failed to note; and now it only remains for me to say good-day and to wish all success to 'Getting Married.' "

To Frederick Jackson

×××

Parknasilla Hotel. Sneem
18th September 1910

My dear Jackson

We are both here—in the only place in the world that makes Tarn Moor a mere dust heap.

Yesterday I left the Kerry coast in an open boat 33 feet long, propelled by ten men at 5 oars. These men started at 49 strokes a minute, a rate which I did not believe they could keep up for five minutes. They kept it without slackening half a second for two hours, at the end of which they landed me on the most fantastic and impossible rock in the world: Skellig Michael, or the Great Skellig, where, in south west gales, the spray knocks stones out of the lighthouse keeper's house, 160 feet above calm sea level. There is a little Skellig covered with gannets—white with them (and their guano)—covered with screaming crowds of them. The Bass rock is a mere lump in comparison: both the Skelligs are pinnacled, crocketed, spired, arched, caverned, minaretted; and these Gothic extravagances are not curiosities of the islands: they *are* the islands: there is nothing else. The rest of the cathedral may be under the sea for all I know: there are 90 fathoms by the chart, out of which the Great Skellig rushes up 700 feet so suddenly that you have to go straight upstairs to the top—over 600 steps. And at the top amazing beehives of flat rubble stones, each overlapping the one below until the circles meet in a dome—cells, oratories, churches, and outside them cemeteries, wells, crosses, all clustering like shells on a prodigious rock pinnacle, with precipices sheer down on every hand, and, lodged on the projecting stones overhanging the deep, huge stone coffins made apparently by giants, and dropped there, God knows how. An incredible, impossible, mad place, which still tempts devotees to make "stations" of every stair landing, and to creep through "needle's eyes" at impossible altitudes, and kiss "stones of pain" jutting out 700 feet above the Atlantic. Most incredible of all, the lighthouse keeper will not take a tip, but sits proud, melancholy and haunted in his kitchen after placing all his pantry at your disposal—will also accompany you down to the desperate little harbor to squeeze the last word out of you before you abandon him, and gives you letters to post like the Flying Dutchman—also his strange address to send newspapers and literature to; for these he will accept.

I tell you the thing does not belong to any world that you and I have ever lived and worked in: it is part of our dream world.

And you talk of your Hindhead! Skellig Michael, sir, is the Forehead.

Then back in the dark, without compass, and the moon invisible in the mist, 49 strokes to the minute striking patines of white fire from the Atlantic, spurting across threatening currents and furious tideraces, pursued by terrors, ghosts from Michael, possibilities of the sea rising making every fresh breeze a fresh fright, impossibilities of being quite sure whither we were heading, two hours and a half before us at best, all the rowers wildly imaginative, superstitious, excitable, and apparently superhuman in energy and endurance, two women sitting with the impenetrable dignity and quiet comeliness of Italian saints and Irish peasant women silent in their shawls with their hands on the quietest part of the oars (next the gunwale) like spirit rappers, keeping the pride of the men at the utmost tension, so that every interval of dogged exhaustion and dropping into sleep (the stroke never slackening, though) would be broken by an explosion of "Up-up-up-keep her up!" "Up Kerry!"; and the captain of the stroke oar—a stranger imported by ourselves, and possessed by ten devils each with a formidable second wind, would respond with a spurt in which he would, with short yelps of "Double it—double it—double it" almost succeed in doubling it, and send the boat charging through the swell.

Three pound ten, my dear Jackson—six shillings a man—

including interest on the price of the boat and wear and
tear of ten oars, was what they demanded. They had thrown
down their farming implements (they dont fish on Satur-
days) to take to the sea for us at the figure.

I hardly feel real again yet.

Hindhead! Pooh! I repeat it in your teeth. POOH!!!

Celt and Saxon—you and me—I mean me and you—or
is it you and I? Meredith and Anatole France!! Is Box Hill
a beehive cell 700 feet up? What does any Parisian know
of Skellig Michael? Get out!

[G.B.S.]

To Mrs. Patrick Campbell

XXXXXXXXXXXXXXXXXXXXXXXXXXXXXXXXXXXXXXXX

Stella Campbell, whom Shaw had in mind when he wrote his Cleopatra role, became the Cleopatra of his own life in 1913, when he put his career and his marriage in jeopardy by offering to run off with her. The assignation at the Guilford Hotel, Sandwich, was aborted when she arrived and then fled, realizing that both of their lives might be ruined. "I had to behave like a man—and a gentleman," she wrote him afterwards, "hadn't I?" Shaw was crushed— for nearly a month. When the abortive affair ended, Shaw was 57 and Stella 48. A year later she played his Eliza Doolittle—age 18—in Pygmalion.

The Guilford Hotel, Sandwich.
11th Aug. 1913

Very well, go: the loss of a woman is not the end of the world. The sun shines: it is pleasant to swim: it is good to work: my soul can stand alone. But I am deeply, deeply, deeply wounded. You have tried me; and you are not comfortable with me: I cannot bring you peace, or rest, or even fun: there is nothing really frank in our comradeship after all. It is I who have been happy, carelessly happy, comfortable, able to walk for miles after dinner at top speed in search of you, singing all the way (I had walked eight miles in the morning, by the way, and written a scene of my play) and to become healthily and humorously sleepy afterwards the moment I saw that you were rather bored and that the wind was in the wrong quarter. Bah! You have no nerve: you have no brain: you are the caricature of an eighteenth century male sentimentalist, a Hedda Gabler titivated with odds and ends from Burne Jones's ragbag: you know nothing, God help you, except what you know all wrong: daylight blinds you: you run after life furtively and run away or huddle up and scream when it turns and opens its arms to you: you are a man's disgrace and infatuation not his crown "above rubies"; instead of adding the world to yourself you detach yourself, extricate yourself, guard yourself: instead of a thousand charms for a thousand different people you have one fascination with which you blunder about—hit or miss—with old and young, servants, children, artists, Philistines: you are a one-part actress and that one not a real part: you are an owl, sickened by two days of my sunshine: I have treated you far too well, idolized, thrown my heart and mind to you (as I throw them to all the world) to make what you could of; and what you make of them is to run away. Go then: the Shavian oxygen burns up your little lungs: seek some stuffiness that suits you. You will not marry George!* At the last moment you will funk him or be ousted by a bolder soul. You have wounded my vanity: an inconceivable audacity, an unpardonable crime.

Farewell, wretch that I loved.

G.B.S.

* George Cornwallis West, who was much younger than Mrs Campbell. They were married in April 1914, while *Pygmalion* was in rehearsal.

To Edmund Gurney

XXXXXXXXXXXXXXXXXXXXXXXXXXXXXXXXXXXXXXXXXX

Gurney was rehearsing the role of the dustman father of Eliza, Alfred Doolittle.

10 Adelphi Terrace, London, W.C.
6th March 1914.

My dear Gurney

Your last act has all gone to the dickens. Possibly you share my opinion, and would like to be fortified with my reasons.

In the first act your whole scene is played on the point of your being one of the undeserving poor. You get the very last inch out of it, and the slightest attempt to come back to it in the last act would be quite fatal. When it is alluded to there, there must be no emphasis whatever on it: you must play the last act altogether on your melancholy downfall as a captive of middle-class morality. When you come on the stage, Higgins will be somewhere—God knows where: if it ever gets settled at all it will probably be settled by Mrs Campbell; but you must not depend on that: for however much she settles it, Higgins will forget all about it and turn up in whatever spot destiny may lead him to. The point for you is that no matter where he is, even if he's in the middle of the stalls (and he's just as likely to be there as anywhere else) go straight to him and have it out with him about the clothes close up nose to nose with him, and make it clear that you are quite oblivious of the presence of Mrs. Higgins. I don't know where she will be; but you can ask Bell before you go on. From the moment she speaks to you, you must adapt your manner to her presence, and throw yourself with instinctive good manners, and the gallantry that has made you a slave to women all your life, on her sympathy. I want it to be clear that the dustman has much more social talent than anybody present.

He and the Colonel are the two considerate gentlemen present; but the Colonel is a bit stiff and conventional, whilst Doolittle is a born genius at the game. Take no notice of Higgins at all except in the speeches which are directly addressed to him, and make the most of your melancholy charm. Be particularly careful to do nothing that Sir Herbert tells you, because Sir Herbert thinks it's a joke to be a dustman. You and I know better. If the dustman is perfectly natural and sincere and unconscious of his being a comic character, he will be enormously entertaining. If he tries on the comic dustman for a moment, he will be a bore and a failure; the audience will guffaw at him for the first three minutes and then get tired of him. If Sir Herbert, who has the best intentions in the world towards you, tries to set you wrong on this point, pull this letter out of your pocket and make him read it. He is quite clever enough to see that I am right, or rather that we are right; for I need not keep up the pretence that all his business of turning round and bawling out the words deserved and undeserved, and so on, has been your own doing. Play the part your own way and it will come right. The truth is, I not only cast you for the part but wrote the part for you; so you may trust yourself in it without any hesitation. Sir Herbert, like most tragedians, thinks that nature intended him for a low comedian; and he thinks that Doolittle is low comedy, whereas it is a piece of straightforward life and very subtle comedy at the same time.

I have to write you this as there is no use in my coming back to the rehearsals until Mrs Campbell is tired of moving the furniture and begins to think about her own part a little; indeed, I may not come back at all. I daresay the play will get produced somehow before Christmas.

Yours sincerely,

G. Bernard Shaw

PYGMALION*
A Romance in Five Acts

XXXXXXXXXXXXXXXXXXXXXXXXXXXXXXXXXXXXXXXXXX

PREFACE: *A Professor of Phonetics*

As will be seen later on, Pygmalion needs, not a preface, but a sequel, which I have supplied in its due place.

The English have no respect for their language, and will not teach their children to speak it. They cannot spell it because they have nothing to spell it with but an old foreign alphabet of which only the consonants—and not all of them—have any agreed speech value. Consequently no man can teach himself what it should sound like from reading it; and it is impossible for an Englishman to open his mouth without making some other Englishman despise him. Most European languages are now accessible in black and white to foreigners: English and French are not thus accessible even to Englishmen and Frenchmen. The reformer we need most today is an energetic phonetic enthusiast: that is why I have made such a one the hero of a popular play.

There have been heroes of that kind crying in the wilderness for many years past. When I became interested in the subject towards the end of the eighteen-seventies, the illustrious Alexander Melville Bell, the inventor of Visible Speech, had emigrated to Canada, where his son invented the telephone; but Alexander J. Ellis was still a London patriarch, with an impressive head always covered by a velvet skull cap, for which he would apologize to public meetings in a very courtly manner. He and Tito Pagliardini, another phonetic veteran, were men whom it was impos-

---

* The text of *Pygmalion* is a hybrid one, created by Shaw after the success of his screenplay in 1938. Combined with the stage play are short scenes and narrative material from the film or to introduce the film segments. Although the lines of narrative added as a result of the film were printed in Roman, Shaw retained italics for stage directions and narrative material from the stage play. The text is printed as Shaw directed.

sible to dislike. Henry Sweet, then a young man, lacked
their sweetness of character: he was about as conciliatory
to conventional mortals as Ibsen or Samuel Butler. His
great ability as a phonetician (he was, I think, the best of
them all at his job) would have entitled him to high official
recognition, and perhaps enabled him to popularize his
subject, but for his Satanic contempt for all academic digni-
taries and persons in general who thought more of Greek
than of phonetics. Once, in the days when the Imperial
Institute rose in South Kensington, and Joseph Chamberlain was booming the Empire, I induced the editor of a
leading monthly review to commission an article from
Sweet on the imperial importance of his subject. When it
arrived, it contained nothing but a savagely derisive attack
on a professor of language and literature whose chair Sweet
regarded as proper to a phonetic expert only. The article,
being libellous, had to be returned as impossible; and I had
to renounce my dream of dragging its author into the limelight. When I met him afterwards, for the first time for
many years, I found to my astonishment that he, who had
been a quite tolerably presentable young man, had actually
managed by sheer scorn to alter his personal appearance
until he had become a sort of walking repudiation of
Oxford and all its traditions. It must have been largely in
his own despite that he was squeezed into something called
a Readership of phonetics there. The future of phonetics
rests probably with his pupils, who all swore by him; but
nothing could bring the man himself into any sort of com-
pliance with the university to which he nevertheless clung
by divine right in an intensely Oxonian way. I daresay his
papers, if he has left any, include some satires that may be
published without too destructive results fifty years hence.
He was, I believe, not in the least an ill-natured man: very
much the opposite, I should say; but he would not suffer
fools gladly; and to him all scholars who were not rabid
phoneticians were fools.

Those who knew him will recognize in my third act the
allusion to the Current Shorthand in which he used to write
postcards. It may be acquired from a four and sixpenny
manual published by the Clarendon Press. The postcards

which Mrs Higgins describes are such as I have received
from Sweet. I would decipher a sound which a cockney
would represent by *zerr*, and a Frenchman by *seu*, and
then write demanding with some heat what on earth it
meant. Sweet, with boundless contempt for my stupidity,
would reply that it not only meant but obviously was the
word Result, as no other word containing that sound, and
capable of making sense with the context, existed in any
language spoken on earth. That less expert mortals should
require fuller indications was beyond Sweet's patience.
Therefore, though the whole point of his Current Shorthand
is that it can express every sound in the language perfectly,
vowels as well as consonants, and that your hand has to
make no stroke except the easy and current ones with
which you write m, n, and u, l, p, and q, scribbling them
at whatever angle comes easiest to you, his unfortunate
determination to make this remarkable and quite legible
script serve also as a shorthand reduced it in his own practice to the most inscrutable of cryptograms. His true objec-
tive was the provision of a full, accurate, legible script for
our language; but he was led past that by his contempt for
the popular Pitman system of shorthand, which he called
the Pitfall system. The triumph of Pitman was a triumph
of business organization: there was a weekly paper to
persuade you to learn Pitman: there were cheap textbooks
and exercise books and transcripts of speeches for you to
copy, and schools where experienced teachers coached you
up to the necessary proficiency. Sweet could not organize
his market in that fashion. He might as well have been the
Sybil who tore up the leaves of prophecy that nobody
would attend to. The four and sixpenny manual, mostly in
his lithographed handwriting, that was never vulgarly
advertized, may perhaps some day be taken up by a syndicate and pushed upon the public as The Times pushed the
Encyclopaedia Britannica; but until then it will certainly
not prevail against Pitman. I have bought three copies of
it during my lifetime; and I am informed by the publishers
that its cloistered existence is still a steady and healthy one.
I actually learned the system two several times; and yet
the shorthand in which I am writing these lines is Pitman's.

And the reason is, that my secretary cannot transcribe Sweet, having been perforce taught in the schools of Pitman. In America I could use the commercially organized Gregg shorthand, which has taken a hint from Sweet by making its letters writable (current, Sweet would have called them) instead of having to be geometrically drawn like Pitman's; but all these systems, including Sweet's, are spoilt by making them available for verbatim reporting, in which complete and exact spelling and word division are impossible. A complete and exact phonetic script is neither practicable nor necessary for ordinary use; but if we enlarge our alphabet to the Russian size, and make our spelling as phonetic as Spanish, the advance will be prodigious.

Pygmalion Higgins is not a portrait of Sweet, to whom the adventure of Eliza Doolittle would have been impossible; still, as will be seen, there are touches of Sweet in the play. With Higgins's physique and temperament Sweet might have set the Thames on fire. As it was, he impressed himself professionally on Europe to an extent that made his comparative personal obscurity, and the failure of Oxford to do justice to his eminence, a puzzle to foreign specialists in his subject. I do not blame Oxford, because I think Oxford is quite right in demanding a certain social amenity from its nurslings (heaven knows it is not exorbitant in its requirements!); for although I well know how hard it is for a man of genius with a seriously underrated subject to maintain serene and kindly relations with the men who underrate it, and who keep all the best places for less important subjects which they profess without originality and sometimes without much capacity for them, still, if he overwhelms them with wrath and disdain, he cannot expect them to heap honors on him.

Of the later generations of phoneticians I know little. Among them towered Robert Bridges, to whom perhaps Higgins may owe his Miltonic sympathies, though here again I must disclaim all portraiture. But if the play makes the public aware that there are such people as phoneticians, and that they are among the most important people in England at present, it will serve its turn.

I wish to boast that Pygmalion has been an extremely

successful play, both on stage and screen, all over Europe and North America as well as at home. It is so intensely and deliberately didactic, and its subject is esteemed so dry, that I delight in throwing it at the heads of the wiseacres who repeat the parrot cry that art should never be didactic. It goes to prove my contention that great art can never be anything else.

Finally, and for the encouragement of people troubled with accents that cut them off from all high employment, I may add that the change wrought by Professor Higgins in the flower-girl is neither impossible nor uncommon. The modern concierge's daughter who fulfils her ambition by playing the Queen of Spain in Ruy Blas at the Théâtre Français is only one of many thousands of men and women who have sloughed off their native dialects and acquired a new tongue. Our West End shop assistants and domestic servants are bi-lingual. But the thing has to be done scientifically, or the last state of the aspirant may be worse than the first. An honest slum dialect is more tolerable than the attempts of phonetically untaught persons to imitate the plutocracy. Ambitious flower-girls who read this play must not imagine that they can pass themselves off as fine ladies by untutored imitation. They must learn their alphabet over again, and different, from a phonetic expert. Imitation will only make them ridiculous.

NOTE FOR TECHNICIANS. A complete representation of the play as printed for the first time in this edition is technically possible only on the cinema screen or on stages furnished with exceptionally elaborate machinery. For ordinary theatrical use the scenes separated by rows of asterisks are to be omitted.

In the dialogue an e upside down indicates the indefinite vowel, sometimes called obscure or neutral, for which, though it is one of the commonest sounds in English speech, our wretched alphabet has no letter.

PYGMALION

ACT I

London at 11.15 p.m. Torrents of heavy summer rain. Cab whistles blowing frantically in all directions. Pedestrians running for shelter into the portico of St Paul's church (not Wren's cathedral but Inigo Jones's. church in Covent Garden vegetable market), among them a lady and her daughter in evening dress. All are peering out gloomily at the rain, except one man with his back turned to the rest, wholly preoccupied with a notebook in which he is writing.

The church clock strikes the first quarter.

THE DAUGHTER [*in the space between the central pillars, close to the one on her left*] I'm getting chilled to the bone. What can Freddy be doing all this time? He's been gone twenty minutes.

THE MOTHER [*on her daughter's right*] Not so long. But he ought to have got us a cab by this.

A BYSTANDER [*on the lady's right*] He wont get no cab not until half-past eleven, missus, when they come back after dropping their theatre fares.

THE MOTHER. But we must have a cab. We cant stand here until half-past eleven. It's too bad.

THE BYSTANDER. Well it aint my fault, missus.

THE DAUGHTER. If Freddy had a bit of gumption, he would have got one at the theatre door.

THE MOTHER. What could he have done, poor boy?

THE DAUGHTER. Other people got cabs. Why couldn't he?

Freddy rushes in out of the rain from the Southampton Street side, and comes between them closing a dripping umbrella. He is a young man of twenty, in evening dress, very wet round the ankles.

THE DAUGHTER. Well, havnt you got a cab?

FREDDY. Theres not one to be had for love or money.

THE MOTHER. Oh, Freddy, there must be one. You cant have tried.

THE DAUGHTER. It's too tiresome. Do you expect us to go and get one ourselves?

FREDDY. I tell you theyre all engaged. The rain was so sudden: nobody was prepared; and everybody had to take a cab. Ive been to Charing Cross one way and nearly to Ludgate Circus the other; and they were all engaged.

THE MOTHER. Did you try Trafalgar Square?

FREDDY. There wasnt one at Trafalgar Square.

THE DAUGHTER. Did you try?

FREDDY. I tried as far as Charing Cross Station. Did you expect me to walk to Hammersmith?

THE DAUGHTER. You havnt tried at all.

THE MOTHER. You really are very helpless, Freddy. Go again; and dont come back until you have found a cab.

FREDDY. I shall simply get soaked for nothing.

THE DAUGHTER. And what about us? Are we to stay here all night in this draught, with next to nothing on? You selfish pig—

FREDDY. Oh, very well: I'll go, I'll go. [*He opens his umbrella and dashes off Strandwards, but comes into colli-
sion with a flower girl who is hurrying in for shelter,
knocking her basket out of her hands. A blinding flash
of lightning, followed instantly by a rattling peal of
thunder, orchestrates the incident*].

THE FLOWER GIRL. Nah then, Freddy: look wh' y' gowin,
deah.

FREDDY. Sorry [*he rushes off*].

THE FLOWER GIRL [*picking up her scattered flowers and replacing them in the basket*] Theres menners f'yer! Tə-oo
banches o voylets trod into the mad. [*She sits down on the
plinth of the column, sorting her flowers, on the lady's
right. She is not at all a romantic figure. She is perhaps
eighteen, perhaps twenty, hardly older. She wears a little
sailor hat of black straw that has long been exposed to
the dust and soot of London and has seldom if ever been
brushed. Her hair needs washing rather badly: its mousy
color can hardly be natural. She wears a shoddy black
coat that reaches nearly to her knees and is shaped to her
waist. She has a brown skirt with a coarse apron. Her
boots are much the worse for wear. She is no doubt as
clean as she can afford to be; but compared to the ladies
she is very dirty. Her features are no worse than theirs;
but their condition leaves something to be desired; and
she needs the services of a dentist*].

THE MOTHER. How do you know that my son's name is
Freddy, pray?

THE FLOWER GIRL. Ow, eez yə-ooa san is e? Wal, fewd
dan y' də-ooty bawmz a mather should, eed now bettern
to spawl a pore gel's flahrzn than ran awy athaht pyin.
Will ye-oo py me f'them? [*Here, with apologies, this desperate attempt to represent her dialect without a phonetic
alphabet must be abandoned as unintelligible outside
London*].

THE DAUGHTER. Do nothing of the sort, mother. The
idea!

THE MOTHER. Please allow me, Clara. Have you any
pennies?

THE DAUGHTER. No. Ive nothing smaller than sixpence.

THE FLOWER GIRL [*hopefully*] I can give you change for a tanner, kind lady.

THE MOTHER [*to Clara*] Give it to me. [*Clara parts reluctantly*]. Now [*to the girl*] This is for your flowers.

THE FLOWER GIRL. Thank you kindly, lady.

THE DAUGHTER. Make her give you the change. These things are only a penny a bunch.

THE MOTHER. Do hold your tongue, Clara. [*To the girl*] You can keep the change.

THE FLOWER GIRL. Oh, thank you, lady.

THE MOTHER. Now tell me how you know that young gentleman's name.

THE FLOWER GIRL. I didnt.

THE MOTHER. I heard you call him by it. Dont try to deceive me.

THE FLOWER GIRL [*protesting*] Who's trying to deceive you? I called him Freddy or Charlie same as you might yourself if you was talking to a stranger and wished to be pleasant.

THE DAUGHTER. Sixpence thrown away! Really, mamma, you might have spared Freddy that. [*She retreats in disgust, behind the pillar*].

An elderly gentleman of the amiable military type rushes into the shelter, and closes a dripping umbrella. He is in the same plight as Freddy, very wet about the ankles. He is in evening dress, with a light overcoat. He takes the place left vacant by the daughter.

THE GENTLEMAN. Phew!

THE MOTHER [*to the gentleman*] Oh, sir, is there any sign of its stopping?

THE GENTLEMAN. I'm afraid not. It started worse than ever about two minutes ago [*he goes to the plinth beside the flower girl; puts up his foot on it; and stoops to turn down his trouser ends*].

THE MOTHER. Oh dear [*She retires sadly and joins her daughter*].

THE FLOWER GIRL [*taking advantage of the military gentleman's proximity to establish friendly relations with him*] If it's worse, it's a sign it's nearly over. So cheer up, Captain; and buy a flower off a poor girl.

THE GENTLEMAN. I'm sorry. I havnt any change.

THE FLOWER GIRL. I can give you change, Captain.

THE GENTLEMAN. For a sovereign? Ive nothing less.

THE FLOWER GIRL. Garn! Oh do buy a flower off me, Captain. I can change half-a-crown. Take this for tuppence.

THE GENTLEMAN. Now dont be troublesome: theres a good girl. [*Trying his pockets*] I really havnt any change— Stop: heres three hapence, if thats any use to you [*he retreats to the other pillar*].

THE FLOWER GIRL [*disappointed, but thinking three halfpence better than nothing*] Thank you, sir.

THE BYSTANDER [*to the girl*] You be careful: give him a flower for it. Theres a bloke here behind taking down every blessed word youre saying. [*All turn to the man who is taking notes*].

THE FLOWER GIRL [*springing up terrified*] I aint done nothing wrong by speaking to the gentleman. Ive a right to sell flowers if I keep off the kerb. [*Hysterically*] I'm a respectable girl: so help me, I never spoke to him except to ask him to buy a flower off me.

General hubbub, mostly sympathetic to the flower girl, but deprecating her excessive sensibility. Cries of Dont start hollerin. Who's hurting you? Nobody's going to touch you. Whats the good of fussing? Steady on. Easy easy, etc., *come from the elderly staid spectators, who pat her comfortingly. Less patient ones bid her shut her head, or ask her roughly what is wrong with her. A remoter group, not knowing what the matter is, crowd in and increase the noise with question and answer*: Whats the row? What-she-do? Where is he? A tec taking her down. What! him? Yes: him over there: Took money off the gentleman, etc.

THE FLOWER GIRL [*breaking through them to the gentleman, crying wildly*] Oh, sir, dont let him charge me. You dunno what it means to me. Theyll take away my character and drive me on the streets for speaking to gentlemen. They—

THE NOTE TAKER [*coming forward on her right, the rest

crowding after him] There! there! there! there! who's
hurting you, you silly girl? What do you take me for?

THE BYSTANDER. It's aw rawt: e's a genleman: look at his
bə-oots. [*Explaining to the note taker*] She thought you
was a copper's nark, sir.

THE NOTE TAKER [*with quick interest*] Whats a copper's
nark?

THE BYSTANDER [*inapt at definition*] It's a—well, it's a copper's nark, as you might say. What else would you call
it? A sort of informer.

THE FLOWER GIRL [*still hysterical*] I take my Bible oath I
never said a word—

THE NOTE TAKER [*overbearing but good-humored*] Oh, shut
up, shut up. Do I look like a policeman?

THE FLOWER GIRL [*far from reassured*] Then what did you
take down my words for? How do I know whether you
took me down right? You just shew me what youve wrote
about me. [*The note taker opens his book and holds it
steadily under her nose, though the pressure of the mob
trying to read it over his shoulders would upset a weaker
man*]. Whats that? That aint proper writing. I cant read
that.

THE NOTE TAKER. I can. [*Reads, reproducing her pronunciation exactly*] "Cheer ap, Keptin; n' baw ya flahr orf a
pore gel."

THE FLOWER GIRL [*much distressed*] It's because I called
him Captain. I meant no harm. [*To the gentleman*] Oh,
sir, dont let him lay a charge agen me for a word like
that. You—

THE GENTLEMAN. Charge! I make no charge. [*To the note
taker*] Really, sir, if you are a detective, you need not
begin protecting me against molestation by young
women until I ask you. Anybody could see that the girl
meant no harm.

THE BYSTANDERS GENERALLY [*demonstrating against police
espionage*] Course they could. What business is it of
yours? You mind your own affairs. He wants promotion,
he does. Taking down people's words! Girl never said a
word to him. What harm if she did? Nice thing a girl

cant shelter from the rain without being insulted, etc., etc., etc. [*She is conducted by the more sympathetic demonstrators back to her plinth, where she resumes her seat and struggles with her emotion*].

THE BYSTANDER. He aint a tec. He's a blooming busybody: thats what he is. I tell you, look at his bə-oots.

THE NOTE TAKER [*turning on him genially*] And how are all your people down at Selsey?

THE BYSTANDER [*suspiciously*] Who told you my people come from Selsey?

THE NOTE TAKER. Never you mind. They did. [*To the girl*] How do you come to be up so far east? You were born in Lisson Grove.

THE FLOWER GIRL [*appalled*] Oh, what harm is there in my leaving Lisson Grove? It wasnt fit for a pig to live in; and I had to pay four-and-six a week. [*In tears*] Oh, boo–hoo–oo—

THE NOTE TAKER. Live where you like; but stop that noise.

THE GENTLEMAN [*to the girl*] Come, come! he cant touch you: you have a right to live where you please.

A SARCASTIC BYSTANDER [*thrusting himself between the note taker and the gentleman*] Park Lane, for instance. I'd like to go into the Housing Question with you, I would.

THE FLOWER GIRL [*subsiding into a brooding melancholy over her basket, and talking very low-spiritedly to herself*] I'm a good girl, I am.

THE SARCASTIC BYSTANDER [*not attending to her*] Do you know where *I* come from?

THE NOTE TAKER [*promptly*] Hoxton.

Titterings. Popular interest in the note taker's performance increases.

THE SARCASTIC ONE [*amazed*] Well, who said I didnt? Bly me! you know everything, you do.

THE FLOWER GIRL [*still nursing her sense of injury*] Aint no call to meddle with me, he aint.

THE BYSTANDER [*to her*] Of course he aint. Dont you stand it from him. [*To the note taker*] See here: what call have you to know about people what never offered to meddle with you?

THE FLOWER GIRL. Let him say what he likes. I dont want
to have no truck with him.

THE BYSTANDER. You take us for dirt under your feet,
dont you? Catch you taking liberties with a gentleman!

THE SARCASTIC BYSTANDER. Yes: tell him where he come
from if you want to go fortune-telling.

THE NOTE TAKER. Cheltenham, Harrow, Cambridge, and
India.

THE GENTLEMAN. Quite right.

Great laughter. Reaction in the note taker's favor.
Exclamations of He knows all about it. Told him proper.
Hear him tell the toff where he come from? *etc.*

THE GENTLEMAN. May I ask, sir, do you do this for your
living at a music hall?

THE NOTE TAKER. Ive thought of that. Perhaps I shall some
day.

The rain has stopped; and the persons on the outside of
the crowd begin to drop off.

THE FLOWER GIRL [*resenting the reaction*] He's no gentleman, he aint, to interfere with a poor girl.

THE DAUGHTER [*out of patience, pushing her way rudely to*
the front and displacing the gentleman, who politely
retires to the other side of the pillar] What on earth is
Freddy doing? I shall get pneumownia if I stay in this
draught any longer.

THE NOTE TAKER [*to himself, hastily making a note of her*
pronunciation of "monia"] Earls Court.

THE DAUGHTER [*violently*] Will you please keep your impertinent remarks to yourself.

THE NOTE TAKER. Did I say that out loud? I didnt mean
to. I beg your pardon. Your mother's Epsom, unmis-
takeably.

THE MOTHER [*advancing between the daughter and the note*
taker] How very curious! I was brought up in Largelady
Park, near Epsom.

THE NOTE TAKER [*uproariously amused*] Ha! ha! What a
devil of a name! Excuse me. [*To the daughter*] You want
a cab, do you?

THE DAUGHTER. Dont dare speak to me.

THE MOTHER. Oh please, please, Clara. [*Her daughter repudiates her with an angry shrug and retires haughtily*]. We should be so grateful to you, sir, if you found us a cab. [*The note taker produces a whistle*]. Oh, thank you. [*She joins her daughter*].

The note taker blows a piercing blast.

THE SARCASTIC BYSTANDER. There! I knowed he was a plain-clothes copper.

THE BYSTANDER. That aint a police whistle: thats a sporting whistle.

THE FLOWER GIRL [*still preoccupied with her wounded feelings*] He's no right to take away my character. My character is the same to me as any lady's.

THE NOTE TAKER. I dont know whether youve noticed it; but the rain stopped about two minutes ago.

THE BYSTANDER. So it has. Why didnt you say so before? and us losing our time listening to your silliness! [*He walks off towards the Strand*].

THE SARCASTIC BYSTANDER. I can tell where you come from. You come from Anwell. Go back there.

THE NOTE TAKER [*helpfully*] *H*anwell.

THE SARCASTIC BYSTANDER [*affecting great distinction of speech*] Thenk you, teacher. Haw haw! So long [*he touches his hat with mock respect and strolls off*].

THE FLOWER GIRL. Frightening people like that! How would he like it himself?

THE MOTHER. It's quite fine now, Clara. We can walk to a motor bus. Come. [*She gathers her skirts above her ankles and hurries off towards the Strand*].

THE DAUGHTER. But the cab— [*her mother is out of hearing*]. Oh, how tiresome! [*She follows angrily*].

All the rest have gone except the note taker, the gentleman, and the flower girl, who sits arranging her basket, and still pitying herself in murmurs.

THE FLOWER GIRL. Poor girl! Hard enough for her to live without being worrited and chivied.

THE GENTLEMAN [*returning to his former place on the note taker's left*] How do you do it, if I may ask?

THE NOTE TAKER. Simply phonetics. The science of speech.

Thats my profession: also my hobby. Happy is the man
who can make a living by his hobby! You can spot an
Irishman or a Yorkshireman by his brogue. *I* can place
any man within six miles. I can place him within two
miles in London. Sometimes within two streets.

THE FLOWER GIRL. Ought to be ashamed of himself, un-
manly coward!

THE GENTLEMAN. But is there a living in that?

THE NOTE TAKER. Oh, yes. Quite a fat one. This is an age
of upstarts. Men begin in Kentish Town with £80 a
year, and end in Park Lane with a hundred thousand.
They want to drop Kentish Town; but they give themselves away every time they open their mouths. Now I
can teach them—

THE FLOWER GIRL. Let him mind his own business and
leave a poor girl—

THE NOTE TAKER [*explosively*] Woman: cease this detestable boohooing instantly; or else seek the shelter of
some other place of worship.

THE FLOWER GIRL [*with feeble defiance*] Ive a right to be
here if I like, same as you.

THE NOTE TAKER. A woman who utters such depressing and
disgusting sounds has no right to be anywhere—no right
to live. Remember that you are a human being with a
soul and the divine gift of articulate speech: that your
native language is the language of Shakespear and
Milton and The Bible; and dont sit there crooning like
a bilious pigeon.

THE FLOWER GIRL [*quite overwhelmed, looking up at him
in mingled wonder and deprecation without daring to
raise her head*] Ah-ah-ah-ow-ow-oo!

THE NOTE TAKER [*whipping out his book*] Heavens! what a
sound! [*He writes; then holds out the book and reads,
reproducing her vowels exactly*] Ah-ah-ah-ow-ow-oo!

THE FLOWER GIRL [*tickled by the performance, and laughing in spite of herself*] Garn!

THE NOTE TAKER. You see this creature with her kerb-stone
English: the English that will keep her in the gutter to
the end of her days. Well, sir, in three months I could

pass that girl off as a duchess at an ambassador's garden party. I could even get her a place as lady's maid or shop assistant, which requires better English.

THE FLOWER GIRL. Whats that you say?

THE NOTE TAKER. Yes, you squashed cabbage leaf, you disgrace to the noble architecture of these columns, you incarnate insult to the English language: I could pass you off as the Queen of Sheba. [*To the Gentleman*] Can you believe that?

THE GENTLEMAN. Of course I can. I am myself a student of Indian dialects; and—

THE NOTE TAKER [*eagerly*] Are you? Do you know Colonel Pickering, the author of Spoken Sanscrit?

THE GENTLEMAN. I am Colonel Pickering. Who are you?

THE NOTE TAKER. Henry Higgins, author of Higgins's Universal Alphabet.

PICKERING [*with enthusiasm*] I came from India to meet you.

HIGGINS. I was going to India to meet you.

PICKERING. Where do you live?

HIGGINS. 27A Wimpole Street. Come and see me tomorrow.

PICKERING. I'm at the Carlton. Come with me now and lets have a jaw over some supper.

HIGGINS. Right you are.

THE FLOWER GIRL [*to Pickering, as he passes her*] Buy a flower, kind gentleman. I'm short for my lodging.

PICKERING. I really havnt any change. I'm sorry [*he goes away*].

HIGGINS [*shocked at the girl's mendacity*] Liar. You said you could change half-a-crown.

THE FLOWER GIRL [*rising in desperation*] You ought to be stuffed with nails, you ought. [*Flinging the basket at his feet*] Take the whole blooming basket for sixpence.

    The church clock strikes the second quarter.

HIGGINS [*hearing in it the voice of God, rebuking him for his Pharisaic want of charity to the poor girl*] A reminder. [*He raises his hat solemnly; then throws a handful of money into the basket and follows Pickering*].

THE FLOWER GIRL [*picking up a half-crown*] Ah-ow-ooh! [*Picking up a couple of florins*] Aaah-ow-ooh! [*Picking up several coins*] Aaaaaah-ow-ooh! [*Picking up a half-sovereign*] Aaaaaaaaaaaah-ow-ooh!!!

FREDDY [*springing out of a taxicab*] Got one at last. Hallo! [*To the girl*] Where are the two ladies that were here?

THE FLOWER GIRL. They walked to the bus when the rain stopped.

FREDDY. And left me with a cab on my hands! Damnation!

THE FLOWER GIRL [*with grandeur*] Never mind, young man. *I*'m going home in a taxi. [*She sails off to the cab. The driver puts his hand behind him and holds the door firmly shut against her. Quite understanding his mistrust, she shews him her handful of money*]. A taxi fare aint no object to me, Charlie. [*He grins and opens the door*]. Here. What about the basket?

THE TAXIMAN. Give it here. Tuppence extra.

LIZA. No: I dont want nobody to see it. [*She crushes it into the cab and gets in, continuing the conversation through the window*] Goodbye, Freddy.

FREDDY [*dazedly raising his hat*] Goodbye.

TAXIMAN. Where to?

LIZA. Bucknam Pellis [Buckingham Palace].

TAXIMAN. What d'ye mean—Bucknam Pellis?

LIZA. Dont you know where it is? In the Green Park, where the King lives. Goodbye, Freddy. Dont let me keep you standing there. Goodbye.

FREDDY. Goodbye [*He goes*].

TAXIMAN. Here? Whats this about Bucknam Pellis? What . business have you at Bucknam Pellis?

LIZA. Of course I havnt none. But I wasnt going to let him know that. You drive me home.

TAXIMAN. And wheres home?

LIZA. Angel Court, Drury Lane, next Meiklejohn's oil shop.

TAXIMAN. That sounds more like it, Judy. [*he drives off*].

*   *   *

Let us follow the taxi to the entrance to Angel Court, a narrow little archway between two shops, one of them Meiklejohn's oil shop. When it stops there, Eliza gets out, dragging her basket with her.

LIZA. How much?

TAXIMAN [*indicating the taximeter*] Cant you read? A shilling.

LIZA. A shilling for two minutes!!

TAXIMAN. Two minutes or ten: it's all the same.

LIZA. Well, I dont call it right.

TAXIMAN. Ever been in a taxi before?

LIZA [*with dignity*] Hundreds and thousands of times, young man.

TAXIMAN [*laughing at her*] Good for you, Judy. Keep the shilling, darling, with best love from all at home. Good luck! [*He drives off*].

LIZA [*humiliated*] Impidence!

She picks up the basket and trudges up the alley with it to her lodging: a small room with very old wall paper hanging loose in the damp places. A broken pane in the window is mended with paper. A portrait of a popular actor and a fashion plate of ladies' dresses, all wildly beyond poor Eliza's means, both torn from newspapers, are pinned up on the wall. A bird-cage hangs in the window; but its tenant died long ago: it remains as a memorial only.

These are the only visible luxuries: the rest is the irreducible minimum of poverty's needs: a wretched bed heaped with all sorts of coverings that have any warmth in them, a draped packing case with a basin and jug on it and a little looking glass over it, a chair and table, the refuse of some suburban kitchen, and an American alarum clock on the shelf above the unused fireplace: the whole lighted with a gas lamp with a penny in the slot meter. Rent: four shillings a week.

Here Eliza, chronically weary, but too excited to go to bed sits, counting her new riches and dreaming and planning what to do with them, until the gas goes out, when she enjoys for the first time the sensation of being able to put in another penny without grudging it. This prodigal mood does not extinguish her gnawing sense of the need for economy sufficiently to prevent her from calculating that she can dream and plan in bed more cheaply and warmly than sitting up without a fire. So she takes off her shawl and skirt and adds them to the miscel-

laneous bedclothes. Then she kicks off her shoes and gets
into bed without any further change.

ACT II

*Next day at 11 a.m. Higgins's laboratory in Wimpole Street.
It is a room on the first floor, looking on the street, and was
meant for the drawing room. The double doors are in the
middle of the back wall; and persons entering find in the
corner to their right two tall file cabinets at right angles to
one another against the walls. In this corner stands a flat
writing-table, on which are a phonograph, a laryngoscope,
a row of tiny organ pipes with a bellows, a set of lamp
chimneys for singing flames with burners attached to a gas
plug in the wall by an indiarubber tube, several tuning-forks
of different sizes, a life-size image of half a human head,
shewing in section the vocal organs, and a box containing
a supply of wax cylinders for the phonograph.*

*Further down the room, on the same side, is a fireplace,
with a comfortable leather-covered easy-chair at the side
of the hearth nearest the door, and a coal-scuttle. There is
a clock on the mantlepiece. Between the fireplace and the
phonograph table is a stand for newspapers.*

*On the other side of the central door, to the left of the
visitor, is a cabinet of shallow drawers. On it is a telephone
and the telephone directory. The corner beyond, and most
of the side wall, is occupied by a grand piano, with the
keyboard at the end furthest from the door, and a bench
for the player extending the full length of the keyboard. On
the piano is a dessert dish heaped with fruit and sweets,
mostly chocolates.*

*The middle of the room is clear. Besides the easy-chair,
the piano bench, and two chairs at the phonograph table,
there is one stray chair. It stands near the fireplace. On the
walls, engravings: mostly Piranesis and mezzotint portraits. No paintings.*

*Pickering is seated at the table, putting down some cards
and a tuning-fork which he has been using. Higgins is
standing up near him, closing two or three file drawers*

*which are hanging out. He appears in the morning light as
a robust, vital, appetizing sort of man of forty or thereabouts, dressed in a professional-looking black frock-coat
with a white linen collar and black silk tie. He is of the
energetic, scientific type, heartily, even violently interested
in everything that can be studied as a scientific subject, and
careless about himself and other people, including their
feelings. He is, in fact, but for his years and size, rather
like a very impetuous baby "taking notice" eagerly and
loudly, and requiring almost as much watching to keep
him out of unintended mischief. His manner varies from
genial bullying when he is in a good humor to stormy
petulance when anything goes wrong; but he is so entirely
frank and void of malice that he remains likeable even in
his least reasonable moments.*

HIGGINS [*as he shuts the last drawer*] Well, I think thats the
   whole show.

PICKERING. It's really amazing. I havent taken half of it in,
   you know.

HIGGINS. Would you like to go over any of it again?

PICKERING [*rising and coming to the fireplace, where he
   plants himself with his back to the fire*] No, thank you:
   not now. I'm quite done up for this morning.

HIGGINS [*following him, and standing beside him on his
   left*] Tired of listening to sounds?

PICKERING. Yes. It's a fearful strain. I rather fancied
   myself because I can pronounce twenty-four distinct
   vowel sounds; but your hundred and thirty beat me. I
   cant hear a bit of difference between most of them.

HIGGINS [*chuckling, and going over to the piano to eat
   sweets*] Oh, that comes with practice. You hear no difference at first; but you keep on listening, and presently you
   find theyre all as different as A from B. [*Mrs Pearce
   looks in: she is Higgins's housekeeper*]. Whats the matter?

MRS PEARCE [*hesitating, evidently perpexed*] A young
   woman asks to see you, sir.

HIGGINS. A young woman! What does she want?

MRS PEARCE. Well, sir, she says youll be glad to see her
   when you know what she's come about. She's quite a

common girl, sir. Very common indeed. I should have
sent her away, only I thought perhaps you wanted her
to talk into your machines. I hope Ive not done wrong;
but really you see such queer people sometimes—youll
excuse me, I'm sure, sir—

HIGGINS. Oh, thats all right, Mrs Pearce. Has she an interesting accent?

MRS PEARCE. Oh, something dreadful, sir, really. I dont
know how you can take an interest in it.

HIGGINS [*to Pickering*] Lets have her up. Shew her up, Mrs
Pearce [*he rushes across to his working table and picks
out a cylinder to use on the phonograph*].

MRS PEARCE [*only half resigned to it*] Very well, sir. It's for
you to say. [*She goes downstairs*].

HIGGINS. This is rather a bit of luck. I'll shew you how I
make records. We'll set her talking; and I'll take it down
first in Bell's Visible Speech; then in broad Romic; and
then we'll get her on the phonograph so that you can
turn her on as often as you like with the written trans-
script before you.

MRS PEARCE [*returning*] This is the young woman, sir.

*The flower girl enters in state. She has a hat with three
ostrich feathers, orange, sky-blue, and red. She has a
nearly clean apron and the shoddy coat has been tidied
a little. The pathos of this deplorable figure, with its
innocent vanity and consequential air, touches Pickering,
who has already straightened himself in the presence of
Mrs Pearce. But as to Higgins, the only distinction he
makes between men and women is that when he is neither
bullying nor exclaiming to the heavens against some
featherweight cross, he coaxes women as a child coaxes
its nurse when it wants to get anything out of her.*

HIGGINS [*brusquely, recognizing her with unconcealed disappointment, and at once, babylike, making an intolerable grievance of it*] Why, this is the girl I jotted down
last night. She's no use: Ive got all the records I want of
the Lisson Grove lingo; and I'm not going to waste
another cylinder on it. [*To the girl*] Be off with you: I
dont want you.

THE FLOWER GIRL. Dont be so saucy. You aint heard

what I come for yet. [*To Mrs Pearce, who is waiting at
the door for further instructions*] Did you tell him I
come in a taxi?

MRS PEARCE. Nonsense, girl! what do you think a gentleman like Mr Higgins cares what you came in?

THE FLOWER GIRL. Oh, we a r e proud! He aint above
giving lessons, not him: I heard him say so. Well, I aint
come here to ask for any compliment; and if my money's
not good enough I can go elsewhere.

HIGGINS. Good enough for what?

THE FLOWER GIRL. Good enough for yə-oo. Now you
know, dont you? I'm come to have lessons, I am. And to
pay for em tə-oo: make no mistake.

HIGGINS [*stupent*] Well!!! [*Recovering his breath with a
gasp*] What do you expect me to say to you?

THE FLOWER GIRL. Well, if you was a gentleman, you
might ask me to sit down, I think. Dont I tell you I'm
bringing you business?

HIGGINS. Pickering: shall we ask this baggage to sit down,
or shall we throw her out of the window?

THE FLOWER GIRL [*running away in terror to the piano,
where she turns at bay*] Ah-ah-oh-ow-ow-ow-oo!
[*Wounded and whimpering*] I wont be called a baggage
when Ive offered to pay like any lady.

   *Motionless, the two men stare at her from the other
   side of the room, amazed.*

PICKERING [*gently*] But what is it you want?

THE FLOWER GIRL. I want to be a lady in a flower shop
'stead of sellin at the corner of Tottenham Court Road.
But they wont take me unless I can talk more genteel. He
said he could teach me. Well, here I am ready to pay him
—not asking any favor—and he treats me zif I was dirt.

MRS PEARCE. How can you be such a foolish ignorant girl
as to think you could afford to pay Mr Higgins?

THE FLOWER GIRL. Why shouldnt I? I know what lessons
cost as well as you do; and I'm ready to pay.

HIGGINS. How much?

THE FLOWER GIRL [*coming back to him, triumphant*] Now
youre talking! I thought youd come off it when you saw
a chance of getting back a bit of what you chucked at me

last night. [*Confidentially*] Youd had a drop in, hadnt you?

HIGGINS [*peremptorily*] Sit down.

THE FLOWER GIRL. Oh, if youre going to make a compliment of it—

HIGGINS [*thundering at her*] Sit down.

MRS PEARCE [*severely*] Sit down, girl. Do as youre told.

THE FLOWER GIRL. *Ah-ah-ah-ow-ow-oo!* [*She stands, half rebellious, half-bewildered*].

PICKERING [*very courteous*] Wont you sit down? [*He places the stray chair near the hearthrug between himself and Higgins*].

LIZA [*coyly*] Dont mind if I do. [*She sits down. Pickering returns to the hearthrug*].

HIGGINS. Whats your name?

THE FLOWER GIRL. Liza Doolittle.

HIGGINS [*declaiming gravely*]

> Eliza, Elizabeth, Betsy and Bess,
> They went to the woods to get a bird's nes':

PICKERING: They found a nest with four eggs in it:

HIGGINS. They took one apiece, and left three in it.

They laugh heartily at their own fun.

LIZA. Oh, dont be silly.

MRS PEARCE [*placing herself behind Eliza's chair*] You mustnt speak to the gentleman like that.

LIZA. Well, why wont he speak sensible to me?

HIGGINS. Come back to business. How much do you propose to pay me for the lessons?

LIZA. Oh, I know whats right. A lady friend of mine gets French lessons for eighteenpence an hour from a real French gentleman. Well, you wouldnt have the face to ask me the same for teaching me my own language as you would for French; so I wont give more than a shilling. Take it or leave it.

HIGGINS [*walking up and down the room, rattling his keys and his cash in his pockets*] You know, Pickering, if you consider a shilling, not as a simple shilling, but as a percentage of this girl's income, it works out as fully equivalent to sixty or seventy guineas from a millionaire.

PICKERING. How so?

HIGGINS. Figure it out. A millionaire has about £150 a day. She earns about half-a-crown.

LIZA [*haughtily*] Who told you I only—

HIGGINS [*continuing*] She offers me two-fifths of her day's income for a lesson. Two-fifths of a millionaire's income for a day would be somewhere about £60. It's handsome. By George, it's enormous! It's the biggest offer I ever had.

LIZA [*rising, terrified*] Sixty pounds! What are you talking about? I never offered you sixty pounds. Where would I get—

HIGGINS. Hold your tongue.

LIZA [*weeping*] But I aint got sixty pounds. Oh—

MRS PEARCE. Dont cry, you silly girl. Sit down. Nobody is going to touch your money.

HIGGINS. Somebody is going to touch you, with a broomstick, if you dont stop snivelling. Sit down.

LIZA [*obeying slowly*] Ah-ah-ah-ow-oo-o! One would think you was my father.

HIGGINS. If I decide to teach you, I'll be worse than two fathers to you. Here [*he offers her his silk handkerchief*]!

LIZA. Whats this for?

HIGGINS. To wipe your eyes. To wipe any part of your face that feels moist. Remember: thats your handkerchief: and thats your sleeve. Dont mistake the one for the other if you wish to become a lady in a shop.

Liza, utterly bewildered, stares helplessly at him.

MRS PEARCE. It's no use talking to her like that, Mr Higgins: she doesnt understand you. Besides, youre quite wrong: she doesnt do it that way at all [*she takes the handkerchief*].

LIZA [*snatching it*] Here! You give me that handkerchief. He gev it to me, not to you.

PICKERING [*laughing*] He did. I think it must be regarded as her property, Mrs Pearce.

MRS PEARCE [*resigning herself*] Serve you right, Mr Higgins.

PICKERING. Higgins: I'm interested. What about the ambassador's garden party? I'll say youre the greatest teacher alive if you make that good. I'll bet you all the

expenses of the experiment you cant do it. And I'll pay
for the lessons.

LIZA. Oh, you are real good. Thank you, Captain.

HIGGINS [*tempted, looking at her*] It's almost irresistible.
She's so deliciously low—so horribly dirty—

LIZA [*protesting extremely*] Ah-ah-ah-ah-ow-ow-oo-oo!!! I
aint dirty: I washed my face and hands afore I come, I
did.

PICKERING. Youre certainly not going to turn her head with
flattery, Higgins.

MRS PEARCE [*uneasy*] Oh, dont say that, sir: theres more
ways than one of turning a girl's head; and nobody can
do it better than Mr Higgins, though he may not always
mean it. I do hope, sir, you wont encourage him to do
anything foolish.

HIGGINS [*becoming excited as the idea grows on him*] What
is life but a series of inspired follies? The difficulty is to
find them to do. Never lose a chance: it doesnt come
every day. I shall make a duchess of this draggletailed
guttersnipe.

LIZA [*strongly deprecating this view of her*] Ah-ah-ah-ow-
ow-oo!

HIGGINS [*carried away*] Yes: in six months—in three if she
has a good ear and a quick tongue—I'll take her anywhere and pass her off as anything. We'll start today:
now! this moment! Take her away and clean her, Mrs
Pearce. Monkey Brand, if it wont come off any other
way. Is there a good fire in the kitchen?

MRS PEARCE [*protesting*] Yes; but—

HIGGINS [*storming on*] Take all her clothes off and burn
them. Ring up Whiteley or somebody for new ones.
Wrap her up in brown paper til they come.

LIZA. Youre no gentleman, youre not, to talk of such
things. I'm a good girl, I am; and I know what the like
of you are, I do.

HIGGINS. We want none of your Lisson Grove prudery
here, young woman. Youve got to learn to behave like a
duchess. Take her away, Mrs Pearce. If she gives you any
trouble, wallop her.

LIZA [*springing up and running between Pickering and Mrs Pearce for protection*] No! I'll call the police, I will.

MRS PEARCE. But Ive no place to put her.

HIGGINS. Put her in the dustbin.

LIZA. Ah-ah-ah-ow-ow-oo!

PICKERING. Oh come, Higgins! be reasonable.

MRS PEARCE [*resolutely*] You must be reasonable, Mr Higgins: really you must. You cant walk over everybody like this.

    Higgins, thus scolded, subsides. The hurricane is succeeded by a zephyr of amiable surprise.

HIGGINS [*with professional exquisiteness of modulation*] I walk over everybody! My dear Mrs Pearce, my dear Pickering, I never had the slightest intention of walking over anyone. All I propose is that we should be kind to this poor girl. We must help her to prepare and fit herself for her new station in life. If I did not express myself clearly it was because I did not wish to hurt her delicacy, or yours.

    Liza, reassured, steals back to her chair.

MRS PEARCE [*to Pickering*] Well, did you ever hear anything like that, sir?

PICKERING [*laughing heartily*] Never, Mrs Pearce: never.

HIGGINS [*patiently*] Whats the matter?

MRS PEARCE. Well, the matter is, sir, that you cant take a girl up like that as if you were picking up a pebble on the beach.

HIGGINS. Why not?

MRS PEARCE. Why not! But you dont know anything about her. What about her parents? She may be married.

LIZA. Garn!

HIGGINS. There! As the girl very properly says, Garn! Married indeed! Dont you know that a woman of that class looks a worn out drudge of fifty a year after she's married?

LIZA. Whood marry me?

HIGGINS [*suddenly resorting to the most thrillingly beautiful low tones in his best elocutionary style*] By George, Eliza, the streets will be strewn with the bodies of men shooting themselves for your sake before Ive done with you.

MRS PEARCE. Nonsense, sir. You mustnt talk like that to her.

LIZA [*rising and squaring herself determinedly*] I'm going away. He's off his chump, he is. I dont want no balmies teaching me.

HIGGINS [*wounded in his tenderest point by her insensibility to his elocution*] Oh, indeed! I'm mad, am I? Very well, Mrs Pearce: you neednt order the new clothes for her. Throw her out.

LIZA [*whimpering*] Nah-ow. You got no right to touch me.

MRS PEARCE. You see now what comes of being saucy. [*Indicating the door*] This way, please.

LIZA [*almost in tears*] I didnt want no clothes. I wouldnt have taken them [*she throws away the handkerchief*]. I can buy my own clothes.

HIGGINS [*deftly retrieving the handkerchief and intercepting her on her reluctant way to the door*] Youre an ungrateful wicked girl. This is my return for offering to take you out of the gutter and dress you beautifully and make a lady of you.

MRS PEARCE. Stop, Mr Higgins. I wont allow it. It's you that are wicked. Go home to your parents, girl; and tell them to take better care of you.

LIZA. I aint got no parents. They told me I was big enough to earn my own living and turned me out.

MRS PEARCE. Wheres your mother?

LIZA. I aint got no mother. Her that turned me out was my sixth stepmother. But I done without them. And I'm a good girl, I am.

HIGGINS. Very well, then, what on earth is all this fuss about? The girl doesnt belong to anybody—is no use to anybody but me. [*He goes to Mrs Pearce and begins coaxing*]. You can adopt her, Mrs Pearce: I'm sure a daughter would be a great amusement to you. Now dont make any more fuss. Take her downstairs; and—

MRS PEARCE. But whats to become of her? Is she to be paid anything? Do be sensible, sir.

HIGGINS. Oh, pay her whatever is necessary: put it down in the housekeeping book. [*Impatiently*] What on earth will she want with money? She'll have her food and her clothes. She'll only drink if you give her money.

LIZA [*turning on him*] Oh you are a brute. It's a lie: nobody
    ever saw the sign of liquor on me. [*To Pickering*] Oh, sir:
    youre a gentleman: dont let him speak to me like that.

PICKERING [*in good-humored remonstrance*] Does it occur
    to you, Higgins, that the girl has some feelings?

HIGGINS [*looking critically at her*] Oh no, I dont think so.
    Not any feeling that we need bother about. [*Cheerily*]
    Have you, Eliza?

LIZA. I got my feelings same as anyone else.

HIGGINS [*to Pickering, reflectively*] You see the difficulty?

PICKERING. Eh? What difficulty?

HIGGINS. To get her to talk grammar. The mere pronun-
    ciation is easy enough.

LIZA. I dont want to talk grammar. I want to talk like a
    lady in a flower-shop.

MRS PEARCE. Will you please keep to the point, Mr Higgins.
    I want to know on what terms the girl is to be here. Is she
    to have any wages? And what is to become of her when
    youve finished your teaching? You must look ahead a
    little.

HIGGINS [*impatiently*] Whats to become of her if I leave her
    in the gutter? Tell me that, Mrs Pearce.

MRS PEARCE. Thats her own business, not yours, Mr
    Higgins.

HIGGINS. Well, when Ive done with her, we can throw her
    back into the gutter; and then it will be her own business
    again; so thats all right.

LIZA. Oh, youve no feeling heart in you: you dont care for
    nothing but yourself. [*She rises and takes the floor reso-
    lutely*]. Here! Ive had enough of this. I'm going [*making
    for the door*]. You ought to be ashamed of yourself, you
    ought.

HIGGINS [*snatching a chocolate cream from the piano, his
    eyes suddenly beginning to twinkle with mischief*] Have
    some chocolates, Eliza.

LIZA [*halting, tempted*] How do I know what might be in
    them? Ive heard of girls being drugged by the like of you.

    *Higgins whips out his penknife; cuts a chocolate in
    two; puts one half into his mouth and bolts it; and offers
    her the other half.*

HIGGINS. Pledge of good faith, Eliza. I eat one half: you eat the other. [*Liza opens her mouth to retort: he pops the half chocolate into it*]. You shall have boxes of them, barrels of them, every day. You shall live on them. Eh?

LIZA [*who has disposed of the chocolate after being nearly choked by it*] I wouldnt have ate it, only I'm too ladylike to take it out of my mouth.

HIGGINS. Listen, Eliza. I think you said you came in a taxi.

LIZA. Well, what if I did? Ive as good a right to take a taxi as anyone else.

HIGGINS. You have, Eliza; and in the future you shall have as many taxis as you want. You shall go up and down and round the town in a taxi every day. Think of that, Eliza.

MRS PEARCE. Mr Higgins: youre tempting the girl. It's not right. She should think of the future.

HIGGINS. At her age! Nonsense! Time enough to think of the future when you havnt any future to think of. No, Eliza: do as this lady does: think of other people's futures; but never think of your own. Think of chocolates, and taxis, and gold, and diamonds.

LIZA. No: I dont want no gold and no diamonds. I'm a good girl, I am. [*She sits down again, with an attempt at dignity*].

HIGGINS. You shall remain so, Eliza, under the care of Mrs Pearce. And you shall marry an officer in the Guards, with a beautiful moustache: the son of a marquis, who will disinherit him for marrying you, but will relent when he sees your beauty and goodness—

PICKERING. Excuse me, Higgins; but I really must interfere. Mrs Pearce is quite right. If this girl is to put herself in your hands for six months for an experiment in teaching, she must understand thoroughly what she's doing.

HIGGINS. How can she? She's incapable of understanding anything. Besides, do any of us understand what we are doing? If we did, would we ever do it?

PICKERING. Very clever, Higgins; but not to the present point. [*To Eliza*] Miss Doolittle—

LIZA [*overwhelmed*] Ah-ah-ow-oo!

HIGGINS. There! Thats all youll get out of Eliza. Ah-ah-ow-oo! No use explaining. As a military man you ought to know that. Give her her orders: thats enough for her. Eliza: you are to live here for the next six months, learning how to speak beautifully, like a lady in a florist's shop. If youre good and do whatever youre told, you shall sleep in a proper bedroom, and have lots to eat, and money to buy chocolates and take rides in taxis. If youre naughty and idle you will sleep in the back kitchen among the black beetles, and be walloped by Mrs Pearce with a broomstick. At the end of six months you shall go to Buckingham Palace in a carriage, beautifully dressed. If the King finds out youre not a lady, you will be taken by the police to the Tower of London, where your head will be cut off as a warning to other presumptuous flower girls. If you are not found out, you shall have a present of seven-and-sixpence to start life with as a lady in a shop. If you refuse this offer you will be a most ungrateful wicked girl; and the angels will weep for you. [*To Pickering*] Now are you satisfied, Pickering? [*To Mrs Pierce*] Can I put it more plainly and fairly, Mrs Pearce?

MRS PEARCE [*patiently*] I think youd better let me speak to the girl properly in private. I dont know that I can take charge of her or consent to the arrangement at all. Of course I know you dont mean her any harm; but when you get what you call interested in people's accents, you never think or care what may happen to them or you. Come with me, Eliza.

HIGGINS. That's all right. Thank you, Mrs Pearce. Bundle her off to the bathroom.

LIZA [*rising reluctantly and suspiciously*] Youre a great bully, you are. I wont stay here if I dont like. I wont let nobody wallop me. I never asked to go to Bucknam Palace, I didnt. I was never in trouble with the police, not me. I'm a good girl—

MRS PEARCE. Dont answer back, girl. You dont understand the gentleman. Come with me. [*She leads the way to the door, and holds it open for Eliza*].

LIZA [*as she goes out*] Well, what I say is right. I wont go near the King, not if I'm going to have my head cut off. If I'd known what I was letting myself in for, I wouldnt

have come here. I always been a good girl; and I never
offered to say a word to him; and dont owe him nothing;
and I dont care; and I wont be put upon; and I have my
feelings the same as anyone else—

*Mrs Pearce shuts the door; and Eliza's plaints are no
longer audible.*

*   *   *

Eliza is taken upstairs to the third floor greatly to her
surprise; for she expected to be taken down to the
scullery. There Mrs Pearce opens a door and takes her
into a spare bedroom.

MRS PEARCE. I will have to put you here. This will be your
bedroom.

LIZA. O-h, I couldnt sleep here, missus. It's too good for the
likes of me. I should be afraid to touch anything. I aint a
duchess yet, you know.

MRS PEARCE. You have got to make yourself as clean as
the room: then you wont be afraid of it. And you must
call me Mrs Pearce, not missus. [*She throws open the
door of the dressing-room, now modernized as a bathroom*].

LIZA. Gawd! whats this? Is this where you wash clothes?
Funny sort of copper I call it.

MRS PEARCE. It is not a copper. This is where we wash
ourselves, Eliza, and where I am going to wash you.

LIZA. You expect me to get into that and wet myself all
over! Not me. I should catch my death. I knew a woman
did it every Saturday night; and she died of it.

MRS PEARCE. Mr Higgins has the gentlemen's bathroom
downstairs; and he has a bath every morning, in cold
water.

LIZA. Ugh! He's made of iron, that man.

MRS PEARCE. If you are to sit with him and the Colonel and
be taught you will have to do the same. They wont like
the smell of you if you dont. But you can have the water
as hot as you like. There are two taps: hot and cold.

LIZA [*weeping*] I couldnt. I dursnt. It's not normal: it would
kill me. Ive never had a bath in my life: not what youd
call a proper one.

MRS PEARCE. Well, dont you want to be clean and sweet and decent, like a lady? You know you cant be a nice girl inside if youre a dirty slut outside.

LIZA. Boohoo!!!!

MRS PEARCE. Now stop crying and go back in to your room and take off all your clothes. Then wrap yourself in this [*taking down a gown from its peg and handing it to her*] and come back to me. I will get the bath ready.

LIZA [*all tears*] I cant. I wont. I'm not used to it. Ive never took off all my clothes before. It's not right: it's not decent.

MRS PEARCE. Nonsense, child. Dont you take off all your clothes every night when you go to bed?

LIZA [*amazed*] No. Why should I? I should catch my death. Of course I take off my skirt.

MRS PEARCE. Do you mean that you sleep in the under-clothes you wear in the daytime?

LIZA. What else have I to sleep in?

MRS PEARCE. You will never do that again as long as you live here. I will get you a proper nightdress.

LIZA. Do you mean change into cold things and lie awake shivering half the night? You want to kill me, you do.

MRS PEARCE. I want to change you from a frowzy slut to a clean respectable girl fit to sit with the gentlemen in the study. Are you going to trust me and do what I tell you or be thrown out and sent back to your flower basket?

LIZA. But you dont know what the cold is to me. You dont know how I dread it.

MRS PEARCE. Your bed wont be cold here: I will put a hot water bottle in it. [*Pushing her into the bedroom*] Off with you and undress.

LIZA. Oh, if only I'd a known what a dreadful thing it is to be clean I'd never have come. I didnt know when I was well off. I— [*Mrs Pearce pushes her through the door, but leaves it partly open lest her prisoner should take to flight*].

Mrs Pearce puts on a pair of white rubber sleeves, and fills the bath, mixing hot and cold, and testing the result with the bath thermometer. She perfumes it with a hand-ful of bath salts and adds a palmful of mustard. She then

*takes a formidable looking long handled scrubbing brush
and soaps it profusely with a ball of scented soap.*

*Eliza comes back with nothing on but the bath gown
huddled tightly round her, a piteous spectacle of abject
terror.*

MRS PEARCE. Now come along. Take that thing off.

LIZA. Oh I couldnt, Mrs Pearce: I reely couldnt. I never
done such a thing.

MRS PEARCE. Nonsense. Here: step in and tell me whether
it's hot enough for you.

LIZA. Ah-oo! Ah-oo! It's too hot.

MRS PEARCE [*deftly snatching the gown away and throwing
Eliza down on her back*] It wont hurt you. [*She sets to
work with the scrubbing brush*].

Eliza's screams are heartrending.

*   *   *

*Meanwhile the Colonel has been having it out with
Higgins about Eliza. Pickering has come from the hearth
to the chair and seated himself astride of it with his arms
on the back to cross-examine him.*

PICKERING. Excuse the straight question, Higgins. Are you
a man of good character where women are concerned?

HIGGINS [*moodily*] Have you ever met a man of good character where women are concerned?

PICKERING. Yes: very frequently.

HIGGINS [*dogmatically, lifting himself on his hands to the
level of the piano, and sitting on it with a bounce*] Well,
I havnt. I find that the moment I let a woman make
friends with me, she becomes jealous, exacting, suspicious, and a damned nuisance. I find that the moment I
let myself make friends with a woman, I become selfish
and tyrannical. Women upset everything. When you let
them into your life, you find that the woman is driving
at one thing and youre driving at another.

PICKERING. At what, for example?

HIGGINS [*coming off the piano restlessly*] Oh, Lord knows! I
suppose the woman wants to live her own life; and the
man wants to live his; and each tries to drag the other on

to the wrong track. One wants to go north and the other south; and the result is that both have to go east, though they both hate the east wind. [*He sits down on the bench at the keyboard*]. So here I am, a confirmed old bachelor, and likely to remain so.

PICKERING [*rising and standing over him gravely*] Come, Higgins! You know what I mean. If I'm to be in this business I shall feel responsible for that girl. I hope it's understood that no advantage is to be taken of her position.

HIGGINS. What! That thing! Sacred, I assure you. [*Rising to explain*] You see, she'll be a pupil; and teaching would be impossible unless pupils were sacred. Ive taught scores of American millionairesses how to speak English: the best looking women in the world. I'm seasoned. They might as well be blocks of wood. *I* might as well be a block of wood. It's—

Mrs. Pearce opens the door. She has Eliza's hat in her hand. Pickering retires to the easy-chair at the hearth and sits down.

HIGGINS [*eagerly*] Well, Mrs Pearce: is it all right?

MRS PEARCE [*at the door*] I just wish to trouble you with a word, if I may, Mr Higgins.

HIGGINS. Yes, certainly. Come in. [*She comes forward*]. Dont burn that, Mrs Pearce. I'll keep it as a curiosity. [*He takes the hat*].

MRS PEARCE. Handle it carefully, sir, please. I had to promise her not to burn it; but I had better put it in the oven for a while.

HIGGINS [*putting it down hastily on the piano*] Oh! thank you. Well, what have you to say to me?

PICKERING. Am I in the way?

MRS PEARCE. Not at all, sir. Mr Higgins: will you please be very particular what you say before the girl?

HIGGINS [*sternly*] Of course. I'm always particular about what I say. Why do you say this to me?

MRS PEARCE [*unmoved*] No sir: youre not at all particular when youve mislaid anything or when you get a little impatient. Now it doesnt matter before me: I'm used to it. But you really must not swear before the girl!

HIGGINS [*indignantly*] *I* swear! [*Most emphatically*] I never swear. I detest the habit. What the devil do you mean?

MRS PEARCE [*stolidly*] Thats what I mean, sir. You swear a great deal too much. I dont mind your damning and blasting, and what the devil and where the devil and who the devil—

HIGGINS. Mrs Pearce: this language from your lips! Really!

MRS PEARCE [*not to be put off*] —but there is a certain word I must ask you not to use. The girl used it herself when she began to enjoy the bath. It begins with the same letter as bath. She knows no better: she learnt it at her mother's knee. But she must not hear it from your lips.

HIGGINS [*loftily*] I cannot charge myself with having ever uttered it, Mrs Pearce. [*She looks at him steadfastly. He adds, hiding an uneasy conscience with a judicial air*] Except perhaps in a moment of extreme and justifiable excitement.

MRS PEARCE. Only this morning, sir, you applied it to your boots, to the butter, and to the brown bread.

HIGGINS. Oh, that! Mere alliteration, Mrs. Peace, natural to a poet.

MRS PEARCE. Well, sir, whatever you choose to call it, I beg you not to let the girl hear you repeat it.

HIGGINS. Oh, very well, very well. Is that all?

MRS PEARCE. No, sir. We shall have to be very particular with this girl as to personal cleanliness.

HIGGINS. Certainly. Quite right. Most important.

MRS PEARCE. I mean not to be slovenly about her dress or untidy in leaving things about.

HIGGINS [*going to her solemnly*] Just so. I intended to call your attention to that. [*He passes on to Pickering, who is enjoying the conversation immensely*]. It is these little things that matter, Pickering. Take care of the pence and the pounds will take care of themselves is as true of personal habits as of money. [*He comes to anchor on the hearthrug, with the air of a man in an unassailable position*].

MRS PEARCE. Yes, sir. Then might I ask you not to come down to breakfast in your dressing-gown, or at any rate not to use it as a napkin to the extent you do, sir. And if

you would be so good as not to eat everything off the
same plate, and to remember not to put the porridge
saucepan out of your hand on the clean tablecloth, it
would be a better example to the girl. You know you
nearly choked yourself with a fishbone in the jam only
last week.

HIGGINS [*routed from the hearthrug and drifting back to the
piano*] I may do these things sometimes in absence of
mind; but surely I dont do them habitually. [*Angrily*] By
the way: my dressing-gown smells most damnably of
benzine.

MRS PEARCE. No doubt it does, Mr Higgins. But if you will
wipe your fingers—

HIGGINS [*yelling*] Oh very well, very well: I'll wipe them in
my hair in future.

MRS PEARCE. I hope youre not offended, Mr Higgins.

HIGGINS [*shocked at finding himself thought capable of an
unamiable sentiment*] Not at all, not at all. Youre quite
right, Mrs Pearce: I shall be particularly careful before
the girl. Is that all?

MRS PEARCE. No, sir. Might she use some of those
Japanese dresses you brought from abroad? I really cant
put her back into her old things.

HIGGINS. Certainly. Anything you like. Is that all?

MRS PEARCE. Thank you, sir. Thats all. [*She goes out*].

HIGGINS. You know, Pickering, that woman has the most
extraordinary ideas about me. Here I am, a shy, diffident
sort of man. Ive never been able to feel really grown-up
and tremendous, like other chaps. And yet she's firmly
persuaded that I'm an arbitrary overbearing bossing kind
of person. I cant account for it.

Mrs Pearce returns.

MRS PEARCE. If you please, sir, the trouble's beginning
already. Theres a dustman downstairs, Alfred Doolittle,
wants to see you. He says you have his daughter here.

PICKERING [*rising*] Phew! I say!

HIGGINS [*promptly*] Send the blackguard up.

MRS PEARCE. Oh, very well, sir. [*She goes out*].

PICKERING. He may not be a blackguard, Higgins.

HIGGINS. Nonsense. Of course he's a blackguard.

PICKERING. Whether he is or not, I'm afraid we shall have some trouble with him.

HIGGINS [*confidently*] Oh no: I think not. If theres any trouble he shall have it with me, not I with him. And we are sure to get something interesting out of him.

PICKERING. About the girl?

HIGGINS. No. I mean his dialect.

PICKERING. Oh!

MRS PEARCE [*at the door*] Doolittle, sir. [*She admits Doolittle and retires*].

Alfred Doolittle is an elderly but vigorous dustman, clad in the costume of his profession, including a hat with a back brim covering his neck and shoulders. He has well marked and rather interesting features, and seems equally free from fear and conscience. He has a remarkably expressive voice, the result of a habit of giving vent to his feelings without reserve. His present pose is that of wounded honour and stern resolution.

DOOLITTLE [*at the door, uncertain which of the two gentlemen is his man*] Professor Iggins?

HIGGINS. Here. Good morning. Sit down.

DOOLITTLE. Morning. Governor. [*He sits down magisterially*] I come about a very serious matter, Governor.

HIGGINS [*to Pickering*] Brought up in Hounslow. Mother Welsh, I should think. [*Doolittle opens his mouth, amazed. Higgins continues*] What do you want, Doolittle?

DOOLITTLE [*menacingly*] I want my daughter: thats what I want. See?

HIGGINS. Of course you do. Youre her father, arnt you? You dont suppose anyone else wants her, do you? I'm glad to see you have some spark of family feeling left. She's upstairs. Take her away at once.

DOOLITTLE [*rising, fearfully taken aback*] What!

HIGGINS. Take her away. Do you suppose I'm going to keep your daughter for you?

DOOLITTLE [*remonstrating*] Now, now, look here, Governor. Is this reasonable? Is it fairity to take advantage of a man like this? The girl belongs to me. You got her. Where do I come in? [*He sits down again*].

HIGGINS. Your daughter had the audacity to come to my

house and ask me to teach her how to speak properly so
that she could get a place in a flower-shop. This gentleman and my housekeeper have been here all the time.
[*Bullying him*] How dare you come here and attempt to
blackmail me? You sent her here on purpose.

DOOLITTLE [*protesting*] No, Governor.

HIGGINS. You must have. How else could you possibly
know that she is here?

DOOLITTLE. Dont take a man up like that, Governor.

HIGGINS. The police shall take you up. This is a plant—a
plot to extort money by threats. I shall telephone for the
police [*he goes resolutely to the telephone and opens the
directory*].

DOOLITTLE. Have I asked you for a brass farthing? I leave
it to the gentleman here: have I said a word about
money?

HIGGINS [*throwing the book aside and marching down on
Doolittle with a poser*] What else did you come for?

DOOLITTLE [*sweetly*] Well, what w o u l d a man come for?
Be human, Governor.

HIGGINS [*disarmed*] Alfred: did you put her up to it?

DOOLITTLE. So help me, Governor, I never did. I take my
Bible oath I aint seen the girl these two months past.

HIGGINS. Then how did you know she was here?

DOOLITTLE [*"most musical, most melancholy"*] I'll tell you,
Governor, if youll only let me get a word in. I'm willing
to tell you. I'm wanting to tell you. I'm waiting to tell
you.

HIGGINS. Pickering: this chap has a certain natural gift of
rhetoric. Observe the rhythm of his native woodnotes
wild. "I'm willing to tell you: I'm wanting to tell you:
I'm waiting to tell you." Sentimental rhetoric! thats the
Welsh strain in him. It also accounts for his mendacity
and dishonesty.

PICKERING. Oh, please, Higgins: I'm west country myself.
[*To Doolittle*] How did you know the girl was here if you
didnt send her?

DOOLITTLE. It was like this, Governor. The girl took a boy
in the taxi to give him a jaunt. Son of her landlady, he is.
He hung about on the chance of her giving him another

ride home. Well, she sent him back for her luggage when she heard you was willing for her to stop here. I met the boy at the corner of Long Acre and Endell Street.

HIGGINS. Public house. Yes?

DOOLITTLE. The poor man's club, Governor: why shouldnt I?

PICKERING. Do let him tell his story, Higgins.

DOOLITTLE. He told me what was up. And I ask you, what was my feelings and my duty as a father? I says to the boy, "You bring me the luggage," I says—

PICKERING. Why didnt you go for it yourself?

DOOLITTLE. Landlady wouldnt have trusted me with it, Governor. She's that kind of woman: you know. I had to give the boy a penny afore he trusted me with it, the little swine. I brought it to her just to oblige you like, and make myself agreeable. Thats all.

HIGGINS. How much luggage?

DOOLITTLE. Musical instrument, Governor. A few pictures, a trifle of jewelry, and a bird-cage. She said she didnt want no clothes. What was I to think from that, Governor? I ask you as a parent what was I to think?

HIGGINS. So you came to rescue her from worse than death eh?

DOOLITTLE [*appreciatively: relieved at being so well understood*] Just so, Governor. Thats right.

PICKERING. But why did you bring her luggage if you intended to take her away?

DOOLITTLE. Have I said a word about taking her away? Have I now?

HIGGINS [*determinedly*] Youre going to take her away, double quick. [*He crosses to the hearth and rings the bell*].

DOOLITTLE [*rising*] No, Governor. Dont say that. I'm not the man to stand in my girl's light. Heres a career opening for her as you might say; and—

Mrs Pearce opens the door and awaits orders.

HIGGINS. Mrs Pearce: this is Eliza's father. He has come to take her away. Give her to him. [*He goes back to the piano, with an air of washing his hands of the whole affair*].

DOOLITTLE. No. This is a misunderstanding. Listen here—

MRS PEARCE. He cant take her away, Mr Higgins: how can he? You told me to burn her clothes.

DOOLITTLE. Thats right. I cant carry the girl through the streets like a blooming monkey, can I? I put it to you.

HIGGINS. You have put it to me that you want your daughter. Take your daughter. If she has no clothes go out and buy her some.

DOOLITTLE [*desperate*] Wheres the old clothes she come in? Did I burn them or did your missus here?

MRS PEARCE. I am the housekeeper, if you please. I have sent for some clothes for your girl. When they come you can take her away. You can wait in the kitchen. This way, please.

Doolittle, much troubled, accompanies her to the door; then hesitates; finally turns confidentially to Higgins.

DOOLITTLE. Listen here, Governor. You and me is men of the world, aint we?

HIGGINS. Oh! Men of the world, are we? Youd better go, Mrs Pearce.

MRS PEARCE. I think so, indeed, sir. [*She goes, with dignity*].

PICKERING. The floor is yours, Mr. Doolittle.

DOOLITTLE [*to Pickering*] I thank you, Governor. [*To Higgins, who takes refuge on the piano bench, a little overwhelmed by the proximity of his visitor; for Doolittle has a professional flavour of dust about him*]. Well, the truth is, Ive taken a sort of fancy to you, Governor; and if you want the girl, I'm not so set on having her back home again but what I might be open to an arrangement. Regarded in the light of a young woman, she's a fine handsome girl. As a daughter she's not worth her keep; and so I tell you straight. All I ask is my rights as a father; and youre the last man alive to expect me to let her go for nothing; for I can see you're one of the straight sort, Governor. Well, whats a five-pound note to you? and whats Eliza to me? [*He turns to his chair and sits down judicially*].

PICKERING. I think you ought to know, Doolittle, that Mr Higgins's intentions are entirely honourable.

DOOLITTLE. Course they are, Governor. If I thought they wasnt, I'd ask for fifty.

HIGGINS [*revolted*] Do you mean to say that you would sell your daughter for £50?

DOOLITTLE. Not in a general way I wouldnt; but to oblige a gentleman like you I'd do a good deal, I do assure you.

PICKERING. Have you no morals, man?

DOOLITTLE [*unabashed*] Cant afford them, Governor. Neither could you if you was as poor as me. Not that I mean any harm, you know. But if Liza is going to have a bit out of this, why not me too?

HIGGINS [*troubled*] I dont know what to do, Pickering. There can be no question that as a matter of morals it's a positive crime to give this chap a farthing. And yet I feel a sort of rough justice in his claim.

DOOLITTLE. Thats it, Governor. Thats all I say. A father's heart, as it were.

PICKERNG. Well, I know the feeling; but really it seems hardly right—

DOOLITTLE. Dont say that, Governor. Dont look at it that way. What am I, Governors both? I ask you, what am I? I'm one of the undeserving poor: thats what I am. Think of what that means to a man. It means that he's up agen middle class morality all the time. If theres anything going, and I put in for a bit of it, it's always the same story: "Youre undeserving; so you cant have it." But my needs is as great as the most deserving widow's that ever got money out of six different charities in one week for the death of the same husband. I dont need less than a deserving man: I need more. I dont eat less hearty than him; and I drink a lot more. I want a bit of amusement, cause I'm a thinking man. I want cheerfulness and a song and a band when I feel low. Well, they charge me just the same for everything as they charge the deserving. What is middle class morality? Just an excuse for never giving me anything. Therefore, I ask, as two gentlemen, not to play that game on me. I'm playing straight with you. I aint pretending to be deserving. I'm undeserving; and I mean to go on being undeserving. I like it;

and thats the truth. Will you take advantage of a man's
nature to do him out of the price of his own daughter
what he's brought up and fed and clothed by the sweat
of his brow until she's growed big enough to be interesting to you two gentlemen? Is five pounds unreasonable?
I put it to you; and I leave it to you.

HIGGINS [*rising, and going over to Pickering*] Pickering: if
we were to take this man in hand for three months, he
could choose between a seat in the Cabinet and a popular
pulpit in Wales.

PICKERING. What do you say to that, Doolittle?

DOOLITTLE. Not me, Governor, thank you kindly. I've heard
all the preachers and all the prime ministers—for I'm a
thinking man and game for politics or religion or social
reform same as all the other amusements—and I tell you
it's a dog's life any way you look at it. Undeserving
poverty is my line. Taking one station in society with
another, it's—it's—well, it's the only one that has any
ginger in it, to my taste.

HIGGINS. I suppose we must give him a fiver.

PICKERING. He'll make a bad use of it, I'm afraid.

DOOLITTLE. Not me, Governor, so help me I wont. Dont
you be afraid that I'll save it and spare it and live idle on
it. There wont be a penny of it left by Monday: I'll have
to go to work same as if I'd never had it. It wont
pauperize me, you bet. Just one good spree for myself
and the missus, giving pleasure to ourselves and employment to others, and satisfaction to you to think it's not
been throwed away. You couldnt spend it better.

HIGGINS [*taking out his pocket book and coming between
Doolittle and the piano*] This is irresistible. Lets give him
ten. [*He offers two notes to the dustman*].

DOOLITTLE. No, Governor. She wouldnt have the heart to
spend ten; and perhaps I shouldnt neither. Ten pounds
is a lot of money: it makes a man feel prudent like; and
then goodbye to happiness. You give me what I ask you,
Governor: not a penny more, and not a penny less.

PICKERING. Why dont you marry that missus of yours? I
rather draw the line at encouraging that sort of immorality.

DOOLITTLE. Tell her so, Governor: tell her so. *I*'m willing. It's me that suffers by it. Ive no hold on her. I got to be agreeable to her. I got to give her presents. I got to buy her clothes something sinful. I'm a slave to that woman, Governor, just because I'm not her lawful husband. And she knows it too. Catch her marrying me! Take my advice, Governor—marry Eliza while she's young and dont know no better. If you dont youll be sorry for it after. If you do, she'll be sorry for it after; but better her than you, because youre a man, and she's only a woman and dont know how to be happy anyhow.

HIGGINS. Pickering: if we listen to this man another minute, we shall have no convictions left. [*To Doolittle*] Five pounds I think you said.

DOOLITTLE. Thank you kindly, Governor.

HIGGINS. Youre sure you wont take ten?

DOOLITTLE. Not now. Another time, Governor.

HIGGINS [*handing him a five-pound note*] Here you are.

DOOLITTLE. Thank you, Governor. Good morning. [*He hurries to the door, anxious to get away with his booty. When he opens it he is confronted with a dainty and exquisitely clean young Japanese lady in a simple blue cotton kimono printed cunningly with small white jasmine blossoms. Mrs Pearce is with her. He gets out of her way deferentially and apologizes*]. Beg pardon, miss.

THE JAPANESE LADY. Garn! Dont you know your own daughter?

DOOLITTLE	exclaiming	Bly me! it's Eliza!
HIGGINS	simul-	Whats that? This!
PICKERING	taneously	By Jove!

LIZA. Dont I look silly?

HIGGINS. Silly?

MRS PEARCE [*at the door*] Now, Mr Higgins, please dont say anything to make the girl conceited about herself.

HIGGINS [*conscientiously*] Oh! Quite right, Mrs Pearce. [*To Eliza*] Yes: damned silly.

MRS PEARCE. Please, sir.

HIGGINS [*correcting himself*] I mean extremely silly.

LIZA. I should look all right with my hat on. [*She takes up*

her hat; puts it on; and walks across the room to the
fireplace with a fashionable air].

HIGGINS. A new fashion, by George! And it ought to look horrible!

DOOLITTLE [*with fatherly pride*] Well, I never thought she'd clean up as good looking as that, Governor. She's a credit to me, aint she?

LIZA. I tell you, it's easy to clean up here. Hot and cold water on tap, just as much as you like, there is. Woolly towels, there is; and a towel horse so hot, it burns your fingers. Soft brushes to scrub yourself, and a wooden bowl of soap smelling like primroses. Now I know why ladies is so clean. Washing's a treat for them. Wish they could see what it is for the like of me!

HIGGINS. I'm glad the bathroom met with your approval.

LIZA. It didnt: not all of it; and I dont care who hears me say it. Mrs Pearce knows.

HIGGINS. What was wrong, Mrs Pearce?

MRS PEARCE [*blandly*] Oh, nothing, sir. It doesnt matter.

LIZA. I had a good mind to break it. I didnt know which way to look. But I hung a towel over it, I did.

HIGGINS. Over what?

MRS PEARCE. Over the looking-glass, sir.

HIGGINS. Doolittle: you have brought your daughter up too strictly.

DOOLITTLE. Me! I never brought her up at all, except to give her a lick of a strap now and again. Dont put it on me, Governor. She aint accustomed to it, you see: thats all. But she'll soon pick up your free-and-easy ways.

LIZA. I'm a good girl, I am; and I wont pick up no free-and-easy ways.

HIGGINS. Eliza: if you say again that youre a good girl, your father shall take you home.

LIZA. Not him. You dont know my father. All he come here for was to touch you for some money to get drunk on.

DOOLITTLE. Well, what else would I want money for? To put into the plate in church, I suppose. [*She puts out her tongue at him. He is so incensed by this that Pickering presently finds it necessary to step between them*]. Dont you give me none of your lip; and dont let me hear you giving this gentleman any of it either, or youll hear from me about it. See?

HIGGINS. Have you any further advice to give her before you go, Doolittle? Your blessing, for instance.

DOOLITTLE. No, Governor: I aint such a mug as to put up my children to all I know myself. Hard enough to hold them in without that. If you want Eliza's mind improved, Governor, you do it yourself with a strap. So long, gentlemen. [He turns to go].

HIGGINS [*impressively*] Stop. Youll come regularly to see your daughter. It's your duty, you know. My brother is a clergyman; and he could help you in your talks with her.

DOOLITTLE [*evasively*] Certainly, I'll come, Governor. Not just this week, because I have a job at a distance. But later on you may depend on me. Afternoon, gentlemen. Afternoon, maam. [*He touches his hat to Mrs Pearce, who disdains the salutation and goes out. He winks at Higgins, thinking him probably a fellow-sufferer from Mrs Pearce's difficult disposition, and follows her*].

LIZA. Dont you believe the old liar. He'd as soon you set a bulldog on him as a clergyman. You wont see him again in a hurry.

HIGGINS. I dont want to, Eliza. Do you?

LIZA. Not me. I dont want never to see him again, I dont. He's a disgrace to me, he is, collecting dust, instead of working at his trade.

PICKERING. What is his trade, Eliza?

LIZA. Talking money out of other people's pockets into his own. His proper trade's a navvy; and he works at it sometimes too—for exercise—and earns good money at it. Aint you going to call me Miss Doolittle any more?

PICKERING. I beg your pardon, Miss Doolittle. It was a slip of the tongue.

LIZA. Oh, I dont mind; only it sounded so genteel. I should just like to take a taxi to the corner of Tottenham Court Road and get out there and tell it to wait for me, just to put the girls in their place a bit. I wouldnt speak to them, you know.

PICKERING. Better wait til we get you something really fashionable.

HIGGINS. Besides, you shouldnt cut your old friends now
that you have risen in the world. Thats what we call
snobbery.

LIZA. You dont call the like of them my friends now, I
should hope. Theyve took it out of me often enough with
their ridicule when they had the chance; and now I mean
to get a bit of my own back. But if I'm to have fashionable clothes, I'll wait. I should like to have some. Mrs
Pearce says youre going to give me some to wear in bed
at night different to what I wear in the daytime; but it do
seem a waste of money when you could get something to
shew. Besides, I never could fancy changing into cold
things on a winter night.

MRS PEARCE [*coming back*] Now, Eliza. The new things
have come for you to try on.

LIZA. *Ah-ow-oo-ooh!* [*She rushes out*].

MRS PEARCE [*following her*] Oh, dont rush about like that,
girl. [*She shuts the door behind her*].

HIGGINS. Pickering: we have taken on a stiff job.

PICKERING [*with conviction*] Higgins: we have.

*   *   *

There seems to be some curiosity as to what Higgins's
lessons to Eliza were like. Well, here is a sample: the first
one.

Picture Eliza, in her new clothes, and feeling her inside
put out of step by a lunch, dinner, and breakfast of a
kind to which it is unaccustomed, seated with Higgins
and the Colonel in the study, feeling like a hospital out-
patient at a first encounter with the doctors.

Higgins, constitutionally unable to sit still, discomposes
her still more by striding restlessly about. But for the
reassuring presence and quietude of her friend the
Colonel she would run for her life, even back to Drury
Lane.

HIGGINS. Say your alphabet.

LIZA. I know my alphabet. Do you think I know nothing?
I dont need to be taught like a child.

HIGGINS [*thundering*] Say your alphabet.

PICKERING. Say it, Miss Doolittle. You will understand

presently. Do what he tells you; and let him teach you in his own way.

LIZA. Oh well, if you put it like that—Ahyee, bəyee, cəyee, dəyee—

HIGGINS [*with the roar of a wounded lion*] Stop. Listen to this, Pickering. This is what we pay for as elementary education. This unfortunate animal has been locked up for nine years in school at our expense to teach her to speak and read the language of Shakespear and Milton. And the result is Ahyee, Bə-yee, Cə-yee, Də-yee. [*To Eliza*] Say A, B, C, D.

LIZA. [*almost in tears*] But I'm sayin it. Ahyee, Bəyee, Cə-yee—

HIGGINS. Stop. Say a cup of tea.

LIZA. A cappətə-ee.

HIGGINS. Put your tongue forward until it squeezes against the top of your lower teeth. Now say cup.

LIZA. C-c-c— I cant. C-Cup.

PICKERING. Good. Splendid, Miss Doolittle.

HIGGINS. By Jupiter, she's done it at the first shot. Pickering: we shall make a duchess of her. [*To Eliza*] Now do you think you could possibly say tea? Not tə-yee, mind: if you ever say bə-yee cə-yee də-yee again you shall be dragged round the room three times by the hair of your head. [*Fortissimo*] T, T, T, T.

LIZA [*weeping*] I cant hear no difference cep that it sounds more genteel-like when you say it.

HIGGINS. Well, if you can hear the difference, what the devil are you crying for? Pickering: give her a chocolate.

PICKERING. No, no. Never mind crying a little, Miss Doolittle: you are doing very well; and the lessons wont hurt. I promise you I wont let him drag you round the room by your hair.

HIGGINS. Be off with you to Mrs Pearce and tell her about it. Think about it. Try to do it by yourself: and keep your tongue well forward in your mouth instead of trying to roll it up and swallow it. Another lesson at half-past four this afternoon. Away with you.

Eliza, still sobbing, rushes from the room.

And that is the sort of ordeal poor Eliza has to go

through for months before we meet her again on her first
appearance in London society of the professional class.

ACT III

*It is Mrs Higgins's at-home day. Nobody has yet arrived.
Her drawing room, in a flat on Chelsea Embankment, has
three windows looking on the river; and the ceiling is not
so lofty as it would be in an older house of the same pretension. The windows are open, giving access to a balcony with
flowers in pots. If you stand with your face to the windows,
you have the fireplace on your left and the door in the
right-hand wall close to the corner nearest the windows.*

*Mrs Higgins was brought up on Morris and Burne Jones;
and her room, which is very unlike her son's room in Wimpole Street, is not crowded with furniture and little tables
and nicknacks. In the middle of the room there is a big
ottoman; and this, with the carpet, the Morris wallpapers,
and the Morris chintz window curtains and brocade covers
of the ottoman and its cushions, supply all the ornament,
and are much too handsome to be hidden by odds and ends
of useless things. A few good oil-paintings from the exhibitions in the Grosvenor Gallery thirty years ago (the Burne
Jones, not the Whistler side of them) are on the walls. The
only landscape is a Cecil Lawson on the scale of a Rubens.
There is a portrait of Mrs Higgins as she was when she
defied the fashion in her youth in one of the beautiful Ros-
settian costumes which, when caricatured by people who
did not understand, led to the absurdities of popular esthet-
icism in the eighteen-seventies.*

*In the corner diagonally opposite the door Mrs Higgins,
now over sixty and long past taking the trouble to dress out
of the fashion, sits writing at an elegantly simple writing-
table with a bell button within reach of her hand. There is
a Chippendale chair further back in the room between her
and the window nearest her side. At the other side of the
room, further forward, is an Elizabethan chair roughly
carved in the taste of Inigo Jones. On the same side a piano
in a decorated case. The corner between the fireplace and*

the window is occupied by a divan cushioned in Morris chintz.

It is between four and five in the afternoon.

The door is opened violently; and Higgins enters with his hat on.

MRS HIGGINS [*dismayed*] Henry! [*Scolding him*] What are you doing here today? It is my at-home day: you promised not to come. [*As he bends to kiss her, she takes his hat off, and presents it to him*].

HIGGINS. Oh bother! [*He throws the hat down on the table*].

MRS HIGGINS. Go home at once.

HIGGINS [*kissing her*] I know, mother. I came on purpose.

MRS HIGGINS. But you mustnt. I'm serious, Henry. You offend all my friends: they stop coming whenever they meet you.

HIGGINS. Nonsense! I know I have no small talk; but people dont mind. [*He sits on the settee*].

MRS HIGGINS. Oh! dont they? Small talk indeed! What about your large talk? Really, dear, you mustnt stay.

HIGGINS. I must. Ive a job for you. A phonetic job.

MRS HIGGINS. No use, dear. I'm sorry; but I cant get round your vowels; and though I like to get pretty postcards in your patent shorthand, I always have to read the copies in ordinary writing you so thoughtfully send me.

HIGGINS. Well, this isnt a phonetic job.

MRS HIGGINS. You said it was.

HIGGINS. Not your part of it. Ive picked up a girl.

MRS HIGGINS. Does that mean that some girl has picked you up?

HIGGINS. Not at all. I dont mean a love affair.

MRS HIGGINS. What a pity!

HIGGINS. Why?

MRS HIGGINS. Well, you never fall in love with anyone under forty-five. When will you discover that there are some rather nice-looking young women about?

HIGGINS. Oh, I cant be bothered with young women. My idea of a lovable woman is somebody as like you as possible. I shall never get into the way of seriously liking young women: some habits lie too deep to be changed.

[*Rising abruptly and walking about, jingling his money and his keys in his trouser pockets*] Besides, theyre all idiots.

MRS HIGGINS. Do you know what you would do if you really loved me, Henry?

HIGGINS. Oh bother! What? Marry, I suppose.

MRS HIGGINS. No. Stop fidgeting and take your hands out of your pockets. [*With a gesture of despair, he obeys and sits down again*]. Thats a good boy. Now tell me about the girl.

HIGGINS. She's coming to see you.

MRS HIGGINS. I dont remember asking her.

HIGGINS. You didnt. *I* asked her. If youd known her you wouldnt have asked her.

MRS HIGGINS. Indeed! Why?

HIGGINS. Well, it's like this. She's a common flower girl. I picked her off the kerbstone.

MRS HIGGINS. And invited her to my at-home!

HIGGINS [*rising and coming to her to coax her*] Oh, thatll be all right. Ive taught her to speak properly; and she has strict orders as to her behavior. She's to keep to two subjects: the weather and everybody's health—Fine day and How do you do, you know—and not to let herself go on things in general. That will be safe.

MRS HIGGINS. Safe! To talk about our health! about our insides! perhaps about our outsides! How could you be so silly, Henry?

HIGGINS [*impatiently*] Well, she must talk about something. [*He controls himself and sits down again*]. Oh, she'll be all right: dont you fuss. Pickering is in it with me. Ive a sort of bet on that I'll pass her off as a duchess in six months. I started on her some months ago; and she's getting on like a house on fire. I shall win my bet. She has a quick ear; and she's been easier to teach than my middle-class pupils because she's had to learn a complete new language. She talks English almost as you talk French.

MRS HIGGINS. Thats satisfactory, at all events.

HIGGINS. Well, it is and it isnt.

MRS HIGGINS. What does that mean?

HIGGINS. You see, Ive got her pronunciation all right; but
you have to consider not only h o w a girl pronounces,
but what she pronounces; and that's where—

*They are interrupted by the parlormaid, announcing
guests.*

THE PARLORMAID. Mrs and Miss Eynsford Hill. [*She withdraws*].

HIGGINS. Oh Lord! [*He rises; snatches his hat from the table;
and makes for the door; but before he reaches it his
mother introduces him*].

*Mrs and Miss Eynsford Hill are the mother and
daughter who sheltered from the rain in Covent Garden.
The mother is well bred, quiet, and has the habitual
anxiety of straitened means. The daughter has acquired
a gay air of being very much at home in society: the
bravado of genteel poverty.*

MRS EYNSFORD HILL [*to Mrs Higgins*] How do you do?
[*They shake hands*].

MISS EYNSFORD HILL. How d'you do? [*She shakes*].

MRS HIGGINS [*introducing*] My son Henry.

MRS EYNSFORD HILL. Your celebrated son! I have so longed
to meet you, Professor Higgins.

HIGGINS [*glumly, making no movement in her direction*] Delighted. [*He backs against the piano and bows brusquely*]·

MISS EYNSFORD HILL [*going to him with confident familiarity*] How do you do?

HIGGINS [*staring at her*] Ive seen you before somewhere. I
havnt the ghost of a notion where; but Ive heard your
voice. [*Drearily*] It doesnt matter. Youd better sit down.

MRS HIGGINS. I'm sorry to say that my celebrated son has
no manners. You mustnt mind him.

MISS EYNSFORD HILL [*gaily*] I dont. [*She sits in the Elizabethan chair*].

MRS EYNSFORD HILL [*a little bewildered*] Not at all. [*She sits
on the ottoman between her daughter and Mrs Higgins,
who has turned her chair away from the writing-table*].

HIGGINS. Oh, have I been rude? I didnt mean to be.

He goes to the central window, through which, with his

*back to the company, he contemplates the river and the
flowers in Battersea Park on the opposite bank as if they
were a frozen desert.*

    The parlormaid returns, ushering in Pickering.

THE PARLORMAID. Colonel Pickering. [*She withdraws*].

PICKERING. How do you do, Mrs Higgins?

MRS HIGGINS. So glad youve come. Do you know Mrs
Eynsford Hill—Miss Eynsford Hill? [*Exchange of bows.
The Colonel brings the Chippendale chair a little forward
between Mrs Hill and Mrs Higgins, and sits down*].

PICKERING. Has Henry told you what weve come for?

HIGGINS [*over his shoulder*] We were interrupted: damn it!

MRS HIGGINS. Oh Henry, Henry, really!

MRS EYNSFORD HILL [*half rising*] Are we in the way?

MRS HIGGINS [*rising and making her sit down again*] No,
no. You couldnt have come more fortunately: we want
you to meet a friend of ours.

HIGGINS [*turning hopefully*] Yes, by George! We want two
or three people. Youll do as well as anybody else.

    The parlormaid returns, ushering Freddy.

THE PARLORMAID. Mr Eynsford Hill.

HIGGINS [*almost audibly, past endurance*] God of Heaven!
another of them.

FREDDY [*shaking hands with Mrs Higgins*] Ahdedo?

MRS HIGGINS. Very good of you to come. [*Introducing*]
Colonel Pickering.

FREDDY [*bowing*] Ahdedo?

MRS HIGGINS. I dont think you know my son, Professor
Higgins.

FREDDY [*going to Higgins*] Ahdedo?

HIGGINS [*looking at him much as if he were a pick-
pocket*] I'll take my oath Ive met you before somewhere.
Where was it?

FREDDY. I dont think so.

HIGGINS [*resignedly*] It dont matter, anyhow. Sit down.

    *He shakes Freddy's hand, and almost slings him on to
the ottoman with his face to the window; then comes
round to the other side of it.*

HIGGINS. Well, here we are, anyhow! [*He sits down on the*

ottoman next Mrs Eynsford Hill, on her left]. And now, what the devil are we going to talk about until Eliza comes?

MRS HIGGINS. Henry: you are the life and soul of the Royal Society's soirées; but really youre rather trying on more commonplace occasions.

HIGGINS. Am I? Very sorry. [*Beaming suddenly*] I suppose I am, you know. [*Uproariously*] Ha, ha!

MISS EYNSFORD HILL [*who considers Higgins quite eligible matrimonially*] I sympathize. *I* havnt any small talk. If people would only be frank and say what they really think!

HIGGINS [*relapsing into gloom*] Lord forbid!

MRS EYNSFORD HILL [*taking up her daughter's cue*] But why?

HIGGINS. What they think they ought to think is bad enough, Lord knows; but what they really think would break up the whole show. Do you suppose it would be really agreeable if I were to come out now with what *I* really think?

MISS EYNSFORD HILL [*gaily*] Is it so very cynical?

HIGGINS. Cynical! Who the dickens said it was cynical? I mean it wouldnt be decent.

MRS EYNSFORD HILL [*seriously*] Oh! I'm sure you dont mean that, Mr. Higgins.

HIGGINS. You see, we're all savages, more or less. We're supposed to be civilized and cultured—to know all about poetry and philosophy and art and science, and so on; but how many of us know even the meanings of these names? [*To Miss Hill*] What do you know of poetry? [*To Mrs Hill*] What do y o u know of science? [*Indicating Freddy*] What does h e know of art or science or anything else? What the devil do you imagine I know of philosophy?

MRS HIGGINS [*warningly*] Or of manners, Henry?

THE PARLORMAID [*opening the door*] Miss Doolittle. [*She withdraws*].

HIGGINS [*rising hastily and running to Mrs Higgins*] Here she is, mother. [*He stands on tiptoe and makes signs over*

*his mother's head to Eliza to indicate to her which lady
is her hostess*].

*Eliza, who is exquisitely dressed, produces an impres-
sion of such remarkable distinction and beauty as she
enters that they all rise, quite fluttered. Guided by Higgins's signals, she comes to Mrs Higgins with studied
grace.*

LIZA [*speaking with pedantic correctness of pronunciation
and great beauty of tone*] How do you do, Mrs Higgins?
[*She gasps slightly in making sure of the H in Higgins,
but is quite successful*]. Mr Higgins told me I might
come.

MRS HIGGINS [*cordially*] Quite right: I'm very glad indeed
to see you.

PICKERING. How do you do, Miss Doolittle?

LIZA [*shaking hands with him*] Colonel Pickering, is it not?

MRS EYNSFORD HILL. I feel sure we have met before, Miss
Doolittle. I remember your eyes.

LIZA. How do you do? [*She sits down on the ottoman grace-
fully in the place just left vacant by Higgins*].

MRS EYNSFORD HILL [*introducing*] My daughter Clara.

LIZA. How do you do?

CLARA [*impulsively*] How do you do? [*She sits down on the
ottoman beside Eliza, devouring her with her eyes*].

FREDDY [*coming to their side of the ottoman*] Ive certainly
had the pleasure.

MRS EYNSFORD HILL [*introducing*] My son Freddy.

LIZA. How do you do?

*Freddy bows and sits down in the Elizabethan chair,
infatuated.*

HIGGINS [*suddenly*] By George, yes: it all comes back to
me! [*They stare at him*]. Covent Garden! [*Lamentably*]
What a damned thing!

MRS HIGGINS. Henry, please! [*He is about to sit on the edge
of the table*] Dont sit on my writing-table: youll break it.

HIGGINS [*sulkily*] Sorry.

*He goes to the divan, stumbling into the fender and
over the fire-irons on his way; extricating himself with
muttered imprecations; and finishing his disastrous journey by throwing himself so impatiently on the divan that*

he almost breaks it. Mrs Higgins looks at him, but controls herself and says nothing.

A long and painful pause ensues.

MRS HIGGINS [*at last, conversationally*] Will it rain, do you think?

LIZA. The shallow depression in the west of these islands is likely to move slowly in an easterly direction. There are no indications of any great change in the barometrical situation.

FREDDY. Ha! ha! how awfully funny!

LIZA. What is wrong with that, young man? I bet I got it right.

FREDDY. Killing!

MRS EYNSFORD HILL. I'm sure I hope it wont turn cold. Theres so much influenza about. It runs right through our whole family regularly every spring.

LIZA [*darkly*] My aunt died of influenza: so they said.

MRS EYNSFORD HILL [*clicks her tongue sympathetically*]!!!

LIZA [*in the same tragic tone*] But it's my belief they done the old woman in.

MRS HIGGINS [*puzzled*] Done her in?

LIZA. Y-e-e-e-es, Lord love you! Why should she die of influenza? She come through diphtheria right enough the year before. I saw her with my own eyes. Fairly blue with it, she was. They all thought she was dead; but my father he kept ladling gin down her throat til she came to so sudden that she bit the bowl off the spoon.

MRS EYNSFORD HILL [*startled*] Dear me!

LIZA [*piling up the indictment*] What call would a woman with that strength in her have to die of influenza? What become of her new straw hat that should have come to me? Somebody pinched it; and what I say is, them as pinched it done her in.

MRS EYNSFORD HILL. What does doing her in mean?

HIGGINS [*hastily*] Oh, thats the new small talk. To do a person in means to kill them.

MRS EYNSFORD HILL [*to Eliza, horrified*] You surely dont believe that your aunt was killed?

LIZA. Do I not! Them she lived with would have killed her for a hat-pin, let alone a hat.

MRS EYNSFORD HILL. But it cant have been right for your father to pour spirits down her throat like that. It might have killed her.

LIZA. Not her. Gin was mother's milk to her. Besides, he'd poured so much down his own throat that he knew the good of it.

MRS EYNSFORD HILL. Do you mean that he drank?

LIZA. Drank! My word! Something chronic.

MRS EYNSFORD HILL. How dreadful for you!

LIZA. Not a bit. It never did him no harm what I could see. But then he did not keep it up regular. [*Cheerfully*] On the burst, as you might say, from time to time. And always more agreeable when he had a drop in. When he was out of work, my mother used to give him fourpence and tell him to go out and not come back until he'd drunk himself cheerful and loving-like. Theres lots of women has to make their husbands drunk to make them fit to live with. [*Now quite at her ease*] You see, it's like this. If a man has a bit of a conscience, it always takes him when he's sober; and then it makes him low-spirited. A drop of booze just takes that off and makes him happy. [*To Freddy, who is in convulsions of suppressed laughter*] Here! what are you sniggering at?

FREDDY. The new small talk. You do it so awfully well.

LIZA. If I was doing it proper, what was you laughing at? [*To Higgins*] Have I said anything I oughtnt?

MRS HIGGINS [*interposing*] Not at all, Miss Doolittle.

LIZA. Well, thats a mercy, anyhow. [*Expansively*] What I always say is—

HIGGINS [*rising and looking at his watch*] Ahem!

LIZA [*looking round at him; taking the hint; and rising*] Well: I must go. [*They all rise. Freddy goes to the door*]. So pleased to have met you. Goodbye. [*She shakes hands with Mrs Higgins*].

MRS HIGGINS. Goodbye.

LIZA. Goodbye, Colonel Pickering.

PICKERING. Goodbye, Miss Doolittle. [*They shake hands*].

LIZA [*nodding to the others*] Goodbye, all.

FREDDY [*opening the door for her*] Are you walking across the Park, Miss Doolittle? If so—

LIZA [*perfectly elegant diction*] Walk! Not bloody likely. [*Sensation*]. I am going in a taxi. [*She goes out*].

Pickering gasps and sits down. Freddy goes out on the balcony to catch another glimpse of Eliza.

MRS EYNSFORD HILL [*suffering from shock*] Well, I really cant get used to the new ways.

CLARA [*throwing herself discontentedly into the Elizabethan chair*] Oh, it's all right, mamma, quite right. People will think we never go anywhere or see anybody if you are so old-fashioned.

MRS EYNSFORD HILL. I daresay I am very old-fashioned; but I do hope you wont begin using that expression, Clara. I have got accustomed to hear you talking about men as rotters, and calling everything filthy and beastly; though I do think it horrible and unladylike. But this last is really too much. Dont you think so, Colonel Pickering?

PICKERING. Dont ask me. Ive been away in India for several years; and manners have changed so much that I sometimes dont know whether I'm at a respectable dinner-table or in a ship's forecastle.

CLARA. It's all a matter of habit. Theres no right or wrong in it. Nobody means anything by it. And it's s o quaint, and gives such a smart emphasis to things that are not in themselves very witty. I find the new small talk delightful and quite innocent.

MRS EYNSFORD HILL [*rising*] Well, after that, I think it's time for us to go.

Pickering and Higgins rise.

CLARA [*rising*] Oh yes: we have three at-homes to go to still. Goodbye, Mrs Higgins. Goodbye, Colonel Pickering. Goodbye, Professor Higgins.

HIGGINS [*coming grimly at her from the divan, and accompanying her to the door*] Goodbye. Be sure you try on that small talk at the three at-homes. Dont be nervous about it. Pitch it in strong.

CLARA [*all smiles*] I will. Goodbye. Such nonsense, all this early Victorian prudery!

HIGGINS [*tempting her*] Such damned nonsense!

CLARA. Such bloody nonsense!

MRS EYNSFORD HILL [*convulsively*] Clara!

CLARA. Ha! Ha! [*She goes out radiant, conscious of being thoroughly up to date, and is heard descending the stairs in a stream of silvery laughter*].

FREDDY [*to the heavens at large*] Well, I ask you— [*He gives it up, and comes to Mrs Higgins*]. Goodbye.

MRS HIGGINS [*shaking hands*] Goodbye. Would you like to meet Miss Doolittle again?

FREDDY [*eagerly*] Yes, I should, most awfully.

MRS HIGGINS. Well, you know my days.

FREDDY. Yes. Thanks awfully. Goodbye. [*He goes out*].

MRS EYNSFORD HILL. Goodbye, Mr Higgins.

HIGGINS. Goodbye. Goodbye.

MRS EYNSFORD HILL [*to Pickering*] It's no use. I shall never be able to bring myself to use that word.

PICKERING. Dont. It's not compulsory, you know. Youll get on quite well without it.

MRS EYNSFORD HILL. Only, Clara is so down on me if I am not positively reeking with the latest slang. Goodbye.

PICKERING. Goodbye [*They shake hands*].

MRS EYNSFORD HILL [*to Mrs Higgins*] You mustnt mind Clara. [*Pickering, catching from her lowered tone that this is not meant for him to hear, discreetly joins Higgins at the window*]. We're so poor! and she gets so few parties, poor child! She doesnt quite know. [*Mrs Higgins, seeing that her eyes are moist, takes her hand sympathetically and goes with her to the door*]. But the boy is nice. Dont you think so?

MRS HIGGINS. Oh, quite nice. I shall always be delighted to see him.

MRS EYNSFORD HILL. Thank you, dear. Goodbye. [*She goes out*].

HIGGINS [*eagerly*] Well? Is Eliza presentable [*he swoops on his mother and drags her to the ottoman, where she sits down in Eliza's place with her son on her left*]?
    Pickering returns to his chair on her right.

MRS HIGGINS. You silly boy, of course she's not presentable. She's a triumph of your art and of her dressmaker's; but if you suppose for a moment that she doesnt give herself away in every sentence she utters, you must be perfectly cracked about her.

PICKERING. But dont you think something might be done? I mean something to eliminate the sanguinary element from her conversation.

MRS HIGGINS. Not as long as she is in Henry's hands.

HIGGINS [*aggrieved*] Do you mean that m y language is improper?

MRS HIGGINS. No, dearest: it would be quite proper—say on a canal barge; but it would not be proper for her at a garden party.

HIGGINS [*deeply injured*] Well I must say—

PICKERING [*interrupting him*] Come, Higgins: you must learn to know yourself. I havnt heard such language as yours since we used to review the volunteers in Hyde Park twenty years ago.

HIGGINS [*sulkily*] Oh, well, if y o u say so, I suppose I dont always talk like a bishop.

MRS HIGGINS [*quieting Henry with a touch*] Colonel Pickering: will you tell me what is the exact state of things in Wimpole Street?

PICKERING [*cheerfully: as if this completely changed the subject*] Well, I have come to live there with Henry. We work together at my Indian Dialects; and we think it more convenient—

MRS HIGGINS. Quite so. I know all about that: it's an excellent arrangement. But where does this girl live?

HIGGINS. With us, of course. Where s h o u l d she live?

MRS HIGGINS. But on what terms? Is she a servant? If not, what is she?

PICKERING [*slowly*] I think I know what you mean, Mrs Higgins.

HIGGINS. Well, dash me if *I* do! Ive had to work at the girl every day for months to get her to her present pitch. Besides, she's useful. She knows where my things are, and remembers my appointments and so forth.

MRS HIGGINS. How does your housekeeper get on with her?

HIGGINS. Mrs Pearce? Oh, she's jolly glad to get so much taken off her hands; for before Eliza came, she used to have to find things and remind me of my appointments. But she's got some silly bee in her bonnet about Eliza.

She keeps saying "You dont t h i n k, sir": doesnt she, Pick?

PICKERING. Yes: thats the formula. "You dont t h i n k, sir." Thats the end of every conversation about Eliza.

HIGGINS. As if I ever stop thinking about the girl and her confounded vowels and consonants. I'm worn out, thinking about her, and watching her lips and her teeth and her tongue, not to mention her soul, which is the quaintest of the lot.

MRS HIGGINS. You certainly are a pretty pair of babies, playing with your live doll.

HIGGINS. Playing! The hardest job I ever tackled: make no mistake about that, mother. But you have no idea how frightfully interesting it is to take a human being and change her into a quite different human being by creating a new speech for her. It's filling up the deepest gulf that separates class from class and soul from soul.

PICKERING [drawing his chair closer to Mrs Higgins and bending over to her eagerly] Yes: it's enormously interesting. I assure you, Mrs Higgins, we take Eliza very seriously. Every week—every day almost—there is some new change. [Closer again] We keep records of every stage—dozens of gramophone disks and photographs—

HIGGINS [assailing her at the other ear] Yes, by George: it's the most absorbing experiment I ever tackled. She regularly fills our lives up: doesnt she, Pick?

PICKERING. We're always talking Eliza.

HIGGINS. Teaching Eliza.

PICKERING. Dressing Eliza.

MRS HIGGINS. What!

HIGGINS. Inventing new Elizas.

HIGGINS.	*speaking*	You know, she has the most extraordinary quickness of ear:
PICKERING.	*together*	I assure you, my dear Mrs Higgins, that girl
HIGGINS.		just like a parrot. Ive tried her with every
PICKERING.		is a genius. She can play the piano quite beautifully.

HIGGINS. ⎫ *speaking* ⎧ possible sort of sound that a human
                              being can make—
PICKERING. ⎬ *together* ⎨ We have taken her to classical con-
                              certs and to music

HIGGINS. ⎫ ⎧ Continental dialects, African dia-
                 lects, Hottentot
PICKERING. ⎬ ⎨ halls; and it's all the same to her:
                 she plays everything

HIGGINS. ⎫ ⎧ clicks, things it took me years to get
                 hold of; and
PICKERING. ⎬ ⎨ she hears right off when she comes
                 home, whether it's

HIGGINS. ⎫ ⎧ she picks them up like a shot, right
                 away, as if she had
PICKERING. ⎬ ⎨ Beethoven and Brahms or Lehar
                 and Lionel Monckton;

HIGGINS. ⎫ ⎧ been at it all her life.
PICKERING. ⎬ ⎨ though six months ago, she'd never
                 as much as touched a piano—

MRS HIGGINS [*putting her fingers in her ears, as they are by this time shouting one another down with an intolerable noise*] Sh-sh-sh-sh! [*They stop*].

PICKERING. I beg your pardon. [*He draws his chair back apologetically*].

HIGGINS. Sorry. When Pickering starts shouting nobody can get a word in edgeways.

MRS HIGGINS. Be quiet, Henry. Colonel Pickering: dont you realize that when Eliza walked into Wimpole Street, something walked in with her?

PICKERING. Her father did. But Henry soon got rid of him.

MRS HIGGINS. It would have been more to the point if her mother had. But as her mother didnt something else did.

PICKERING. But what?

MRS HIGGINS [*unconsciously dating herself by the word*] A problem.

PICKERING. Oh I see. The problem of how to pass her off as a lady.

HIGGINS. I'll solve that problem. Ive half solved it already.

MRS HIGGINS. No, you two infinitely stupid male creatures: the problem of what is to be done with her afterwards.

HIGGINS. I dont see anything in that. She can go her own way, with all the advantages I have given her.

MRS HIGGINS. The advantages of that poor woman who was here just now! The manners and habits that disqualify a fine lady from earning her own living without giving her a fine lady's income! Is that what you mean?

PICKERING [*indulgently, being rather bored*] Oh, that will be all right, Mrs Higgins. [*He rises to go*].

HIGGINS [*rising also*] We'll find her some light employment.

PICKERING. She's happy enough. Dont you worry about her. Goodbye. [*He shakes hands as if he were consoling a frightened child, and makes for the door*].

HIGGINS. Anyhow, theres no good bothering now. The thing's done. Goodbye, mother. [*He kisses her, and follows Pickering*].

PICKERING [*turning for a final consolation*] There are plenty of openings. We'll do whats right. Goodbye.

HIGGINS [*to Pickering as they go out together*] Lets take her to the Shakespear exhibition at Earls Court.

PICKERING. Yes: lets. Her remarks will be delicious.

HIGGINS. She'll mimic all the people for us when we get home.

PICKERING. Ripping. [*Both are heard laughing as they go downstairs*].

MRS HIGGINS [*rises with an impatient bounce, and returns to her work at the writing-table. She sweeps a litter of disarranged papers out of the way; snatches a sheet of paper from her stationery case; and tries resolutely to write. At the third time she gives it up; flings down her pen; grips the table angrily and exclaims*] Oh, men! men! men!! men!!!

*   *   *

Clearly Eliza will not pass as a duchess yet; and Higgins's bet remains unwon. But the six months are not yet exhausted; and just in time Eliza does actually pass as a princess. For a glimpse of how she did it imagine an Embassy in London one summer evening after dark. The hall door has an awning and a carpet across the sidewalk to the kerb, because a grand reception is in progress. A small crowd is lined up to see the guests arrive.

A Rolls-Royce car drives up. Pickering in evening dress, with medals and orders, alights, and hands out Eliza, in opera cloak, evening dress, diamonds, fan, flowers and all accessories. Higgins follows. The car drives off; and the three go up the steps and into the house, the door opening for them as they approach.

Inside the house they find themselves in a spacious hall from which the grand staircase rises. On the left are the arrangements for the gentlemen's cloaks. The male guests are depositing their hats and wraps there.

On the right is a door leading to the ladies' cloakroom. Ladies are going in cloaked and coming out in splendor. Pickering whispers to Eliza and points out the ladies' room. She goes into it. Higgins and Pickering take off their overcoats and take tickets for them from the attendant.

One of the guests, occupied in the same way, has his back turned. Having taken his ticket, he turns round and reveals himself as an important looking young man with an astonishingly hairy face. He has an enormous moustache, flowing out into luxuriant whiskers. Waves of hair cluster on his brow. His hair is cropped closely at the back and glows with oil. Otherwise he is very smart. He wears several worthless orders. He is evidently a foreigner, guessable as a whiskered Pandour from Hungary; but in spite of the ferocity of his moustache he is amiable and genially voluble.

Recognizing Higgins, he flings his arms wide apart and approaches him enthusiastically.

WHISKERS. Maestro, maestro [*he embraces Higgins and kisses him on both cheeks*]. You remember me?

HIGGINS. No I dont. Who the devil are you?

WHISKERS. I am your pupil: your first pupil, your best and greatest pupil. I am little Nepommuck, the marvelous boy. I have made your name famous throughout Europe. You teach me phonetic. You cannot forget ME.

HIGGINS. Why dont you shave?

NEPOMMUCK. I have not your imposing appearance, your

chin, your brow. Nobody notice me when I shave. Now
I am famous: they call me Hairy Faced Dick.

HIGGINS. And what are you doing here among all these
swells?

NEPOMMUCK. I am interpreter. I speak 32 languages. I am
indispensable at these international parties. You are great
cockney specialist: you place a man anywhere in London
the moment he open his mouth. I place any man in
Europe.

*A footman hurries down the grand staircase and comes
to Nepommuck.*

FOOTMAN. You are wanted upstairs. Her Excellency cannot understand the Greek gentleman.

NEPOMMUCK. Thank you, yes, immediately.

The footman goes and is lost in the crowd.

NEPOMMUCK [*to Higgins*] This Greek diplomatist pretends
he cannot speak nor understand English. He cannot
deceive me. He is the son of a Clerkenwell watchmaker.
He speaks English so villainously that he dare not utter
a word of it without betraying his origin. I help him to
pretend; but I make him pay through the nose. I make
them all pay. Ha ha! [*He hurries upstairs*].

PICKERING. Is this fellow really an expert? Can he find out
Eliza and blackmail her?

HIGGINS. We shall see. If he finds her out I lose my bet.

Eliza comes from the cloakroom and joins them.

PICKERING. Well, Eliza, now for it. Are you ready?

LIZA. Are you nervous, Colonel?

PICKERING. Frightfully. I feel exactly as I felt before my
first battle. It's the first time that frightens.

LIZA. It is not the first time for me, Colonel. I have done
this fifty times—hundreds of times—in my little piggery
in Angel Court in my day-dreams. I am in a dream now.
Promise me not to let Professor Higgins wake me; for if
he does I shall forget everything and talk as I used to in
Drury Lane.

PICKERING. Not a word, Higgins. [*To Eliza*] Now ready?

LIZA. Ready.

PICKERING. Go.

They mount the stairs, Higgins last. Pickering whispers to the footman on the first landing.

FIRST LANDING FOOTMAN. Miss Doolittle, Colonel Pickering, Professor Higgins.

SECOND LANDING FOOTMAN. Miss Doolittle, Colonel Pickering, Professor Higgins.

At the top of the staircase the Ambassador and his wife, with Nepommuck at her elbow, are receiving.

HOSTESS [*taking Eliza's hand*] How d'ye do?

HOST [*same play*] How d'ye do? How d'ye do, Pickering?

LIZA [*with a beautiful gravity that awes her hostess*] How do you do? [*She passes on to the drawing room*].

HOSTESS. Is that your adopted daughter, Colonel Pickering? She will make a sensation.

PICKERING. Most kind of you to invite her for me. [*He passes on*].

HOSTESS [*to Nepommuck*] Find out all about her.

NEPOMMUCK [*bowing*] Excellency— [*he goes into the crowd*].

HOST. How d'ye do, Higgins? You have a rival here tonight. He introduced himself as your pupil. Is he any good?

HIGGINS. He can learn a language in a fortnight—knows dozens of them. A sure mark of a fool. As a phonetician, no good whatever.

HOSTESS. How d'ye do, Professor?

HIGGINS. How do you do? Fearful bore for you this sort of thing. Forgive my part in it. [*He passes on*].

In the drawing room and its suite of salons the reception is in full swing. Eliza passes through. She is so intent on her ordeal that she walks like a somnambulist in a desert instead of a débutante in a fashionable crowd. They stop talking to look at her, admiring her dress, her jewels, and her strangely attractive self. Some of the younger ones at the back stand on their chairs to see.

The Host and Hostess come in from the staircase and mingle with their guests. Higgins, gloomy and contemptuous of the whole business, comes into the group where they are chatting.

HOSTESS. Ah, here is Professor Higgins: he will tell us. Tell us all about the wonderful young lady, Professor.

HIGGINS [*almost morosely*] What wonderful young lady?

HOSTESS. You know very well. They tell me there has been nothing like her in London since people stood on their chairs to look at Mrs Langtry.

Nepommuck joins the group, full of news.

HOSTESS. Ah, here you are at last, Nepommuck. Have you found out all about the Doolittle lady?

NEPOMMUCK. I have found out all about her. She is a fraud.

HOSTESS. A fraud! Oh no.

NEPOMMUCK. YES, yes. She cannot deceive me. Her name cannot be Doolittle.

HIGGINS. Why?

NEPOMMUCK. Because Doolittle is an English name. And she is not English.

HOSTESS. Oh, nonsense! She speaks English perfectly.

NEPOMMUCK. Too perfectly. Can you shew me any English woman who speaks English as it should be spoken? Only foreigners who have been taught to speak it speak it well.

HOSTESS. Certainly she terrified me by the way she said How d'ye do. I had a schoolmistress who talked like that; and I was mortally afraid of her. But if she is not English what is she?

NEPOMMUCK. Hungarian.

ALL THE REST. Hungarian!

NEPOMMUCK. Hungarian. And of royal blood. I am Hungarian. My blood is royal.

HIGGINS. Did you speak to her in Hungarian?

NEPOMMUCK. I did. She was very clever. She said "Please speak to me in English: I do not understand French." French! She pretends not to know the difference between Hungarian and French. Impossible: she knows both.

HIGGINS. And the blood royal? How did you find that out?

NEPOMMUCK. Instinct, maestro, instinct. Only the Magyar races can produce that air of the divine right, those resolute eyes. She is a princess.

HOST. What do you say, Professor?

HIGGINS. I say an ordinary London girl out of the gutter

and taught to speak by an expert. I place her in Drury Lane.

NEPOMMUCK. Ha ha ha! Oh, maestro, maestro, you are mad on the subject of cockney dialects. The London gutter is the whole world for you.

HIGGINS [*to the hostess*] What does your Excellency say?

HOSTESS. Oh, of course I agree with Nepommuck. She must be a princess at least.

HOST. Not necessarily legitimate, of course. Morganatic perhaps. But that is undoubtedly her class.

HIGGINS. I stick to my opinion.

HOSTESS. Oh, you are incorrigible.

The group breaks up, leaving Higgins isolated. Pickering joins him.

PICKERING. Where is Eliza? We must keep an eye on her.

Eliza joins them.

LIZA. I dont think I can bear much more. The people all stare so at me. An old lady has just told me that I speak exactly like Queen Victoria. I am sorry if I have lost your bet. I have done my best; but nothing can make me the same as these people.

PICKERING. You have not lost it, my dear. You have won it ten times over.

HIGGINS. Let us get out of this. I have had enough of chattering to these fools.

PICKERING. Eliza is tired; and I am hungry. Let us clear out and have supper somewhere.

ACT IV

The Wimpole Street laboratory. Midnight. Nobody in the room. The clock on the mantlepiece strikes twelve. The fire is not alight: it is a summer night.

Presently Higgins and Pickering are heard on the stairs.

HIGGINS [*calling down to Pickering*] I say, Pick: lock up, will you? I shant be going out again.

PICKERING. Right. Can Mrs Pearce go to bed? We dont want anything more, do we?

HIGGINS. Lord, no!

Eliza opens the door and is seen on the lighted landing in all the finery in which she has just won Higgins's bet for him. She comes to the hearth, and switches on the electric lights there. She is tired: her pallor contrasts strongly with her dark eyes and hair; and her expression is almost tragic. She takes off her cloak; puts her fan and gloves on the piano; and sits down on the bench, brooding and silent. Higgins, in evening dress, with overcoat and hat, comes in, carrying a smoking jacket which he has picked up downstairs. He takes off the hat and overcoat; throws them carelessly on the newspaper stand; disposes of his coat in the same way; puts on the smoking jacket; and throws himself wearily into the easy-chair at the hearth. Pickering, similarly attired, comes in. He also takes off his hat and overcoat, and is about to throw them on Higgins's when he hesitates.

PICKERING. I say: Mrs Pearce will row if we leave these things lying about in the drawing room.

HIGGINS. Oh, chuck them over the banisters into the hall. She'll find them there in the morning and put them away all right. She'll think we were drunk.

PICKERING. We are, slightly. Are there any letters?

HIGGINS. I didnt look. [*Pickering takes the overcoats and hats and goes downstairs. Higgins begins half singing half yawning an air from La Fanciulla del Golden West. Suddenly he stops and exclaims*] I wonder where the devil my slippers are!

Eliza looks at him darkly; then rises suddenly and leaves the room.

Higgins yawns again, and resumes his song.

Pickering returns, with the contents of the letter-box in his hand.

PICKERING. Only circulars, and this coroneted billet-doux for you. [*He throws the circulars into the fender, and posts himself on the hearthrug, with his back to the grate*].

HIGGINS [*glancing at the billet-doux*] Money-lender. [*He throws the letter after the circulars*].

Eliza returns with a pair of large down-at-heel

slippers. She places them on the carpet before Higgins,
and sits as before without a word.

HIGGINS [*yawning again*] Oh Lord! What an evening! What
a crew! What a silly tomfoolery! [*He raises his shoe to
unlace it, and catches sight of the slippers. He stops un-
lacing and looks at them as if they had appeared there
of their own accord*]. Oh! Theyre there, are they?

PICKERING [*stretching himself*] Well, I feel a bit tired. It's
been a long day. The garden party, a dinner party, and
the reception! Rather too much of a good thing. But
youve won your bet, Higgins. Eliza did the trick, and
something to spare, eh?

HIGGINS [*fervently*] Thank God it's over!

Eliza flinches violently; but they take no notice of her;
and she recovers herself and sits stonily as before.

PICKERING. Were you nervous at the garden party? *I* was.
Eliza didnt seem a bit nervous.

HIGGINS. Oh, s h e wasnt nervous. I knew she'd be all right.
No: it's a strain of putting the job through all these
months that has told on me. It was interesting enough at
first, while we were at the phonetics; but after that I got
deadly sick of it. If I hadnt backed myself to do it I
should have chucked the whole thing up two months ago.
It was a silly notion: the whole thing has been a bore.

PICKERING. Oh come! the garden party was frightfully exciting. My heart began beating like anything.

HIGGINS. Yes, for the first three minutes. But when I saw
we were going to win hands down, I felt like a bear in a
cage, hanging about doing nothing. The dinner was
worse: sitting gorging there for over an hour, with nobody but a damned fool of a fashionable woman to talk
to! I tell you, Pickering, never again for me. No more
artificial duchesses. The whole thing has been simple
purgatory.

PICKERING. Youve never been broken in properly to the
social routine. [*Strolling over to the piano*] I rather enjoy
dipping into it occasionally myself: it makes me feel
young again. Anyhow, it was a great success: an immense
success. I was quite frightened once or twice because
Eliza was doing it so well. You see, lots of the real people

cant do it at all: theyre such fools that they think style
comes by nature to people in their position; and so they
never learn. Theres always something professional about
doing a thing superlatively well.

HIGGINS. Yes: thats what drives me mad: the silly people
dont know their own silly business. [*Rising*] However,
it's over and done with; and now I can go to bed at last
without dreading tomorrow.

Eliza's beauty becomes murderous.

PICKERING. I think I shall turn in too. Still, it's been a
great occasion: a triumph for you. Goodnight. [*He goes*].

HIGGINS [*following him*] Goodnight. [*Over his shoulder, at
the door*] Put out the lights, Eliza; and tell Mrs Pearce
not to make coffee for me in the morning: I'll take tea.
[*He goes out*].

*Eliza tries to control herself and feel indignant as she
rises and walks across to the hearth to switch off the
lights. By the time she gets there she is on the point of
screaming. She sits down in Higgins's chair and holds on
hard to the arms. Finally she gives way and flings herself
furiously on the floor, raging.*

HIGGINS [*in despairing wrath outside*] What the devil have
I done with my slippers? [*He appears at the door*].

LIZA [*snatching up the slippers, and hurling them at him
one after the other with all her force*] There are your
slippers. And there. Take your slippers; and may you
never have a day's luck with them!

HIGGINS [*astounded*] What on earth—! [*He comes to her*].
Whats the matter? Get up. [*He pulls her up*]. Anything
wrong?

LIZA [*breathless*] Nothing wrong—with you. Ive won your
bet for you, havnt I? Thats enough for you. *I* dont
matter, I suppose.

HIGGINS. You won my bet! You! Presumptuous insect! *I*
won it. What did you throw those slippers at me for?

LIZA. Because I wanted to smash your face. I'd like to kill
you, you selfish brute. Why didnt you leave me where
you picked me out of—in the gutter? You thank God it's
all over, and that now you can throw me back again
there, do you? [*She crisps her fingers frantically*].

HIGGINS [*looking at her in cool wonder*] The creature is nervous, after all.

LIZA. [*gives a suffocated scream of fury, and instinctively darts her nails at his face*]!!

HIGGINS [*catching her wrists*] Ah! would you? Claws in, you cat. How dare you shew your temper to me? Sit down and be quiet. [*He throws her roughly into the easy-chair*].

LIZA [*crushed by superior strength and weight*] Whats to become of me? Whats to become of me?

HIGGINS. How the devil do I know whats to become of you? What does it matter what becomes of you?

LIZA. You dont care. I know you dont care. You wouldnt care if I was dead. I'm nothing to you—not so much as them slippers.

HIGGINS [*thundering*] T h o s e slippers.

LIZA [*with bitter submission*] Those slippers. I didnt think it made any difference now.

A pause. Eliza hopeless and crushed. Higgins a little uneasy.

HIGGINS [*in his loftiest manner*] Why have you begun going on like this? May I ask whether you complain of your treatment here?

LIZA. No.

HIGGINS. Has anybody behaved badly to you? Colonel Pickering? Mrs Pearce? Any of the servants?

LIZA. No.

HIGGINS. I presume you dont pretend that *I* have treated you badly?

LIZA. No.

HIGGINS. I am glad to hear it. [*He moderates his tone*]. Perhaps youre tired after the strain of the day. Will you have a glass of champagne? [*He moves towards the door*].

LIZA. No [*Recollecting her manners*] Thank you.

HIGGINS [*good-humored again*] This has been coming on you for some days. I suppose it was natural for you to be anxious about the garden party. But thats all over now. [*He pats her kindly on the shoulder. She writhes*]. Theres nothing more to worry about.

LIZA. No. Nothing more for you to worry about. [*She suddenly rises and gets away from him by going to the piano bench, where she sits and hides her face*]. Oh God! I wish I was dead.

HIGGINS [*staring after her in sincere surprise*] Why? In heaven's name, why? [*Reasonably, going to her*] Listen to me, Eliza. All this irritation is purely subjective.

LIZA. I dont understand. I'm too ignorant.

HIGGINS. It's only imagination. Low spirits and nothing else: Nobody's hurting you. Nothing's wrong. You go to bed like a good girl and sleep it off. Have a little cry and say your prayers: that will make you comfortable.

LIZA. I heard y o u r prayers. "Thank God it's all over!"

HIGGINS [*impatiently*] Well, dont you thank God it's all over? Now you are free and can do what you like.

LIZA. [*pulling herself together in desperation*] What am I fit for? What have you left me fit for? Where am I to go? What am I to do? Whats to become of me?

HIGGINS [*enlightened, but not at all impressed*] Oh, thats whats worrying you, is it? [*He thrusts his hands into his pockets, and walks about in his usual manner, rattling the contents of his pockets, as if condescending to a trivial subject out of pure kindness*]. I shoudnt bother about it if I were you. I should imagine you wont have much difficulty in settling yourself somewhere or other, though I hadnt quite realized that you were going away. [*She looks quickly at him: he does not look at her, but examines the dessert stand on the piano and decides that he will eat an apple*]. You might marry, you know. [*He bites a large piece out of the apple and munches it noisily*]. You see, Eliza, all men are not confirmed old bachelors like me and the Colonel. Most men are the marrying sort (poor devils!); and youre not bad-looking: it's quite a pleasure to look at you sometimes—not now, of course, because youre crying and looking as ugly as the very devil; but when youre all right and quite yourself, youre what I should call attractive. That is, to the people in the marrying line, you understand. You go to bed and have a good nice rest; and then get up and look at yourself in the glass; and you wont feel so cheap.

Eliza again looks at him, speechless, and does not stir.

The look is quite lost on him: he eats his apple with a dreamy expression of happiness, as it is quite a good one.

HIGGINS [*a genial afterthought occurring to him*] I daresay my mother could find some chap or other who would do very well.

LIZA. We were above that at the corner of Tottenham Court Road.

HIGGINS [*waking up*] What do you mean?

LIZA. I sold flowers. I didnt sell myself. Now youve made a lady of me I'm not fit to sell anything else. I wish youd left me where you found me.

HIGGINS [*slinging the core of the apple decisively into the grate*] Tosh, Eliza. Dont you insult human relations by dragging all this cant about buying and selling into it. You neednt marry the fellow if you dont like him.

LIZA. What else am I to do?

HIGGINS. Oh, lots of things. What about your old idea of a florist's shop? Pickering could set you up in one: he has lots of money. [*Chuckling*] He'll have to pay for all those togs you have been wearing today; and that, with the hire of the jewellery, will make a big hole in two hundred pounds. Why, six months ago you would have thought it the millennium to have a flower shop of your own. Come! youll be all right. I must clear off to bed: I'm devilish sleepy. By the way, I came down for something: I forgot what it was.

LIZA. Your slippers.

HIGGINS. Oh yes, of course. You shied them at me. [*He picks them up, and is going out when she rises and speaks to him*].

LIZA. Before you go, sir—

HIGGINS [*dropping the slippers in his surprise at her calling him Sir*] Eh?

LIZA. Do my clothes belong to me or to Colonel Pickering?

HIGGINS [*coming back into the room as if her question were the very climax of unreason*] What the devil use would they be to Pickering?

LIZA. He might want them for the next girl you pick up to experiment on.

HIGGINS [*shocked and hurt*] Is that the way you feel towards us?

LIZA. I dont want to hear anything more about that. All I want to know is whether anything belongs to me. My own clothes were burnt.

HIGGINS. But what does it matter? Why need you start bothering about that in the middle of the night?

LIZA. I want to know what I may take away with me. I dont want to be accused of stealing.

HIGGINS [*now deeply wounded*] Stealing! You shouldnt have said that, Eliza. That shews a want of feeling.

LIZA. I'm sorry. I'm only a common ignorant girl; and in my station I have to be careful. There cant be any feelings between the like of you and the like of me. Please will you tell me what belongs to me and what doesnt?

HIGGINS [*very sulky*] You may take the whole damned houseful if you like. Except the jewels. Theyre hired. Will that satisfy you? [*He turns on his heel and is about to go in extreme dudgeon*].

LIZA [*drinking in his emotion like nectar, and nagging him to provoke a further supply*] Stop, please. [*She takes off her jewels*]. Will you take these to your room and keep them safe? I dont want to run the risk of their being missing.

HIGGINS [*furious*] Hand them over. [*She puts them into his his hands*]. If these belonged to me instead of to the jeweller, I'd ram them down your ungrateful throat. [*He perfunctorily thrusts them into his pockets, unconsciously decorating himself with the protruding ends of the chains*].

LIZA [*taking a ring off*] This ring isnt the jeweller's: it's the one you bought me in Brighton. I dont want it now. [*Higgins dashes the ring violently into the fireplace, and turns on her so threateningly that she crouches over the piano with her hands over her face, and exclaims*] Dont you hit me.

HIGGINS. Hit you! You infamous creature, how dare you accuse me of such a thing? It is you who have hit me. You have wounded me to the heart.

LIZA [*thrilling with hidden joy*] I'm glad. Ive got a little of
my own back anyhow.

HIGGINS [*with dignity, in his finest professional style*] You
have caused me to lose my temper: a thing that has
hardly ever happened to me before. I prefer to say nothing more tonight. I am going to bed.

LIZA [*pertly*] Youd better leave a note for Mrs Pearce about
the coffee; for she wont be told by me.

HIGGINS [*formally*] Damn Mrs Pearce; and damn the coffee;
and damn you; and [*wildly*] damn my own folly in having
lavished my hard-earned knowledge and the treasure of
my regard and intimacy on a heartless guttersnipe. [*He
goes out with impressive decorum, and spoils it by
slamming the door savagely*].

*Eliza goes down on her knees on the hearthrug to look
for the ring. When she finds it she considers for a
moment what to do with it. Finally she flings it down on
the dessert stand and goes upstairs in a tearing rage.*

*   *   *

*The furniture of Eliza's room has been increased by a
big wardrobe and a sumptuous dressing-table. She comes
in and switches on the electric light. She goes to the
wardrobe; opens it; and pulls out a walking dress, a hat,
and a pair of shoes, which she throws on the bed. She
takes off her evening dress and shoes; then takes a
padded hanger from the wardrobe; adjusts it carefully in
the evening dress and hangs it in the wardrobe, which
she shuts with a slam. She puts on her walking shoes, her
walking dress, and hat. She takes her wrist watch from
the dressing-table and fastens it on. She pulls on her
gloves; takes her vanity bag; and looks into it to see that
her purse is there before hanging it on her wrist. She
makes for the door. Every movement expresses her
furious resolution.*

She takes a last look at herself in the glass.

*She suddenly puts out her tongue at herself; then
leaves the room, switching off the electric light at the door.*

Meanwhile, in the street outside, Freddy Eynsford

*Hill, lovelorn, is gazing up at the second floor, in which
one of the windows is still lighted.*

The light goes out.

FREDDY. Goodnight, darling, darling, darling.

*Eliza comes out, giving the door a considerable bang
behind her.*

LIZA. Whatever are you doing here?

FREDDY. Nothing. I spend most of my nights here. It's the
only place where I'm happy. Dont laugh at me, Miss
Doolittle.

LIZA. Dont you call me Miss Doolittle, do you hear? Liza's
good enough for me. [*She breaks down and grabs him by
the shoulders*] Freddy: you dont think I'm a heartless
guttersnipe, do you?

FREDDY. Oh no, no, darling: how can you imagine such a
thing? You are the loveliest, dearest—

*He loses all self-control and smothers her with kisses.
She, hungry for comfort, responds. They stand there in
one another's arms.*

An elderly police constable arrives.

CONSTABLE [*scandalized*] Now then! Now then!! Now
then!!!

They release one another hastily.

FREDDY. Sorry, constable. Weve only just become engaged.

They run away.

The constable shakes his head, reflecting on his own
courtship and on the vanity of human hopes. He moves
off in the opposite direction with slow professional
steps.

The flight of the lovers takes them to Cavendish
Square. There they halt to consider their next move.

LIZA [*out of breath*] He didnt half give me a fright, that
copper. But you answered him proper.

FREDDY. I hope I havnt taken you out of your way. Where
were you going?

LIZA. To the river.

FREDDY. What for?

LIZA. To make a hole in it.

FREDDY [*horrified*] Eliza, darling. What do you mean?
Whats the matter?

LIZA. Never mind. It doesnt matter now. Theres nobody in the world now but you and me, is there?

FREDDY. Not a soul.

They indulge in another embrace, and are again surprised by a much younger constable.

SECOND CONSTABLE. Now then, you two! Whats this? Where do you think you are? Move along here, double quick.

FREDDY. As you say, sir, double quick.

They run away again, and are in Hanover Square before they stop for another conference.

FREDDY. I had no idea the police were so devilishly prudish.

LIZA. It's their business to hunt girls off the streets.

FREDDY. We must go somewhere. We cant wander about the streets all night.

LIZA. Cant we? I think it'd be lovely to wander about for ever.

FREDDY. Oh, darling.

They embrace again, oblivious of the arrival of a crawling taxi. It stops.

TAXIMAN. Can I drive you and the lady anywhere, sir?

They start asunder.

LIZA. Oh, Freddy, a taxi. The very thing.

FREDDY. But, damn it, Ive no money.

LIZA. I have plenty. The Colonel thinks you should never go out without ten pounds in your pocket. Listen. We'll drive about all night; and in the morning I'll call on old Mrs Higgins and ask her what I ought to do. I'll tell you all about it in the cab. And the police wont touch us there.

FREDDY. Righto! Ripping. [*To the Taximan*] Wimbledon Common. [*They drive off*].

ACT V

Mrs Higgins's drawing room. She is at her writing-table as before. The parlormaid comes in.

THE PARLORMAID [*at the door*] Mr Henry, maam, is downstairs with Colonel Pickering.

MRS HIGGINS. Well, shew them up.

THE PARLORMAID. Theyre using the telephone, maam. Telephoning to the police, I think.

MRS HIGGINS. What!

THE PARLORMAID [*coming further in and lowering her voice*] Mr Henry is in a state, maam. I thought I'd better tell you.

MRS HIGGINS. If you had told me that Mr Henry was not in a state it would have been more surprising. Tell them to come up when theyve finished with the police. I suppose he's lost something.

THE PARLORMAID. Yes, maam [*going*].

MRS HIGGINS. Go upstairs and tell Miss Doolittle that Mr Henry and the Colonel are here. Ask her not to come down til I send for her.

THE PARLORMAID. Yes, maam.

    Higgins bursts in. He is, as the parlormaid has said, in a state.

HIGGINS. Look here, mother: heres a confounded thing!

MRS HIGGINS. Yes, dear. Good morning. [*He checks his impatience and kisses her, whilst the parlormaid goes out*]. What is it?

HIGGINS. Eliza's bolted.

MRS HIGGINS [*calmly continuing her writing*] You must have frightened her.

HIGGINS. Frightened her! Nonsense! She was left last night, as usual, to turn out the lights and all that; and instead of going to bed she changed her clothes and went right off: her bed wasnt slept in. She came in a cab for her things before seven this morning; and that fool Mrs Pearce let her have them without telling me a word about it. What am I to do?

MRS HIGGINS. Do without, I'm afraid, Henry. The girl has a perfect right to leave if she chooses.

HIGGINS [*wandering distractedly across the room*] But I cant find anything. I dont know what appointments Ive got. I'm— [*Pickering comes in. Mrs Higgins puts down her pen and turns away from the writing-table*].

PICKERING [*shaking hands*] Good morning, Mrs Higgins. Has Henry told you? [*He sits down on the ottoman*].

HIGGINS. What does that ass of an inspector say? Have you offered a reward?

MRS HIGGINS [*rising in indignant amazement*] You dont mean to say you have set the police after Eliza?

HIGGINS. Of course. What are the police for? What else could we do? [*He sits in the Elizabethan chair*].

PICKERING. The inspector made a lot of difficulties. I really think he suspected us of some improper purpose.

MRS HIGGINS. Well, of course he did. What right have you to go to the police and give the girl's name as if she were a thief, or a lost umbrella, or something? Really! [*She sits down again, deeply vexed*].

HIGGINS. But we want to find her.

PICKERING. We cant let her go like this, you know, Mrs Higgins. What were we to do?

MRS HIGGINS. You have no more sense, either of you, than two children. Why—

The parlormaid comes in and breaks off the conversation.

THE PARLORMAID. Mr Henry: a gentleman wants to see you very particular. He's been sent on from Wimpole Street.

HIGGINS. Oh, brother! I cant see anyone now. Who is it?

THE PARLOMAID. A Mr Doolittle, sir.

PICKERING. Doolittle! Do you mean the dustman?

THE PARLORMAID. Dustman! Oh no, sir: a gentleman.

HIGGINS [*springing up excitedly*] By George, Pick, it's some relative of hers that she's gone to. Somebody we know nothing about. [*To the parlormaid*] Send him up, quick.

THE PARLORMAID. Yes, sir. [*She goes*].

HIGGINS [*eagerly, going to his mother*] Genteel relatives! now we shall hear something. [*He sits down in the Chippendale chair*].

MRS HIGGINS. Do you know any of her people?

PICKERING. Only her father: the fellow we told you about.

THE PARLORMAID [*announcing*] Mr Doolittle. [*She withdraws*].

Doolittle enters. He is resplendently dressed as for a fashionable wedding, and might, in fact, be the bridegroom. A flower in his buttonhole, a dazzling silk hat, and patent leather shoes complete the effect. He is too

concerned with the business he has come on to notice
Mrs Higgins. He walks straight to Higgins, and accosts
him with vehement reproach.

DOOLITTLE [indicating his own person] See here! Do you see
this? Y o u done this.

HIGGINS. Done what, man?

DOOLITTLE. This, I tell you. Look at it. Look at this hat.
Look at this coat.

PICKERING. Has Eliza been buying you clothes?

DOOLITTLE. Eliza! Not she. Why would she buy me clothes?

MRS HIGGINS. Good morning, Mr Doolittle. Wont you sit
down?

DOOLITTLE [taken aback as he becomes conscious that he
has forgotten his hostess] Asking your pardon, maam.
[He approaches her and shakes her proffered hand].
Thank you. [He sits down on the ottoman, on Pickering's
right]. I am that full of what has happened to me that I
cant think of anything else.

HIGGINS. What the dickens has happened to you?

DOOLITTLE. I shouldnt mind if it had only happened to me:
anything might happen to anybody and nobody to blame
but Providence, as you might say. But this is something
that y o u done to me: yes, y o u, Enry Iggins.

HIGGINS. Have you found Eliza?

DOOLITTLE. Have you lost her?

HIGGINS. Yes.

DOOLITTLE. You have all the luck, you have. I aint found
her; but she'll find me quick enough now after what you
done to me.

MRS HIGGINS. But what has my son done to you, Mr.
Doolittle?

DOOLITTLE. Done to me! Ruined me. Destroyed my happiness. Tied me up and delivered me into the hands of
middle class morality.

HIGGINS [rising intolerantly and standing over Doolittle]
Youre raving. Youre drunk. Youre mad. I gave you five
pounds. After that I had two conversations with you, at
half-a-crown an hour. Ive never seen you since.

DOOLITTLE. Oh! Drunk am I? Mad am I? Tell me this. Did
you or did you not write a letter to an old blighter in

America that was giving five millions to found Moral
Reform Societies all over the world, and that wanted you
to invent a universal language for him?

HIGGINS. What! Ezra D. Wannafeller! He's dead. [*He sits
down again carelessly*].

DOOLITTLE. Yes: he's dead; and I'm done for. Now did
you or did you not write a letter to him to say that the
most original moralist at present in England, to the best
of your knowledge, was Alfred Doolittle, a common
dustman?

HIGGINS. Oh, after your first visit I remember making some
silly joke of the kind.

DOOLITTLE. Ah! You may well call it a silly joke. It put the
lid on me right enough. Just give him the chance he
wanted to shew that Americans is not like us: that they
reckonize and respect merit in every class of life, however
humble. Them words is in his blooming will, in which,
Henry Higgins, thanks to your silly joking, he leaves me
a share in his Pre-digested Cheese Trust worth three
thousand a year on condition that I lecture for his
Wannafeller Moral Reform World League as often as
they ask me up to six times a year.

HIGGINS. The devil he does! Whew! [*Brightening suddenly*]
What a lark!

PICKERING. A safe thing for you, Doolittle. They wont ask
you twice.

DOOLITTLE. It aint the lecturing I mind. I'll lecture them
blue in the face, I will, and not turn a hair. It's making a
gentleman of me that I object to. Who asked him to make
a gentleman of me? I was happy. I was free. I touched
pretty nigh everybody for money when I wanted it, same
as I touched you, Enry Iggins. Now I am worried; tied
neck and heels; and everybody touches m e for money.
It's a fine thing for you, says my solicitor. Is it? says I.
You mean it's a good thing for you, I says. When I was
a poor man and had a solicitor once when they found a
pram in the dust cart, he got me off, and got shut of me
and got me shut of him as quick as he could. Same with
the doctors: used to shove me out of the hospital before
I could hardly stand on my legs, and nothing to pay. Now

they finds out that I'm not a healthy man and cant live
unless they looks after me twice a day. In the house I'm
not let do a hand's turn for myself: somebody else must
do it and touch me for it. A year ago I hadnt a relative
in the world except two or three that wouldnt speak to
me. Now Ive fifty, and not a decent week's wages among
the lot of them. I have to live for others and not for myself: thats middle class morality. Y o u talk of losing
Eliza. Dont you be anxious: I bet she's on my doorstep
by this: she that could support herself easy by selling
flowers if I wasnt respectable. And the next one to touch
me will be you, Enry Iggins. I'll have to learn to speak
middle class language from you, instead of speaking
proper English. Thats where youll come in; and I daresay
thats what you done it for.

MRS HIGGINS. But, my dear Mr Doolittle, you need not
suffer all this if you are really in earnest. Nobody can
force you to accept this bequest. You can repudiate it.
Isnt that so, Colonel Pickering?

PICKERING. I believe so.

DOOLITTLE [*softening his manner in deference to her sex*]
Thats the tragedy of it, maam. It's easy to say chuck it;
but I havnt the nerve. Which of us has? We're all intimidated. Intimidated, maam: thats what we are. What is
there for me if I chuck it but the workhouse in my old
age? I have to dye my hair already to keep my job as a
dustman. If I was one of the deserving poor, and had
put by a bit, I could chuck it; but then why should I,
acause the deserving poor might as well be millionaires
for all the happiness they ever has. They dont know what
happiness is. But I, as one of the undeserving poor, have
nothing between me and the pauper's uniform but this
here blasted three thousand a year that shoves me into
the middle class. (Excuse the expression, maam; youd
use it yourself if you had my provocation.) Theyve got
you every way you turn: it's a choice between the Skilly
of the workhouse and the Char Bydis of the middle class;
and I havnt the nerve for the workhouse. Intimidated:
thats what I am. Broke. Bought up. Happier men than
me will call for my dust, and touch me for their tip; and

I'll look on helpless, and envy them. And thats what your son has brought me to. [*He is overcome by emotion*].

MRS HIGGINS. Well, I'm very glad youre not going to do anything foolish, Mr Doolittle. For this solves the problem of Eliza's future. You can provide for her now.

DOOLITTLE [*with melancholy resignation*] Yes, maam: I'm expected to provide for everyone now, out of three thousand a year.

HIGGINS [*jumping up*] Nonsense! he cant provide for her. He shant provide for her. She doesnt belong to him. I paid him five pounds for her. Doolittle: either youre an honest man or a rogue.

DOOLITTLE [*tolerantly*] A little of both, Henry, like the rest of us: a little of both.

HIGGINS. Well, you took that money for the girl; and you have no right to take her as well.

MRS HIGGINS. Henry: dont be absurd. If you want to know where Eliza is, she is upstairs.

HIGGINS [*amazed*] Upstairs!!! Then I shall jolly soon fetch her downstairs. [*He makes resolutely for the door*].

MRS HIGGINS [*rising and following him*] Be quiet, Henry. Sit down.

HIGGINS. I—

MRS HIGGINS. Sit down, dear; and listen to me.

HIGGINS. Oh very well, very well, very well. [*He throws himself ungraciously on the ottoman, with his face towards the windows*]. But I think you might have told us this half an hour ago.

MRS HIGGINS. Eliza came to me this morning. She told me of the brutal way you two treated her.

HIGGINS [*bounding up again*] What!

PICKERING [*rising also*] My dear Mrs Higgins, she's been telling you stories. We didnt treat her brutally. We hardly said a word to her; and we parted on particularly good terms. [*Turning on Higgins*] Higgins: did you bully her after I went to bed?

HIGGINS. Just the other way about. She threw my slippers in my face. She behaved in the most outrageous way. I never gave her the slightest provocation. The slippers

came bang into my face the moment I entered the room
—before I had uttered a word. And [she] used perfectly
awful language.

PICKERING [*astonished*] But why? What did we do to her?

MRS HIGGINS. I think I know pretty well what you did. The
girl is naturally rather affectionate, I think. Isnt she, Mr
Doolittle?

DOOLITTLE. Very tender-hearted, maam. Takes after me.

MRS HIGGINS. Just so. She had become attached to you
both. She worked very hard for you, Henry. I dont think
you quite realize what anything in the nature of brain
work means to a girl of her class. Well, it seems that
when the great day of trial came, and she did this
wonderful thing for you without making a single mistake,
you two sat there and never said a word to her, but
talked together of how glad you were that it was all over
and how you had been bored with the whole thing. And
then you were surprised because she threw your slippers
at you! *I* should have thrown the fire-irons at you.

HIGGINS. We said nothing except that we were tired and
wanted to go to bed. Did we, Pick?

PICKERING [*shrugging his shoulders*] That was all.

MRS HIGGINS [*ironically*] Quite sure?

PICKERING. Absolutely. Really, that was all.

MRS HIGGINS. You didnt thank her, or pet her, or admire
her, or tell her how splendid she'd been.

HIGGINS [*impatiently*] But she knew all about that. We
didnt make speeches to her, if thats what you mean.

PICKERING [*conscience stricken*] Perhaps we were a little inconsiderate. Is she very angry?

MRS HIGGINS [*returning to her place at the writing-table*]
Well, I'm afraid she wont go back to Wimpole Street,
especially now that Mr Doolittle is able to keep up the
position you have thrust on her; but she says she is quite
willing to meet you on friendly terms and to let bygones
be bygones.

HIGGINS [*furious*] Is she, by George? Ho!

MRS HIGGINS. If you promise to behave yourself, Henry, I'll
ask her to come down. If not, go home; for you have
taken up quite enough of my time.

HIGGINS. Oh, all right. Very well. Pick: you behave your-self. Let us put on our best Sunday manners for this creature that we picked out of the mud. [*He flings him-self sulkily into the Elizabethan chair*].

DOOLITTLE [*remonstrating*] Now, now, Enry Iggins! Have some consideration for my feelings as a middle class man.

MRS HIGGINS. Remember your promise, Henry. [*She presses the bell-button on the writing-table*]. Mr Doolittle: will you be so good as to step out on the balcony for a moment. I dont want Eliza to have the shock of your news until she has made it up with these two gentlemen. Would you mind?

DOOLITTLE. As you wish, lady. Anything to help Henry to keep her off my hands. [*He disappears through the window*].

The parlormaid answers the bell. Pickering sits down in Doolittle's place.

MRS HIGGINS. Ask Miss Doolittle to come down, please.

THE PARLORMAID. Yes, maam. [*She goes out*].

MRS HIGGINS. Now, Henry: be good.

HIGGINS. I am behaving myself perfectly.

PICKERING. He is doing his best, Mrs Higgins.

A pause. Higgins throws back his head; stretches out his legs and begins to whistle.

MRS HIGGINS. Henry, dearest, you dont look at all nice in that attitude.

HIGGINS [*pulling himself together*] I was not trying to look nice, mother.

MRS HIGGINS. It doesnt matter, dear. I only wanted to make you speak.

HIGGINS. Why?

MRS HIGGINS. Because you cant speak and whistle at the same time.

Higgins groans. Another very tiring pause.

HIGGINS [*springing up, out of patience*] Where the devil is that girl? Are we to wait here all day?

Eliza enters, sunny, self-possessed, and giving a stag-geringly convincing exhibition of ease of manner. She carries a little work-basket, and is very much at home. Pickering is too much taken aback to rise.

LIZA. How do you do, Professor Higgins? Are you quite
well?

HIGGINS [*choking*] Am I— [*He can say no more*].

LIZA. But of course you are: you are never ill. So glad to
see you again, Colonel Pickering. [*He rises hastily; and
they shake hands*]. Quite chilly this morning, isnt it? [*She
sits down on his left. He sits beside her*].

HIGGINS. Dont you dare try this game on me. I taught it to
you; and it doesnt take me in. Get up and come home;
and dont be a fool.

> *Eliza takes a piece of needlework from her basket, and
> begins to stitch at it, without taking the least notice of
> this outburst.*

MRS HIGGINS. Very nicely put, indeed, Henry. No woman
could resist such an invitation.

HIGGINS. You let her alone, mother. Let her speak for herself. You will jolly soon see whether she has an idea that
I havnt put into her head or a word that I havnt put into
her mouth. I tell you I have created this thing out of the
squashed cabbage leaves of Covent Garden; and now she
pretends to play the fine lady with me.

MRS HIGGINS [*placidly*] Yes, dear; but youll sit down, wont
you?

> *Higgins sits down again, savagely.*

LIZA [*to Pickering, taking no apparent notice of Higgins,
and working away deftly*] Will y o u drop me altogether
now that the experiment is over, Colonel Pickering?

PICKERING. Oh dont. You mustnt think of it as an experiment. It shocks me, somehow.

LIZA. Oh, I'm only a squashed cabbage leaf—

PICKERING [*impulsively*] No.

LIZA [*continuing quietly*] —but I owe so much to you that
I should be very unhappy if you forgot me.

PICKERING. It's very kind of you to say so, Miss Doolittle.

LIZA. It's not because you paid for my dresses. I know you
are generous to everybody with money. But it was from
you that I learnt really nice manners; and that is what
makes one a lady, isnt it? You see it was so very difficult
for me with the example of Professor Higgins always
before me. I was brought up to be just like him, unable

to control myself, and using bad language on the slightest provocation. And I should never have known that ladies and gentlemen didnt behave like that if you hadnt been there.

HIGGINS. Well!!

PICKERING. Oh, thats only his way, you know. He doesnt mean it.

LIZA. Oh, *I* didnt mean it either, when I was a flower girl. It was only my way. But you see I did it; and thats what makes the difference after all.

PICKERING. No doubt. Still, he taught you to speak; and I couldnt have done that, you know.

LIZA [*trivially*] Of course: that is his profession.

HIGGINS. Damnation!

LIZA [*continuing*] It was just like learning to dance in the fashionable way: there was nothing more than that in it. But do you know what began my real education?

PICKERING. What?

LIZA [*stopping her work for a moment*] Your calling me Miss Doolittle that day when I first came to Wimpole Street. That was the beginning of self-respect for me. [*She resumes her stitching*]. And there were a hundred little things you never noticed, because they came naturally to you. Things about standing up and taking off your hat and opening doors—

PICKERING. Oh, that was nothing.

LIZA. Yes: things that shewed you thought and felt about me as if I were something better than a scullery-maid; though of course I know you would have been just the same to a scullery-maid if she had been let into the drawing room. Y o u never took off your boots in the dining room when I was there.

PICKERING. You mustnt mind that. Higgins takes off his boots all over the place.

LIZA. I know. I am not blaming him. It is his way, isnt it? But it made s u c h a difference to me that you didnt do it. You see, really and truly, apart from the things anyone can pick up (the dressing and the proper way of speaking, and so on), the difference between a lady and a flower girl is not how she behaves, but how she's

treated. I shall always be a flower girl to Professor
Higgins, because he always treats me as a flower girl, and
always will; but I know I can be a lady to you, because
you always treat me as a lady, and always will.

MRS HIGGINS. Please dont grind your teeth, Henry.

PICKERING. Well, this really is very nice of you, Miss
Doolittle.

LIZA. I should like you to call me Eliza, now, if you would.

PICKERING. Thank you. Eliza, of course.

LIZA. And I should like Professor Higgins to call me Miss
Doolittle.

HIGGINS. I'll see you damned first.

MRS HIGGINS. Henry! Henry!

PICKERING [*laughing*] Why dont you slang back at him?
Dont stand it. It would do him a lot of good.

LIZA. I cant. I could have done it once but now I cant go
back to it. You told me, you know, that when a child is
brought to a foreign country, it picks up the language in
a few weeks, and forgets its own. Well, I am a child in
your country. I have forgotten my own language, and
can speak nothing but yours. Thats the real break-off
with the corner of Tottenham Court Road. Leaving
Wimpole Street finishes it.

PICKERING [*much alarmed*] Oh! but youre coming back to
Wimpole Street, arnt you? Youll forgive Higgins?

HIGGINS [*rising*] Forgive! Will she, by George! Let her go.
Let her find out how she can get on without us. She will
relapse into the gutter in three weeks without me at her
elbow.

   *Doolittle appears at the centre window. With a look of
   dignified reproach at Higgins, he comes slowly and
   silently to his daughter, who, with her back to the
   window, is unconscious of his approach.*

PICKERING. He's incorrigible, Eliza. You wont relapse, will
you?

LIZA. No: not now. Never again. I have learnt my lesson. I
dont believe I could utter one of the old sounds if I tried.
[*Doolittle touches her on her left shoulder. She drops
her work, losing her self-possession utterly at the spectacle of her father's splendor*] A-a-a-a-a-ah-ow-ooh!

HIGGINS [*with a crow of triumph*] Aha! Just so. A-a-a-a-ahowooh! A-a-a-a-ahowooh! A-a-a-a-ahowooh! Victory! Victory! [*He throws himself on the divan, folding his arms, and spraddling arrogantly*].

DOOLITTLE. Can you blame the girl? Dont look at me like that, Eliza. It aint my fault. Ive come into some money.

LIZA. You must have touched a millionaire this time, dad.

DOOLITTLE. I have. But I'm dressed something special today. I'm going to St George's, Hanover Square. Your stepmother is going to marry me.

LIZA [*angrily*] Youre going to let yourself down to marry that low common woman!

PICKERING [*quietly*] He ought to, Eliza. [*To Doolittle*] Why has she changed her mind?

DOOLITTLE [*sadly*] Intimidated, Governor. Intimidated. Middle class morality claims its victim. Wont you put on your hat, Liza, and come and see me turned off?

LIZA. If the Colonel says I must, I— I'll [*almost sobbing*] I'll demean myself. And get insulted for my pains, like enough.

DOOLITTLE. Dont be afraid: she never comes to words with anyone now, poor woman! respectability has broke all the spirit out of her.

PICKERING [*squeezing Eliza's elbow gently*] Be kind to them, Eliza. Make the best of it.

LIZA [*forcing a little smile for him through her vexation*] Oh well, just to shew theres no ill feeling. I'll be back in a moment. [*She goes out*].

DOOLITTLE [*sitting down beside Pickering*] I feel uncommon nervous about the ceremony, Colonel. I wish youd come and see me through it.

PICKERING. But youve been through it before, man. You were married to Eliza's mother.

DOOLITTLE. Who told you that, Colonel?

PICKERING. Well, nobody told me. But I concluded— naturally—

DOOLITTLE. No: that aint the natural way, Colonel: it's only the middle class way. My way was always the undeserving way. But dont say nothing to Eliza. She dont know: I always had a delicacy about telling her.

PICKERING. Quite right. We'll leave it so, if you dont mind.

DOOLITTLE. And youll come to the church, Colonel, and put me through straight?

PICKERING. With pleasure. As far as a bachelor can.

MRS HIGGINS. May I come, Mr Doolittle? I should be very sorry to miss your wedding.

DOOLITTLE. I should indeed be honored by your condenscension, maam; and my poor old woman would take it as a tremenjous compliment. She's been very low, thinking of the happy days that are no more.

MRS HIGGINS [*rising*] I'll order the carriage and get ready. [*The men rise, except Higgins*]. I shant be more than fifteen minutes. [*As she goes to the door Eliza comes in, hatted and buttoning her gloves*]. I'm going to the church to see your father married, Eliza. You had better come in the brougham with me. Colonel Pickering can go on with the bridegroom.

    Mrs Higgins goes out. Eliza comes to the middle of the room between the centre window and the ottoman. Pickering joins her.

DOOLITTLE. Bridegroom! What a word! It makes a man realize his position, somehow. [*He takes up his hat and goes towards the door*].

PICKERING. Before I go, Eliza, do forgive Higgins and come back to us.

LIZA. I dont think dad would allow me. Would you, dad?

DOOLITTLE [*sad but magnanimous*] They played you off very cunning, Eliza, them two sportsmen. If it had been only one of them, you could have nailed him. But you see, there was two; and one of them chaperoned the other, as you might say. [*To Pickering*] It was artful of you, Colonel; but I bear no malice: I should have done the same myself. I been the victim of one woman after another all my life, and I dont grudge you two getting the better of Liza. I shant interfere. It's time for us to go, Colonel. So long, Henry. See you in St George's, Eliza. [*He goes out*].

PICKERING [*coaxing*] Do stay with us, Eliza. [*He follows Doolittle*].

    Eliza goes out on the balcony to avoid being alone

with Higgins. He rises and joins her there. She immediately comes back into the room and makes for the door; but he goes along the balcony quickly and gets his back to the door before she reaches it.

HIGGINS. Well, Eliza, youve had a bit of your own back, as you call it. Have you had enough? and are you going to be reasonable? Or do you want any more?

LIZA. You want me back only to pick up your slippers and put up with your tempers and fetch and carry for you.

HIGGINS. I havnt said I wanted you back at all.

LIZA. Oh, indeed. Then what are we talking about?

HIGGINS. About you, not about me. If you come back I shall treat you just as I have always treated you. I cant change my nature; and I dont intend to change my manners. My manners are exactly the same as Colonel Pickering's.

LIZA. Thats not true. He treats a flower girl as if she was a duchess.

HIGGINS. And I treat a duchess as if she was a flower girl.

LIZA. I see. [*She turns away composedly, and sits on the ottoman, facing the window*]. The same to everybody.

HIGGINS. Just so.

LIZA. Like father.

HIGGINS [*grinning, a little taken down*] Without accepting the comparison at all points, Eliza, it's quite true that your father is not a snob, and that he will be quite at home in any station of life to which his eccentric destiny may call him. [*Seriously*] The great secret, Eliza, is not having bad manners or good manners or any other particular sort of manners, but having the same manner for all human souls: in short, behaving as if you were in Heaven, where there are no third-class carriages, and one soul is as good as another.

LIZA. Amen. You are a born preacher.

HIGGINS [*irritated*] The question is not whether I treat you rudely, but whether you ever heard me treat anyone else better.

LIZA [*with sudden sincerity*] I dont care how you treat me. I dont mind your swearing at me. I shouldnt mind a black eye: Ive had one before this. But [*standing up and facing him*] I wont be passed over.

HIGGINS. Then get out of my way; for I wont stop for you. You talk about me as if I were a motor bus.

LIZA. So you are a motor bus: all bounce and go, and no consideration for anyone. But I can do without you: dont think I cant.

HIGGINS. I know you can. I told you you could.

LIZA [*wounded, getting away from him to the other side of the ottoman with her face to the hearth*] I know you did, you brute. You wanted to get rid of me.

HIGGINS. Liar.

LIZA. Thank you. [*She sits down with dignity*].

HIGGINS. You never asked yourself, I suppose, whether *I* could do without y o u.

LIZA [*earnestly*] Dont you try to get round me. Youll have to do without me.

HIGGINS [*arrogant*] I can do without anybody. I have my own soul: my own spark of divine fire. But [*with sudden humility*] I shall miss you, Eliza. [*He sits down near her on the ottoman*]. I have learnt something from your idiotic notions: I confess that humbly and gratefully. And I have grown accustomed to your voice and appearance. I like them, rather.

LIZA. Well, you have both of them on your gramophone and in your book of photographs. When you feel lonely without me, you can turn the machine on. It's got no feelings to hurt.

HIGGINS. I cant turn your soul on. Leave me those feelings; and you can take away the voice and the face. They are not you.

LIZA. Oh, you a r e a devil. You can twist the heart in a girl as easy as some could twist her arms to hurt her. Mrs Pearce warned me. Time and again she has wanted to leave you; and you always got round her at the last minute. And you dont care a bit for her. And you dont care a bit for me.

HIGGINS. I care for life, for humanity; and you are a part of it that has come my way and been built into my house. What more can you or anyone ask?

LIZA. I wont care for anybody that doesnt care for me.

HIGGINS. Commercial principles, Eliza. Like [*reproducing*

*her Covent Garden pronunciation with professional
exactness]* s'yollin voylets [selling violets], isnt it?

LIZA. Dont sneer at me. It's mean to sneer at me.

HIGGINS. I have never sneered in my life. Sneering doesnt
become either the human face or the human soul. I am
expressing my righteous contempt for Commercialism. I
dont and wont trade in affection. You call me a brute
because you couldnt buy a claim on me by fetching my
slippers and finding my spectacles. You were a fool: I
think a woman fetching a man's slippers is a disgusting
sight: did I ever fetch y o u r slippers? I think a good deal
more of you for throwing them in my face. No use
slaving for me and then saying you want to be cared for:
who cares for a slave? If you come back, come back for
the sake of good fellowship; for youll get nothing else.
Youve had a thousand times as much out of me as I
have out of you; and if you dare to set up your little
dog's tricks of fetching and carrying slippers against my
creation of a Duchess Eliza, I'll slam the door in your
silly face.

LIZA. What did you do it for if you didnt care for me?

HIGGINS [*heartily*] Why, because it was my job.

LIZA. You never thought of the trouble it would make for
me.

HIGGINS. Would the world ever have been made if its maker
had been afraid of making trouble? Making life means
making trouble. Theres only one way of escaping trouble;
and thats killing things. Cowards, you notice, are always
shrieking to have troublesome people killed.

LIZA. I'm no preacher: I dont notice things like that. I
notice that you dont notice me.

HIGGINS [*jumping up and walking about intolerantly*] Eliza:
youre an idiot. I waste the treasures of my Miltonic mind
by spreading them before you. Once for all, understand
that I go my way and do my work without caring two-
pence what happens to either of us. I am not intimidated,
like your father and your stepmother. So you can come
back or go to the devil: which you please.

LIZA. What am I to come back for?

HIGGINS [*bounding up on his knees on the ottoman and*

leaning over it to her] For the fun of it. Thats why I took you on.

LIZA [*with averted face*] And you may throw me out tomorrow if I dont do everything you want me too?

HIGGINS. Yes; and you may walk out tomorrow if I dont do everything y o u want me to.

LIZA. And live with my stepmother?

HIGGINS. Yes, or sell flowers.

LIZA. Oh! if I only c o u l d go back to my flower basket! I should be independent of both you and father and all the world! Why did you take my independence from me? Why did I give it up? I'm a slave now, for all my fine clothes.

HIGGINS. Not a bit. I'll adopt you as my daughter and settle money on you if you like. Or would you rather marry Pickering?

LIZA [*looking fiercely round at him*] I wouldnt marry y o u if you asked me; and youre nearer my age than what he is.

HIGGINS [*gently*] Than he is: not "than what he is."

LIZA [*losing her temper and rising*] I'll talk as I like. Youre not my teacher now.

HIGGINS [*reflectively*] I dont suppose Pickering would, though. He's as confirmed an old bachelor as I am.

LIZA. Thats not what I want; and dont you think it. Ive always had chaps enough wanting me that way. Freddy Hill writes to me twice and three times a day, sheets and sheets.

HIGGINS [*disagreeably surprised*] Damn his impudence! [*He recoils and finds himself sitting on his heels*].

LIZA. He has a right to if he likes, poor lad. And he does love me.

HIGGINS [*getting off the ottoman*] You have no right to encourage him.

LIZA. Every girl has a right to be loved.

HIGGINS. What! By fools like that?

LIZA. Freddy's not a fool. And if he's weak and poor and wants me, maybe he'd make me happier than my betters that bully me and dont want me.

HIGGINS. Can he make anything of you? Thats the point.

LIZA. Perhaps I could make something of him. But I never
thought of us making anything of one another; and you
never think of anything else. I only want to be natural.

HIGGINS. In short, you want me to be as infatuated about
you as Freddy? Is that it?

LIZA. No I dont. Thats not the sort of feeling I want from
you. And dont you be too sure of yourself or of me. I
could have been a bad girl if I'd liked. Ive seen more of
some things than you, for all your learning. Girls like me
can drag gentlemen down to make love to them easy
enough. And they wish each other dead the next minute.

HIGGINS. Of course they do. Then what in thunder are we
quarrelling about?

LIZA [*much troubled*] I want a little kindness. I know I'm a
common ignorant girl, and you a book-learned gentleman; but I'm not dirt under your feet. What I done
[*correcting herself*] what I did was not for the dresses and
the taxis: I did it because we were pleasant together and
I come—came—to care for you; not to want you to make
love to me, and not forgetting the difference between us,
but more friendly like.

HIGGINS. Well, of course. Thats just how I feel. And how
Pickering feels. Eliza: youre a fool.

LIZA. Thats not a proper answer to give me [*she sinks on the
chair at the writing-table in tears*].

HIGGINS. It's all youll get until you stop being a common
idiot. If youre going to be a lady, youll have to give up
feeling neglected if the men you know dont spend half
their time snivelling over you and the other half giving
you black eyes. If you cant stand the coldness of my sort
of life, and the strain of it, go back to the gutter. Work til
youre more a brute than a human being; and then cuddle
and squabble and drink til you fall asleep. Oh, it's a fine
life, the life of the gutter. It's real: it's warm: it's violent:
you can feel it through the thickest skin: you can taste it
and smell it without any training or any work. Not like
Science and Literature and Classical Music and Philo-
osphy and Art. You find me cold, unfeeling, selfish, dont
you? Very well: be off with you to the sort of people you
like. Marry some sentimental hog or other with lots of

money, and a thick pair of lips to kiss you with and a
thick pair of boots to kick you with. If you cant appreciate what youve got, youd better get what you can
appreciate.

LIZA [*desperate*] Oh, you a r e a cruel tyrant. I cant talk to
you: you turn everything against me: I'm always in the
wrong. But you know very well all the time that youre
nothing but a bully. You know I cant go back to the
gutter, as you call it, and that I have no real friends in
the world but you and the Colonel. You know well I
couldnt bear to live with a low common man after you
two; and it's wicked and cruel of you to insult me by
pretending I could. You think I must go back to Wimpole
Street because I have nowhere else to go but father's.
But dont be too sure that you have me under your feet
to be trampled on and talked down. I'll marry Freddy, I
will, as soon as I'm able to support him.

HIGGINS [*thunderstruck*] Freddy!!! that young fool! That
poor devil who couldnt get a job as an errand boy even if
he had the guts to try for it! Woman: do you not understand that I have made you a consort for a king?

LIZA. Freddy loves me: that makes him king enough for
me. I dont want him to work: he wasnt brought up to it
as I was. I'll go and be a teacher.

HIGGINS. Whatll you teach, in heaven's name?

LIZA. What you taught me. I'll teach phonetics.

HIGGINS. Ha! ha! ha!

LIZA. I'll offer myself as an assistant to that hairyfaced
Hungarian.

HIGGINS [*rising in a fury*] What! That impostor! that humbug! that toadying ignoramus! Teach him my methods!
my discoveries! You take one step in his direction and
I'll wring your neck. [*He lays his hands on her*]. Do you
hear?

LIZA [*defiantly non-resistant*] Wring away. What do I care?
I knew youd strike me some day. [*He lets her go, stamping with rage at having forgotten himself, and recoils so
hastily that he stumbles back into his seat on the ottoman*].
Aha! Now I know how to deal with you. What a fool I
was not to think of it before! You cant take away the

knowledge you gave me. You said I had a finer ear than
you. And I can be civil and kind to people, which is more
than you can. Aha! [*Purposely dropping her aitches to
annoy him*] Thats done you, Enry Iggins, it az. Now I
dont care that [*snapping her fingers*] for your bullying
and your big talk. I'll advertize it in the papers that your
duchess is only a flower girl that you taught, and that
she'll teach anybody to be a duchess just the same in six
months for a thousand guineas. Oh, when I think of
myself crawling under your feet and being trampled on
and called names, when all the time I had only to lift up
my finger to be as good as you, I could just kick myself.

HIGGINS [*wondering at her*] You damned impudent slut,
you! But it's better than snivelling; better than fetching
slippers and finding spectacles, isn't it? [*Rising*] By
George, Eliza, I said I'd make a woman of you; and I
have. I like you like this.

LIZA. Yes: you turn round and make up to me now that
I'm not afraid of you, and can do without you.

HIGGINS. Of course I do, you little fool. Five minutes ago
you were like a millstone round my neck. Now youre a
tower of strength: a consort battleship. You and I and
Pickering will be three old bachelors instead of only two
men and a silly girl.

*Mrs Higgins returns, dressed for the wedding. Eliza
instantly becomes cool and elegant.*

MRS HIGGINS. The carriage is waiting, Eliza. Are you ready?

LIZA. Quite. Is the Professor coming?

MRS HIGGINS. Certainly not. He cant behave himself in
church. He makes remarks out loud all the time on the
clergyman's pronunciation.

LIZA. Then I shall not see you again, Professor. Goodbye.
[*She goes to the door*].

MRS HIGGINS [*coming to Higgins*] Goodbye, dear.

HIGGINS. Goodbye, mother. [*He is about to kiss her, when
he recollects something*]. Oh, by the way, Eliza, order a
ham and a Stilton cheese, will you? And buy me a pair of
reindeer gloves, number eights, and a tie to match that
new suit of mine. You can choose the color. [*His cheerful, careless, vigorous voice shews that he is incorrigible*].

LIZA [*disdainfully*] Number eights are too small for you if
you want them lined with lamb's wool. You have three
new ties that you have forgotten in the drawer of your
washstand. Colonel Pickering prefers double Gloucester
to Stilton; and you dont notice the difference. I telephoned Mrs Pearce this morning not to forget the ham.
What you are to do without me I cannot imagine. [*She
sweeps out*].

MRS HIGGINS. I'm afraid youve spoilt that girl, Henry. I
should be uneasy about you and her if she were less fond
of Colonel Pickering.

HIGGINS. Pickering! Nonsense: she's going to marry Freddy.
Ha ha! Freddy! Freddy!! Ha ha ha ha ha!!!!! [*He roars*
with laughter as the play ends].

*   *   *

The rest of the story need not be shewn in action, and indeed, would hardly need telling if our imaginations were
not so enfeebled by their lazy dependence on the ready-
mades and reach-me-downs of the ragshop in which Romance keeps its stock of 'happy endings' to misfit all
stories. Now, the history of Eliza Doolittle, though called
a romance because the transfiguration it records seems
exceedingly improbable, is common enough. Such trans-
figurations have been achieved by hundreds of resolutely
ambitious young women since Nell Gwynne set them the
example by playing queens and fascinating kings in the
theatre in which she began by selling oranges. Nevertheless, people in all directions have assumed, for no other
reason than that she became the heroine of a romance,
that she must have married the hero of it. This is unbearable, not only because her little drama, if acted on such
a thoughtless assumption, must be spoiled, but because the
true sequel is patent to anyone with a sense of human
nature in general, and of feminine instinct in particular.

Eliza, in telling Higgins she would not marry him if he
asked, was not coquetting: she was announcing a well-
considered decision. When a bachelor interests, and domi-

nates, and teaches, and becomes important to a spinster, as
Higgins with Eliza, she always, if she has character enough
to be capable of it, considers very seriously indeed whether
she will play for becoming that bachelor's wife, especially if
he is so little interested in marriage that a determined and
devoted woman might capture him if she set herself resolutely to do it. Her decision will depend a good deal on
whether she is really free to choose; and that, again, will
depend on her age and income. If she is at the end of her
youth, and has no security for her livelihood, she will
marry him because she must marry anybody who will provide for her. But at Eliza's age a good-looking girl does
not feel that pressure: she feels free to pick and choose.
She is therefore guided by her instinct in the matter. Eliza's
instinct tells her not to marry Higgins. It does not tell her
to give him up. It is not in the slightest doubt as to his
remaining one of the strongest personal interests in her
life. It would be very sorely strained if there was another
woman likely to supplant her with him. But as she feels
sure of him on that last point, she has no doubt at all as
to her course, and would not have any, even if the difference of twenty years in age, which seems so great to youth,
did not exist between them.

As our own instincts are not appealed to by her conclusion, let us see whether we cannot discover some reason
in it. When Higgins excused his indifference to young
women on the ground that they had an irresistible rival
in his mother, he gave the clue to his inveterate old-
bachelordom. The case is uncommon only to the extent
that remarkable mothers are uncommon. If an imaginative
boy has a sufficiently rich mother who has intelligence,
personal grace, dignity of character without harshness, and
a cultivated sense of the best art of her time to enable her
to make her house beautiful, she sets a standard for him
against which very few women can struggle, besides effect-
ing for him a disengagement of his affections, his sense of
beauty, and his idealism from his specifically sexual impulses. This makes him a standing puzzle to the huge
number of uncultivated people who have been brought up
in tasteless homes by commonplace or disagreeable par-

ents, and to whom, consequently, literature, painting, sculpture, music, and affectionate personal relations come as modes of sex if they come at all. The word passion means nothing else to them; and that Higgins could have a passion for phonetics and idealize his mother instead of Eliza, would seem to them absurd and unnatural. Nevertheless, when we look round and see that hardly anyone is too ugly or disagreeable to find a wife or a husband if he or she wants one, whilst many old maids and bachelors are above the average in quality and culture, we cannot help suspecting that the disentanglement of sex from the associations with which it is so commonly confused, a disentanglement which persons of genius achieve by sheer intellectual analysis, is sometimes produced or aided by parental fascination.

Now, though Eliza was incapable of thus explaining to herself Higgins's formidable powers of resistance to the charm that prostrated Freddy at the first glance, she was instinctively aware that she could never obtain a complete grip of him, or come between him and his mother (the first necessity of the married woman). To put it shortly, she knew that for some mysterious reason he had not the makings of a married man in him, according to her conception of a husband as one to whom she would be his nearest and fondest and warmest interest. Even had there been no mother-rival, she would still have refused to accept an interest in herself that was secondary to philosophic interests. Had Mrs Higgins died, there would still have been Milton and the Universal Alphabet. Landor's remark that to those who have the greatest power of loving, love is a secondary affair, would not have recommended Landor to Eliza. Put that along with her resentment of Higgins's domineering superiority, and her mistrust of his coaxing cleverness in getting round her and evading her wrath when he had gone too far with his impetuous bullying, and you will see that Eliza's instinct had good grounds for warning her not to marry her Pygmalion.

And now, whom did Eliza marry? For if Higgins was a predestinate old bachelor, she was most certainly not a predestinate old maid. Well, that can be told very shortly to those who have not guessed it from the indications she has herself given them.

Almost immediately after Eliza is stung into proclaiming her considered determination not to marry Higgins, she mentions the fact that young Mr Frederick Eynsford Hill is pouring out his love for her daily through the post. Now Freddy is young, practically twenty years younger than Higgins: he is a gentleman (or, as Eliza would qualify him, a toff), and speaks like one. He is nicely dressed, is treated by the Colonel as an equal, loves her unaffectedly, and is not her master, nor ever likely to dominate her in spite of his advantage of social standing. Eliza has no use for the foolish romantic tradition that all women love to be mastered, if not actually bullied and beaten. 'When you go to women' says Nietzsche 'take your whip with you.' Sensible despots have never confined that precaution to women: they have taken their whips with them when they have dealt with men, and been slavishly idealized by the men over whom they have flourished the whip much more than by women. No doubt there are slavish women as well as slavish men; and women, like men, admire those that are stronger than themselves. But to admire a strong person and to live under that strong person's thumb are two different things. The weak may not be admired and hero-worshipped; but they are by no means disliked or shunned; and they never seem to have the least difficulty in marrying people who are too good for them. They may fail in emergencies; but life is not one long emergency: it is mostly a string of situations for which no exceptional strength is needed, and with which even rather weak people can cope if they have a stronger partner to help them out. Accordingly, it is a truth everywhere in evidence that strong people, masculine or feminine, not only do not marry stronger people, but do not shew any preference for them in selecting their friends. When a lion meets another with a louder roar 'the first lion thinks the last a bore'. The man or woman who feels strong enough for two, seeks for every other quality in a partner than strength.

The converse is also true. Weak people want to marry

strong people who do not frighten them too much; and this often leads them to make the mistake we describe metaphorically as 'biting off more than they can chew'. They want too much for too little; and when the bargain is unreasonable beyond all bearing, the union becomes impossible: it ends in the weaker party being either discarded or borne as a cross, which is worse. People who are not only weak, but silly or obtuse as well, are often in these difficulties.

This being the state of human affairs, what is Eliza fairly sure to do when she is placed between Freddy and Higgins? Will she look forward to a lifetime of fetching Higgins's slippers or to a lifetime of Freddy fetching hers? There can be no doubt about the answer. Unless Freddy is biologically repulsive to her, and Higgins biologically attractive to a degree that overwhelms all her other instincts, she will, if she marries either of them, marry Freddy.

And that is just what Eliza did.

Complications ensued; but they were economic, not romantic. Freddy had no money and no occupation. His mother's jointure, a last relic of the opulence of Largelady Park, had enabled her to struggle along in Earls Court with an air of gentility, but not to procure any serious secondary education for her children, much less give the boy a profession. A clerkship at thirty shillings a week was beneath Freddy's dignity, and extremely distasteful to him besides. His prospects consisted of a hope that if he kept up appearances somebody would do something for him. The something appeared vaguely to his imagination as a private secretaryship or a sinecure of some sort. To his mother it perhaps appeared as a marriage to some lady of means who could not resist her boy's niceness. Fancy her feelings when he married a flower girl who had become disclassed under extraordinary circumstances which were now notorious!

It is true that Eliza's situation did not seem wholly ineligible. Her father, though formerly a dustman, and now fantastically disclassed, had become extremely popular in the smartest society by a social talent which triumphed over every prejudice and every disadvantage. Rejected by

the middle class, which he loathed, he had shot up at once
into the highest circles by his wit, his dustmanship (which
he carried like a banner), and his Nietzschean transcend-
ence of good and evil. At intimate ducal dinners he sat on
the right hand of the Duchess; and in country houses he
smoked in the pantry and was made much of by the butler
when he was not feeding in the dining room and being consulted by cabinet ministers. But he found it almost as hard
to do all this on four thousand a year as Mrs Eynsford Hill
to live in Earls Court on an income so pitiably smaller that
I have not the heart to disclose its exact figure. He absolutely refused to add the last straw to his burden by con-
tributing to Eliza's support.

Thus Freddy and Eliza, now Mr and Mrs Eynsford
Hill, would have spent a penniless honeymoon but for a
wedding present of £500 from the Colonel to Eliza. It
lasted a long time because Freddy did not know how to
spend money, never having had any to spend, and Eliza,
socially trained by a pair of old bachelors, wore her clothes
as long as they held together and looked pretty, without
the least regard to their being many months out of fashion.
Still, £500 will not last two young people for ever; and
they both knew, and Eliza felt as well, that they must shift
for themselves in the end. She could quarter herself on
Wimpole Street because it had come to be her home; but
she was quite aware that she ought not to quarter Freddy
there, and that it would not be good for his character if
she did.

Not that the Wimpole Street bachelors objected. When
she consulted them, Higgins declined to be bothered about
her housing problem when that solution was so simple.
Eliza's desire to have Freddy in the house with her seemed
of no more importance than if she had wanted an extra
piece of bedroom furniture. Pleas as to Freddy's character,
and the moral obligation on him to earn his own living,
were lost on Higgins. He denied that Freddy had any character, and declared that if he tried to do any useful work
some competent person would have the trouble of undoing
it: a procedure involving a net loss to the community, and
great unhappiness to Freddy himself, who was obviously

intended by Nature for such light work as amusing Eliza,
which, Higgins declared, was a much more useful and
honorable occupation than working in the city. When Eliza
referred again to her project of teaching phonetics, Higgins
abated not a jot of his violent opposition to it. He said she
was not within ten years of being qualified to meddle with
his pet subject; and as it was evident that the Colonel
agreed with him, she felt she could not go against them in
this grave matter, and that she had no right, without Higgins's consent, to exploit the knowledge he had given her;
for his knowledge seemed to her as much his private
property as his watch: Eliza was no communist. Besides,
she was superstitiously devoted to them both, more entirely
and frankly after her marriage than before it.

It was the Colonel who finally solved the problem, which
had cost him much perplexed cogitation. He one day asked
Eliza, rather shyly, whether she had quite given up her
notion of keeping a flower shop. She replied that she had
thought of it, but had put it out of her head, because the
Colonel had said, that day at Mrs Higgin's, that it would
never do. The Colonel confessed that when he said that, he
had not quite recovered from the dazzling impression of
the day before. They broke the matter to Higgins that
evening. The sole comment vouchsafed by him very nearly
led to a serious quarrel with Eliza. It was to the effect that
she would have in Freddy an ideal errand boy.

Freddy himself was next sounded on the subject. He
said he had been thinking of a shop himself; though it had
presented itself to his pennilessness as a small place in
which Eliza should sell tobacco at one counter whilst he
sold newspapers at the opposite one. But he agreed that it
would be extraordinarily jolly to go early every morning
with Eliza to Covent Garden and buy flowers on the scene
of their first meeting: a sentiment which earned him many
kisses from his wife. He added that he had always been
afraid to propose anything of the sort, because Clara
would make an awful row about a step that must damage
her matrimonial chances, and his mother could not be
expected to like it after clinging for so many years to that
step of the social ladder on which retail trade is impossible.

This difficulty was removed by an event highly unexpected by Freddy's mother. Clara, in the course of her incursions into those artistic circles which were the highest within her reach, discovered that her conversational qualifications were expected to include a grounding in the novels of Mr H. G. Wells. She borrowed them in various directions so energetically that she swallowed them all within two months. The result was a conversion of a kind quite common today. A modern Acts of the Apostles would fill fifty whole Bibles if anyone were capable of writing it.

Poor Clara, who appeared to Higgins and his mother as a disagreeable and ridiculous person, and to her own mother as in some inexplicable way a social failure, had never seen herself in either light; for, though to some extent ridiculed and mimicked in West Kensington like everybody else there, she was accepted as a rational and normal—or shall we say inevitable?—sort of human being. At worst they called her The Pusher; but to them no more than to herself had it ever occurred that she was pushing the air, and pushing it in a wrong direction. Still, she was not happy. She was growing desperate. Her one asset, the fact that her mother was what the Epsom greengrocer called a carriage lady, had no exchange value, apparently. It had prevented her from getting educated, because the only education she could have afforded was education with the Earls Court greengrocer's daughter. It had led her to seek the society of her mother's class; and that class simply would not have her, because she was much poorer than the greengrocer, and, far from being able to afford a maid, could not afford even a housemaid, and had to scrape along at home with an illiberally treated general servant. Under such circumstances nothing could give her an air of being a genuine product of Largelady Park. And yet its tradition made her regard a marriage with anyone within her reach as an unbearable humiliation. Commercial people and professional people in a small way were odious to her. She ran after painters and novelists; but she did not charm them; and her bold attempts to pick up and practise artistic and literary talk irritated them. She was, in short, an utter failure, an ignorant, incompetent, pretentious, unwelcome, penniless, useless little snob; and though she did not admit these disqualifications (for nobody ever faces unpleasant truths of this kind until the possibility of a way out dawns on them) she felt their effects too keenly to be satisfied with her position.

Clara had a startling eyeopener when, on being suddenly wakened to enthusiasm by a girl of her own age who dazzled her and produced in her a gushing desire to take her for a model, and gain her friendship, she discovered that this exquisite apparition had graduated from the gutter in a few months time. It shook her so violently, that when Mr H. G. Wells lifted her on the point of his puissant pen, and placed her at the angle of view from which the life she was leading and the society to which she clung appeared in its true relation to real human needs and worthy social structure, he effected a conversion and a conviction of sin comparable to the most sensational feats of General Booth or Gypsy Smith. Clara's snobbery went bang. Life suddenly began to move with her. Without knowing how or why, she began to make friends and enemies. Some of the acquaintances to whom she had been a tedious or indifferent or ridiculous affliction, dropped her: others became cordial. To her amazement she found that some 'quite nice' people were saturated with Wells, and that this accessibility to ideas was the secret of their niceness. People she had thought deeply religious, and had tried to conciliate on that tack with disastrous results, suddenly took an interest in her, and revealed a hostility to conventional religion which she had never conceived possible except among the most desperate characters. They made her read Galsworthy; and Galsworthy exposed the vanity of Largelady Park and finished her. It exasperated her to think that the dungeon in which she had languished for so many unhappy years had been unlocked all the time, and that the impulses she had so carefully struggled with and stifled for the sake of keeping well with society, were precisely those by which alone she could have come into any sort of sincere human contact. In the radiance of these discoveries, and the tumult of their reaction, she made a fool of herself as freely and conspicuously as when she so rashly adopted Eliza's expletive in Mrs Higgins's drawing room; for the new-born Wellsian had to find her bearings almost as ridiculously as a baby; but nobody hates a baby for its ineptitudes, or thinks the worse of it for trying to eat the matches; and Clara lost no friends by her follies. They laughed at her to her face this time; and she had to defend herself and fight it out as best she could.

When Freddy paid a visit to Earls Court (which he never did when he could possibly help it) to make the desolating announcement that he and his Eliza were thinking of blackening the Largelady scutcheon by opening a shop, he found the little household already convulsed by a prior announcement from Clara that she also was going to work in an old furniture shop in Dover Street, which had been started by a fellow Wellsian. This appointment Clara owed, after all, to her old social accomplishment of Push. She had made up her mind that, cost what it might, she would see Mr Wells in the flesh; and she had achieved her end at a garden party. She had better luck than so rash an enterprise deserved. Mr Wells came up to her expectations. Age had not withered him, nor could custom stale his infinite variety in half an hour. His pleasant neatness and compactness, his small hands and feet, his teeming ready brain, his unaffected accessibility, and a certain fine apprehensiveness which stamped him as susceptible from his topmost hair to his tipmost toe, proved irresistible. Clara talked of nothing else for weeks and weeks afterwards. And as she happened to talk to the lady of the furniture shop, and that lady also desired above all things to know Mr Wells and sell pretty things to him, she offered Clara a job on the chance of achieving that end through her.

And so it came about that Eliza's luck held, and the expected opposition to the flower shop melted away. The shop is in the arcade of a railway station not very far from the Victoria and Albert Museum; and if you live in that neighbourhood you may go there any day and buy a buttonhole from Eliza.

Now here is a last opportunity for romance. Would you not like to be assured that the shop was an immense success, thanks to Eliza's charms and her early business experience in Covent Garden? Alas! the truth is the truth: the shop did not pay for a long time, simply because Eliza and her Freddy did not know how to keep it. True, Eliza had not to begin at the very beginning: she knew the names and prices of the cheaper flowers; and her elation was unbounded when she found that Freddy, like all youths educated at cheap, pretentious, and thoroughly inefficient schools, knew a little Latin. It was very little, but enough to make him appear to her a Porson or Bentley, and to put him at his ease with botanical nomenclature. Unfortunately he knew nothing else; and Eliza, though she could count money up to eighteen shillings or so, and had acquired a certain familiarity with the language of Milton from her struggles to qualify herself for winning Higgins's bet, could not write out a bill without utterly disgracing the establishment. Freddy's power of stating in Latin that Balbus built a wall and that Gaul was divided into three parts did not carry with it the slightest knowledge of accounts or business: Colonel Pickering had to explain to him what a cheque book and a bank account meant. And the pair were by no means easily teachable. Freddy backed up Eliza in her obstinate refusal to believe that they could save money by engaging a bookkeeper with some knowledge of the business. How, they argued, could you possibly save money by going to extra expense when you already could not make both ends meet? But the Colonel, after making the ends meet over and over again, at last gently insisted; and Eliza, humbled to the dust by having to beg from him so often, and stung by the uproarious derision of Higgins, to whom the notion of Freddy succeeding at anything was a joke that never palled, grasped the fact that business, like phonetics, has to be learned.

On the piteous spectacle of the pair spending their evenings in shorthand schools and polytechnic classes, learning bookkeeping and typewriting with incipient junior clerks, male and female, from the elementary schools, let me not dwell. There were even classes at the London School of Economics, and a humble personal appeal to the director of that institution to recommend a course bearing on the flower business. He, being a humorist, explained to them the method of the celebrated Dickensian essay on Chinese Metaphysics by the gentleman who read an article on China and an article on Metaphysics and combined the information. He suggested that they should combine the London School with Kew Gardens. Eliza, to whom the procedure of the Dickensian gentleman seemed perfectly correct (as in fact it was) and not in the least funny (which was only her ignorance), took the advice with entire gravity. But the effort that cost her the deepest humiliation was a request to Higgins, whose pet artistic fancy, next to Milton's verse, was caligraphy, and who himself wrote a most beautiful Italian hand, that he would teach her to write. He declared that she was congenitally incapable of forming a single letter worthy of the least of Milton's words; but she persisted; and again he suddenly threw himself into the task of teaching her with a combination of stormy intensity, concentrated patience, and occasional bursts of interesting disquisition on the beauty and nobility, the august mission and destiny, of human handwriting. Eliza ended by acquiring an extremely uncommercial script which was a positive extension of her personal beauty, and spending three times as much on stationery as anyone else because certain qualities and shapes of paper became indispensable to her. She could not even address an envelope in the usual way because it made the margins all wrong.

Their commercial schooldays were a period of disgrace and despair for the young couple. They seemed to be learning nothing about flower shops. At last they gave it up as hopeless, and shook the dust of the shorthand schools, and the polytechnics, and the London School of Economics from their feet for ever. Besides, the business was in some mysterious way beginning to take care of itself. They had somehow forgotten their objections to employing other people. They came to the conclusion that their own way was the best, and that they had really a remarkable talent for business. The Colonel, who had been compelled for some years to keep a sufficient sum on current account at his bankers to make up their deficits, found that the provision was unnecessary: the young couple were prospering.

It is true that there was not quite fair play between them
and their competitors in trade. Their week-ends in the
country cost them nothing, and saved them the price of
their Sunday dinners; for the motor car was the Colonel's;
and he and Higgins paid the hotel bills. Mr F. Hill, florist
and greengrocer (they soon discovered that there was
money in asparagus; and asparagus led to other vegeta-
bles), had an air which stamped the business as classy;
and in private life he was still Frederick Eynsford Hill,
Esquire. Not that there was any swank about him: nobody
but Eliza knew that he had been christened Frederick
Challoner. Eliza herself swanked like anything.

That is all. That is how it has turned out. It is astonishing
how much Eliza still manages to meddle in the housekeeping at Wimpole Street in spite of the shop and her
own family. And it is notable that though she never nags
her husband, and frankly loves the Colonel as if she were
his favorite daughter, she has never got out of the habit
of nagging Higgins that was established on the fatal night
when she won his bet for him. She snaps his head off on the
faintest provocation, or on none. He no longer dares to
tease her by assuming an abysmal inferiority of Freddy's
mind to his own. He storms and bullies and derides; but
she stands up to him so ruthlessly that the Colonel has to
ask her from time to time to be kinder to Higgins; and it
is the only request of his that brings a mulish expression
into her face. Nothing but some emergency or calamity
great enough to break down all likes and dislikes, and
throw them both back on their common humanity—and
may they be spared any such trial!—will ever alter this.
She knows that Higgins does not need her, just as her
father did not need her. The very scrupulousness with
which he told her that day that he had become used to
having her there, and dependent on her for all sorts of
little services, and that he should miss her if she went
away (it would never have occurred to Freddy or the
Colonel to say anything of the sort) deepens her inner certainty that she is 'no more to him than them slippers'; yet
she has a sense, too, that his indifference is deeper than
the infatuation of commoner souls. She is immensely inter-

ested in him. She has even secret mischievous moments in which she wishes she could get him alone, on a desert island, away from all ties and with nobody else in the world to consider, and just drag him off his pedestal and see him making love like any common man. We all have private imaginations of that sort. But when it comes to business, to the life that she really leads as distinguished from the life of dreams and fancies, she likes Freddy and she likes the Colonel; and she does not like Higgins and Mr Doolittle. Galatea never does quite like Pygmalion: his relation to her is too godlike to be altogether agreeable.

To Beatrice and Sidney Webb

Clifford Sharp was editor of The New Statesman, *which Shaw and the Webbs were instrumental in founding. The* Lusitania *had been torpedoed by a German submarine in May 1915, and Shaw had commented that the sinking was no more a war crime than the sending of hundreds of thousands of young men to certain death in the trenches of France. The German Zeppelin downed near Ayot St Lawrence on 1 October 1916 was the L-31, commanded by the daring former destroyer skipper Heinrich Mathy. Shaw used the episode to end* Heartbreak House, *which he was then in the process of writing.*

Ayot St Lawrence, Welwyn, Herts
5 October 1916

As I have got on poor Sharp's nerves, which have been in indifferent tune since the Lusitania torpedo got him, it is mere cruelty to animals remaining on the Statesman Board. I have therefore written formally to the secretary to convey my resignation to the next meeting and regard me in the future as a simple shareholder. My withdrawal will be a great relief to everybody, probably; and as everything that cannot be done without me would not be done anyhow, it will do no harm. Anyhow, I am always accessible if I am wanted. . . .

The oddest thing about the whole business is that no Englishman seems to have any real concern for the future of England provided his immediate passions are gratified. It seems to me plain enough that Germany is going to be smashed to the extent of completely eliminating from European diplomacy that dread of her which has dominated the continent for years and produced and held together the Alliance. Nothing is more plainly printed across the skies than that the removal of that dread will operate on the Alliance like the removal of the string from a faggot; and that Germany, forced to relinquish her dream of a Pax Germanica and to seek alliances like other human species, will seek them either in the east with Russia or in the west with America. Also that the dread of Germany will be succeeded by the no less formidable bogey of the British Empire. Our position will then be an extremely critical one; and if our pro-Japs (perhaps led by you in your oriental enthusiasm) prevent us from the obvious solution of a western alliance to which both Britain and Germany will be parties, and from which France could then hardly withdraw, we may at last get what we deserve; and a more fearful fate could hardly be imagined. Already Grey, with instinctive folly, is letting himself be encouraged by our Somme successes to bully Sweden, which simply spits in his face, knowing that he can do nothing now to her, as any fool could have told him beforehand. Blatchford and the Jingoes are already trying to repeat their success over warnings of war with Germany by warnings of war with America, without whose friendship we shall be caught in such an *Einkreisung* as will make the German one seem a joke. But as there is no passionate satisfaction in contemplating these possibilities and providing for them, they stare us in the face in vain; and Sharp writes proposals for the disarmament of Germany and then calmly tells me that this is the policy of the Fabian Society as formulated by me. The prospect fills me with genuine concern. It only bores you, because diplomacy and history are not your Fach.*

I must stop this ridiculously long letter, which, however, will roughly convey to you my private mind. The Potters Bar Zeppelin manoeuvred over the Welwyn valley for about half an hour before it came round and passed Londonwards with the nicest precision over our house straight along our ridge tiles. It made a magnificent noise the whole time; and not a searchlight touched it, as it was the night-out of the Essenden and Luton [search] lights. And not a shot was fired at it. I was amazed at its impunity and

* German: *department, province, business, profession.*

audacity. It sailed straight for London and must have got past Hatfield before they woke up and brought it down. The commander was such a splendid personage that the divisional surgeon and an officer who saw him grieved as for an only son. At two o'clock another Zeppelin passed over Ayot; but we have no telephone, and nobody bothered. I went to see the wreck on my motor bicycle. The police were in great feather, as there is a strict cordon, which means that you cant get in without paying. The charges are not excessive, as I guess; for I created a ducal impression by a shilling. Corpses are extra, no doubt; but I did not intrude on the last sleep of the brave. What is hardly credible, but true, is that the sound of the Zepp's engines was so fine, and its voyage through the stars so enchanting, that I positively caught myself hoping next night that there would be another raid. I grieve to add that after seeing the Zepp fall like a burning newspaper, with its human contents roasting for some minutes (it was frightfully slow) I went to bed and was comfortably asleep in ten minutes. One is so pleased at having seen the show that the destruction of a dozen people or so in hideous terror and torment does not count. "I didn't half cheer, I tell you" said a damsel at the wreck. Pretty lot of animals we are!

Yours ever,

G.B.S.

HEARTBREAK HOUSE: A Fantasia in the Russian Manner on English Themes

×××××××××××××××××××××××××××××××××××××

HEARTBREAK HOUSE AND HORSEBACK HALL

WHERE HEARTBREAK HOUSE STANDS

Heartbreak House is not merely the name of the play which follows this preface. It is cultured, leisured Europe before the war. When the play was begun not a shot had been fired; and only the professional diplomatists and the very few amateurs whose hobby is foreign policy even knew that the guns were loaded. A Russian playwright, Tchekov, had produced four fascinating dramatic studies of Heartbreak House, of which three, The Cherry Orchard, Uncle Vanya, and The Seagull, had been performed in England. Tolstoy, in his Fruits of Enlightenment, had shewn us through it in his most ferociously contemptuous manner. Tolstoy did not waste any sympathy on it: it was to him the house in which Europe was stifling its soul; and he knew that our utter enervation and futilization in that over-heated drawing-room atmosphere was delivering the world over to the control of ignorant and soulless cunning and energy, with the frightful consequences which have now overtaken it. Tolstoy was no pessimist: he was not disposed to leave the house standing if he could bring it down about the ears of its pretty and amiable voluptuaries; and he wielded the pickaxe with a will. He treated the case of the inmates as one of opium poisoning, to be dealt with by seizing the patients roughly and exercising them violently until they were broad awake. Tchekov, more of a fatalist, had no faith in these charming people extricating themselves. They would, he thought, be sold up and sent adrift by the bailiffs; therefore he had no scruple in exploiting and even flattering their charm.

THE INHABITANTS

Tchekov's plays, being less lucrative than swings and roundabouts, got no further in England, where theatres are only ordinary commercial affairs, than a couple of performances by the Stage Society. We stared and said, "How Russian!" They did not strike me in that way. Just as Ibsen's intensely Norwegian plays exactly fitted every middle and professional class suburb in Europe, these intensely Russian plays fitted all the country houses in Europe in which the pleasures of music, art, literature, and the theatre had supplanted hunting, shooting, fishing, flirting, eating, and drinking. The same nice people, the same utter futility. The nice people could read; some of them could write; and they were the only repositories of culture who had social opportunities of contact with our politicians, administrators, and newspaper proprietors, or any chance of sharing or influencing their activities. But they shrank from that contact. They hated politics. They did not wish to realize Utopia for the common people: they wished to realize their favorite fictions and poems in their own lives; and, when they could, they lived without scruple on incomes which they did nothing to earn. The women in their girlhood made themselves look like variety theatre stars, and settled down later into the types of beauty imagined by the previous generation of painters. They took the only part of our society in which there was leisure for high culture, and made it an economic, political, and, as far as practicable, a moral vacuum; and as Nature, abhorring the vacuum, immediately filled it up with sex and with all sorts of refined pleasures, it was a very delightful place at its best for moments of relaxation. In other moments it was disastrous. For prime ministers and their like, it was a veritable Capua.

HORSEBACK HALL

But where were our front benchers to nest if not here? The alternative to Heartbreak House was Horseback Hall, consisting of a prison for horses with an annex for the ladies and gentlemen who rode them, hunted them, talked about them, bought them and sold them, and gave nine-

tenths of their lives to them, dividing the other tenth
between charity, churchgoing (as a substitute for religion),
and conservative electioneering (as a substitute for politics). It is true that the two establishments got mixed at
the edges. Exiles from the library, the music room, and
the picture gallery would be found languishing among the
stables, miserably discontented; and hardy horsewomen
who slept at the first chord of Schumann were born, horribly misplaced, into the garden of Klingsor; but sometimes
one came upon horsebreakers and heartbreakers who could
make the best of both worlds. As a rule, however, the two
were apart and knew little of one another; so the prime
minister folk had to choose between barbarism and Capua.
And of the two atmospheres it is hard to say which was
the more fatal to statesmanship.

REVOLUTION ON THE SHELF

Heartbreak House was quite familiar with revolutionary
ideas on paper. It aimed at being advanced and freethink-
ing, and hardly ever went to church or kept the Sabbath
except by a little extra fun at week-ends. When you spent
a Friday to Tuesday in it you found on the shelf in your
bedroom not only the books of poets and novelists, but of
revolutionary biologists and even economists. Without at
least a few plays by myself and Mr Granville Barker, and
a few stories by Mr H. G. Wells, Mr Arnold Bennett, and
Mr John Galsworthy, the house would have been out of
the movement. You would find Blake among the poets,
and beside him Bergson, Butler, Scott Haldane, the poems
of Meredith and Thomas Hardy, and, generally speaking,
all the literary implements for forming the mind of the
perfect modern Socialist and Creative Evolutionist. It was
a curious experience to spend Sunday in dipping into
these books, and on Monday morning to read in the daily
paper that the country had just been brought to the verge
of anarchy because a new Home Secretary or chief of
police, without an idea in his head that his great-grand-
mother might not have had to apologize for, had refused
to "recognize" some powerful Trade Union, just as a
gondola might refuse to recognize a 20,000-ton liner.

In short, power and culture were in separate compartments. The barbarians were not only literally in the saddle, but on the front bench in the House of Commons, with nobody to correct their incredible ignorance of modern thought and political science but upstarts from the counting-house, who had spent their lives furnishing their pockets instead of their minds. Both, however, were practised in dealing with money and with men, as far as acquiring the one and exploiting the other went; and although this is as undesirable an expertness as that of the medieval robber baron, it qualifies men to keep an estate or a business going in its old routine without necessarily understanding it, just as Bond Street tradesmen and domestic servants keep fashionable society going without any instruction in sociology.

THE CHERRY ORCHARD

The Heartbreak people neither could nor would do anything of the sort. With their heads as full of the Anticipations of Mr H. G. Wells as the heads of our actual rulers were empty even of the anticipations of Erasmus or Sir Thomas More, they refused the drudgery of politics, and would have made a very poor job of it if they had changed their minds. Not that they would have been allowed to meddle anyhow, as only through the accident of being a hereditary peer can any one in these days of Votes for Everybody [fail to] get into parliament if handicapped by a [lack of] serious modern cultural equipment; but if they had, their habit of living in a vacuum would have left them helpless and ineffective in public affairs. Even in private life they were often helpless wasters of their inheritance, like the people in Tchekov's Cherry Orchard. Even those who lived within their incomes were really kept going by their solicitors and agents, being unable to manage an estate or run a business without continual prompting from those who have to learn how to do such things or starve.

From what is called Democracy no corrective to this state of things could be hoped. It is said that every people has the Government it deserves. It is more to the point that every Government has the electorate it deserves; for the orators of the front bench can edify or debauch an ignorant electorate at will. Thus our democracy moves in a vicious circle of reciprocal worthiness and unworthiness.

NATURE'S LONG CREDITS

Nature's way of dealing with unhealthy conditions is unfortunately not one that compels us to conduct a solvent hygiene on a cash basis. She demoralizes us with long credits and reckless overdrafts, and then pulls us up cruelly with catastrophic bankruptcies. Take, for example, common domestic sanitation. A whole city generation may neglect it utterly and scandalously, if not with absolute impunity, yet without any evil consequences that anyone thinks of tracing to it. In a hospital two generations of medical students may tolerate dirt and carelessness, and then go out into general practice to spread the doctrine that fresh air is a fad, and sanitation an imposture set up to make profits for plumbers. Then suddenly Nature takes her revenge. She strikes at the city with a pestilence and at the hospital with an epidemic of hospital gangrene, slaughtering right and left until the innocent young have paid for the guilty old, and the account is balanced. And then she goes to sleep again and gives another period of credit, with the same result.

This is what has just happened in our political hygiene. Political science has been as recklessly neglected by Governments and electorates during my lifetime as sanitary science was in the days of Charles the Second. In international relations diplomacy has been a boyishly lawless affair of family intrigues, commercial and territorial brigandage, torpors of pseudo-goodnature produced by laziness, and spasms of ferocious activity produced by terror. But in these islands we muddled through. Nature gave us a longer credit than she gave to France or Germany or Russia. To British centenarians who died in their beds in 1914, any dread of having to hide underground in London from the shells of an enemy seemed more remote and fantastic than a dread of the appearance of a colony of cobras and rattlesnakes in Kensington Gardens. In the prophetic works of Charles Dickens we were warned against many evils which have since come to pass; but of the evil of being slaughtered by a foreign foe on our own doorsteps there was no shadow. Nature gave us a very long credit; and we abused it to the utmost. But when she struck at last she struck with a vengeance. For four years she smote our firstborn and heaped on us plagues of which Egypt never dreamed. They were all as preventible as the great Plague of London, and came solely because they had not been prevented. They were not undone by winning the war. The earth is still bursting with the dead bodies of the victors.

THE WICKED HALF CENTURY

It is difficult to say whether indifference and neglect are worse than false doctrine; but Heartbreak House and Horseback Hall unfortunately suffered from both. For half a century before the war civilization had been going to the devil very precipitately under the influence of a pseudo-science as disastrous as the blackest Calvinism. Calvinism taught that as we are predestinately saved or damned, nothing that we do can alter our destiny. Still, as Calvinism gave the individual no clue as to whether he had drawn a lucky number or an unlucky one, it left him a fairly strong interest in encouraging his hopes of salvation and allaying his fear of damnation by behaving as one of the elect might be expected to behave rather than as one of the reprobate. But in the middle of the nineteenth century naturalists and physicists assured the world, in the name of Science, that salvation and damnation are all nonsense, and that predestination is the central truth of religion, inasmuch as human beings are produced by their environment, their sins and good deeds being only a series of chemical and mechanical reactions over which they have no control. Such figments as mind, choice, purpose, conscience, will, and so forth, are, they taught, mere illusions, produced because they are useful in the continual struggle of the human machine to maintain its environment in a favourable condition, a process incidentally involving the ruthless destruction or subjection of its competitors for the supply (assumed to be limited) of subsistence available. We taught Prussia this religion; and Prussia bettered our instruction so effectively that we presently found ourselves confronted with the necessity of destroying Prussia to prevent Prussia destroying us. And that has just ended in each destroying the other to an extent doubtfully reparable in our time.

It may be asked how so imbecile and dangerous a creed ever came to be accepted by intelligent beings. I will answer that question more fully in my next volume of plays, which will be entirely devoted to the subject. For the present I will only say that there were better reasons than the obvious one that such sham science as this opened a scientific career to very stupid men, and all the other careers to shameless rascals, provided they were industrious enough. It is true that this motive operated very powerfully; but when the new departure in scientific doctrine which is associated with the name of the great naturalist Charles Darwin began, it was not only a reaction against a barbarous pseudo-evangelical teleology intolerably obstructive to all scientific progress, but was accompanied, as it happened, by discoveries of extraordinary interest in physics, chemistry, and that lifeless method of evolution which its investigators called Natural Selection. Howbeit, there was only one result possible in the ethical sphere, and that was the banishment of conscience from human affairs, or, as Samuel Butler vehemently put it, "of mind from the universe."

HYPOCHONDRIA

Now Heartbreak House, with Butler and Bergson and Scott Haldane alongside Blake and the other major poets on its shelves (to say nothing of Wagner and the tone poets), was not so completely blinded by the doltish materialism of the laboratories as the uncultured world outside. But being an idle house it was a hypochondriacal house, always running after cures. It would stop eating meat, not on valid Shelleyan grounds, but in order to get rid of a bogey called Uric Acid; and it would actually let you pull all its teeth out to exorcize another demon named Pyorrhea. It was superstitious, and addicted to table-rapping, materialization séances, clairvoyance, palmistry, crystal-gazing and the like to such an extent that it may be doubted whether ever before in the history of the world did soothsayers, astrologers, and unregistered therapeutic specialists of all sorts flourish as they did during this half century of the drift to the abyss. The registered doctors and surgeons were hard put to it to compete with the unregistered. They were not clever enough to appeal to the imagination and sociability of the Heartbreakers by the arts of the actor, the orator, the poet, the winning conversationalist. They had to fall back coarsely on the terror of infection and death. They prescribed inoculations and operations. Whatever part of a human being could be cut out without necessarily killing him they cut out; and he often died (unnecessarily of course) in consequences. From such trifles as uvulas and tonsils they went on to ovaries and appendices until at last no one's inside was safe. They explained that the human intestine was too long, and that nothing could make a child of Adam healthy except short circuiting the pylorus by cutting a length out of the lower intestine and fastening it directly to the stomach. As their mechanist theory taught them that medicine was the business of the chemist's laboratory, and surgery of the carpenter's shop, and also that Science (by which they meant their practices) was so important that no consideration for the interests of any individual creature, whether frog or philosopher, much less the vulgar commonplaces of sentimental ethics, could weigh for a moment against the remotest off-chance of an addition to the body of scientific knowledge, they operated and vivisected and inoculated and lied on a stupendous scale, clamoring for and actually acquiring such legal powers over the bodies of their fellow-citizens as neither king, pope, nor parliament dare ever have claimed. The Inquisition itself was a Liberal institution compared to the General Medical Council.

THOSE WHO DO NOT KNOW HOW TO LIVE
MUST MAKE A MERIT OF DYING

Heartbreak House was far too lazy and shallow to extricate itself from this palace of evil enchantment. It rhapsodized about love; but it believed in cruelty. It was afraid of the cruel people; and it saw that cruelty was at least effective. Cruelty did things that made money, whereas Love did nothing but prove the soundness of Larochefoucauld's saying that very few people would fall in love if they had never read about it. Heartbreak House, in short, did not know how to live, at which point all that was left to it was the boast that at least it knew how to die: a melancholy accomplishment which the outbreak of war presently gave it practically unlimited opportunities of displaying. Thus were the firstborn of Heartbreak House smitten; and the young, the innocent, the hopeful expiated the folly and worthlessness of their elders.

WAR DELIRIUM

Only those who have lived through a first-rate war, not in the field, but at home, and kept their heads, can possibly understand the bitterness of Shakespear and Swift, who both went through this experience. The horror of Peer Gynt in the madhouse, when the lunatics, exalted by illusions of splendid talent and visions of a dawning millennium, crowned him as their emperor, was tame in comparison. I do not know whether anyone really kept his head completely except those who had to keep it because they had to conduct the war at first hand. I should not have kept my own (as far as I did keep it) if I had not at once understood that as a scribe and speaker I too was under the most serious public obligation to keep my grip on realities; but this did not save me from a considerable degree of hyperaesthesia. There were of course some happy people to whom the war meant nothing: all political and general matters lying outside their little circle of interest. But the ordinary war-conscious civilian went mad, the main symptom being a conviction that the whole order of nature had been reversed. All foods, he felt, must now be adulterated. All schools must be closed. No advertisements must be sent to the newspapers, of which new editions must appear and be bought up every ten minutes. Travelling must be stopped, or, that being impossible, greatly hindered. All pretences about fine art and culture and the like must be flung off as an intolerable affectation; and the picture galleries and museums and schools at once occupied

by war workers. The British Museum itself was saved only
by a hairsbreadth. The sincerity of all this, and of much
more which would not be believed if I chronicled it, may be
established by one conclusive instance of the general crazi-
ness. Men were seized with the illusion that they could win
the war by giving away money. And they not only subscribed millions to Funds of all sorts with no discoverable
object, and to ridiculous voluntary organizations for doing
what was plainly the business of the civil and military
authorities, but actually handed out money to any thief
in the street who had the presence of mind to pretend
that he (or she) was "collecting" it for the annihilation
of the enemy. Swindlers were emboldened to take offices;
label themselves Anti-Enemy Leagues; and simply pocket
the money that was heaped on them. Attractively dressed
young women found that they had nothing to do but
parade the streets, collecting-box in hand, and live gloriously on the profits. Many months elapsed before, as a first
sign of returning sanity, the police swept an Anti-Enemy
secretary into prison *pour encourager les autres,* and the
passionate penny collecting of the Flag Days was brought
under some sort of regulation.

MADNESS IN COURT

The demoralization did not spare the Law Courts. Soldiers were acquitted, even on fully proved indictments for
wilful murder, until at last the judges and magistrates had
to announce that what was called the Unwritten Law,
which meant simply that a soldier could do what he liked
with impunity in civil life, was not the law of the land,
and that a Victoria Cross did not carry with it a perpetual
plenary indulgence. Unfortunately the insanity of the juries
and magistrates did not always manifest itself in indulgence. No person unlucky enough to be charged with any
sort of conduct, however reasonable and salutary, that did
not smack of war delirium had the slightest chance of
acquittal. There was in the country, too, a certain number
of people who had conscientious objections to war as
criminal or unchristian. The Act of Parliament introducing
Compulsory Military Service thoughtlessly exempted these

persons, merely requiring them to prove the genuineness
of their convictions. Those who did so were very ill-advised
from the point of view of their own personal interest; for
they were persecuted with savage logicality in spite of the
law; whilst those who made no pretence of having any
objection to war at all, and had not only had military training in Officers' Training Corps, but had proclaimed on
public occasions that they were perfectly ready to engage
in civil war on behalf of their political opinions, were
allowed the benefit of the Act on the ground that they did
not approve of this particular war. For the Christians
there was no mercy. In cases where the evidence as to their
being killed by ill treatment was so unequivocal that the
verdict would certainly have been one of wilful murder had
the prejudice of the coroner's jury been on the other side,
their tormentors were gratuitously declared to be blameless.
There was only one virtue, pugnacity: only one vice, paci-
fism. That is an essential condition of war; but the
Government had not the courage to legislate accordingly;
and its law was set aside for Lynch law.

The climax of legal lawlessness was reached in France.
The greatest Socialist statesman in Europe, Jaurés, was shot
and killed by a gentleman who resented his efforts to avert
the war. M. Clemenceau was shot by another gentleman of
less popular opinions, and happily came off no worse than
having to spend a precautionary couple of days in bed.
The slayer of Jaurés was recklessly acquitted: the would-be
slayer of M. Clemenceau was carefully found guilty. There
is no reason to doubt that the same thing would have happened in England if the war had begun with a successful
attempt to assassinate Keir Hardie, and ended with an
unsuccessful one to assassinate Mr Lloyd George.

THE LONG ARM OF WAR

The pestilence which is the usual accompaniment of war
was called influenza. Whether it was really a war pestilence
or not was made doubtful by the fact that it did its worst
in places remote from the battle-fields, notably on the west
coast of North America and in India. But the moral pestilence, which was unquestionably a war pestilence, repro-

duced this phenomenon. One would have supposed that the war fever would have raged most furiously in the countries actually under fire, and that the others would be more reasonable. Belgium and Flanders, where over large districts literally not one stone was left upon another as the opposed armies drove each other back and forward over it after terrific preliminary bombardments, might have been pardoned for relieving their feelings more emphatically than by shrugging their shoulders and saying *"C'est la guerre."* England, inviolate for so many centuries that the swoop of war on her homesteads had long ceased to be more credible than a return of the Flood, could hardly be expected to keep her temper sweet when she knew at last what it was to hide in cellars and underground railway stations, or lie quaking in bed, whilst bombs crashed, houses crumbled, and aircraft guns distributed shrapnel on friend and foe alike until certain shop windows in London, formerly full of fashionable hats, were filled with steel helmets. Slain and mutilated women and children, and burnt and wrecked dwellings, excuse a good deal of violent language, and produce a wrath on which many suns go down before it is appeased. Yet it was in the United States of America, where nobody slept the worse for the war, that the war fever went beyond all sense and reason. In European Courts there was vindictive illegality: in American Courts there was raving lunacy. It is not for me to chronicle the extravagances of an Ally: let some candid American do that. I can only say that to us sitting in our gardens in England, with the guns in France making themselves felt by a throb in the air as unmistakeable as an audible sound, or with tightening hearts studying the phases of the moon in London in their bearing on the chances whether our houses would be standing or ourselves alive next morning, the newspaper accounts of the sentences American Courts were passing on young girls and old men alike for the expression of opinions which were being uttered amid thundering applause before huge audiences in England, and the more private records of the methods by which the American War Loans were raised, were so amazing that they would put the guns and the possibilities of a raid clean out of our heads for the moment.

THE RABID WATCHDOGS OF LIBERTY

Not content with these rancorous abuses of the existing law, the war maniacs made a frantic rush to abolish all constitutional guarantees of liberty and well-being. The ordinary law was superseded by Acts under which newspapers were seized and their printing machinery destroyed by simple police raids à la Russe, and persons arrested and shot without any pretence of trial by jury or publicity of procedure or evidence. Though it was urgently necessary that production should be increased by the most scientific organization and economy of labor, and though no fact was better established than that excessive duration and intensity of toil reduces production heavily instead of increasing it, the factory laws were suspended, and men and women recklessly overworked until the loss of their efficiency became too glaring to be ignored. Remonstrances and warnings were met either with an accusation of pro-Germanism or the formula, "Remember that we are at war now." I have said that men assumed that war had reversed the order of nature, and that all was lost unless we did the exact opposite of everything we had found necessary and beneficial in peace. But the truth was worse than that. The war did not change men's minds in any such impossible way. What really happened was that the impact of physical death and destruction, the one reality that every fool can understand, tore off the masks of education, art, science, and religion from our ignorance and barbarism, and left us glorying grotesquely in the license suddenly accorded to our vilest passions and most abject terrors. Ever since Thucydides wrote his history, it has been on record that when the angel of death sounds his trumpet the pretences of civilization are blown from men's heads into the mud like hats in a gust of wind. But when this scripture was fulfilled among us, the shock was not the less appalling because a few students of Greek history were not surprised by it. Indeed these students threw themselves into the orgy as shamelessly as the illiterate. The Christian priest joining in the war dance without even throwing off his cassock first, and the respectable school governor expelling the German professor with insult and bodily violence, and declaring that no English child should ever again be taught the language of Luther and Goethe, were kept in countenance by the most impudent repudiations of every decency of civilization and every lesson of political experience on the part of the very persons who, as university professors, historians, philosophers, and men of science, were the accredited custodians of culture. It was crudely natural, and perhaps necessary for recruiting purposes, that German militarism and German dynastic ambition should be painted by journalists and recruiters in black and red as European dangers (as in fact they are), leaving it to be inferred that our own militarism and our own political constitution are millennially democratic (which they certainly are not); but when it came to frantic denunciations of German chemistry, German biology, German poetry, German music, German literature, German philosophy, and even German engineering, as malignant abominations standing towards British and French chemistry and so forth in the relation of heaven to hell, it was clear that the utterers of such barbarous ravings had never really understood or cared for the arts and sciences they professed and were profaning, and were only the appallingly degenerate descendants of the men of the seventh and eighteenth centuries who, recognizing no national frontiers in the great realm of the human mind, kept the European comity of that realm loftily and even ostentatiously above the rancors of the battle-field. Tearing the Garter from the Kaiser's leg, striking the German dukes from the roll of our peerage, changing the King's illustrious and historically appropriate surname for that of a traditionless locality, was not a very dignified business; but the erasure of German names from the British rolls of science and learning was a confession that in England the little respect paid to science and learning is only an affectation which hides a savage contempt for both. One felt that the figure of St George and the Dragon on our coinage should be replaced by that of the soldier driving his spear through Archimedes. But by that time there was no coinage: only paper money in which ten shillings called itself a pound as confidently as the people who were disgracing their country called themselves patriots.

THE SUFFERINGS OF THE SANE

The mental distress of living amid the obscene din of all these carmagnoles and corobberies was not the only burden that lay on sane people during the war. There was also the emotional strain, complicated by the offended economic sense, produced by the casualty lists. The stupid, the selfish, the narrow-minded, the callous and unimaginative were spared a great deal. "Blood and destruction shall be so in use that mothers shall but smile when they behold their infants quartered by the hands of war," was a Shakespearean prophecy that very nearly came true; for when nearly every house had a slaughtered son to mourn, we should all have gone quite out of our senses if we had taken our own and our friends' bereavements at their peace value. It became necessary to give them a false value; to proclaim the young life worthily and gloriously sacrificed to redeem the liberty of mankind, instead of to expiate the heedlessness and folly of their fathers, and expiate it in vain. We had even to assume that the parents and not the children had made the sacrifice, until at last the comic papers were driven to satirize fat old men, sitting comfortably in club chairs, and boasting of the sons they had "given" to their country.

No one grudged these anodynes to acute personal grief; but they only embittered those who knew that the young men were having their teeth set on edge because their parents had eaten sour political grapes. Then think of the young men themselves! Many of them had no illusions about the policy that led to the war: they went clear-sighted to a horribly repugnant duty. Men essentially gentle and essentially wise, with really valuable work in hand, laid it down voluntarily and spent months forming fours in the barrack yard, and stabbing sacks of straw in the public eye, so that they might go out to kill and maim men as

gentle as themselves. These men, who were perhaps, as a
class, our most efficient soldiers (Frederick Keeling, for
example), were not duped for a moment by the hypocritical
melodrama that consoled and stimulated the others. They
left their creative work to drudge at destruction, exactly as
they would have left it to take their turn at the pumps in
a sinking ship. They did not, like some of the conscientious
objectors, hold back because the ship had been neglected
by its officers and scuttled by its wreckers. The ship had
to be saved, even if Newton had to leave his fluxions and
Michael Angelo his marbles to save it; so they threw away
the tools of their beneficent and ennobling trades, and took
up the bloodstained bayonet and the murderous bomb,
forcing themselves to pervert their divine instinct for perfect artistic execution to the effective handling of these
diabolical things, and their economic faculty for organization to the contriving of ruin and slaughter. For it gave
an ironic edge to their tragedy that the very talents they
were forced to prostitute made the prostitution not only
effective, but even interesting; so that some of them were
rapidly promoted, and found themselves actually becoming artists in war, with a growing relish for it, like Napoleon and all the other scourges of mankind, in spite of
themselves. For many of them there was not even this
consolation. They "stuck it," and hated it, to the end.

EVIL IN THE THRONE OF GOOD

This distress of the gentle was so acute that those who
shared it in civil life, without having to shed blood with
their own hands, or witness destruction with their own
eyes, hardly cared to obtrude their own woes. Nevertheless,
even when sitting at home in safety, it was not easy for
those who had to write and speak about the war to throw
away their highest conscience, and deliberately work to a
standard of inevitable evil instead of the ideal of life more
abundant. I can answer for at least one person who found
the change from the wisdom of Jesus and St Francis to
the morals of Richard III and the madness of Don Quixote
extremely irksome. But that change had to be made; and

we are all the worse for it, except those for whom it was not really a change at all, but only a relief from hypocrisy.

Think, too, of those who, though they had neither to write nor to fight, and had no children of their own to lose, yet knew the inestimable loss to the world of four years of the life of a generation wasted on destruction. Hardly one of the epoch-making works of the human mind might not have been aborted or destroyed by taking their authors away from their natural work for four critical years. Not only were Shakespears and Platos being killed outright; but many of the best harvests of the survivors had to be sown in the barren soil of the trenches. And this was no mere British consideration. To the truly civilized man, to the good European, the slaughter of the German youth was as disastrous as the slaughter of the English. Fools exulted in "German losses." They were our losses as well. Imagine exulting in the death of Beethoven because Bill Sykes dealt him his death blow!

STRAINING AT THE GNAT AND SWALLOWING THE CAMEL

But most people could not comprehend these sorrows. There was a frivolous exultation in death for its own sake, which was at bottom an inability to realize that the deaths were real deaths and not stage ones. Again and again, when an air raider dropped a bomb which tore a child and its mother limb from limb, the people who saw it, though they had been reading with great cheerfulness of thousands of such happenings day after day in their newspapers, suddenly burst into furious imprecations on "the Huns" as murderers, and shrieked for savage and satisfying vengeance. At such moments it became clear that the deaths they had not seen meant no more to them than the mimic deaths of the cinema screen. Sometimes it was not necessary that death should be actually witnessed: it had only to take place under circumstances of sufficient novelty and proximity to bring it home almost as sensationally and effectively as if it had been actually visible.

For example, in the spring of 1915 there was an appalling

slaughter of our young soldiers at Neuve Chapelle and at
the Gallipoli landing. I will not go so far as to say that our
civilians were delighted to have such exciting news to read
at breakfast. But I cannot pretend that I noticed either in
the papers, or in general intercourse, any feeling beyond
the usual one that the cinema show at the front was going
splendidly, and that our boys were the bravest of the brave.
Suddenly there came the news that an Atlantic liner, the
Lusitania, had been torpedoed, and that several well-known
first class passengers, including a famous theatrical manager and the author of a popular farce, had been drowned,
among others. The others included Sir Hugh Lane; but as
he had only laid the country under great obligations in the
sphere of the fine arts, no great stress was laid on that loss.

Immediately an amazing frenzy swept through the
country. Men who up to that time had kept their heads
now lost them utterly. "Killing saloon passengers! What
next?" was the essence of the whole agitation; but it is far
too trivial a phrase to convey the faintest notion of the rage
which possessed us. To me, with my mind full of the hideous cost of Neuve Chapelle, Ypres, and the Gallipoli landing, the fuss about the Lusitania seemed almost a heartless
impertinence, though I was well acquainted personally with
the three best-known victims, and understood, better perhaps than most people, the misfortune of the death of Lane.
I even found a grim satisfaction, very intelligible to all
soldiers, in the fact that the civilians who found the war
such splendid British sport should get a sharp taste of what
it was to the actual combatants. I expressed my impatience
very freely, and found that my very straightforward and
natural feeling in the matter was received as a monstrous
and heartless paradox. When I asked those who gaped at
me whether they had anything to say about the holocaust
of Festubert, they gaped wider than before, having totally
forgotten it, or rather, having never realized it. They were
not heartless any more than I was; but the big catastrophe
was too big for them to grasp, and the little one had been
just the right size for them. I was not surprised. Have I not
seen a public body for just the same reason pass a vote
for £30,000 without a word, and then spend three special

meetings, prolonged into the night, over an item of seven
shillings for refreshments?

LITTLE MINDS AND BIG BATTLES

Nobody will be able to understand the vagaries of public
feeling during the war unless they bear constantly in mind
that the war in its entire magnitude did not exist for the
average civilian. He could not conceive even a battle, much
less a campaign. To the suburbs the war was nothing but a
suburban squabble. To the miner and navvy it was only a
series of bayonet fights between German champions and
English ones. The enormity of it was quite beyond most of
us. Its episodes had to be reduced to the dimensions of a
railway accident or a shipwreck before it could produce any
effect on our minds at all. To us the ridiculous bombardments of Scarborough and Ramsgate were colossal tragedies, and the battle of Jutland a mere ballad. The words
"after thorough artillery preparation" in the news from the
front meant nothing to us; but when our seaside trippers
learned that an elderly gentleman at breakfast in a week-end
marine hotel had been interrupted by a bomb dropping
into his egg-cup, their wrath and horror knew no bounds.
They declared that this would put a new spirit into the
army, and had no suspicion that the soldiers in the trenches
roared with laughter over it for days, and told each other
that it would do the blighters at home good to have a
taste of what the army was up against. Sometimes the
smallness of view was pathetic. A man would work at
home regardless of the call "to make the world safe for
democracy." His brother would be killed at the front.
Immediately he would throw up his work and take up the
war as a family blood feud against the Germans. Sometimes it was comic. A wounded man, entitled to his discharge, would return to the trenches with a grim determination to find the Hun who had wounded him and pay him
out for it.

It is impossible to estimate what proportion of us, in
khaki or out of it, grasped the war and its political anteced-
ents as a whole in the light of any philosophy of history or
knowledge of what war is. I doubt whether it was as high

as our proportion of higher mathematicians. But there can be no doubt that it was prodigiously outnumbered by the comparatively ignorant and childish. Remember that these people had to be stimulated to make the sacrifices demanded by the war, and that this could not be done by appeals to a knowledge which they did not possess, and a comprehension of which they were incapable. When the armistice at last set me free to tell the truth about the war at the following general election, a soldier said to a candidate whom I was supporting "If I had known all that in 1914, they would never have got me into khaki." And that, of course, was precisely why it had been necessary to stuff him with a romance that any diplomatist would have laughed at. Thus the natural confusion of ignorance was increased by a deliberately propagated confusion of nursery bogey stories and melodramatic nonsense, which at last overreached itself and made it impossible to stop the war before we had not only achieved the triumph of vanquishing the German army and thereby overthrowing its militarist monarchy, but made the very serious mistake of ruining the centre of Europe, a thing that no sane European State could afford to do.

THE DUMB CAPABLES AND THE NOISY INCAPABLES

Confronted with this picture of insensate delusion and folly, the critical reader will immediately counterplead that England all this time was conducting a war which involved the organization of several millions of fighting men and of the workers who were supplying them with provisions, munitions, and transport, and that this could not have been done by a mob of hysterical ranters. This is fortunately true. To pass from the newspaper offices and political platforms and club fenders and suburban drawing-rooms to the Army and the munition factories was to pass from Bedlam to the busiest and sanest of workaday worlds. It was to rediscover England, and find solid ground for the faith of those who still believed in her. But a necessary condition of this efficiency was that those who were efficient should give all their time to their business and leave the rabble raving to its heart's content. Indeed the raving was useful to the efficient, because, as it was always wide of the mark, it often distracted attention very conveniently from operations that would have been defeated or hindered by publicity. A precept which I endeavored vainly to popularize early in the war, "If you have anything to do go and do it: if not, for heaven's sake get out of the way," was only half carried out. Certainly the capable people went and did it; but the incapables would by no means get out of the way: they fussed and bawled and were only prevented from getting very seriously into the way by the blessed fact that they never knew where the way was. Thus whilst all the efficiency of England was silent and invisible, all its imbecility was deafening the heavens with its clamor and blotting out the sun with its dust. It was also unfortunately intimidating the Government by its blusterings into using the irresistible powers of the State to intimidate the sensible people, thus enabling a despicable minority of would-be lynchers to set up a reign of terror which could at any time have been broken by a single stern word from a responsible minister. But our ministers had not that sort of courage: neither Heartbreak House nor Horseback Hall had bred it, much less the suburbs. When matters at last came to the looting of shops by criminals under patriotic pretexts, it was the police force and not the Government that put its foot down. There was even one deplorable moment, during the submarine scare, in which the Government yielded to a childish cry for the maltreatment of naval prisoners of war, and, to our great disgrace, was forced by the enemy to behave itself. And yet behind all this public blundering and misconduct and futile mischief, the effective England was carrying on with the most formidable capacity and activity. The ostensible England was making the empire sick with its incontinences, its ignorances, its ferocities, its panics, and its endless and intolerable blarings of Allied national anthems in season and out. The esoteric England was proceeding irresistibly to the conquest of Europe.

THE PRACTICAL BUSINESS MEN

From the beginning the useless people set up a shriek for "practical business men." By this they meant men who had become rich by placing their personal interests before those of the country, and measuring the success of every activity by the pecuniary profit it brought to them and to those on whom they depended for their supplies of capital. The pitiable failure of some conspicuous samples from the first batch we tried of these poor devils helped to give the whole public side of the war an air of monstrous and hopeless farce. They proved not only that they were useless for public work, but that in a well-ordered nation they would never have been allowed to control private enterprise.

HOW THE FOOLS SHOUTED THE WISE MEN DOWN

Thus, like a fertile country flooded with mud, England shewed no sign of her greatness in the days when she was putting forth all her strength to save herself from the worst consequences of her littleness. Most of the men of action, occupied to the last hour of their time with urgent practical work, had to leave to idler people, or to professional rhetoricians, the presentation of the war to the reason and imagination of the country and the world in speeches, poems, manifestos, picture posters, and newspaper articles. I have had the privilege of hearing some of our ablest commanders talking about their work; and I have shared the common lot of reading the accounts of that work given to the world by the newspapers. No two experiences could be more different. But in the end the talkers obtained a dangerous ascendancy over the rank and file of the men of action; for though the great men of action are always inveterate talkers and often very clever writers, and therefore cannot have their minds formed for them by others, the average man of action, like the average fighter with the bayonet, can give no account of himself in words even to himself, and is apt to pick up and accept what he reads about himself and other people in the papers, except when the writer is rash enough to commit himself on technical points. It was not uncommon during the war to hear a soldier, or a civilian engaged on war work, describing events within his own experience that reduced to utter absurdity the ravings and maunderings of his daily paper, and yet echo the opinions of that paper like a parrot. Thus, to escape from the prevailing confusion and folly it was not enough to seek the company of the ordinary man of action: one had to get into contact with the master spirits. This was a privilege which only a handful of people could enjoy. For the unprivileged citizen there was no escape. To him the whole country seemed mad, futile, silly, incompetent, with no hope of victory except the hope that the enemy might be just as mad. Only by very resolute reflection and reasoning could he reassure himself that if there was nothing more solid beneath these appalling appearances the war could not possibly have gone on for a single day without a total breakdown of its organization.

THE MAD ELECTION

Happy were the fools and the thoughtless men of action in those days. The worst of it was that the fools were very strongly represented in parliament, as fools not only elect fools, but can persuade men of action to elect them too. The election that immediately followed the armistice was perhaps the maddest that has ever taken place. Soldiers who had done voluntary and heroic service in the field were defeated by persons who had apparently never run a risk or spent a farthing that they could avoid, and who even had in the course of the election to apologize publicly for bawling Pacifist or Pro-German at their opponent. Party leaders seek such followers, who can always be depended on to walk tamely into the lobby at the party whip's orders, provided the leader will make their seats safe for them by the process which was called, in derisive reference to the war rationing system, "giving them the coupon." Other incidents were so grotesque that I cannot mention them without enabling the reader to identify the parties, which would not be fair, as they were no more to blame than thousands of others who must necessarily be nameless. The general result was patently absurd; and the electorate, disgusted at its own work, instantly recoiled to the opposite extreme, and cast out all the coupon candidates at the earliest bye-elections by equally silly majorities. But the mischief of the general election could not be undone; and the Government had not only to pretend to abuse its

European victory as it had promised, but actually to do it
by starving the enemies who had thrown down their arms.
It had, in short, won the election by pledging itself to be
thriftlessly wicked, cruel, and vindictive; and it did not find
it as easy to escape from this pledge as it had from nobler
ones. The end, as I write, is not yet; but it is clear that
this thoughtless savagery will recoil on the heads of the
Allies so severely that we shall be forced by the sternest
necessity to take up our share of healing the Europe we
have wounded almost to death instead of attempting to
complete her destruction.

THE YAHOO AND THE ANGRY APE

Contemplating this picture of a state of mankind so
recent that no denial of its truth is possible, one understands Shakespear comparing Man to an angry ape, Swift
describing him as a Yahoo rebuked by the superior virtue
of the horse, and Wellington declaring that the British can
behave themselves neither in victory nor defeat. Yet none
of the three had seen war as we have seen it. Shakespear
blamed great men, saying that "Could great men thunder
as Jove himself does Jove would ne'er be quiet; for every
pelting petty officer would use his heaven for thunder:
nothing but thunder." What would Shakespear have said
if he had seen something far more destructive than thunder
in the hand of every village laborer, and found on the
Messines Ridge the craters of the nineteen volcanoes that
were let loose there at the touch of a finger that might
have been a child's finger without the result being a whit
less ruinous? Shakespear may have seen a Stratford cottage struck by one of Jove's thunderbolts, and have helped
to extinguish the lighted thatch and clear away the bits of
the broken chimney. What would he have said if he had
seen Ypres as it is now, or returned to Stratford, as French
peasants are returning to their homes today, to find the
old familiar signpost inscribed "To Stratford, 1 mile," and
at the end of the mile nothing but some holes in the ground
and a fragment of a broken churn here and there? Would
not the spectacle of the angry ape endowed with powers of

destruction that Jove never pretended to, have beggared even his command of words?

And yet, what is there to say except that war puts a strain on human nature that breaks down the better half of it, and makes the worse half a diabolical virtue? Better for us if it broke it down altogether; for then the warlike way out of our difficulties would be barred to us, and we should take greater care not to get into them. In truth, it is, as Byron said, "not difficult to die," and enormously difficult to live: that explains why, at bottom, peace is not only better than war, but infinitely more arduous. Did any hero of the war face the glorious risk of death more bravely than the traitor Bolo faced the ignominious certainty of it? Bolo taught us all how to die: can we say that he taught us all how to live? Hardly a week passes now without some soldier who braved death in the field so recklessly that he was decorated or specially commended for it, being haled before our magistrates for having failed to resist the paltriest temptations of peace, with no better excuse than the old one that "a man must live." Strange that one who, sooner than do honest work, will sell his honor for a bottle of wine, a visit to the theatre, and an hour with a strange woman, all obtained by passing a worthless cheque, could yet stake his life on the most desperate chances of the battle-field! Does it not seem as if, after all, the glory of death were cheaper than the glory of life? If it is not easier to attain, why do so many more men attain it? At all events it is clear that the kingdom of the Prince of Peace has not yet become the kingdom of this world. His attempts at invasion have been resisted far more fiercely than the Kaiser's. Successful as that resistance has been, it has piled up a sort of National Debt that is not the less oppressive because we have no figures for it and do not intend to pay it. A blockade that cuts off "the grace of our Lord" is in the long run less bearable than the blockades which merely cut off raw materials; and against that blockade our Armada is impotent. In the blockader's house, he has assured us, there are many mansions; but I am afraid they do not include either Heartbreak House or Horseback Hall.

PLAGUE ON BOTH YOUR HOUSES!

Meanwhile the Bolshevist picks and petards are at work on the foundations of both buildings; and though the Bolshevists may be buried in the ruins, their deaths will not save the edifices. Unfortunately they can be built again. Like Doubting Castle, they have been demolished many times by successive Greathearts, and rebuilt by Simple, Sloth, and Presumption, by Feeble Mind and Much Afraid, and by all the jurymen of Vanity Fair. Another generation of "secondary education" at our ancient public schools and the cheaper institutions that ape them will be quite sufficient to keep the two going until the next war.

For the instruction of that generation I leave these pages as a record of what civilian life was during the war: a matter on which history is usually silent. Fortunately it was a very short war. It is true that the people who thought it could not last more than six months were very signally refuted by the event. As Sir Douglas Haig has pointed out, its Waterloos lasted months instead of hours. But there would have been nothing surprising in its lasting thirty years. If it had not been for the fact that the blockade achieved the amazing feat of starving out Europe, which it could not possibly have done had Europe been properly organized for war, or even for peace, the war would have lasted until the belligerents were so tired of it that they could no longer be compelled to compel themselves to go on with it. Considering its magnitude, the war of 1914–18 will certainly be classed as the shortest in history. The end came so suddenly that the combatants literally stumbled over it; and yet it came a full year later than it should have come if the belligerents had not been far too afraid of one another to face the situation sensibly. Germany, having failed to provide for the war she began, failed again to surrender before she was dangerously exhausted. Her opponents, equally improvident, went as much too close to bankruptcy as Germany to starvation. It was a bluff at which both were bluffed. And, with the usual irony of war, it remains doubtful whether Germany and Russia, the defeated, will not be the gainers; for the victors are already

busy fastening on themselves the chains they have struck
from the limbs of the vanquished.

HOW THE THEATRE FARED

Let us now contract our view rather violently from the
European theatre of war to the theatre in which the fights
are sham fights, and the slain, rising the moment the curtain has fallen, go comfortably home to supper after washing off their rosepink wounds. It is nearly twenty years since
I was last obliged to introduce a play in the form of a
book for lack of an opportunity of presenting it in its
proper mode by a performance in a theatre. The war has
thrown me back on this expedient. Heartbreak House has
not yet reached the stage. I have withheld it because the war
has completely upset the economic conditions which formerly enabled serious drama to pay its way in London. The
change is not in the theatres nor in the management of
them, nor in the authors and actors, but in the audiences.
For four years the London theatres were crowded every
night with thousands of soldiers on leave from the front.
These soldiers were not seasoned London playgoers. A
childish experience of my own gave me a clue to their
condition. When I was a small boy I was taken to the
opera. I did not then know what an opera was, though I
could whistle a good deal of opera music. I had seen in
my mother's album photographs of all the great opera singers, mostly in evening dress. In the theatre I found myself
before a gilded balcony filled with persons in evening dress
whom I took to be the opera singers. I picked out one mas-
sive dark lady as Alboni, and wondered how soon she would
stand up and sing. I was puzzled by the fact that I was
made to sit with my back to the singers instead of facing
them. When the curtain went up, my astonishment and
delight were unbounded.

THE SOLDIER AT THE THEATRE FRONT

In 1915 I saw in the theatres men in khaki in just the
same predicament. To everyone who had my clue to their
state of mind it was evident that they had never been in a

theatre before and did not know what it was. At one of our great variety theatres I sat beside a young officer, not at all a rough specimen, who, even when the curtain rose and enlightened him as to the place where he had to look for his entertainment, found the dramatic part of it utterly incomprehensible. He did not know how to play his part of the game. He could understand the people on the stage singing and dancing and performing gymnastic feats. He not only understood but intensely enjoyed an artist who imitated cocks crowing and pigs squeaking. But the people who pretended that they were somebody else, and that the painted picture behind them was real, bewildered him. In his presence I realized how very sophisticated the natural man has to become before the conventions of the theatre can be easily acceptable, or the purpose of the drama obvious to him.

Well, from the moment when the routine of leave for our soldiers was established, such novices, accompanied by damsels (called flappers) often as innocent as themselves, crowded the theatres to the doors. It was hardly possible at first to find stuff crude enough to nurse them on. The best music-hall comedians ransacked their memories for the older quips and the most childish antics to avoid carrying the military spectators out of their depth. I believe that this was a mistake as far as the novices were concerned. Shakespear, or the dramatized histories of George Barnwell, Maria Martin, or the Demon Barber of Fleet Street, would probably have been quite popular with them. But the novices were only a minority after all. The cultivated soldier, who in time of peace would look at nothing theatrical except the most advanced post-Ibsen plays in the most artistic settings, found himself, to his own astonishment, thirsting for silly jokes, dances, and brainlessly sensuous exhibitions of pretty girls. The author of some of the most grimly serious plays of our time told me that after enduring the trenches for months without a glimpse of the female of his species, it gave him an entirely innocent but delightful pleasure merely to see a flapper. The reaction from the battle-field produced a condition of hyperaesthesia in which all the theatrical values were altered. Trivial things gained intensity and stale things novelty. The actor, instead of having to coax his audiences out of the boredom which had driven them to the theatre in an ill humor to seek some sort of distraction, had only to exploit the bliss of smiling men who were no longer under fire and under military discipline, but actually clean and comfortable and in a mood to be pleased with anything and everything that a bevy of pretty girls and a funny man, or even a bevy of girls pretending to be pretty and a man pretending to be funny, could do for them.

Then could be seen every night in the theatres old-fashioned farcical comedies, in which a bedroom, with four doors on each side and a practicable window in the middle, was understood to resemble exactly the bedroom in the flats beneath and above, all three inhabited by couples consumed with jealousy. When these people came home drunk at night; mistook their neighbors' flats for their own; and in due course got into the wrong beds, it was not only the novices who found the resulting complications and scandals exquisitely ingenious and amusing, nor their equally verdant flappers who could not help squealing in a manner that astonished the oldest performers when the gentleman who had just come in drunk through the window pretended to undress, and allowed glimpses of his naked person to be descried from time to time. Men who had just read the news that Charles Wyndham was dying, and were thereby sadly reminded of Pink Dominos and the torrent of farcical comedies that followed it in his heyday until every trick of that trade had become so stale that the laughter they provoked turned to loathing: these veterans also, when they returned from the field, were as much pleased by what they knew to be stale and foolish as the novices by what they thought fresh and clever.

COMMERCE IN THE THEATRE

Wellington said that an army moves on its belly. So does a London theatre. Before a man acts he must eat. Before he performs plays he must pay rent. In London we have no theatres for the welfare of the people: they are all for the sole purpose of producing the utmost obtainable rent for the proprietor. If the twin flats and twin beds produce a guinea more than Shakespear, out goes Shakespear, and in come the twin flats and the twin beds. If the brainless bevy of pretty girls and the funny man outbid Mozart, out goes Mozart.

UNSER SHAKESPEAR

Before the war an effort was made to remedy this by establishing a national theatre in celebration of the tercentenary of the death of Shakespear. A committee was formed; and all sorts of illustrious and influential persons lent their names to a grand appeal to our national culture. My play, The Dark Lady of The Sonnets, was one of the incidents of that appeal. After some years of effort the result was a single handsome subscription from a German gentleman. Like the celebrated swearer in the anecdote when the cart containing all his household goods lost its tailboard at the top of the hill and let its contents roll in ruin to the bottom, I can only say, "I cannot do justice to this situation," and let it pass without another word.

THE HIGHER DRAMA PUT OUT OF ACTION

The effect of the war on the London theatres may now be imagined. The beds and the bevies drove every higher form of art out of it. Rents went up to an unprecedented figure. At the same time prices doubled everywhere except at the theatre payboxes, and raised the expenses of management to such a degree that unless the houses were quite full every night, profit was impossible. Even bare solvency could not be attained without a very wide popularity. Now what had made serious drama possible to a limited extent before the war was that a play could pay its way even if the theatre were only half full until Saturday and three-quarters full then. A manager who was an enthusiast and a desperately hard worker, with an occasional grant-in-aid from an artisticaly disposed millionaire, and a due proportion of those rare and happy accidents by which plays of the higher sort turn out to be potboilers as well, could hold out for some years, by which time a relay might arrive in the person of another enthusiast. Thus and not otherwise

occurred that remarkable revival of the British drama at the
beginning of the century which made my own career as a
playwright possible in England. In America I had already
established myself, not as part of the ordinary theatre
system, but in association with the exceptional genius of
Richard Mansfield. In Germany and Austria I had no difficulty: the system of publicly aided theatres there, Court
and Municipal, kept drama of the kind I dealt in alive; so
that I was indebted to the Emperor of Austria for magnificent productions of my works at a time when the sole
official attention paid me by the British Court was the
announcement to the English-speaking world that certain
plays of mine were unfit for public performance, a substantial set-off against this being that the British Court, in
the course of its private playgoing, paid no regard to the
bad character given me by the chief officer of its household.

Howbeit, the fact that my plays effected a lodgment on
the London stage, and were presently followed by the plays
of Granville Barker, Gilbert Murray, John Masefield, St
John Hankin, Laurence Housman, Arnold Bennett, John
Galsworthy, John Drinkwater, and others which would in
the nineteenth century have stood rather less chance of production at a London theatre than the Dialogues of Plato,
not to mention revivals of the ancient Athenian drama, and
a restoration to the stage of Shakespear's plays as he wrote
them, was made economically possible solely by a supply of
theatres which could hold nearly twice as much money as it
cost to rent and maintain them. In such theatres work appealing to a relatively small class of cultivated persons, and
therefore attracting only from half to three-quarters as
many spectators as the more popular pastimes, could nevertheless keep going in the hands of young adventurers who
were doing it for its own sake, and had not yet been forced
by advancing age and responsibilities to consider the commercial value of their time and energy too closely. The war
struck this foundation away in the manner I have just
described. The expenses of running the cheapest west-end
theatres rose to a sum which exceeded by twenty-five per
cent the utmost that the higher drama can, as an ascertained
matter of fact, be depended on to draw. Thus the higher

Heartbreak House

drama, which has never really been a commercially sound speculation, now became an impossible one. Accordingly, attempts are being made to provide a refuge for it in suburban theatres in London and repertory theatres in the provinces. But at the moment when the army has at last disgorged the survivors of the gallant band of dramatic pioneers whom it swallowed, they find that the economic conditions which formerly made their work no worse than precarious now put it out of the question altogether, as far as the west end of London is concerned.

CHURCH AND THEATRE

I do not suppose many people care particularly. We are not brought up to care; and a sense of the national importance of the theatre is not born in mankind: the natural man, like so many of the soldiers at the beginning of the war, does not know what a theatre is. But please note that all these soldiers who did not know what a theatre was, knew what a church was. And they had been taught to respect churches. Nobody had ever warned them against a church as a place where frivolous women paraded in their best clothes; where stories of improper females like Potiphar's wife, and erotic poetry like the Song of Songs, were read aloud; where the sensuous and sentimental music of Schubert, Mendelssohn, Gounod, and Brahms was more popular than severe music by greater composers; where the prettiest sort of pretty pictures of pretty saints assailed the imagination and senses through stained-glass windows; and where sculpture and architecture came to the help of painting. Nobody ever reminded them that these things had sometimes produced such developments of erotic idolatry that men who were not only enthusiastic amateurs of literature, painting, and music, but famous practitioners of them, had actually exulted when mobs and even regular troops under express command had mutilated church statues, smashed church windows, wrecked church organs, and torn up the sheets from which the church music was read and sung. When they saw broken statues in churches, they were told that this was the work of wicked godless rioters, instead of, as it was, the work partly of zealots bent on driving the world, the flesh, and the devil out of the temple, and partly of insurgent men who had become intolerably poor because the temple had become a den of thieves. But all the sins and perversions that were so carefully hidden from them in the history of the Church were laid on the shoulders of the Theatre: that stuffy, uncomfortable place of penance in which we suffer so much inconvenience on the slenderest chance of gaining a scrap of food for our starving souls. When the Germans bombed the Cathedral of Rheims the world rang with the horror of the sacrilege. When they bombed the Little Theatre in the Adelphi, and narrowly missed bombing two writers of plays who lived within a few yards of it, the fact was not even mentioned in the papers. In point of appeal to the senses no theatre ever built could touch the fane at Rheims: no actress could rival its Virgin in beauty, nor any operatic tenor look otherwise than a fool beside its David. Its picture glass was glorious even to those who had seen the glass of Chartres. It was wonderful in its very grotesques: who would look at the Blondin Donkey after seeing its leviathans? In spite of the Adam-Adelphian decoration on which Miss Kingston had lavished so much taste and care, the Little Theatre was in comparison with Rheims the gloomiest of little conventicles: indeed the cathedral must, from the Puritan point of view, have debauched a million voluptuaries for every one whom the Little Theatre had sent home thoughtful to a chaste bed after Mr Chesterton's Magic or Brieux's Les Avariés. Perhaps that is the real reason why the Church is lauded and the Theatre reviled. Whether or no, the fact remains that the lady to whose public spirit and sense of the national value of the theatre I owed the first regular public performance of a play of mine had to conceal her action as if it had been a crime, whereas if she had given the money to the Church she would have worn a halo for it. And I admit, as I have always done, that this state of things may have been a very sensible one. I have asked Londoners again and again why they pay half a guinea to go to a theatre when they can go to St Paul's or Westminster Abbey for nothing. Their only possible reply is that they want to see something new and possibly something wicked; but the theatres mostly disappoint both hopes. If ever a revolution makes me Dictator, I shall establish a heavy charge for admission to our churches. But everyone who pays at the church door shall receive a ticket entitling him or her to free admission to one performance at any theatre he or she prefers. Thus shall the sensuous charms of the church service be made to subsidize the sterner virtue of the drama.

THE NEXT PHASE

The present situation will not last. Although the newspaper I read at breakfast this morning before writing these words contains a calculation that no less than twenty-three wars are at present being waged to confirm the peace, England is no longer in khaki; and a violent reaction is setting in against the crude theatrical fare of the four terrible years. Soon the rents of theatres will once more be fixed on the assumption that they cannot always be full, nor even on the average half full week in and week out. Prices will change. The higher drama will be at no greater disadvantage than it was before the war; and it may benefit, first, by the fact that many of us have been torn from the fools' paradise in which the theatre formerly traded, and thrust upon the sternest realities and necessities until we have lost both faith in and patience with the theatrical pretences that had no root either in reality or necessity; second, by the startling change made by the war in the distribution of income. It seems only the other day that a millionaire was a man with £50,000 a year. Today, when he has paid his income tax and super tax, and insured his life for the amount of his death duties, he is lucky if his net income is £10,000, though his nominal property remains the same. And this is the result of a Budget which is called "a respite for the rich." At the other end of the scale millions of persons have had regular incomes for the first time in their lives; and their men have been regularly clothed, fed, lodged, and taught to make up their minds that certain things have to be done, also for the first time in their lives. Hundreds of thousands of women have been taken out of their domestic cages and tasted both discipline and independence. The thoughtless and snobbish middle classes have been pulled up short by the very unpleasant experience of being ruined to an unprecedented extent. We have all had a tremendous jolt; and although the widespread notion that the shock of the war would automatically make a new heaven and a new earth, and that the dog would never go back to his vomit nor the sow to her wallowing in the mire, is already seen to be a delusion, yet we are far more conscious of our condition than we were, and far less disposed to submit to it. Revolution, lately only a sensational chapter in history or a demagogic claptrap, is now a possibility so imminent that hardly by trying to suppress it in other countries by arms and defamation, and calling the process anti-Bolshevism, can our Government stave it off at home.

Perhaps the most tragic figure of the day is the American President who was once a historian. In those days it became his task to tell us how, after that great war in America which was more clearly than any other war of our time a war for an idea, the conquerors, confronted with a heroic task of reconstruction, turned recreant, and spent fifteen years in abusing their victory under cover of pretending to accomplish the task they were doing what they could to make impossible. Alas! Hegel was right when he said that we learn from history that men never learn anything from history. With what anguish of mind the President sees that we, the new conquerors, forgetting everything we professed to fight for, are sitting down with watering mouths to a good square meal of ten years revenge upon and humiliation of our prostrate foe, can only be guessed by those who know, as he does, how hopeless is remonstrance, and how happy Lincoln was in perishing from the earth before his inspired messages became scraps of paper. He knows well that from the Peace Conference will come, in spite of his utmost, no edict on which he will be able, like Lincoln, to invoke "the considerate judgment of mankind, and the gracious favor of Almighty God." He led his people to destroy the militarism of Zabern; and the army they rescued is busy in Cologne imprisoning every German who does not salute a British officer; whilst the Government at home,

asked whether it approves, replies that it does not propose
even to discontinue this Zabernism when the Peace is concluded, but in effect looks forward to making Germans
salute British officers until the end of the world. That is
what war makes of men and women. It will wear off; and
the worst it threatens is already proving impracticable; but
before the humble and contrite heart ceases to be despised,
the President and I, being of the same age, will be dotards.
In the meantime there is, for him, another history to write;
for me, another comedy to stage. Perhaps, after all, that is
what wars are for, and what historians and playwrights
are for. If men will not learn until their lessons are written
in blood, why, blood they must have, their own for preference.

THE EPHEMERAL THRONES AND THE ETERNAL THEATRE

To the theatre it will not matter. Whatever Bastilles fall,
the theatre will stand. Apostolic Hapsburg has collapsed;
All Highest Hohenzollern languishes in Holland, threatened
with trial on a capital charge of fighting for his country
against England; Imperial Romanoff, said to have perished
miserably by a more summary method of murder, is
perhaps alive or perhaps dead: nobody cares more than if
he had been a peasant; the lord of Hellas is level with his
lackeys in republican Switzerland; Prime Ministers and
Commanders-in-Chief have passed from a brief glory as
Solons and Cæsars into failure and obscurity as closely on
one another's heels as the descendants of Banquo; but
Euripides and Aristophanes, Shakespear and Molière,
Goethe and Ibsen remain fixed in their everlasting seats.

HOW WAR MUZZLES THE DRAMATIC POET

As for myself, why, it may be asked, did I not write two
plays about the war instead of two pamphlets on it? The
answer is significant. You cannot make war on war and on
your neighbor at the same time. War cannot bear the terrible castigation of comedy, the ruthless light of laughter
that glares on the stage. When men are heroically dying for
their country, it is not the time to shew their lovers and

wives and fathers and mothers how they are being sacrificed to the blunders of boobies, the cupidity of capitalists, the ambition of conquerors, the electioneering of demagogues, the Pharisaism of patriots, the lusts and lies and rancors and bloodthirsts that love war because it opens their prison doors, and sets them in the thrones of power and popularity. For unless these things are mercilessly exposed they will hide under the mantle of the ideals on the stage just as they do in real life.

And though there may be better things to reveal, it may not, and indeed cannot, be militarily expedient to reveal them whilst the issue is still in the balance. Truth telling is not compatible with the defence of the realm. We are just now reading the revelations of our generals and admirals, unmuzzled at last by the armistice. During the war, General A, in his moving despatches from the field, told how General B had covered himself with deathless glory in such and such a battle. He now tells us that General B came within an ace of losing us the war by disobeying his orders on that occasion, and fighting instead of running away as he ought to have done. An excellent subject for comedy now that the war is over, no doubt; but if General A had let this out at the time, what would have been the effect on General B's soldiers? And had the stage made known what the Prime Minister and the Secretary of State for War who overruled General A thought of him, and what he thought of them, as now revealed in raging controversy, what would have been the effect on the nation? That is why comedy, though sorely tempted, had to be loyally silent; for the art of the dramatic poet knows no patriotism; recognizes no obligation but truth to natural history; cares not whether Germany or England perish; is ready to cry with Brynhild, *"Lass' uns verderben, lachend zu Grunde geh'n"* sooner than deceive or be deceived; and thus becomes in time of war a greater military danger than poison, steel, or trinitrotoluene. That is why I had to withhold Heartbreak House from the footlights during the war; for the Germans might on any night have turned the last act from play into earnest, and even then might not have waited for their cues.

June 1919

HEARTBREAK HOUSE

ACT I

*The hilly country in the middle of the north edge of Sussex,
looking very pleasant on a fine evening at the end of September, is seen through the windows of a room which has
been built so as to resemble the after part of an old-fashioned high-pooped ship with a stern gallery; for the windows are ship built with heavy timbering, and run right
across the room as continuously as the stability of the wall
allows. A row of lockers under the windows provides an
unupholstered window-seat interrupted by twin glass doors,
respectively halfway between the stern post and the sides.
Another door strains the illusion a little by being apparently
in the ship's port side, and yet leading, not to the open sea,
but to the entrance hall of the house. Between this door and
the stern gallery are bookshelves. There are electric light
switches beside the door leading to the hall and the glass
doors in the stern gallery. Against the starboard wall is a
carpenter's bench. The vice has a board in its jaws; and the
floor is littered with shavings, overflowing from a waste-
paper basket. A couple of planes and a centrebit are on
the bench. In the same wall, between the bench and the
windows, is a narrow doorway with a half door, above
which a glimpse of the room beyond shews that it is a
shelved pantry with bottles and kitchen crockery.*

*On the starboard side, but close to the middle, is a plain
oak drawing-table with drawing-board, T-square, straight-
edges, set squares, mathematical instruments, saucers of
water color, a tumbler of discolored water, Indian ink, pen-
cils, and brushes on it. The drawing-board is set so that the
draughtsman's chair has the window on its left hand. On
the floor at the end of the table, on his right, is a ship's
fire bucket. On the port side of the room, near the bookshelves, is a sofa with its back to the windows. It is a sturdy
mahogany article, oddly upholstered in sailcloth, including
the bolster, with a couple of blankets hanging over the back.*

*Between the sofa and the drawing-table is a big wicker
chair, with broad arms and a low sloping back, with its
back to the light. A small but stout table of teak, with a
round top and gate legs, stands against the port wall between the door and the bookcase. It is the only article in
the room that suggests (not at all convincingly) a woman's
hand in the furnishing. The uncarpeted floor of narrow
boards is caulked and holystoned like a deck.*

*The garden to which the glass doors lead dips to the
south before the landscape rises again to the hills. Emerging
from the hollow is the cupola of an observatory. Between
the observatory and the house is a flagstaff on a little
esplanade, with a hammock on the east side and a long
garden seat on the west.*

*A young lady, gloved and hatted, with a dust coat on, is
sitting in the window-seat with her body twisted to enable
her to look out at the view. One hand props her chin: the
other hangs down with a volume of the Temple Shakespear
in it, and her finger stuck in the page she has been reading.*

A clock strikes six.

*The young lady turns and looks at her watch. She rises
with an air of one who waits and is almost at the end of
her patience. She is a pretty girl, slender, fair, and intelligent
looking, nicely but not expensively dressed, evidently not a
smart idler.*

*With a sigh of weary resignation she comes to the
draughtsman's chair; sits down; and begins to read Shakespear. Presently the book sinks to her lap; her eyes close;
and she dozes into a slumber.*

*An elderly womanservant comes in from the hall with
three unopened bottles of rum on a tray. She passes through
and disappears in the pantry without noticing the young
lady. She places the bottles on the shelf and fills her tray
with empty bottles. As she returns with these, the young
lady lets her book drop, awakening herself, and startling the
womanservant so that she all but lets the tray fall.*

THE WOMANSERVANT. God bless us! [*The young lady picks
up the book and places it on the table*]. Sorry to wake

you, miss, I'm sure; but you are a stranger to me. What might you be waiting here for now?

THE YOUNG LADY. Waiting for somebody to shew some signs of knowing that I have been invited here.

THE WOMANSERVANT. Oh, youre invited, are you? And has nobody come? Dear! Dear!

THE YOUNG LADY. A wild-looking old gentleman came and looked in at the window; and I heard him calling out "Nurse: there is a young and attractive female waiting in the poop. Go and see what she wants." Are you the nurse?

THE WOMANSERVANT. Yes, miss: I'm Nurse Guinness. That was old Captain Shotover, Mrs Hushabye's father. I heard him roaring; but I thought it was for something else. I suppose it was Mrs Hushabye that invited you, ducky?

THE YOUNG LADY. I understood her to do so. But really I think I'd better go.

NURSE GUINNESS. Oh, dont think of such a thing, miss. If Mrs Hushabye has forgotten all about it, it will be a pleasant surprise for her to see you, wont it?

THE YOUNG LADY. It has been a very unpleasant surprise to me to find that nobody expects me.

NURSE GUINNESS. Youll get used to it, miss: this house is full of surprises for them that dont know our ways.

CAPTAIN SHOTOVER [*looking in from the hall suddenly: an ancient but still hardy man with an immense white beard, in a reefer jacket with a whistle hanging from his neck*] Nurse: there is a hold-all and a handbag on the front steps for everybody to fall over. Also a tennis racquet. Who the devil left them there?

THE YOUNG LADY. They are mine, I'm afraid.

THE CAPTAIN [*advancing to the drawing-table*] Nurse: who is this misguided and unfortunate young lady?

NURSE GUINNESS. She says Miss Hessy invited her, sir.

THE CAPTAIN. And had she no friend, no parents, to warn her against my daughter's invitations? This is a pretty sort of house, by heavens! A young and attractive lady is invited here. Her luggage is left on the steps for hours;

and she herself is deposited in the poop and abandoned, tired and starving. This is our hospitality. These are our manners. No room ready. No hot water. No welcoming hostess. Our visitor is to sleep in the toolshed, and to wash in the duckpond.

NURSE GUINNESS. Now it's all right, Captain: I'll get the lady some tea; and her room shall be ready before she has finished it. [*To the young lady*] Take off your hat, ducky; and make yourself at home [*she goes to the door leading to the hall*].

THE CAPTAIN [*as she passes him*] Ducky! Do you suppose, woman, that because this young lady has been insulted and neglected, you have the right to address her as you address my wretched children, whom you have brought up in ignorance of the commonest decencies of social intercourse?

NURSE GUINNESS. Never mind him, doty. [*Quite unconcerned, she goes out into the hall on her way to the kitchen*].

THE CAPTAIN. Madam: will you favor me with your name? [*He sits down in the big wicker chair*].

THE YOUNG LADY. My name is Ellie Dunn.

THE CAPTAIN. Dunn! I had a boatswain whose name was Dunn. He was originally a pirate in China. He set up as a ship's chandler with stores which I have every reason to believe he stole from me. No doubt he became rich. Are you his daughter?

ELLIE [*indignant*] No: certainly not. I am proud to be able to say that though my father has not been a successful man, nobody has ever had one word to say against him. I think my father is the best man I have ever known.

THE CAPTAIN. He must be greatly changed. Has he attained the seventh degree of concentration?

ELLIE. I dont understand.

THE CAPTAIN. But how could he, with a daughter! I, madam, have two daughters. One of them is Hesione Hushabye, who invited you here. I keep this house: she upsets it. I desire to attain the seventh degree of concentration: she invites visitors and leaves me to entertain them. [*Nurse Guinness returns with the tea-tray, which she places on the teak table*]. I have a second daughter, who is, thank God, in a remote part of the Empire with her numskull of a husband. As a child she thought the figure-head of my ship, the Dauntless, the most beautiful thing on earth. He resembled it. He had the same expression: wooden yet enterprising. She married him, and will never set foot in this house again.

NURSE GUINNESS [*carrying the table, with the tea-things on it, to Ellie's side*] Indeed you never were more mistaken. She is in England this very moment. You have been told three times this week that she is coming home for a year for her health. And very glad you should be to see your own daughter again after all these years.

THE CAPTAIN. I am not glad. The natural term of the affection of the human animal for its offspring is six years. My daughter Ariadne was born when I was forty-six. I am now eighty-eight. If she comes, I am not at home. If she wants anything, let her take it. If she asks for me, let her be informed that I am extremely old, and have totally forgotten her.

NURSE GUINNESS. Thats no talk to offer to a young lady. Here, ducky, have some tea; and dont listen to him [*she pours out a cup of tea*].

THE CAPTAIN [*rising wrathfully*] Now before high heaven they have given this innocent child Indian tea: the stuff they tan their own leather insides with. [*He seizes the cup and the tea-pot and empties both into the leathern bucket*].

ELLIE [*almost in tears*] Oh, please! I am so tired. I should have been glad of anything.

NURSE GUINNESS. Oh, what a thing to do! The poor lamb is ready to drop.

THE CAPTAIN. You shall have some of my tea. Do not touch that fly-blown cake: nobody eats it here except the dogs. [*He disappears into the pantry*].

NURSE GUINNESS. Theres a man for you! They say he sold himself to the devil in Zanzibar before he was a captain; and the older he grows the more I believe them.

A WOMAN'S VOICE [*in the hall*] Is anyone at home? Hesione!

Nurse! Papa! Do come, somebody; and take in my
luggage.

Thumping heard, as of an umbrella, on the wainscot.

NURSE GUINNESS. My gracious! It's Miss Addie, Lady
Utterword, Mrs Hushabye's sister: the one I told the
Captain about. [*Calling*] Coming, Miss, coming.

*She carries the table back to its place by the door, and
is hurrying out when she is intercepted by Lady Utterword, who bursts in much flustered. Lady Utterword, a
blonde, is very handsome, very well dressed, and so
precipitate in speech and action that the first impression
(erroneous) is one of comic silliness.*

LADY UTTERWORD. Oh, is that you, Nurse? How are you?
You dont look a day older. Is anybody at home? Where
is Hesione? Doesnt she expect me? Where are the
servants? Whose luggage is that on the steps? Wheres
Papa? Is everybody asleep? [*Seeing Ellie*] Oh! I beg your
pardon. I suppose you are one of my nieces. [*Approaching her with outstretched arms*] Come and kiss your aunt,
darling.

ELLIE. I'm only a visitor. It is my luggage on the steps.

NURSE GUINNESS. I'll go get you some fresh tea, ducky. [*She
takes up the tray*].

ELLIE. But the old gentleman said he would make some
himself.

NURSE GUINNESS. Bless you! he's forgotten what he went
for already. His mind wanders from one thing to another.

LADY UTTERWORD. Papa, I suppose?

NURSE GUINNESS. Yes, Miss.

LADY UTTERWORD [*vehemently*] Dont be silly, nurse. Dont
call me Miss.

NURSE GUINNESS [*placidly*] No, lovey [*she goes out with the
tea-tray*].

LADY UTTERWORD [*sitting down with a flounce on the sofa*]
I know what you must feel. Oh, this house, this house! I
come back to it after twenty-three years; and it is just the
same: the luggage lying on the steps, the servants spoilt
and impossible, nobody at home to receive anybody, no
regular meals, nobody ever hungry because they are
always gnawing bread and butter or munching apples,

and, what is worse, the same disorder in ideas, in talk, in feeling. When I was a child I was used to it: I had never known anything better, though I was unhappy, and longed all the time—oh, how I longed!—to be respectable, to be a lady, to live as others did, not to have to think of everything for myself. I married at nineteen to escape from it. My husband is Sir Hastings Utterword, who has been governor of all the crown colonies in succession. I have always been the mistress of Government House. I have been so happy: I had forgotten that people could live like this. I wanted to see my father, my sister, my nephews and nieces (one ought to, you know), and I was looking forward to it. And now the state of the house! the way I'm received! the casual impudence of that woman Guinness, our old nurse! really Hesione might at least have been here: s o m e preparation might have been made for me. You must excuse my going on in this way; but I am really very much hurt and annoyed and disillusioned: and if I had realized it was to be like this, I wouldnt have come. I have a great mind to go away without another word [*she is on the point of weeping*].

ELLIE [*also very miserable*] Nobody has been here to receive me either. I thought I ought to go away too. But how can I, Lady Utterword? My luggage is on the steps; and the station fly has gone.

The Captain emerges from the pantry with a tray of Chinese lacquer and a very fine tea-set on it. He rests it provisionally on the end of the table; snatches away the drawing-board, which he stands on the floor against the table legs; and puts the tray in the space thus cleared. Ellie pours out a cup greedily.

THE CAPTAIN. Your tea, young lady. What! another lady! I must fetch another cup [*he makes for the pantry*].

LADY UTTERWORD [*rising from the sofa, suffused with emotion*] Papa! Dont you know me? I'm your daughter.

THE CAPTAIN. Nonsense! my daughter's upstairs asleep. [*He vanishes through the half door*].

Lady Utterword retires to the window to conceal her tears.

ELLIE [*going to her with the cup*] Dont be so distressed.
Have this cup of tea. He is very old and very strange: he
has been just like that to me. I know how dreadful it
must be: my own father is all the world to me. Oh, I'm
sure he didnt mean it.

The Captain returns with another cup.

THE CAPTAIN. Now we are complete. [*He places it on the
tray*].

LADY UTTERWORD [*hysterically*] Papa: you cant have forgotten me. I am Ariadne. I'm little Paddy Patkins. Wont
you kiss me? [*She goes to him and throws her arms round
his neck*].

THE CAPTAIN [*woodenly enduring her embrace*] How can you
be Ariadne? You are a middle-aged woman: well preserved, madam, but no longer young.

LADY UTTERWORD. But think of all the years and years I
have been away, Papa. I have had to grow old, like other
people.

THE CAPTAIN [*disengaging himself*] You should grow out of
kissing strange men: they may be striving to attain the
seventh degree of concentration.

LADY UTTERWORD. But I'm your daughter. You havnt seen
me for years.

THE CAPTAIN. So much the worse! When our relatives are
at home, we have to think of all their good points or it
would be impossible to endure them. But when they are
away, we console ourselves for their absence by dwelling
on their vices. That is how I have come to think my
absent daughter Ariadne a perfect fiend; so do not try to
ingratiate yourself here by impersonating her [*he walks
firmly away to the other side of the room*].

LADY UTTERWORD. Ingratiating myself indeed! [*With dignity*] Very well, papa. [*She sits down at the drawing-table
and pours out tea for herself*].

THE CAPTAIN. I am neglecting my social duties. You remember Dunn? Billy Dunn?

LADY UTTERWORD. Do you mean that villainous sailor who
robbed you?

THE CAPTAIN [*introducing Ellie*] His daughter. [*He sits down
on the sofa*].

ELLIE [*protesting*] No—

Nurse Guinness returns with fresh tea.

THE CAPTAIN. Take that hogwash away. Do you hear?

NURSE. Youve actually remembered about the tea! [*To Ellie*] O, miss, he didnt forget you after all! You h a v e made an impression.

THE CAPTAIN [*gloomily*] Youth, beauty! novelty! They are badly wanted in this house. I am excessively old. Hesione is only moderately young. Her children are not youthful.

LADY UTTERWORD. How can children be expected to be youthful in this house? Almost before we could speak we were filled with notions that might have been all very well for pagan philosophers of fifty, but were certainly quite unfit for respectable people of any age.

NURSE. You were always for respectability, Miss Addy.

LADY UTTERWORD. Nurse: will you please remember that I am Lady Utterword, and not Miss Addy, nor lovey, nor darling, nor doty? Do you hear?

NURSE. Yes, ducky: all right. I'll tell them all they must call you my lady. [*She takes her tray out with undisturbed placidity*].

LADY UTTERWORD. What comfort? what sense is there in having servants with no manners?

ELLIE [*rising and coming to the table to put down her empty cup*] Lady Utterword: do you think Mrs Hushabye really expects me?

LADY UTTERWORD. Oh, dont ask me. You can see for yourself that Ive just arrived; her only sister, after twenty-three years absence! and it seems that *I* am not expected.

THE CAPTAIN. What does it matter whether the young lady is expected or not? She is welcome. There are beds: there is food. I'll find a room for her myself [*he makes for the door*].

ELLIE [*following him to stop him*] Oh please— [*he goes out*]. Lady Utterword: I dont know what to do. Your father persists in believing that my father is some sailor who robbed him.

LADY UTTERWORD. You had better pretend not to notice it. My father is a very clever man; but he always forgot things; and now that he is old, of course he is worse. And

I must warn you that it is sometimes very hard to feel quite sure that he really forgets.

Mrs Hushabye bursts into the room tempestuously, and embraces Ellie. She is a couple of years older than Lady Utterword and even better looking. She has magnificent black hair, eyes like the fishpools of Heshbon, and a nobly modelled neck, short at the back and low between her shoulders in front. Unlike her sister she is uncorseted and dressed anyhow in a rich robe of black pile that shews off her white skin and statuesque contour.

MRS HUSHABYE. Ellie, my darling, my pettikins [*kissing her*]: how long have you been here? Ive been at home all the time: I was putting flowers and things in your room; and when I just sat down for a moment to try how comfortable the armchair was I went off to sleep. Papa woke me and told me you were here. Fancy you finding no one, and being neglected and abandoned. [*Kissing her again*]. My poor love! [*She deposits Ellie on the sofa. Meanwhile Ariadne has left the table and come over to claim her share of attention*]. Oh! youve brought someone with you. Introduce me.

LADY UTTERWORD: Hesione; is it possible that y o u dont know me?

MRS HUSHABYE [*conventionally*] Of course I remember your face quite well. Where have we met?

LADY UTTERWORD. Didnt Papa tell you I was here? Oh! this is really too much. [*She throws herself sulkily into the big chair*].

MRS HUSHABYE. Papa!

LADY UTTERWORD. Yes: Papa. O u r papa, you unfeeling wretch. [*Rising angrily*] I'll go straight to a hotel.

MRS HUSHABYE [*seizing her by the shoulders*] My goodness gracious goodness, you dont mean to say that youre Addy!

LADY UTTERWORD. I certainly am Addy; and I dont think I can be so changed that you would not have recognized me if you had any real affection for me. And Papa didnt think me even worth mentioning!

MRS HUSHABYE. What a lark! Sit down [*she pushes her back*

*into the chair instead of kissing her, and posts herself
behind it*]. You do look a swell. Youre much handsomer
than you used to be. Youve made the acquaintance of
Ellie, of course. She is going to marry a perfect hog of a
millionaire for the sake of her father, who is as poor as a
church mouse; and you must help me to stop her.

ELLIE. Oh p l e a s e, Hesione.

MRS HUSHABYE. My pettikins, the man's coming here today
with your father to begin persecuting you; and everybody
will see the state of the case in ten minutes; so whats
the use of making a secret of it?

ELLIE. He is not a hog, Hesione. You dont know how
wonderfully good he was to my father, and how deeply
grateful I am to him.

MRS HUSHABYE [*to Lady Utterword*] Her father is a very
remarkable man, Addy. His name is Mazzini Dunn.
Mazzini was a celebrity of some kind who knew Ellie's
grandparents. They were both poets, like the Brownings;
and when her father came into the world Mazzini said
·"Another soldier born for freedom!" So they christened
him Mazzini; and he has been fighting for freedom in his
quiet way ever since. Thats why he is so poor.

ELLIE. I am proud of his poverty.

MRS HUSHABYE. Of course you are, pettikins. Why not
leave him in it, and marry someone you love?

LADY UTTERWORD. [*rising suddenly and explosively*]
Hesione: are you going to kiss me or are you not?

MRS HUSHABYE. What do you want to be kissed for?

LADY UTTERWORD. I dont want to be kissed; but I do want
you to behave properly and decently. We are sisters. We
have been separated for twenty-three years. You ought
to kiss me.

MRS HUSHABYE. Tomorrow morning, dear, before you make
up. I hate the smell of powder.

LADY UTTERWORD. Oh! you unfeeling— [*she is interrupted
by the return of the captain*].

THE CAPTAIN [*to Ellie*] Your room is ready. [*Ellie rises*].
The sheets were damp; but I have changed them [*he
makes for the garden door on the port side*].

LADY UTTERWORD. Oh! What about my sheets?

THE CAPTAIN [*halting at the door*] Take my advice: air them; or take them off and sleep in blankets. You shall sleep in Ariadne's old room.

LADY UTTERWORD. Indeed I shall do nothing of the sort. That little hole! I am entitled to the best spare room.

THE CAPTAIN [*continuing unmoved*] She married a numskull. She told me she would marry anyone to get away from home.

LADY UTTERWORD. You are pretending not to know me on purpose. I will leave the house.

Mazzini Dunn enters from the hall. He is a little elderly man with bulging credulous eyes and an earnest manner. He is dressed in a blue serge jacket suit with an unbuttoned mackintosh over it, and carries a soft black hat of clerical cut.

ELLIE. At last! Captain Shotover: here is my father.

THE CAPTAIN. This! Nonsense! not a bit like him [*he goes away through the garden, shutting the door sharply behind him*].

LADY UTTERWORD. I will not be ignored and pretended to be somebody else. I will have it out with papa now, this instant. [*To Mazzini*] Excuse me. [*She follows the Captain out, making a hasty bow to Mazzini, who returns it*].

MRS HUSHABYE [*hospitably, shaking hands*] How good of you to come, Mr Dunn! You dont mind papa, do you? He is as mad as a hatter, you know, but quite harmless, and extremely clever. You will have some delightful talks with him.

MAZZINI. I hope so. [*To Ellie*] So here you are, Ellie dear. [*He draws her arm affectionately through his*]. I must thank you, Mrs Hushabye, for your kindness to my daughter. I'm afraid she would have had no holiday if you had not invited her.

MRS HUSHABYE. Not at all. Very nice of her to come and attract young people to the house for us.

MAZZINI [*smiling*] I'm afraid Ellie is not interested in young men, Mrs Hushabye. Her taste is on the graver, solider side.

MRS HUSHABYE [*with a sudden rather hard brightness in her*

manner] Wont you take off your overcoat, Mr Dunn? You will find a cupboard for coats and hats and things in the corner of the hall.

MAZZINI [*hastily releasing Ellie*] Yes—thank you—I had better— [*he goes out*].

MRS HUSHABYE [*emphatically*] The old brute!

ELLIE. Who?

MRS HUSHABYE. Who! Him. He. It [*pointing after Mazzini*]. "Graver, solider tastes," indeed!

ELLIE [*aghast*] You dont mean that you were speaking like that of my father!

MRS HUSHABYE. I was. You know I was.

ELLIE [*with dignity*] I will leave your house at once. [*She turns to the door*].

MRS HUSHABYE. If you attempt it, I'll tell your father why.

ELLIE [*turning again*] Oh! How can you treat a visitor like this, Mrs Hushabye?

MRS HUSHABYE. I thought you were going to call me Hesione.

ELLIE. Certainly not now?

MRS HUSHABYE. Very well: I'll tell your father.

ELLIE [*distressed*] Oh!

MRS HUSHABYE. If you turn a hair—if you take his part against me and against your own heart for a moment, I'll give that born soldier of freedom a piece of my mind that will stand him on his selfish old head for a week.

ELLIE. Hesione! My father selfish! How little you know—
    She is interrupted by Mazzini, who returns, excited and perspiring.

MAZZINI. Ellie: Mangan has come: I thought youd like to know. Excuse me, Mrs Hushabye: the strange old gentleman—

MRS HUSHABYE. Papa. Quite so.

MAZZINI. Oh, I beg your pardon· of course: I was a little confused by his manner. He is making Mangan help him with something in the garden; and he wants me too—
    A powerful whistle is heard.

THE CAPTAIN'S VOICE. Bosun ahoy! [*the whistle is repeated*].

MAZZINI [*flustered*] Oh dear! I believe he is whistling for me. [*He hurries out*].

MRS HUSHABYE. Now my father is a wonderful man if you like.

ELLIE. Hesione: listen to me. You dont understand. My father and Mr Mangan were boys together. Mr Ma—

MRS HUSHABYE. I dont care what they were: we must sit down if you are going to begin as far back as that [*She snatches at Ellie's waist, and makes her sit down on the sofa beside her*]. Now, pettikins: tell me all about Mr Mangan. They call him Boss Mangan, dont they? He is a Napoleon of industry and disgustingly rich, isn't he? Why isnt your father rich?

ELLIE. My poor father should never have been in business. His parents were poets; and they gave him the noblest ideas; but they could not afford to give him a profession.

MRS HUSHABYE. Fancy your grandparents, with their eyes in fine frenzy rolling! And so your poor father had to go into business. Hasnt he succeeded in it?

ELLIE. He always used to say he could succeed if he only had some capital. He fought his way along, to keep a roof over our heads and bring us up well; but it was always a struggle: always the same difficulty of not having capital enough. I dont know how to describe it to you.

MRS HUSHABYE. Poor Ellie! I know. Pulling the devil by the tail.

ELLIE [*hurt*] Oh no. Not like that. It was at least dignified.

MRS HUSHABYE. That made it all the harder, didnt it? *I* shouldnt have pulled the devil by the tail with dignity. I should have pulled hard— [*between her teeth*] hard. Well? Go on.

ELLIE. At last it seemed that all our troubles were at an end. Mr Mangan did an extraordinarily noble thing out of pure friendship for my father and respect for his character. He asked him how much capital he wanted, and gave it to him. I dont mean that he lent it to him, or that he invested it in his business. He just simply made him a present of it. Wasnt that splendid of him?

MRS HUSHABYE. On condition that you married him?

ELLIE. Oh no, no, no. This was when I was a child. He had never even seen me: he never came to our house. It was absolutely disinterested. Pure generosity.

MRS HUSHABYE. Oh! I beg the gentleman's pardon. Well, what became of the money?

ELLIE. We all got new clothes and moved into another house. And I went to another school for two years.

MRS HUSHABYE. Only two years?

ELLIE. That was all; for at the end of two years my father was utterly ruined.

MRS HUSHABYE. How?

ELLIE. I dont know. I never could understand. But it was dreadful. When we were poor my father had never been in debt. But when he launched out into business on a large scale, he had to incur liabilities. When the business went into liquidation he owed more money than Mr Mangan had given him.

MRS HUSHABYE. Bit off more than he could chew, I suppose.

ELLIE. I think you are a little unfeeling about it

MRS HUSHABYE. My pettikins: you musnt mind my way of talking. I was quite as sensitive and particular as you once; but I have picked up so much slang from the children that I am really hardly presentable. I suppose your father had no head for business, and made a mess of it.

ELLIE. Oh, that just shews how entirely you are mistaken about him. The business turned out a great success. It now pays forty-four per cent after deducting the excess profits tax.

MRS HUSHABYE. Then why arnt you rolling in money?

ELLIE. I dont know. It seems very unfair to me. You see, my father was made bankrupt. It nearly broke his heart, because he had persuaded several of his friends to put money into the business. He was sure it would succeed; and events proved that he was quite right. But they all lost their money. It was dreadful. I dont know what we should have done but for Mr Mangan.

MRS HUSHABYE. What! Did the Boss come to the rescue again, after all his money being thrown away?

ELLIE. He did indeed, and never uttered a reproach to my father. He bought what was left of the business—the buildings and the machinery and things—from the official

trustee for enough money to enable my father to pay six
and eightpence in the pound and get his discharge. Everyone pitied papa so much, and saw so plainly that he was
an honorable man, that they let him off at six-and-eight-
pence instead of ten shillings. Then Mr Mangan started a
company to take up the business, and made my father a
manager in it to save us from starvation; for I wasnt
earning anything then.

MRS HUSHABYE. Quite a romance. And when did the Boss
develop the tender passion?

ELLIE. Oh, that was years after, quite lately. He took the
chair one night at a sort of people's concert. I was singing
there. As an amateur, you know: half a guinea for expenses and three songs with three encores. He was so
pleased with my singing that he asked might he walk
home with me. I never saw anyone so taken aback as he
was when I took him home and introduced him to my
father: his own manager. It was then that my father told
me how nobly he had behaved. Of course it was considered a great chance for me, as he is so rich. And—
and—we drifted into a sort of understanding—I suppose
I should call it an engagement— [*she is distressed and
cannot go on*].

MRS HUSHABYE [*rising and marching about*] You may have
drifted into it; but you will bounce out of it, my pettikins,
if I am to have anything to do with.

ELLIE [*hopelessly*] No: it's no use. I am bound in honor and
gratitude. I will go through with it.

MRS HUSHABYE [*behind the sofa, scolding down at her*] You
know, of course, that it's not honorable or grateful to
marry a man you dont love. Do you love this Mangan
man?

ELLIE. Yes. At least—

MRS HUSHABYE. I dont want to know about "the least": I
want to know the worst. Girls of your age fall in love
with all sorts of impossible people, especially old people.

ELLIE. I like Mr Mangan very much; and I shall always
be—

MRS HUSHABYE [*impatiently completing the sentence and*

prancing away intolerantly to starboard] —grateful to
him for his kindness to dear father. I know. Anybody
else?

ELLIE. What do you mean?

MRS HUSHABYE. Anybody else? Are you in love with anybody else?

ELLIE. Of course not.

MRS HUSHABYE. Humph! [*The book on the drawing-table
catches her eye. She picks it up, and evidently finds the
title very unexpected. She looks at Ellie, and asks,
quaintly*]. Quite sure youre not in love with an actor?

ELLIE. No, no. Why? What put such a thing into your head?

MRS HUSHABYE. This is yours, isnt it? Why else should you
be reading Othello?

ELLIE. My father taught me to love Shakespear.

MRS HUSHABYE [*flinging the book down on the table*] Really!
your father does seem to be about the limit.

ELLIE [*naïvely*] Do you never read Shakespear, Hesione?
That seems to me so extraordinary. I like Othello.

MRS HUSHABYE. Do you indeed? He was jealous, wasnt he?

ELLIS. Oh, not that. I think all the part about jealousy is
horrible. But dont you think it must have been a wonderful experience for Desdemona, brought up so quietly at
home, to meet a man who had been out in the world
doing all sorts of brave things and having terrible adventures, and yet finding something in her that made him
love to sit and talk with her and tell her about them?

MRS HUSHABYE. Thats your idea of romance, is it?

ELLIE. Not romance, exactly. It might really happen.

*Ellie's eyes shew that she is not arguing, but in a day-
dream. Mrs Hushabye, watching her inquisitively, goes
deliberately back to the sofa and resumes her seat beside
her.*

MRS HUSHABYE. Ellie darling: have you noticed that some
of those stories that Othello told Desdemona couldnt
have happened?

ELLIE. Oh no. Shakespear thought they could have
happened.

MRS HUSHABYE. Hm! Desdemona thought they could have
happened. But they didnt.

ELLIE. Why do you look so enigmatic about it? You are such a sphinx: I never know what you mean.

MRS HUSHABYE. Desdemona would have found him out if she had lived, you know. I wonder was that why he strangled her!

ELLIE. Othello was not telling lies.

MRS HUSHABYE. How do you know?

ELLIE. Shakespear would have said if he was. Hesione: there are men who have done wonderful things: men like Othello, only, of course, white, and very handsome, and—

MRS HUSHABYE. Ah! Now we're coming to it. Tell me all about him. I knew there must be somebody, or youd never have been so miserable about Mangan: youd have thought it quite a lark to marry him.

ELLIE [*blushing vividly*] Hesione: you are dreadful. But I dont want to make a secret of it, though of course I dont tell everybody. Besides, I dont know him.

MRS HUSHABYE. Dont know him! What does that mean?

ELLIE. Well, of course I know him to speak to.

MRS HUSHABYE. But you want to know him ever so much more intimately, eh?

ELLIE. No no: I know him quite—almost intimately.

MRS HUSHABYE. You dont know him; and you know him almost intimately. How lucid!

ELLIE. I mean that he does not call on us. I—I got into conversation with him by chance at a concert.

MRS HUSHABYE. You seem to have rather a gay time at your concerts, Ellie.

ELLIE. Not at all: we talk to everyone in the green-room waiting for our turns. I thought he was one of the artists: he looked so splendid. But he was only one of the committee. I happened to tell him that I was copying a picture at the National Gallery. I make a little money that way. I cant paint much; but as it's always the same picture I can do it pretty quickly and get two or three pounds for it. It happened that he came to the National Gallery one day.

MRS HUSHABYE. One student's day. Paid sixpence to stumble about through a crowd of easels, when he might have come in next day for nothing and found the floor clear! Quite by accident?

ELLIE [*triumphantly*] No. On purpose. He liked talking to me. He knows lots of the most splendid people. Fashionable women who are all in love with him. But he ran away from them to see me at the National Gallery and persuade me to come with him for a drive round Richmond Park in a taxi.

MRS HUSHABYE. My pettikins, you have been going it. It's wonderful what you good girls can do without anyone saying a word.

ELLIE. I am not in society, Hesione. If I didnt make acquaintances in that way I shouldnt have any at all.

MRS HUSHABYE. Well, no harm if you know how to take care of yourself. May I ask his name?

ELLIE [*slowly and musically*] Marcus Darnley.

MRS HUSHABYE [*echoing the music*] Marcus Darnley! What a splendid name!

ELLIE. Oh, I'm so glad you think so. I think so too; but I was afraid it was only a silly fancy of my own.

MRS HUSHABYE. Hm! Is he one of the Aberdeen Darnleys?

ELLIE. Nobody knows. Just fancy! He was found in an antique chest—

MRS HUSHABYE. A what?

ELLIE. An antique chest, one summer morning in a rose garden, after a night of the most terrible thunderstorm.

MRS HUSHABYE. What on earth was he doing in the chest? Did he get into it because he was afraid of the lightning?

ELLIE. Oh no, no: he was a baby. The name Marcus Darnley was embroidered on his babyclothes. And five hundred pounds in gold.

MRS HUSHABYE [*looking hard at her*] Ellie!

ELLIE. The garden of the Viscount—

MRS HUSHABYE.— de Rougement?

ELLIE [*innocently*] No: de Larochejaquelin. A French family. A vicomte. His life has been one long romance. A tiger—

MRS HUSHABYE. Slain by his own hand?

ELLIE. Oh no: nothing vulgar like that. He saved the life of the tiger from a hunting party: one of King Edward's hunting parties in India. The King was furious: that was why he never had his military services properly recognized. But he doesnt care. He is a Socialist and despises rank, and has been in three revolutions fighting on the barricades.

MRS HUSHABYE. How can you sit there telling me such lies? You, Ellie, of all people! And I thought you were a perfectly simple, straightforward, good girl.

ELLIE [*rising, dignified but very angry*] Do you mean to say you dont believe me?

MRS HUSHABYE. Of course I dont believe you. Youre inventing every word of it. Do you take me for a fool?

Ellie stares at her. Her candor is so obvious that Mrs Hushabye is puzzled.

ELLIE. Goodbye, Hesione. I'm very sorry. I see now that it sounds very improbable as I tell it. But I cant stay if you think that way about me.

MRS HUSHABYE [*catching her dress*] You shant go. I couldnt be so mistaken: I know too well what liars are like. Somebody has really told you all this.

ELLIE [*flushing*] Hesione: dont say that you dont believe h i m. I couldnt bear that.

MRS HUSHABYE [*soothing her*] Of course I believe him, dearest. But you shouldnt have broken it to me by degrees. [*Drawing her back to the seat*] Now tell me all about him. Are you in love with him?

ELLIE. Oh no, I'm not so foolish. I dont fall in love with people. I'm not so silly as you think.

MRS HUSHABYE. I see. Only something to think about—to give some interest and pleasure to life.

ELLIE. Just so. Thats all, really.

MRS HUSHABYE. It makes the hours go fast, doesnt it? No tedious waiting to go to sleep at nights and wondering whether you will have a bad night. How delightful it makes waking up in the morning! How much better than the happiest dream! All life transfigured! No more wishing one had an interesting book to read, because life is so much happier than any book! No desire but to be alone and not have to talk to anyone: to be alone and just think about it.

ELLIE [*embracing her*] Hesione: you are a witch. How do
you know? Oh, you are the most sympathetic woman in
the world.

MRS HUSHABYE [*caressing her*] Pettikins, my pettikins: how
I envy you! and how I pity you!

ELLIE. Pity me! Oh, why?

*A very handsome man of fifty, with mousquetaire
moustaches, wearing a rather dandified curly brimmed
hat, and carrying an elaborate walking-stick, comes into
the room from the hall, and stops short at sight of the
women on the sofa.*

ELLIE [*seeing him and rising in glad surprise*]. Oh! Hesione:
this is Mr Marcus Darnley.

MRS HUSHABYE [*rising*] What a lark! He is my husband.

ELLIE. But how— [*she stops suddenly; then turns pale and
sways*].

MRS HUSHABYE [*catching her and sitting down with her on
the sofa*] Steady, my pettikins.

THE MAN [*with a mixture of confusion and effrontery, depositing his hat and stick on the teak table*] My real
name, Miss Dunn, is Hector Hushabye. I leave you to
judge whether that is a name any sensitive man would
care to confess to. I never use it when I can possibly help
it. I have been away for nearly a month; and I had no
idea you knew my wife, or that you were coming here. I
am none the less delighted to find you in our little house.

ELLIE [*in great distress*] I dont know what to do. Please,
may I speak to papa? Do leave me. I cant bear it.

MRS HUSHABYE. Be off, Hector.

HECTOR. I—

MRS HUSHABYE. Quick, quick. Get out.

HECTOR. If you think it better— [*he goes out, taking his hat
with him but leaving the stick on the table*].

MRS HUSHABYE [*laying Ellie down at the end of the sofa*]
Now, pettikins, he is gone. Theres nobody but me. You
can let yourself go. Dont try to control yourself. Have a
good cry.

ELLIE [*raising her head*] Damn!

MRS HUSHABYE. Splendid! Oh, what a relief! I thought you

were going to be broken-hearted. Never mind me. Damn
him again.

ELLIE. I am not damning him: I am damning myself for
being such a fool. [*Rising*] How could I let myself be
taken in so? [*She begins prowling to and fro, her bloom
gone, looking curiously older and harder*].

MRS HUSHABYE [*cheerfully*] Why not, pettikins? Very few
young women can resist Hector. I couldnt when I was
your age. He is really rather splendid, you know.

ELLIE [*turning on her*] Splendid! Yes: splendid l o o k i n g,
of course. But how can you love a liar?

MRS HUSHABYE. I dont know. But you can, fortunately.
Otherwise there wouldnt be much love in the world.

ELLIE. But to lie like that! To be a boaster! a coward!

MRS HUSHABYE [*rising in alarm*] Pettikins: none of that, if
you please. If you hint the slightest doubt of Hector's
courage he will go straight off and do the most horribly
dangerous things to convince himself that he isnt a
coward. He has a dreadful trick of getting out of one
third-floor window and coming in at another, just to test
his nerve. He has a whole drawerful of Albert Medals for
saving people's lives.

ELLIE. He never told me that.

MRS HUSHABYE. He never boasts of anything he really did:
he cant bear it; and it makes him shy if anyone else does.
All his stories are made-up stories.

ELLIE [*coming to her*] Do you mean that he is really brave,
and really has adventures, and yet tells lies about things
that he never did and that never happened?

MRS HUSHABYE. Yes, pettikins, I do. People dont have their
virtues and vices in sets: they have them anyhow: all
mixed.

ELLIE [*staring at her thoughtfully*] Theres something odd
about this house, Hesione, and even about you. I dont
know why I'm talking to you so calmly. I have a horrible
fear that my heart is broken, but that heartbreak is not
like what I thought it must be.

MRS HUSHABYE [*fondling her*] It's only life educating you,
pettikins. How do you feel about Boss Mangan now?

ELLIE [*disengaging herself with an expression of distaste*]
Oh, how can you remind me of him, Hesione?

MRS HUSHABYE. Sorry, dear. I think I hear Hector coming
back. You dont mind now, do you, dear?

ELLIE. Not in the least. I am quite cured.

Mazzini Dunn and Hector come in from the hall.

HECTOR [*as he opens the door and allows Mazzini to pass
in*] One second more, and she would have been a dead
woman!

MAZZINI. Dear! dear! what an escape! Ellie, my love: Mr
Hushabye has just been telling me the most extraordinary—

ELLIE. Yes: Ive heard it [*She crosses to the other side of the
room*].

HECTOR [*following her*] Not this one: I'll tell it to you after
dinner. I think youll like it. The truth is, I made it up for
you, and I was looking forward to the pleasure of telling
it to you. But in a moment of impatience at being turned
out of the room, I threw it away on your father.

ELLIE [*turning at bay with her back to the carpenter's
bench, scornfully self-possessed*] It was not thrown away.
He believes it. I should not have believed it.

MAZZINI [*benevolently*] Ellie is very naughty, Mr Hushabye.
Of course she does not really think that. [*He goes to the
bookshelves, and inspects the titles of the volumes*].

*Boss Mangan comes in from the hall, followed by the
Captain. Mangan, carefully frock-coated as for church
or for a directors' meeting, is about fifty-five, with a careworn, mistrustful expression, standing a little on an entirely imaginary dignity, with a dull complexion, straight,
lustreless hair, and features so entirely commonplace that
it is impossible to describe them.*

CAPTAIN SHOTOVER [*to Mrs Hushabye, introducing the newcomer*] Says his name is Mangan. Not ablebodied.

MRS HUSHABYE [*graciously*] How do you do, Mr Mangan?

MANGAN [*shaking hands*] Very pleased.

CAPTAIN SHOTOVER. Dunn's lost his muscle, but recovered
his nerve. Men seldom do after three attacks of delirium
tremens [*he goes into the pantry*].

MRS HUSHABYE. I congratulate you, Mr Dunn.

MAZZINI [*dazed*] I am a lifelong teetotaler.

MRS HUSHABYE. You will find it far less trouble to let papa have his own way than try to explain.

MAZZINI. But three attacks of delirium tremens, really!

MRS HUSHABYE [*to Mangan*] Do you know my husband, Mr Mangan [*she indicates Hector*].

MANGAN [*going to Hector, who meets him with outstretched hand*] Very pleased. [*Turning to Ellie*] I hope, Miss Ellie, you have not found the journey down too fatiguing. [*They shake hands*].

MRS HUSHABYE. Hector: shew Mr Dunn his room.

HECTOR. Certainly. Come along, Mr Dunn. [*He takes Mazzini out*].

ELLIE. You havnt shewn me my room yet, Hesione.

MRS HUSHABYE. How stupid of me! Come along. Make yourself quite at home, Mr Mangan. Papa will entertain you. [*She calls to the Captain in the pantry*] Papa: come and explain the house to Mr Mangan.

    She goes out with Ellie. The Captain comes from the pantry.

CAPTAIN SHOTOVER. Youre going to marry Dunn's daughter. Dont. Youre too old.

MANGAN [*staggered*] Well! Thats fairly blunt, Captain.

CAPTAIN SHOTOVER. It's true.

MANGAN. She doesnt think so.

CAPTAIN SHOTOVER. She does.

MANGAN. Older men than I have—

CAPTAIN SHOTOVER [*finishing the sentence for him*] —made fools of themselves. That, also, is true.

MANGAN [*asserting himself*] I dont see that this is any business of yours.

CAPTAIN SHOTOVER. It is everybody's business. The stars in their courses are shaken when such things happen.

MANGAN. I'm going to marry her all the same.

CAPTAIN SHOTOVER. How do you know?

MANGAN [*playing the strong man*] I intend to. I mean to. See? I never made up my mind to do a thing yet that I didnt bring it off. Thats the sort of man I am; and there will be a better understanding between us when you make up your mind to that, Captain.

CAPTAIN SHOTOVER. You frequent picture palaces.

MANGAN. Perhaps I do. Who told you?

CAPTAIN SHOTOVER. Talk like a man, not like a movy. You mean that you make a hundred thousand a year.

MANGAN. I dont boast. But when I meet a man that makes a hundred thousand a year, I take off my hat to that man, and stretch out my hand to him and call him brother.

CAPTAIN SHOTOVER. Then you also make a hundred thousand a year, hey?

MANGAN. No. I cant say that. Fifty thousand, perhaps.

CAPTAIN SHOTOVER. His half brother only [*he turns away from Mangan with his usual abruptness, and collects the empty tea-cups on the Chinese tray*].

MANGAN [*irritated*] See here, Captain Shotover. I dont quite understand my position here. I came here on your daughter's invitation. Am I in her house or in yours?

CAPTAIN SHOTOVER. You are beneath the dome of heaven, in the house of God. What is true within these walls is true outside them. Go out on the seas; climb the mountains; wander through the valleys. She is still too young.

MANGAN [*weakening*] But I'm very little over fifty.

CAPTAIN SHOTOVER. You are still less under sixty. Boss Mangan: you will not marry the pirate's child [*he carries the tray away into the pantry*].

MANGAN [*following him to the half door*] What pirate's child? What are you talking about?

CAPTAIN SHOTOVER [*in the pantry*] Ellie Dunn. You will not marry her.

MANGAN. Who will stop me?

CAPTAIN SHOTOVER [*emerging*] My daughter [*he makes for the door leading to the hall*].

MANGAN [*following him*] Mrs Hushabye! Do you mean to say she brought me down here to break it off?

CAPTAIN SHOTOVER [*stopping and turning on him*] I know nothing more than I have seen in her eye. She will break it off. Take my advice: marry a West Indian negress: they make excellent wives. I was married to one myself for two years.

MANGAN. Well, I am damned!

CAPTAIN SHOTOVER. I thought so. I was, too, for many years. The negress redeemed me.

MANGAN [*feebly*] This is queer. I ought to walk out of this house.

CAPTAIN SHOTOVER. Why?

MANGAN. Well, many men would be offended by your style of talking.

CAPTAIN SHOTOVER. Nonsense! It's the other sort of talking that makes quarrels. Nobody ever quarrels with me.

A gentleman, whose firstrate tailoring and frictionless manners proclaim the wellbred West Ender, comes in from the hall. He has an engaging air of being young and unmarried, but on close inspection is found to be at least over forty.

THE GENTLEMAN. Excuse my intruding in this fashion; but there is no knocker on the door; and the bell does not seem to ring.

CAPTAIN SHOTOVER. Why should there be a knocker? Why should the bell ring? The door is open.

THE GENTLEMAN. Precisely. So I ventured to come in.

CAPTAIN SHOTOVER. Quite right. I will see about a room for you [*he makes for the door*].

THE GENTLEMAN [*stopping him*] But I'm afraid you dont know who I am.

CAPTAIN SHOTOVER. Do you suppose that at my age I make distinctions between one fellowcreature and another? [*He goes out. Mangan and the newcomer stare at one another*].

MANGAN. Strange character, Captain Shotover, sir.

THE GENTLEMAN. Very.

CAPTAIN SHOTOVER [*shouting outside*] Hesione: another person has arrived and wants a room. Man about town, well dressed, fifty.

THE GENTLEMAN. Fancy Hesione's feelings! May I ask are you a member of the family?

MANGAN. No.

THE GENTLEMAN. I am. At least a connexion.

Mrs Hushabye comes back.

MRS HUSHABYE. How do you do? How good of you to come!

THE GENTLEMAN. I am very glad indeed to make your acquaintance, Hesione. [*Instead of taking her hand he kisses her. At the same moment the Captain appears in the doorway*]. You will excuse my kissing your daughter, Captain, when I tell you that—

CAPTAIN SHOTOVER. Stuff! Everyone kisses my daughter. Kiss her as much as you like [*he makes for the pantry*].

THE GENTLEMAN. Thank you. One moment. Captain. [*The Captain halts and turns. The gentleman goes to him affably*]. Do you happen to remember—but probably you dont, as it occurred many years ago—that your younger daughter married a numskull.

CAPTAIN SHOTOVER. Yes. She said she'd marry anybody to get away from this house. I should not have recognized you: your head is no longer like a walnut. Your aspect is softened. You have been boiled in bread and milk for years and years, like other married men. Poor devil! [*He disappears into the pantry*].

MRS HUSHABYE [*going past Mangan to the gentleman and scrutinizing him*] I dont believe you are Hastings Utterword.

THE GENTLEMAN. I am not.

MRS HUSHABYE. Then what business had you to kiss me?

THE GENTLEMAN. I thought I would like to. The fact is, I am Randall Utterword, the unworthy younger brother of Hastings. I was abroad diplomatizing when he was married.

LADY UTTERWORD [*dashing in*] Hesione: where is the key of the wardrobe in my room? My diamonds are in my dressing-bag: I must lock it up— [*recognizing the stranger with a shock*] Randall: how dare you? [*She marches at him past Mrs Hushabye, who retreats and joins Mangan near the sofa*].

RANDALL. How dare I what? I am not doing anything.

LADY UTTERWORD. Who told you I was here?

RANDALL. Hastings. You had just left when I called on you at Claridge's; so I followed you down here. You are looking extremely well.

LADY UTTERWORD. Dont presume to tell me so.

MRS HUSHABYE. What is wrong with Mr Randall, Addy?

LADY UTTERWORD [*recollecting herself*] Oh, nothing. But he
has no right to come bothering you and papa without
being invited [*she goes to the window-seat and sits down,
turning away from them ill-humoredly and looking into
the garden, where Hector and Ellie are now seen strolling
together*].

MRS HUSHABYE. I think you have not met Mr Mangan,
Addy.

LADY UTTERWORD [*turning her head and nodding coldly to
Mangan*] I beg your pardon. Randall: you have flustered
me so: I made a perfect fool of myself.

MRS HUSHABYE. Lady Utterword. My sister. My younger
sister.

MANGAN [*bowing*] Pleased to meet you, Lady Utterword.

LADY UTTERWORD [*with marked interest*] Who is that gentleman walking in the garden with Miss Dunn?

MRS HUSHABYE. I dont know. She quarrelled mortally with
my husband only ten minutes ago; and I didnt know
anyone else had come. It must be a visitor. [*She goes to
the window to look*]. Oh, it i s Hector. Theyve made it up.

LADY UTTERWORD. Your husband! That handsome man?

MRS HUSHABYE. Well, why shouldnt my husband be a
handsome man?

RANDALL [*joining them at the window*] One's husband never
is, Ariadne [*he sits by Lady Utterword, on her right*].

MRS HUSHABYE. One's sister's husband always is, Mr.
Randall.

LADY UTTERWORD. Dont be vulgar, Randall. And you,
Hesione, are just as bad.

*Ellie and Hector come in from the garden by the star-
board door. Randall rises. Ellie retires into the corner
near the pantry. Hector comes forward; and Lady Utterword rises looking her very best.*

MRS HUSHABYE. Hector: this is Addy.

HECTOR [*apparently surprised*] Not this lady.

LADY UTTERWORD [*smiling*] Why not?

HECTOR [*looking at her with a piercing glance of deep but
respectful admiration, his moustache bristling*] I thought

— [*pulling himself together*] I beg your pardon, Lady Utterword. I am extremely glad to welcome you at last under our roof [*he offers his hand with grave courtesy*].

MRS HUSHABYE. She wants to be kissed, Hector.

LADY UTTERWORD. Hesione! [*but she still smiles*].

MRS HUSHABYE. Call her Addy; and kiss her like a good brother-in-law; and have done with it. [*She leaves them to themselves*].

HECTOR. Behave yourself, Hesione. Lady Utterword is entitled not only to hospitality but to civilization.

LADY UTTERWORD [*gratefully*] Thank you, Hector. [*They shake hands cordially*].

   Mazzini Dunn is seen crossing the garden from starboard to port.

CAPTAIN SHOTOVER [*coming from the pantry and addressing Ellie*] Your father has washed himself.

ELLIE [*quite self-possessed*] He often does, Captain Shotover.

CAPTAIN SHOTOVER. A strange conversion! I saw him through the pantry window.

   Mazzini Dunn enters through the port window door, newly washed and brushed, and stops, smiling benevolently, between Mangan and Mrs Hushabye.

MRS HUSHABYE [*introducing*] Mr Mazzini Dunn, Lady Ut— oh, I forgot: youve met. [*Indicating Ellie*] Miss Dunn.

MAZZINI [*walking across the room to take Ellie's hand, and beaming at his own naughty irony*] I have met Miss Dunn also. She is my daughter. [*He draws her arm through his caressingly*].

MRS HUSHABYE. Of course: how stupid! Mr Utterword, my sister's—er—

RANDALL [*shaking hands agreeably*] Her brother-in-law, Mr Dunn. How do you do?

MRS HUSHABYE. This is my husband.

HECTOR. We have met, dear. Dont introduce us any more. [*He moves away to the big chair, and adds*] Wont you sit down, Lady Utterword? [*She does so very graciously*].

MRS HUSHABYE. Sorry. I hate it: it's like making people shew their tickets.

MAZZINI [*sententiously*] How little it tells us, after all! The great question is, not who we are, but what we are.

CAPTAIN SHOTOVER. Ha! What are you?

MAZZINI [*taken aback*] What am I?

CAPTAIN SHOTOVER. A thief, a pirate, and a murderer.

MAZZINI. I assure you you are mistaken.

CAPTAIN SHOTOVER. An adventurous life; but what does it end in? Respectability. A ladylike daughter. The language and appearance of a city missionary. Let it be a warning to all of you [*he goes out through the garden*].

DUNN. I hope nobody here believes that I am a thief, a pirate, or a murderer. Mrs Hushabye: will you excuse me a moment? I must really go and explain. [*He follows the Captain*].

MRS HUSHABYE [*as he goes*] It's no use. Youd really better— [*but Dunn has vanished*]. We had better all go out and look for some tea. We never have regular tea; but you can always get some when you want: the servants keep it stewing all day. The kitchen veranda is the best place to ask. May I shew you? [*She goes to the starboard door*].

RANDALL [*going with her*] Thank you, I dont think I'll take any tea this afternoon. But if you will shew me the garden— ?

MRS HUSHABYE. Theres nothing to see in the garden except papa's observatory, and a gravel pit with a cave where he keeps dynamite and things of that sort. However, it's pleasanter out of doors; so come along.

RANDALL. Dynamite! Isn't that rather risky?

MRS HUSHABYE. Well, we dont sit in the gravel pit when theres a thunderstorm.

LADY UTTERWORD. Thats something new. What is the dynamite for?

HECTOR. To blow up the human race if it goes too far. He is trying to discover a psychic ray that will explode all the explosives at the will of a Mahatma.

ELLIE. The Captain's tea is delicious, Mr Utterword.

MRS HUSHABYE [*stopping in the doorway*] Do you mean to say that youve had some of my father's tea? that you got round him before you were ten minutes in the house?

ELLIE. I did.

MRS HUSHABYE. You little devil! [*She goes out with Randall*].

MANGAN. Wont you come, Miss Ellie?

ELLIE. I'm too tired. I'll take a book up to my room and rest a little. [*She goes to the bookshelf*].

MANGAN. Right. You cant do better. But I'm disappointed. [*He follows Randall and Mrs Hushabye*].

　　Ellie, Hector, and Lady Utterword are left. Hector is close to Lady Utterword. They look at Ellie, waiting for her to go.

ELLIE [*looking at the title of a book*] Do you like stories of adventure, Lady Utterword?

LADY UTTERWORD [*patronizingly*] Of course, dear.

ELLIE. Then I'll leave you to Mr Hushabye. [*She goes out through the hall*].

HECTOR. That girl is mad about tales of adventure. The lies I have to tell her!

LADY UTTERWORD [*not interested in Ellie*] When you saw me what did you mean by saying that you thought, and then stopping short? What did you think?

HECTOR [*folding his arms and looking down at her magnetically*] May I tell you?

LADY UTTERWORD. Of course.

HECTOR. It will not sound very civil. I was on the point of saying "I thought you were a plain woman."

LADY UTTERWORD. Oh for shame, Hector! What right had you to notice whether I am plain or not?

HECTOR. Listen to me, Ariadne. Until today I have seen only photographs of you; and no photograph can give the strange fascination of the daughters of that supernatural old man. There is some damnable quality in them that destroys men's moral sense, and carries them beyond honor and dishonor. You know that, dont you?

LADY UTTERWORD. Perhaps I do, Hector. But let me warn you once for all that I am a rigidly conventional woman. You may think because I'm a Shotover that I'm a Bohemian, because we are all so horribly Bohemian. But I'm not. I hate and loathe Bohemianism. No child brought up in a strict Puritan household ever suffered from Puritanism as I suffered from our Bohemianism.

HECTOR. Our children are like that. They spend their holidays in the houses of their respectable schoolfellows.

LADY UTTERWORD. I shall invite them for Christmas.

HECTOR. Their absence leaves us both without our natural chaperons.

LADY UTTERWORD. Children are certainly very inconvenient sometimes. But intelligent people can always manage, unless they are Bohemians.

HECTOR. You are no Bohemian; but you are no Puritan either: your attraction is alive and powerful. What sort of woman do you count yourself?

LADY UTTERWORD. I am a woman of the world, Hector; and I can assure you that if you will only take the trouble always to do the perfectly correct thing, and to say the perfectly correct thing, you can do just what you like. An ill-conducted, careless woman gets simply no chance. An ill-conducted, careless man is never allowed within arm's length of any woman worth knowing.

HECTOR. I see. You are neither a Bohemian woman nor a Puritan woman. You are a dangerous woman.

LADY UTTERWORD. On the contrary, I am a safe woman.

HECTOR. You are a most accursedly attractive woman. Mind: I am not making love to you. I do not like being attracted. But you had better know how I feel if you are going to stay here.

LADY UTTERWORD. You are an exceedingly clever ladykiller, Hector. And terribly handsome. I am quite a good player, myself, at that game. Is it quite understood that we are only playing?

HECTOR. Quite. I am deliberately playing the fool, out of sheer worthlessness.

LADY UTTERWORD [*rising brightly*] Well, you are my brother-in-law. Hesione asked you to kiss me. [*He seizes her in his arms, and kisses her strenuously*]. Oh! that was a little more than play, brother-in-law. [*She pushes him suddenly away*]. You shall not do that again.

HECTOR. In effect, you got your claws deeper into me than I intended.

MRS HUSHABYE [*coming in from the garden*] Dont let me disturb you: I only want a cap to put on daddiest. The sun is setting; and he'll catch cold [*she makes for the door leading to the hall*].

LADY UTTERWORD. Your husband is quite charming, darling. He has actually condescended to kiss me at last. I shall go into the garden: it's cooler now [*she goes out by the port door*].

MRS HUSHABYE. Take care, dear child. I dont believe any man can kiss Addy without falling in love with her. [*She goes into the hall*].

HECTOR [*striking himself on the chest*] Fool! Goat!

Mrs Hushabye comes back with the Captain's cap.

HECTOR. Your sister is an extremely enterprising old girl. Wheres Miss Dunn!

MRS HUSHABYE. Mangan says she has gone up to her room for a nap. Addy wont let you talk to Ellie: she marked you for her own.

HECTOR. She has the diabolical family fascination. I began making love to her automatically. What am I to do? I cant fall in love; and I cant hurt a woman's feelings by telling her so when she falls in love with me. And as women are always falling in love with my moustache I get landed in all sorts of tedious and terrifying flirtations in which I'm not a bit in earnest.

MRS HUSHABYE. Oh, neither is Addy. She has never been in love in her life, though she has always been trying to fall in head over ears. She is worse than you, because you had one real go at least, with me.

HECTOR. That was a confounded madness. I cant believe that such an amazing experience is common. It has left its mark on me. I believe that is why I have never been able to repeat it.

MRS HUSHABYE [*laughing and caressing his arm*] We were frightfully in love with one another, Hector. It was such an enchanting dream that I have never been able to grudge it to you or anyone else since. I have invited all sorts of pretty women to the house on the chance of giving you another turn. But it has never come off.

HECTOR. I dont know that I want it to come off. It was damned dangerous. You fascinated me; but I loved you;

so it was heaven. This sister of yours fascinates me; but I hate her; so it is hell. I shall kill her if she persists.

MRS HUSHABYE. Nothing will kill Addy: she is as strong as a horse. [*Releasing him*] Now *I* am going off to fascinate somebody.

HECTOR. The Foreign Office toff? Randall?

MRS HUSHABYE. Goodness gracious, no! Why should I fascinate him?

HECTOR. I presume you dont mean the bloated capitalist, Mangan?

MRS HUSHABYE. Hm! I think he had better be fascinated by me than by Ellie. [*She is going into the garden when the Captain comes in from it with some sticks in his hand*]. What have you got there, daddiest?

CAPTAIN SHOTOVER. Dynamite.

MRS HUSHABYE. Youve been to the gravel pit. Dont drop it about the house: theres a dear. [*She goes into the garden, where the evening light is now very red*].

HECTOR. Listen, O sage. How long dare you concentrate on a feeling without risking having it fixed in your consciousness all the rest of your life?

CAPTAIN SHOTOVER. Ninety minutes. An hour and a half. [*He goes into the pantry*].

Hector, left alone, contracts his brows, and falls into a daydream. He does not move for some time. Then he folds his arms. Then, throwing his hands behind him, and gripping one with the other, he strides tragically once to and fro. Suddenly he snatches his walking-stick from the teak table, and draws it; for it is a sword-stick. He fights a desperate duel with an imaginary antagonist, and after many vicissitudes runs him through the body up to the hilt. He sheathes his sword and throws it on the sofa, falling into another reverie as he does so. He looks straight into the eyes of an imaginary woman; seizes her by the arms; and says in a deep and thrilling tone "Do you love me!" The Captain comes out of the pantry at this moment; and Hector, caught with his arms stretched out and his fists clenched, has to account for his attitude by going through a series of gymnastic exercises.

CAPTAIN SHOTOVER. That sort of strength is no good. You will never be as strong as a gorilla.

HECTOR. What is the dynamite for?

CAPTAIN SHOTOVER. To kill fellows like Mangan.

HECTOR. No use. They will always be able to buy more dynamite than you.

CAPTAIN SHOTOVER. I will make a dynamite that he cannot explode.

HECTOR. And that you can, eh?

CAPTAIN SHOTOVER. Yes: when I have attained the seventh degree of concentration.

HECTOR. Whats the use of that? You never do attain it.

CAPTAIN SHOTOVER. What then is to be done? Are we to be kept for ever in the mud by these hogs to whom the universe is nothing but a machine for greasing their bristles and filling their snouts?

HECTOR. Are Mangan's bristles worse than Randall's love-locks?

CAPTAIN SHOTOVER. We must win powers of life and death over them both. I refuse to die until I have invented the means.

HECTOR. Who are we that we should judge them?

CAPTAIN SHOTOVER. What are they that they should judge us? Yet they do, unhesitatingly. There is enmity between our seed and their seed. They know it and act on it, strangling our souls. They believe in themselves. When we believe in ourselves, we shall kill them.

HECTOR. It is the same seed. You forget that your pirate has a very nice daughter. Mangan's son may be a Plato: Randall's a Shelley. What was my father?

CAPTAIN SHOTOVER. The damndest scoundrel I ever met. [*He replaces the drawing-board; sits down at the table; and begins to mix a wash of color*].

HECTOR. Precisely. Well, dare you kill his innocent grand-children?

CAPTAIN SHOTOVER. They are mine also.

HECTOR. Just so. We are members one of another. [*He throws himself carelessly on the sofa*]. I tell you I have often thought of this killing of human vermin. Many men have thought of it. Decent men are like Daniel in the lion's den: their survival is a miracle; and they do not always survive. We live among the Mangans and Randalls and Billie Dunns as they, poor devils, live among the disease germs and the doctors and the lawyers and the parsons and the restaurant chefs and the tradesmen and the servants and all the rest of the parasites and blackmailers. What are our terrors to theirs? Give me the power to kill them; and I'll spare them in sheer—

CAPTAIN SHOTOVER [*cutting in sharply*] Fellow feeling?

HECTOR. No. I should kill myself if I believed that. I must believe that my spark, small as it is, is divine, and that the red light over their door is hell fire. I should spare them in simple magnanimous pity.

CAPTAIN SHOTOVER. You cant spare them until you have the power to kill them. At present they have the power to kill you. There are millions of blacks over the water for them to train and let loose on us. Theyre going to do it. Theyre doing it already.

HECTOR. They are too stupid to use their power.

CAPTAIN SHOTOVER [*throwing down his brush and coming to the end of the sofa*] Do not deceive yourself: they do use it. We kill the better half of ourselves every day to propitiate them. The knowledge that these people are there to render all our aspirations barren prevents us having the aspirations. And when we are tempted to seek their destruction they bring forth demons to delude us, disguised as pretty daughters, and singers and poets and the like, for whose sake we spare them.

HECTOR [*sitting up and leaning towards him*] May not Hesione be such a demon, brought forth by you lest I should slay you?

CAPTAIN SHOTOVER. That is possible. She has used you up, and left you nothing but dreams, as some women do.

HECTOR. Vampire women, demon women.

CAPTAIN SHOTOVER. Men think the world well lost for them, and lose it accordingly. Who are the men that do things? The husbands of the shrew and of the drunkard, the men with the thorn in the flesh. [*Walking distractedly away towards the pantry*] I must think these things out. [*Turning suddenly*] But I go on with the dynamite none the

less. I will discover a ray mightier than any X-ray: a
mind ray that will explode the ammunition in the belt of
my adversary before he can point his gun at me. And I
must hurry. I am old: I have no time to waste in talk
[*he is about to go into the pantry, and Hector is making
for the hall, when Hesione comes back*].

MRS HUSHABYE. Daddiest: you and Hector must come and
help me to entertain all these people. What on earth were
you shouting about?

HECTOR [*stopping in the act of turning the doorhandle*] He
is madder than usual.

MRS HUSHABYE. We all are.

HECTOR. I must change [*he resumes his door opening*].

MRS HUSHABYE. Stop, stop. Come back, both of you. Come
back. [*They return, reluctantly*]. Money is running
short.

HECTOR. Money! Where are my April dividends?

MRS HUSHABYE. Where is the snow that fell last year?

CAPTAIN SHOTOVER. Where is all the money you had for
that patent lifeboat I invented?

MRS HUSHABYE. Five hundred pounds; and I have made it
last since Easter!

CAPTAIN SHOTOVER. Since Easter! Barely four months!
Monstrous extravagance! I could live for seven years on
£500.

MRS HUSHABYE. Not keeping open house as we do here,
daddiest.

CAPTAIN SHOTOVER. Only £500 for that lifeboat! I got
twelve thousand for the invention before that.

MRS HUSHABYE. Yes, dear; but that was for the ship with
the magnetic keel that sucked up submarines. Living at
the rate we do, you cannot afford life-saving inventions.
Cant you think of something that will murder half
Europe at one bang?

CAPTAIN SHOTOVER. No. I am ageing fast. My mind does
not dwell on slaughter as it did when I was a boy. Why
doesnt your husband invent something? He does nothing
but tell lies to women.

HECTOR. Well, that is a form of invention, is it not? However, you are right: I ought to support my wife.

MRS HUSHABYE. Indeed you shall do nothing of the sort: I should never see you from breakfast to dinner. I want my husband.

HECTOR [*bitterly*] I might as well be your lapdog.

MRS HUSHABYE. Do you want to be my breadwinner, like the other poor husbands?

HECTOR. No, by thunder! What a damned creature a husband is anyhow!

MRS HUSHABYE [*to the Captain*] What about that harpoon cannon?

CAPTAIN SHOTOVER. No use. It kills whales, not men.

MRS HUSHABYE. Why not? You fire the harpoon out of a cannon. It sticks in the enemy's general; you wind him in; and there you are.

HECTOR. You are your father's daughter, Hesione.

CAPTAIN SHOTOVER. There is something in it. Not to wind in generals: they are not dangerous. But one could fire a grapnel and wind in a machine gun or even a tank. I will think it out.

MRS HUSHABYE [*squeezing the Captain's arm affectionately*] Saved! You a r e a darling, daddiest. Now we must go back to these dreadful people and entertain them.

CAPTAIN SHOTOVER. They have had no dinner. Dont forget that.

HECTOR. Neither have I. And it is dark: it must be all hours.

MRS HUSHABYE. Oh, Guinness will produce some sort of dinner for them. The servants always take jolly good care that there is food in the house.

CAPTAIN SHOTOVER [*raising a strange wail in the darkness*] What a house! What a daughter!

MRS HUSHABYE [*raving*] What a father!

HECTOR [*following suit*] What a husband!

CAPTAIN SHOTOVER. Is there no thunder in heaven?

HECTOR. Is there no beauty, no bravery, on earth?

MRS HUSHABYE. What do men want? They have their food, their firesides, their clothes mended, and our love at the end of the day. Why are they not satisfied? Why do they envy us the pain with which we bring them into the world, and make strange dangers and torments for themselves to be even with us?

CAPTAIN SHOTOVER [*weirdly chanting*]

> I built a house for my daughters, and opened the
>   doors thereof,
> That men might come for their choosing, and their
>   betters spring from their love;
> But one of them married a numskull;

HECTOR [*taking up the rhythm*]

>   The other a liar wed;

MRS HUSHABYE [*completing the stanza*]

> And now must she lie beside him, even as she made
>   her bed.

LADY UTTERWORD [*calling from the garden*] Hesione! Hesione! Where are you?

HECTOR. The cat is on the tiles.

MRS HUSHABYE. Coming, darling, coming [*she goes quickly
into the garden*].

> *The Captain goes back to his place at the table.*

HECTOR [*going into the hall*] Shall I turn up the lights for
you?

CAPTAIN SHOTOVER. No. Give me deeper darkness. Money
is not made in the light.

ACT II

*The same room, with the lights turned up and the curtains
drawn. Ellie comes in, followed by Mangan. Both are
dressed for dinner. She strolls to the drawing-table. He
comes between the table and the wicker chair.*

MANGAN. What a dinner! I dont call it a dinner: I call it
a meal.

ELLIE. I am accustomed to meals, Mr Mangan, and very
lucky to get them. Besides, the captain cooked some mac-
aroni for me.

MANGAN [*shuddering liverishly*] Too rich: I cant eat such
things. I suppose it's because I have to work so much with
my brain. Thats the worst of being a man of business:
you are always thinking, thinking, thinking. By the way,
now that we are alone, may I take the opportunity to
come to a little understanding with you?

ELLIE [*settling into the draughtsman's seat*] Certainly. I should like to.

MANGAN [*taken aback*] Should you? That surprises me; for I thought I noticed this afternoon that you avoided me all you could. Not for the first time either.

ELLIE. I was very tired and upset. I wasnt used to the ways of this extraordinary house. Please forgive me.

MANGAN. Oh, thats all right: I dont mind. But Captain Shotover has been talking to me about you. You and me, you know.

ELLIE [*interested*] The Captain! What did he say?

MANGAN. Well, he noticed the difference between our ages.

ELLIE. He notices everything.

MANGAN. You dont mind, then?

ELLIE. Of course I know quite well that our engagement—

MANGAN. Oh! you call it an engagement.

ELLIE. Well, isnt it?

MANGAN. Oh, yes, yes: no doubt it is if you hold to it. This is the first time youve used the word; and I didnt quite know where we stood: thats all. [*He sits down in the wicker chair; and resigns himself to allow her to lead the conversation*]. You were saying— ?

ELLIE. Was I? I forget. Tell me. Do you like this part of the country? I heard you ask Mr Hushabye at dinner whether there are any nice houses to let down here.

MANGAN. I like the place. The air suits me. I shouldnt be surprised if I settled down here.

ELLIE. Nothing would please me better. The air suits me too. And I want to be near Hesione.

MANGAN [*with growing uneasiness*] The air may suit us; but the question is, should we suit one another? Have you thought about that?

ELLIE. Mr Mangan: we must be sensible, mustnt we? It's no use pretending that we are Romeo and Juliet. But we can get on very well together if we choose to make the best of it. Your kindness of heart will make it easy for me.

MANGAN [*leaning forward, with the beginning of something like deliberate unpleasantness in his voice*] Kindness of heart, eh? I ruined your father, didnt I?

ELLIE. Oh, not intentionally.

MANGAN. Yes I did. Ruined him on purpose.

ELLIE. On purpose!

MANGAN. Not out of ill-nature, you know. And youll admit
that I kept a job for him when I had finished with him.
But business is business; and I ruined him as a matter of
business.

ELLIE. I dont understand how that can be. Are you trying
to make me feel that I need not be grateful to you, so that
I may choose freely?

MANGAN [*rising aggressively*] No. I mean what I say.

ELLIE. But how could it possibly do you any good to ruin
my father? The money he lost was yours.

MANGAN [*with a sour laugh*] W a s mine! It i s mine, Miss
Ellie, and all the money the other fellows lost too. [*He
shoves his hands into his pockets and shews his teeth*]. I
just smoked them out like a hive of bees. What do you
say to that? A bit of a shock, eh?

ELLIE. It would have been, this morning. Now! you cant
think how little it matters. But it's quite interesting. Only,
you must explain it to me. I dont understand it. [*Propping
her elbows on the drawing-board and her chin on her
hands, she composes herself to listen with a combination
of conscious curiosity with unconscious contempt which
provokes him to more and more unpleasantness, and an
attempt at patronage of her ignorance*].

MANGAN. Of course you dont understand: what do you
know about business? You just listen and learn. Your
father's business was a new business; and I dont start
new businesses: I let other fellows start them. They put
all their money and their friends' money into starting
them. They wear out their souls and bodies trying to
make a success of them. Theyre what you call enthusiasts.
But the first dead lift of the thing is too much for them;
and they havnt enough financial experience. In a year
or so they have either to let the whole show go bust, or
sell out to a new lot of fellows for a few deferred ordinary shares: that is, if theyre lucky enough to get anything at all. As likely as not the very same thing happens
to the new lot. They put in more money and a couple

of years more work; and then perhaps they have to sell out to a third lot. If it's really a big thing the third lot will have to sell out too, and leave t h e i r work and their money behind them. And thats where the real business man comes in: where I come in. But I'm cleverer than some: I dont mind dropping a little money to start the process. I took your father's measure. I saw that he had a sound idea, and that he would work himself silly for it if he got the chance. I saw that he was a child in business, and was dead certain to outrun his expenses and be in too great a hurry to wait for his market. I knew that the surest way to ruin a man who doesnt know how to handle money is to give him some. I explained my idea to some friends in the city, and they found the money; for I take no risks in ideas, even when theyre my own. Your father and the friends that ventured their money with him were no more to me than a heap of squeezed lemons. Youve been wasting your gratitude: my kind heart is all rot. I'm sick of it. When I see your father beaming at me with his moist, grateful eyes, regularly wallowing in gratitude, I sometimes feel I must tell him the truth or burst. What stops me is that I know he wouldnt believe me. He'd think it was my modesty, as you did just now. He'd think anything rather than the truth, which is that he's a blamed fool, and I am a man that knows how to take care of himself. [*He throws himself back into the big chair with large self-approval*]. Now what do you think of me, Miss Ellie?

ELLIE [*dropping her hands*] How strange! that my mother, who knew nothing at all about business, should have been quite right about you! She always said—not before papa, of course, but to us children—that you were just that sort of man.

MANGAN [*sitting up, much hurt*] Oh! did she? And yet she'd have let you marry me.

ELLIE. Well, you see, Mr Mangan, my mother married a very good man—for whatever you may think of my father as a man of business, he is the soul of goodness—and she is not at all keen on my doing the same.

MANGAN. Anyhow, you dont want to marry me now, do
you?

ELLIE [*very calmly*] Oh, I think so. Why not?

MANGAN [*rising aghast*] Why not!

ELLIE. I dont see why we shouldnt get on very well together.

MANGAN. Well, but look here, you know— [*he stops, quite
at a loss*].

ELLIE [*patiently*] Well?

MANGAN. Well, I thought you were rather particular about
people's characters.

ELLIE. If we women were particular about men's characters, we should never get married at all, Mr Mangan.

MANGAN. A child like you talking of "we women"! What
next! Youre not in earnest?

ELLIE. Yes I am. Arnt you?

MANGAN. You mean to hold me to it?

ELLIE. Do you wish to back out of it?

MANGAN. Oh no. Not exactly back out of it.

ELLIE. Well?

*He has nothing to say. With a long whispered whistle,
he drops into the wicker chair and stares before him like
a beggared gambler. But a cunning look soon comes into
his face. He leans over towards her on his right elbow,
and speaks in a low steady voice.*

MANGAN. Suppose I told you I was in love with another
woman!

ELLIE [*echoing him*] Suppose I told you I was in love with
another man!

MANGAN [*bouncing angrily out of his chair*] I'm not
joking.

ELLIE. Who told you *I* was?

MANGAN. I tell you I'm serious. Youre too young to be
serious; but youll have to believe me. I want to be near
your friend Mrs Hushabye. I'm in love with her. Now
the murder's out.

ELLIE. I want to be near your friend Mr Hushabye. I'm in
love with him. [*She rises and adds with a frank air*] Now
we are in one another's confidence, we shall be real
friends. Thank you for telling me.

MANGAN [*almost beside himself*] Do you think I'll be made a convenience of like this?

ELLIE. Come, Mr Mangan! you made a business convenience of my father. Well, a woman's business is marriage. Why shouldnt I make a domestic convenience of you?

MANGAN. Because I dont choose, see? Because I'm not a silly gull like your father. Thats why.

ELLIE [*with serene contempt*] You are not good enough to clean my father's boots, Mr Mangan; and I am paying you a great compliment in condescending to make a convenience of you, as you call it. Of course you are free to throw over our engagement if you like; but, if you do, youll never enter Hesione's house again: I will take care of that.

MANGAN [*gasping*] You little devil, youve done me [*On the point of collapsing into the big chair again he recovers himself*] Wait a bit, though: youre not so cute as you think. You cant beat Boss Mangan as easy as that. Suppose I go straight to Mrs Hushabye and tell her that youre in love with her husband.

ELLIE. She knows it.

MANGAN. You told her!!!

ELLIE. She told me.

MANGAN [*clutching at his bursting temples*] Oh, this is a crazy house. Or else I'm going clean off my chump. Is she making a swop with you—she to have your husband and you to have hers?

ELLIE. Well, you dont want us both, do you?

MANGAN [*throwing himself into the chair distractedly*] My brain wont stand it. My head's going to split. Help! Help me to hold it. Quick: hold it: squeeze it. Save me. [*Ellie comes behind his chair; claps his head hard for a moment; then begins to draw her hands from his forehead back to his ears*]. Thank you. [*Drowsily*] Thats very refreshing. [*Waking a little*] Dont you hypnotize me, though. Ive seen men made fools of by hypnotism.

ELLIE [*steadily*] Be quiet. Ive seen men made fools of without hypnotism.

MANGAN [*humbly*] You dont dislike touching me, I hope.
You never touched me before, I noticed.

ELLIE. Not since you fell in love naturally with a grown-up
nice woman, who will never expect you to make love
to her. And I will never expect him to make love to me.

MANGAN. He may, though.

ELLIE [*making her passes rhythmically*] Hush. Go to sleep.
Do you hear? You are to go to sleep, go to sleep, go to
sleep; be quiet, deeply deeply quiet; sleep, sleep, sleep,
sleep, sleep.

> *He falls asleep. Ellie steals away; turns the light out;
> and goes into the garden.*

> *Nurse Guinness opens the door and is seen in the light
> which comes in from the hall.*

GUINNESS [*speaking to someone outside*] Mr Mangan's not
here, ducky: theres no one here. It's all dark.

MRS HUSHABYE [*without*] Try the garden. Mr Dunn and I
will be in my boudoir. Shew him the way.

GUINNESS. Yes, ducky. [*She makes for the garden door in
the dark; stumbles over the sleeping Mangan; and
screams*] Ahoo! Oh Lord, sir! I beg your pardon, I'm
sure: I didnt see you in the dark. Who is it? [*She goes
back to the door and turns on the light*]. Oh, Mr Mangan,
sir, I hope I havnt hurt you plumping into your lap like
that. [*Coming to him*] I was looking for you, sir. Mrs
Hushabye says will you please—[*noticing that he remains
quite insensible*] Oh, my good Lord, I hope I havnt
killed him. Sir! Mr Mangan! Sir! [*She shakes him; and
he is rolling inertly off the chair on the floor when she
holds him up and props him against the cushion*]. Miss
Hessy! Miss Hessy! Quick, doty darling. Miss Hessy!
[*Mrs Hushabye comes in from the hall, followed by
Mazzini Dunn*]. Oh, Miss Hessy, Ive been and killed him.

> *Mazzini runs round the back of the chair to Mangan's
> right hand, and sees that the nurse's words are apparently
> only too true.*

MAZZINI. What tempted you to commit such a crime,
woman?

MRS HUSHABYE [*trying not to laugh*] Do you mean you did
it on purpose?

GUINNESS. Now is it likely I'd kill any man on purpose. I fell over him in the dark; and I'm a pretty tidy weight. He never spoke nor moved until I shook him; and then he would have dropped dead on the floor. Isnt it tiresome?

MRS HUSHABYE [*going past the nurse to Mangan's side, and inspecting him less credulously than Mazzini*] Nonsense! he is not dead: he is only asleep. I can see him breathing.

GUINNESS. But why wont he wake?

MAZZINI [*speaking very politely into Mangan's ear*] Mangan! My dear Mangan! [*he blows into Mangan's ear*].

MRS HUSHABYE. Thats no good [*she shakes him vigorously*]. Mr Mangan: wake up. Do you hear? [*He begins to roll over*]. Oh! Nurse, nurse: he's falling: help me.

Nurse Guinness rushes to the rescue. With Mazzini's assistance, Mangan is propped safely up again.

GUINNESS [*behind the chair; bending over to test the case with her nose*] Would he be drunk, do you think, pet?

MRS HUSHABYE. Had he any of papa's rum?

MAZZINI. It cant be that: he is most abstemious. I am afraid he drank too much formerly, and has to drink too little now. You know, Mrs Hushabye, I really think he has been hypnotized.

GUINNESS. Hip no what, sir?

MAZZINI. One evening at home, after we had seen a hypnotizing performance, the children began playing at it; and Ellie stroked my head. I assure you I went off dead asleep; and they had to send for a professional to wake me up after I had slept eighteen hours. They had to carry me upstairs; and as the poor children were not very strong, they let me slip; and I rolled right down the whole flight and never woke up. [*Mrs Hushabye splutters*]. Oh, you may laugh, Mrs Hushabye; but I might have been killed.

MRS HUSHABYE. I couldnt have helped laughing even if you had been, Mr Dunn. So Ellie has hypnotized him. What fun!

MAZZINI. Oh no, no, no. It was such a terrible lesson to her: nothing would induce her to try such a thing again.

MRS HUSHABYE. Then who did it? *I* didnt.

MAZZINI. I thought perhaps the Captain might have done it unintentionally. He is so fearfully magnetic: I feel vibrations whenever he comes close to me.

GUINNESS. The Captain will get him out of it anyhow, sir: I'll back him for that. I'll go fetch him [*she makes for the pantry*].

MRS HUSHABYE. Wait a bit. [*To Mazzini*] You say he is all right for eighteen hours?

MAZZINI. Well, *I* was asleep for eighteen hours.

MRS HUSHABYE. Were you any the worse for it?

MAZZINI. I dont quite remember. They had poured brandy down my throat, you see; and—

MRS HUSHABYE. Quite. Anyhow, you survived. Nurse, darling: go and ask Miss Dunn to come to us here. Say I want to speak to her particularly. You will find her with Mr Hushabye probably.

GUINNESS. I think not, ducky: Miss Addy is with him. But I'll find her and send her to you. [*She goes out into the garden*].

MRS HUSHABYE [*calling Mazzini's attention to the figure on the chair*] Now, Mr Dunn, look. Just look. Look hard. Do you still intend to sacrifice your daughter to that thing?

MAZZINI [*troubled*] You have completely upset me, Mrs Hushabye, by all you have said to me. That anyone could imagine that I—*I*, a consecrated soldier of freedom, if I may say so—could sacrifice Ellie to anybody or anyone, or that I should ever have dreamed of forcing her inclinations in any way, is a most painful blow to my—well, I suppose you would say to my good opinion of myself.

MRS HUSHABYE [*rather stolidly*] Sorry.

MAZZINI [*looking forlornly at the body*] What is your objection to poor Mangan, Mrs Hushabye? He looks all right to me. But then I am so accustomed to him.

MRS HUSHABYE. Have you no heart? Have you no sense? Look at the brute! Think of poor weak innocent Ellie in the clutches of this slavedriver, who spends his life making thousands of rough violent workmen bend to his will and sweat for him: a man accustomed to have great

masses of iron beaten into shape for him by steam-
hammers! to fight with women and girls over a halfpenny an hour ruthlessly! a captain of industry, I think
you call him, dont you? Are you going to fling your
delicate, sweet, helpless child into such a beast's claws
just because he will keep her in an expensive house and
make her wear diamonds to shew how rich he is?

MAZZINI [*staring at her in wide-eyed amazement*] Bless you,
dear Mrs Hushabye, what romantic ideas of business
you have! Poor dear Mangan isnt a bit like that.

MRS HUSHABYE [*scornfully*] Poor dear Mangan indeed!

MAZZINI. But he doesnt know anything about machinery.
He never goes near the men: he couldnt manage them:
he is afraid of them. I never can get him to take the least
interest in the works: he hardly knows more about them
than you do. People are cruelly unjust to Mangan: they
think he is all rugged strength just because his manners
are bad.

MRS HUSHABYE. Do you mean to tell me he isnt strong
enough to crush poor little Ellie?

MAZZINI. Of course it's very hard to say how any marriage
will turn out; but speaking for myself, I should say that
he wont have a dog's chance against Ellie. You know,
Ellie has remarkable strength of character. I think it is
because I taught her to like Shakespear when she was
very young.

MRS HUSHABYE [*contemptuously*] Shakespear! The next
thing you will tell me is that you could have made a
great deal more money than Mangan. [*She retires to the
sofa, and sits down at the port end of it in the worst of
humors*].

MAZZINI [*following her and taking the other end*] No: I'm
no good at making money. I dont care enough for it,
somehow. I'm not ambitious! that must be it. Mangan
is wonderful about money: he thinks of nothing else. He
is so dreadfully afraid of being poor. I am always thinking of other things: even at the works I think of the
things we are doing and not of what they cost. And the
worst of it is, poor Mangan doesnt know what to do with
his money when he gets it. He is such a baby that he

doesnt know even what to eat and drink: he has ruined his liver eating and drinking the wrong things; and now he can hardly eat at all. Ellie will diet him splendidly. You will be surprised when you come to know him better: he is really the most helpless of mortals. You get quite a protective feeling towards him.

MRS HUSHABYE. Then who manages his business, pray?

MAZZINI. I do. And of course other people like me.

MRS HUSHABYE. Footling people, you mean.

MAZZINI. I suppose youd think us so.

MRS HUSHABYE. And pray why dont you do without him if youre all so much cleverer?

MAZZINI. Oh, we couldnt: we should ruin the business in a year. I've tried; and I know. We should spend too much on everything. We should improve the quality of the goods and make them too dear. We should be sentimental about the hard cases among the workpeople. But Mangan keeps us in order. He is down on us about every extra halfpenny. We could never do without him. You see, he will sit up all night thinking of how to save sixpence. Wont Ellie make him jump, though, when she takes his house in hand!

MRS HUSHABYE. Then the creature is a fraud even as a captain of industry!

MAZZINI. I am afraid all the captains of industry are what you call frauds, Mrs Hushabye. Of course there are some manufacturers who really do understand their own works; but they dont make as high a rate of profit as Mangan does. I assure you Mangan is quite a good fellow in his way. He means well.

MRS HUSHABYE. He doesnt look well. He is not in his first youth, is he?

MAZZINI. After all, no husband is in his first youth for very long, Mrs Hushabye. And men cant afford to marry in their first youth nowadays.

MRS HUSHABYE. Now if *I* said that, it would sound witty. Why cant y o u say it wittily? What on earth is the matter with you? Why dont you inspire everybody with confidence? with respect?

MAZZINI [*humbly*] I think that what is the matter with me is

that I am poor. You dont know what that means at home.
Mind: I dont say they have ever complained. Theyve all
been wonderful: theyve been proud of my poverty.
Theyve even joked about it quite often. But my wife has
had a very poor time of it. She has been quite resigned—

MRS HUSHABYE [*shuddering involuntarily*]!!

MAZZINI. There! You see, Mrs Hushabye. I dont want Ellie
to live on resignation.

MRS HUSHABYE. Do you want her to have to resign herself
to living with a man she doesnt love?

MAZZINI [*wistfully*] Are you sure that would be worse than
living with a man she did love, if he was a footling person?

MRS HUSHABYE [*relaxing her contemptuous attitude, quite
interested in Mazzini now*] You know, I really think you
must love Ellie very much; for you become quite clever
when you talk about her.

MAZZINI. I didnt know I was so very stupid on other
subjects.

MRS HUSHABYE. You are, sometimes.

MAZZINI [*turning his head away; for his eyes are wet*] I
have learnt a good deal about myself from you, Mrs
Hushabye; and I'm afraid I shall not be the happier for
your plain speaking. But if you thought I needed it to
make me think of Ellie's happiness you were very much
mistaken.

MRS HUSHABYE [*leaning towards him kindly*] Have I been
a beast?

MAZZINI [*pulling himself together*] It doesnt matter about
me, Mrs Hushabye. I think you like Ellie; and that is
enough for me.

MRS HUSHABYE. I'm beginning to like you a little. I perfectly loathed you at first. I thought you the most
odious, self-satisfied, boresome elderly prig I ever met.

MAZZINI [*resigned, and now quite cheerful*] I daresay I am
all that. I never have been a favorite with gorgeous
women like you. They always frighten me.

MRS HUSHABYE [*pleased*] Am I a gorgeous woman, Mazzini?
I shall fall in love with you presently.

MAZZINI [*with placid gallantry*] No you wont, Hesione. But

you would be quite safe. Would you believe it that quite a lot of women have flirted with me because I am quite safe? But they get tired of me for the same reason.

MRS HUSHABYE [*mischievously*] Take care. You may not be so safe as you think.

MAZZINI. Oh yes, quite safe. You see, I have been in love really: the sort of love that only happens once. [*Softly*] Thats why Ellie is such a lovely girl.

MRS HUSHABYE. Well, really, you a r e coming out. Are you quite sure you wont let me tempt you into a second grand passion?

MAZZINI. Quite. It wouldnt be natural. The fact is, you dont strike on my box, Mrs Hushabye; and I certainly dont strike on yours.

MRS HUSHABYE. I see. Your marriage was a safety match.

MAZZINI. What a very witty application of the expression I used! I should never have thought of it.

    Ellie comes in from the garden, looking anything but happy.

MRS HUSHABYE [*rising*] Oh! here is Ellie at last. [*She goes behind the sofa*].

ELLIE [*on the threshold of the starboard door*] Guinness said you wanted me: you and papa.

MRS HUSHABYE. You have kept us waiting so long that it almost came to—well, never mind. Your father is a very wonderful man [*she ruffles his hair affectionately*]: the only one I ever met who could resist me when I made myself really agreeable. [*She comes to the big chair, on Mangan's left*]. Come here. I have something to shew you. [*Ellie strolls listlessly to the other side of the chair*]. Look.

ELLIE [*contemplating Mangan without interest*] I know. He is only asleep. We had a talk after dinner; and he fell asleep in the middle of it.

MRS HUSHABYE. You did it, Ellie. You put him asleep.

MAZZINI [*rising quickly and coming to the back of the chair*] Oh, I hope not. Did you, Ellie?

ELLIE [*wearily*] He asked me to.

MAZZINI. But it's dangerous. You know what happened to me.

ELLIE [*utterly indifferent*] Oh, I daresay I can wake him. If not, somebody else can.

MRS HUSHABYE. It doesnt matter, anyhow, because I have at last persuaded your father that you dont want to marry him.

ELLIE [*suddenly coming out of her listlessness, much vexed*] But why did you do that, Hesione? I d o want to marry him. I fully intend to marry him.

MAZZINI. Are you quite sure, Ellie? Mrs Hushabye has made me feel that I may have been thoughtless and selfish about it.

ELLIE [*very clearly and steadily*] Papa. When Mrs Hushabye takes it on herself to explain to you what I think or dont think, shut your ears tight; and shut your eyes too. Hesione knows nothing about me: she hasnt the least notion of the sort of person I am, and never will. I promise you I wont do anything I dont want to do and mean to do for my own sake.

MAZZINI. You are quite, quite sure?

ELLIE. Quite, quite sure. Now you must go away and leave me to talk to Mrs Hushabye.

MAZZINI. But I should like to hear. Shall I be in the way?

ELLIE [*inexorable*] I had rather talk to her alone.

MAZZINI [*affectionately*] Oh, well, I know what a nuisance parents are, dear. I will be good and go. [*He goes to the garden door*]. By the way, do you remember the address of that professional who woke me up? Dont you think I had better telegraph to him.

MRS HUSHABYE [*moving towards the sofa*] It's too late to telegraph tonight.

MAZZINI. I suppose so. I do hope he'll wake up in the course of the night. [*He goes out into the garden*].

ELLIE [*turning vigorously on Hesione the moment her father is out of the room*] Hesione: what the devil do you mean by making mischief with my father about Mangan?

MRS HUSHABYE [*promptly losing her temper*] Dont you dare speak to me like that, you little minx. Remember that you are in my house.

ELLIE. Stuff! Why dont you mind your own business? What is it to you whether I choose to marry Mangan or not?

MRS HUSHABYE. Do you suppose you can bully me, you miserable little matrimonial adventurer?

ELLIE. Every woman who hasnt any money is a matrimonial adventurer. It's easy for you to talk: you have never known what it is to want money; and you can pick up men as if they were daisies. I am poor and respectable—

MRS HUSHABYE [*interrupting*] Ho! respectable! How did you pick up Mangan? How did you pick up my husband? You have the audacity to tell me that I am a—a—a—

ELLIE. A siren. So you are. You were born to lead men by the nose: if you werent, Marcus would have waited for me, perhaps.

MRS HUSHABYE [*suddenly melting and half laughing*] Oh, my poor Ellie, my pettikins, my unhappy darling! I am so sorry about Hector. But what can I do? It's not my fault: I'd give him to you if I could.

ELLIE. I dont blame you for that.

MRS HUSHABYE. What a brute I was to quarrel with you and call you names! Do kiss me and say youre not angry with me.

ELLIE [*fiercely*] Oh, dont slop and gush and be sentimental. Dont you see that unless I can be hard—as hard as nails—I shall go mad. I dont care a damn about your calling me names: do you think a woman in my situation can feel a few hard words?

MRS HUSHABYE. Poor little woman! Poor little situation!

ELLIE. I suppose you think youre being sympathetic. You are just foolish and stupid and selfish. You see me getting a smasher right in the face that kills a whole part of my life: the best part that can never come again; and you think you can help me over it by a little coaxing and kissing. When I want all the strength I can get to lean on: something iron, something stony, I dont care how cruel it is, you go all mushy and want to slobber over me. I'm not angry; I'm not unfriendly; but for God's sake do pull yourself together; and dont think that because youre on velvet and always have been, women who are in hell can take it as easily as you.

MRS HUSHABYE [*shrugging her shoulders*] Very well. [*She*

sits down on the sofa in her old place]. But I warn you
that when I am neither coaxing and kissing nor laughing,
I am just wondering how much longer I can stand living
in this cruel, damnable world. You object to the siren:
well, I drop the siren. You want to rest your wounded
bosom against a grindstone. Well [*folding her arms*], here
is the grindstone.

ELLIE [*sitting down beside her, appeased*] Thats better: you
really have the trick of falling in with everyone's mood;
but you dont understand, because you are not the sort of
woman for whom there is only one man and only one
chance.

MRS HUSHABYE. I certainly dont understand how your
marrying that object [*indicating Mangan*] will console
you for not being able to marry Hector.

ELLIE. Perhaps you dont understand why I was quite a nice
girl this morning, and am now neither a girl nor particularly nice.

MRS HUSHABYE. Oh yes I do. It's because you have made
up your mind to do something despicable and wicked.

ELLIE. I dont think so, Hesione. I must make the best of
my ruined house.

MRS HUSHABYE. Pooh! Youll get over it. Your house isnt
ruined.

ELLIE. Of course I shall get over it. You dont suppose I'm
going to sit down and die of a broken heart, I hope, or
be an old maid living on a pittance from the Sick and
Indigent Roomkeepers' Association. But my heart is
broken, all the same. What I mean by that is that I know
that what has happened to me with Marcus will not happen to me ever again. In the world for me there is Marcus
and a lot of other men of whom one is just the same
as another. Well, if I cant have love, thats no reason
why I should have poverty. If Mangan has nothing else,
he has money.

MRS HUSHABYE. And are there no young men with money?

ELLIE. Not within my reach. Besides, a young man would
have the right to expect love from me, and would perhaps
leave me when he found I could not give it to him. Rich
young men can get rid of their wives, you know, pretty

cheaply. But this object, a⁰ you call him, can expect nothing more from me than I am prepared to give him.

MRS HUSHABYE. He will be your owner, remember. If he buys you, he will make the bargain pay him and not you. Ask your father.

ELLIE [*rising and strolling to the chair to contemplate their subject*] You need not trouble on that score, Hesione. I have more to give Boss Mangan than he has to give me: it is I who am buying him, and at a pretty good price too, I think. Women are better at that sort of bargain than men. I have taken the Boss's measure; and ten Boss Mangans shall not prevent me doing far more as I please as his wife than I have ever been able to do as a poor girl. [*Stooping to the recumbent figure*] Shall they, Boss? I think not. [*She passes on to the drawing-table, and leans against the end of it, facing the windows*]. I shall not have to spend most of my time wondering how long my gloves will last, anyhow.

MRS HUSHABYE [*rising superbly*] Ellie: you are a wicked sordid little beast. And to think that I actually condescended to fascinate that creature there to save you from him! Well, let me tell you this: if you make this disgusting match, you will never see Hector again if I can help it.

ELLIE [*unmoved*] I nailed Mangan by telling him that if he did not marry me he should never see y o u again [*she lifts herself on her wrists and seats herself on the end of the table*].

MRS HUSHABYE [*recoiling*] Oh!

ELLIE. So you see I am not unprepared for your playing that trump against me. Well, you just try it: thats all. I should have made a man of Marcus, not a household pet.

MRS HUSHABYE [*flaming*] You dare!

ELLIE [*looking almost dangerous*] Set him thinking about me if you dare.

MRS HUSHABYE. Well, of all the impudent little fiends I ever met! Hector says there is a certain point at which the only answer you can give to a man who breaks all the rules is to knock him down. What would you say if I were to box your ears?

ELLIE [*calmly*] I should pull your hair.

MRS HUSHABYE [*mischievously*] That wouldnt hurt me. Perhaps it comes off at night.

ELLIE [*so taken aback that she drops off the table and runs to her*] Oh, you dont mean to say, Hesione, that your beautiful black hair is false?

MRS HUSHABYE [*patting it*] Dont tell Hector. He believes in it.

ELLIE [*groaning*] Oh! Even the hair that ensnared him false! Everything false!

MRS HUSHABYE. Pull it and try. Other women can snare men in their hair; but I can swing a baby on mine. Aha! you cant do that, Goldylocks.

ELLIE [*heartbroken*] No. You have stolen my babies.

MRS HUSHABYE. Pettikins: dont make me cry. You know, what you said about my making a household pet of him is a little true. Perhaps he ought to have waited for you. Would any other woman on earth forgive you?

ELLIE. Oh, what right had you to take him all for yourself! [*Pulling herself together*] There! You couldnt help it: neither of us could help it. He couldnt help it. No: dont say anything more: I cant bear it. Let us wake the object. [*She begins stroking Mangan's head, reversing the movement with which she put him to sleep*]. Wake up, wake up, wake—

MANGAN [*bouncing out of the chair in a fury and turning on them*] Wake up! So you think Ive been asleep, do you? [*He kicks the chair violently out of his way, and gets between them*]. You throw me into a trance so that I cant move hand or foot—I might have been buried alive! it's a mercy I wasnt—and then you think I was only asleep. If youd let me drop the two times you rolled me about, my nose would have been flattened for life against the floor. But Ive found you all out, anyhow. I know the sort of people I'm among now. Ive heard every word youve said, you and your precious father, and [*to Mrs Hushabye*] you too. So I'm an object, am I? I'm a thing, am I? I'm a fool that hasnt sense enough to feed myself properly, am I? I'm afraid of the men that would starve if it werent for the wages I give them,

am I? I'm nothing but a disgusting old skinflint to be
made a convenience of by designing women and fool
managers of my works, am I? I'm—

MRS HUSHABYE [*with the most elegant aplomb*] Sh-sh-sh-sh-
sh! Mr Mangan: you are bound in honor to obliterate
from your mind all you heard while you were pretending
to be asleep. It was not meant for you to hear.

MANGAN. Pretending to be asleep! Do you think if I was
only pretending that I'd have sprawled there helpless,
and listened to such unfairness, such lies, such injustice
and plotting and backbiting and slandering of me, if I
could have up and told you what I thought of you! I
wonder I didnt burst.

MRS HUSHABYE [*sweetly*] You dreamt it all, Mr Mangan.
We were only saying how beautifully peaceful you looked
in your sleep. That was all, wasnt it, Ellie? Believe me,
Mr Mangan, all those unpleasant things came into your
mind in the last half second before you woke. Ellie
rubbed your hair the wrong way; and the disagreeable
sensation suggested a disagreeable dream.

MANGAN [*doggedly*] I believe in dreams.

MRS HUSHABYE. So do I. But they go by contraries, dont
they?

MANGAN [*depths of emotion suddenly welling up in him*] I
shant forget, to my dying day, that when you gave me the
glad eye that time in the garden, you were making a fool
of me. That was a dirty low mean thing to do. You had
no right to let me come near you if I disgusted you. It
isnt my fault if I'm old and havnt a moustache like a
bronze candlestick as your husband has. There are things
no decent woman would do to a man—like a man hitting
a woman in the breast.

*Hesione, utterly shamed, sits down on the sofa and
covers her face with her hands. Mangan sits down also
on his chair and begins to cry like a child. Ellie stares at
them. Mrs Hushabye, at the distressing sound he makes,
takes down her hands and looks at him. She rises and
runs to him.*

MRS HUSHABYE. Dont cry: I cant bear it. Have I broken
your heart? I didnt know you had one. How could I?

MANGAN. I'm a man aint I?

MRS HUSHABYE [*half coaxing, half rallying, altogether tenderly*] Oh no: not what I call a man. Only a Boss: just that and nothing else. What business has a Boss with a heart?

MANGAN. Then youre not a bit sorry for what you did, nor ashamed?

MRS HUSHABYE. I was ashamed for the first time in my life when you said that about hitting a woman in the breast, and I found out what I'd done. My very bones blushed red. Youve had your revenge, Boss. Arnt you satisfied?

MANGAN. Serve you right! Do you hear? Serve you right! Youre just cruel. Cruel.

MRS HUSHABYE. Yes: cruelty would be delicious if one could only find some sort of cruelty that didnt really hurt. By the way [*sitting down beside him on the arm of the chair*], whats your name? It's not really Boss, is it?

MANGAN [*shortly*] If you want to know, my name's Alfred.

MRS HUSHABYE [*springing up*] Alfred!! Ellie: he was christened after Tennyson!!!

MANGAN [*rising*] I was christened after my uncle, and never had a penny from him, damn him! What of it?

MRS HUSHABYE. It comes to me suddenly that you are a real person: that you had a mother, like anyone else. [*Putting her hands on his shoulders and surveying him*] Little Alf!

MANGAN. Well, you have a nerve.

MRS HUSHABYE. And you have a heart, Alfy, a whimpering little heart, but a real one. [*Releasing him suddenly*] Now run and make it up with Ellie. She has had time to think what to say to you, which is more than I had [*she goes out quickly into the garden by the port door*].

MANGAN. That woman has a pair of hands that go right through you.

ELLIE. Still in love with her, in spite of all we said about you?

MANGAN. Are all women like you two? Do they never think of anything about a man except what they can get out of him? Y o u werent even thinking that about me. You were only thinking whether your gloves would last.

ELLIE. I shall not have to think about that when we are married.

MANGAN. And you think I am going to marry you after what I heard there!

ELLIE. You heard nothing from me that I did not tell you before.

MANGAN. Perhaps you think I cant do without you.

ELLIE. I think you would feel lonely without us all now, after coming to know us so well.

MANGAN [*with something like a yell of despair*] Am I never to have the last word?

CAPTAIN SHOTOVER [*appearing at the starboard garden door*] There is a soul in torment here. What is the matter?

MANGAN. This girl doesnt want to spend her life wondering how long her gloves will last.

CAPTAIN SHOTOVER [*passing through*] Dont wear any. I never do [*he goes into the pantry*].

LADY UTTERWORD [*appearing at the port garden door, in a handsome dinner dress*] Is anything the matter?

ELLIE. This gentleman wants to know is he never to have the last word?

LADY UTTERWORD [*coming forward to the sofa*] I should let him have it, my dear. The important thing is not to have the last word, but to have your own way.

MANGAN. She wants both.

LADY UTTERWORD. She wont get them, Mr Mangan. Providence always has the last word.

MANGAN [*desperately*] Now y o u are going to come religion over me. In this house a man's mind might as well be a football. I'm going. [*He makes for the hall, but is stopped by a hail from the Captain, who has just emerged from his pantry*].

CAPTAIN SHOTOVER. Whither away, Boss Mangan?

MANGAN. To hell out of this house: let that be enough for you and all here.

CAPTAIN SHOTOVER. You were welcome to come: you are free to go. The wide earth, the high seas, the spacious skies are waiting for you outside.

LADY UTTERWORD. But your things, Mr Mangan. Your bags, your comb and brushes, your pyjamas—

HECTOR [*who has just appeared in the port doorway in a handsome Arab costume*] Why should the escaping slave take his chains with him?

MANGAN. Thats right, Hushabye. Keep the pyjamas, my lady; and much good may they do you.

HECTOR [*advancing to Lady Utterword's left hand*] Let us all go out into the night and leave everything behind us.

MANGAN. You stay where you are, the lot of you. I want no company, especially female company.

ELLIE. Let him go. He is unhappy here. He is angry with us.

CAPTAIN SHOTOVER. Go, Boss Mangan; and when you have found the land where there is happiness and where there are no women, send me its latitude and longitude; and I will join you there.

LADY UTTERWORD. You will certainly not be comfortable without your luggage, Mr Mangan.

ELLIE [*impatient*] Go, go: why dont you go? It is a heavenly night: you can sleep on the heath. Take my waterproof to lie on: it is hanging up in the hall.

HECTOR. Breakfast at nine, unless you prefer to breakfast with the Captain at six.

ELLIE. Good night, Alfred.

HECTOR. Alfred! [*He runs back to the door and calls into the garden*] Randall: Mangan's Christian name i s Alfred.

RANDALL [*appearing in the starboard doorway in evening dress*] Then Hesione wins her bet.

Mrs Hushabye appears in the port doorway. She throws her left arm round Hector's neck; draws him with her to the back of the sofa; and throws her right arm round Lady Utterword's neck.

MRS HUSHABYE. They wouldnt believe me, Alf.

They contemplate him.

MANGAN. Is there any more of you coming in to look at me, as if I was the latest thing in a menagerie.

MRS HUSHABYE. You a r e the latest thing in this menagerie.

Before Mangan can retort, a fall of furniture is heard from upstairs; then a pistol shot, and a yell of pain. The staring group breaks up in consternation.

MAZZINI'S VOICE [*from above*] Help! A burglar! Help!

HECTOR [*his eyes blazing*] A burglar!!!

MRS HUSHABYE. No, Hector: youll be shot [*but it is too late: he has dashed out past Mangan, who hastily moves towards the bookshelves out of his way*].

CAPTAIN SHOTOVER [*blowing his whistle*] All hands aloft! [*He strides out after Hector*].

LADY UTTERWORD. My diamonds! [*She follows the Captain*].

RANDALL [*rushing after her*] No, Ariadne. Let me.

ELLIE. Oh, is papa shot? [*she runs out*].

MRS HUSHABYE. Are you frightened, Alf?

MANGAN. No. It aint my house, thank God.

MRS HUSHABYE. If they catch a burglar, shall we have to go into court as witnesses, and be asked all sorts of questions about our private lives?

MANGAN. You wont be believed if you tell the truth.

> *Mazzini, terribly upset, with a dueling pistol in his hand, comes from the hall, and makes his way to the drawing-table.*

MAZZINI. Oh, my dear Mrs Hushabye, I might have killed him [*He throws the pistol on the table and staggers round to the chair*]. I hope you wont believe I really intended to.

> *Hector comes in, marching an old and villainous looking man before him by the collar. He plants him in the middle of the room and releases him.*

> *Ellie follows, and immediately runs across to the back of her father's chair, and pats his shoulders.*

RANDALL [*entering with a poker*] Keep your eye on this door, Mangan. I'll look after the other [*he goes to the starboard door and stands on guard there*].

> *Lady Utterword comes in after Randall, and goes between Mrs Hushabye and Mangan.*

> *Nurse Guinness brings up the rear, and waits near the door, on Mangan's left.*

MRS HUSHABYE. What has happened?

MAZZINI. Your housekeeper told me there was somebody upstairs, and gave me a pistol that Mr Hushabye had been practising with. I thought it would frighten him; but it went off at a touch.

THE BURGLAR. Yes, and took the skin off my ear. Precious near took the top off my head. Why dont you have a proper revolver instead of a thing like that, that goes off if you as much as blow on it?

HECTOR. One of my duelling pistols. Sorry.

MAZZINI. He put his hands up and said it was a fair cop.

THE BURGLAR. So it was. Send for the police.

HECTOR. No, by thunder! It was not a fair cop. We were four to one.

MRS HUSHABYE. What will they do to him?

THE BURGLAR. Ten years. Beginning with solitary. Ten years off my life. I shant serve it all: I'm too old. It will see me out.

LADY UTTERWORD. You should have thought of that before you stole my diamonds.

THE BURGLAR. Well, youve got them back, lady: havnt you? Can you give me back the years of my life you are going to take from me?

MRS HUSHABYE. Oh, we cant bury a man alive for ten years for a few diamonds.

THE BURGLAR. Ten little shining diamonds! Ten long black years!

LADY UTTERWORD. Think of what it is for us to be dragged through the horrors of a criminal court, and have all our family affairs in the papers! If you were a native, and Hastings could order you a good beating and send you away, I shouldnt mind; but here in England there is no real protection for any respectable person.

THE BURGLAR. I'm too old to be giv a hiding, lady. Send for the police and have done with it. It's only just and right you should.

RANDALL [who has relaxed his vigilance on seeing the burglar so pacifically disposed, and comes forward swinging the poker between his fingers like a well-folded umbrella] It is neither just nor right that we should be put to a lot of inconvenience to gratify your moral enthusiasm, my friend. You had better get out, while you have the chance.

THE BURGLAR [inexorably] No. I must work my sin off my

conscience. This has come as a sort of call to me. Let me spend the rest of my life repenting in a cell. I shall have my reward above.

MANGAN [*exasperated*] The very burglars cant behave naturally in this house.

HECTOR. My good sir: you must work out your salvation at somebody else's expense. Nobody here is going to charge you.

THE BURGLAR. Oh, you wont charge me, wont you?

HECTOR. No. I'm sorry to be inhospitable; but will you kindly leave the house?

THE BURGLAR. Right. I'll go to the police station and give myself up. [*He turns resolutely to the door; but Hector stops him*].

HECTOR. ⎞ ⎛ Oh no. You mustnt do that.
RANDALL. ⎬ ⎨ No, no. Clear out, man, cant you; and
⎟ ⎜   dont be a fool.
MRS HUSHABYE. ⎠ ⎝ Dont be so silly. Cant you repent at
   home?

LADY UTTERWORD. You will have to do as you are told.

THE BURGLAR. It's compounding a felony, you know.

MRS HUSHABYE. This is utterly ridiculous. Are we to be forced to prosecute this man when we dont want to?

THE BURGLAR. Am I to be robbed of my salvation to save you the trouble of spending a day at the sessions? Is that justice? Is it right? Is it fair to me?

MAZZINI [*rising and leaning across the table persuasively as if it were a pulpit desk or a shop counter*] Come, come! let me shew you how you can turn your very crimes to account. Why not set up as a locksmith? You must know more about locks than most honest men?

THE BURGLAR. Thats true, sir. But I couldnt set up as a locksmith under twenty pounds.

RANDALL. Well, you can easily steal twenty pounds. You will find it in the nearest bank.

THE BURGLAR [*horrified*] Oh what a thing for a gentleman to put into the head of a poor criminal scrambling out of the bottomless pit as it were! Oh, shame on you, sir! Oh, God forgive you! [*He throws himself into the big chair and covers his face as if in prayer*].

LADY UTTERWORD. Really, Randall!

HECTOR. It seems to me that we shall have to take up a collection for this inopportunately contrite sinner.

LADY UTTERWORD. But twenty pounds is ridiculous.

THE BURGLAR [*looking up quickly*] I shall have to buy a lot of tools, lady.

LADY UTTERWORD. Nonsense: you have your burgling kit.

THE BURGLAR. Whats a jemmy and a centrebit and an acetylene welding plant and a bunch of skelton keys? I shall want a forge, and a smithy, and a shop, and fittings. I cant hardly do it for twenty.

HECTOR. My worthy friend, we havnt got twenty pounds.

THE BURGLAR [*now master of the situation*] You can raise it among you, cant you?

MRS HUSHABYE. Give him a sovereign, Hector; and get rid of him.

HECTOR [*giving him a pound*] There! Off with you.

THE BURGLAR [*rising and taking the money very ungratefully*] I wont promise nothing. You have more on you than a quid: all the lot of you, I mean.

LADY UTTERWORD [*vigorously*] Oh, let us prosecute him and have done with it. I have a conscience too, I hope; and I do not feel at all sure that we have any right to let him go, especially if he is going to be greedy and impertinent.

THE BURGLAR [*quickly*] All right, lady, all right. I've no wish to be anything but agreeable. Good evening, ladies and gentlemen; and thank you kindly.

He is hurrying out when he is confronted in the doorway by Captain Shotover.

CAPTAIN SHOTOVER [*fixing the burglar with a piercing regard*] What's this? Are there two of you?

THE BURGLAR [*falling on his knees before the Captain in abject terror*] Oh my good Lord, what have I done? Dont tell me it's y o u r house Ive broken into, Captain Shotover.

The Captain seizes him by the collar; drags him to his feet; and leads him to the middle of the group, Hector falling back beside his wife to make way for them.

CAPTAIN SHOTOVER [*turning him towards Ellie*] Is that your daughter? [*He releases him*].

THE BURGLAR. Well, how do I know, Captain? You know
the sort of life you and me has led. Any young lady of
that age might be my daughter anywhere in the wide
world, as you might say.

CAPTAIN SHOTOVER [*to Mazzini*] You are not Billy Dunn.
This is Billy Dunn. Why have you imposed on me?

THE BURGLAR [*indignantly to Mazzini*] Have you been giving yourself out to be me? You, that nigh blew my head
off! Shooting yourself, in a manner of speaking!

MAZZINI. My dear Captain Shotover, ever since I came into
this house I have done hardly anything else but assure
you that I am not Mr William Dunn, but Mazzini Dunn,
a very different person.

THE BURGLAR. He dont belong to my branch, Captain.
Theres two sets in the family: the thinking Dunns and
the drinking Dunns, each going their own ways. I'm a
drinking Dunn: he's a thinking Dunn. But that didnt give
him any right to shoot me.

CAPTAIN SHOTOVER. So youve turned burglar, have you?

THE BURGLAR. No, Captain: I wouldnt disgrace our old sea
calling by such a thing. I am no burglar.

LADY UTTERWORD. What were you doing with my diamonds?

GUINNESS. What did you break into the house for if youre
no burglar?

RANDALL. Mistook the house for your own and came in by
the wrong window, eh?

THE BURGLAR. Well, it's no use my telling you a lie: I can
take in most captains, but not Captain Shotover, because
he sold himself to the devil in Zanzibar, and can divine
water, spot gold, explode a cartridge in your pocket with
a glance of his eye, and see the truth hidden in the
heart of man. But I'm no burglar.

CAPTAIN SHOTOVER. Are you an honest man?

THE BURGLAR. I dont set up to be better than my fellow-
creatures, and never did, as you well know, Captain.
But what I do is innocent and pious. I enquire about for
houses where the right sort of people live. I work it on
them same as I worked it here. I break into the house;

put a few spoons or diamonds in my pocket; make a noise; get caught; and take up a collection. And you wouldnt believe how hard it is to get caught when youre actually trying to. I have knocked over all the chairs in a room without a soul paying any attention to me. In the end I have had to walk out and leave the job.

RANDALL. When that happens, do you put back the spoons and diamonds?

THE BURGLAR. Well, I dont fly in the face of Providence, if thats what you want to know.

CAPTAIN SHOTOVER. Guinness: you remember this man?

GUINNESS. I should think I do, seeing I was married to him, the blackguard!

HESIONE   ⎞ *exclaiming* ⎛Married to him!
LADY UTTERWORD ⎠ *together*   ⎝Guinness!!

THE BURGLAR. It wasnt legal. Ive been married to no end of women. No use coming that over me.

CAPTAIN SHOTOVER. Take him to the forecastle [*he flings him to the door with a strength beyond his years*].

GUINNESS. I suppose you mean the kitchen. They wont have him there. Do you expect servants to keep company with thieves and all sorts?

CAPTAIN SHOTOVER. Land-thieves and water-thieves are the same flesh and blood. I'll have no boatswain on my quarter-deck. Off with you both.

THE BURGLAR. Yes, Captain. [*He goes out humbly*].

MAZZINI. Will it be safe to have him in the house like that?

GUINNESS. Why didnt you shoot him, sir? If I'd known who he was, I'd have shot him myself. [*She goes out*].

MRS HUSHABYE. Do sit down, everybody. [*She sits down on the sofa*].

They all move except Ellie. Mazzini resumes his seat. Randall sits down in the window seat near the starboard door, again making a pendulum of his poker, and studying it as Galileo might have done. Hector sits on his left, in the middle. Mangan, forgotten, sits in the port corner. Lady Utterword takes the big chair. Captain Shotover goes into the pantry in deep abstraction. They all look after him; and Lady Utterword coughs unconsciously.

MRS HUSHABYE. So Billy Dunn was poor nurse's little romance. I knew there had been somebody.

RANDALL. They will fight their battles over again and enjoy themselves immensely.

LADY UTTERWORD [*irritably*] You are not married; and you know nothing about it, Randall. Hold your tongue.

RANDALL. Tyrant!

MRS HUSHABYE. Well, we have had a very exciting evening. Everything will be an anticlimax after it. We'd better all go to bed.

RANDALL. Another burglar may turn up.

MAZZINI. Oh, impossible! I hope not.

RANDALL. Why not? There is more than one burglar in England.

MRS HUSHABYE. What do you say, Alf?

MANGAN [*huffily*] Oh, I dont matter. I'm forgotten. The burglar has put my nose out of joint. Shove me into a corner and have done with me.

MRS HUSHABYE [*jumping up mischievously, and going to him*] Would you like a walk on the heath, Alfred? With me?

ELLIE. Go, Mr Mangan. It will do you good. Hesione will soothe you.

MRS HUSHABYE [*slipping her arm under his and pulling him upright*] Come, Alfred. There is a moon: it's like the night in Tristan and Isolde. [*She caresses his arm and draws him to the port garden door*].

MANGAN [*writhing but yielding*] How you can have the face—the heart— [*he breaks down and is heard sobbing as she takes him out.*]

LADY UTTERWORD. What an extraordinary way to behave! What is the matter with the man?

ELLIE [*in a strangely calm voice, staring into an imaginary distance*] His heart is breaking: that is all. [*The Captain appears at the pantry door, listening*]. It is a curious sensation: the sort of pain that goes mercifully beyond our powers of feeling. When your heart is broken, your boats are burned: nothing matters any more. It is the end of happiness and the beginning of peace.

LADY UTTERWORD [*suddenly rising in a rage, to the astonish-ment of the rest*] How dare you?

HECTOR. Good heavens! Whats the matter?

RANDALL [*in a warning whisper*] Tch—tch—tch! Steady.

ELLIE [*surprised and haughty*] I was not addressing you particularly, Lady Utterword. And I am not accustomed to be asked how dare I.

LADY UTTERWORD. Of course not. Anyone can see how badly you have been brought up.

MAZZINI. Oh, I hope not, Lady Utterword. Really!

LADY UTTERWORD. I know very well what you meant. The impudence!

ELLIE. What on earth do you mean?

CAPTAIN SHOTOVER [*advancing to the table*] She means that her heart will not break. She has been longing all her life for someone to break it. At last she has become afraid she has none to break.

LADY UTTERWORD [*flinging herself on her knees and throw-ing her arms round him*] Papa: dont say you think Ive no heart.

CAPTAIN SHOTOVER [*raising her with grim tenderness*] If you had no heart how could you want to have it broken, child?

HECTOR [*rising with a bound*] Lady Utterword: you are not to be trusted. You have made a scene [*he runs out into the garden through the starboard door*].

LADY UTTERWORD. Oh! Hector, Hector! [*she runs out after him*].

RANDALL. Only nerves, I assure you. [*He rises and fol-lows her, waving the poker in his agitation*] Ariadne! Ariadne! For God's sake be careful. You will— [*he is gone*].

MAZZINI [*rising*] How distressing! Can I do anything, I wonder?

CAPTAIN SHOTOVER [*promptly taking his chair and setting to work at the drawing-board*] No. Go to bed. Goodnight.

MAZZINI [*bewildered*] Oh! Perhaps you are right.

ELLIE. Good night, dearest. [*She kisses him*].

MAZZINI Good night, love. [*He makes for the door, but*

turns aside to the bookshelves]. I'll just take a book [*he takes one*]. Goodnight. [*He goes out, leaving Ellie alone with the Captain*].

The Captain is intent on his drawing. Ellie, standing sentry over his chair, contemplates him for a moment.

ELLIE. Does nothing ever disturb you, Captain Shotover?

CAPTAIN SHOTOVER. Ive stood on the bridge for eighteen hours in a typhoon. Life here is stormier; but I can stand it.

ELLIE. Do you think I ought to marry Mr Mangan?

CAPTAIN SHOTOVER [*never looking up*] One rock is as good as another to be wrecked on.

ELLIE. I am not in love with him.

CAPTAIN SHOTOVER. Who said you were?

ELLIE. You are not surprised?

CAPTAIN SHOTOVER. Surprised! At m y age!

ELLIE. It seems to me quite fair. He wants me for one thing: I want him for another.

CAPTAIN SHOTOVER. Money?

ELLIE. Yes.

CAPTAIN SHOTOVER. Well, one turns the cheek; the other kisses it. One provides the cash: the other spends it.

ELLIE. Who will have the best of the bargain, I wonder?

CAPTAIN SHOTOVER. You. These fellows live in an office all day. You will have to put up with him from dinner to breakfast; but you will both be asleep most of that time. All day you will be quit of him; and you will be shopping with his money. If that is too much for you, marry a seafaring man: you will be bothered with him only three weeks in the year, perhaps.

ELLIE. That would be best of all, I suppose.

CAPTAIN SHOTOVER. It's a dangerous thing to be married right up to the hilt, like my daughter's husband. The man is at home all day, like a damned soul in hell.

ELLIE. I never thought of that before.

CAPTAIN SHOTOVER. If youre marrying for business, you cant be too businesslike.

ELLIE. Why do women always want other women's husbands?

CAPTAIN SHOTOVER. Why do horse-thieves prefer a horse that is broken-in to one that is wild?

ELLIE [*with a short laugh*] I suppose so. What a vile world it is!

CAPTAIN SHOTOVER. It doesnt concern me. I'm nearly out of it.

ELLIE. And I'm only just beginning.

CAPTAIN SHOTOVER. Yes; so look ahead.

ELLIE. Well, I think I am being very prudent.

CAPTAIN SHOTOVER. I didnt say prudent. I said look ahead.

ELLIE. Whats the difference?

CAPTAIN SHOTOVER. It's prudent to gain the whole world and lose your own soul. But dont forget that your soul sticks to you if you stick to it; but the world has a way of slipping through your fingers.

ELLIE [*wearily, leaving him and beginning to wander restlessly about the room*] I'm sorry, Captain Shotover; but it's no use talking like that to me. Old-fashioned people are no use to me. Old-fashioned people think you can have a soul without money. They think the less money you have, the more soul you have. Young people nowadays know better. A soul is a very expensive thing to keep: much more so than a motor car.

CAPTAIN SHOTOVER. Is it? How much does your soul eat?

ELLIE. Oh, a lot. It eats music and pictures and books and mountains and lakes and beautiful things to wear and nice people to be with. In this country you cant have them without lots of money: that is why our souls are so horribly starved.

CAPTAIN SHOTOVER. Mangan's soul lives on pigs' food.

ELLIE. Yes: money is thrown away on him. I suppose his soul was starved when he was young. But it will not be thrown away on me. It is just because I want to save my soul that I am marrying for money. All the women who are not fools do.

CAPTAIN SHOTOVER. There are other ways of getting money. Why dont you steal it?

ELLIE. Because I dont want to go to prison.

CAPTAIN SHOTOVER. Is that the only reason? Are you quite sure honesty has nothing to do with it?

ELLIE. Oh, you are very very old-fashioned, Captain. Does any modern girl believe that the legal and illegal ways of getting money are the honest and dishonest ways? Mangan robbed my father and my father's friends. I should rob all the money back from Mangan if the police would let me. As they wont, I must get it back by marrying him.

CAPTAIN SHOTOVER. I cant argue: I'm too old: my mind is made up and finished. All I can tell you is that, old-fashioned or new-fashioned, if you sell yourself, you deal your soul a blow that all the books and pictures and concerts and scenery in the world wont heal [*he gets up suddenly and makes for the pantry*].

ELLIE [*running after him and seizing him by the sleeve*] Then why did you sell yourself to the devil in Zanzibar?

CAPTAIN SHOTOVER [*stopping, startled*] What?

ELLIE. You shall not run away before you answer. I have found out that trick of yours. If you sold yourself, why shouldnt I?

CAPTAIN SHOTOVER. I had to deal with men so degraded that they wouldnt obey me unless I swore at them and kicked them and beat them with my fists. Foolish people took young thieves off the streets; flung them into a training ship where they were taught to fear the cane instead of fearing God; and thought theyd make men and sailors of them by private subscription. I tricked these thieves into believing I'd sold myself to the devil. It saved my soul from the kicking and swearing that was damning me by inches.

ELLIE [*releasing him*] I shall pretend to sell myself to Boss Mangan to save my soul from the poverty that is damning m e by inches.

CAPTAIN SHOTOVER. Riches will damn you ten times deeper. Riches wont save even your body.

ELLIE. Old-fashioned again. We know now that the soul is the body, and the body the soul. They tell us they are different because they want to persuade us that we can keep our souls if we let them make slaves of our bodies. I am afraid you are no use to me, Captain.

CAPTAIN SHOTOVER. What did you expect? A Savior, eh? Are you old-fashioned enough to believe in that?

ELLIE. No. But I thought you were very wise, and might help me. Now I have found you out. You pretend to be busy, and think of fine things to say, and run in and out to surprise people by saying them, and get away before they can answer you.

CAPTAIN SHOTOVER. It confuses me to be answered. It discourages me. I cannot bear men and women. I h a v e to run away. I must run away now [*he tries to*].

ELLIE [*again seizing his arm*] You shall not run away from me. I can hypnotize you. You are the only person in the house I can say what I like to. I know you are fond of me. Sit down. [*She draws him to the sofa*].

CAPTAIN SHOTOVER [*yielding*] Take care: I am in my dotage. Old men are dangerous: it doesnt matter to them what is going to happen to the world.

They sit side by side on the sofa. She leans affectionately against him with her head on his shoulder and her eyes half closed.

ELLIE [*dreamily*] I should have thought nothing else mattered to old men. They cant be very interested in what is going to happen to themselves.

CAPTAIN SHOTOVER. A man's interest in the world is only the overflow from his interest in himself. When you are a child your vessel is not yet full; so you care for nothing but your own affairs. When you grow up, your vessel overflows; and you are a politician, a philosopher, or an explorer and adventurer. In old age the vessel dries up: there is no overflow: you are a child again. I can give you the memories of my ancient wisdom: mere scraps and leavings; but I no longer really care for anything but my own little wants and hobbies. I sit here working out my old ideas as a means of destroying my fellow-creatures. I see my daughters and their men living foolish lives of romance and sentiment and snobbery. I see you, the younger generation, turning from their romance and sentiment and snobbery to money and comfort and hard common sense. I was ten times happier on the bridge in the typhoon, or frozen into Arctic ice for months in

darkness, than you or they have ever been. You are
looking for a rich husband. At your age I looked for
hardship, danger, horror, and death, that I might feel
the life in me more intensely. I did not let the fear of
death govern my life; and my reward was, I had my life.
You are going to let the fear of poverty govern your life;
and your reward will be that you will eat, but you will
not live.

ELLIE [*sitting up impatiently*] But what can I do? I am not
a sea captain: I cant stand on bridges in typhoons, or go
slaughtering seals and whales in Greenland's icy mountains. They wont let women be captains. Do you want me
to be a stewardess?

CAPTAIN SHOTOVER. There are worse lives. The stewardesses
could come ashore if they liked; but they sail and sail
and sail.

ELLIE. What could they do ashore but marry for money? I
dont want to be a stewardess: I am too bad a sailor.
Think of something else for me.

CAPTAIN SHOTOVER. I cant think so long and continuously.
I am too old. I must go in and out. [*He tries to rise*].

ELLIE [*pulling him back*] You shall not. You are happy
here, arnt you?

CAPTAIN SHOTOVER. I tell you it's dangerous to keep me.
I cant keep awake and alert.

ELLIE. What do you run away for? To sleep?

CAPTAIN SHOTOVER. No. To get a glass of rum.

ELLIE [*frightfully disillusioned*] Is t h a t it? How disgusting! Do you like being drunk?

CAPTAIN SHOTOVER. No: I dread being drunk more than
anything in the world. To be drunk means to have
dreams; go soft; to be easily pleased and deceived; to
fall into the clutches of women. Drink does that for you
when you are young. But when you are old: very very
old, like me, the dreams come by themselves. You dont
know how terrible that is: you are young: you sleep
at night only, and sleep soundly. But later on you will
sleep in the afternoon. Later still you will sleep even
in the morning; and you will awake tired, tired of life.
You will never be free from dozing and dreams: the

dreams will steal upon your work every ten minutes
unless you can awaken yourself with rum. I drink now
to keep sober; but the dreams are conquering: rum is
not what it was: I have had ten glasses since you came;
and it might be so much water. Go get me another:
Guinness knows where it is. You had better see for
yourself the horror of an old man drinking.

ELLIE. You shall not drink. Dream. I like you to dream.
You must never be in the real world when we talk
together.

CAPTAIN SHOTOVER. I am too weary to resist or too weak.
I am in my second childhood. I do not see you as you
really are. I cant remember what I really am. I feel
nothing but the accursed happiness I have dreaded all
my life long: the happiness that comes as life goes, the
happiness of yielding and dreaming instead of resisting
and doing, the sweetness of the fruit that is going
rotten.

ELLIE. You dread it almost as much as I used to dread
losing my dreams and having to fight and do things. But
that is all over for me: m y dreams are dashed to pieces.
I should like to marry a very old, very rich man. I should
like to marry you. I had much rather marry you than
marry Mangan. Are you very rich?

CAPTAIN SHOTOVER. No. Living from hand to mouth. And
I have a wife somewhere in Jamaica: a black one. My
first wife. Unless she's dead.

ELLIE. What a pity! I feel so happy with you. [*She takes his
hand, almost unconsciously, and pats it*]. I thought I
should never feel happy again.

CAPTAIN SHOTOVER. Why?

ELLIE. Dont you know?

CAPTAIN SHOTOVER. No.

ELLIE. Heartbreak. I fell in love with Hector, and didnt
know he was married.

CAPTAIN SHOTOVER. Heartbreak? Are you one of those who
are so sufficient to themselves that they are only happy
when they are stripped of everything, even of hope?

ELLIE [*gripping the hand*] It seems so; for I feel now as if
there was nothing I could not do, because I want nothing.

CAPTAIN SHOTOVER. Thats the only real strength. Thats genius. Thats better than rum.

ELLIE [*throwing away his hand*] Rum! Why did you spoil it?
Hector and Randall come in from the garden through the starboard door.

HECTOR. I beg your pardon. We did not know there was anyone here.

ELLIE [*rising*] That means that you want to tell Mr Randall the story about the tiger. Come, Captain: I want to talk to my father; and you had better come with me.

CAPTAIN SHOTOVER [*rising*] Nonsense! the man is in bed.

ELLIE. Aha! Ive caught you. My real father has gone to bed; but the father you gave me is in the kitchen. You knew quite well all along. Come. [*She draws him out into the garden with her through the port door*].

HECTOR. Thats an extraordinary girl. She has the Ancient Mariner on a string like a Pekinese dog.

RANDALL. Now that they have gone, shall we have a friendly chat?

HECTOR. You are in what is supposed to be my house. I am at your disposal.
Hector sits down in the draughtsman's chair, turning it to face Randall, who remains standing, leaning at his ease against the carpenter's bench.

RANDALL. I take it that we may be quite frank. I mean about Lady Utterword.

HECTOR. You may. I have nothing to be frank about. I never met her until this afternoon.

RANDALL [*straightening up*] What! But you are her sister's husband.

HECTOR. Well, if you come to that, you are her husband's brother.

RANDALL. But you seem to be on intimate terms with her.

HECTOR. So do you.

RANDALL. Yes; but I a m on intimate terms with her. I have known her for years.

HECTOR. It took her years to get to the same point with you that she got to with me in five minutes, it seems.

RANDALL [*vexed*] Really, Ariadne is the limit [*he moves away huffishly towards the windows*].

HECTOR [*coolly*] She is, as I remarked to Hesione, a very enterprising woman.

RANDALL [*returning, much troubled*] You see, Hushabye, you are what women consider a good-looking man.

HECTOR. I cultivated that appearance in the days of my vanity; and Hesione insists on my keeping it up. She makes me wear these ridiculous things [*indicating his Arab costume*] because she thinks me absurd in evening dress.

RANDALL. Still, you do keep it up, old chap. Now, I assure you I have not an atom of jealousy in my disposition—

HECTOR. The question would seem to be rather whether your brother has any touch of that sort.

RANDALL. What! Hastings! Oh, dont trouble about Hastings. He has the gift of being able to work sixteen hours a day at the dullest detail, and actually likes it. That gets him to the top wherever he goes. As long as Ariadne takes care that he is fed regularly, he is only too thankful to anyone who will keep her in good humor for him.

HECTOR. And as she has all the Shotover fascination, there is plenty of competition for the job, eh?

RANDALL [*angrily*] She encourages them. Her conduct is perfectly scandalous. I assure you, my dear fellow, I havnt an atom of jealousy in my composition; but she makes herself the talk of every place she goes to by her thoughtlessness. It's nothing more: she doesnt really care for the men she keeps hanging about her; but how is the world to know that? It's not fair to Hastings. It's not fair to me.

HECTOR. Her theory is that her conduct is so correct—

RANDALL. Correct! She does nothing but make scenes from morning til night. You be careful, old chap. She will get you into trouble: that is, she would if she really cared for you.

HECTOR. Doesnt she?

RANDALL. Not a scrap. She may want your scalp to add to her collection; but her true affection has been engaged years ago. You had really better be careful.

HECTOR. Do you suffer much from this jealousy?

RANDALL. Jealousy! I jealous! My dear fellow, havnt I told
you that there is not an atom of—

HECTOR. Yes. And Lady Utterword told me she never
made scenes. Well, dont waste your jealousy on my
moustache. Never waste jealousy on a real man: it is
the imaginary hero that supplants us all in the long run.
Besides, jealousy does not belong to your easy man-of-
the world pose, which you carry so well in other respects.

RANDALL. Really, Hushabye, I think a man may be allowed
to be a gentleman without being accused of posing.

HECTOR. It is a pose like any other. In this house we know
all the poses: our game is to find out the man under the
pose. The man under your pose is apparently Ellie's
favorite, Othello.

RANDALL. Some of your games in this house are damned
annoying, let me tell you.

HECTOR. Yes: I have been their victim for many years. I
used to writhe under them at first; but I became accustomed to them. At last I learned to play them.

RANDALL. If it's all the same to you, I had rather you didnt
play them on me. You evidently dont quite understand
my character, or my notions of good form.

HECTOR. Is it your notion of good form to give away Lady
Utterword?

RANDALL [a childishly plaintive note breaking into his huff]
I have not said a word against Lady Utterword. This is
just the conspiracy over again.

HECTOR. What conspiracy?

RANDALL. You know very well, sir. A conspiracy to make
me out to be pettish and jealous and childish and everything I am not. Everyone knows I am just the opposite.

HECTOR [rising] Something in the air of the house has upset
you. It often does have that effect. [He goes to the garden
door and calls Lady Utterword with commanding em-
phasis] Ariadne!

LADY UTTERWORD [at some distance] Yes.

RANDALL. What are you calling her for? I want to speak—

LADY UTTERWORD [arriving breathless] Yes. You really are
a terribly commanding person. Whats the matter?

HECTOR. I do not know how to manage your friend Randall.
No doubt you do.

LADY UTTERWORD. Randall: have you been making yourself ridiculous, as usual? I can see it in your face. Really,
you are the most pettish creature.

RANDALL. You know quite well, Ariadne, that I have not
an ounce of pettishness in my disposition. I have made
myself perfectly pleasant here. I have remained absolutely cool and imperturbable in the face of a burglar.
Imperturbability is almost too strong a point of mine. But
[*putting his foot down with a stamp, and walking angrily
up and down the room*] I insist on being treated with a
certain consideration. I will not allow Hushabye to take
liberties with me. I will not stand your encouraging people as you do.

HECTOR. The man has a rooted delusion that he is your
husband.

LADY UTTERWORD. I know. He is jealous. As if he had any
right to be! He compromises me everywhere. He makes
scenes all over the place. Randall: I will not allow it. I
simply will not allow it. You had no right to discuss me
with Hector. I will not be discussed by men.

HECTOR. Be reasonable, Ariadne. Your fatal gift of beauty
forces men to discuss you.

LADY UTTERWORD. Oh indeed! what about y o u r fatal gift
of beauty?

HECTOR. How can I help it?

LADY UTTERWORD. You could cut off your moustache: I
cant cut off my nose. I get my whole life messed up with
people falling in love with me. And then Randall says I
run after men.

RANDALL. I—

LADY UTTERWORD. Yes you do: you said it just now. Why
cant you think of something else than women? Napoleon
was quite right when he said that women are the occupation of the idle man. Well, if ever there was an idle man
on earth, his name is Randall Utterword.

RANDALL. Ariad—

LADY UTTERWORD [*overwhelming him with a torrent of*

words] O h yes you are: it's no use denying it. What
have you ever done? What good are you? You are as
much trouble in the house as a child of three. You
couldnt live without your valet.

RANDALL. This is—

LADY UTTERWORD. Laziness! You are laziness incarnate.
You are selfishness itself. You are the most uninteresting
man on earth. You cant even gossip about anything but
yourself and your grievances and your ailments and the
people who have offended you. [*Turning to Hector*] Do
you know what they call him, Hector?

HECTOR.   ) *speaking* (Please dont tell me.
RANDALL.   ) *together* (I'll not stand it—

LADY UTTERWORD. Randall the Rotter: that is his name in
good society.

RANDALL [*shouting*] I'll not bear it, I tell you. Will you listen to me, you infernal— [*he chokes*].

LADY UTTERWORD. Well: go on. What were you going to
cal me? An infernal what? Which unpleasant animal is it
to be this time?

RANDALL [*foaming*] There is no animal in the world so hateful as a woman can be. You are a maddening devil.
Hushabye: you will not believe me when I tell you that
I have loved this demon all my life; but God knows I
have paid for it [*he sits down in the draughtsman's chair,
weeping*].

LADY UTTERWORD [*standing over him with triumphant contempt*] Cry-baby!

HECTOR [*gravely, coming to him*] My friend: the Shotover
sisters have two strange powers over men. They can
make them love; and they can make them cry. Thank
your stars that you are not married to one of them.

LADY UTTERWORD [*haughtily*] And pray, Hector—

HECTOR [*suddenly catching her round the shoulders; swinging her right round him and away from Randall; and
gripping her throat with the other hand*] Ariadne: if you
attempt to start on me, I'll choke you: do you hear? The
cat-and-mouse game with the other sex is a good game;
but I can play your head off at it. [*He throws her, not
at all gently, into the big chair, and proceeds, less fiercely*

but firmly] It is true that Napoleon said that woman is
the occupation of the idle man. But he added that she
is the relaxation of the warrior. Well, *I* am the warrior.
So take care.

LADY UTTERWORD [*not in the least put out, and rather
pleased by his violence*] My dear Hector: I have only
done what you asked me to do.

HECTOR. How do you make that out, pray?

LADY UTTERWORD. You called me in to manage Randall,
didnt you? You said you couldnt manage him yourself.

HECTOR. Well, what if I did? I did not ask you to drive the
man mad.

LADY UTTERWORD. He isnt mad. Thats the way to manage him. If you were a mother, youd understand.

HECTOR. Mother! What are you up to now?

LADY UTTERWORD. It's quite simple. When the children got
nerves and were naughty, I smacked them just enough
to give them a good cry and a healthy nervous shock.
They went to sleep and were quite good afterwards. Well,
I cant smack Randall: he is too big; so when he gets
nerves and is naughty, I just rag him til he cries. He
will be all right now. Look: he is half asleep already
[*which is quite true*].

RANDALL [*waking up indignantly*] I'm not. You are most
cruel, Ariadne. [*Sentimentally*] But I suppose I must
forgive you, as usual [*he checks himself in the act of
yawning*].

LADY UTTERWORD [*to Hector*] Is the explanation satisfactory, dread warrior?

HECTOR. Some day I shall kill you, if you go too far. I
thought you were a fool.

LADY UTTERWORD [*laughing*] Everybody does, at first. But
I am not such a fool as I look. [*She rises complacently*].
Now, Randall: go to bed. You will be a good boy in
the morning.

RANDALL [*only very faintly rebellious*] I'll go to bed when I
like. It isnt ten yet.

LADY UTTERWORD. It is long past ten. See that he goes to
bed at once, Hector. [*She goes into the garden*].

HECTOR. Is there any slavery on earth viler than this slavery of men to women?

RANDALL [*rising resolutely*] I'll not speak to her for another week. I'll give her s u c h a lesson. I'll go straight to bed without bidding her goodnight. [*He makes for the door leading to the hall*].

HECTOR. You are under a spell, man. Old Shotover sold himself to the devil in Zanzibar. The devil gave him a black witch for a wife; and these two demon daughters are their mystical progeny. I am tied to Hesione's apronstring; but I'm her husband; and if I did go stark staring mad about her, at least we became man and wife. But why should you let yourself be dragged about and beaten by Ariadne as a toy donkey is dragged about and beaten by a child? What do you get by it? Are you her lover?

RANDALL. You must not misunderstand me. In a higher sense—in a Platonic sense—

HECTOR. Psha! Platonic sense! She makes you her servant; and when pay-day comes round, she bilks you: that is what you mean.

RANDALL [*feebly*] Well, if I dont mind, I dont see what business it is of yours. Besides, I tell you I am going to punish her. You shall see: *I* know how to deal with women. I'm really very sleepy. Say goodnight to Mrs Hushabye for me, will you, like a good chap. Goodnight. [*He hurries out*].

HECTOR. Poor wretch! Oh women! women! women! [*He lifts his fists in invocation to heaven*] Fall. Fall and crush. [*He goes out into the garden*].

ACT III

In the garden, Hector, as he comes out through the glass door of the poop, finds Lady Utterword lying voluptuously in the hammock on the east side of the flagstaff, in the circle of light cast by the electric arc, which is like a moon in its opal globe. Beneath the head of the hammock, a campstool. On the other side of the flagstaff, on the long garden seat,

Captain Shotover is asleep with Ellie beside him, leaning affectionately against him on his right hand. On his left is a deck chair. Behind them in the gloom, Hesione is strolling about with Mangan. It is a fine still night, moonless.

LADY UTTERWORD. What a lovely night! It seems made for us.

HECTOR. The night takes no interest in us. What are we to the night? [*He sits down moodily in the deck chair*].

ELLIE [*dreamily, nestling against the Captain*] Its beauty soaks into my nerves. In the night there is peace for the old and hope for the young.

HECTOR. Is that remark your own?

ELLIE. No. Only the last thing the Captain said before he went to sleep.

CAPTAIN SHOTOVER. I'm not asleep.

HECTOR. Randall is. Also Mr Mazzini Dunn. Mangan too, probably.

MANGAN. No.

HECTOR. Oh, you are there. I thought Hesione would have sent you to bed by this time.

MRS HUSHABYE. [*coming to the back of the garden seat, into the light, with Mangan*] I think I shall. He keeps telling me he has a presentiment that he is going to die. I never met a man so greedy for sympathy.

MANGAN [*plaintively*] But I have a presentiment. I really have. And you wouldnt listen.

MRS HUSHABYE. I was listening for something else. There was a sort of splendid drumming in the sky. Did none of you hear it? It came from a distance and then died away.

MANGAN. I tell you it was a train.

MRS HUSHABYE. And *I* tell you, Alf, there is no train at this hour. The last is nine forty-five.

MANGAN. But a goods train.

MRS HUSHABYE. Not on our little line. They tack a truck on to the passenger train. What can it have been, Hector?

HECTOR. Heaven's threatening growl of disgust at us useless futile creatures. [*Fiercely*] I tell you, one of two things must happen. Either out of that darkness some new creation will come to supplant us as we have supplanted the animals, or the heavens will fall in thunder and destroy us.

LADY UTTERWORD [*in a cool instructive manner, wallowing comfortably in her hammock*] We have not supplanted the animals, Hector. Why do you ask heaven to destroy this house, which could be made quite comfortable if Hesione had any notion of how to live? Dont you know what is wrong with it?

HECTOR. We are wrong with it. There is no sense in us. We are useless, dangerous, and ought to be abolished.

LADY UTTERWORD. Nonsense! Hastings told me the very first day he came here, nearly twenty-four years ago, what is wrong with the house.

CAPTAIN SHOTOVER. What! The numskull said there was something wrong with my house!

LADY UTTERWORD. I said Hastings said it; and he is not in the least a numskull.

CAPTAIN SHOTOVER. Whats wrong with my house?

LADY UTTERWORD. Just what is wrong with a ship, papa. Wasnt it clever of Hastings to see that?

CAPTAIN SHOTOVER. The man's a fool. Theres nothing wrong with a ship.

LADY UTTERWORD. Yes there is.

MRS HUSHABYE. But what is it? Dont be aggravating, Addy.

LADY UTTERWORD. Guess.

HECTOR. Demons. Daughters of the witch of Zanzibar. Demons.

LADY UTTERWORD. Not a bit. I assure you, all this house needs to make it a sensible, healthy, pleasant house, with good appetites and sound sleep in it, is horses.

MRS HUSHABYE. Horses! What rubbish!

LADY UTTERWORD. Yes: horses. Why have we never been able to let this house? Because there are no proper stables. Go anywhere in England where there are natural, wholesome, contented, and really nice English people; and what do you always find? That the stables are the real centre of the household; and that if any visitor wants to play the piano the whole room has to be upset before it can be opened, there are so many things piled on it. I never lived until I learned to ride; and I shall never ride really well because I didnt begin as a child. There are only two classes in good society in England: the equestrian classes and the neurotic classes. It isnt mere convention: everybody can see that the people who hunt are the right people and the people who dont are the wrong ones.

CAPTAIN SHOTOVER. There is some truth in this. My ship made a man of me; and a ship is the horse of the sea.

LADY UTTERWORD. Exactly how Hastings explained your being a gentleman.

CAPTAIN SHOTOVER. Not bad for a numskull. Bring the man here with you next time: I must talk to him.

LADY UTTERWORD. Why is Randall such an obvious rotter? He is well bred; he has been at a public school and a university; he has been in the Foreign Office; he knows the best people and has lived all his life among them. Why is he so unsatisfactory, so contemptible? Why cant he get a valet to stay with him longer than a few months? Just because he is too lazy and pleasure-loving to hunt and shoot. He strums the piano, and sketches, and runs after married women, and reads literary books and poems. He actually plays the flute; but I never let him bring it into my house. If he would only— [*she is interrupted by the melancholy strains of a flute coming from an open window above. She raises herself indignantly in the hammock*]. Randall: you have not gone to bed. Have you been listening? [*The flute replies pertly:*]

How vulgar! Go to bed instantly, Randall: how dare you? [*The window is slammed down. She subsides*]. How can anyone care for such a creature!

MRS HUSHABYE. Addy: do you think Ellie ought to marry poor Alfred merely for his money?

MANGAN [*much alarmed*] Whats that? Mrs Hushabye: are my affairs to be discussed like this before everybody?

LADY UTTERWORD. I dont think Randall is listening now.

MANGAN. Everybody is listening. It isnt right.

MRS HUSHABYE. But in the dark, what does it matter? Ellie doesnt mind. Do you, Ellie?

ELLIE. Not in the least. What is your opinion, Lady Utterword? You have so much good sense.

MANGAN. But it isnt right. It— [*Mrs Hushabye puts her hand on his mouth*]. Oh, very well.

LADY UTTERWORD. How much money have you, Mr Mangan?

MANGAN. Really— No: I cant stand this.

LADY UTTERWORD. Nonsense, Mr Mangan! It all turns on your income, doesnt it?

MANGAN. Well, if you come to that, how much money has she?

ELLIE. None.

LADY UTTERWORD. You are answered, Mr Mangan. And now, as you have made Miss Dunn throw her cards on the table, you cannot refuse to shew your own.

MRS HUSHABYE. Come, Alf! out with it! How much?

MANGAN [*baited out of all prudence*] Well, if you want to know, I have no money and never had any.

MRS HUSHABYE. Alfred: you mustnt tell naughty stories.

MANGAN. I'm not telling you stories. I'm telling you the raw truth.

LADY UTTERWORD. Then what do you live on, Mr Mangan?

MANGAN. Travelling expenses. And a trifle of commission.

CAPTAIN SHOTOVER. What more have any of us but travelling expenses for our life's journey?

MRS HUSHABYE. But you have factories and capital and things?

MANGAN. People think I have. People think I'm an industrial Napoleon. Thats why Miss Ellie wants to marry me. But I tell you I have nothing.

ELLIE. Do you mean that the factories are like Marcus's tigers? That they dont exist?

MANGAN. They exist all right enough. But theyre not mine. They belong to syndicates and shareholders and all sorts of lazy good-for-nothing capitalists. I get money from such people to start the factories. I find people like Miss

Dunn's father to work them, and keep a tight hand so as to make them pay. Of course I make them keep me going pretty well; but it's a dog's life; and I dont own anything.

MRS HUSHABYE. Alfred, Alfred: you are making a poor mouth of it to get out of marrying Ellie.

MANGAN. I'm telling the truth about my money for the first time in my life; and it's the first time my word has ever been doubted.

LADY UTTERWORD. How sad! Why dont you go in for politics, Mr Mangan?

MANGAN. Go in for politics! Where have you been living? I a m in politics.

LADY UTTERWORD. I'm sure I beg your pardon. I never heard of you.

MANGAN. Let me tell you, Lady Utterword, that the Prime Minister of this country asked me to join the Government without even going through the nonsense of an election, as the dictator of a great public department.

LADY UTTERWORD. As a Conservative or a Liberal?

MANGAN. No such nonsense. As a practical business man. [*They all burst out laughing*]. What are you all laughing at?

MRS HUSHABYE. Oh, Alfred, Alfred!

ELLIE. You! who have to get my father to do everything for you!

MRS HUSHABYE. You! who are afraid of your own workmen!

HECTOR. You! with whom three women have been playing cat and mouse all the evening!

LADY UTTERWORD. You must have given an immense sum to the party funds, Mr Mangan.

MANGAN. Not a penny out of my own pocket. The syndicate found the money: they knew how useful I should be to them in the Government.

LADY UTTERWORD. This is most interesting and unexpected, Mr Mangan. And what have your administrative achievements been, so far?

MANGAN. Achievements? Well, I dont know what you call achievements; but Ive jolly well put a stop to the games of the other fellows in the other departments. Every man of them thought he was going to save the country all by

himself, and do me out of the credit and out of my
chance of a title. I took good care that if they wouldnt let
me do it they shouldnt do it themselves either. I may not
know anything about my own machinery; but I know
how to stick a ramrod into the other fellow's. And now
they all look the biggest fools going.

HECTOR. And in heaven's name, what do y o u look like?

MANGAN. I look like the fellow that was too clever for all
the others, dont I? If that isnt a triumph of practical business, what is?

HECTOR. Is this England, or is it a madhouse?

LADY UTTERWORD. Do you expect to save the country, Mr
Mangan?

MANGAN. Well, who else will? Will your Mr Randall save
it?

LADY UTTERWORD. Randall the Rotter! Certainly not.

MANGAN. Will your brother-in-law save it with his moustache and his fine talk.

HECTOR. Yes, if they will let me.

MANGAN [*sneering*] Ah! W i l l they let you?

HECTOR. No. They prefer you.

MANGAN. Very well then, as youre in a world where I'm
appreciated and youre not, youd best be civil to me,
hadnt you? Who else is there but me?

LADY UTTERWORD. There is Hastings. Get rid of your
ridiculous sham democracy; and give Hastings the necessary powers, and a good supply of bamboo to bring the
British native to his senses: h e will save the country with
the greatest ease.

CAPTAIN SHOTOVER. It had better be lost. Any fool can
govern with a stick in his hand. *I* could govern that way.
It is not God's way. The man is a numskull.

LADY UTTERWORD. The man is worth all of you rolled into
one. What do y o u say, Miss Dunn?

ELLIE. I think my father would do very well if people did
not put upon him and cheat him and despise him because
he is so good.

MANGAN [*contemptuously*] I think I see Mazzini Dunn
getting into parliament or pushing his way into the

Government. Weve not come to that yet, thank God!
What do you say, Mrs Hushabye?

MRS HUSHABYE. Oh, *I* say it matters very little which of you
governs the country so long as we govern you.

HECTOR. We? Who is we, pray?

MRS HUSHABYE. The devil's granddaughters, dear. The
lovely women.

HECTOR [*raising his hands as before*] Fall, I say; and deliver
us from the lures of Satan!

ELLIE. There seems to be nothing real in the world except
my father and Shakespear. Marcus's tigers are false; Mr
Mangan's millions are false; there is nothing really strong
and true about Hesione but her beautiful black hair; and
Lady Utterword's is too pretty to be real. The one thing
that was left to me was the Captain's seventh degree of
concentration; and that turns out to be—

LADY UTTERWORD [*placidly*] A good deal of my hair is quite
genuine. The Duchess of Dithering offered me fifty
guineas for this [*touching her forehead*] under the impression that it was a transformation; but it is all natural
except the color.

MANGAN [*wildly*] look here: I'm going to take off all my
clothes [*he begins tearing off his coat*].

LADY UTTERWORD.		Mr Mangan!
CAPTAIN SHOTOVER.	*in*	Whats that?
HECTOR.	*consternation*	Ha! ha; Do. Do.
ELLIE		Please dont.

MRS HUSHABYE [*catching his arm and stopping him*] Alfred:
for shame! Are you mad?

MANGAN. Shame! What shame is there in this house? Let's
all strip stark naked. We may as well do the thing
thoroughly when we're about it. Weve stripped ourselves
morally naked: well, let us strip ourselves physically
naked as well, and see how we like it. I tell you I cant
bear this. I was brought up to be respectable. I dont mind
the women dyeing their hair and the men drinking: it's
human nature. But it's not human nature to tell everybody about it. Every time one of you opens your mouth
I go like this [*he cowers as if to avoid a missile*] afraid of

what will come next. How are we to have any self-respect
if we dont keep it up that we're better than we really are?

LADY UTTERWORD. I quite sympathize with you, Mr. Mangan. I have been through it all; and I know by experience
that men and women are delicate plants and must be
cultivated under glass. Our family habit of throwing
stones in all directions and letting the air in is not only
unbearably rude, but positively dangerous. Still, there is
no use catching physical colds as well as moral ones; so
please keep your clothes on.

MANGAN. I'll do as I like: not what you tell me. Am I a
child or a grown man? I wont stand this mothering
tyranny. I'll go back to the city, where I'm respected and
made much of.

MRS HUSHABYE. Goodbye, Alf. Think of us sometimes in
the city. Think of Ellie's youth!

ELLIE. Think of Hesione's eyes and hair!

CAPTAIN SHOTOVER. Think of this garden in which you are
not a dog barking to keep the truth out!

HECTOR. Think of Lady Utterword's beauty! her good sense!
her style!

LADY UTTERWORD. Flatterer. Think, Mr Mangan, whether
you can really do any better for yourself elsewhere: that
is the essential point, isnt it?

MANGAN [*surrendering*] All right: all right. I'm done. Have
it your own way. Only let me alone. I dont know whether
I'm on my head or my heels when you all start on me like
this. I'll stay. I'll marry her. I'll do anything for a quiet
life. Are you satisfied now?

ELLIE. No. I never really intended to make you marry me,
Mr Mangan. Never in the depths of my soul. I only
wanted to feel my strength: to know that you could not
escape if I chose to take you.

MANGAN [*indignantly*] What! Do you mean to say you are
going to throw me over after my acting so handsome?

LADY UTTERWORD. I should not be too hasty, Miss Dunn.
You can throw Mr Mangan over at any time up to the
last moment. Very few men in his position go bankrupt.
You can live very comfortably on his reputation for immense wealth.

ELLIE. I cannot commit bigamy, Lady Utterword.

MRS HUSHABYE.		Bigamy! Whatever on earth are you talking about, Ellie?
LADY UTTERWORD.	*exclaiming all together*	Bigamy! What do you mean, Miss Dunn?
MANGAN.		Bigamy! Do you mean to say youre married already?
HECTOR.		Bigamy! This is some enigma.

ELLIE. Only half an hour ago I became Captain Shotover's white wife.

MRS HUSHABYE. Ellie! What nonsense! Where?

ELLIE. In heaven, where all true marriages are made.

LADY UTTERWORD. Really, Miss Dunn! Really, papa!

MANGAN. He told me *I* was too old! And him a mummy!

HECTOR [*quoting Shelley*]

> Their altar the grassy earth outspread,
> And their priest the muttering wind.

ELLIE. Yes: I, Ellie Dunn, give my broken heart and my strong sound soul to its natural captain, my spiritual husband and second father.

She draws the Captain's arm through hers, and pats his hand. The Captain remains fast asleep.

MRS HUSHABYE. Oh, thats very clever of you, pettikins. V e r y clever. Alfred: you could never have lived up to Ellie. You must be content with a little share of me.

MANGAN [*sniffing and wiping his eyes*] It isnt kind— [*his emotion chokes him*].

LADY UTTERWORD. You are well out of it, Mr Mangan. Miss Dunn is the most conceited young woman I have met since I came back to England.

MRS HUSHABYE. Oh, Ellie isnt conceited. Are you pettikins?

ELLIE. I know my strength now, Hesione.

MANGAN. Brazen, I call you. Brazen.

MRS HUSHABYE. Tut tut, Alfred: dont be rude. Dont you feel how lovely this marriage night is, made in heaven? Arnt you happy, you and Hector? Open your eyes: Addy and Ellie look beautiful enough to please the most

fastidious man: we live and love and have not a care in
the world. We women have managed all that for you.
Why in the name of common sense do you go on as if
you were two miserable wretches?

CAPTAIN SHOTOVER. I tell you happiness is no good. You
can be happy when you are only half alive. I am happier
now I am half dead than ever I was in my prime. But
there is no blessing on my happiness.

ELLIE [*her face lighting up*] Life with a blessing! that is what
I want. Now I know the real reason why I couldnt marry
Mr Mangan: there would be no blessing on our marriage.
There is a blessing on my broken heart. There is a
blessing on your beauty, Hesione. There is a blessing on
your father's spirit. Even on the lies of Marcus there is
a blessing; but on Mr Mangan's money there is none.

MANGAN. I dont understand a word of that.

ELLIE. Neither do I. But I know it means something.

MANGAN. Dont say there was any difficulty about the
blessing. I was ready to get a bishop to marry us.

MRS HUSHABYE. Isnt he a fool, pettikins?

HECTOR [*fiercely*] Do not scorn the man. We are all fools.
*Mazzini, in pyjamas and a richly colored silk dressing-
gown, comes from the house, on Lady Utterword's side.*

MRS HUSHABYE. Oh! here comes the only man who ever
resisted me. Whats the matter, Mr Dunn? Is the house on
fire?

MAZZINI. Oh no: nothing's the matter; but really it's impossible to go to sleep with such an interesting conversation going on under one's window, and on such a beautiful night too. I just had to come down and join you all.
What has it all been about?

MRS HUSHABYE. Oh, wonderful things, soldier of freedom.

HECTOR. For example, Mangan, as a practical business man,
has tried to undress himself and has failed ignominiously;
whilst you, as an idealist, have succeeded brilliantly.

MAZZINI. I hope you dont mind my being like this, Mrs
Hushabye. [*He sits down on the campstool*].

MRS HUSHABYE. On the contrary, I could wish you always
like that.

LADY UTTERWORD. Your daughter's match is off, Mr Dunn. It seems that Mr Mangan, whom we all supposed to be a man of property, owns absolutely nothing.

MAZZINI. Well of course I knew that, Lady Utterword. But if people believe in him and are always giving him money, whereas they dont believe in me and never give me any, how can I ask poor Ellie to depend on what I can do for her?

MANGAN. Dont you run away with this idea that I have nothing. I—

HECTOR. Oh, dont explain. We understand. You have a couple of thousand pounds in exchequer bills, 50,000 shares worth tenpence a dozen, and half a dozen tabloids of cyanide of potassium to poison yourself with when you are found out. Thats the reality of your millions.

MAZZINI. Oh no, no, no. He is quite honest: the businesses are genuine and perfectly legal.

HECTOR [disgusted] Yah! Not even a great swindler!

MANGAN. So you think. But Ive been too many for some honest men, for all that.

LADY UTTERWORD. There is no pleasing you, Mr Mangan. You are determined to be neither rich nor poor, honest nor dishonest.

MANGAN. There you go again. Ever since I came into this silly house I have been made to look like a fool, though I'm as good a man in this house as in the city.

ELLIE [musically] Yes: this silly house, this strangely happy house, this agonizing house, this house without foundations. I shall call it Heartbreak House.

MRS HUSHABYE. Stop, Ellie; or I shall howl like an animal.

MANGAN [breaks into a low snivelling]!!!

MRS HUSHABYE. There! you have set Alfred off.

ELLIE. I like him best when he is howling.

CAPTAIN SHOTOVER. Silence! [Mangan subsides into silence]. I say, let the heart break in silence.

HECTOR. Do you accept that name for your house?

CAPTAIN SHOTOVER. It is not my house: it is only my kennel.

HECTOR. We have been too long here. We do not live in this house: we haunt it.

LADY UTTERWORD [*heart torn*] It is dreadful to think how you have been here all these years while I have gone round the world. I escaped young; but it has drawn me back. It wants to break my heart too. But it shant. I have left you and it behind. It was silly of me to come back. I felt sentimental about papa and Hesione and the old place. I felt them calling to me.

MAZZINI. But what a very natural and kindly and charming human feeling, Lady Utterword!

LADY UTTERWORD. So I thought, Mr Dunn. But I know now that it was only the last of my influenza. I found that I was not remembered and not wanted.

CAPTAIN SHOTOVER. You left because you did not want us. Was there no heartbreak in that for your father? You tore yourself up by the roots; and the ground healed up and brought forth fresh plants and forgot you. What right had you to come back and probe old wounds?

MRS HUSHABYE. You were a complete stranger to me at first, Addy; but now I feel as if you had never been away.

LADY UTTERWORD. Thank you, Hesione; but the influenza is quite cured. The place may be Heartbreak House to you, Miss Dunn, and to this gentleman from the city who seems to have so little self-control; but to me it is only a very ill-regulated and rather untidy villa without any stables.

HECTOR. Inhabited by— ?

ELLIE. A crazy old sea captain and a young singer who adores him.

MRS HUSHABYE. A sluttish female, trying to stave off a double chin and an elderly spread, vainly wooing a born soldier of freedom.

MAZZINI. Oh, really, Mrs Hushabye—

MANGAN. A member of His Majesty's Government that everybody sets down as a nincompoop: dont forget him, Lady Utterword.

LADY UTTERWORD. And a very fascinating gentleman whose chief occupation is to be married to my sister.

HECTOR. All heartbroken imbeciles.

MAZZINI. Oh no. Surely, if I may say so, rather a favorable specimen of what is best in our English culture. You are very charming people, most advanced, unprejudiced, frank, humane, unconventional, democratic, free-thinking, and everything that is delightful to thoughtful people.

MRS HUSHABYE. You do us proud, Mazzini.

MAZZINI. I am not flattering, really. Where else could I feel perfectly at ease in my pyjamas? I sometimes dream that I am in very distinguished society, and suddenly I have nothing on but my pyjamas! Sometimes I havnt even pyjamas. And I always feel overwhelmed with confusion. But here, I dont mind in the least: it seems quite natural.

LADY UTTERWORD. An infallible sign that you are not now in really distinguished society, Mr Dunn. If you were in my house, you would feel embarrassed.

MAZZINI. I shall take particular care to keep out of your house, Lady Utterword.

LADY UTTERWORD. You will be quite wrong, Mr Dunn. I should make you very comfortable; and you would not have the trouble and anxiety of wondering whether you should wear your purple and gold or your green and crimson dressing-gown at dinner. You complicate life instead of simplifying it by doing these ridiculous things.

ELLIE. Y o u r house is not Heartbreak House: is it, Lady Utterword?

HECTOR. Yet she breaks hearts, easy as her house is. That poor devil upstairs with his flute howls when she twists his heart, just as Mangan howls when my wife twists his.

LADY UTTERWORD. That is because Randall has nothing to do but have his heart broken. It is a change from having his head shampooed. Catch anyone breaking Hastings' heart!

CAPTAIN SHOTOVER. The numskull wins, after all.

LADY UTTERWORD. I shall go back to my numskull with the greatest satisfaction when I am tired of you all, clever as you are.

MANGAN [huffily] I never set up to be clever.

LADY UTTERWORD. I forgot you, Mr Mangan.

MANGAN. Well, I dont see that quite, either.

LADY UTTERWORD. You may not be clever, Mr Mangan; but you are successful.

MANGAN. But I dont want to be regarded merely as a successful man. I have an imagination like anyone else. I have a presentiment—

MRS HUSHABYE. Oh, you are impossible, Alfred. Here I am devoting myself to you; and you think of nothing but your ridiculous presentiment. You bore me. Come and talk poetry to me under the stars. [*She drags him away into the darkness*].

MANGAN [*tearfully, as he disappears*] Yes: it's all very well to make fun of me; but if you only knew—

HECTOR [*impatiently*] How is all this going to end?

MAZZINI. It wont end, Mr Hushabye. Life doesnt end: it goes on.

ELLIE. Oh, it cant go on for ever. I'm always expecting something. I dont know what it is; but life must come to a point sometime.

LADY UTTERWORD. The point for a young woman of your age is a baby.

HECTOR. Yes, but damn it, I have the same feeling; and *I* cant have a baby.

LADY UTTERWORD. By deputy, Hector.

HECTOR. But I have children. All that is over and done with for me: and yet I too feel that this cant last. We sit here talking, and leave everything to Mangan and to chance and to the devil. Think of the powers of destruction that Mangan and his mutual admiration gang wield! It's madness: it's like giving a torpedo to a badly brought up child to play at earthquakes with.

MAZZINI. I know. I used often to think about that when I was young.

HECTOR. Think! Whats the good of thinking about it? Why didnt you do something?

MAZZINI. But I did. I joined societies and made speeches and wrote pamphlets. That was all I could do. But, you know, though the people in the societies thought they knew more than Mangan, most of them wouldnt have joined if they had known as much. You see they had never had any money to handle or any men to manage. Every year I expected a revolution, or some frightful smash-up: it seemed impossible that we could blunder and muddle on any longer. But nothing happened, except, of course, the usual poverty and crime and drink that we are used to. Nothing ever does happen. It's amazing how well we get along, all things considered.

LADY UTTERWORD. Perhaps somebody cleverer than you and Mr Mangan was at work all the time.

MAZZINI. Perhaps so. Though I was brought up not to believe in anything, I often feel that there is a great deal to be said for the theory of an overruling Providence, after all.

LADY UTTERWORD. Providence! I meant Hastings.

MAZZINI. Oh, I b e g your pardon, Lady Utterword.

CAPTAIN SHOTOVER. Every drunken skipper trusts to Providence. But one of the ways of Providence with drunken skippers is to run them on the rocks.

MAZZINI. Very true, no doubt, at sea. But in politics, I assure you, they only run into jellyfish. Nothing happens.

CAPTAIN SHOTOVER. At sea nothing happens to the sea. Nothing happens to the sky. The sun comes up from the east and goes down to the west. The moon grows from a sickle to an arc lamp, and comes later and later until she is lost in the light as other things are lost in the darkness. After the typhoon, the flying-fish glitter in the sunshine like birds. It's amazing how t h e y get along, all things considered. Nothing happens, except something not worth mentioning.

ELLIE. What is that, O Captain, my captain?

CAPTAIN SHOTOVER. [*savagely*] Nothing but the smash of the drunken skipper's ship on the rocks, the splintering of her rotten timbers, the tearing of her rusty plates, the drowning of the crew like rats in a trap.

ELLIE. Moral: dont take rum.

CAPTAIN SHOTOVER [*vehemently*] That is a lie, child. Let a man drink ten barrels of rum a day, he is not a drunken skipper until he is a drifting skipper. Whilst he can lay his course and stand on his bridge and steer it, he is no drunkard. It is the man who lies drinking in his bunk and trusts to Providence that I call the drunken skipper, though he drank nothing but the waters of the River Jordan.

ELLIE. Splendid! And you havnt had a drop for an hour. You see you dont need it: your own spirit is not dead.

CAPTAIN SHOTOVER. Echoes: nothing but echoes. The last shot was fired years ago.

HECTOR. And this ship we are all in? This soul's prison we call England?

CAPTAIN SHOTOVER. The captain is in his bunk, drinking bottled ditch-water; and the crew is gambling in the forecastle. She will strike and sink and split. Do you think the laws of God will be suspended in favor of England because you were born in it?

HECTOR. Well, I didnt mean to be drowned like a rat in a trap. I still have the will to live. What am I to do?

CAPTAIN SHOTOVER. Do? Nothing simpler. Learn your business as an Englishman.

HECTOR. And what may my business as an Englishman be, pray?

CAPTAIN SHOTOVER. Navigation. Learn it and live; or leave it and be damned.

ELLIE. Quiet, quiet; youll tire yourself.

MAZZINI. I thought all that once, Captain; but I assure you nothing will happen.

A dull distant explosion is heard.

HECTOR [*starting up*] What was that?

CAPTAIN SHOTOVER. Something happening [*he blows his whistle*]. Breakers ahead!

The light goes out.

HECTOR [*furiously*] Who put that light out? Who dared put that light out?

NURSE GUINNESS [*running in from the house to the middle of the esplanade*] I did, sir. The police have telephoned to say we'll be summoned if we dont put that light out: it can be seen for miles.

HECTOR. It shall be seen for a hundred miles [*he dashes into the house*].

NURSE GUINNESS. The rectory is nothing but a heap of bricks, they say. Unless we can give the rector a bed he has nowhere to lay his head this night.

CAPTAIN SHOTOVER. The Church is on the rocks, breaking

up. I told him it would unless it headed for God's open sea.

NURSE GUINNESS. And you are all to go down to the cellars.

CAPTAIN SHOTOVER. Go there yourself, you and all the crew. Batten down the hatches.

NURSE GUINNESS. And hide beside the coward I married! I'll go on the roof first. [*The lamp lights up again*]. There! Mr Hushabye's turned it on again.

THE BURGLAR [*hurrying in and appealing to Nurse Guinness*] Here: wheres the way to that gravel pit? The boot-boy says theres a cave in the gravel pit. Them cellars is no use. Wheres the gravel pit, Captain?

NURSE GUINNESS. Go straight on past the flagstaff until you fall into it and break your dirty neck. [*She pushes him contemptuously towards the flagstaff, and herself goes to the foot of the hammock and waits there, as it were by Ariadne's cradle*].

Another and louder explosion is heard. The burglar stops and stands trembling.

ELLIE [*rising*] That was nearer.

CAPTAIN SHOTOVER. The next one will get us. [*He rises*]. Stand by, all hands, for judgment.

THE BURGLAR. Oh my Lordy God! [*He rushes away frantically past the flagstaff into the gloom*].

MRS HUSHABYE [*emerging panting from the darkness*] Who was that running away? [*She comes to Ellie*]. Did you hear the explosions? And the sound in the sky: it's splendid: it's like an orchestra: it's like Beethoven.

ELLIE. By thunder, Hesione: it is Beethoven.

She and Hesione throw themselves into one another's arms in wild excitement. The light increases.

MAZZINI [*anxiously*] The light is getting brighter.

NURSE GUINNESS [*looking up at the house*] It's Mr Hushabye turning on all the lights in the house and tearing down the curtains.

RANDALL [*rushing in in his pyjamas, distractedly waving a flute*] Ariadne: my soul, my precious, go down to the cellars: I beg and implore you, go down to the cellars!

LADY UTTERWORD [*quite composed in her hammock*] The

governor's wife in the cellars with the servants! Really, Randall!

RANDALL. But what shall I do if you are killed?

LADY UTTERWORD. You will probably be killed, too, Randall. Now play your flute to shew that you are not afraid; and be good. Play us Keep the home fires burning.

NURSE GUINNESS [*grimly*] Theyll keep the home fires burning for us: them up there.

RANDALL [*having tried to play*] My lips are trembling. I cant get a sound.

MAZZINI. I hope poor Mangan is safe.

MRS HUSHABYE. He is hiding in the cave in the gravel pit.

CAPTAIN SHOTOVER. My dynamite drew him there. It is the hand of God.

HECTOR [*returning from the house and striding across to his former place*] There is not half light enough. We should be blazing to the skies.

ELLIE [*tense with excitement*] Set fire to the house, Marcus.

MRS HUSHABYE. My house! No.

HECTOR. I thought of that; but it would not be ready in time.

CAPTAIN SHOTOVER. The judgment has come. Courage will not save you; but it will shew that your souls are still alive.

MRS HUSHABYE. Sh-sh! Listen: do you hear it now? It's magnificent.

They all turn away from the house and look up, listening.

HECTOR [*gravely*] Miss Dunn: you can do no good here. We of this house are only moths flying into the candle. You had better go down to the cellar.

ELLIE [*scornfully*] I d o n t think.

MAZZINI. Ellie, dear, there is no disgrace in going to the cellar. An officer would order his soldiers to take cover. Mr Hushabye is behaving like an amateur. Mangan and the burglar are acting very sensibly; and it is they who will survive.

ELLIE. Let them. I shall behave like an amateur. But why should you run any risk?

MAZZINI. Think of the risk those poor fellows up there are running!

NURSE GUINNESS. Think of t h e m, indeed, the murdering blackguards! What next?

A terrific explosion shakes the earth. They reel back into their seats, or clutch the nearest support. They hear the falling of the shattered glass from the windows.

MAZZINI. Is anyone hurt?

HECTOR. Where did it fall?

NURSE GUINNESS [*in hideous triumph*] Right in the gravel pit: I seen it. Serve un right! I seen it [*she runs away towards the gravel pit, laughing harshly*].

HECTOR. One husband gone.

CAPTAIN SHOTOVER. Thirty pounds of good dynamite wasted.

MAZZINI. Oh, poor Mangan!

HECTOR. Are you immortal that you need pity him? Our turn next.

They wait in silence and intense expectation. Hesione and Ellie hold each other's hands tight.

A distant explosion is heard.

MRS HUSHABYE [*relaxing her grip*] Oh! they have passed us.

LADY UTTERWORD. The danger is over, Randall. Go to bed.

CAPTAN SHOTOVER. Turn in, all hands. The ship is safe. [*He sits down and goes asleep*].

ELLIE [*disappointedly*] Safe!

HECTOR [*disgustedly*] Yes, safe. And how damnably dull the world has become again suddenly! [*He sits down*].

MAZZINI [*sitting down*] I was quite wrong, after all. It is we who have survived; and Mangan and the burglar—

HECTOR. —the two burglars—

LADY UTTERWORD. —the two practical men of business—

MAZZINI. —both gone. And the poor clergyman will have to get a new house.

MRS HUSHABYE. But what a glorious experience! I hope theyll come again tomorrow night.

ELLIE [*radiant at the prospect*] Oh, I hope so.

Randall at last succeeds in keeping the home fires burning on his flute.

To J. B. Fagan

Fagan was producing Heartbreak House *at the Royal Court Theatre, London.*

✕✕✕✕✕✕✕✕✕✕✕✕✕✕✕✕✕✕✕✕✕✕✕✕✕✕✕✕✕✕✕✕✕✕✕✕

10 Adelphi Terrace, W.C.2
20th Oct. 1921

My dear Fagan

Take a blue pencil and a copy of H. H.; and mark the
following cuts in Act III.

p 97—*Lady U*—I quite sympathize with you, Mr. Mangan. (cut 5 lines) Still, there is no &c &c

98—line 5. *Lady U*—I should not be too hasty, Miss
Dunn (cut the next two lines). You can live very
comfortably on Mr. Mangan's reputation &c.

p 100—*Mr. H.*—Oh, wonderful things, soldier of freedom
(cut the next 3 speeches), Lady U—Your daughter's match &c . . . absolutely nothing. (cut the
rest of the page and the first 2 lines of p 101).
Mangan—There you go again &c.

p 102—9th speech—*Hector*—All heartbroken imbeciles
(cut the rest of the page, and the first two
speeches on 103). *Ellie*—Your house is not H. H.
&c.

p 105—line 9. *Mazz. Very true &c.* . . . Nothing happens
(cut the next 7½ lines) *Shotover*—Except something not worth mentioning.

I hope this last cut will not hurt Brember [Wills]'s feelings;
but I think he will be glad of it, because for some reason
the speech has always bothered him: he has never visual-
ized it. Probably he never saw a flying fish. This gets rid
of 65 lines of print, and improves the scene: at least I
think you will find it so, I never cut anything merely to
save time: it is never worth saving at the cost of the play,
but here it ought to help the play. There are always lines
which are dud lines with a given cast. Change the cast and

you get other lines dud. The line which strikes on A's box will only bother B. Besides, there are in this act a few passages which are first act passages: that is, they require first act patience, which is much thicker than last act patience. Also a lash or two at dead horses.

I have been rather unhappy because I let the play go before it was safely ready and before we had polished it. It needed, for Shotover, Ellie & Hesione, another week, three days of which they should have spent at home studying. But the strained financial situation, the doubt whether a week would be enough, the staleness of the easy parts, and perhaps my own exhaustion (the cat & mouse watching of every word uses up one's nerve), determined me to relieve you of *your* strain and let it go, trusting to its very unpreparedness to give a certain agonized intensity to the performance—which, by the Lord, it *did*. Still, it was a risk; and it cost us some bad notices. Ellie & Hesione kept going splendidly; but Shotover was terribly slow and bewildered: he dragged the scene with Ellie almost beyond endurance; and it missed fire in consequence. That was serious, as the whole play depends on it for its balance of effect. Ellie was very clear and competent, and did not miss a stroke. at no point did she seem to be muddled or to do anything she did not intend to do; but he was like a drowning man, or rather like a man sitting on Wells's Time Machine, and ageing ten years every minute, which was all the more alarming as he started at 99 instead of 88. However he will get over this. His first act is all right; but he must knock 20 years off the rest.

You will find a great improvement all round when they at last get clear about the meaning of their lines and master the train of thought. Until then do not hurry them too much; for if you make an actor speak faster than he can think, his part will be like nothing at all, and you will lose the play to save the lost train. I calculate that it will take a fortnight to get the more difficult parts really slick.

Mary [Grey] astonished all the people who said she couldn't act [Hesione]; but she needed a good night's sleep to get her full bloom on. You must pamper her for all you are worth: those three hours on the stage must be paid for by a worthless, luxurious, lie-a-bed, lazy spoilt life during the other 21.

[Arnold] Bennett & Nigel [Playfair] are sticking to their anti-O'Mallegism. A.B. is sure the play will fail because he & N.P. did not produce it with someone else in the part. They know that Ellie [O'Malley] is unexciting and disappointing as an ingenue, and have never found out that she is not an ingenue at all (nor ever was) but a heavy. Ellie is the heavy lead, and Hesione is the siren, to whom, by the way, give the author's love.

G.B.S.

P.S. The article has gone to the Sunday Herald. It goes beyond all the worst notices in its description of the audience on the rock.

PPS I forgot to say that in Act III, the horses speech is for the stalls: it means nothing to the poor.

To Lawrence Langner

XXXXXXXXXXXXXXXXXXXXXXXXXXXXXXXXXXXXXXX

Langner was director of the Theatre Guild, which was planning the first New York production of Back to Methuselah. *Shaw talks of* In the Beginning *as both the first play in the cycle as well as the prologue to it. The second play,* The Gospel of the Brothers Barnabas, *had thinly veiled caricatures in it of England's First World War prime ministers, H. H. Asquith and David Lloyd George.*

Shapespeare Hotel, Stratford-on-Avon
3 May 1921

My dear Langner

I have been travelling about for more than a month, delivering political orations; trying to recover from the too long spell of unbroken work that *Methuselah* brought on me; and writing nothing but the most urgently necessary letters on picture postcards. Hence my delay in replying to the letter you wrote on the Aquitania on the 18th March.

The second play will not mean Asquith and Lloyd George to your public; and so far it will not produce the effect it will produce here on the few people who have any sense of political personalities. But in *Fanny's First Play*, the American public knew nothing about Walkley, Gilbert Cannan, and A. E. Vaughan (for that matter very few people outside a little ring in London were any better informed). Nevertheless Trotter, Gunn, and Vaughan went down just as well in America as here. I therefore believe that if Joyce Burge and Lubin fail here, they will fail everywhere; and if they succeed here they will succeed just as well in America. However that may be, the thing must stay as it is now. The job did itself that way, and I cannot pull it to pieces and do it some other way.

As to the first play, it produced such an astonishing effect when I read it to an audience consisting mostly of women that I never ventured on the experiment again. I gather that it missed fire with you. It may be so with your public; but I assure you it *can* explode with shattering consequences. To play it and the second play at the same performance is impossible. You will have to make up your mind to the three evenings and the two matinees. You must sell the tickets in batches of five, all five tickets on one sheet with perforated card divisions. If people buy them that way they will not throw them away. They may be bothered and disappointed by the first two plays as you expect; but their bewilderment will not take the form of throwing their tickets into the fire, especially if you charge enough for them. You can warn them that the prologue in the Garden of Eden will last only an hour (or perhaps 50 minutes; you can time it at rehearsal) and that no assumptions must be made as to the duration of each part of the play. Mark: each part of the play, not each play. The wording of your programmes and announcements must always rub in the fact that what the public is going to see is one play, with sections of various lengths.

Later on we can see about giving separate performances of the sections; but for the first ten performances (say) it must be impossible to take less than the whole dose.

The book will be published on the first of June or thereabouts. I note your calm suggestion that it should be held back until you are ready to produce. I told you you wanted the earth. If you want to produce simultaneously with the publication you must hurry up very smartly indeed.

I scrawl this in great haste in a hotel after a day's driving.

Yours as always,
G. Bernard Shaw

BACK TO METHUSELAH (conclusion from the preface, "The Infidel Half Century")

×××××××××××××××××××××××××××××××××××××××

A TOUCHSTONE FOR DOGMA

The test of a dogma is its universality. Any doctrine that the British churchgoer, the Brahman, the Jainist, the Buddhist, the Mussulman cannot hold in common, however varied their rituals, is an obstruction to the fellowship of the Holy Ghost. The only frontier to the currency of a sound dogma as such is the frontier of capacity for understanding it.

This does not mean that we should throw away legend and parable and drama: they are the natural vehicles of dogma; but woe to the Churches and rulers who substitute the legend for the dogma, the parable for the history, the drama for the religion! Better by far declare the throne of God empty than set a liar and a fool on it. What are called wars of religion are always wars to destroy religion by affirming the historical truth or material substantiality of some legend, and killing those who refuse to accept it as historical or substantial. But who has ever refused to accept a good legend with delight as a legend? The legends, the parables, the dramas, are among the choicest treasures of mankind. No one is ever tired of stories of miracles. In vain did Mahomet repudiate the miracles ascribed to him: in vain did Christ furiously scold those who asked him to give them an exhibition as a conjurer: in vain did the saints declare that God chose them not for their powers but for their weaknesses; that the humble might be exalted, and the proud rebuked. People will have their miracles, their stories, their heroes and heroines and saints and martyrs and divinities to exercise their gifts of affection, admiration, wonder, and worship, and their Judases and devils to enable them to be angry and yet feel that they do well to be angry. Every one of these legends is the common heritage of the human race; and there is only one inexorable condition attached to their healthy enjoyment, which is that no one shall believe them literally. The reading of stories and delighting in them made Don Quixote a gentleman: the believing them literally made him a madman who slew lambs instead of feeding them. In England today good books of Eastern religious legends are read eagerly; and Protestants and Atheists read legends of the saints with pleasure. Sceptical Freethinkers read the Bible: indeed they seem to be its only readers now except the parsons at the Church lecterns. This is because the imposition of the legends as literal truths at once changes them from legends into falsehoods. The feeling against the Bible has become so strong at last that educated people will not tolerate even the chronicles of King David, which may be historical, and are certainly more candid than the official biographies of our contemporary monarchs.

WHAT TO DO WITH THE LEGENDS

What we should do, then, is to pool our legends and make a delightful stock of religious folk-lore on an honest basis for all children. With our minds freed from pretence and falsehood we could enter into the heritage of all the faiths. China would share her sages with Spain, and Spain her saints with China. The Belfast Orangemen who gives his son a thrashing if the boy is so tactless as to ask how the evening and the morning could be the first day before the sun was created, or to betray an innocent calf-love for the Virgin Mary, would buy him a bookful of legends of the creation and of mothers of God from all parts of the world, and be very glad to find his laddie as interested in such things as in marbles or Police and Robbers. That would be better than beating all good feeling towards religion out of the child, and blackening his mind by teaching him that the worshippers of the holy virgins, whether of the Parthenon or St Peter's, are fire-doomed heathens and idolaters. All the sweetness of religion is conveyed to children by the hands of storytellers and image-makers. Without their fictions the truths of religion would for the multitude be neither intelligible nor even apprehen-

sible; and the prophets would prophesy and the philosophers cerebrate in vain. And nothing stands between the
people and the fictions except the silly falsehood that the
fictions are literal truths, and that there is nothing in
religion but fiction.

A LESSON FROM SCIENCE TO THE CHURCHES

Let the Churches ask themselves why there is no revolt
against the dogmas of mathematics though there is one
against the dogmas of religion. It is not that the mathematical dogmas are more comprehensible. The law of inverse
squares is as incomprehensible to the common man as the
Athanasian creed. It is not that science is free from legends,
witchcraft, miracles, biographic boostings of quacks as
heroes and saints, and of barren scoundrels as explorers and
discoverers. On the contrary, the inconography and hagiol-
ogy of Scientism are as copious as they are mostly squalid.
But no student of science has yet been taught that specific
gravity consists in the belief that Archimedes jumped out
of his bath and ran naked through the streets of Syracuse
shouting Eureka, Eureka, or that the law of inverse squares
must be discarded if anyone can prove that Newton was
never in an orchard in his life. When some unusually
conscientious or enterprising bacteriologist reads the pamphlets of Jenner, and discovers that they might have been
written by an ignorant but curious and observant nursery-
maid, and could not possibly have been written by any
person with a scientifically trained mind, he does not feel
that the whole edifice of science has collapsed and crumbled, and that there is no such thing as smallpox. . . . But
in fact it is the mind of Europe that has shrunk, being, as
we have seen, wholly preoccupied with a busy spring-
cleaning to get rid of its superstitions before readjusting
itself to the creative conception of Evolution.

EVOLUTION IN THE THEATRE

On the stage (and here I come at last to my own particular function in the matter), Comedy, as a destructive,
derisory, critical, negative art, kept the theatre open when
sublime tragedy perished. From Molière to Oscar Wilde

we had a line of comedic playwrights who, if they had nothing fundamentally positive to say, were at least in revolt against falsehood and imposture, and were not only, as they claimed, "chastening morals by ridicule," but, in Johnson's phrase, clearing our minds of cant, and thereby shewing an uneasiness in the presence of error which is the surest symptom of intellectual vitality. Meanwhile the name of Tragedy was assumed by plays in which everyone was killed in the last act, just as, in spite of Molière, plays in which everyone was married in the last act called themselves comedies. Now neither tragedies nor comedies can be produced according to a prescription which gives only the last moments of the last act.

Ever since Shakespear, playwrights have been struggling with their lack of positive religion. Many of them were forced to become mere pandars and sensation-mongers because, though they had higher ambitions, they could find no better subject matter. From Congreve to Sheridan they were so sterile in spite of their wit that they did not achieve between them the output of Molière's single lifetime; and they were all (not without reason) ashamed of their profession, and preferred to be regarded as mere men of fashion with a rakish hobby. Goldsmith's was the only saved soul in that pandemonium. Consider the great exception of Goethe. He is Olympian: the other giants are infernal in everything but their veracity and their repudiation of the irreligion of their time: that is, they are bitter and hopeless. It is not a question of mere dates. Goethe was an Evolutionist in 1830: many modern playwrights, even young ones, are still untouched by Creative Evolution. Even Ibsen was Darwinized to the extent of exploiting heredity on the stage much as the ancient Athenian playwrights exploited the Eumenides. Evolution as a poetic aspiration is plain enough in his Emperor as Galilean; but it is one of Ibsen's distinctions that nothing was valid for him but science; and he left that vision of the future which his Roman seer calls "the third Empire" behind him when he settled down to his serious grapple with realities in those plays of nineteenth century life with which he over-

came Europe, and broke the dusty windows of every dry-
rotten theatre in it from Moscow to Manchester.

MY OWN PART IN THE MATTER

In my own activities as a playwright I found this state
of things intolerable. The fashionable theatre prescribed
one serious subject: clandestine adultery: the dullest of all
subjects for a serious author, whatever it may be for audiences who read the police intelligence and skip the reviews
and leading articles. I tried slum-landlordism, doctrinaire
Free Love (pseudo-Ibsenism), prostitution, militarism,
marriage, history, current politics, natural Christianity,
national and individual character, paradoxes of conventional society, husband-hunting, questions of conscience,
professional delusions and impostures, all worked into a
series of comedies of manners in the classic fashion, which
was then very much out of fashion, the mechanical tricks
of Parisian "construction" being held obligatory in the
theatre. But this, though it occupied me and established me
professionally, did not constitute me an iconographer of
the religion of my time, fulfilling my natural function as
an artist. I knew that civilization needs a religion as a
matter of life or death; and as the conception of Creative
Evolution developed I saw that we were at last within reach
of a faith which complied with the first condition of all
the religions that have ever taken hold of humanity:
namely, that it must be, first and fundamentally, a science
of metabiology. This was a crucial point with me; for I
had seen Bible fetishism, after standing up to all the
rationalistic batteries of Hume, Voltaire, and the rest, collapse before the onslaught of much less gifted Evolutionists,
solely because they discredited it as a biological document;
so that from that moment it lost its hold, and left literate
Christendom faithless. My own Irish eighteenth-centuryism
made it impossible for me to believe anything until I could
conceive it as a scientific hypothesis, even though the
abominations, quackeries, impostures, venalities, credulities,
and delusions of the camp followers of science, and the
brazen lies and priestly pretensions of the pseudo-scientific

cure-mongers, all sedulously inculcated by modern "secondary education," were so monstrous that I was sometimes forced to make a verbal distinction between science
and knowledge lest I should mislead my readers. But I
never forgot that without knowledge even wisdom is more
dangerous than mere opportunist ignorance, and that somebody must take the Garden of Eden in hand and weed it
properly.

Accordingly, in 1901, I took the legend of Don Juan
in its Mozartian form and made it a dramatic parable of
Creative Evolution. But being then at the height of my
invention and comedic talent, I decorated it too brilliantly
and lavishly. I surrounded it with a comedy of which it
formed only one act, and that act was so completely episodical (it was a dream which did not affect the action of
the piece) that the comedy could be detached and played
by itself. Also I supplied the published work with an
imposing framework consisting of a preface, an appendix
called The Revolutionist's Handbook, and a final display of
aphoristic fireworks. The effect was so vertiginous, apparently, that nobody noticed the new religion in the centre
of the intellectual whirlpool. Now I protest I did not cut
these cerebral capers in mere inconsiderate exuberance. I
did it because the worst convention of the criticism of the
theatre current at that time was that intellectual seriousness
is out of place on the stage; that the theatre is a place of
shallow amusement; that people go there to be soothed
after the enormous intellectual strain of a day in the city:
in short, that a playwright is a person whose business it
is to make unwholesome confectionery out of cheap emotions. My answer to this was to put all my intellectual
goods in the shop window under the sign of Man and
Superman. That part of my design succeeded. By good luck
and acting, the comedy triumphed on the stage; and the
book was a good deal discussed. But as its tale of a
husband huntress obscured its evolutionary doctrine I try
again with this cycle of plays that keep to the point and
through. I abandon the legend of Don Juan with its erotic
associations, and go back to the legend of the Garden of
Eden. I exploit the external interest of the philosopher's

stone which enables men to live for ever. I am not, I hope, under more illusion than is humanly inevitable as to my contribution to the scriptures of Creative Evolution. It is my hope that a hundred parables by young hands will soon leave mine as far behind as the religious pictures of the fifteenth century left behind the first attempts of the early Christians at iconography. In that hope I withdraw and ring up the curtain.

AYOT SAINT LAWRENCE, 1921
Revised, 1944

BACK TO METHUSELAH

P A R T   I   *In the Beginning*

ACT I

The Garden of Eden. Afternoon. An immense serpent is sleeping with her head buried in a thick bed of Johnswort, and her body coiled in apparently endless rings through the branches of a tree, which is already well grown; for the days of creation have been longer than our reckoning. She is not yet visible to anyone unaware of her presence, as her colors of green and brown make a perfect camouflage. Near her head a low rock shews above the Johnswort.

The rock and tree are on the border of a glade in which lies a dead fawn all awry, its neck being broken. Adam, crouching with one hand on the rock, is staring in consternation at the dead body. He has not noticed the serpent on his left hand. He turns his face to his right and calls excitedly.

ADAM. Eve! Eve!
EVE'S VOICE. What is it, Adam?
ADAM. Come here. Quick. Something has happened.
EVE [*running in*] What? Where? [*Adam points to the fawn*].
   Oh! [*She goes to it; and he is emboldened to go with her*].

What is the matter with its eyes?

ADAM. It is not only its eyes. Look. [*He kicks it*].

EVE. Oh dont! Why doesnt it wake?

ADAM. I dont know. It is not asleep.

EVE. Not asleep?

ADAM. Try.

EVE [*trying to shake it and roll it over*] It is stiff and cold.

ADAM. Nothing will wake it.

EVE. It has a queer smell. Pah! [*She dusts her hands, and draws away from it*]. Did you find it like that?

ADAM. No. It was playing about; and it tripped and went head over heels. It never stirred again. Its neck is wrong [*he stoops to lift the neck and shew her*].

EVE. Dont touch it. Come away from it.

    They both retreat, and contemplate it from a few steps' distance with growing repulsion.

EVE. Adam.

ADAM. Yes?

EVE. Suppose you were to trip and fall, would you go like that?

ADAM. Ugh! [*He shudders and sits down on the rock*].

EVE [*throwing herself on the ground beside him, and grasping his knee*] You must be careful. Promise me you will be careful.

ADAM. What is the good of being careful? We have to live here for ever. Think of what for ever means! Sooner or later I shall trip and fall. It may be tomorrow; it may be after as many days as there are leaves in the garden and grains of sand by the river. No matter: some day I shall forget and stumble.

EVE. I too.

ADAM [*horrified*] Oh no, no. I should be alone. Alone for ever. You must never put yourself in danger of stumbling. You must not move about. You must sit still. I will take care of you and bring you what you want.

EVE [*turning away from him with a shrug, and hugging her ankles*] I should soon get tired of that. Besides, if it happened to you, *I* should be alone. I could not sit still then. And at last it would happen to me too.

ADAM. And then?

EVE. Then we should be no more. There would be only the things on all fours, and the birds, and the snakes.

ADAM. That must not be.

EVE. Yes: that must not be. But it might be.

ADAM. No. I tell you it must not be. I know that it must not be.

EVE. We both know it. How do we know it?

ADAM. There is a voice in the garden that tells me things.

EVE. The garden is full of voices sometimes. They put all sorts of thoughts into my head.

ADAM. To me there is only one voice. It is very low; but it is so near that it is like a whisper from within myself. There is no mistaking it for any voice of the birds or beasts, or for your voice.

EVE. It is strange that I should hear voices from all sides and you only one from within. But I have some thoughts that come from within me and not from the voices. The thought that we must not cease to be comes from within.

ADAM [*despairingly*] But we s h a l l cease to be. We shall fall like the fawn and be broken. [*Rising and moving about in his agitation*]. I cannot bear this knowledge. I will not have it. It must not be, I tell you. Yet I do not know how to prevent it.

EVE. That is just what I feel; but it is very strange that you should say so: there is no pleasing you. You change your mind so often.

ADAM [*scolding her*] Why do you say that? How have I changed my mind?

EVE. You say we must not cease to exist. But you used to complain of having to exist always and for ever. You sometimes sit for hours brooding and silent, hating me in your heart. When I ask you what I have done to you, you say you are not thinking of me, but of the horror of having to be here for ever. But I know very well that what you mean is the horror of having to be here with me for ever.

ADAM. Oh! That is what you think, is it? Well, you are wrong. [*He sits down again, sulkily*]. It is the horror of having to be with myself for ever. I like you; but I do not like myself. I want to be different; to be better, to begin again and again; to shed myself as a snake sheds its skin. I am tired of myself. And yet I must endure myself, not for a day or for many days, but for ever. That is a dreadful thought. That is what makes me sit brooding and silent and hateful. Do you never think of that?

EVE. No: I do not think about myself: what is the use? I am what I am: nothing can alter that. I think about you.

ADAM. You should not. You are always spying on me. I can never be alone. You always want to know what I have been doing. It is a burden. You should try to have an existence of your own, instead of occupying yourself with my existence.

EVE. I h a v e to think about you. You are lazy: you are dirty: you neglect yourself: you are always dreaming: you would eat bad food and become disgusting if I did not watch you and occupy myself with you. And now some day, in spite of all my care, you will fall on your head and become dead.

ADAM. Dead? What word is that?

EVE [*pointing to the fawn*] Like that. I call it dead.

ADAM [*rising and approaching it slowly*] There is something uncanny about it.

EVE [*joining him*] Oh! It is changing into little white worms.

ADAM. Throw it into the river. It is unbearable.

EVE. I dare not touch it.

ADAM. Then I must, though I loathe it. It is poisoning the air. [*He gathers its hooves in his hand and carries it away in the direction from which Eve came, holding it as far from him as possible*].

> *Eve looks after them for a moment; then, with a shiver of disgust, sits down on the rock, brooding. The body of the serpent becomes visible, glowing with wonderful new colors. She rears her head slowly from the bed of Johnswort, and speaks into Eve's ear in a strange seductively musical whisper.*

THE SERPENT. Eve.

EVE [*startled*] Who is that?

THE SERPENT. It is I. I have come to shew you my beautiful new hood. See [*she spreads a magnificent amethystine hood*]!

EVE [*admiring it*] Oh! But who taught you to speak?

THE SERPENT. You and Adam. I have crept through the grass, and hidden, and listened to you.

EVE. That was wonderfully clever of you.

THE SERPENT. I am the most subtle of all the creatures of the field.

EVE. Your hood is most lovely. [*She strokes it and pets the serpent*]. Pretty thing! Do you love your godmother Eve?

THE SERPENT. I adore her. [*She licks Eve's neck with her double tongue*].

EVE [*petting her*] Eve's wonderful darling snake. Eve will never be lonely now that her snake can talk to her.

THE SNAKE. I can talk of many things. I am very wise. It was I who whispered the word to you that you did not know. Dead. Death. Die.

EVE [*shuddering*] Why do you remind me of it? I forgot it when I saw your beautiful hood. You must not remind me of unhappy things.

THE SERPENT. Death is not an unhappy thing when you have learnt how to conquer it.

EVE. How can I conquer it?

THE SERPENT. By another thing, called birth.

EVE. What? [*Trying to pronounce it*] B-birth?

THE SERPENT. Yes, birth.

EVE. What is birth?

THE SERPENT. The serpent never dies. Some day you shall see me come out of this beautiful skin, a new snake with a new and lovelier skin. That is birth.

EVE. I have seen that. It is wonderful.

THE SERPENT. If I can do that, what can I not do? I tell you I am very subtle. When you and Adam talk, I hear you say "Why?" Always "Why?" You see things; and you say "Why?" But I dream things that never were; and I say "Why not?" I made the word dead to describe my old skin that I cast when I am renewed. I call that renewal being born.

EVE. Born is a beautiful word.

THE SERPENT. Why not be born again and again as I am, new and beautiful every time?

EVE. I! It does not happen: that is why.

THE SERPENT. That is how; but it is not why. Why not?

EVE. But I should not like it. It would be nice to be new again; but my old skin would lie on the ground looking just like me; and Adam would see it shrivel up and—

THE SERPENT. No. He need not. There is a second birth.

EVE. A second birth?

THE SERPENT. Listen. I will tell you a great secret. I am very subtle; and I have thought and thought and thought. And I am very wilful, and must have what I want; and I have willed and willed and willed. And I have eaten strange things: stones and apples that you are afraid to eat.

EVE. You dared!

THE SERPENT. I dared everything. And at last I found a way of gathering together a part of the life in my body—

EVE. What is the life?

THE SERPENT. That which makes the difference between the dead fawn and the live one.

EVE. What a beautiful word! And what a wonderful thing! Life is the loveliest of all the new words.

THE SERPENT. Yes: it was by meditating on Life that I gained the power to do miracles.

EVE. Miracles? Another new word.

THE SERPENT. A miracle is an impossible thing that is nevertheless possible. Something that never could happen, and yet does happen.

EVE. Tell me some miracle that you have done.

THE SERPENT. I gathered a part of the life in my body, and shut it into a tiny white case made of the stones I had eaten.

EVE. And what good was that?

THE SERPENT. I shewed the little case to the sun, and left it in its warmth. And it burst; and a little snake came out; and it became bigger and bigger from day to day until it was as big as I. That was the second birth.

EVE. Oh! That is too wonderful. It stirs inside me. It hurts.

THE SERPENT. It nearly tore me asunder. Yet I am alive, and can burst my skin and renew myself as before. Soon there will be as many snakes in Eden as there are scales on my body. Then death will not matter: this snake and that snake will die; but the snakes will live.

EVE. But the rest of us will die sooner or later, like the fawn. And then there will be nothing but snakes, snakes, snakes everywhere.

THE SERPENT. That must not be. I worship you, Eve. I must have something to worship. Something quite different to myself, like you. There must be something greater than the snake.

EVE. Yes: it must not be. Adam must not perish. You are very subtle: tell me what to do.

THE SERPENT. Think. Will. Eat the dust. Lick the white stone: bite the apple you dread. The sun will give life.

EVE. I do not trust the sun. I will give life myself. I will tear another Adam from my body if I tear my body to pieces in the act.

THE SERPENT. Do. Dare it. Everything is possible: everything. Listen. I am old. I am the old serpent, older than Adam, older than Eve. I remember Lilith, who came before Adam and Eve. I was her darling as I am yours. She was alone: there was no man with her. She saw death as you saw it when the fawn fell; and she knew then that she must find out how to renew herself and cast the skin like me. She had a mighty will: she strove and strove and willed and willed for more moons than there are leaves on all the trees of the garden. Her pangs were terrible: her groans drove sleep from Eden. She said it must never be again: that the burden of renewing life was past bearing: that it was too much for one. And when she cast the skin, lo! there was not one new Lilith but two: one like herself, the other like Adam. You were the one: Adam was the other.

EVE. But why did she divide into two, and make us different?

THE SERPENT. I tell you the labor is too much for one. Two must share it.

EVE. Do you mean that Adam must share it with me? He will not. He cannot bear pain, nor take trouble with his body.

THE SERPENT. He need not. There will be no pain for him. He will implore you to let him do his share. He will be in your power through his desire.

EVE. Then I will do it. But how? How did Lilith work this miracle?

THE SERPENT. She imagined it.

EVE. What is imagined?

THE SERPENT. She told it to me as a marvellous story of something that never happened to a Lilith that never was. She did not know then that imagination is the beginning of creation. You imagine what you desire; you will what you imagine; and at last you create what you will.

EVE. How can I create out of nothing?

THE SERPENT. Everything must have been created out of nothing. Look at that thick roll of hard flesh on your strong arm! That was not always there: you could not climb a tree when I first saw you. But you willed and tried and willed and tried; and your will created out of nothing the roll on your arm until you had your desire, and could draw yourself up with one hand and seat yourself on the bough that was above your head.

EVE. That was practice.

THE SERPENT. Things wear out by practice: they do not grow by it. Your hair streams in the wind as if it were trying to stretch itself further and further. But it does not grow longer for all its practice in streaming, because you have not willed it so. When Lilith told me what she had imagined in our silent language (for there were no words then) I bade her desire it and will it; and then, to our great wonder, the thing she had desired and willed created itself in her under the urging of her will. Then I too willed to renew myself as two instead of one; and after many days the miracle happened, and I burst from my skin another snake interlaced with me; and now there are two imaginations, two desires, two wills to create with.

EVE. To desire, to imagine, to will, to create. That is too

long a story. Find me one word for it all: you, who are
so clever at words.

THE SERPENT. In one word, to conceive. That is the word
that means both the beginning in imagination and the
end in creation.

EVE. Find me a word for the story Lilith imagined and
told you in your silent language: the story that was too
wonderful to be true, and yet came true.

THE SERPENT. A poem.

EVE. Find me another word for what Lilith was to me.

THE SERPENT. She was your mother.

EVE. And Adam's mother?

THE SERPENT. Yes.

EVE [*about to rise*] I will go and tell Adam to conceive.

THE SERPENT [*laughs*]!!!

EVE [*jarred and startled*] What a hateful noise! What is the
matter with you? No one has ever uttered such a sound
before.

THE SERPENT. Adam cannot conceive.

EVE. Why?

THE SERPENT. Lilith did not imagine him so. He can imagine: he can will: he can desire: he can gather his life
together for a great spring towards creation: he can
create all things except one; and that one is his own kind.

EVE. Why did Lilith keep this from him?

THE SERPENT. Because if he could do that he could do
without Eve.

EVE. That is true. It is I who must conceive.

THE SERPENT. Yes. By that he is tied to you.

EVE. And I to him!

THE SERPENT. Yes, until you create another Adam.

EVE. I had not thought of that. You are very subtle. But
if I create another Eve he may turn to her and do
without me. I will not create any Eves, only Adams.

THE SERPENT. They cannot renew themselves without Eves.
Sooner or later you will die like the fawn; and the new
Adams will be unable to create without new Eves. You
can imagine such an end; but you cannot desire it,
therefore cannot will it, therefore cannot create Adams
only.

EVE. If I am to die like the fawn, why should not the rest die too? What do I care?

THE SERPENT. Life must not cease. That comes before everything. It is silly to say you do not care. You do care. It is that care that will prompt your imagination; inflame your desires; make your will irresistible; and create out of nothing.

EVE [*thoughtfully*] There can be no such thing as nothing. The garden is full, not empty.

THE SERPENT. That is true. Darling Eve: this is a great thought. Yes: there is no such thing as nothing, only things we cannot see. The chameleon eats the air.

EVE. I have another thought: I must tell it to Adam. [*Calling*] Adam! Adam! Coo-ee!

ADAM'S VOICE. Coo-ee!

EVE. This will please him, and cure his fits of melancholy.

THE SERPENT. Do not tell him yet. I have not told you the great secret.

EVE. What more is there to tell? It is I who have to do the miracle.

THE SERPENT. No: he, too, must desire and will. But he must give his desire and his will to you.

EVE. How?

THE SERPENT. That is the great secret. Hush! he is coming.

ADAM [*returning*] Is there another voice in the garden besides our voices and the Voice? I heard a new voice.

EVE [*rising and running to him*] Only think, Adam! Our snake has learnt to speak by listening to us.

ADAM [*delighted*] Is it so? [*He goes past her to the stone, and fondles the serpent*].

THE SERPENT [*responding affectionately*] It is so, dear Adam.

EVE. But I have more wonderful news than that. Adam: we need not live for ever.

ADAM [*dropping the snake's head in his excitement*] What! Eve: do not play with me about this. If only there may be an end some day, and yet no end! If only I can be relieved of the horror of having to endure myself for ever! If only the care of this terrible garden may pass on to some other gardener! If only the sentinel set by

the Voice can be relieved! If only the rest and sleep
that enable me to bear it from day to day could grow
after many days into an eternal rest, an eternal sleep,
then I could face my days, however long they may last.
Only, there must be some end, some end: I am not
strong enough to bear eternity.

THE SERPENT. You need not live to see another summer;
and yet there shall be no end.

ADAM. That cannot be.

THE SERPENT. It can be.

EVE. It shall be.

THE SERPENT. It is. Kill me; and you will find another
snake in the garden tomorrow. You will find more
snakes than there are fingers on your hands.

EVE. I will make other Adams, other Eves.

ADAM. I tell you you must not make up stories about this.
It cannot happen.

THE SERPENT. I can remember when you were yourself a
thing that could not happen. Yet you are.

ADAM [struck] That must be true. [He sits down on the
stone].

THE SERPENT. I will tell Eve the secret; and she will tell
it to you.

ADAM. The secret! [He turns quickly towards the serpent,
and in doing so puts his foot on something sharp]. Oh!

EVE. What is it?

ADAM [rubbing his foot] A thistle. And there, next to it, a
briar. And nettles, too! I am tired of pulling these things
up to keep the garden pleasant for us for ever.

THE SERPENT. They do not grow very fast. They will not
overrun the whole garden for a long time: not until
you have laid down your burden and gone to sleep for
ever. Why should you trouble yourself? Let the new
Adams clear a place for themselves.

ADAM. That is very true. You must tell us your secret. You
see, Eve, what a splendid thing it is not to have to live
for ever.

EVE [throwing herself down discontentedly and plucking at
the grass] That is so like a man. The moment you find
we need not last for ever, you talk as if we were going

to end today. You must clear away some of those horrid
things, or we shall be scratched and stung whenever we
forget to look where we are stepping.

ADAM. Oh yes, some of them, of course. But only some.
I will clear them away tomorrow.

THE SERPENT [*laughs*]!!!

ADAM. That is a funny noise to make. I like it.

EVE. I do not. Why do you make it again?

THE SERPENT. Adam has invented something new. He has
invented tomorrow. You will invent things every day
now that the burden of immortality is lifted from you.

EVE. Immortality? What is that?

THE SERPENT. My new word for having to live for ever.

EVE. The serpent has made a beautiful word for being.
Living.

ADAM. Make me a beautiful word for doing things tomorrow; for that surely is a great and blessed invention.

THE SERPENT. Procrastination.

EVE. That is a sweet word. I wish I had a serpent's tongue.

THE SERPENT. That may come too. Everything is possible.

ADAM [*springing up in sudden terror*] Oh!

EVE. What is the matter now?

ADAM. My rest! My escape from life!

THE SERPENT. Death. That is the word.

ADAM. There is a terrible danger in this procrastination.

EVE. What danger?

ADAM. If I put off death until tomorrow, I shall never die.
There is no such day as tomorrow, and never can be.

THE SERPENT. I am very subtle; but Man is deeper in his
thought than I am. The woman knows that there is no
such thing as nothing: the man knows that there is no
such day as tomorrow. I do well to worship them.

ADAM. If I am to overtake death, I must appoint a real
day, not a tomorrow. When shall I die?

EVE. You may die when I have made another Adam. Not
before. But then, as soon as you like. [*She rises, and passing behind him, strolls off carelessly to the tree and leans
against it, stroking a ring of the snake*].

ADAM. There need be no hurry even then.

EVE. I see you will put it off until tomorrow.

ADAM. And you? Will you die the moment you have made a new Eve?

EVE. Why should I? Are you eager to be rid of me? Only just now you wanted me to sit still and never move lest I should stumble and die like the fawn. Now you no longer care.

ADAM. It does not matter so much now.

EVE [*angrily to the snake*] This death that you have brought into the garden is an evil thing. He wants me to die.

THE SERPENT [*to Adam*] Do you want her to die?

ADAM. No. It is I who am to die. Eve must not die before me. I should be lonely.

EVE. You could get one of the new Eves.

ADAM. That is true. But they might not be quite the same. They could not: I feel sure of that. They would not have the same memories. They would be—I want a word for them.

THE SERPENT. Strangers.

ADAM. Yes: that is a good hard word. Strangers.

EVE. When there are new Adams and new Eves we shall live in a garden of strangers. We shall need each other. [*She comes quickly behind him and turns up his face to her*]. Do not forget that, Adam. Never forget it.

ADAM. Why should I forget it? It is I who have thought of it.

EVE. I, too, have thought of something. The fawn stumbled and fell and died. But you could come softly up behind me and [*she suddenly pounces on his shoulders and throws him forward on his face*] throw me down so that I should die. I should not dare to sleep if there were no reason why you should not make me die.

ADAM [*scrambling up in horror*] Make you die!!! What a frightful thought!

THE SERPENT. Kill, kill, kill, kill. That is the word.

EVE. The new Adams and Eves might kill us. I shall not make them. [*She sits on the rock and pulls him down beside her, clasping him to her with her right arm*].

THE SERPENT. You must. For if you do not there will be an end.

ADAM. No: they will not kill us: they will feel as I do.

There is something against it. The Voice in the garden
will tell them that they must not kill, as it tells me.

THE SERPENT. The voice in the garden is your own voice.

ADAM. It is; and it is not. It is something greater than me:
I am only a part of it.

EVE. The Voice does not tell me not to kill you. Yet I do
not want you to die before me. No voice is needed to
make me feel that.

ADAM [*throwing his arm round her shoulder with an expression of anguish*] Oh no: that is plain without any
voice. There is something that holds us together, something that has no word—

THE SERPENT. Love. Love. Love.

ADAM. That is too short a word for so long a thing.

THE SERPENT [*laughs*]!!!

EVE [*turning impatiently to the snake*] That heart-biting
sound again! Do not do it. Why do you do it?

THE SERPENT. Love may be too long a word for so short
a thing soon. But when it is short it will be very sweet.

ADAM [*ruminating*] You puzzle me. My old trouble was
heavy; but it was simple. These wonders that you promise
to do may tangle up my being before they bring me the
gift of death. I was troubled with the burden of eternal
being; but I was not confused in my mind. If I did not
know that I loved Eve, at least I did not know that she
might cease to love me, and come to love some other
Adam and desire my death. Can you find a name for
that knowledge?

THE SERPENT. Jealousy. Jealousy. Jealousy.

ADAM. A hideous word.

EVE [*shaking him*] Adam: you must not brood. You think
too much.

ADAM [*angrily*] How can I help brooding when the future
has become uncertain? Anything is better than uncertainty. Life has become uncertain. Love is uncertain.
Have you a word for this new misery?

THE SERPENT. Fear. Fear. Fear.

ADAM. Have you a remedy for it?

THE SERPENT. Yes. Hope. Hope. Hope.

ADAM. What is hope?

THE SERPENT. As long as you do not know the future you do not know that it will not be happier than the past. That is hope.

ADAM. It does not console me. Fear is stronger in me than hope. I must have certainty. [*He rises threateningly*]. Give it to me; or I will kill you when next I catch you asleep.

EVE [*throwing her arms round the serpent*] My beautiful snake. Oh no. How can you even think such a horror?

ADAM. Fear will drive me to anything. The serpent gave me fear. Let it now give me certainty or go in fear of me.

THE SERPENT. Bind the future by your will. Make a vow.

ADAM. What is a vow?

THE SERPENT. Choose a day for your death; and resolve to die on that day. Then death is no longer uncertain but certain. Let Eve vow to love you until your death. Then love will be no longer uncertain.

ADAM. Yes: that is splendid: that will bind the future.

EVE [*displeased, turning away from the serpent*] But it will destroy hope.

ADAM [*angrily*] Be silent, woman. Hope is wicked. Happiness is wicked. Certainty is blessed.

THE SERPENT. What is wicked? You have invented a word.

ADAM. Whatever I fear to do is wicked. Listen to me, Eve; and you, snake, listen too, that your memory may hold my vow. I will live a thousand sets of the four seasons—

THE SERPENT. Years. Years.

ADAM. I will live a thousand years; and then I will endure no more: I will die and take my rest. And I will love Eve all that time and no other woman.

EVE. And if Adam keeps his vow I will love no other man until he dies.

THE SERPENT. You have both invented marriage. And what he will be to you and not to any other woman is husband; and what you will be to him and not to any other man is wife.

ADAM [*instinctively moving his hand towards her*] Husband and wife.

EVE [*slipping her hand into his*] Wife and husband.

THE SERPENT [*laughs*]!!!

EVE [*snatching herself loose from Adam*] Do not make that odious noise, I tell you.

ADAM. Do not listen to her: the noise is good: it lightens my heart. You are a jolly snake. But you have not made a vow yet. What vow do you make?

THE SERPENT. I make no vows. I take my chance.

ADAM. Chance? What does that mean?

THE SERPENT. It means that I fear certainty as you fear uncertainty. It means that nothing is certain but uncertainty. If I bind the future I bind my will. If I bind my will I strangle creation.

EVE. Creation must not be strangled. I tell you I will create, though I tear myself to pieces in the act.

ADAM. Be silent, both of you. I w i l l bind the future. I will be delivered from fear. [*To Eve*] We have made our vows; and if you must create, you shall create within the bonds of those vows. You shall not listen to that snake any more. Come [*he seizes her by the hair to drag her away*].

EVE. Let me go, you fool. It has not yet told me the secret.

ADAM [*releasing her*] That is true. What is a fool?

EVE. I do not know: the word came to me. It is what you are when you forget and brood and are filled with fear. Let us listen to the snake.

ADAM. No: I am afraid of it. I feel as if the ground were giving way under my feet when it speaks. Do you stay and listen to it.

THE SERPENT [*laughs*]!!!

ADAM [*brightening*] That noise takes away fear. Funny. The snake and the woman are going to whisper secrets. [*He chuckles and goes away slowly, laughing his first laugh*].

EVE. Now the secret. The secret. [*She sits on the rock and throws her arms round the serpent, who begins whispering to her*].

    Eve's face lights up with intense interest, which increases until an expression of overwhelming repugnance takes its place. She buries her face in her hands.

ACT II

*A few centuries later. Morning. An oasis in Mesopotamia.
Close at hand the end of a log house abuts on a kitchen
garden. Adam is digging in the middle of the garden. On
his right, Eve sits on a stool in the shadow of a tree by
the doorway, spinning flax. Her wheel, which she turns by
hand, is a large disc of heavy wood, practically a fly-wheel.
At the opposite side of the garden is a thorn brake with a
passage through it barred by a hurdle.*

*The two are scantily and carelessly dressed in rough linen
and leaves. They have lost their youth and grace; and
Adam has an unkempt beard and jaggedly cut hair; but
they are strong and in the prime of life. Adam looks worried, like a farmer. Eve, better humored (having given up
worrying), sits and spins and thinks.*

A MAN'S VOICE. Hallo, mother!

EVE [*looking across the garden towards the hurdle*] Here
is Cain.

ADAM [*uttering a grunt of disgust*]!!! [*He goes on digging
without raising his head*].

*Cain kicks the hurdle out of his way, and strides into
the garden. In pose, voice, and dress he is insistently warlike. He is equipped with huge spear and broad brassbound leather shield; his casque is a tiger's head with
bull's horns; he wears a scarlet cloak with gold brooch
over a lion's skin with the claws dangling; his feet are
in sandals with brass ornaments; his shins are in brass
greaves; and his bristling military moustache glistens
with oil. To his parents he has the self-assertive, not-
quite-at-ease manner of a revolted son who knows that
he is not forgiven nor approved of.*

CAIN [*to Adam*] Still digging? Always dig, dig, dig. Sticking in the old furrow. No progress! no advanced ideas!
no adventures! What should I be if I had stuck to
the digging you taught me?

ADAM. What are you now, with your shield and spear, and

your brother's blood crying from the ground against
you?

CAIN. I am the first murderer: you are only the first man.
Anybody could be the first man: it is as easy as to be
the first cabbage. To be the first murderer one must be
a man of spirit.

ADAM. Begone. Leave us in peace. The world is wide
enough to keep us apart.

EVE. Why do you want to drive him away? He is mine.
I made him out of my own body. I want to see my
work sometimes.

ADAM. You made Abel also. He killed Abel. Can you bear
to look at him after that?

CAIN. Whose fault was it that I killed Abel? Who invented
killing? Did *I*? No: he invented it himself. I followed
your teaching. I dug and dug and dug. I cleared away
the thistles and briars. I ate the fruits of the earth. I
lived in the sweat of my brow, as you do. I was a fool.
But Abel was a discoverer, a man of ideas, of spirit:
a true Progressive. He was the discoverer of blood. He
was the inventor of killing. He found out that the fire
of the sun could be brought down by a dewdrop. He
invented the altar to keep the fire alive. He changed the
beasts he killed into meat by the fire on the altar. He
kept himself alive by eating meat. His meal cost him
a day's glorious health-giving sport and an hour's amusing play with the fire. You learnt nothing from him:
you drudged and drudged and drudged, and dug and dug
and dug, and made me do the same. I envied his happiness, his freedom. I despised myself for not doing as he
did instead of what you did. He became so happy that
he shared his meal with the Voice that had whispered
all his inventions to him. He said that the Voice was
the voice of the fire that cooked his food, and that the
fire that could cook could also eat. It was true: I saw
the fire consume the food on his altar. Then I, too,
made an altar, and offered my food on it, my grains,
my roots, my fruit. Useless: nothing happened. He
laughed at me; and then came my great idea: why not

kill him as he killed the beasts? I struck; and he died,
just as they did. Then I gave up your old silly drudging
ways, and lived as he had lived, by the chase, by the
killing, and by the fire. Am I not better than you?
stronger, happier, freer?

ADAM. You are not stronger: you are shorter in the wind:
you cannot endure. You have made the beasts afraid of
us; and the snake has invented poison to protect herself
against you. I fear you myself. If you take a step towards
your mother with that spear of yours I will strike you
with my spade as you struck Abel.

EVE. He will not strike me. He loves me.

ADAM. He loved his brother. But he killed him.

CAIN. I do not want to kill women. I do not want to kill
my mother. And for her sake I will not kill you, though
I could send this spear through you without coming
within reach of your spade. But for her, I could not resist
the sport of trying to kill you, in spite of my fear that
you would kill me. I have striven with a boar and with
a lion as to which of us should kill the other. I have
striven with a man: spear to spear and shield to shield. It
is terrible; but there is no joy like it. I call it fighting.
He who has never fought has never lived. That is
what has brought me to my mother today.

ADAM. What have you to do with one another now? She
is the creator, you the destroyer.

CAIN. How can I destroy unless she creates? I want her to
create more and more men: aye, and more and more
women, that they may in turn create more men. I have
imagined a glorious poem of many men, of more men
than there are leaves on a thousand trees. I will divide
them into two great hosts. One of them I will lead; and
the other will be led by the man I fear most and desire
to fight and kill most. And each host shall try to kill
the other host. Think of that! all those multitudes of
men fighting, fighting, killing, killing! The four rivers
running with blood! The shouts of triumph! the howls
of rage! the curses of despair! the shrieks of torment!
That will be life indeed: life lived to the very marrow:

burning, overwhelming life. Every man who has not
seen it, heard it, felt it, risked it, will feel a humbled
fool in the presence of the man who has.

EVE. And I! I am to be a mere convenience to make men
for you to kill!

ADAM. Or to kill you, you fool.

CAIN. Mother: the making of men is your right, your risk,
your agony, your glory, your triumph. You make my
father here your mere convenience, as you call it, for
that. He has to dig for you, sweat for you, plod for you,
like the ox who helps him to tear up the ground or the
ass who carries his burdens for him. No woman shall
make me live my father's life. I will hunt: I will fight
and strive to the very bursting of my sinews. When I
have slain the boar at the risk of my life, I will throw
it to my woman to cook, and give her a morsel of it for
her pains. She shall have no other food; and that will
make her my slave. And the man that slays me shall
have her for his booty. Man shall be the master of
Woman, not her baby and her drudge.

*Adam throws down his spade, and stands looking
darkly at Eve.*

EVE. Are you tempted, Adam? Does this seem a better
thing to you than love between us?

CAIN. What does he know of love? Only when he has
fought, when he has faced terror and death, when he
has striven to the spending of the last rally of his
strength, can he know what it is to rest in love in the
arms of a woman. Ask that woman whom you made,
who is also my wife, whether she would have me as I
was in the days when I followed the ways of Adam,
and was a digger and a drudge?

EVE [*angrily throwing down her distaff*] What! You dare
come here boasting about that good-for-nothing Lua, the
worst of daughters and the worst of wives! You her
master! You are more her slave than Adam's ox or your
own sheepdog. Forsooth, when you have slain the boar
at the risk of your life, you will throw her a morsel of
it for her pains! Ha! Poor wretch: do you think I do not

know her, and know you, better than that? Do you risk
your life when you trap the ermine and the sable and
the blue fox to hang on her lazy shoulders and make
her look more like an animal than a woman? When you
have to snare the little tender birds because it is too
much trouble for her to chew honest food, how much
of a great warrior do you feel then? You slay the tiger
at the risk of your life; but who gets the striped skin
you have run that risk for? She takes it to lie on, and
flings you the carrion flesh you cannot eat. You fight
because you think that your fighting makes her admire
and desire you. Fool: she makes you fight because you
bring her the ornaments and the treasures of those you
have slain, and because she is courted and propitiated
with power and gold by the people who fear you. You
say that I make a mere convenience of Adam: *I* who spin
and keep the house, and bear and rear children, and am
a woman and not a pet animal to please men and prey
on them! What are you, you poor slave of a painted
face and a bundle of skunk's fur? You were a man-child
when I bore you. Lua was a woman-child when I bore
her. What have you made of yourselves?

CAIN [*letting his spear fall into the crook of his shield arm,
and twirling his moustache*] There is something higher
than man. There is hero and superman.

EVE. Superman! You are no superman: you are Anti-Man:
you are to other men what the stoat is to the rabbit; and
she is to you what the leech is to the stoat. You despise
your father; but when he dies the world will be the richer
because he lived. When you die, men will say, "He was a
great warrior; but it would have been better for the
world if he had never been born." And of Lua they will
say nothing; but when they think of her they will spit.

CAIN. She is a better sort of woman to live with than you.
If Lua nagged at me as you are nagging, and as you nag
at Adam, I would beat her black and blue from head
to foot. I have done it too, slave as you say I am.

EVE. Yes, because she looked at another man. And then
you grovelled at her feet, and cried, and begged her to

forgive you, and were ten times more her slave than
ever; and she, when she had finished screaming and the
pain went off a little, she forgave you, did she not?

CAIN. She loved me more than ever. That is the true
nature of woman.

EVE [*now pitying him maternally*] Love! You call that love!
You call that the nature of woman! My boy: this is
neither man nor woman nor love nor life. You have no
real strength in your bones nor sap in your flesh.

CAIN. Ha! [*he seizes his spear and swings it muscularly*].

EVE. Yes: you have to twirl a stick to feel your strength:
you cannot taste life without making it bitter and boiling
hot: you cannot love Lua until her face is painted, nor
feel the natural warmth of her flesh until you have stuck
a squirrel's fur on it. You can feel nothing but a
torment, and believe nothing but a lie. You will not
raise your head to look at all the miracles of life that
surround you; but you will run ten miles to see a fight
or a death.

ADAM. Enough said. Let the boy alone.

CAIN. Boy! Ha! ha!

EVE [*to Adam*] You think, perhaps, that his way of life may
be better than yours after all. You are still tempted. Well,
will you pamper me as he pampers his woman? Will you
kill tigers and bears until I have a heap of their skins to
lounge on? Shall I paint my face and let my arms waste
into pretty softness, and eat partridges and doves, and
the flesh of kids whose milk you will steal for me?

ADAM. You are hard enough to bear with as you are. Stay
as you are; and I will stay as I am.

CAIN. You neither of you know anything about life. You
are simple country folk. You are the nurses and valets of
the oxen and dogs and asses you have tamed to work
for you. I can raise you out of that. I have a plan. Why
not tame men and women to work for us? Why not bring
them up from childhood never to know any other lot,
so that they may believe that we are gods, and that they
are here only to make life glorious for us?

ADAM [*impressed*] That is a great thought, certainly.

EVE [*contemptuously*] Great thought!

ADAM. Well, as the serpent used to say, why not?

EVE. Because I would not have such wretches in my house. Because I hate creatures with two heads, or with withered limbs, or that are distorted and perverted and unnatural. I have told Cain already that he is not a man and that Lua is not a woman: they are monsters. And now you want to make still more unnatural monsters, so that you may be utterly lazy and worthless, and that your tamed human animals may find work a blasting curse. A fine dream, truly! [*To Cain*] Your father is a fool skin deep; but you are a fool to your very marrow; and your baggage of a wife is worse.

ADAM. Why am I a fool? How am I a greater fool than you?

EVE. You said there would be no killing because the Voice would tell our children that they must not kill. Why did it not tell Cain that?

CAIN. It did; but I am not a child to be afraid of a Voice. The Voice thought I was nothing but my brother's keeper. It found that I was myself, and that it was for Abel to be himself also, and look to himself. He was not my keeper any more than I was his: why did he not kill me? There was no more to prevent him than there was to prevent me: it was man to man; and I won. I was the first conqueror.

ADAM. What did the Voice say to you when you thought all that?

CAIN. Why, it gave me right. It said that my deed was as a mark on me, a burnt-in mark such as Abel put on his sheep, that no man should slay me. And here I stand unslain, whilst the cowards who have never slain, the men who are content to be their brothers' keepers instead of their masters, are despised and rejected, and slain like rabbits. He who bears the brand of Cain shall rule the earth. When he falls, he shall be avenged sevenfold: the Voice has said it; so beware how you plot against me, you and all the rest.

ADAM. Cease your boasting and bullying, and tell the truth.

Does not the Voice tell you that as no man dare slay
you for murdering your brother, you ought to slay
yourself?

CAIN. No.

ADAM. Then there is no such thing as divine justice, unless
you are lying.

CAIN. I am not lying: I dare all truths. There is divine
justice. For the Voice tells me that I must offer myself to
every man to be killed if he can kill me. Without danger
I cannot be great. That is how I pay for Abel's blood.
Danger and fear follow my steps everywhere. Without
them courage would have no sense. And it is courage,
courage, courage, that raises the blood of life to crimson splendor.

ADAM [*picking up his spade and preparing to dig again*]
Take yourself off then. This splendid life of yours does
not last for a thousand years; and I must last for a
thousand years. When you fighters do not get killed in
fighting one another or fighting the beasts, you die from
mere evil in yourselves. Your flesh ceases to grow like
man's flesh: it grows like a fungus on a tree. Instead of
breathing you sneeze, or cough up your insides, and
wither and perish. Your bowels become rotten; your hair
falls from you; your teeth blacken and drop out; and
you die before your time, not because you will, but
because you must. I will dig, and live.

CAIN. And pray, what use is this thousand years of life to
you, you old vegetable? Do you dig any better because
you have been digging for hundreds of years? I have not
lived as long as you; but I know all there is to be known
of the craft of digging. By quitting it I have set myself
free to learn nobler crafts of which you know nothing.
I know the craft of fighting and of hunting: in a word,
the craft of killing. What certainty have you of your
thousand years? I could kill both of you; and you
could no more defend yourselves than a couple of sheep.
I spare you; but others may kill you. Why not live
bravely, and die early and make room for others? Why,
I—I! that know many more crafts than either of you,
am tired of myself when I was not fighting or hunting.

Sooner than face a thousand years of it I should kill myself, as the Voice sometimes tempts me to do already.

ADAM. Liar: you denied just now that it called on you to pay for Abel's life with your own.

CAIN. The Voice does not speak to me as it does to you. I am a man: you are only a grown-up child. One does not speak to a child as to a man. And a man does not listen and tremble in silence. He replies: he makes the Voice respect him: in the end he dictates what the Voice shall say.

ADAM. May your tongue be accurst for such blasphemy!

EVE. Keep a guard on your own tongue; and do not curse my son. It was Lilith who did wrong when she shared the labor of creation so unequally between man and wife. If you, Cain, had had the trouble of making Abel, or had had to make another man to replace him when he was gone, you would not have killed him: you would have risked your own life to save his. That is why all this empty talk of yours, which tempted Adam just now when he threw down his spade and listened to you for a while, went by me like foul wind that has passed over a dead body. That is why there is enmity between Woman the creator and Man the destroyer. I know you: I am your mother. You are idle: you are selfish. It is long and hard and painful to create life: it is short and easy to steal the life others have made. When you dug, you made the earth live and bring forth as I live and bring forth. It was for that that Lilith set you free from the travail of women, not for theft and murder.

CAIN. The Devil thank her for it! I can make better use of my time than to play the husband to the clay beneath my feet.

ADAM. Devil? What new word is that?

CAIN. Hearken to me, old fool. I have never in my soul listened willingly when you have told me of the Voice that whispers to you. There must be two Voices: one that gulls and despises you, and another that trusts and respects me. I call yours the Devil. Mine I call the Voice of God.

ADAM. Mine is the Voice of Life: yours the Voice of Death.

CAIN. Be it so. For it whispers to me that death is not really death: that it is the gate of another life: a life: infinitely splendid and intense: a life of the soul alone: a life without clods or spades, hunger or fatigue—

EVE. Selfish and idle, Cain. I know.

CAIN. Selfish, yes: a life in which no man is his brother's keeper, because his brother can keep himself. But am I idle? In rejecting your drudgery, have I not embraced evils and agonies of which you know nothing? The arrow is lighter in the hand than the spade; but the energy that drives it through the breast of a fighter is as fire to water compared with the strength that drives the spade into the harmless dirty clay. My strength is as the strength of ten because my heart is pure.

ADAM. What is that word? What is pure?

CAIN. Turned from the clay. Turned upward to the sun, to the clear clean heavens.

ADAM. The heavens are empty, child. The earth is fruitful. The earth feeds us. It gives us the strength by which we made you and all mankind. Cut off from the clay which you despise, you would perish miserably.

CAIN. I revolt against the clay. I revolt against the food. You say it gives us strength: does it not also turn into filth and smite us with diseases? I revolt against these births that you and mother are so proud of. They drag us down to the level of the beasts. If that is to be the last thing as it has been the first, let mankind perish. If I am to eat like a bear, if Lua is to bring forth cubs like a bear, then I had rather be a bear than a man; for the bear is not ashamed: he knows no better. If you are content, like the bear, I am not. Stay with the woman who gives you children: I will go to the woman who gives me dreams. Grope in the ground for your food: I will bring it from the skies with my arrows, or strike it down as it roams the earth in the pride of its life. If I must have food or die, I will at least have it at as far a remove from the earth as I can. The ox shall make it something nobler than grass before it comes to me. And as the man is nobler than the ox, I shall some day let my enemy eat the ox; and then I will slay and eat him.

ADAM. Monster! You hear this, Eve?

EVE. So that is what comes of turning your face to the clean clear heavens! Man-eating! Child-eating! For that is what it would come to, just as it came to lambs and kids when Abel began with sheep and goats. You are a poor silly creature after all. Do you think I never have these thoughts: I! who have the labor of the child-bearing: I! who have the drudgery of preparing the food? I thought for a moment that perhaps this strong brave son of mine, who could imagine something better, and could desire what he imagined, might also be able to will what he desired until he created it. And all that comes of it is that he wants to be a bear and eat children. Even a bear would not eat a man if it could get honey instead.

CAIN. I do not want to be a bear. I do not want to eat children. I do not know what I want, except that I want to be something higher and nobler than this stupid old digger whom Lilith made to help you to bring me into the world, and whom you despise now that he has served your turn.

ADAM [in sullen rage] I have half a mind to show you that my spade can split your undutiful head open, in spite of your spear.

CAIN. Undutiful! Ha! ha! [Flourishing his spear] Try it, old everybody's father. Try a taste of fighting.

EVE. Peace, peace, you two fools. Sit down and be quiet; and listen to me. [Adam, with a weary shrug, throws down his spade. Cain, with a laughing one, throws down his shield and spear. Both sit on the ground]. I hardly know which of you satisfies me least, you with your dirty digging, or he with his dirty killing. I cannot think it was for either of these cheap ways of life that Lilith set you free. [To Adam] You dig roots and coax grains out of the earth: why do you not draw down a divine sustenance from the skies? He steals and kills for his

food; and makes up idle poems of life after death; and
dresses up his terror-ridden life with fine words and his
disease-ridden body with fine clothes, so that men may
glorify and honor him instead of cursing him as murderer and thief. All you men, except only Adam, are my
sons, or my sons' sons, or my sons' sons' sons: you all
come to see me: you all shew off before me: all your
little wisdoms and accomplishments are trotted out
before mother Eve. The diggers come: the fighters and
killers come: they are both very dull; for they either
complain to me of the last harvest, or boast to me of
the last fight; and one harvest is just like another, and
the last fight only a repetition of the first. Oh, I have
heard it all a thousand times. They tell me too of their
last-born: the clever thing the darling child said yesterday, and how much more wonderful or witty or quaint
it is than any child that ever was born before. And I
have to pretend to be surprised, delighted, interested;
though the last child is like the first, and has said and
done nothing that did not delight Adam and me when
you and Abel said it. For you were the first children in
the world, and filled us with such wonder and delight
as no couple can ever again feel while the world lasts.
When I can bear no more, I go to our old garden, that is
now a mass of nettles and thistles, in the hope of finding the serpent to talk to. But you have made the serpent
our enemy: she has left the garden, or is dead: I never
see her now. So I have to come back and listen to Adam
saying the same thing for the ten-thousandth time, or to
receive a visit from the last great-great-grandson who
has grown up and wants to impress me with his importance. Oh, it is dreary, dreary! And there is yet
nearly seven hundred years of it to endure.

CAIN. Poor mother! You see, life is too long. One tires of
everything. There is nothing new under the sun.

ADAM [to Eve, grumpily] Why do you live on, if you can
find nothing better to do than complain?

EVE. Because there is still hope.

CAIN. Of what?

EVE. Of the coming true of your dreams and mine. Of
newly created things. Of better things. My sons and my
sons' sons are not all diggers and fighters. Some of
them will neither dig nor fight: they are more useless
than either of you: they are weaklings and cowards: they
are vain; yet they are dirty and will not take the trouble
to cut their hair. They borrow and never pay; but one
gives them what they want, because they tell beautiful
lies in beautiful words. They can remember their dreams.
They can dream without sleeping. They have not will
enough to create instead of dreaming; but the serpent
said that every dream could be willed into creation by
those strong enough to believe in it. There are others
who cut reeds of different lengths and blow through
them, making lovely patterns of sound in the air; and
some of them can weave the patterns together, sounding
three reeds at the same time, and raising my soul to
things for which I have no words. And others make
little mammoths out of clay, or make faces appear on
flat stones, and ask me to create women for them with
such faces. I have watched those faces and willed; and
then I have made a woman-child that has grown up
quite like them. And others think of numbers without
having to count on their fingers, and watch the sky at
night, and give names to the stars, and can foretell when
the sun will be covered with a black saucepan lid. And
there is Tubal, who made this wheel for me which has
saved me so much labor. And there is Enoch, who walks
on the hills, and hears the Voice continually, and has
given up his will to do the will of the Voice, and has
some of the Voice's greatness. When they come, there
is always some new wonder, or some new hope: something to live for. They never want to die, because they
are always learning and always creating either things or
wisdom, or at least dreaming of them. And then you,
Cain, come to me with your stupid fighting and destroying, and your foolish boasting; and you want me to tell
you that it is all splendid, and that you are heroic, and
that nothing but death or the dread of death makes life

worth living. Away with you, naughty child; and do you,
Adam, go on with your work and not waste your time
listening to him.

CAIN. I am not, perhaps, very clever; but—

EVE [*interrupting him*] Perhaps not; but do not begin to
boast of that. It is no credit to you.

CAIN. For all that, mother, I have an instinct which tells
me that death plays its part in life. Tell me this: who
invented death?

*Adam springs to his feet. Eve drops her distaff. Both
shew the greatest consternation.*

CAIN. What is the matter with you both?

ADAM. Boy: you have asked us a terrible question.

EVE. You invented murder. Let that be enough for you.

CAIN. Murder is not death. You know what I mean. Those
whom I slay would die if I spared them. If I am not
slain, yet I shall die. Who put this upon me? I say,
who invented death?

ADAM. Be reasonable, boy. Could you bear to live for ever?
You think you could, because you know that you will
never have to make your thought good. But I have
known what it is to sit and brood under the terror of
eternity, of immorality. Think of it, man: to have no
escape! to be Adam, Adam, Adam through more days
than there are grains of sand by the two rivers, and
then be as far from the end as ever! I, who have so
much in me that I hate and long to cast off! Be thankful
to your parents, who enabled you to hand on your
burden to new and better men, and won for you an
eternal rest; for it was we who invented death.

CAIN [*rising*] You did well: I, too, do not want to live for
ever. But if you invented death, why do you blame me,
who am a minister of death?

ADAM. I do not blame you. Go in peace. Leave me to my
digging, and your mother to her spinning.

CAIN. Well, I will leave you to it, though I have shewn you
a better way. [*He picks up his shield and spear*]. I will
go back to my brave warrior friends and their splendid
women. [*He strides to the thorn brake*]. When Adam

delved and Eve span, where was then the gentle man?
[*He goes away roaring with laughter, which ceases as
he cries from the distance*] Goodbye, mother.

ADAM [*grumbling*] He might have put the hurdle back,
lazy hound! [*He replaces the hurdle across the passage*].

EVE. Through him and his like, death is gaining on life.
Already most of our grandchildren die before they have
sense enough to know how to live.

ADAM. No matter. [*He spits on his hands, and takes up the
spade again*]. Life is still long enough to learn to dig,
short as they are making it.

EVE [*musing*] Yes, to dig. And to fight. But is it long enough
for the other things, the great things? Will they live long
enough to eat manna?

ADAM. What is manna?

EVE. Food drawn down from heaven, made out of the air,
not dug dirtily from the earth. Will they learn all the
ways of all the stars in their little time? It took Enoch
two hundred years to learn to interpret the will of the
Voice. When he was a mere child of eighty, his babyish
attempts to understand the Voice were more dangerous
than the wrath of Cain. If they shorten their lives, they
will dig and fight and kill and die; and their baby
Enochs will tell them that it is the will of the Voice
that they should dig and fight and kill and die for
ever.

ADAM. If they are lazy and have a will towards death I
cannot help it. I will live my thousand years: if they will
not, let them die and be damned.

EVE. Damned? What is that?

ADAM. The state of them that love death more than life. Go
on with your spinning; and do not sit there idle while
I am straining my muscles for you.

EVE [*slowly taking up her distaff*] If you were not a fool
you would find something better for both of us to live
by than this spinning and digging.

ADAM. Go on with your work, I tell you; or you shall go
without bread.

EVE. Man need not always live by bread alone. There is

something else. We do not yet know what it is; but some day we shall find out; and then we will live on that alone; and there shall be no more digging nor spinning, nor fighting nor killing.

She spins resignedly; he digs impatiently.

To H. K. Ayliff

XXXXXXXXXXXXXXXXXXXXXXXXXXXXXXXXXXXXXXXXXX

Ayliff was producer of the first English performances of
Back to Methuselah.

Parknasilla. Kenmare. Co. Kerry.
29th Aug. 1923.

Dear Ayliff
No property head that the clumsiest pantomime property
man could perpetrate could be half so fatal as Edith
Evans's torso offering itself as the voice that breathed oer
Eden.

You must get an artist (or get Sir Whitworth Wallis to
choose one) to design a very slender snake's head and
neck to rise out of the Johnswort and quiver there while
Edith, sunk in the cut with her head just above the level
of the stage, and hidden by the Johnswort, speaks the lines.
She must stand on something resonant, not on anything
solid, and tick out her words with deadly distinctness in
a tone that suggests a whisper, but isnt.

The hood may be practicable or may not. The serpents
neck should be vibrant, not rigid. It is impossible to say
more without experiments on the spot, and a real artist
doing the design and coloring and lighting.

If I had known Edith was to be in it I would have written in a proper part for her. Why dont you make her play
the Envoy's wife? she would lift it to a leading part at once.
Anybody can play the oracle. She is going to play Lady
Utterword in Heartbreak House, I hope.

ever
G.B.S.

To the Editor of *The Weekly Westminster*

✕✕✕✕✕✕✕✕✕✕✕✕✕✕✕✕✕✕✕✕✕✕✕✕✕✕✕✕✕✕✕✕

A discussion in the letters column on the means of sexual reproduction Shaw intended to satirize in In the Beginning *led to the playwright's own response in the issue of 5 April 1924.*

Sir, —

Eve's wry face is simply a criticism of the *method* of reproduction, which offends her sense of human dignity and decency. Making all possible allowance for the artificiality of civilised prudery, it remains true that if the extraordinary emotion and intensification of life which makes reproduction so irresistible could be dissociated from a physical procedure which is common to mankind and the lower forms of evolutionary creation, we should no longer be so ashamed of it that no sober person can be induced to face it in the presence of a third party.

G. Bernard Shaw

To T. E. Lawrence ("of Arabia")

>>>><<<<>>>><<<<>>>><<<<>>>><<<<>>>><<<<>>>><<<<>>>><<<<

*Ex-colonel Lawrence (as "J. H. Ross") had just been dis-
covered by the newspapers as a recruit in the R.A.F., which
in the aftermath of the publicity felt compelled to discharge him. He was still dubious about publishing his
masterpiece,* Seven Pillars of Wisdom, *and G.B.S. was
pressing him to use his unexpected leisure to prepare it
for publication. Lawrence did so, but only after he enlisted
again as a recruit, hiding this time in the Army as Private
T. E. Shaw.*

10, Adelphi Terrace, London WC 2
4 January 1923

Dear Lawrence

Like all heroes, and, I must add, all idiots, you greatly
exaggerate your power of moulding the universe to your
personal convictions. You have just had a crushing demonstration of the utter impossibility of hiding or disguising
the monster you have created. It is useless to protest that
Lawrence is not your real name. That will not save you.
You may be registered as Higg the son of Snell or Brian
de Bois Guilbert or anything else; and if you had only
stuck to it or else kept quiet, you might be Higg or Brian
still. But you masqueraded as Lawrence and didnt keep quiet;
and now Lawrence you will be to the end of your days,
and thereafter to the end of what we call modern history.
Lawrence may be as great a nuisance to you sometimes as
G.B.S. is to me, or as Frankenstein found the man he
had manufactured; but you created him, and must now
put up with him as best you can.

As to the book, bear two things in mind about me. First,
I am an old and hardened professional; and you are still

apparently a palpitating amateur in literature, wondering
whether your first MS is good enough to be published, and
whether you have a style or not. Second, I am entitled to
a reasonable construction; and when I say, as I do, that
the work must be published unabridged I do not mean
that it shall be published with the passages which would
force certain people either to take an action against you
or throw up their jobs. The publisher would take jolly
good care of that if you were careless about it. But these
passages are few, and can be omitted or paraphrased without injury or misrepresentation.

As to style, what have you to do with such dilettanti
rubbish, any more than I have? You have something to
say; and you say it as accurately and vividly as you can;
and when you have done that you do not go fooling with
your statement with the notion that if you do it over again
five or six times you will do it five or six times better.
You get it set up, and correct its inevitable slips in proof.
Then you get a revise and go over your corrections to see
that they fit in properly and that you have not dropped
one stitch in mending another. Then you pass for press;
and there you are. The result has a certain melody and a
certain mannerism which is your style, of which you are
no more aware than you are of the taste of the water that
is always in your mouth. You can, however, try an experiment. Copy out half a page of the work of some other man,
and you will find your hand so rebelling against his particular melody and mannerism that you will have to look at the
original after every second or third word to prevent yourself from getting off his track on to your own. The moment
you are conscious of style in your own work, you are
quoting or imitating or tom-fooling in some way or other.
So much for style.

Now as to the book just as it is. You will no more be
able to get rid of it, or to play about with it, than with
Lawrence. It is another Frankenstein monster; and you
must make up your mind to do the will of Allah, in whose
hand you were only a pen. You say that to publish anything now might look as though you were using the R.A.F.

as an advertizing stunt. Considering that you have already used the whole Arab race and the New Testament and the entire armies of all the countries engaged in the war to advertize yourself (since you take that view of it), I do not see why you should have a sudden fit of the bashfulness of the lady in reduced circumstances who cried laces in the street but hoped nobody heard her. A long deceased friend of mine, a parson, once told a drunken carpenter that there was once a carpenter who gave his life to save him. "If so," replied the reprobate, "you may bet that he did it to get his name up." You must get used to the limelight. I am naturally a pitiably nervous, timid man, born with a whole plume of white feathers; but nowadays this only gives a zest to the fun of swanking at every opportunity. If you read my works with the attention they deserve they would have cured you of this misplaced modesty, which is precisely what makes Rahab assure you that she is only a clergyman's daughter. The officer who saw a first rate advertisement for the R.A.F. in your enlistment shewed a much finer appreciation of the situation. And the people have their rights too, in this matter. They want you to appear always in glory, crying, "This is I, Lawrence, Prince of Mecca!" To live under a cloud is to defame God.

Moral: do your duty by the book; and arrange for its publication at once. It will not bounce out in five minutes, you know. You have the whole publishing world at your feet, as keen as Constables, who have perhaps more capital than Cape. Subject to that limitation you can choose where you will.

The other day Sidney Webb stayed with me for a week end. I put the book into his hand and said "Read a couple of pages of that and tell me how it strikes you." As he reads a book almost as fast as he can turn the pages, he took quite a large dose in ten minutes, and then said "George Borrow—not that I ever read George Borrow." "What do you mean by that?" said I. "He describes every blade of grass he walked over" said Webb. I told Mrs Webb that there was something in it about her nephew Meinertzhagen. She did not find it; but she gave me his South African dossier. Funny, your meeting at the Colonial Office!

Forgive the length of this; but as you never think unless you are down with dysentery in an Arab tent with the thermometer 100° above the temperature of hell, I must do your thinking for you. That is the worst of the Army: a soldier stops thinking instinctively. If he didnt he wouldn't be a soldier. With which gibe, farewell until your next folly.

Ever
G.B.S.

To Charles Graves

4, Whitehall Court (130) London, S.W.1
14th December, 1929

My dear Charles

My attendance at your wedding, or at anybody's wedding, is out of the question. I have within the last week or so stoutly absented myself from similar ceremonies of such pressing importance that if I made an exception in your case I could not look some of my best friends in the face again.

Besides, I have not the proper clothes—on purpose.

I have ascertained that a correct outfit at my tailors would cost me fifteen guineas; and it would be of no use to me subsequently, as I never dress correctly in daylight. But it would be of considerable use to you, as you earn your living by going into society. Therefore, as I suppose I ought to give you a wedding present, it is clear that the sensible solution of our problem is to give you the suit in which I should have graced your nuptials if I were a normal person.

You will therefore hand the enclosed cheque to your tailor and order him to do the best he can for you to that amount.

And if there is a list of presents see to it that I am entered as "Bernard Shaw: suit of clothes." If there is an exhibition of presents the tailor will lend you a dummy.

I celebrate the passing of your youth and irresponsibility with a melancholy shake-hands. I am sorry for Peggy; but you can assure her that any other man would be an equal disappointment after a week or so.

As for you, it is too late to run away now. You are for it, Charles.

faithfully
G. Bernard Shaw

To Frank Harris

×××××××××××××××××××××××××××××××××××××

When "G.B.S." was drama critic on the Saturday Review, *his editor was the notorious Frank Harris. Harris had since fallen on evil days. He had tried to recoup his fortunes with biographical sketches and his almost unprintable* My Life and Loves, *and finally with a full-length life of Shaw, which Shaw, knowing Harris to be poor and ill, cooperated in bringing to completion.*

London, 24th June, 1930

Dear Frank Harris,

First, O Biographer, get it clear in your mind that you can learn nothing about your sitter (or Biograph*ee*) from a mere record of his copulations. You have no such record in the case of Shakespear, and a pretty full one for a few years in the case of Pepys: but you know much more about Shakespear than about Pepys. The explanation is that the relation between the parties in copulation is not a personal relation. It can be irresistibly desired and rapturously executed between persons who could not endure one another for a day in any other relation. If I were to tell you every such adventure that I have enjoyed you would be none the wiser as to my personal, nor even as to my sexual history. You would know only what you already know: that I am a human being. If you have any doubts as to my normal virility, dismiss them from your mind. I was not impotent: I was not sterile; I was not homosexual; and I was extremely, though not promiscuously susceptible.

Also I was entirely free from the neurosis (as it seems to me) of Original Sin. I never associated sexual intercourse with delinquency. I associated it always with delight, and had no scruples nor remorses nor misgivings of conscience. Of course I had scruples, and effectively inhibitive ones too, about getting women into trouble (or rather letting them get themselves into it with me) or cuckolding my friends; and I understand that chastity can be a passion just as intellect is a passion; but St Paul's was to me always a pathological case. Sexual experience seemed a necessary completion of human growth; and I was not attracted by virgins as such. I preferred women who knew what they were doing.

As I have told you, my corporeal adventures began when I was twenty-nine. But it would be a prodigious mistake to take that as the date of the beginning of my sexual life. Do not misunderstand this: I was perfectly continent except for the involuntary incontinences of dreamland, which were very unfrequent. But as between Oscar Wilde, who gave 16 as the age at which sex begins, and Rousseau, who declared that his blood boiled with sensuality from his birth (but wept when Madame de Warens initiated him) my experience confirms Rousseau and is amazed at Wilde. Just as I cannot remember any time when I could not read and write, so I cannot remember any time when I did not exercise my overwhelming imagination in telling myself stories about women.

I was, as all young people should be, a votary of the Uranian Venus. I was steeped in romantic music from my childhood. I knew all the pictures and statues in the National Gallery of Ireland (a very good one) by heart. I read everything I could lay my hands on. Dumas père made French history like an opera by Meyerbeer for me. From our cottage on Dalkey Hill I contemplated an eternal Shelleyan vision of sea, sky and mountain. Real life was only a squalid interruption to an imaginary paradise. I was overfed on honey dew. The Uranian Venus was beautiful.

The difficulty about the Uranian Venus is that though she saves you from squalid debaucheries and enables you to prolong your physical virginity long after your adolescence, she may sterilise you by giving you imaginary amours on the plains of heaven with goddesses and angels and even devils so enchanting that they spoil you for real women or—if you are a woman—for real men. You be-

come inhuman through a surfeit of beauty and an excess
of voluptuousness. You end as an ascetic, a saint, an old
bachelor, an old maid (in short, a celibate) because, like
Heine, you cannot ravish the Venus de Milo or be ravished
by the Hermes of Praxiteles. Your love poems are like
Shelley's Epipsychidion, irritating to *terre à terre* sensual
women, who know at once that you are making them
palatable by pretending they are something that they are
not, and cannot stand comparison with.

Now you know how I lived, a continent virgin, until I
was 29, and ran away even when the handkerchief was
thrown me.

From that time until my marriage there was always
some lady at my disposal, and I tried all the experiments
and learned what there was to be learnt from them. They
were "all for love"; for I had no spare money: I earned
enough to keep me on a second floor, and took the rest
out, not in money, but in freedom to preach Socialism.

When at last I could afford to dress presentably I soon
became accustomed to find women falling in love with me.
I did not need to pursue women: I was pursued by them.

Here again do not jump at conclusions. All the pur-
suers did not want sexual intercourse. They wanted company and friendship. Some were happily married, and
were affectionately appreciative of my understanding
that sex was barred. Some were prepared to buy friendship with pleasure, having made up their minds that
men were made that way. Some were sexual geniuses,
quite unbearable in any other capacity. No two cases were
alike: William Morris's dictum "that all taste alike" was
not, as Longfellow puts it, "spoken of the soul."

I found sex hopeless as a basis for permanent relations,
and never dreamt of marriage in connection with it. I put
everything else before it, and never refused or broke an
engagement to speak on Socialism to pass a gallant evening.
I liked sexual intercourse because of its amazing power
of producing a celestial flood of emotion and exaltation of
existence which, however momentary, gave me a sample
of what may one day be the normal state of being for
mankind in intellectual ecstasy. I always gave the wildest

expression to this in a torrent of words, partly because I felt it due to the woman to know what I felt in her arms, and partly because I wanted her to share it. But except perhaps on one occasion I never felt quite convinced that I had carried the lady more than half as far as she had carried me: the capacity for it varies like any other capacity. I remember one woman who had a sort of affectionate worship for me, explaining that she had to leave her husband because sexual intercourse felt as she put it "like someone sticking a finger into my eye." Between her and the heroine of my first adventure, who was sexually insatiable, there is an enormous range of sensation; and the range of celestial exaltation must be still greater.

When I married I was too experienced to make the frightful mistake of simply setting up a permanent whore; nor was my wife making the complementary mistake. There was nothing whatever to prevent us from satisfying our sexual needs without paying that price for it; and it was for other considerations that we became man and wife. In permanence and seriousness my consummated love affairs count for nothing beside the ones that were either unconsummated or ended by discarding that relation.

Do not forget that all marriages are different, and that a marriage between two young people followed by parentage cannot be lumped in with a childless partnership between two middle-aged people who have passed the age at which it is safe to bear a first child.

And now, no romance and above all no pornography.

G.B.S.

To Mabel Shaw

×××××××××××××××××××××××××××××××××××××××

*A year after G.B.S. wrote the following letter he told
Nancy Astor (12 May 1930) that he had invited to lunch
"a certain Miss Mabel Shaw (no relation), a woman with a
craze for self-torture, who broke off her engagement with
a clergyman (he died of it) to bury herself in the wilds of
Africa and lead negro children to Christ. She has a very
graphic pen; and some of her letters were shewn to me. She
has come home on a missionary-furlough. . . ." Not long
afterward G.B.S. was visiting in South Africa; and when
the visit was prolonged because Charlotte was injured in
an auto accident, he used his enforced leisure to write*
The Black Girl, *which appears to owe much of its inspiration to Mabel Shaw.*

*Margaret Macmillan administered an innovative and ef-
ficient nursery school program.*

Ayot St. Lawrence, Welwyn, Herts
30 January 1928

Dear Miss Shaw

A friend of yours has shewn me some of your letters, and
asked me—as I found them interesting—to let you know
whether I thought you qualified to take up literature as
a profession.

As far as mere literary faculty is concerned I should say
decidedly Yes. You have evidently no difficulty in putting
into writing anything you want to say or describe, and in
such a way that the reader reads willingly and expectantly.
No more than this is required of the greatest authors as
professional qualification.

But success in literature depends on what you have to
say as well as on how you say it. For instance, of Bunyan's

two romances, The Pilgrim's Progress and The Holy War, the second is, if anything, more skilfully written than the first, the hand being more experienced. But the first is universally readable by people whose tastes rise above the football page of the evening paper; and the second ends by making theology ridiculous and unreadable even to a specialist of Bunyan's own persuasion.

Whether you are enough of a freethinker to be successful in literature outside your own sect I cannot say. We are none of us complete freethinkers (least of all sometimes the professed ones): we all have our superstitions and our complexes, the difference between a rather mad writer like Saint Paul and a rather sane one like Voltaire being only one of degree. One can only say that it would have been better for the world if Paul had never been born, and that it would have been a great misfortune—a religious misfortune—to have missed Voltaire, who at least loved justice and did mercy and walked humbly with his God, and believed that no further theology was required of him. Also he certainly loved mercy and, as far as his temperament would let him, tried to do justly. That is why he is still so readable. Besides, as the wickednesses which he exposed and which he called on the world's conscience to renounce were too frightful to be contemplated without some sort of anaesthetic, he used his sense of fun to make people come to scoff, knowing that that was the only chance of getting them to remain to pray.

Now it is clear from what you have written that you are one of the would-be saviors, like Bunyan and Voltaire. Having found happiness with God (so to speak) you wish to bring others to him. Jesus, who was strongly anti-missionary, as his warning about the tares and the wheat shews, would probably tell you to mind your own business and suffer little children to find their own way to God even if it were a black way; but he certainly would not demur to your describing your own pilgrimage and testifying that you had found God in your own white way. That is, if he had any patience with you after discovering that you had set up in the virgin forest the horrible emblem of

Roman cruelty and Roman terrorism as an emblem of Christianity. Even Rome itself would have set up the image of a mother and child.

The question is, then, would your descriptions of your own discovery of God please a sufficient number of book-buyers to make a profit for a publisher and bookseller and a living for you. I think it quite likely they would. I have found your scraps interesting; and I am not in sympathy with you at all. I am not in the least what modern psychologists call a masochist: that is, a person with a queer lust for being tortured; so that when your parents no longer tortured you you tortured yourself. You are not satiated even with the horrible things they did to Christ: you must heap on him a broken body, though the story insists so strongly on the fact that his body was not broken as the bodies of the thieves were. You meet a young man with whom you fall in love, and who falls in love with you. There was nothing to prevent you making him and yourself happy by naturally and unaffectedly marrying him and filling your lap with babies. But no: that would not have been any fun for you: you must break his heart and break your own (if you have one) on the ridiculous pretext that the negro children needed you, though your own country was swarming with little white heathens who needed you as badly as they need Margaret Macmillan in Deptford. And then comes your artistic impulse. You must write about it and make a propaganda of voluptuous agony. Well, there are plenty of people who find agony voluptuous on paper; and they will make a reading public for you. But I, who loathe torture, and object most strongly to being tortured, my lusts being altogether normal, should take you and shake you were it not that you are out of my reach and that you would rather enjoy being shaken if it hurt you enough.

It may be that this psychosis (pardon the jargon) will pass away as your glands mature. At the bottom of this African business there may be a young woman with a healthy taste for travel, novelty, adventure, and salutary hardening hardship. You may not really have wanted that unfortunate young parson whom you smashed up. You are, after all, the granddaughter of your delightful old humbug of a grandmother as well as the daughter of your (as I gather) detestable parents. I call your grandmother a humbug in the friendliest sense because she made child happy by flattering God, and pretending that he had not a great deal to answer for. She spoilt you; but she saved your soul alive for the time when you will be strong enough to face adult life and grow out of the pastime of playing with the souls of little children as your soul was played with.

And that is all I have to say to you on the little information I have about you. You may think I have said a great deal too much; but I assure you the question of becoming a professional writer is a pretty deep one when the intention behind it extends to becoming a prophet as well. I am in that line myself; and I KNOW.

And anyhow you brought it on yourself. I wonder what you expected me to say.

faithfully

G. Bernard Shaw

THE ADVENTURES OF THE BLACK GIRL IN HER SEARCH FOR GOD*

×××××××××××××××××××××××××××××××××××××

"Where is God?" said the black girl to the missionary who had converted her.

"He has said 'Seek and ye shall find me'" said the missionary.

The missionary was a small white woman, not yet thirty: an odd little body who had found no satisfaction for her soul with her very respectable and fairly well-to-do family in her native England, and had settled down in the African forest to teach little African children to love Christ and adore the Cross. She was a born apostle of love. At school she had adored one or other of her teachers with an idolatry that was proof against all snubbing, but had never cared much for girls of her own age and standing. At eighteen she began falling in love with earnest clergymen, and actually became engaged to six of them in succession. But when it came to the point she always broke it off; for these love affairs, full at first of ecstatic happiness and hope, somehow became unreal and eluded her in the end. The clergymen thus suddenly and unaccountably disengaged did not always conceal their sense of relief and escape, as if they too had discovered that the dream was only a dream, or a sort of metaphor by which they had striven to express the real thing, but not itself the real thing.

* In 1934 Shaw altered the original text in two places, changing "minus x" to "minus one," and "Myna's sex" to "Myna's one." Shaw had first summed up the mystery of existence in the equation "the square root of minus x." From the equation he created the Black Girl's misconstruing of the concept, which she identified with the sex of the goddess Myna, thus innocently suggesting a female divinity. When charged with inaccuracy in his use of Einstein's Relativity theory, Shaw altered the equation and weakened the pun. In this edition and future editions authorized by the Shaw Estate, art will be granted precedence over mathematics and the original pun preserved.

One of the jilted, however, committed suicide; and this tragedy gave her an extraordinary joy. It seemed to take her from a fool's paradise of false happiness into a real region in which intense suffering became transcendent rapture.

But it put an end to her queer marriage engagements. Not that it was the last of them. But a worldly cousin, of whose wit she was a little afraid, and who roundly called her a coquette and a jilt, one day accused her of playing in her later engagements for another suicide, and told her that many a woman had been hanged for less. And though she knew in a way that this was not true, and that the cousin, being a woman of this world, did not understand; yet she knew also that in the worldly way it was true enough, and that she must give up this strange game of seducing men into engagements which she now knew she would never keep. So she jilted the sixth clergyman and went to plant the cross in darkest Africa; and the last stirring in her of what she repudiated as sin was a flash of rage when he married the cousin, through whose wit and worldly wisdom he at last became a bishop in spite of himself.

The black girl, a fine creature, whose satin skin and shining muscles made the white missionary folk seem like ashen ghosts by contrast, was an interesting but unsatisfactory convert; for instead of taking Christianity with sweet docility exactly as it was administered to her, she met it with unexpected interrogative reactions which forced her teacher to improvize doctrinal replies and invent evidence on the spur of the moment to such an extent that at last she could not conceal from herself that the life of Christ, as she narrated it, had accreted so many circumstantial details and such a body of homemade doctrine that the Evangelists would have been amazed and confounded if they had been alive to hear it all put forward on their authority. Indeed the missionary's choice of a specially remote station, which had been at first an act of devotion, very soon became a necessity, as the appearance of a rival missionary would have led to the discovery that though some of the finest plums in the gospel pudding concocted by her had been picked out of the Bible, and the scenery and *dramatis personae* borrowed from it, yet the resultant religion was, in spite of this element of compilation, really a product of the missionary's own direct inspiration. Only as a solitary pioneer missionary could she be her own Church and determine its canon without fear of being excommunicated as a heretic.

But she was perhaps rash when, having taught the black girl to read, she gave her a bible on her birthday. For when the black girl, receiving her teacher's reply very literally, took her knobkerry and strode off into the African forest in search of God, she took the bible with her as her guidebook.

The first thing she met was a mamba snake, one of the few poisonous snakes that will attack mankind if crossed. Now the missionary, who was fond of making pets of animals because they were affectionate and never asked questions, had taught the black girl never to kill anything if she could help it, and never to be afraid of anything. So she grasped her knobkerry a little tighter and said to the mamba "I wonder who made you, and why he gave you the will to kill me and the venom to do it with."

The mamba immediately beckoned her by a twist of its head to follow it, and led her to a pile of rocks on which sat enthroned a well-built aristocratic looking white man with handsome regular features, an imposing beard and luxuriant wavy hair, both as white as isinglass, and a ruthlessly severe expression. He had in his hand a staff which seemed a combination of sceptre, big stick, and great assegai; and with this he immediately killed the mamba, who was approaching him humbly and adoringly.

The black girl, having been taught to fear nothing, felt her heart harden against him, partly because she thought strong men ought to be black, and only missionary ladies white, partly because he had killed her friend the snake, and partly because he wore a ridiculous white nightshirt, and thereby rubbed her up on the one point on which her teacher had never been able to convert her, which was the duty of being ashamed of her person and wearing petticoats. There was a certain contempt in her voice as she addressed him.

"I am seeking God" she said. "Can you direct me?"

"You have found him" he replied. "Kneel down and worship me this very instant, you presumptuous creature, or dread my wrath. I am the Lord of Hosts: I made the heavens and the earth and all that in them is. I made the poison of the snake and the milk in your mother's breast. In my hand are death and all the diseases, the thunder and lightning, the storm and the pestilence, and all the other proofs of my greatness and majesty. On your knees, girl; and when you next come before me, bring me your favorite child and slay it here before me as a sacrifice; for I love the smell of newly spilled blood."

"I have no child" said the black girl. "I am a virgin."

"Then fetch your father and let him slay you" said the Lord of Hosts. "And see that your relatives bring me plenty of rams and goats and sheep to roast before me as offerings to propitiate me, or I shall certainly smite them with the most horrible plagues so that they may know that I am God."

"I am not a piccaninny, nor even a grown up ninny, to believe such wicked nonsense" said the black girl; "and in the name of the true God whom I seek I will scotch you as you scotched that poor mamba." And she bounded up the rocks at him, brandishing her knobkerry.

But when she reached the top there was nothing there. This so bewildered her that she sat down and took out her bible for guidance. But whether the ants had got at it, or, being a very old book, it had perished by natural decay, all the early pages had crumbled to dust which blew away when she opened it.

So she sighed and got up and resumed her search. Presently she disturbed a sort of cobra called a ringhals, which spat at her and was gliding away when she said "You no dare spit at me. I want to know who made you, and why you are so unlike me. The mamba's God was no use: he wasnt real when I tried him with my knobkerry. Lead me to yours."

On that, the ringhals came back and beckoned her to follow him, which she did.

He led her to a pleasant glade in which an oldish gentleman with a soft silvery beard and hair, also in a white nightshirt, was sitting at a table covered with a white cloth and strewn with manuscript poems and pens made of angels' quills. He looked kindly enough; but his turned up moustaches and eyebrows expressed a self-satisfied cunning which the black girl thought silly.

"Good little Spitty-spitty" he said to the snake. "You have brought somebody to argue with me." And he gave the snake an egg, which it carried away joyfully into the forest.

"Do not be afraid of me" he said to the black girl. "I am not a cruel god: I am a reasonable one. I do nothing worse than argue. I am a Nailer at arguing. Dont worship me. Reproach me. Find fault with me. Dont spare my feelings. Throw something in my teeth; so that I can argue about it."

"Did you make the world?" said the black girl.

"Of course I did" he said.

"Why did you make it with so much evil in it?" she said.

"Splendid!" said the god. "That is just what I wanted you to ask me. You are a clever intelligent girl. I had a servant named Job once to argue with; but he was so modest and stupid that I had to shower the most frightful misfortunes on him before I could provoke him to complain. His wife told him to curse me and die; and I dont wonder at the poor woman; for I gave him a terrible time, though I made it all up to him afterwards. When at last I got him arguing, he thought a lot of himself. But I soon shewed him up. He acknowledged that I had the better of him. I took him down handsomely, I tell you."

"I do not want to argue" said the black girl. "I want to know why, if you really made the world, you made it so badly."

"Badly!" cried the Nailer. "Ho! You set yourself up to call me to account! Who are you, pray, that you should criticize me? Can you make a better world yourself? Just try: thats all. Try to make one little bit of it. For instance, make a whale. Put a hook in its nose and bring it to me when you have finished. Do you realize, you ridiculous little insect, that I not only made the whale, but made the sea for him to swim in? The whole mighty ocean, down to its bottomless depths and up to the top of the skies. You think that was easy, I suppose. You think you could do it better yourself. I tell you what, young woman: you want the conceit taken out of you. You couldnt make a mouse; and you set yourself up against me, who made a megatherium. You couldnt make a pond; and you dare talk to me, the maker of the seven seas. You will be ugly and old and dead in fifty years, whilst my majesty will endure for ever; and here you are taking me to task as if you were my aunt. You think, dont you, that you are better than God? What have you to say to that argument?"

"It isnt an argument: it's a sneer" said the black girl. "You dont seem to know what an argument is."

"What! I who put down Job, as all the world admits, not know what an argument is! I simply laugh at you, child" said the old gentleman, considerably huffed, but too astonished to take the situation in fully.

"I dont mind your laughing at me" said the black girl; "but you have not told me why you did not make the world all good instead of a mixture of good and bad. It is no answer to ask me whether I could have made it any better myself. If I were God there would be no tsetse flies. My people would not fall down in fits and have dreadful swellings and commit sins. Why did you put a bag of poison in the mamba's mouth when other snakes can live as well without it? Why did you make the monkeys so ugly and the birds so pretty?"

"Why shouldnt I?" said the old gentleman. "Answer me that."

"Why should you? unless you have a taste for mischief" said the black girl.

"Asking conundrums is not arguing" he said. "It is not playing the game."

"A God who cannot answer my questions is no use to

me" said the black girl. "Besides, if you had really made everything you would know why you made the whale as ugly as he is in the pictures."

"If I chose to amuse myself by making him look funny, what is that to you?" he said. "Who are you to dictate to me how I shall make things?"

"I am tired of you" said the black girl. "You always come back to the same bad manners. I dont believe you ever made anything. Job must have been very stupid not to find you out. There are too many old men pretending to be gods in this forest."

She sprang at him with her knobkerry uplifted; but he dived nimbly under the table, which she thought must have sunk into the earth; for when she reached it there was nothing there. And when she resorted to her bible again the wind snatched thirty more pages out of it and scattered them in dust over the trees.

After this adventure the black girl felt distinctly sulky. She had not found God; her bible was half spoilt; and she had lost her temper twice without any satisfaction whatever. She began to ask herself whether she had not overrated white beards and old age and nightshirts as divine credentials. It was lucky that this was her mood when she came upon a remarkably good looking clean shaven white young man in a Greek tunic. She had never seen anything like him before. In particular there was a lift and twist about the outer corners of his brows that both interested and repelled her.

"Excuse me, baas" she said. "You have knowing eyes. I am in search of God. Can you direct me?"

"Do not trouble about that" said the young man. "Take the world as it comes; for beyond it there is nothing. All roads end at the grave, which is the gate of nothingness; and in the shadow of nothingness everything is vanity. Take my advice and seek no further than the end of your nose. You will always know that there is something beyond that; and in that knowledge you will be hopeful and happy."

"My mind ranges further" said the black girl. "It is not

right to shut one's eyes. I desire a knowledge of God more than happiness or hope. God is my happiness and my hope."

"How if you find that there is no God?" said the young man.

"I should be a bad woman if I did not know that God exists" said the black girl.

"Who told you that?" said the young man. "You should not let people tie up your mind with such limitations. Besides, why should you not be a bad woman?"

"That is nonsense" said the black girl. "Being a bad woman means being something you ought not to be."

"Then you must find out what you ought to be before you can tell whether you are a good woman or a bad one."

"That is true" said the black girl. "But I know I ought to be a good woman even if it is bad to be good."

"There is no sense in that" said the young man.

"Not your sort of sense but God's sort of sense" she said. "I want to have that sort of sense; and I feel that when I have got it I shall be able to find God."

"How can you tell what you shall find?" he said. "My counsel to you is to do all the work that comes to you as well as you can while you can, and so fill up with use and honor the days that remain to you before the inevitable end, when there will be neither counsel nor work, neither doing nor knowing, nor even being."

"There will be a future when I am dead" said the black girl. "If I cannot live it I can know it."

"Do you know the past?" said the young man. "If the past, which has really happened, is beyond your knowledge, how can you hope to know the future, which has not yet happened?"

"Yet it will happen; and I know enough of it to tell you that the sun will rise every day" said the black girl.

"That also is vanity" said the young sage. "The sun is burning and must some day burn itself out."

"Life is a flame that is always burning itself out; but it catches fire again every time a child is born. Life is greater than death, and hope than despair. I will do the work that comes to me only if I know that it is good work; and to know that, I must know the past and the future, and must know God."

"You mean that you must *be* God" he said, looking hard at her.

"As much as I can" said the black girl. "Thank you. We who are young are the wise ones: I have learned from you that to know God is to be God. You have strengthened my soul. Before I leave you, tell me who you are."

"I am Koheleth, known to many as Ecclesiastes the preacher" he replied. "God be with you if you can find him! He is not with me. Learn Greek: it is the language of wisdom. Farewell."

He made a friendly sign and passed on. The black girl went the opposite way, thinking harder than ever; but the train of thought he had started in her became so puzzling and difficult that at last she fell asleep and walked steadily on in her sleep until she smelt a lion, and, waking suddenly, saw him sitting in the middle of her path, sunning himself like a cat before the hearth: a lion of the kind they call maneless because its mane is handsome and orderly and not like a touzled mop.

"In God's name, Dicky" she said, giving his throat as she passed him a caressing little pull with her fingers which felt as if she had pulled at a warm tuft of moss on a mountain.

King Richard beamed graciously, and followed her with his eyes as if he had an impulse to go for a walk with her; but she left him too decisively for that; and she, remembering that there are many less amiable and even stronger creatures in the forest than he, proceeded more warily until she met a dark man with wavy black hair, and a number six nose. He had nothing on but a pair of sandals. His face was very much wrinkled; but the wrinkles were those of pity and kindliness, though the number six nose had large courageous nostrils, and the corners of his mouth were resolute. She heard him before she saw him; for he was making strange roaring and hooting noises and seemed in great trouble. When he saw her he stopped roaring and tried to look ordinary and unconcerned.

"Say, baas" said the black girl: "are you the prophet

that goes stripped and naked, wailing like the dragons and mourning like the owls?"

"I do a little in that line" he said apologetically. "Micah is my name: Micah the Morasthite. Can I do anything for you?"

"I seek God" she answered.

"And have you found Him?" said Micah.

"I found an old man who wanted me to roast animals for him because he loved the smell of cooking, and to sacrifice my children on his altar."

At this Micah uttered such a lamentable roar that King Richard hastily took cover in the forest and sat watching there with his tail slashing.

"He is an impostor and a horror" roared Micah. "Can you see yourself coming before the high God with burnt calves of a year old? Would He be pleased with thousands of rams or rivers of oil or the sacrifice of your first born, the fruit of your body, instead of the devotion of your soul? God has shewed your soul what is good; and your soul has told you that He speaks the truth. And what does He require of you but to do justice and love mercy and walk humbly with Him?"

"This is a third God" she said; "and I like him much better than the one who wanted sacrifices and the one who wanted me to argue with him so that he might sneer at my weakness and ignorance. But doing justice and shewing mercy is only a small part of life when one is not a baas or a judge. And what is the use of walking humbly if you dont know where you are walking to?"

"Walk humbly and God will guide you" said the Prophet. "What is it to you whither He is leading you?"

"He gave me eyes to guide myself" said the black girl. "He gave me a mind and left me to use it. How can I now turn on him and tell him to see for me and to think for me?"

Micah's only reply was such a fearful roar that King Richard fairly bolted and ran for two miles without stopping. And the black girl did the same in the opposite direction. But she ran only a mile.

"What am I running away from?" she said to herself,

pulling herself up. "I'm not afraid of that dear noisy old man."

"Your fears and hopes are only fancies" said a voice close to her, proceeding from a very shortsighted elderly man in spectacles who was sitting on a gnarled log. "In running away you were acting on a conditioned reflex. It is quite simple. Having lived among lions you have from your childhood associated the sound of a roar with deadly danger. Hence your precipitate flight when that superstitious old jackass brayed at you. This remarkable discovery cost me twenty-five years of devoted research, during which I cut out the brains of innumerable dogs, and observed their spittle by making holes in their cheeks for them to salivate through instead of through their tongues. The whole scientific world is prostrate at my feet in admiration of this colossal achievement and gratitude for the light it has shed on the great problems of human conduct."

"Why didnt you ask me?" said the black girl. "I could have told you in twenty-five seconds without hurting those poor dogs."

"Your ignorance and presumption are unspeakable" said the old myop. "The fact was known of course to every child; but it had never been proved experimentally in the laboratory; and therefore it was not scientifically known at all. It reached me as an unskilled conjecture: I handed it on as science. Have you ever performed an experiment may I ask?"

"Several" said the black girl. "I will perform one now. Do you know what you are sitting on?"

"I am sitting on a log grey with age, and covered with an uncomfortable rugged bark" said the myop.

"You are mistaken" said the black girl. "You are sitting on a sleeping crocodile."

With a yell which Micah himself might have envied, the myop rose and fled frantically to a neighboring tree, up which he climbed catlike with an agility which in so elderly a gentleman was quite superhuman.

"Come down" said the black girl. "You ought to know that crocodiles are only to be found near rivers. I was only trying an experiment. Come down."

"How am I to come down?" said the myop trembling. "I should break my neck."

"How did you get up?" said the black girl.

"I dont know" he replied, almost in tears. "It is enough to make a man believe in miracles. I couldnt have climbed this tree; and yet here I am and shall never be able to get down again."

"A very interesting experiment, wasnt it?" said the black girl.

"A shamefully cruel one, you wicked girl" he moaned. "Pray did it occur to you that you might have killed me? Do you suppose you can give a delicate physiological organism like mine a violent shock without the most serious and quite possibly fatal reactions on the heart? I shall never be able to sit on a log again as long as I live. I believe my pulse is quite abnormal, though I cannot count it; for if I let go of this branch I shall drop like a stone."

"If you can cut half a dog's brain out without causing any reactions on its spittle you need not worry" she said calmly. "I think African magic much more powerful than your divining by dogs. By saying one word to you I made you climb a tree like a cat. You confess it was a miracle."

"I wish you would say another word and get me safely down again, confound you for a black witch" he grumbled.

"I will" said the black girl. "There is a tree snake smelling at the back of your neck."

The myop was on the ground in a jiffy. He landed finally on his back; but he scrambled to his feet at once and said "You did not take me in: dont think it. I knew perfectly well you were inventing that snake to frighten me."

"And yet you were as frightened as if it had been a real snake" said the black girl.

"I was not" said the myop indignantly. "I was not frightened in the least."

"You nipped down the tree as if you were" said the black girl.

"That is what is so interesting" said the myop, recovering his self-possession now that he felt safe. "It was a conditioned reflex. I wonder could I make a dog climb a tree."

"What for?" said the black girl.

"Why, to place this phenomenon on a scientific basis" said he.

"Nonsense!" said the black girl. "A dog cant climb a tree."

"Neither can I without the stimulus of an imaginary crocodile" said the professor. "How am I to make a dog imagine a crocodile?"

"Introduce him to a few real ones to begin with" said the black girl.

"That would cost a great deal" said the myop, wrinkling his brows. "Dogs are cheap if you buy them from professional dog-stealers, or lay in a stock when the dog tax becomes due; but crocodiles would run into a lot of money. I must think this out carefully."

"Before you go" said the black girl "tell me whether you believe in God."

"God is an unnecessary and discarded hypothesis" said the myop. "The universe is only a gigantic system of reflexes reproduced by shocks. If I give you a clip on the knee you will wag your ankle."

"I will also give you a clip with my knobkerry; so dont do it" said the black girl.

"For scientific purposes it is necessary to inhibit such secondary and apparently irrelevant reflexes by tying the subject down" said the professor. "Yet they also are quite relevant as examples of reflexes produced by association of ideas. I have spent twenty-five years studying their effects."

"Effects on what?" said the black girl.

"On a dog's saliva" said the myop.

"Are you any the wiser?" she said.

"I am not interested in wisdom" he replied: "in fact I do not know what it means and have no reason to believe that it exists. My business is to learn something that was not known before. I impart that knowledge to the world, and thereby add to the body of ascertained scientific truth."

"How much better will the world be when it is all knowledge and no mercy?" said the black girl. "Havnt you brains enough to invent some decent way of finding out what you want to know?"

"Brains!" cried the myop, as if he could hardly believe his ears. "You must be an extraordinarily ignorant young woman. Do you not know that men of science are all brains from head to foot?"

"Tell that to the crocodile" said the black girl. "And tell me this. Have you ever considered the effect of your experiments on other people's minds and characters? Is it worth while losing your own soul and damning everybody else's to find out something about a dog's spittle?"

"You are using words that have no meaning" said the myop. "Can you demonstrate the existence of the organ you call a soul on the operating table or in the dissecting room? Can you reproduce the operation you call damning in the laboratory?"

"I can turn a live body with a soul into a dead one without it with a whack of my knobkerry" said the black girl "and you will soon see the difference and smell it. When people damn their souls by doing something wicked, you soon see the difference too."

"I have seen a man die: I have never seen one damn his soul" said the myop.

"But you have seen him go to the dogs" said the black girl. "You have gone to the dogs yourself, havnt you?"

"A quip; and an extremely personal one" said the myop haughtily. "I leave you."

So he went his way trying to think of some means of making a dog climb a tree in order to prove scientifically that he himself could climb one; and the black girl went her opposite way until she came to a hill on the top of which stood a huge cross guarded by a Roman soldier with a spear. Now in spite of all the teachings of the missionary, who found in the horrors of the crucifixion the same strange joy she had found in breaking her own heart and those of her lovers, the black girl hated the cross and thought it a great pity that Jesus had not died peacefully and painlessly and naturally, full of years and wisdom, protecting his granddaughters (her imagination always completed the picture with at least twenty promising black granddaughters) against the selfishness and violence of their parents. So she was averting her head from the cross with an expression of disgust when the Roman soldier sprang at her with his spear at the charge and shouted fiercely "On your knees, blackamoor, before the instrument and symbol of Roman justice, Roman law, Roman order and Roman peace."

But the black girl side-stepped the spear and swung her knobkerry so heartily on the nape of his neck that he went down sprawling and trying vainly to co-ordinate the movement of his legs sufficiently to rise. "That is the blackamoor instrument and symbol of all those fine things" said the black girl, shewing him the knobkerry. "How do you like it?"

"Hell!" groaned the soldier. "The tenth legion rabbit punched by a black bitch! This is the end of the world." And he ceased struggling and lay down and cried like a child.

He recovered before she had gone very far; but being a Roman soldier he could not leave his post to gratify his feelings. The last she saw of him before the brow of the hill cut off their view of one another was the shaking of his fist at her; and the last she heard from him need not be repeated here.

Her next adventure was at a well where she stopped to drink, and suddenly saw a man whom she had not noticed before sitting beside it. As she was about to scoop up some water in her hand he produced a cup from nowhere and said

"Take this and drink in remembrance of me."

"Thank you, baas" she said, and drank. "Thank you kindly."

She gave him back the cup; and he made it disappear like a conjurer, at which she laughed and he laughed too. "That was clever, baas" she said. "Great magician, you. You perhaps tell black woman something. I am in search of God. Where is he?"

"Within you" said the conjurer. "Within me too."

"I think so" said the girl. "But what is he?"

"Our father" said the conjurer.

The black girl made a wry face and thought for a moment. "Why not our mother?" she said then.

It was the conjurer's turn to make a wry face; and he made it. "Our mothers would have us put them before God" he said. "If I had been guided by my mother I should perhaps have been a rich man instead of an outcast and a wanderer; but I should not have found God."

"My father beat me from the time I was little until I was big enough to lay him out with my knobkerry" said the black girl; "and even after that he tried to sell me to a white baas-soldier who had left his wife across the seas. I have always refused to say 'Our father which art in heaven.' I always say 'Our grandfather.' I will not have a God who is my father."

"That need not prevent us loving one another like brother and sister" said the conjurer smiling; for the grandfather amendment tickled his sense of humor. Besides, he was a goodnatured fellow who smiled whenever he could.

"A woman does not love her brother" said the black girl. "Her heart turns from her brother to a stranger as my heart turns to you."

"Well: let us drop the family: it is only a metaphor" said the conjurer. "We are members of the same body of mankind, and therefore members one of another. Let us leave it at that."

"I cannot, baas" she said. "God tells me that he has nothing to do with bodies, and fathers and mothers, and sisters and brothers."

"It is a way of saying love one another: that is all" said the conjurer. "Love them that hate you. Bless them that curse you. Never forget that two blacks do not make a white."

"I do not want everyone to love me" said the black girl. "I cannot love everybody. I do not want to. God tells me that I must not hit people with my knobkerry merely because I dislike them, and that their dislike of me—if they happen to dislike me—gives them no right to hit me. But God makes me dislike many people. And there are people who must be killed like snakes, because they rob and kill other people."

"I wish you would not remind me of these people" said the conjurer. "They make me very unhappy."

"It makes things very nice to forget about the unpleasant things" said the black girl; "but it does not make them believable; and it does not make them right. Do you really and truly love me, baas?"

The conjurer shrank, but immediately smiled kindly as he replied "Do not let us make a personal matter of it."

"But it has no sense if it is not a personal matter" said the black girl. "Suppose I tell you I love you, as you tell me I ought! Do you not feel that I am taking a liberty with you?"

"Certainly not" said the conjurer. "You must not think that. Though you are black and I am white we are equal before God who made us so."

"I am not thinking about that at all" said the black girl. "I forgot when I spoke that I am black and that you are only a poor white. Think of me as a white queen and of yourself as a white king. What is the matter? Why did you start?"

"Nothing. Nothing" said the conjurer. "Or—Well, I am the poorest of poor whites; yet I have thought of myself as a king. But that was when the wickedness of men had driven me crazy."

"I have seen worse kings" said the black girl; "so you need not blush. Well, let you be King Solomon and let me be Queen of Sheba, same as in the bible. I come to you and say that I love you. That means I have come to take possession of you. I come with the love of a lioness and eat you up and make you a part of myself. From this time you will have to think, not of what pleases you, but of what pleases me. I will stand between you and yourself, between you and God. Is not that a terrible tyranny? Love is a devouring thing. Can you imagine heaven with love in it?"

"In my heaven there is nothing else. What else is heaven but love?" said the conjurer, boldly but uncomfortably.

"It is glory. It is the home of God and of his thoughts: there is no billing and cooing there, no clinging to one another like a tick to a sheep. The missionary, my teacher, talks of love; but she has run away from all her lovers to do God's work. The whites turn their eyes away from me lest they should love me. There are companies of men and women who have devoted themselves to God's work; but though they call themselves brotherhoods and sisterhoods they do not speak to one another."

"So much the worse for them" said the conjurer.

"It is silly, of course" said the black girl. "We have to live with people and must make the best of them. But does it not shew that our souls need solitude as much as our bodies need love? We need the help of one another's bodies and the help of one another's minds; but our souls need to be alone with God; and when people come loving you and wanting your soul as well as your mind and body, you cry 'Keep your distance: I belong to myself, not to you.' This 'love one another' of yours is worse mockery to me who am in search of God than it is to the warrior who must fight against murder and slavery, or the hunter who must slay or see his children starve."

"Shall I then say 'This commandment I give unto you: that you kill one another'?" said the conjurer.

"It is only the other one turned inside out" said the black girl. "Neither is a rule to live by. I tell you these cure-all commandments of yours are like the pills the cheap jacks sell us: they are useful once in twenty times perhaps, but in the other nineteen they are no use. Besides, I am not seeking commandments. I am seeking God."

"Continue your search; and God be with you" said the conjurer. "To find him, such as you must go past me." And with that he vanished.

"That is perhaps your best trick" said the black girl; "though I am sorry to lose you; for to my mind you are a lovable man and mean well."

A mile further on she met an ancient fisherman carrying an enormous cathedral on his shoulders.

"Take care: it will break your poor old back" she cried, running to help him.

"Not it" he replied cheerfully. "I am the rock on which this Church is built."

"But you are not a rock; and it is too heavy for you!" she said, expecting every moment to see him crushed by its weight.

"No fear" he said, grinning pleasantly at her. "It is made entirely of paper." And he danced past her, making all the bells in the cathedral tinkle merrily.

Before he was out of sight several others, dressed in different costumes of black and white and all very carefully soaped and brushed, came along carrying smaller and mostly much uglier paper Churches. They all cried to her "Do not believe the fisherman. Do not listen to those other fellows. Mine is the true Church." At last she had to turn aside into the forest to avoid them; for they began throwing stones at one another; and as their aim was almost as bad as if they were blind, the stones came flying all over the road. So she concluded that she would not find God to her taste among them.

When they had passed, or rather when the battle had rolled by, she returned to the road, where she found a very old wandering Jew, who said to her "Has He come?"

"Has who come?" said the black girl.

"He who promised to come" said the Jew. "He who said that I must tarry til He comes. I have tarried beyond all reason. If He does not come soon now it will be too late; for men learn nothing except how to kill one another in greater and greater numbers."

"That wont be stopped by anybody coming" said the black girl.

"But He will come in glory, sitting on the right hand of God" cried the Jew. "He said so. He will set everything right."

"If you wait for other people to come and set everything right" said the black girl "you will wait for ever." At that the Jew uttered a wail of despair; spat at her; and tottered away.

She was by this time quite out of conceit with old men; so she was glad to shake him off. She marched on until she came to a shady bank by the wayside; and here she found fifty of her own black people, evidently employed as bearers, sitting down to enjoy a meal at a respectful distance from a group of white gentlemen and ladies. As the ladies wore breeches and sunhelmets the black girl knew that they were explorers, like the men. They had just finished eating. Some of them were dozing: others were writing in note books.

"What expedition is this?" said the black girl to the leader of the bearers.

"It is çalled the Caravan of the Curious" he replied.

"Are they good whites or bad?" she asked.

"They are thoughtless, and waste much time quarreling about trifles" he said. "And they ask questions for the sake of asking questions."

"Hi! you there" cried one of the ladies. "Go about your business: you cannot stop here. You will upset the men."

"No more than you" said the black girl.

"Stuff, girl" said the lady: "I am fifty. I am a neuter. Theyre used to me. Get along with you."

"You need not fear: they are not white men" said the black girl rather contemptuously. "Why do you call your-selves the Caravan of the Curious? What are you curious about? Are you curious about God?"

There was such a hearty laugh at this that those who were having a nap woke up and had to have the joke repeated to them.

"Many hundred years have passed since there has been any curiosity on that subject in civilized countries" said one of the gentlemen.

"Not since the fifteenth century, I should say" said another. "Shakespear is already quite Godless."

"Shakespear was not everybody" said a third. "The national anthem belongs to the eighteenth century. In it you find us ordering God about to do our political dirty work."

"Not the same God" said the second gentleman. "In the middle ages God was conceived as ordering us about and keeping our noses to the grindstone. With the rise of the bourgeoisie and the shaking off by the feudal aristoc-racy of the duties that used to be the price of their privileges you get a new god, who is ordered about and has his nose kept to the grindstone by the upper classes. 'Confound their politics; frustrate their knavish tricks' and so forth."

"Yes" said the first gentleman; "and also a third god of the petty bourgeoisie, whose job it is, when they have filled the recording angel's slate with their trade dishonesties for the week, to wipe the slate clean with his blood on Sunday."

"Both these gods are still going strong" said the third gentleman. "If you doubt it, try to provide a decent second verse for the national anthem; or to expunge the Atonement from the prayerbook."

"That makes six gods that I have met or heard of in my search; but none of them is the God I seek" said the black girl.

"Are you in search of God?" said the first gentleman. "Had you not better be content with Mumbo Jumbo, or whatever you call the god of your tribe? You will not find any of ours an improvement on him."

"We have a very miscellaneous collection of Mumbo Jumbos" said the third gentleman, "and not one that we can honestly recommend to you."

"That may be so" said the black girl. "But you had better be careful. The missionaries teach us to believe in your gods. It is all the instruction we get. If we find out that you do not believe in them and are their enemies we may come and kill you. There are millions of us; and we can shoot as well as you."

"There is something in that" said the second gentleman. "We have no right to teach these people what we do not believe. They may take it in deadly earnest. Why not tell them the simple truth that the universe has occurred through Natural Selection, and that God is a fable."

"It would throw them back on the doctrine of the survival of the fittest" said the first gentleman dubiously; "and it is not clear that we are the fittest to survive in competition with them. That girl is a fine specimen. We have had to give up employing poor whites for the work of our expedition: the natives are stronger, cleaner, and more intelligent."

"Besides having much better manners" said one of the ladies.

"Precisely" said the first gentleman. "I should really prefer to teach them to believe in a god who would give us a chance against them if they started a crusade against European atheism."

"You cannot teach these people the truth about the universe" said a spectacled lady. "It is, we now know, a mathematical universe. Ask that girl to divide a quantity by the square root of minus x, and she will not have the faintest notion what you mean. Yet division by the square root of minus x is the key to the universe."

"A skeleton key" said the second gentleman. "To me the square root of minus x is flat nonsense. Natural Selection—"

"What is the use of all this?" groaned a depressed gentleman. "The only thing we know for certain is that the sun is losing its heat, and that we shall presently die of cold. What does anything matter in the face of that fact?"

"Cheer up, Mr Croker" said a lively young gentleman. "As chief physicist to this expedition I am in a position to inform you authoritatively that unless you reject cosmic radiation and tidal retardation you have just as much reason to believe that the sun is getting hotter and hotter and will eventually cremate us all alive."

"What comfort is there in that?" said Mr Croker. "We perish anyhow."

"Not necessarily" said the first gentleman.

"Yes, necessarily" said Mr Croker rudely. "The elements of temperature within which life can exist are ascertained and unquestionable. You cannot live at the temperature of frozen air and you cannot live at the temperature of a cremation furnace. No matter which of these temperatures the earth reaches we perish."

"Pooh!" said the first gentleman. "Our bodies, which are the only part of us to which your temperatures are fatal, will perish in a few years, mostly in well ventilated bedrooms kept at a comfortable temperature. But what of the something that makes the difference between the live body and the dead one? Is there a rag of proof, a ray of probability even, that it is in any way dependent on temperature? It is certainly not flesh nor blood nor bone, though it has the curious property of building bodily organs for itself in those forms. It is incorporeal: if you try to figure it at all you must figure it as an electromagnetic wave, as a rate of vibration, as a vortex in the ether if there be an ether; that is to say as something that, if it exists at all—and who can question its existence?—can exist on the coldest of the dead stars or in the hottest crater of the sun."

"Besides" said one of the ladies, "how do you know that the sun is hot?"

"You ask that in Africa!" said Mr Croker scornfully. "I feel it to be hot: that is how I know."

"You feel pepper to be hot" said the lady, returning his scorn with interest; "but you cannot light a match at it."

"You feel that a note at the right end of the piano keyboard is higher than a note at the left; yet they are both on the same level" said another lady.

"You feel that a macaw's coloring is loud; but it is really as soundless as a sparrow's" said yet another lady.

"You need not condescend to answer such quibbles" said an authoritative gentleman. "They are on the level of the three card trick. I am a surgeon; and I know, as a matter of observed fact, that the diameter of the vessels which supply blood to the female brain is excessive according to the standard set by the male brain. The resultant surcharge of blood both overstimulates and confuses the imagination, and so produces an iconosis in which the pungency of pepper suggests heat, the scream of a soprano height, and the flamboyancy of a macaw noise."

"Your literary style is admirable, Doctor" said the first gentleman; "but it is beside my point, which is that whether the sun's heat is the heat of pepper or the heat of flame, whether the moon's cold is the coldness of ice or the coldness of a snub to a poor relation, they are just as likely to be inhabited as the earth."

"The coldest parts of the earth are not inhabited" said Mr Croker.

"The hottest are" said the first gentleman. "And the

coldest probably would be if there were not plenty of accommodation on earth for us in more congenial climates. Besides, there are Emperor penguins in the Antarctic. Why should there not be Emperor salamanders in the sun? Our great grandmothers, who believed in a brimstone hell, knew that the soul, as they called the thing that leaves the body when it dies and makes the difference between life and death, could live eternally in flames. In that they were much more scientific than my friend Croker here."

"A man who believes in hell could believe in anything" said Mr Croker, "even in the inheritance of acquired habits."

"I thought you believed in evolution, Croker" said a gentleman who was naturalist to the expedition.

"I *do* believe in evolution" said Mr Croker warmly. "Do you take me for a fundamentalist?"

"If you believe in evolution" said the naturalist "you must believe that all habits are both acquired and inherited. But you all have the Garden of Eden in your blood still. The way you fellows take in new ideas without ever thinking of throwing out the old ones makes you public dangers. You are all fundamentalists with a top dressing of science. That is why you are the stupidest of conservatives and reactionists in politics and the most bigoted of obstructionists in science itself. When it comes to getting a move on you are all of the same opinion: stop it, flog it, hang it, dynamite it, stamp it out."

"All of the same opinion!" exclaimed the first lady. "Have they ever agreed on any subject?"

"They are all looking in the same direction at present!" said a lady with a sarcastic expression.

"What direction?" said the first lady.

"That direction" said the sarcastic lady, pointing to the black girl.

"Are you there still?" said the first lady. "You were told to go. Get along with you."

The black girl did not reply. She contemplated the lady gravely and let the knobkerry swing slowly between her fingers. Then she looked at the mathematical lady and said "Where does it grow?"

"Where does what grow?" said the mathematical lady.

"The root you spoke of" said the black girl. "The square root of Myna's sex."

"It grows in the mind" said the lady. "It is a number. Can you count forwards from one?"

"One, two, three, four, five, do you mean?" said the black girl, helping herself by her fingers.

"Just so" said the lady. "Now count backwards from one."

"One, one less, two less, three less, four less."

They all clapped their hands. "Splendid!" cried one. "Newton!" said another. "Leibniz!" said a third. "Einstein!" said a fourth. And then altogether, "Marvellous! marvellous!"

"I keep telling you" said a lady who was the ethnologist of the expedition "that the next great civilization will be a black civilization. The white man is played out. He knows it, too, and is committing suicide as fast as he can."

"Why are you surprised at a little thing like that?" said the black girl. "Why cannot you white people grow up and be serious as we blacks do? I thought glass beads marvellous when I saw them for the first time; but I soon got used to them. You cry marvellous every time one of you says something silly. The most wonderful things you have are your guns. It must be easier to find God than to find out how to make guns. But you do not care for God: you care for nothing but guns. You use your guns to make slaves of us. Then, because you are too lazy to shoot, you put the guns into our hands and teach us to shoot for you. You will soon teach us to make the guns because you are too lazy to make them yourselves. You have found out how to make drinks that make men forget God, and put their consciences to sleep and make murder seem a delight. You sell these drinks to us and teach us how to make them. And all the time you steal the land from us and starve us and make us hate you as we hate the snakes. What will be the end of that? You will kill one another so fast that those who are left will be too few to resist when our warriors fill themselves with your magic drink and kill you with your own guns. And then our warriors will kill one another as you do, unless they are prevented by God. Oh that I knew where I might find Him! Will none of you help me in my search? Do none of you care?"

"Our guns have saved you from the man-eating lion and the trampling elephant, have they not?" said a huffy gentleman, who had hitherto found the conversation too deep for him.

"Only to deliver us into the hands of the man-beating slave-driver and the trampling baas" said the black girl. "Lion and elephant shared the land with us. When they ate or trampled on our bodies they spared our souls. When they had enough they asked for no more. But nothing will satisfy your greed. You work generations of us to death until you have each of you more than a hundred of us could eat or spend; and yet you go on forcing us to work harder and harder and longer and longer for less and less food and clothing. You do not know what enough means for yourselves, or less than enough for us. You are for ever grumbling because we have no money to buy the goods you trade in; and your only remedy is to give us less money: This must be because you serve false gods. You are heathens and savages. You know neither how to live nor let others live. When I find God I shall have the strength of mind to destroy you and to teach my people not to destroy themselves."

"Look!" cried the first lady. "She is upsetting the men. I told you she would. They have been listening to her seditious rot. Look at their eyes. They are dangerous. I shall put a bullet through her if none of you men will."

And the lady actually drew a revolver, she was so frightened. But before she could get it out of its leather case the black girl sprang at her; laid her out with her favorite knobkerry stroke; and darted away into the forest. And all the black bearers went into extasies of merriment.

"Let us be thankful that she has restored good humor" said the first gentleman. "Things looked ugly for a moment. Now all is well. Doctor: will you see to poor Miss Fitzjones's cerebellum."

"The mistake we made" said the naturalist "was in not offering her some of our food."

The black girl hid herself long enough to make sure that she was not being pursued. She knew that what she had done was a flogging matter, and that no plea of defence would avail a black defendant against a white plaintiff. She did not worry about the mounted police; for in that district they were very scarce. But she did not want to have to dodge the caravan continuously; and as one direction was as good as another for her purpose, she turned back on her tracks (for the caravan had been going her way) and so found herself towards evening at the well where she had talked with the conjurer. There she found a booth with many images of wood, plaster, or ivory set out for sale; and lying on the ground beside it was a big wooden cross on which the conjurer was lying with his ankles crossed and his arms stretched out. And the man who kept the booth was carving a statue of him in wood with great speed and skill. They were watched by a handsome Arab gentleman in a turban, with a scimitar in his sash, who was sitting on the coping of the well, and combing his beard.

"Why do you do this, my friend?" said the Arab gentleman. "You know that it is a breach of the second commandment given by God to Moses. By rights I should smite you dead with my scimitar; but I have suffered and sinned all my life through an infirmity of spirit which renders me incapable of slaying any animal, even a man, in cold blood. Why do you do it?"

"What else can I do if I am not to starve?" said the conjurer. "I am so utterly rejected of men that my only means of livelihood is to sit as a model to this compassionate artist who pays me sixpence an hour for stretching myself on this cross all day. He himself lives by selling images of me in this ridiculous position. People idolize me as the Dying Malefactor because they are interested in nothing but the police news. When he has laid in a sufficient stock of images, and I have saved a sufficient number of sixpences, I take a holiday and go about giving people good advice and telling them wholesome truths. If they would only listen to me they would be ever so much happier and better. But they refuse to believe me unless I do conjuring tricks for them; and when I do them they only throw me coppers and sometimes tickeys, and say what a wonderful man I am, and that there has been nobody like me ever on earth; but they go on being foolish and wicked and cruel all the same. It makes me feel that God has forsaken me sometimes."

"What is a tickey?" said the Arab, rearranging his robe in more becoming folds.

"A threepenny bit" said the conjurer. "It is coined because proud people are ashamed to be seen giving me coppers, and they think sixpence too much."

"I should not like people to treat me like that" said the Arab. "I also have a message to deliver. My people, if left to themselves, would fall down and worship all the images in that booth. If there were no images they would worship stones. My message is that there is no majesty and no might save in Allah the glorious, the great, the one and only. Of Him no mortal has ever dared to make an image: if anyone attempted such a crime I should forget that Allah is merciful, and overcome my infirmity to the extremity of slaying him with my own hand. But who could conceive the greatness of Allah in a bodily form? Not even an image of the finest horse could convey a notion of His beauty and greatness. Well, when I tell them this, they ask me, too, to do conjuring tricks; and when I tell them that I am a man like themselves and that not Allah Himself can violate His own laws—if one could conceive Him as doing anything unlawful—they go away and pretend that I am working miracles. But they believe; for if they doubt I have them slain by those who believe. That is what you should do, my friend."

"But my message is that they should not kill one another" said the conjurer. "One has to be consistent."

"That is quite right as far as their private quarrels are concerned" said the Arab. "But we must kill those who are unfit to live. We must weed the garden as well as water it."

"Who is to be the judge of our fitness to live?" said the

conjurer. "The highest authorities, the imperial governors and the high priests, find that I am unfit to live. Perhaps they are right."

"Precisely the same conclusion was reached concerning myself" said the Arab. "I had to run away and hide until I had convinced a sufficient number of athletic young men that their elders were mistaken about me: that, in fact, the boot was on the other leg. Then I returned with the athletic young men, and weeded the garden."

"I admire your courage and practical sagacity" said the conjurer; "but I am not built that way."

"Do not admire such qualities" said the Arab. "I am somewhat ashamed of them. Every desert chieftain displays them abundantly. It is on the superiority of my mind, which has made me the vehicle of divine inspiration, that I value myself. Have you ever written a book?"

"No" said the conjurer sadly: "I wish I could; for then I could make money enough to come off this tiresome cross and send my message in print all over the world. But I am no author. I have composed a handy sort of short prayer with, I hope, all the essentials in it. But God inspires me to speak, not to write."

"Writing is useful" said the Arab. "I have been inspired to write many chapters of the word of Allah, praised be His name! But there are fellows in his world with whom Allah cannot be expected to trouble Himself. His word means nothing to them; so when I have to deal with them I am no longer inspired, and have to rely on my own invention and my own wit. For them I write terrible stories of the Day of Judgment, and of the hell in which evildoers will suffer eternally. I contrast these horrors with enchanting pictures of the paradise maintained for those who do the will of Allah. Such a paradise as will tempt them, you understand: a paradise of gardens and perfumes and beautiful women."

"And how do you know what is the will of Allah?" said the conjurer.

"As they are incapable for understanding it, my will must serve them for it instead" said the Arab. "They can understand my will, which is indeed truly the will of

Allah at second hand, a little soiled by my mortal passions and necessities, no doubt, but the best I can do for them. Without it I could not manage them at all. Without it they would desert me for the first chief who promised them a bigger earthly plunder. But what other chief can write a book and promise them an eternity of bliss after their death with all the authority of a mind which can surround its own inventions with the majesty of authentic inspiration?"

"You have every qualification for success" said the conjurer politely, and a little wistfully.

"I am the eagle and the serpent" said the Arab. "Yet in my youth I was proud to be the servant of a widow and drive her camels. Now I am the humble servant of Allah and drive men for Him. For in no other do I recognize majesty and might; and with Him I take refuge from Satan and his brood."

"What is all this majesty and might without a sense of beauty and the skill to embody it in images that time cannot change into corruption?" said the wood carver, who had been working and listening in silence. "I have no use for your Allah, who forbids the making of images."

"Know, dog of an unbeliever," said the Arab, "that images have a power of making men fall down and worship them, even when they are images of beasts."

"Or of the sons of carpenters" interjected the conjurer.

"When I drove the camels" continued the Arab, not quite catching the interruption, "I carried in my pack idols of men seated on thrones with the heads of hawks on their shoulders and scourges in their hands. The Christians who began by worshipping God in the form of a man, now worship Him in the form of a lamb. This is the punishment decreed by Allah for the sin of presuming to imitate the work of His hands. But do not on that account dare to deny Allah His sense of beauty. Even your model here who is sharing your sin will remind you that the lilies of Allah are more lovely than the robes of Solomon in all his glory. Allah makes the skies His pictures and His children His statues, and does not withhold them from our earthly vision. He permits you to make lovely robes and saddles and trappings, and carpets to kneel on before Him, and windows like flower beds of precious stones. Yet you will be meddling in the work He reserves for Himself, and making idols. For ever be such sin forbidden to my people!"

"Pooh!" said the sculptor "your Allah is a bungler; and he knows it. I have in my booth in a curtained-off corner some Greek gods so beautiful that Allah himself may well burst with envy when he compares them with his own amateur attempts. I tell you Allah made this hand of mine because his own hands are too clumsy, if indeed he have any hands at all. The artist-god is himself an artist, never satisfied with His work, always perfecting it to the limit of His powers, always aware that though He must stop when He reaches that limit, yet there is a further perfection without which the picture has no meaning. Your Allah can make a woman. Can he make the Goddess of Love? No: only an artist can do that. See!" he said, rising to go into his booth. "Can Allah make *her*?" And he brought from the curtained corner a marble Venus and placed her on the counter.

"Her limbs are cold" said the black girl, who had been listening all this time unnoticed.

"Well said!" cried the Arab. "A living failure is better than a dead masterpiece; and Allah is justified against this most presumptuous idolater, whom I must have slain with a blow had you not slain him with a word."

"I still live" said the artist, unabashed. "That girl's limbs will one day be colder than any marble. Cut my goddess in two: she is still white marble to the core. Cut that girl in two with your scimitar, and see what you will find there."

"Your talk no longer interests me" said the Arab. "Maiden: there is yet room in my house for another wife. You are beautiful: your skin is like black satin: you are full of life."

"How many wives have you?" said the black girl.

"I have long since ceased to count them" replied the Arab; "but there are enough to shew you that I am an experienced husband and know how to make women as happy as Allah permits."

"I do not seek happiness: I seek God" said the black girl.

"Have you not found Him yet?" said the conjurer.

"I have found many gods" said the black girl. "Everyone I meet has one to offer me; and this image maker here has a whole shopful of them. But to me they are all half dead, except the ones that are half animals like this one on the top shelf, playing a mouth organ, who is half a goat and half a man. That is very true to nature; for I myself am half a goat and half a woman, though I should like to be a goddess. But even these gods who are half goats are half men. Why are they never half women?"

"What about this one?" said the image maker, pointing to Venus.

"Why is her lower half hidden in a sack?" said the black girl. "She is neither a goddess nor a woman: she is ashamed of half her body, and the other half of her is what the white people call a lady. She is ladylike and beautiful; and a white Governor General would be glad to have her at the head of his house; but to my mind she has no conscience; and that makes her inhuman without making her godlike. I have no use for her."

"The Word shall be made flesh, not marble" said the conjurer. "You must not complain because these gods have the bodies of men. If they did not put on humanity for you, how could you, who are human, enter into any communion with them? To make a link between Godhood and Manhood, some god must become man."

"Or some woman become God" said the black girl. "That would be far better, because the god who condescends to be human degrades himself; but the woman who becomes God exalts herself."

"Allah be my refuge from all troublesome women" said the Arab. "This is the most troublesome woman I have ever met. It is one of the mysterious ways of Allah to make women troublesome when he makes them beautiful. The more reason he gives them to be content, the more dissatisfied they are. This one is dissatisfied even with Allah Himself, in whom is all majesty and all might. Well, maiden, since Allah the glorious and great cannot please you, what god or goddess can?"

"There is a goddess of whom I have heard, and of whom I would know more" said the black girl. "She is named Myna; and I feel there is something about her that none of the other gods can give."

"There is no such goddess" said the image maker. "There are no other gods or goddesses except those I make; and I have never made a goddess named Myna."

"She most surely exists" said the black girl; "for the white missy spoke of her with reverence, and said that the key to the universe was the root of her womanhood and that it was bodiless like number, which has neither end nor beginning; for you can count one less and less and less and never come to a beginning; and you can count one more and more and more and never come to an end: thus it is through numbers that you find eternity."

"Eternity in itself and by itself is nothing" said the Arab. "What is eternity to me if I cannot find eternal truth?"

"Only the truth of number is eternal" said the black girl. "Every other truth passes away or becomes error, like the fancies of our childhood; but one and one are two and one and nine ten and always will be. Therefore I feel that there is something godlike about numbers."

"You cannot eat and drink numbers" said the image maker. "You cannot marry them."

"God has provided other things for us to eat and drink; and we can marry one another" said the black girl.

"Well, you cannot draw nor mould them; and that is enough for me" said the image maker.

"We Arabs can; and in this sign we shall conquer the world. See!" said the Arab. And he stooped and drew figures in the sand.

"The missionary says that God is a magic number that is three in one and one in three" said the black girl.

"That is simple" said the Arab; "for I am the son of

my father and the father of my sons and myself to boot: three in one and one in three. Man's nature is manifold; Allah alone is one. He is unity. He is the core of the onion, the bodiless centre without which there could be no body. He is the number of the innumerable stars, the weight of the imponderable air, the—"

"You are a poet, I believe" said the image maker.

The Arab, thus interrupted, colored deeply; sprang to his feet; and drew his scimitar. "Do you dare accuse me of being a lewd balladmonger?" he said. "This is an insult to be wiped out in blood."

"Sorry" said the image maker. "I meant no offence. Why are you ashamed to make a ballad which outlives a thousand men, and not ashamed to make a corpse, which any fool can make, and which he has to hide in the earth when he has made it lest it stink him to death?"

"That is true" said the Arab, sheathing his weapon, and sitting down again. "It is one of the mysteries of Allah that when Satan makes impure verses Allah sends a divine tune to cleanse them. Nevertheless I was an honest cameldriver, and never took money for singing, though I confess I was much addicted to it."

"I too have not been righteous overmuch" said the conjurer. "I have been called a gluttonous man and a winebibber. I have not fasted. I have broken the sabbath. I have been kind to women who were no better than they should be. I have been unkind to my mother and shunned my family; for a man's true household is that in which God is the father and we are all His children, and not the belittling house and shop in which he must stay within reach of his mother's breast until he is weaned."

"A man needs many wives and a large household to prevent this cramping of his mind" said the Arab. "He should distribute his affection. Until he has known many women he cannot know the value of any; for value is a matter of comparison. I did not know what an old angel I had in my first wife until I found what I had in my last."

"And your wives?" said the black girl. "Are they also to know many men in order that they may learn your value?"

"I take refuge with Allah against this black daughter of Satan" cried the Arab vehemently. "Learn to hold your peace, woman, when men are talking and wisdom is their topic. God made Man before he made Woman."

"Second thoughts are best" said the black girl. "If it is as you say, God must have created Woman because He found Man insufficient. By what right do you demand fifty wives and condemn each of them to one husband?"

"Had I my life to live over again" said the Arab "I would be a celibate monk and shut my door upon women and their questions. But consider this. If I have only one wife I deny all other women any share in me, though many women will desire me in proportion to my excellence and their discernment. The enlightened woman who desires the best father for her children will ask for a fiftieth share in me rather than a piece of human refuse all to herself. Why should she suffer this injustice when there is no need for it?"

"But how is she to know your value unless she has known fifty men to compare with you?" said the black girl.

"The child who has fifty fathers has no father" cried the Arab.

"What matter if it have a mother?" said the black girl. "Besides, what you say is not true. One of the fifty will be its father."

"Know then" said the Arab "that there are many shameless women who have known men without number; but they do not bear children, whereas I, who covet and possess every desirable woman my eyes light on, have a large posterity. And from this it plainly appears that injustice to women is one of the mysteries of Allah, against whom it is vain to rebel. Allah is great and glorious; and in him alone is there majesty and might; but his justice is beyond our understanding. My wives, who pamper themselves too much, bring forth their children in torments that wring my heart when I hear their cries; and these torments we men are spared. This is not just; but if you have no better remedy for such injustice than to let women do what men do and men do what women do, will you tell me to lie in and bear children? I can reply only that Allah will not have it so. It is against nature."

"I know that we cannot go against nature" said the black girl. "You cannot bear children; but a woman could have several husbands and could still bear children provided she had no more than one husband at a time."

"Among the other injustices of Allah" said the Arab "is His ordinance that a woman must have the last word. I am dumb."

"What happens" said the image maker "when fifty women assemble round one man, and each must have the last word?"

"The hell in which the one man expiates all his sins and takes refuges with Allah the merciful" said the Arab, with deep feeling.

"I shall not find God where men are talking about women" said the black girl, turning to go.

"Nor where women are talking about men" shouted the image maker after her.

She waved her hand in assent and left them. Nothing particular happened after that until she came to a prim little villa with a very amateurish garden which was being cultivated by a wizened old gentleman whose eyes were so striking that his face seemed all eyes, his nose so remarkable that his face seemed all nose, and his mouth so expressive of a comically malicious relish that his face seemed all mouth until the black girl combined these three incompatibles by deciding that his face was all intelligence.

"Excuse me, baas" she said: "may I speak to you?"

"What do you want?" said the old gentleman.

"I want to ask my way to God" she said; "and as you have the most knowing face I have ever seen, I thought I would ask you."

"Come in" said he. "I have found, after a good deal of consideration, that the best place to seek God is in a garden. You can dig for Him here."

"That is not my idea of seeking for God at all" said the black girl, disappointed. "I will go on, thank you."

"Has your own idea, as you call it, led you to Him yet?"

"No" said the black girl, stopping: "I cannot say that it has. But I do not like your idea."

"Many people who have found God have not liked Him and have spent the rest of their lives running away from Him. Why do you suppose you would like Him?"

"I dont know" said the black girl. "But the missionary has a line of poetry that says that we needs must love the highest when we see it."

"That poet was a fool" said the old gentleman. "We hate it; we crucify it; we poison it with hemlock; we chain it to a stake and burn it alive. All my life I have striven in my little way to do God's work and teach His enemies to laugh at themselves; but if you told me God was coming down the road I should creep into the nearest mousehole and not dare to breathe until He had passed. For if He saw me or smelt me, might He not put His foot on me and squelch me, as I would squelch any venomous little thing that broke my commandments? These fellows who run after God crying 'Oh that I knew where I might find Him' must have a tremendous opinion of themselves to think that they could stand before Him. Has the missionary ever told you the story of Jupiter and Semele?"

"No" said the black girl. "What is that story?"

"Jupiter is one of the names of God" said the old gentleman. "You know that He has many names, dont you?"

"The last man I met called Him Allah," she said.

"Just so" said the old gentleman. "Well, Jupiter fell in love with Semele, and was considerate enough to appear and behave just like a man to her. But she thought herself good enough to be loved by a god in all the greatness of his godhood. So she insisted on His coming to her in the full panoply of His divinity."

"What happened when He did?" asked the black girl.

"Just what she might have known would happen if she had had any sense" said the old gentleman. "She shrivelled up and cracked like a flea in the fire. So take care. Do not be a fool like Semele. God is at your elbow, and He has been there all the time; but in His divine mercy He has not revealed Himself to you lest too full a knowledge of Him should drive you mad. Make a little garden for yourself: dig and plant and weed and prune; and be content if He jogs your elbow when you are gardening unskilfully, and blesses you when you are gardening well."

"And shall we never be able to bear His full presence?" said the black girl.

"I trust not" said the old philosopher. "For we shall never be able to bear His full presence until we have fulfilled all His purposes and become gods ourselves. But as His purposes are infinite, and we are most briefly finite, we shall never, thank God, be able to catch up with His purposes. So much the better for us. If our work were done we should be of no further use: that would be the end of us; for He would hardly keep us alive for the pleasure of looking at us, ugly and ephemeral insects as we are. Therefore come in and help to cultivate this garden to His glory. The rest you had better leave to Him."

So she laid down her knobkerry and went in and gardened with him. And from time to time other people came in and helped. At first this made the black girl jealous; but she hated feelings like that, and soon got used to their comings and goings.

One day she found a redhaired Irishman laboring in the back garden where they grew the kitchen stuff.

"Who let you in here?" she said.

"Faith, I let myself in" said the Irishman. "Why wouldnt I?"

"But the garden belongs to the old gentleman" said the black girl.

"I'm a Socialist" said the Irishman "and dont admit that gardens belong to annybody. That oul' fella is cracked and past his work and needs somewan to dig his podatoes for him. Theres a lot been found out about podatoes since he learnt to dig them."

"Then you did not come in to search for God?" said the black girl.

"Divvle a search" said the Irishman. "Sure God can search for me if He wants me. My own belief is that He's

not all that He sets up to be. He's not properly made
and finished yet. Theres somethin in us thats dhrivin at
Him, and somethin out of us thats dhrivin at Him: thats
certain; and the only other thing thats certain is that the
somethin makes plenty of mistakes in thryin to get there.
We'v got to find out its way for it as best we can, you
and I; for theres a hell of a lot of other people thinkin
of nothin but their own bellies." And he spat on his
hands and went on digging.

Both the black girl and the old gentleman thought the
Irishman rather a coarse fellow (as indeed he was) but
as he was useful and would not go away, they did their
best to teach him nicer habits and refine his language.
But nothing would ever persuade him that God was anything more solid and satisfactory than an eternal but as
yet unfulfilled purpose, or that it could ever be fulfilled
if the fulfillment were not made reasonably easy and hopeful by Socialism.

Still, when they had taught him manners and cleanliness they got used to him and even to his dreadful jokes.
One day the old gentleman said to her "It is not right
that a fine young woman like you should not have a
husband and children. I am much too old for you: so
you had better marry that Irishman."

As she had become very devoted to the old gentleman
she was fearfully angry at first at his wanting her to
marry anyone else, and even spent a whole night planning to drive the Irishman out of the place with her
knobkerry. She could not bring herself to admit that the
old gentleman had been born sixty years too early for
her, and must in the course of nature die and leave her
without a companion. But the old gentleman rubbed these
flat facts into her so hard that at last she gave in and
the two went together into the kitchen garden and told
the Irishman that she was going to marry him.

He snatched up his spade with a yell of dismay and
made a dash for the garden gate. But the black girl
had taken the precaution to lock it; and before he could
climb it they overtook him and held him fast.

"Is it me marry a black heathen niggerwoman?" he cried piteously, forgetting all his lately acquired refinements of speech. "Lemme go, will yous. I dont want to marry annywan."

But the black girl held him in a grip of iron (softly padded, however); and the old gentleman pointed out to him that if he ran away he would only fall into the clutches of some strange woman who cared nothing about searching for God, and who would have a pale ashy skin instead of the shining black satin he was accustomed to. At last, after half an hour or so of argument and coaxing, and a glass of the old gentleman's best burgundy to encourage him, he said "Well, I dont mind if I do."

So they were married; and the black girl managed the Irishman and the children (who were charmingly coffee-colored) very capably, and even came to be quite fond of them. Between them and the garden and mending her husband's clothes (which she could not persuade him to leave off wearing) she was kept so busy that her search for God was crowded out of her head most of the time; but there were moments, especially when she was drying her favorite piccaninny, who was very docile and quiet, after his bath, in which her mind went back to her search; only now she saw how funny it was that an unsettled girl should start off to pay God a visit, thinking herself the centre of the universe, and taught by the missionary to regard God as somebody who had nothing better to do than to watch everything she did and worry himself about her salvation. She even tickled the piccaninny and asked him "Suppose I had found God at home what should I have done when He hinted that I was staying too long and that He had other things to attend to?" It was a question which the piccaninny was quite unable to answer: he only chuckled hysterically and tried to grab her wrists. It was only when the piccaninnies grew up and became independent of her, and the Irishman had become an unconscious habit of hers, as if he were a part of herself, that they ceased to take her away from herself and she was left once more with the leisure and loneliness that threw her back on such questions. And by that time her strengthened mind had taken her far beyond the stage at which there is any fun in smashing idols with knob-kerries.

To Sister Laurentia McLachlan

××××××××××××××××××××××××××××××××××××

Dame Laurentia, of Stanbrook Abbey in Worcestershire, had become acquainted with Shaw at about the time of the writing of Saint Joan. *Rarely have such conflicting views formed the basis for so long a friendship and so deep a mutual respect as that between G.B.S. and the Abbess, and rarely was the friendship so strained as following Shaw's publication of his Voltairesque* The Black Girl. *Their remarkable correspondence continued until Shaw's death, three years before her own, in 1950.*

The Malvern Hotel, Great Malvern
24 July 1933

You are the most unreasonable woman I ever knew. You want me to go out and collect 100,000 copies of *The Black Girl*, which have all been read and the mischief, if any, done; and then you want me to announce publicly that my idea of God Almighty is the anti-vegetarian deity who, after trying to exterminate the human race by drowning it, was coaxed out of finishing the job by a gorgeous smell of roast meat. Laurentia: has it never occurred to you that I might possibly have a more exalted notion of divinity, and that I dont as a matter of fact believe that Noah's deity ever existed or ever could exist? How could it possibly comfort you if I declared that I believed in him? It would simply horrify you. I know much better than you what you really believe. You think you believe the eighth chapter of Genesis; and I know you dont: if you did I would never speak to you again. You think you believe that Micah, when he wrote the eighth verse of his sixth chapter, was a liar and a blasphemer; but I know that you agree heartily with Micah, and that if you caught one of your nuns offering rams and calves and her first-born (if she had one)

as a sacrifice to Jehovah you would have her out of the
convent and into the nearest lunatic asylum before she
could say Hail, Mary. You think you are a better Catholic
than I; but my view of the Bible is the view of the Fathers
of the Church; and yours is that of a Belfast Protestant to
whom the Bible is a fetish and religion entirely irrational.
You think you believe that God did not know what he was
about when he made me and inspired me to write *The
Black Girl*. For what happened was that when my wife
was ill in Africa God came to me and said "These women
in Worcester plague me night and day with their prayers
for you. What are you good for, anyhow?" So I said I
could write a bit but was good for nothing else. God said
then "Take your pen and write what I shall put into your
silly head." When I had done so, I told you about it,
thinking that you would be pleased, as it was the answer
to your prayers. But you were not pleased at all, and
peremptorily forbade me to publish it. So I went to God
and said "The Abbess is displeased." And God said, "I
am God; and I will not be trampled on by any Abbess
that ever walked. Go and do as I have ordered you." . . .
"Well," I said, "I suppose I must publish the book if you
are determined that I shall; but it will get me into trouble
with the Abbess; for she is an obstinate woman who will
never let me take her out in my car; and there is no use
your going to have a talk with her; for you might as well
talk to the wall unless you let her have everything all her
own way just as they taught it to her when she was a
child." So I leave you to settle it with God and his Son
as best you can; but you must go on praying for me,
however surprising the results may be.

                                  Your incorrigible
                                  G. Bernard Shaw

"School"

(B.B.C. radio talk to Sixth-Form students, delivered 11 June 1937. *The Listener,* 23 June 1937)

XXXXXXXXXXXXXXXXXXXXXXXXXXXXXXXXXXXXXXXXXXXX

Hallo, Sixth Forms! I have been asked to speak to you because I have become celebrated through my eminence in the profession of Eschylus, Sophocles, Euripides, and Shakespear. Eschylus wrote in school Greek, and Shakespear is "English Literature," which is a school subject. In French schools I am English Literature. Consequently, all the sixth forms in France shudder when they hear my name. However, do not be alarmed: I am not going to talk to you about English literature. To me there is nothing in writing a play: anyone can write one if he has the necessary natural turn for it; and if he hasnt he cant: that is all there is to it.

However, I have another trick for imposing on the young. I am old: over eighty, in fact. Also I have a white beard; and these two facts are somehow associated in people's minds with wisdom. That is a mistake. If a person is a born fool, the folly will get worse, not better, by a long life's practice. Having lived four times as long as you gives me only one advantage over you. I have carried small boys and girls in my arms, and seen them grow into sixth-form scholars, then into young men and women in the flower of youth and beauty, then into brides and bridegrooms who think one another much better and lovelier than they really are, then into middleaged paterfamiliases and anxious mothers with elderly spreads, and finally I have attended their cremations.

Now you may not think much of this; but just consider. Some of your schoolfellows may surprise you by getting hanged. Others, of whom you may have the lowest opinion, will turn out to be geniuses, and become the great men of your time. Therefore, always be nice to young people. Some little beast who is no good at games and whose head you may possibly have clouted for indulging a sarcastic wit and a sharp tongue at your expense may grow into a tremendous swell, like Rudyard Kipling. You never can tell.

It is no use reading about such things or being told about them by your father. You must have known the people personally, as I have. That is what makes a difference between your outlook on the world and mine. When I was as young as you the world seemed to me to be unchangeable, and a year seemed a long time. Now the years fly past before I have time to look round. I am an old man before I have quite got out of the habit of thinking of myself as a boy. You have fifty years before you, and therefore must think carefully about your future and about your conduct. I have no future and need not care what I say or do.

You all think, dont you, that you are nearly grown up. I thought so when I was your age; and now, after eighty-one years of that expectation, I have not grown up yet. The same thing will happen to you. You will escape from school only to discover that the world is a bigger school, and that you are back again in the first form. Before you can work your way up into the sixth form again you will be as old as I am.

The hardest part of schooling is, fortunately, the early part when you are a very small kid and have to be turned into a walking ready reckoner. You have to know up to twelve times twelve, and how many shillings there are in any number of pence up to 144 without looking at a book. And you must understand a printed page just as you understand people talking to you. That is a stupendous feat of sheer learning: much the most difficult I have ever achieved; yet I have not the faintest recollection of being put through it, though I remember the governess who did it. I cannot remember any time at which a printed page was unintelligible to me, nor at which I did not know without counting that fifty-six pence make four and eight-pence. This seems so magical to me now that I sometimes regret that she did not teach me the whole table of logarithms and the binomial theorem and all the other mathematical short cuts and ready reckonings as well. Perhaps she would have if she had known them herself. It is strange that if you learn anything when you are young you remember it forever. Now that I am old I forget everything in a few seconds, and everybody five minutes after they have been introduced to me. That is a great happiness, as I dont want to be bothered with new things and new people; but I still cannot get on without remembering what my governess taught me. So cram in all you can while you are young.

But I am rambling. Let us get back to your escape from your school or your university into the great school of the world; and remember that you will not be chased and brought back. You will just be chucked out neck and crop and the door slammed behind you.

What makes school life irksome until you get used to it, and easy when you do get used to it, is that it is a routine. You have to get up at a fixed hour, wash and dress, take your meals, and do your work all at fixed hours. Now the worst of a routine is that, though it is supposed to suit everybody, it really suits nobody. Sixth-form scholars are like other people: they are all different. Each of you is what is called an individual case, needing individual attention. But you cannot have it at school. Nobody has time enough nor money enough to provide each of you with a separate teacher and a special routine carefully fitted to your individual personality, like your clothes and your boots.

I can remember a time when English people going to live in Germany were astonished to find that German boots were not divided into rights and lefts: a boot was a boot and it did not matter which foot you put it on, your foot had to make the best of it. You may think that funny; but let me ask how many of you have your socks knitted as rights and lefts? I have had mine knitted that way for the last fifty years. Some knitters of socks actually refuse my order and say that it cant be done. Just think of that! We are able to make machines that can fly round the world and instruments that can talk round the world, yet we think we cannot knit socks as rights and lefts, and I am considered a queer sort of fellow because

I want it done and insist that it can be done. Well, school routines are like the socks and the old German boots: they are neither rights or lefts, and consequently they dont fit any human being properly. But we have to manage with them somehow.

And when we escape from school into the big adult world, we have to choose between a lot of routines: the college routine, the military routine, the naval routine, the court routine, the civil service routine, the legal routine, the clerical routine, the theatrical routine, or the parliamentary routine, which is the worst of the lot. To get properly stuck into one of these grooves you have to pass examinations; and this you must set about very clearheadedly or you will fail. You must not let yourself get interested in the subjects or be overwhelmed by the impossibility of anyone mastering them all even at the age of five hundred, much less twenty. The scholar who knows everything is like the little child who is perfectly obedient and perfectly truthful: it doesnt exist and never will. Therefore you must go to a crammer. Now, what is a crammer? A crammer is a person whose whole life is devoted to doing something you have not time to do for yourself: that is, to study all the old examination papers and find out what are the questions that are actually asked, and what are the answers expected by the examiners and officially recognized as correct. You must be very careful not to suppose that these answers are always the true answers. Your examiners will be elderly gentlemen, and their knowledge is sure to be more or less out-of-date. Therefore begin by telling yourself this story.

Imagine yourself a young student early in the fifteenth century being examined as to your knowledge of the movements of the sun and moon, the planets and stars. Imagine also that your father happens to know Copernicus, and that you have learnt from his conversation that the planets go round not in circles but in ellipses. Imagine that you have met the painter Leonardo da Vinci, and been allowed to peep at his funny notebook, and, by holding it up to a mirror, read the words "the earth is a moon of the sun." Imagine that on being examined you gave the answers of Copernicus and Leonardo, believing them to be the true answers. Instead of passing at the head of the successful list you would have been burnt alive for heresy. Therefore you would have taken good care to say that the stars and the sun move in perfect circles, because the circle is a perfect figure and therefore answers to the perfection of the Creator. You would have said that the motion of the sun round the earth was proved by the fact that Joshua saw it move in Gibeon and stopped it. All your answers would be wrong, but you would pass and be patted on the head as a young marvel of Aristotelian science.

Now, passing examinations today is just what it was in the days of Copernicus. If you at twenty years of age go up to be examined by an elderly gentleman of fifty, you must find out what people were taught thirty years ago and stuff him with that, and not with what you are taught today.

But, you will say, how are you possibly to find out what questions are to be asked and what answers are expected? Well, you cannot; but a good crammer can. He cannot get a peep at the papers beforehand, but he can study the old examination papers until he knows all the questions that the examiners have to keep asking over and over again; for, after all, their number is not infinite. If only you will swot hard enough to learn them all you will pass with flying colors. Of course, you will not be able to learn them all, but your chances will be good in proportion to the number you can learn.

The danger of being plucked for giving up-to-date answers to elderly examiners is greatest in the technical professions. If you want to get into the navy, or practise medicine, you must get specially trained for some months in practices that are quite out of date. If you dont you will be turned down by admirals dreaming of the Nelson touch, and surgical baronets brought up on the infallibility of Jenner and Lister and Pasteur. But this does not apply to all examinations. Take the classics, for instance. Homer's Greek and Virgil's Latin, being dead languages, do not change as naval and medical practice changes. Suppose you want to be a clergyman. The Greek of the New Testament does not change. The creeds do not change. The Thirty-nine Articles do not change, though they ought to, for some of them are terribly out of date. You can cram yourself with these subjects and save your money for lessons in elocution.

In any case you may take it as a safe rule that if you happen to have any original ideas about examination subjects you must not air them in your examination papers. You may very possibly know better than your examiners, but do not let them find out that you think so.

Once you are safely through your examinations you will begin life in earnest. You will then discover that your education has been very defective. You will find yourself uninstructed as to eating and drinking and sleeping and breathing. Your notions of keeping yourself fit will consist mostly of physical exercises which will shorten your life by twenty years or so. You may accept me as an educated man because I have earned my living for sixty years by work which only an educated man, and even a highly educated one, could do. Yet the subjects that educated me were never taught in my schools. As far as I know, my schoolmasters were utterly and barbarously ignorant of them. School was to me a sentence of penal servitude. You see, I was born with what people call an artistic temperament. I could read all the masterpieces of English poets, playwrights, historians, and scientific pioneers, but I could not read schoolbooks, because they are written by people who do not know how to write. To me a person who knew nothing of all the great musicians from Palestrina to Edward Elgar, or of the great painters from Giotto to Burne-Jones, was a savage and an ignoramus even if he were hung all over with gold medals for school classics. As to mathematics, to be imprisoned in an ugly room and set to do sums in algebra without ever having had the meaning of mathematics explained to me, or its relation to science, was enough to make me hate mathematics all the rest of my life, as so many literary men do. So do not expect too much from your school achievements. You may win the Ireland scholarship and then find that none of the great business houses will employ a university don on any terms.

As to your general conduct and prospects, all I have time to say is that if you do as everyone does and think as everyone thinks you will get on very well with your neighbors, but you will suffer from all their illnesses and stupidities. If you think and act otherwise you must suffer their dislike and persecution. I was taught when I was young that if people would only love one another, all would be well with the world. This seemed simple and very nice; but I found when I tried to put it in practice not only that other people were seldom lovable, but that I was not very lovable myself. I also found that to love anyone is to take a liberty with them which is quite unbearable unless they happen to return your affection, which you have no right to expect. What you have to learn if you are to be a good citizen of the world is that, though you will certainly dislike many of your neighbors, and differ from some of them so strongly that you could not possibly live in the same house with them, that does not give you the smallest right to injure them or even to be personally uncivil to them. You must not attempt to do good to those who hate you: for they do not need your officious services, and would refuse to be under any obligation to you. Your difficulty will be how to behave to those whom you dislike, and cannot help disliking for no reason whatever, simply because you were born with an antipathy to that sort of person. You must just keep out of their way as much as you can; and when you cannot, deal as honestly and civilly with them as with your best friend. Just think what the world would be like if everyone who disliked you were to punch your head.

The oddest thing about it is that you will find yourself making friends with people whose opinions are the very opposite to your own, whilst you cannot bear the sight of others who share all your beliefs. You may love your dog and find your nearest relatives detestable. So dont waste your time arguing whether you *ought* to love all your neighbors. You cant help yourself, and neither can they.

You may find yourself completely dissatisfied with all your fellow creatures as they exist at present and with all their laws and institutions. Then there is nothing to be done but to set to work to find out exactly what is wrong with them, and how to set them right. That is perhaps the best fun of all; but perhaps I think so only because I am a little in that line myself. I could tell you a lot more about this, but time is up, and I am warned that I must stop. I hope you are sorry.

To Hesketh Pearson

><<<<<<<<<<<<<<<<<<<<<<<<<<<<<<<<<<<<<<<<<<<<<

Pearson was the last major biographer of Shaw to have the playwright's biographical assistance, which proliferated into dozens of letters answering questions, many of which Pearson merely paraphrased into the third person, others of which he used verbatim. When this letter was written, the Second World War was only a fortnight old.

13 September 1939

My dear Pearson

"Into which of your works had you felt you had poured most of your inmost self, your spiritual passion? That was what I meant. But as you seem unwilling to answer, I do not press it."

This, honest Injun! does not describe any process of which I have been conscious. I hammer away as a smith makes horseshoes. When I write *As Far As Thought Can Reach* I argue out the statements until I reach a verdict. The fact that I desire to get at a right verdict and that the search for it is a pleasurable activity and its achievement a satisfaction convinces me that intellect is as much a passion as sex, with less intensity but lifelong permanency, and that in the course of evolution it may become so intense that life will be much happier and free from the revulsions of sex, which will become less tyrannous and finally have its reproduction function fulfilled in a less unpresentable way.

There is a passage at the end of *Too True To Be Good* which caused the then Dean of Worcester (Moore Ede) to preach an impassioned sermon on it. I scribbled it down at rehearsal because we could not get the curtain down at the right instant to choke off Cedric Hardwicke's oration; and I had to provide some lines for him to go on with in case of need. Lilith's "great" speech at the end of *Methuselah* was ground out as pure argument, as Lilith wasnt anybody, and there was no character to express. You may take it that Shakespear wrote "The cloud capt towers" and "There's a divinity" just as he wrote "Now is the bawdy hand of the dial upon the prick of noon," all in the day's work. . . .

We are in the thick of this evacuation idiocy. Indescribable. Our first terrified attempts at Military Communism are beyond words.

What a comfort to know that if we kill 20 millions or so of one another, we'll none of us be missed!

G.B.S.

To Molly Tompkins

XXXXXXXXXXXXXXXXXXXXXXXXXXXXXXXXXXXXXXXXXXXX

*Shaw's correspondence with the American actress Mary
(Molly) Tompkins covered three decades, while he unsuc-
cessfully played Higgins to her Eliza. She was never much
good as a leading lady. Lawrence is her husband and Peter
her son. Shaw was in his ninetieth year.*

Ayot St Lawrence, Herts
30 October 1945

My dear Molly

I have just received your letter with its proposal to come
across the ocean to live with me. The same idea has occurred to other women. Put it out of your very inconsiderate head at once and forever, as they have had to. No
woman shall ever live with me again in that sense.

I am a Great Man, living in dignified retirement in a
village in a house which I have given to the National Trust
to keep as a memorial of my life here with Charlotte and
my death in a solitude which let nobody dare to profane.
It is kept for me by a treasure of a stern Scottish housekeeper who is quite indispensable to me. If you arrived
and proposed to settle in for a single night she would leave
me instantly; and our devoted Irish Catholic housemaid
would follow her and make the house uninhabitable. The
scandal in the village, the degradation to Literature, the
insult to Charlotte's memory would be such that I should
be justified in shooting you if there were no other way of
preventing you from crashing my gates.

If you nevertheless try, it will not be necessary to shoot
you; but the Irish maid will say "Not at home"; and you
will never see me or hear from me again.

Why have you not known all this without my having
to tell you? You are no longer a young savage: you are

a mature woman. If you ever think of old men of ninety, you must realize that they do not wish to be made ridiculous, much less disgraced before all the world. Anyhow, dear Molly, you know now; so enough of the subject.

You have left me no time to say more. You never tell me anything about Lawrence's career as a sculptor, as to which I am interested and curious. And though Peter turns up in your letters at moments I cannot make out where he is nor what he is nor anything definite. Still it is cheering to know that you are painting away busily, as this implies that you may be making a success of it artistically if not commercially. There are worse places to live in than a barge. Let me know sometimes how you are getting on; but no more atomic bombs, please.

G.B.S.

SHAKES VERSUS SHAV

XXXXXXXXXXXXXXXXXXXXXXXXXXXXXXXXXXXXXXXXX

PREFACE

This in all actuarial probability is my last play and the
climax of my eminence, such as it is. I thought my career
as a playwright was finished when Waldo Lanchester of
the Malvern Marionette Theatre, our chief living puppet
master, sent me figures of two puppets, Shakespear and
myself, with a request that I should supply one of my
famous dramas for them, not to last longer than ten
minutes or thereabouts. I accomplished this feat, and was
gratified by Mr. Lanchester's immediate approval.

I have learnt part of my craft as conductor of rehearsals
(producer, they call it) from puppets. Their unvarying
intensity of facial expression, impossible for living actors,
keeps the imagination of the spectators continuously
stimulated. When one of them is speaking or tumbling
and the rest left aside, these, though in full view, are
invisible, as they should be. Living actors have to learn
that they too must be invisible while the protagonists are
conversing, and therefore must not move a muscle nor
change their expression, instead of, as beginners mostly do,
playing to them and robbing them of the audience's undivided attention.

Puppets have also a fascination of their own, because
there is nothing wonderful in a living actor moving and
speaking, but that wooden headed dolls should do so is
a marvel that never palls.

And they can survive treatment that would kill live
actors. When I first saw them in my boyhood nothing
delighted me more than when all the puppets went up
in a balloon and presently dropped from the skies with
an appalling crash on the floor.

Nowadays the development of stagecraft into film-craft may destroy the idiosyncratic puppet charm. Televised puppets could enjoy the scenic backgrounds of the cinema. Sound recording could enable the puppet master to give all his attention to the strings he is manipulating, the dialogue being spoken by a company of first-rate speakers as in the theatre. The old puppet master spoke all the parts himself in accents which he differentiated by Punch-and-Judy squeaks and the like. I can imagine the puppets simulating living performers so perfectly that the spectators will be completely illuded. The result would be the death of puppetry; for it would lose its charm with its magic. So let reformers beware.

Nothing can extinguish my interest in Shakespear. It began when I was a small boy, and extends to Stratford-upon-Avon, where I have attended so many bardic festivals that I have come to regard it almost as a supplementary birthplace of my own.

No year passes without the arrival of a batch of books contending that Shakespear was somebody else. The argument is always the same. Such early works as Venus and Adonis, Lucrece, and Love's Labour's Lost, could not possibly have been written by an illiterate clown and poacher who could hardly write his own name. This is unquestionably true. But the inference that Shakespear did not write them does not follow. What does follow is that Shakespear was not an illiterate clown but a well read grammar-schooled son in a family of good middle-class standing, cultured enough to be habitual playgoers and private entertainers of the players.

This, on investigation, proves to be exactly what Shakespear was. His father, John Shakespear, Gent, was an alderman who demanded a coat of arms which was finally granted. His mother was of equal rank and social pretension. John finally failed commercially, having no doubt let his artistic turn get the better of his mercantile occupation, and leave him unable to afford a university education for William, had he ever wanted to make a professional scholar of him.

These circumstances interest me because they are just

like my own. They were a considerable cut above those of
Bunyan and Cobbett, both great masters of language,
who nevertheless could not have written Venus and
Adonis nor Love's Labour's Lost. One does not forget
Bunyan's "The Latin I borrow." Shakespear's standing was
nearer to Ruskin's, whose splendid style owes much more
to his mother's insistence on his learning the Bible by
heart than to his Oxford degree.

So much for Bacon-Shakespear and all the other fables
founded on that entirely fictitious figure Shaxper or Shag-
sper the illiterate bumpkin.

Enough too for my feeling that the real Shakespear might
have been myself, and for the shallow mistaking of it
for mere professional jealousy.

AYOT SAINT LAWRENCE, 1949

---

*Shakes enters and salutes the audience with a flourish of
his hat.*

SHAKES. Now is the winter of our discontent
Made glorious summer by the Malvern sun.
I, William Shakes, was born in Stratford town,
Where every year a festival is held
To honour my renown not for an age
But for all time. Hither I raging come
An infamous impostor to chastize,
Who in an ecstasy of self-conceit
Shortens my name to Shav, and dares pretend
Here to reincarnate my very self,
And in your stately playhouse to set up
A festival, and plant a mulberry
In most presumptuous mockery of mine.
Tell me, ye citizens of Malvern,
Where I may find this caitiff. Face to face
Set but this fiend of Ireland and myself;

And leave the rest to me. [*Shav enters*]. Who are thou?

That rearst a forehead almost rivalling mine?

SHAV. Nay, who art thou, that knowest not these features

Pictured throughout the globe? Who should I be

But G.B.S.?

SHAKES. What! Stand, thou shameless fraud.

For one or both of us the hour is come.

Put up your hands.

SHAV. Come on.

They spar. Shakes knocks Shav down with a straight left and begins counting him out, stooping over him and beating the seconds with his finger.

SHAKES. Hackerty-backerty one, Hackerty-backerty two,

Hackerty-backerty three . . . Hackerty-backerty nine—

At the count of nine Shav springs up and knocks Shakes down with a right to the chin.

SHAV [*counting*] Hackerty-backerty one, . . . Hackerty-
    backerty ten. Out.

SHAKES. Out! And by thee! Never. [*He rises*]. Younger
    you are

By full three hundred years, and therefore carry

A heavier punch than mine; but what of that?

Death will soon finish you; but as for me,

Not marble nor the gilded monuments

Of princes—

SHAV.   —shall outlive your powerful rhymes.

So you have told us: I have read your sonnets.

SHAKES. Couldst write Macbeth?

SHAV. No need. He has been bettered

By Walter Scott's Rob Roy. Behold, and blush.

Rob Roy and Macbeth appear, Rob in Highland tartan and kilt with claymore, Macbeth in kingly costume.

MACBETH. Thus far into the bowels of the land

Have we marched on without impediment.

Shall I still call you Campbell?

ROB [*in a strong Scotch accent*] Caumill me no Caumills.

Ma fet is on ma native heath: ma name's Macgregor.

MACBETH. I have no words. My voice is in my sword. Lay
    on, Rob Roy;

And damned be he that proves the smaller boy.

*He draws and stands on guard. Rob draws; spins round
several times like a man throwing a hammer; and finally
cuts off Macbeth's head at one stroke.*

ROB. Whaur's your Wullie Shaxper the noo?

Bagpipe and drum music, to which Rob dances off.

MACBETH [*headless*] I will return to Stratford: the hotels
Are cheaper there. [*He picks up his head, and goes off with
it under his arm to the tune of British Grenadiers*].

SHAKES. Call you this cateran
Better than my Macbeth, one line from whom
Is worth a thousand of your piffling plays.

SHAV. Quote one. Just one. I challenge thee. One line.

SHAKES. "The shardborne beetle with his drowsy hum."

SHAV. Hast never heard of Adam Lindsay Gordon?*

SHAKES. A name that sings. What of him?

SHAV.   He eclipsed
Thy shardborne beetle. Hear his mighty lines.
   [*Reciting*]
"The beetle booms adown the glooms
And bumps among the clumps."

SHAKES. [*roaring with laughter*] Ha ha! Ho ho! My lungs
   like chanticleer
Must crow their fill. This fellow hath an ear.
How does it run? "The beetle booms—

SHAV. Adown the glooms—

SHAKES. And bumps—

SHAV. Among the clumps." Well done, Australia!

Shav laughs.

SHAKES. Laughest thou at thyself? Pullst thou my leg?

SHAV. There is more fun in heaven and earth, sweet William,
Than is dreamt of in your philosophy.

SHAKES. Where is thy Hamlet? Couldst thou write King
   Lear?

SHAV. Aye, with his daughters all complete. Couldst thou
Have written Heartbreak House? Behold my Lear.

A transparency is suddenly lit up, shewing Captain

---

* Minor Australian poet (1833–70) once so the subject of adula-
tion for his jingling rhymes that his bust was placed in the Poets'
Corner in Westminster Abbey.

*Shotover seated, as in Millais' picture called North-West
Passage, with a young woman of virginal beauty.*

SHOTOVER [*raising his hand and intoning*] I built a house
  for my daughters and opened the doors thereof
That men might come for their choosing, and their betters
  spring from their love;
But one of them married a numskull: the other a liar wed;
And now she must lie beside him even as she made her bed.
THE VIRGIN. "Yes: this silly house, this strangely happy
house, this agonizing house, this house without founda-
tions. I shall call it Heartbreak House."
SHOTOVER. Enough. Enough. Let the heart break in silence.
    The picture vanishes.

SHAKES. You stole that word from me: did I not write
"The heartache and the thousand natural woes
That flesh is heir to"?
SHAV.   You were not the first
To sing of broken hearts. I was the first
That taught your faithless Timons how to mend them.
SHAKES. Taught what you could not know. Sing if you can
My cloud capped towers, my gorgeous palaces,
My solemn temples. The great globe itself,
Yea, all which it inherit, shall dissolve—
SHAV.   —and like this foolish little show of our
Leave not a wrack behind. So you have said.
I say the world will long outlast our day.
Tomorrow and tomorrow and tomorrow
We puppets shall replay our scene. Meanwhile,
Immortal William dead and turned to clay
May stop a hole to keep the wind away.
Oh that that earth which kept the world in awe
Should patch a wall t' expel the winter's flaw!
SHAKES. These words are mine, not thine.
SHAV.   Peace, jealous Bard:
We both are mortal. For a moment suffer
My glimmering light to shine.
    A light appears between them.
SHAKES. Out, out, brief candle! [*He puffs it out*].
    Darkness. The play ends.

SOURCES AND ACKNOWLEDGMENTS

The text of the plays and prefaces is based on the *Bodley Head Bernard Shaw* as revised and corrected. The Program note to *Don Juan in Hell* and the two self-interviews are also from the Bodley Head edition. Texts of the letters through 1910 are from the *Collected Letters*, I and II, ed. Dan H. Laurence. Music and play reviews are from the *Collected Edition*. "Trials of a Military Dramatist" appeared in the (London) *Review of the Week*, 4 November 1899. "The New Theology" is from *The Religious Speeches of Bernard Shaw*, ed. W. S. Smith. "School" is from *Platform and Pulpit*, ed. Dan H. Laurence. *The Adventures of the Black Girl in Her Search for God* is from the final Standard Edition (1947) as textually corrected in 1977.

I am indebted to the collections, scholars and publications identified below for the post-1910 letters. For more complete references to some of the letters, see the Bibliographical Notes. Shaw's letter to Mrs. Campbell, 11 August 1913 is from Dent. His letter to Edmund Gurney is from the *Boston Evening Transcript*, 14 August 1914, where it appeared as "The Gospel of Play-Acting According to Shaw." The letter to the Webbs, 5 October 1916, is from Henderson's 1956 biography. That to J. B. Fagan, 20 October 1921, is from the autograph letter in the Burgunder Collection, Cornell University. The letter to Lawrence Langner, 3 May 1921, is from Langner's *G.B.S. and the Lunatic* (1964). The letter to H. K. Ayliff, 29 August 1923, is from a photostat in the possession of Dan H. Laurence. The letter to the editor of *The Weekly Westminster* is from the issue of 5 April 1924. The letter to T. E. Lawrence, 4 January 1923, is from A. W. Lawrence, ed., *Letters to T. E. Lawrence* (1962). That to Charles Graves, 14 December 1929, is from the autograph letter in

the Burgunder Collection. The letter to Frank Harris, 24
June 1930, is from the original signed typescript in the
Humanities Research Center, University of Texas at
Austin. GBS bowdlerized it for publication in Harris's
Bernard Shaw. That to Mabel Shaw, 30 January 1928, is
from the signed typescript letter in the Mugar Memorial
Library, Boston University. The letter to Dame Laurentia,
24 July 1933, is from *In a Great Tradition*. That to Hesketh Pearson, 13 September 1939, is from the 1961 version
of his biography. The letter to Molly Tompkins, 30 October 1945, is from the Peter Tompkins edition of Shaw's
letters to his mother.

Several of the notes to the early letters utilize editorial
matter from the *Collected Letters* volumes copyright by
Dan H. Laurence, and adapted from this volume with his
authorization.